Captain Moon

THE TOWER AND THE CURSE OF CARDOZA

HARRY LAUGHLIN

Glue Pot Press

Cover and Interior Design: Max Marbles
Publisher: Glue Pot Press
First Edition
Printed in U.S.A

ISBN-10:
0-9898392-6-5
ISBN-13:
978-0-9898392-6-6

DEDICATION

I dedicate this book to my friend, Lisa Rowland, who inspired its creation.

CHAPTER 1

"And they said to one another, Go to, let us make brick and burn them thoroughly. And they had brick for stone, and slime for mortar. And they said, Go to, let us build a city, and a Tower, whose top may reach unto heaven; and let us make us a name." (Gen. 11:4) And the name of the Tower was Babel and it was three hundred and twenty five feet tall, with the same measure at the base. All that is left of the Tower today is a hole in the ground where the foundations use to be. There are no shortcuts to Heaven.

In the summer of 1939, Charley Manchester was celebrating his sixth birthday. He was living with his parents, Grace and Charles Manchester. His sister, Audrey, lived with them. They lived in a rented house in Antioch, California, a stone throw from the banks of the wandering Sacramento River.

Charley's father was on one of his trips. He was on one most of the time because he was a world class, deep-sea diver, one of the best in the business. Charles had his own equipment and went wherever he was needed. On this trip, he was in Nevada trying to get a man's body out of a mineshaft. The shaft was over two hundred feet deep and was full of water.

Charley had seen his father in a diving suit one time on a dock in San Francisco. His father had looked like some kind of alien invader, wearing that big brass helmet. The helmet had windows so he could see and the brass boots had lead in them to weigh him down and keep his feet under him. The air pump he used was hand operated.

The wheel that made it function was brass and was about three feet in diameter. The air was pumped through a hose to the helmet. Charles had to have a man to run the pump, believing a man to be more dependable than a motor. The air that is pumped to the diver was not just for breathing; it was

1

also needed to equalize the pressure on the inside of the suit with that on the outside. A loss of pressure while in a deep dive could crush a diver to death.

Charles was a big man, over six feet tall. He weighed over two hundred pounds. The body in the shaft was about the same size and partly decomposed. The shaft was narrow, and straight down. It was not known how long it would take to get the body out.

Charley was not concerned about how long his father was going to be gone because he was having a birthday party and was not overly fond of his father anyway. If it were not for him, Charley would be able to sleep with his mother. He often did when his father was gone.

Charley's mother had baked him a cake. It was his favorite, a pineapple upside down cake. It had lots of brown sugar and walnuts on it. It was not the kind to put candles on, but it had six of them. They were lit and waiting to be blown out. Charley closed his eyes and wished he could be a Cowboy. He opened his eyes and blew the candles out with one mighty blow.

Audrey, who was a year younger than Charley, clapped her hands with glee. She was about as excited as Charley wondering what was in the box. Pictures of cowboys, horses, and Indians were all over the paper covering the box.

There were only two other children at the party, Debbie and her brother, Josh. Debbie was a cute girl, but Charley was not yet interested in girls, although he was curious because he had seen his sister naked. He was aware she was different. The children had never had a big party. They had not lived in one place long enough to make many friends. The Manchester family was a nomadic one, they followed the diver's trade winds. They had lived all over California and Oregon.

Charley was a little fellow and his sister was almost as big as he was. She had weighed eight pounds at birth while he had weighed only five and a half pounds. His mother could hold him with his head in her hands with his feet touching the inside of her elbow.

Charley was pretty for a boy. His hair was dark and a little curly. It was usually hanging across his broad forehead. His hazel eyes were innocent and he was meek as a lamb. Charley had long eyelashes that were dark like his arched brows. His lips were full and his smile was sweet. His Lips had a tendency to tremble if he was upset, or afraid. His sister was his opposite; she was brave as a lion.

Charley was frail. His mother had to be careful with his diet. Many things made him ill. He had trouble with any kind of milk products except goat milk. His formula had been made with it since he was a baby. Every evil germ that visited the neighborhood found a home In Charley.

His mother's panacea for all disease was the enema. Charley hated the enema but was sure his mother knew what was best for him. Charley was prone to earaches and there were not many days when he did not have cotton in one ear or both. Charley's right ear was hurting a little and it was also itching inside. With his little finger, he moved the cotton around in an effort to relieve the itching. It helped, but not enough. In exasperation, he jiggled the cotton almost furiously. He did this until it hurt and then stopped. His ear still itched and felt like wax was running out of it.

Charley forgot about his ear when his mother asked him if he wanted to open the box. He never said a word but ran to the box. In haste, he tore at the wrapping until it was scattered on the floor. Charley tore open the top of the box. His eyes got wide as a cowboy hat was exposed. Charley giggled in anticipation as he took the hat out to see if there was anything underneath it. Charley jumped when he spotted the pistols. There were two silver pistols with black holsters. The holsters and the belt had silver studs.

"Oh, boy!" Charley exclaimed, "I'll look just like Hopalong Cassidy." Charley looked into the box again and discovered the caps for the pistols. He loaded both pistols and shot everyone at the party, including his mother.

"Bang, bang!" he yelled, "You are all dead." The aroma of gunpowder flared his nostrils as he opened the rest of his presents, but there was not much there to hold his interest; some socks from his aunt May; a shirt from his grandmother; a sweater from another aunt and some cards came from various places. Children don't care about cards unless they had money in them, he thought to himself. But the Great Depression was still going on and not many families had money to put in cards.

After the fun was over, Grace declared it was time for cake, ice cream, and sodas. It was a hot muggy day and all the children were ready. The cake was moist and some of the brown sugar had turned into thick syrup. The mixed flavors were so good Charley could not stop eating until the first piece was in his stomach. He belched and ate another piece almost as fast, along with some ice cream and root beer.

Charley was full up to his esophagus. It was a good time to remember he had not shot all of his caps. Charley loaded up and killed everyone again. He ran out of caps about the same time his mother ran out of patience. Grace sent the other children home and her own to take a nap.

Grace started to clean up the party mess but found she was out of energy. She decided to take a nap while she had the chance. Grace tried but sleep resisted her. She got up and went to peek at the children. They were sound asleep looking like angels. Grace smiled to herself knowing they were not always little angels. Sometimes they were, but mostly when asleep.

Grace went back to clean up the mess. She felt happy and peaceful. She was just as happy when her husband was on one of his trips as she was when he was home, even more peaceful when he was gone. Grace loved Charles, but life was more harmonious when he was gone. He was handsome, exciting and fun but she needed a periodic rest from him.

Charles was a rascal, and Grace knew it. She knew he lied to her and knew he wasn't always faithful when he was drinking. He was such a charming rascal though, and she had always been unable to withhold her forgiveness. Grace had booted him out a few times, once when he had favored a prostitute with his charms and her partner had rolled him of seven hundred dollars.

Grace was cleaning as she hummed an old, Italian song, one she sometimes played on her accordion. Grace could do a fair job playing her accordion, but she was a little hard of hearing. Sometimes, while practicing a new song, Grace would miss a note without knowing it. She would miss that same note every time she played the song. Charley would wait for the note with disdain.

Grace was happy by nature, optimistic. All she needed from life was for someone to love her and need her. Material things meant little to her, although if a gift was given to her she would treasure it, but it was never the gift that made her happy, it was the giving.

Grace was a pretty woman. Her hair was brunette and curly. Soft ringlets hung across her wide forehead. Her eyes were blue and innocent. There was no guile in Grace. Her lashes were long, but light in color. Grace had to use mascara for them to show. Her eyebrows were like Charley's, shaped so fine. Her nose was straight and prominent, just right for her face. Grace had lips that were full and ready to smile. She was small and graceful, weighing no more than a hundred and five pounds. She stood five feet and two inches tall.

After cleaning up, Grace took another peek at her children. Finding them still in slumber, she decided she would try again to take a nap. As soon as her head had touched the pillow she was sound asleep. Grace slept the sleep of the pure in heart. There was a smile on her face. No sooner had Grace fallen asleep than Charley woke up. He was wide-awake and immediately bored. Charley looked at his sister, who was still asleep. He did not want to play alone so he nudged her. Charley had to do it again to get her to open her eyes. Yawning, she rubbed her eyes and looked at Charley.

"Hi, Jooner," she greeted sweetly. Everyone in the family called Charley Junior, except Grace, who affectionately called him Son. Audrey called him Jooner, being unable to pronounce Junior. It made no difference to Charley since he hated his name no matter how it was said. It sounded like a little kid's name to him.

"Let's go play", suggested Charley. "Okay, Jooner", replied Audrey. Charley put his pistols on and the children skedaddled out of their room. Before they went outside Charley took a peek at his mother. She was still asleep. "Goody!" exclaimed Charley and he sucked in his breath between his teeth because he thought he had said it too loud. His mother stirred, but did not wake. Charley let his breath out easy. All was well.

Outside, the children squinted and rubbed their eyes. The sun was very bright from them having been asleep. They shielded them with their hands as they looked at the gulls that were flying around aimlessly, making their hungry haunting sounds. The sounds were beckoning Charley to the river like a siren song. Charley almost never disobeyed his mother. She had told him many times to stay away from the river. His mother had explained to him why it was dangerous, but this was the very thing that made him want to go there. Charley tried, but could not resist the temptation.

"Let's go down to the river", suggested Charley, and Audrey shook her head in the negative. A worried look passed across her pretty face. "It will be alright" soothed Charley and with a more mature tone he added, "You will be safe with me." Charley took his sister by the hand and led her toward the river.

The ground was flat and parched almost white from the sun. They walked over a small knoll and descended to the river to the boat landing. There was no one there but themselves and the gulls. That was okay with Charley as there would be no one to tell them.

The landing was made of lumber and it sat flat on the water. There was no rail. It was in a cove where the river was almost still. Charley walked out on the landing with Audrey following reluctantly. The landing was about fifteen feet, square with ramps going out in both directions, parallel with the river. Most of the moored boats were small.

The children stood in the middle of the landing and watched the gulls. They both were afraid of the river. Neither of them could swim. It was exciting to do things they were not supposed to do, even more so when it was dangerous.

The children stood there until the fear dissipated some. They were just about ready to go down one of the ramps to look at the boats when a mischievous gust of wind removed Charley's hat from his head and placed it out on the water, about a yard from the landing.

Charley was afraid but had to get his hat. He walked to within a yard from the edge of the landing and got on his knees. He knew he would not be able to reach the hat from that position so he laid flat on his stomach. Charley's guns were uncomfortable so he took them off and scooted to the edge and rested his chin on it. Fear had made a knot in his stomach.

Charley had to lie still for a moment to regain his courage. Meekly, he stretched out his arm but wasn't close enough. It looked like the hat was moving closer. Charley slid his body out a little further and reached again, but still couldn't touch it. His whole head was off the landing now. Charley looked down at the river, which was just inches from his face and gulped.

Charley was frozen with fear, but he had to have his hat. Charley slid out a little further. He tried to reach the hat with his left hand while holding on to the landing with his right but there wasn't much to hang on to. Charley slid out a little further until his chest was on the edge. Charley looked down at the water and closed his eyes in fear. When he opened them he focused on his hat. Charley held his breath and stretched for the hat. He could almost reach it. Charley strained to make his arm longer and could almost touch it. He slid a little further and his fingertip touched the brim.

For a moment Charley was elated but felt his body move out on its own. He tried to move back but failed. Charley tried to get a hold of the landing but suddenly there was nothing. Charley heard his sister scream as the cold water hit his face and he slid into the river like a crocodile.

The river was murky and Charley could not see a thing, not even his hand in front of his face. Charley sunk into a world he wanted no part of. He had never been totally alone before except in his mother's womb and Charley could not remember that. He remembered his mother and screamed for her. Charley screamed as loud as he could but he heard nothing. He choked and then breathed in water like it was air.

Charley didn't think about death, he knew nothing about it. He couldn't think at all, his mind was frozen with fear. Charley reached frantically for something to grab. He was clutching at the water with both hands. Charley touched something and clutched it, trying to hold on to it, not knowing it was his face. Charley was scratching his face but was too cold to feel it. He felt himself land on the bottom of the river.

Audrey just stood there, sobbing, waiting for Jooner to come back up. She didn't know what to do. She was only five years old. Audrey watched the hat as it sat on the water. A fisherman, who had seen the children before, walked down to the landing. The children were usually together, so he wondered why Audrey was alone, crying. His blood turned cold when he saw the hat. The fisherman asked Audrey where her brother was.

"Jooner is under the hat," she wailed. The fisherman's stomach churned as he wondered how long the boy had been under. His first impulse was to jump in, but stopped himself, knowing he would not be able to see anything in the murky water. His mind raced for an idea of what to do.

The fisherman thought of the pipe pole. It was a long pole with a hook on the end of it and was used for pulling in boats that had floated out of reach. The fisherman ran for the pole; it was hanging on a piling nearby. Grabbing it, he ran over by the hat and put the pole in the water, searching for Charley, praying he would not poke the boy's eye out in the process. Even that would be better than the boy drowning, he thought to himself.

Suddenly, Grace came running down to the landing. Charley's silent scream had reached her through her sixth sense. It had awakened her with a start, and she had bolted to a sitting position. She got up, and ran to the children's room and they were both gone. She could not find them outside so she ran to the river. Her heart jumped into her throat when she saw the hat and the fisherman fishing around in the water with the pole. Grace ran to Audrey and picked her up in her arms.

"How long has he been in the water?" Grace asked the fisherman. "I don't know," he replied without looking at her; intent on what he was doing. "I don't know," he answered again in despair.

Charley was wearing a pair of wide, button down suspenders on his trousers. He was on the bottom of the river on his knees, crawling. The hook on the end of the pole caught in his suspenders right at the cross where they come together in the back. The boy felt the tug at the same time the fisherman felt the weight on the end of the pole. He didn't know what it was but couldn't help but feel elated.

The fisherman pulled the weight and the first thing they saw was the stretched suspenders. Grace almost fainted and then they saw Charley. At first, they didn't know if he was alive and then he was kicking his feet, gasping for breath.

"Oh my God!" was all Grace could exclaim. The fisherman was weeping with joy and relief. His hands were shaking as he pulled the drenched boy out of the river. It was a miracle that Charley was still alive. He had been under a long time. It was, even more, a miracle that he was conscious.

Charley's face was full of fright. When he saw his mother the fright left and he started to wail. If anyone had a right to wail it was Charley, but his lungs were full of water and he started choking. The fisherman turned him over and pumped the water out of him. When he had finished Charley stood up on shaky feet. His face was pale and translucent as if his body had been changing to cross over to the spirit world. Charley looked out on the river at his hat. His mother hugged and kissed him while Audrey was trying to do the same. She was so glad to have him back; she had felt lost without him.

"I want my hat!" cried Charley through his tears. The fisherman fished it out with the pole and handed it to him. It was wet but Charley didn't care, he had gone through a lot for that hat. Charley put it on his head and forced a weak grin. He started walking off the landing. Charley never wanted to see that place again. He never wanted to see water again. Grace tried to stop Charley, he looked pale and ill, but he wanted to walk and was stubborn about it.

Although Charley felt sick, when it came to suffering, he had a will of iron; his constant earaches had forged it and it was his will to walk. It was Charley's rebellion against suffering. Charley walked back to the house and went to the toilet to vomit, then passed out.

They took him to the hospital where he spent the night. After an examination the next morning, Charley was found to be physically all right and was allowed to go home. He was not all right emotionally, though. For months Charley had nightmares about sinking into the dark and he could not go to sleep without a light. A light had to be left on in the bathroom in case Charley had to go in the middle of the night. Charley was afraid to be outside at night. There seemed to be danger in every shadow. After many months Charley forgot about his close call with death, but the terror of it was locked in his subconscious forever.

CHAPTER 2

Charley was eight years old and living with his family in El Granada, California. It was small fishing village about twenty-six miles south of San Francisco on Highway One. They had been living in a house on a steep hill by Twin Peaks in San Francisco. His parents had been buying the house, but some hard times had caused them to lose it to the bank.

Big Charles had run out of diving jobs and was working as a commercial fisherman. The boat he was working on was harbored in Princeton, which was walking distance from El Granada. It was a trawler less than forty feet long. Charles, and the owner, Dago Pete were the only ones working the boat. Charles was getting a percentage of the profit.

The house they had moved into was a small one, not near as big, or as nice as the one they had moved out of. It had three bedrooms while the one they moved into had two. Now the children had to share a bedroom. The little house had a living room, kitchen, one bath and a back porch. There was a small dinette set in the kitchen. The Interior walls were plywood brushed with shellac. Time had turned them to an orange color. The ceilings were the same.

The floors were varnished pine, except for the kitchen, bath and back porch. Those rooms were covered with ugly linoleum in a floral pattern. The back porch contained the hot water tank, laundry sink and an old wringer washing machine. The door on the porch had a window, the California type that slid up and down.

The door opened to the driveway at the rear of the house. There was a garage off to the left. The house had imitation log siding on the exterior. It had been painted gray many moons ago. It had sliding casement French windows and they were white. The house was a rectangle, but close to being square, laying north and south. The back of the house faced west, where one could see the ocean.

9

One could see the mansion from the west side of the house. Everyone called it the mansion. It sat on the bluff next to the beach. Erosion had brought the bluff within thirty feet of the mansion. In not many years erosion would claim the mansion.

The mansion was the biggest house in the area. It had at least thirty rooms. It was a contemporary design, with a flat roof. A white fascia hid the rafter ends all around the house. There were many white French windows and doors. The exterior walls were tongue and groove redwood and painted a light blue.

Charley never saw the people who lived in the mansion. He had heard that the old couple who lived there were eccentric. He had no idea what that meant, but had deduced it meant they were different in some way. In what way he had not a clue.

One could not miss the dog that lived in the mansion. She was the biggest dog Charley had ever seen. A little bigger and she could have been a strange looking horse. She was a Saint Bernard and she was a bitch in more ways than one. Her name was "Lady," but she was no lady. She was mean and she ran loose.

Charley was afraid of her, but Smokey was not. Smokey was Charley's dog. She was small, not more than twelve pounds. She had long gray fur; it was in her eyes like a sheep dog. She had black twinkling eyes and a black nose. Her bark was more of a yap and she always looked like she was smiling.

Lady did not like Smokey and the feeling was mutual. Almost every time Charley took her to the beach, Lady would try to interfere and this always led to her frustration and humiliation. Lady could not scare Smokey. Smokey would just get under Lady and bite her legs and feet. Smokey was too fast for Lady. In the end the big dog would pull in her tail and skedaddle for home. Smokey was always proud after one of these confrontations. She would hold her head up and prance.

There were fields on both sides of the road that went by Charley's house. Just before the road got to the mansion it made a right turn and headed north. On the south end of Charley's house there was a creek. It was dry except when it rained; then the water would rush in from a culvert under the road.

On the east side of the house the road ran north and south and here were other houses and some boat yards. Some of the boat yards were small, like in people's back yards. Everywhere one looked were skeletons of boats being built and some that had been given up. Some made of metal were rusted.

Blackberries grew in plenty by the creek. Wild horseradish, licorice, spinach and spearmint grew in the fields. The spearmint leaves gave off a pleasant aroma when rubbed between fingers.

Charley had learned to inspect the beach before taking Smokey there. She loved to roll in dead things. Rolling in dead things would put her in a frenzy of ecstasy and her eyes would roll around in their sockets. Who could understand it? Only God could.

Smokey would go for a dead thing like a bee goes to honey. She would roll around in it with abandon and then Charley would have to give her a bath. Once she rolled in a dead whale that had washed up on the beach. She had nasty stuff all over her. It was a stench straight from Hell. It was a devilish assault on the olfactory nerves. Charley had to bathe her three times to get rid of it.

Most of the time, Audrey would go with Charley when he went anywhere, but sometimes he liked to be alone. Audrey had some girl friends; they liked to kiss Charley, but he was shy and didn't always want to be kissed. But there was one of the girls he liked to kiss almost any time. Charley had a kind of crush on her. She was a pretty Portuguese girl and her name was Bernice. Her skin was dark and beautiful. She was tall, slender and graceful. Bernice was the daughter of a fisherman, who was a friend of the family.

Charley had more family in El Granada other than his parents. His grandparents on his mother's side lived there. Captain Cassidy was his grandfather. He was called "Cap" by just about everyone. He was a fisherman and he had Captain's papers. Cap was a real captain. He had captained tugboats at one time, but now had his own party boat. Captain Cassidy took people out for pleasure fishing for a fee.

Rosella, Charley's grandmother lived with the Captain. They lived in a cottage in the woods. It looked like one you would see on a picture post card. Uncle Horace lived with them; he had diabetes and had to get a shot in the arm every day. Grandma gave it to him.

Uncle George also lived in El Granada with his wife, Aunt Elizabeth. Georgia was their daughter. She was a couple years younger than Charley. Georgia was a spoiled brat. She sassed her mother right in front of everyone. Sometimes, if she did not get her way, she would hold her breath and it usually worked for her.

Charley was always surprised by her attitude, he would never dream of acting in such a way. Once, at the drug store, Georgia had asked for an ice cream cone and Aunt Elizabeth had denied her. The bad seed had stomped her foot and had called her mother a nasty name. Charley had been aghast at hearing such a thing. The naughty girl had left the drug store licking her ice cream cone.

The Captain had been an ocean person since he was thirteen years old. His stepmother had kicked him out and he had gone to sea as a cabin boy. The Captain had been all over the world and had a lot of tales to tell. Charley loved to listen to them. He loved his grandfather, but his grandfather loved Audrey more than he loved Charley. Charley understood because Audrey was pretty and who wouldn't love her more.

The Captain was a large heavy man. Cap had hair like a bear, all over, except on the top of his head. He loved to eat grandma's cooking. He loved potatoes any way, even raw. After a meal was over he loved to sit and pick at what was left. It was a rare occasion when there was any leftovers, left over.

The Captain loved cake and chocolate was his favorite. Sometimes, after he ate a piece, he would eat slivers of it until the whole cake was gone. Cap loved frankfurters. He could eat a whole pound of them at a sitting without even heating them. Most people eat to live, but Cap lived to eat. Eating was not the only thing Cap loved. He loved Rosella more than life. She could not walk past him without him touching her. Cap complimented her constantly.

"Is that a new dress?" he would ask, "You look so pretty in it." "It is old and you know it," she would answer. "You look good in anything, or nothing," Cap would retort. She would give him that loving smile that made one feel good all over. Rosella was a lovely woman, tall straight and proud. She loved Cap just as much as he loved her. She was always running her hand over his head where hair once was.

Cap also loved his children, but none of them more than he loved Audrey; he adored her. His pet name for Audrey was, "Brownie." Cap called her that because it was the color of her hair and eyes. Even as young as Charley was he understood why Cap loved her more and he was not jealous. Cap was Charley's idol but Cap would not let Charley be close. Charley did not know how to be close to him, anyway. He had never been close to any man.

Charley went fishing with Cap one time and this was before Cap had the party boat. The boat had been small, rigged for trawling. It was not much longer than twenty feet. The boat had a small cabin in the middle with an engine that was not covered. Cap had built the boat himself and with few creature comforts. It was a workboat.

Charley had been wearing two pair of pants, two pair of wool socks, a wool shirt, wool sweater and a wool jacket. He also had on a wool skullcap. Charley had been unable to get warm. The Captain had been wearing a short sleeved, shirt.

Charley had tried to get close to the engine to get warm, but had got too close to the exhaust manifold. He had burned a hole in his pants. Cap had got a rag and had dipped it in the ocean to cool Charley's pants. His big body had been shaking with laughter. Charley had never gone fishing with Cap again. Charley had not liked getting up at three in the morning and didn't like being laughed at.

A lot of men who lived in the area were fishermen. One lived across the street from Charley. He was a big man, fat and jovial. His name was "Tiny." He had a metal plate in his head and was not always operating with all his faculties. Tiny was a reader and a collector of comic books. He had trunks and boxes full of them. Tiny had all the action heroes and the funny ones.

Tiny wouldn't loan his comic books out. The children called them "Funny Books." Charley and the other kids could only read them when Tiny was home. That didn't happen often because Tiny liked to frequent the local taverns. When Tiny was home there was always an array of kids there reading his comic books.

Tiny had a small boat. It was rigged for trawling. He was out fishing for bass one day. About five miles out he had engine trouble. Tiny must also have had trouble with the plate in his head because he did a foolish thing. Tiny was frightened because he couldn't get the engine started and he abandoned his boat.

Tiny didn't have a skiff, so he jumped overboard. Tiny was a good swimmer and made it to shore, but his boat was not so lucky. It was battered to bits on a reef. Tiny never lived that dumb trick down; the other fishermen wouldn't let him. They were not a cruel lot; it was like Tiny had broken some kind of moral code. He was teased so much he had to sell his place and move away. Tiny took his comic books with him.

Sometimes, if the weather was inclement, or the fish were not biting, or they were between seasons, Cap, his sons and friends would get together and talk shop. They would usually do it at Cap's place. This day Charley's dad was with them and so was James Bettencourt, a friend of the family.

A lot of people in the area had the name Bettencourt. They were of Portuguese stock. They were hard working, honest and fun loving people. Most of the men were fishermen or farmers. If the weather would permit the men would gather outside to work on their nets or crab pots. This day they were helping Cap mend his nets. Charley was there. He loved to watch the men work and swap tales. He loved to watch their hands as they worked.

Most of the men, especially the older ones, had gnarled, rough, tough looking hands, weathered from salt water and hard work. They were leathery from layers of healed blisters. Most of the men had to pull their lines in by hand, with the lines wearing a trail in their palms.

Charley's dad was weaving a line through a torn section of net. He was using a hand made tool made of ironwood. Charles was skilled with his hands and Charley loved to watch him work. Sometimes he made beautiful belts out of white line. They were made with intricate knots. Charles wore one and he gave them to friends. Charley had one. Charles handed the mended end of the net to Cap and he inspected it.

"Hunky dory," commented Cap, in a pleased tone. "What is a hunky dory?" questioned Charley and Cap smiled. He had wondered when Charley was going to get around to asking him; he had used the term around him before. Cap appreciated the boy's inquisitiveness, because children who do not ask questions do not learn well.

Cap loved Charley but did not know how to express it. Cap Told Charley that a hunky dory was a safe, rowboat, sometimes used as a lifeboat and hunky just meant good. "Oh," replied Charley, thinking this was a hunky day.

Cap pulled the long, slender, orange box out of his shirt pocket. It had black trim and writing on it. Charley had never seen Cap without that box. Cap opened the box and Charley caught a whiff of the pungent smell. It was rock hard, black licorice. It was not sweet; it was like a medicinal type.

Cap pulled the licorice out of the box; it was about the size of a cigar. It was flat at one end with writing on the flat part. Charley's mouth watered as Cap pulled a knife out of his pocket; he cut a small piece off the end of the licorice. It was hard and brittle. It had to be cut with a sharp knife. To try to bite it would be at the risk of breaking teeth. Cap put the little piece in his mouth and moved it around on his tongue, dissolving the delicious piece, making faces of pleasure.

Cap smiled at Charley and cut another piece off the stick. Cap started to put the piece in his mouth, watching the longing and disappointment on Charley's face. He just loved to tease Charley. Cap laughed and to the boys delight, he handed the piece to him. Charley put it in his mouth savoring the bitter flavor as it dissolved in his mouth. It had a lasting flavor, lingering long after its substance was gone.

One day Charley went to the beach with Audrey and one of her girl friends. Smokey went with them. The girl's name was Caterina and she was Portuguese. She was the same age as Audrey and she was pretty. She liked to kiss Charley and he was getting the hang of it. They had swimsuits on and were riding the breakers in with a fish box they had found on the beach. None of the children could swim. Grace believed Charley's fear of the water would keep him out of it and she knew Audrey was afraid of it. Charley was still afraid of the water but it had been a long time since his narrow escape and his fear wasn't bad as long as he had something to hang on to.

The children rode the breakers until they tired of it. They played in the sand and when they tired of that they played some kissing games, which was Caterina's idea. Charley liked the games but it was a little embarrassing kissing his sister. He liked kissing Caterina, though, because she had a pretty mouth. There was something about the way she held her lips, slightly parted.

Kissing was all they knew how to do. They had not learned about anything else, not for certain. They had heard some things about sex and they did know their bodies were different. They had learned some naughty words, but had not yet correlated things.

The sand was dirty and when the children had finished the kissing games they went back to the ocean to wash off. They had finished the games because they were all hungry. The children laughed and splashed water on each other and then ran all the way back to the house.

Smokey had won the race. She was sitting, wagging her tail and laughing at them for being so slow. Dogs do laugh you know, they just do it different.

Grace had gone across the street to confab with one of her neighbor ladies, so the children were alone. They were soaking wet. They were dripping on the floor making it dirty with their dirty little feet. Audrey, feeling naughty, took off her suit and started drying herself with a towel that was hanging on the washer.

Charley and Caterina watched her, glancing at each other, confused, not sure of what to do. Audrey giggled like a naughty girl; she was not embarrassed. Charley had seen her naked lots of times. Caterina got brave next and took her suit off. The naked girls stood there looking at Charley, waiting for him to follow. Charley's face got red. Audrey was the only girl who had seen him naked and she was the only one he had seen that way.

Caterina was more interesting to look at than his sister but he had no idea why. All children love to be naked, so Charley took off his suit and stood there, the only one who was different. The children looked at each other and broke out with laughter and then they started to dry each other.

Grace came in and found them that way. She was shocked at first and then upset at finding them naked together and cavorting. That was the way it looked to her. Grace could see that they were looking at each other over. She didn't want to make a big deal of it because that would only impress them.

"Come children," she told them casually. "Let's get our clothes on; it's not nice to run around without our clothes on." She knew she had made a mistake as the words had left her mouth. "Why is it not nice?" asked Audrey, who had been a rebel from the day she was born. "It is just not nice for boys and girls to be naked together," replied Grace. "Is it because Charley has a prick and we don't?" asked Audrey, and both girls giggled. "Shame on you!" scolded Grace and she gave Audrey a slap on her bare fanny, leaving a red mark on one cheek. She pulled the girls out of the room, telling Charley to put on his clothes. Then she remembered his clothes were where she was taking the girls. She told Charley to wait and she brought his clothes to him.

Dago Pete and Charles had made a good catch of rock cod and it put some extra money in their pockets. Money burned a hole in the big diver's pocket so he bought an old car for an investment. The auto was a Buick, a 1929 model, and a black sedan. It had hardwood spokes in the wheel; they had a varnish finish.

In the morning Charles went to work, leaving the Buick in the driveway. Charles liked to walk to work; it was a short walk to the harbor. For some unknown reason Charley thought the wheels would look better if they were white. Having nothing better to do, he thought he would get in good with his dad by painting them. He found some paint and a brush and he painted all four wheels white. Charley painted them as well as he could, but not very good.

"Oh, Oh my God!" exclaimed Grace, after her horrid discovery. That was all she could say, or do. It was too late to do anything before her husband got home from work. A half hour later Charles did come home and when he saw the wheels, the feces hit the fan. Charles had every intention of whipping the boys behind, but Grace got between them.

Charley was frightened by his father's anger. He thought he had been doing his father a favor. Charley had a spell of courage because his mother was protecting him. Charley called him a name that was fighting words for all black people everywhere.

Although Charles was dark, he was not that dark and he resented the inference. With fury he almost broke his wife's guard. It became clear to Charles right away that he was going to have to beat the hell out of his wife to get to Charley. Instead, he decided to leave and get drunk, which was lucky for Charley.

Grace had a friend since high school. Her name was Irene Galecos, but Grace called her "Reenie." Her form was generous, and rounded. Reenie had a pretty face. She had tried to lose weight but her husband had not liked the idea. He liked her the way she had always been, so she stayed that way and they were both happy.

Reenie and her husband, Jess, had a son. His name was Lonnie. He was high-strung and not bright. They had a lot of trouble with Lonnie and needed no help for more trouble. Lonnie was about a year younger than Audrey.

One day the three children were riding in the back seat of Reenie's car. Grace was sitting in the front seat with Reenie. Reenie was driving to Half Moon Bay to do some shopping; it was only a few miles. Charley and Audrey were having fun. They were trying to teach Lonnie the "F" word. Of course, he picked it up right away.

Children learn nasty words right away. If children were spanked and told that all words were nasty, they would all have a large vocabulary. Lonnie had no idea what the word meant. Charley and Audrey didn't know either, but they thought it would be funny if Lonnie said the word to his mother.

While Reenie was asking Grace what she would like to do first the children were giggling in the back seat. Reenie looked in the rear view mirror and asked the children what they would like to do and Lonnie answered with the "F" word. He had answered after a poke in the ribs by Audrey. Grace was aghast and silent.

Reenie stopped the car and turned around to face the children. Her face was red going on purple and it looked like steam was ready to come out of her ears. Reenie was about as mad as she could get. Other than that, she was relatively calm. Reenie was a good Catholic. She told the children that God hated nasty words.

She had a firm, male like voice. It would have been no chore for her to strangle her friend's children. Grace was still flabbergasted; she said nothing. Sometimes it is work to maintain a friendship.

Charley and Audrey started school at Moss Beach, a wide spot in the road a few miles north of El Granada. The school had only one room. The children were of divers ages grades and ancestral origin, but many were Portuguese.

There was one teacher "Old Iron Ass" behind her back and "Miss Fry," to her face. Neither Charley nor Audrey knew anyone there and were treated like aliens. The children there were of purer stock than Charley and Audrey. They stuck together in little racial groups. They did not like mongrels like Grace's children.

These children were all bigger and tougher than Charley. It gave them pleasure to tease, torment and beat on him every day. Charley never cried, he just gritted his teeth and took it just like he did the earaches. They never bothered Audrey. She was not meek like Charley; she was a tough little mongrel.

Grace complained and had her children transferred to the Half Moon Bay School. Charley fared better there because there were more mongrels there. Bernice was there and so was Caterina and he had seen her naked. He would never tell because she had seen him naked and he wouldn't want anyone to know that. He hoped Audrey wouldn't say anything.

Often, Charley was not feeling well and he missed a lot of school. If he had the slightest temperature, Grace would make him stay home. If Charley said he didn't feel good enough to go, he didn't have to go. If there were something at school he didn't want to face, like a bully or a teacher, Charley would will himself to be sick. Charley missed a lot of school, but was always smart enough to pass, sometimes by the skin of his teeth, though.

When Charley ate at a restaurant he often got sick. Rich things made him ill; spicy things did the same, sometimes combinations did. Once, his mother sent him two sandwiches in his lunch, one tuna fish, the other, peanut butter. Charley got cramps so bad he could not get out of his chair.

They had to carry him out to Cap's pickup in a chair.

Charley was always spraining his ankle. Once he was running as fast as he could down the sidewalk and he sprained his ankle. He fell flat on his face and slid into a concrete wall. It had knocked him dizzy. Charley had seen stars that no one else had seen.

Then he was riding a friend's tricycle on a porch. The porch was about four feet above the sidewalk. He rode it off the porch backward, landing on his head on the sidewalk. Charley's mother found him walking in a circle; he had fractured his skull. Later, Charley got an infection inside his skull and they had to drill a hole to drain it. Being Charley's mother was hard and she smoked a lot of cigarettes.

One of the neighbor's dogs got a knot on the end of his pecker while it was inside of Smokey. There was no way to get her loose before he had spermed her. Smokey had three pups. Grace kept one for Charley and gave the rest away. He named his pup "Scooter" because he had short legs and was slung low like Charley's scooter.

Grandma killed Scooter. It was an accident. Scooter ran under Grandma's car while she was backing out of the driveway. Grace almost had her arm run over trying to stop it but the tire pinched Scooter's tummy and he died a few days later. Scooter died in Charley's arms. Charley watched the glaze of death come into Scooter's eyes.

Smokey loved to chase gophers and there were gopher holes all over the fields. The grass was taller than Smokey. So she hopped around like a rabbit trying to see the gophers. They don't stay under ground all of the time.

A farmer on a spike wheel tractor was plowing the grass under with a gang of plows. He was making a lot of noise, but Smokey was hard of hearing and so intent on what she was doing she didn't hear him. She couldn't see him because she had her nose in a gopher hole. The farmer didn't see her and ran over her with one of the plows. She was cut pretty bad but managed to crawl home to die. Grace cried along with Charley and Audrey while she helped Charley put Smokey in a box and bury her. They gave her a Christian burial. Three people were there.

CHAPTER 3

Some years later, the Manchester family was living near Fort Bragg, California in a small town on the Coast of Mendocino County. They lived about a couple of miles south of Fort Bragg. There was a fishing harbor between where they lived and Fort Bragg. It was at the mouth of the Noyo River and was called "Noyo Harbor." The children went to school in Fort Bragg. They went by bus.

Charley's family had followed Cap there and so had Uncle Horace. Cap had bought some acreage and had built a house and shop out of redwood. The exterior was natural with a spar varnish finish. Cap was a versatile man; he could do just about anything that was needed. Along with having Captain's papers, he was also a journeyman machinist. Cap was also an excellent carpenter, electrician, and plumber. The Great Depression spawned this kind of person. The captain was still operating his party boat and was doing well.

Uncle Horace had a small fishing boat and he was not doing so well. Along with the diabetes, he was having some trouble with alcohol. It did not go well with the insulin he had to take every day. On top of that, Horace liked sweet drinks. He liked port wine and rock and rye whiskey, which had more alcohol and sugar. Horace was a serious introvert. He loved people, but he could not deal with them without the support of alcohol. Horace had set his course for disaster.

When Cap was not on his party boat, he was at home in the house with his wife or in the shop with his tools. Cap was always building something, or taking something apart. He had his own welder and made his own crab pots to replace lost or stolen ones. Sometimes he made them to sell. Cap was never out of money; he could do just about anything and do it well. He was not a "Jack of all trades, master of none." He was master of all he did.

Horace was still living with Cap and Rosella. He could not get by without his mother and Cap shouldered the burden without complaint. Cap understood that Horace was not a well man and would never be one. He was even worse off now, after the accident in Half Moon Bay. Gas fumes had collected in the hold of his boat. A spark had caused an explosion that had blown the cabin clear off the boat with Horace in it. It left him with third degree burns on much of his body. It had been a miracle that Horace had survived the burns, as diabetics have trouble healing.

Horace was nervous as a fly caught in a spider's web and alcohol was his panacea for all ills. If Horace drank too much and had a hangover, he would take an extra shot of Insulin to make him feel better. His compass was set on a steady course of self-destruction.

Horace was short and stocky. His hair was fair and so was his skin. Years on the ocean had not given Horace a tan. He had a laugh that was more like a giggle. He got it from his mother. When Horace laughed he sounded just like her. The genetic code is a strange vehicle; some of its passengers are good some are not.

Horace was still a fisherman but his health wouldn't let him work every day. Sometimes a friend would help him fish. When Horace wasn't fishing and felt well enough he helped around Cap's place. He did plowing, gardening, painting and things like that.

Cap had a Fordson tractor, an old one with spike wheels, just like the one that had killed Smokey. Horace did the plowing with It. Horace and Charley got along so well together. Horace taught him things, like how to drive the tractor. This was great fun for Charley but the tractor had no brakes.

Cap's property was flat as a pancake and the weight of the tractor with its huge iron wheels usually stopped it. Hooking a trailer to the hitch of the tractor and Horace asked Charley to drive the tractor and back it up for him. Charley let the clutch out too fast and knocked the tongue of the trailer out of Horace's grasp. The tongue pushed in the middle of Charley's back.

Charley pushed the clutch in to stop the tractor. But it was sitting on a mound of dirt and it kept rolling back. The tongue kept digging into Charley's back and he was getting scared. Horace jumped on the tractor, put the tractor in forward gear and stepped on the gas. The tractor jumped forward and Charley was saved.

Rosella made a great garden in the black soil that her son had plowed. Although she did have a green thumb, she just could not get her tomatoes to turn red. The sun was lazy in Fort Bragg and just would not do the job. Rosella still grew all the vegetables her family needed, plus some for her neighbors. She made relish and sauce out of the green tomatoes.

The Manchesters lived in a rented, two storied, Cape Cod type of a house. It was on a parcel of land next to Cap's place. The house had two bedrooms upstairs on opposite sides of the house. It had dormers in each bedroom. Downstairs was the living room, kitchen, dining room, one bathroom and the back porch. It housed the laundry facilities.

The children were sharing a bedroom again and they were at the age where it was not a good idea. It had not been long since Charley had his first sexual experience. He had experienced it by himself through accidental self-gratification.

Charley had been taking a shower and had washed his erection more than was necessary and his first orgasm and ejaculation had surprised him. It had filled him with awe. It had felt so good he now had to do it every time he took a bath. And no one had to tell him to take a bath. Charley then discovered there were other times and places to pleasure his self.

Charley had a temptation resistance quotient of zero. He suspected what he was doing was nasty. Though he did not know why and he could not stop himself and he did not want to. Charley knew other boys did it; he could tell by the way they joked about it. And they called it, "Jacking off." Charley suspected that girls did it too after watching his sister caress herself. She did not know he was watching.

One day, while waiting for the school bus, the children had been standing around in a group. A girl from an upper class was there. She was talking to some boys and Charley was one of them. She was a flirty girl and the conversation had turned to sex and then to masturbation.

"I have heard," she commented in all seriousness, "if a boy jacks off too often hair will grow on the palm of his hand." Without thinking, all the boys looked at their palms. The boy's faces all turned red when they realized they had been had. The girl laughed with knowing eyes and left them. She had a Cheshire cat grin on her wise face.

That embarrassing episode did not keep Charley from his self-indulgence. He started collecting pictures of pretty girls to fantasize with. Charley would cut them out and go into the bathroom to do his thing. He was going to wear his family maker out with Old Lady Five Fingers before he ever got it into a girl.

Audrey was turning into a lovely girl. Her body was starting to curve in all the right places. She had the biggest, brownest eyes there ever was and she had long eyelashes. Audrey's lips were full and ready to smile. She was gregarious and was making many friends.

Charley was shy and not gregarious but was making a few friends. Paul Lightle was one of them. His parents owned the Harbor Inn. Paul was sweet natured, full of humor. He had an unusual humility for one so young. It was next to Impossible to make Paul angry. Charley did so, once. In the gym he snapped Paul's bare bottom with a towel. It hurt and Paul got so mad he wanted to fight but Charley wouldn't fight him. Instead, he gave Paul the towel to snap him in the same bare place, and Paul did.

Fort Bragg was a good place to live and go to school. There were wild berries of every kind, even strawberries. The strawberries grew out on the sandy slopes that led to the beach. Grace, and Rosella turned some of the berries into lushes pies. Picking the berries was a fun job they all did together. Many berries were eaten as the picking was being done. Not the huckleberries, though, they were bitter until cooked with a lot of sugar.

The first day of school was a bad one for Charley. His sister had been angry with him for something. A Mexican kid picked a fight with him and Audrey laughed while he was getting his butt kicked. The bell rang and ended the fight. Audrey told him she was sorry that she had laughed at him. They were close, and it was Charley and Audrey against the world.

Charley and Paul got along good. Paul was taller than Charley by about two inches. He had the same kind of build as Charley, slender and muscular. Paul's arms were longer, but Charley could out box him.

Paul was shy and humble, but if pushed too far his stubborn streak would shine through. Although he was a follower, he would not do what he did not want to do. Paul had blond hair and it was straight. His eyes were bright blue. He had a grin on his face almost all the time. Paul was never sick and never missed school. Charley wanted to be that way because he was starting to like school; he did not want the other kids to think he was a pansy.

There were some pretty girls at school, but Anna was beautiful. She was a fair-haired Italian girl. She had a peaches and cream complexion. Anna had rosy cheeks that got more so when she when pleased or embarrassed. She had a slender, pretty body. Her hair, which was almost blond, had traces of red.

Charley had a mad crush on Anna and would have followed her like a puppy, but she wouldn't let him. She was afraid people would talk, and she already had a boy friend. He was older and bigger than Charley and was Italian like Anna. Charley had never seen him and came from a wealthy family, as did Anna.

Her boy friend called her "Noony" but Charley never found out why. Charley had overheard Anna telling this to one of her girl friends, Sicilia. It seemed to be a source of embarrassment to Anna, so Charley never asked her about it. Charley never knew the boy friend's name, but he did often wish he would vanish.

About a year later the Williams brothers moved to town. Charley, Paul and the Williams brothers soon became fast friends. The brothers, David and Richard were both tall and skinny. Richard was the tallest and skinniest. He was also the oldest by a couple of years. Richard was six feet four inches tall and weighed a hundred and forty pounds, all legs and feet. Richard was very smart and very silly, prone to giggling. David was six foot tall, not as smart and not as silly. He had red hair, and Richard was blond.

The Harbor Inn was built on the banks of the Noyo River early in the nineteen twenties. Situated in the harbor area, it was a three-story structure. The natural wood finish was probably linseed oil. The lumber was cedar. The Inn had its own boat dock.

Paul lived in the Inn with his parents, two sisters, one brother and the United States Coast Guard. The Guard had made the Inn its base since the start of World War Two. The Inn had other guest but most of it was home for the Guard and Paul's family. And so it was with the dock. P. T. Boats are bigger than they look in the movies.

The Inn rested on the north side of the river and was up the river from the two-lane suspension bridge that crossed Noyo River. On the other side of the bridge, in the direction of the mouth of the river, was the boats and fishing industry. Fish buyers and processors were on both sides of the river. Restaurants were on both sides. The boat yards and the store were on the north side.

At the mouth of the river was a cement jetty. Sometimes Cap would take Charley fishing off the jetty. They would catch flat, saucer shaped fish. One time Charley caught a fish and wanted to throw it back in, but Cap wouldn't let him, he thought it was foolish. After his puppy was killed, Charley hated to see any thing die. Charley would not go fishing with Cap anymore. Charley had caught the fish; he thought he should be able to throw it back if he wanted to.

A lot of wild pussycats lived on the harbor flats, rats also. They lived off the scraps from the fish cannery. For some reason the scraps were not good for the cats. They were sick looking, with dull looking fur. It was a fine diet for the rats, though; some of them were bigger than the cats. Rats can live on almost anything they can chew.

One day Charley and Paul borrowed a boat. The owner of the boat was not there. They didn't know him anyway, so they just borrowed it. The boat wasn't a skiff like they had wanted, but it was handy. It was a small motorboat minus the motor. It had a covered bow, oars, and oarlocks. It was about ten feet long.

It was a clear, calm day and the boys wanted to row out to the bell buoy, a few miles out on the ocean. Rowing out was fun and easy. Rowing back was another story. They rowed around the buoy a few times to look it over. It was a metal ball with a frame on top; it housed the bell. The buoy was attached with a cable to an anchor on the ocean floor. Its purpose was to warn mariners they were in the area of the entrance channel.

The boys rowed close enough to the buoy to touch it; then they started to head back. Going back in was not as easy as going out. With disdain the boys realized the tide was going out, and they had not thought of it.

The boat the boys were rowing was not built for rowing; it was for motoring. The hull was deep in the water, and they did not have the power to overcome the drag. Power would lift the bow and part of the hull, allowing it to skim on top of the water. They had no motor; all they had was arms and oars. The boys had four arms but only two oars. One boy would row as long and as hard as he could and then the other would take over. They rowed and rowed, but did not seem to get anywhere.

The boys were drifting toward a bed of kelp, with breakers breaking on a reef. They knew that if the got into the bed of kelp they would be done for. Both boys were frightened, but tried not to show it, but they read it on each other's face.

The boys were getting exhausted. Their arms were feeling like lead. The boys did not know how to swim and the water was awful cold to swim in anyway. It looked bad for them. They were running out of energy and it looked like their luck was running out.

The boys had been moving in, though, it just hadn't looked that way. Suddenly, they felt the tide let go of the boat and they laughed hysterically. They rowed on, maneuvered past the jetty and moved into the safety of the harbor. They were a couple of worn out, glad to be alive, kids. One trip to the bell buoy in a lifetime would be enough.

The next weekend the two decided they would row up the river and camp overnight. They would row far enough to get away from people. The boys started early in the afternoon and rowed until dark. The boys went ashore and vacated the Skiff with sleeping bags and a bag of grub. It was dark as the inside of a coffin and the boys had forgotten to bring a flashlight, or even matches.

It wasn't light enough to do anything so they decided to scare each other with ghost stories. After they were bored with that, they decided they were tired. The boys had done a lot of rowing. The area the boys were standing on was a flat area, so without further investigation, they laid out their sleeping bags. After they climbed into them the boys talked for a while about girls and sex and Paul fell asleep.

Charley needed to have sex with himself, but was afraid Paul would catch him at it and he finally fell asleep. The boys slept for a while, but something awakened Charley. It was the noise, the vibration and the light. Paul awoke right after Charley. A pair of bright lights headed straight for the two. Charley had not the time to get out of the bag and he rolled in the bag, out of the way of the approaching lights. After Charley was clear, he looked to see if Paul had made it and he had. Then Charley saw the taillights of the car moving away. Evidently the driver had not seen them.

"Holy Shit!" exclaimed Paul, "Where in the fuck did he come from?" "Fuck if I know!" answered Charley. The boys could swear as much as they wanted out in the boonies. They swore like a bunch of drunken sailors when they were together, with no adults around. It was the right thing to do. And then the time for thinking had come.

A chill went up Charley's spine as he thought about what could have happened had he not woke up. Visions of images went through his head, like tires running over his head, squashing it, popping his eye out, with his brains running out of his ears. There was his body, all flattened out, with his guts running out of his ass and lots of blood.

With some investigation the boys found they had laid their bags in the middle of a dirt road. They moved their bags to what felt like a grassy area and got back into them. The rest of the night was uneventful. When it was light enough for the boys to find the skiff, they put their gear back into it and rowed back down the river.

The Hare Creek Bridge was a tall one, at least seventy feet. It was built of wooden timbers on the underneath side. Charley was trying to persuade Audrey into climbing out on the timbers with him, but she was not inclined to do so, because she was afraid of heights. So was Charley, but once you start something you have to finish it.

"Don't be a chicken!" he scolded, "Don't look down." he told her as she started to do so as she carefully stepped out on the timber. Audrey was pursing her lips, and holding her breath as she eased one foot forward on the beam. It was a twelve by twelve. She held on to the vertical one as long as she could and then the one that went up at an angle.

Audrey had to let go of it and go without anything for a short span to get to the next angled one. Charley held his breath until she had hold of the next beam and then she had a hold on him and it was a death grip she had. Audrey was stiff as a board. Her eyes were wide open, like she had seen a ghost. She was afraid to blink or take a breath.

Charley was facing Audrey and had one hand on a vertical beam. She had let go of the angled beam and now had a hold on nothing but him. Audrey's left foot had been right on the edge of the timber and had slipped a little. It panicked her. She had not lost her balance, but fear of doing so had caused Audrey to pull on Charley and he almost lost his balance.

Audrey's face was white. Charley knew he would have to get her to turn around. He knew he could go no further in either direction. Audrey did not want to turn around; she didn't want to do anything. Charley was afraid, but knew he had to do something. He couldn't get her to turn around, so he backed up until she could hang on to the vertical beam. Charley turned and pretended he was going to cross to the other side.

"Where are you going?" cried Audrey, frantically," do not leave me here alone!" "I have to get off the bridge," he answered as calm as he could," And you wont turn around." "You are not going to leave me here alone!" she exclaimed, defiantly. "You will have to turn around then," scolded Charley, not liking where he was either. Audrey gritted he teeth and turned around and he moved in behind her.

"Don't push!" she scolded as he touched her back. Audrey made her way across with him right behind her. "That was fun," she told him after she had jumped over to the ground. "Yeah," agreed Charley," We can do it again tomorrow." Audrey's eyes were wide as she shook her head in the negative.

The children walked down the bank to get to the beach. It was more like a cliff than a bank, but not very steep. They were able to climb down without anything to hang onto. Hare Greek, which was no more than ten feet across, except in a storm, was in a small valley and most of it was beach. The bridge spanned the valley. It went from the cliffs on one side to the cliffs on the other side. The creek emptied in the ocean.

The children took off their shoes to cross the creek; it was shallow, not more than a foot deep. They rolled their pants up and splashed across, laughing and kicking the water after they had crossed. Audrey kicked some sand on Charley and ran from him. Charley chased her, and he caught her by diving at her, catching her by her ankle. Audrey fell and they wrestled in the sand. Charley kidded her and ended up on top of her, between her legs. She giggled out of control.

"Stop!" she exclaimed and giggled some more. "Get off me!" She giggled some more. "You can't do it to me, I'm your sister." "I'd like to have a real girl in this position," retorted Charley. "I'm not a boy, you know," answered Audrey, petulantly. "I know," he replied," But you may as well be." He got off her and lay on his back on the sand.

"What would you have done if I had been another girl?" Audrey asked. She had started her period and was very curious about sex. Grace had told her next to nothing. She had explained her period to her and told her not to fool around with boys, or she would get pregnant, but she had already known that.

"I would have kissed her," replied Charley, amused at this line of questions. "And then what?" Audrey asked, and he thought a bit, "I would have felt her breast," Charley answered, and held back a chuckle. "And then what?" "I would have felt between her legs." His face was getting red. "And then what?" asked a relentless Audrey. "I would have pulled her under pants off," Charley replied, not certain that he would have. "And then what?" "I guess I would look at her stuff," he answered, sheepishly, his face getting redder as he was getting flustered.

"Would you take your pants off?" Audrey asked, and he giggled. "I guess I would have to if I was going to do anything to her." "What would you do next?" "I would screw her if she would let me." "Have you ever done it?" his sister asked, as if she would believe his every word. "Sure I have." he exclaimed. "What does It feel like?" she asked, squeezing his arm impatiently. "It feels good," lied Charley and he got up and ran. "You Lie!" exclaimed Audrey, as she chased after him, " You lie!" she repeated, "You ain't never done it." Charley laughed and ran all the way to the ocean. He had an erection and was embarrassed by it. Charley splashed in the water and before Audrey could catch up with him, he ran back up the beach, cleared the creek with one leap and ran all the way back up the cliff.

Charley was sitting, waiting for her when she got to the top. Audrey was out of breath, but he had got his back. Charley was playing with a caterpillar. The creature was climbing his fingers, bridging from one finger to the next. He wondered how caterpillars had sex.

"Come on Charley?" his sister pleaded, as she sat next to him, "Tell me the truth...Have you ever done it?" "No," Charley admitted, "But I would sure like to." "First you have to have a girl, you know," replied Audrey and she giggled. "I know," he agreed, and rose to his feet. He gave her his hand and pulled her to her feet. They walked hand in hand back to the house, quiet in thought, loving each other.

The Williams brothers lived in a very large, old house. It was a two storied, wooden structure with dormers on the upstairs bedrooms. The brothers had their bedroom on the upper floor. The boys lived with their parents, Zen and Velda. They also had a younger sister about Audrey's age. Her name was Abigail. She was tall, blond and very pretty. Abigail's eyes were blue and her features delicate. Her neck was long and slender and so were her legs. Her breasts were developing nicely, so Charley thought.

One night, Charley was staying overnight with the brothers. It was getting late when Charley heard Abigail tell her mother she was going to take a bath. The brothers told their mother they were going up to their room for the night. They motioned for Charley to follow.

The mother said she was going to the library. She was going to her library; she had enough books to be a library. She was an odd little person and she was a Rosicrucian. After the boys got into the bedroom and David closed the door, both brothers got a suspicious look on their face.

"Shhhh" whispered David, as he put his fingers to his lips. "Follow me," he whispered and the brothers went into their closet. They pulled the clothes back, exposing a small door on the wall. It opened to attic space, which was used for storage. There was not much storage there, but there was a lot of space.

Charley started to speak, but David motioned for him to be quiet. The brothers tiptoed further into the space and Charley followed. The light in the closet made enough light for them to see. David went to a cardboard box; he picked it up and moved it out of the way. He was on his stomach with his face to the floor sideways.

Charley could tell David was looking intently at something. He could also see he was trying to stifle a giggle, and his brother was having the same problem; his eyes were rolling lasciviously. With great effort David pulled his face from the floor. He motioned for Charley to take a look. When Charley looked at the spot on the floor, he saw that it was a small hole.

When he looked through the hole, he sucked his breath in between his teeth.

Charley had never felt so naughty and had never seen anything so beguiling. The hole was in the ceiling of the bathroom and he was witnessing Abigail taking a bath. She was in a tub full of bubble bath. Charley could not see much, but her feminine movements gave him an erection right away. The way she soaped her arms was lovely, but soaping her leg was even more exciting. She pulled one up, and washed her dainty foot, and then the other.

When Abigail rose out of the tub, he held his breath in anticipation of seeing even more. She had the prettiest rump he had ever seen and Charley wondered what it would be like to touch it. His erection became even more erect as she moved to a chair and sat on it. As Abigail pulled a foot up to dry it she revealed everything to Charley. His heart was in his mouth and his eyes bulged in an effort to see more, but there was no more to see. He had seen it all. Charley had seen her secret place, the cleft in her loins. Charley felt blessed above all boys.

Abigail was only about ten feet away, but he wished he could get closer, close enough to touch her. She started looking around, uneasy like. He sensed she could feel him looking at her and he felt ashamed. It was an effort to pull his eyes away from her. Every time he saw Abigail after that, he would blush, seeing her naked again, in his mind's eye.

The Williams had a puppy. He was black, with little, reddish eyebrows. His feet were the same color, causing him to look like he had socks on. He was a trusting little soul like most baby things.

David took half a peach, put it in a bowl and covered it with some of Zen's whiskey. He let it soak for a few days and fed the peach it to the pup. The pup got so drunk he could hardly stand up. The poor little tyke got sick and puked it up. He tried to eat it again, but Charley put a stop to it. He felt so sorry for him it put a lump in his throat.

The months went by and the only one it showed on was Audrey, She was starting to have a womanly form. Her body was getting curves that were pretty to look at. She had a short waist, but her legs were long and slender. Her feet were small, with a high arch, pretty, and most people's are not. Her bottom was nicely rounded and moved pretty.

One afternoon Charles senior was chopping wood by the woodshed, which was about a hundred feet from the house. Grace was visiting her mother and Charley was in the house building a model airplane. He was building the kind you put the plans on a table, pin the balsa strips to the diagram and then glue them together. After the glue dried one would have a section of the plane. When the sections were glued together, one would have the skeleton of the plane. Then the plane would be covered with paper and dope.

The sun was hot and Audrey was wearing shorts. They were tight and her cute little ass looked good. She had nothing to do. She couldn't talk to Charley while he was working on the plane because he had a one-track mind and there would be a good chance for him to cut himself if she did.

Audrey went out to watch her dad work. Charles had a bottle of whiskey behind the woodshed and he had drunk enough of it to make him horny and stupid. As Audrey was watching him cut wood he was watching her out of the corner of his eye. Charles was sweating profusely from the booze, heat and exertion. His loins were on fire and he was blinded by lust.

Charles had an erection and he had a compulsion to show it to Audrey. He went into the woodshed out of Audrey's sight. Charles unbuttoned his pants, pulled his swollen member out and played with it, trying to get rid of the lust, but making it worse. He called Audrey to come into the woodshed. Charles told her he had something to show her. He had his back to Audrey when she came in.

Charles had his undershirt off, tucked into his pants, hanging over his member. He turned around and took her by the hand, lifted his undershirt and put her hand on his swollen member. It was ugly and angry looking to her. She was aghast, shocked and frozen. He put his hand between her thighs and fondled her. She bolted like a frightened deer and ran for all her worth.

Charley heard Audrey bolt through the door. He heard her running up the stairs and then she was in the room. Charley had never seen his sister so upset. He could see she was afraid, but there was something else. Her face was flushed and she was sobbing. Audrey ran to Charley and he put his arms around her. She buried her face in his chest, sobbing, clinging to him. Charley hugged her to him, caressing her hair, trying to console her. After she had calmed some, he asked her what had happened.

"Daddy put my hand on his prick!" she exclaimed, with a bewildered look. Charley was aghast. What he had heard was incomprehensible. Charley was shaken, he even felt faint. His sister was trembling. Charley led her to the bed and they both sat on the edge of it. He couldn't think of anything to say. His mind was boggled. It was hard for him to believe his dad had done such a thing, yet he knew in his heart it was true, the evidence was shaking next to him. There was still a part of Charley that did not want to believe his father could do such a disgusting thing. "Just what did he do?" he asked his sobbing sister, a little defensively, almost like he felt guilty for asking.

"Oh, God!" she exclaimed and a shudder went through her, a shudder of revulsion. "He had his big cock out and he put my hand on it." She shuddered again, her eyes got wider as she continued. "I didn't know cocks were so big, and so ugly. Ugh! He squeezed my cunt and then I ran." Charley held her while she whimpered quietly. She had stopped sobbing.

Charley felt helpless, impotent, his rage burning his innards. He wished he could hate his father, but he could not, for hate was not in him, it was an emotion he just did not have. By this time Charley had found a release for his confused emotions and he was crying. Charley felt guilty for not hating his father. He was hurt to sickness.

"I will have to tell mother," Charley said it like it was a questionable thing to do. Audrey had not thought of it and the thought caused her more distress. She turned to Charley and started to reply. Her look was negative, but she said nothing. Audrey got a blank look. Her eyes were red and her face was streaked with tears.

The children heard the car door shut and then the engine started. The car drove out of the driveway and away. "Charles just left," said Charley. He would never call him father again. "You are safe now," he told his sister, "I am going after Mom." Audrey clutched him as he made a move to go. "It's alright," he told her, gently," He is gone and I have to tell mom what happened."

Audrey lay on the bed as Charley left the room. He went out the door and headed for Cap's place and met his mother about halfway. She was on her way home to find out where her husband had gone. She knew he had been drinking. When Charley met her he had a look on his face that caused her trepidation.

"What happened?" His mother asked and her face blanched as Charley told her. She ran the rest of the way to Audrey and Charley followed. When they got to the house Grace ran up the stairs and Charley followed. Audrey had heard them and she was standing, facing the door; waiting. Grace stopped when she saw her. Mother looked at daughter and daughter at mother. Silent words were said through their eyes and then they ran to each other's arms. For a long time they said nothing, they just cried. Charley cried, too. It was like the end of the world had come.

Charles never returned. He wrote Grace a letter telling how sorry he was. He asked her to ship his things to him in San Francisco. He had gone straight there and had signed up for a diving job in the South Pacific. Grace was crushed, for she had loved Charles dearly. And that was not all, he had left only a few hundred dollars in the bank and there was no job for her in Fort Bragg.

Grace wanted to get away from there, anyway. She had been married to Charles for eight years and wanted to forget him. Grace had spent some time in Eureka when she was a girl. They would go there and she would look for a job. The children were not happy to leave their new friends.

CHAPTER 4

Eureka was cold in the winter. Some board sidewalks were still around. Early in the morning they would have frost on them, making them slippery as cat poop. It was damp even when it wasn't raining. Trees were rarely planted close to a house because it would cause mildew on the inside wall.

There are few sounds as lonesome as a foghorn. It was not a new sound to Charley; there was one in Fort Bragg and Half Moon Bay. The sound is even more lonesome when one is lonely. Charley missed his friends; he missed Anna and her rosy cheeks and her flirty ways. Charley missed his grand parents, his school and the beach that had been so close.

As soon as they had moved into their upstairs apartment mother told him something. Charles was not his real father. Also, Charles had not adopted him. His legal name was not Charley Manchester it was Vincent Ricardo Cardoza. Charley missed his name.

Grace told him his real father was Castilian and his name was Fernando Cardoza. Grace told him his father was a merchant seaman. His mother also told him she wanted him to start using his real name immediately. She did not want to hear the name Charles ever again. She wanted to forget that name forever.

Changing his name seemed like an adventurous thing at the time and Charley went along with it. What else could he do? Implementing the change was not as easy as talking about it. It was difficult to use a new name. Charley had a hard time remembering to use it.

When his new teacher would call out "Vincent" he would forget it was he. He would sit like a dunce until the second call, or even the third. He finally got the hang of it and soon it was old hat. School was the most help in learning his real name. The girls all called him Vincent and the guys called him Cardoza. It was easy for Audrey, she only had to change her last name and she liked her new last name. She thought it had a romantic sound.

The apartment they moved into was not a bad one; it was just small; it was all Grace could afford. Having only one bedroom left Vincent on a cot in the kitchen. Some cockroaches sharing the space with him kept him from being lonely.

The front side of the apartment faced G Street. There was a view of rooftops from the living room widow. This room was small, with room only for a couch, easy chair, a floor lamp and a small coffee table. A floor furnace took up the rest of the wall space. The walls and ceiling were of vintage plaster of the cracked kind and painted many times, but not recently.

Vincent had his cot against the kitchen wall to save space. There was not much of it to be saved. And that was why it needed to be saved. One night, he felt something crawling on his chest. Half awake and flat on his back, Vincent reached up and touched the thing that had caused the sensation. Vincent awoke the rest of the way with a start. The thing on his chest felt awful and alien. He brushed the thing off his chest and jumped off the cot.

Vincent turned on the light; he was looking for whatever it was. He saw the grand daddy of all cockroaches and it was sprinting for a dark place. Roaches don't like the light; neither do vampires. It was the most ugly repulsive thing he had ever seen. He grabbed his shoe and clobbered it with the heel. He lifted the heel and the king of roaches quivered. Vincent hit it again and the king was juicy and dead. He scooped it up with a napkin and trashed it. Vincent never again slept with his bed against the wall.

Vincent liked the school he was going to. He was learning to smoke there. In the back of the school was a forest of pine trees. At recess and at the lunch hour, some of the guys would go there and smoke, among other things. Vincent became one the guys. He had tried smoking before. His mother had always smoked Camels and on some occasions he had stolen some out her pack. He hadn't liked smoking; in fact they had always made him dizzy. But now he had some incentive, a reason to learn how. He wanted to be like the rest of the guys and what could be wrong with that? After all, his mother smoked.

There was much talking, bragging and telling lies in the forest. They also told raunchy jokes and talked about sex. One of the things Vincent learned was one could catch the clap by screwing girls. If one caught the clap puss would run out one's dick and then it would rot and fall off. Most of the guys said they would take a chance, anyway.

With all this talking, bragging and lying there would sometimes be disagreements. Sometimes the disagreements would progress into violent activity. One of these times Jack broke his leg. Jack was an Indian kid and one of Vincent's new friends. Jack was tougher than shoe leather. He was short, stocky and dark. His hair was black and it was straight. Jack loved to fight, but he didn't look for trouble, it came looking for him.

Jack had a cute little sister. One of the guys made a remark about squaws, about how they just laid there when they were doing it. Squaw talk was fighting talk to Jack. Jack didn't hesitate, or anticipate, he just fisticated. Jack knew only two kinds of punches and they were both roundhouses. The other kid was bigger than Jack, but one of Jack's punches hit him on the side of his jaw. The punch knocked the kid dizzy, and he fell. He grabbed Jack and Jack fell with him.

Vincent was no more than six feet away and he heard Jack's leg break. It made a cracking sound, like a stick broken. It hurt Jack so bad all he could do was roll on the ground and moan. Some of the faculty came and put Jack on a stretcher. The forest was policed for a while and then went back to the way it had been.

Frenchy had long, black, wavy hair. He was small, slender and had dark flashing eyes. He liked the girls and the girls liked him. Frenchy had a temper and no one messed with him, not even the teacher. One teacher, Miss Thatcher, had rapped him on his knuckles with the edge of her ruler for something Frenchy had said. He socked her on the jaw with his fist. It knocked her on her behind. Miss Thatcher sat there for a while with her legs spread awry, looking foolish. Frenchy was kicked out of school for three weeks.

Frenchy seemed to be made out of rubber. When they played touch football no one could touch him. He was fast as greased baby poop and hardly anyone could catch him. And even if they could, it wouldn't do them any good. Just a split second before they could touch him, he would bend his back and head in another direction, with nothing touched but air.

Vincent and an Irish kid hit it off right away. Shaun Cooper was his name. He was about the same size as Vincent and had an easygoing way about him. Shaun had a twinkle in his dark, Irish eyes and mischief in his soul. He had wavy dark hair and an infectious smile.

Shaun lived in a rural area with his parents, an older brother and various livestock. The biggest of the stock was a cow named Florence. Florence liked to kick over the milk bucket every chance she got. The boys would get her mad by getting into a teat fight when they milked her and squirt milk on each other and her. That was when she would kick the bucket.

Shaun had an older brother named Mickey. He liked to fiddle with old cars and he usually had the ranch looking like a junkyard. Mickey also liked to drink spirited beverages and when he did, he liked to fight. When a fight didn't come to Mickey, he went looking for one. He was inclined to be foolish in other ways too. One time Mickey shot flies off the ceiling with a twenty-two rifle. They don't make big holes but they were big enough to make his parents unhappy. They took his rifle away from him and demoted him to a fly swatter.

The two boys made another friend and his name was Granville Jones. The name sounded like two last names. Who ever heard of a first name like Granville? All the guys were called by their last name, but not Granville. No one was kind enough to call him Jones. Granville was shorter than Cooper or Cardoza by an inch or so. He had light, thin hair and a big head. Granville had a Bogart grin on half of his face. He would say, "Yeah, sure," with a grin when he was skeptical over someone's line of blarney. Granville walked with a swagger and had a bit of a New York accent that made him sound like a hood. Granville lived with his parents and some younger brothers and sisters.

His parents owned the house they lived in. It was about ten city blocks from where Vincent lived. The house was a vintage structure covered with clapboard siding. The house had suffered from deferred maintenance for decades. The house sat forlorn looking on a corner lot. There was a garage at the side of the house. It looked as if it was built for a horseless carriage. There was a rope and tire swing in the back yard. Crab grass had conquered the yard.

The boys had a sometimes, friend. He was older and bigger. His name was Dirk and his father was a big wheel of some kind. His father entertained often with parties that required large quantities of social lubricants. He bought his booze by the case. His main booze was Puerto Rican rum. It was the color of piss. Dirk lifted a quart of the pissy looking stuff from his father's stash and brought it to the boys.

It was Vincent's introduction to hard booze, but not Shaun's. Dirk brought the booze to Vincent's place. Then the boys rode bikes to Granville's place knowing his parents would not be there until after five. Vincent didn't have a bike yet, so he rode on Shaun's handlebars.

The boys started drinking the rum in the back yard. Dirk didn't drink much; he was already familiar with the demon. The others got drunk in a hurry. They had not had the time or the opportunity to cultivate a tolerance. Vincent got so intoxicated he kept falling off the swing. He borrowed Granville's bike to go home, but was too, drunk to ride, and he was certainly too drunk to walk.

When Granville's father got home he gave the boys a lecture on the evil of demon rum. He put Vincent and Shaun in his car and took them home. Granville's father dropped Vincent off at the curb in front of Vincent's apartment building. The landlady saw it all. Vincent stood on the sidewalk as the car left. He tried his best to look normal.

Vincent had seen the landlady watching him through the curtain. Vincent tried to smile, but what manifested was a ludicrous leer. He tried to move his two left feet forward as well as he could and made it to the first flight of stairs. Vincent's feet thought the risers were lower than his eyes thought. He stumbled, banging his knee on the corner of the stair. He muttered a vile sentence. Vincent managed to get up and make it to the landing and through the front door. The effort had taken most of the oxygen from his brain leaving him befuddled.

Vincent had to climb the rest of the way up the stairs on his hands and knees to the landing to his door. He had a hard time with his key as he was trying to get it into the lock upside down. When he realized it he giggled. Vincent giggled some more as he tried to get it in right side up. He remembered something he had heard and it was a miracle he could remember anything. He repeated it.

"If there was a little hair around it," he giggled some more and continued, "I could find the hole." Nothing pleases a drunken boy more than to be crude. Vincent had a fit of giggles and fell to the floor. He giggled until he ran out of them and then he just lied there. He almost went to sleep, but came back to awareness with a start. Vincent took hold of the doorknob and pulled himself to his knees. He put the key in the lock and opened the door. The boy was pleased and amazed by his dexterity.

"Ah ha!" Vincent exclaimed and that was all he could put together. He went through the door and left it open, leaving his key in the lock. The drunken boy made it to his bed; he flopped on it and was unconscious as his face hit the pillow.

When Grace came home and found the door open, she also smelled the spirits he was exhaling. At first she was appalled and then indignant. She went quickly to her son and shook him. Vincent awoke to a world of discomfort.

"Son!" exclaimed the exasperated mother, "You have been drinking!" To Vincent, in his world of hurt, this seemed like an asinine thing to say and it made him scornful. "It didn't take a brain surgeon to figure that one out." Vincent retorted.

"Do you want to be like your father?" snapped Grace, without thinking. "I don't know," answered Vincent, scornfully," I never met the guy." Grace cooled, realized she was more fearful than angry, fearful her son would have the curse. "I don't want you to meet your father. He is a violent person and he has the curse, the curse I don't want you to get," answered Grace, fearfully, almost in tears.

"What curse?" asked her son, still in scorn, but now intrigued. "The Cardoza Curse!" she exclaimed," Most of your father's ancestors had it and you must not drink alcohol or you will have it. "What is this curse?" he asked, sobering some. "Genetic alcoholism," she answered," Your father's sister died from it and many of his relatives. And to make it even worse, there is much of it on my side of the family. Your uncle Horace is an alcoholic and if he won't stop drinking it is going to kill him. It killed your real grandfather. He was a drunken Welshman and he was violent just like your father."

"Cap is not my grandfather?" asked Vincent, surprised, and not happy about the news. "Only by marriage is he your grandfather; you have none of his blood and I wish with all my heart that you did because he is the best person I know." Grace was crying now, and her son was feeling guilty for causing her to do so. He was also feeling nausea caused by the rum.

"Promise me you will leave alcohol alone," pleaded his mother. Nausea made it easy. "I promise," he answered and went to the bathroom to vomit. Grace thought it good that he should suffer; it might be the only defense for the curse. After he finished vomiting, Vincent went back to sleep it off.

It was Vincent's night to go to the fights. He loved to watch the pugilist pound each other to a pulp. The last fight he watched the face of one of the fighters had got so bloody it became hard to see that it was a face. When Vincent awoke from his nap he felt close to being human again. Grace, feeling it was her responsibility to punish him for getting drunk, informed him he would have to miss his night at the fights. Vincent was in a foul mood; it is often caused by withdrawal from alcohol.

"Son of a bitch," Vincent muttered under his breath. Although Grace was hard of hearing, she almost always heard what she was not supposed to hear. She heard him and thought he had called her that. The disappointment and anger she had felt finding him drunk and her resolve to punish him for it dissolved and turned into hurt. It reflected in her face immediately and her tear ducts filled and overflowed.

Vincent was dismayed by what he had caused and he felt penitent. He apologized profusely and assured her he would never call her names; he could not call her names because he loved her more than anyone. After all the fuss she told Vincent he could go ahead and go to the fights. Vincent felt humbled by her goodness.

Dirk talked Vincent and Shaun into helping him roll a queer wino. The boys thought it would be all right being as the guy was a dirty queer. Queers shouldn't have any rights. That was what Dirk told them. Dirk told the boys he would talk the old queer into giving them all a blowjob. While he was doing it to one of them, he would clobber the guy in the head and they would take his money.

It turned out the old geezer was pretty tough. He wasn't any taller than Dirk, but he had a big frame with lots of meat on it, plus generous portions of fat. The old guy wore Frisco Jeans with wide suspenders to hold them up. His big belly hung out over his belt. He had a big head, a big nose and a big walrus mustache. The old guy's face was ruddy from too much wine.

Dirk and the boys followed him to his apartment, which was above a cafe. The stairs were steep and the old boy was huffing and puffing by the time he got to his landing. There was only the one apartment; his door was right at the landing. He unlocked his door and went in, the boys followed. The door opened to a kitchen, just like Vincent's. He pulled a bottle of red wine from his cupboard, opened it and poured himself a drink into a white cup. It looked like it might belong to the cafe below. The old guy offered the bottle to the boys, but they declined, not wanting any association with anything that had touched his lips.

Dirk must have made a mistake about the old duffer because he got indignant when Dirk made the lewd suggestion. Dirk hit him on the side of his head with his fist, but it didn't faze him. The old guy was stout as a bull. He tried to get hold of Dirk, but wasn't fast enough, lucky for Dirk. Vincent and Shaun fled the scene as fast as their feet would go. Dirk came running down the stairs after them, laughing all the way.

"Tough old son of a bitch wasn't he?" he commented, excitedly. Dirk was just a little too bad for the boys and they tried to stay away from him. But temptation is a powerful foe. Dirk taught the boys how to shop lift. Vincent knew it was wrong, but it was so exciting. The boys had dozens of cigarette lighters.

They would go into a store and look at lighters; the ones that came in a box, like the world famous "Zippo." They were usually stacked on a table or shelf. The boys would work as a team. One of the boys would pick up a box. He would pretend to read the label while the others were looking at something else. The boy with the box would watch the shopkeeper and when his eye went to the others, the boy would slip the lighter out of the box and into his pocket. The boy would then put the empty box back. The same method worked with a lot of other items. The boys had dozens of jack knives. And they never got caught shoplifting.

Grace had been saving money for Vincent. It was not an easy thing to do with the pittance she received for her labor in the diet kitchen at the County Hospital. The administration had tried to elevate her to a higher position. But she had declined, fearing she would not have enough time left for the children. Grace managed to save enough to buy Vincent the bike he had wanted. It was not new, but had been restored as good as new by the bike shop. It cost Grace forty-five dollars. It was a beautiful bike with balloon tires, whitewalls and now it was Shaun's turn to ride on the handlebars.

Shaun had ruined the front wheel on his bike. Shaun had ridden up the driveway of the Eureka Inn, going way too, fast. Vincent was on the handlebars. When they went back on the street they ran into the side door of a car. The car had a sheriff's sign on the door they hit. The deputy had been unhappy, but only enough to cause a lecture.

Vincent and Granville thought it would be nice and fun to get a front wheel for Shaun. They would have to steal it; it would be no fun to buy one and they had no money, anyway. Broad daylight was a fun time to do it, more daring. In front of the Eureka Theater, during an afternoon matinee, the boys pulled the evil deed.

Some foolish boy had left his bike in the rack with no lock on it. Granville parked his bike on the sidewalk side of the coveted bike and Vincent parked his on the street, partially blocking the view. With the tools he had in his back pocket, Vincent quickly removed the front wheel. The boys rode off with the wheel on Vincent's handlebars.

Shaun was elated about getting a wheel for his bike and couldn't wait to use it. He should have waited at least until the heat was off; or he could have painted it the same color as his other wheel. But Shaun just had to ride it to school the next day. The bike's former owner recognized his wheel. He had a mark on it to prove it. Vincent wouldn't let his buddy take the rap alone, so they both ended in front of the chief of police. The Chief looked hard as flint as he spoke.

"You hoods ever been in jail before?" he asked, in a bored monotone, with a bored look. Both boys were shaking in their shoes. "No, Sir," they replied in unison. "Do you want to go to jail?" asked the Chief in the same tone. "No, Sir," answered the "boys, meekly, in unison. "You guys sound like a couple of trained parrots," commented the Chief, wryly and he almost smiled, if he ever did that sort of thing. The boys just stood with their anus sucking in like a dying bird's ass while the Chief continued.

"Where did you boys learn to pull such a sophisticated caper?" the Chief asked. "We didn't learn it anywhere," answered Vincent, he was regaining his courage. "It just came naturally," smirked the Chief, "I ought to give you bread and water for life," he said sternly. "But your mother would come down here and cry and my wife would put me in the dog house." He stopped and pointed his finger at the boys. "But if I ever see you in here again I'm going to put you where there is no daylight." And his voice softened, "Go home to your moms."

Vincent was so relieved he almost relieved his bladder. He managed to hold it until he was shown where the john was by a rookie cop. "I thought our ass had had it," commented Vincent, trying to sound nonchalant. "You ain't the Lone Ranger," replied Shaun, and he laughed. "And I still don't have a wheel," he added. "I guess we better figure out a way to buy one," suggested Vincent. "You got that right," replied Shaun.

Around the corner from the building Vincent lived there was a store. The back of the store faced the back of Vincent's building. The exterior of the store was dilapidated due to years of deferred maintenance. All the paint had oxidized and peeled off, leaving the boards a dark, grayish color. The inside of the store was dark. Harry liked to keep the electric bill down.

Harry Orick was the owner and his only clerk. Harry's uniform was coveralls, the bibbed ones and a gray shirt. He wore the kind of half boots that poor farmers wore, with Cats Paw half soles.

Harry was an eccentric old geezer and his store reflected this quality. The store was strange and one could smell the strangeness. There was nothing alive in the store except Harry, and whoever walked in. What I mean is there is nothing in there that had died recently, like meat, fruit, or vegetables. There was nothing fresh.

Nothing in the store was in order. The only one who could find anything was Harry. You had to tell him what you wanted and he would find it for you. Most things were still in boxes they came in, usually cardboard. The penny candy was where you could see it, though, and was part of the strange aroma. Wooden floors, cardboard boxes, bulk grain, beans, pasta, gunny sacks, coal oil, leather, licorice and horehound drops were just some of the things that caused the strange aroma. It was strange, but there was something delightful about it. It was like a trip back in time.

Harry was strange himself, but he was a good strange. He never hurt anyone, or anything in his whole life; he just kept to himself. Harry probably had the first dollar he ever earned; it was probably a shrine. To save money he had a garden in back of the store. Harry spent a lot of time in his garden.

Harry had a cowbell hooked to a rope on the front door of the store. The bell would clang when someone entered the store. Harry used a long handled shovel in the garden. When the bell would clang, he would shove the shovel into the ground, leaving the long handle sticking up so not to have to look for it later.

For his thirteenth birthday, Grace bought her son a firearm, a twenty-two rifle. Only God knows what possessed her to do such a thing. After all, how much temptation can one expect a boy of thirteen to resist?

The shovel handle was sticking out of the ground and Vincent was alone. He was looking out the back window with his rifle in his hands. Vincent was looking at the shovel handle; he was possessed by its lonesomeness. The rifle seemed to raise its self and Vincent saw the shovel handle in his sights. Vincent watched it for a while, knowing he shouldn't do it. His finger squeezed the trigger slowly; it was working on its own, just like his heart.

Vincent was surprised when the rifle fired. He was delighted when the handle split right down the middle. He giggled and for a second felt pride for such a good shot, but the elated feeling was short lived. The bullet ricochet after it had split the handle and had crashed through one of Harry's windows. The bullet had spent its self in a hundred pound sack of flour. Harry shuffled out the back door in a hurry. He had a shuffle like Charley Chaplin's tramp. He was looking for what had broken his window. Out of the corner of his eye Harry saw Vincent pull the rifle away from the window and Harry was mad as a cheated whore.

Harry didn't turn Vincent in to the authorities, but did tell Grace. She wanted to pay for the window, but Harry wouldn't let her. Harry told Vincent he should pay for it if he ever got any money. Grace scolded Vincent and took his rifle away for two weeks. Grace had never been able to punish her children severely.

Once they had lived in an apartment in a wooden Victorian building in Oakland. The building was run down and in a poor neighborhood. It had a basement where Vincent and Audrey liked to play. It was kind of a secret place, with rooms and Vincent had a skeleton key for the doors. Most of the rooms were empty, but one had cardboard boxes and old newspapers.

One day it had been cold in the basement and Vincent had built a little fire with the newspapers so he and his sister could get warm. Of course he had been forbidden to play with matches. Vincent wasn't playing though; he had been building a fire to get warm. When the smoke had drifted up into the apartments there had been considerable excitement. The tenants and the fire chief had not been happy and Vincent's mother had been criticized.

"This will hurt me more than you," Vincent's mother had told him when she had spanked him and it had been true. She had laid him across her lap and she had spanked him with a paint stirring stick. A butterfly could have ridden on it in complete safety. Grace had cried, but Vincent had not.

After Vincent had his rifle privileges returned, he took the rifle to the beach. He saw a seagull resting on an abandoned piling that was sticking out of the sand. There had been a wharf there at one time. Vincent was a long way from the gull and the gull didn't seem that real. He aimed at the gull and squeezed the trigger.

The whole thing seemed unreal. He felt detached, somehow, until the rifle fired and then it was real. At first Vincent thought he had missed the gull and was glad he had. As he got closer he saw the bird was trying to puke up the bullet. The bird tried this for what seemed like a long time. Vincent felt awful as he watched the gull fall off the piling and die. Vincent's throat hurt with the pain of regret. He wished to God he hadn't done it, but nothing could be more final than death. Vincent picked up the gull. It was soft, warm and dead. Vincent cried as he dug a hole in the sand. He buried the bird. He walked home with his thoughts of death for a companion.

Shaun's brother had a bunch of old cars, but only one would run. The car was not complete, but it would run. It had no body, no doors and things like that, not even a windshield. This was unfortunate because the gravity tank had no lid to keep the gas from spilling. Whenever a hard bump was hit gas would splash on the passengers.

All that was topside was the front seat, dash and steering wheel and all the stuff that needed to make it go. Other than that, it was a good vehicle. Vincent wanted the car and Shaun's brother wanted Vincent's rifle. A trade was inevitable. It mattered not to Vincent that there were no legal papers for the car. A bill of sale was good enough for him. Vincent handed the rifle over to its new owner and the deal done. Vincent and Shaun got on the car; there was nothing there to get into. Vincent got on the pilot's seat.

Vincent had never driven his own car before. In fact, he had never driven any car before. While Vincent handled the Clutch brake and gas pedal, Shaun operated the gearshift. The boys drove off in a cloud of dust and shouts of glee.

Oh, God! What fun it is to drive your own car for the first time, especially when you have no windshield and the wind is in your face. And no driver's license, no plates on the car and no brakes, almost none.

"Holy Shit!" exclaimed Vincent, as he pushed in the brake pedal to the floor with no reaction from the wheels. How exciting it is to come to a stop sign and discover you have no brakes, well, almost none. Shaun pulled the emergency brake and one wheel stopped spinning. The car slid to a stop on the opposite side of the intersection. Lucky there were no other cars. An emergency brake was a good thing on this car, for every stop was an emergency.

The old car had a flat head, six-cylinder engine. One of the spark plug wires had wiggled off the plug. The engine was greasy, and dirty. The car hit a hard bump. Gas splashed out of the gravity tank onto the hot engine head. The loose spark plug wire danced across the head leaving a trail of sparks. The sparks ignited the gas and the fire from it ignited the grease.

Shaun pulled the emergency brake and the boys waited for the car to stop. There was no traffic and no water, so the boys urinated on the fire. They had to stand on the car to do it because they couldn't urinate high enough. It made an awful skunk like smell and didn't put out the fire. Finally, Vincent had to smother the fire with his Jacket, ruining it.

Much to Vincent's surprise and vexation, his mother did not like his car. She did not like it at all. In fact, she had the gall to tell him he had to give the car back. He had nothing to say about it. His mother was a most unreasonable woman at times.

One night the boys broke into an old movie theater. They went through a window in the alley. It was dark and creepy. Granville turned on his penlight. This was one of many penlights the boys had gained possession of, illegally. The boys wanted to get into the camera room to see what made it work. They couldn't gain access to the room because the door was locked.

There was a stairwell to the balcony on both sides of the building. This created a space between the balcony and the window to the camera room. The space was about six feet across with the stairwell below. It looked a long way to the bottom of the well. They searched, and found a board about ten inches wide, and eight feet long. Vincent laid it across the balcony to the window.

The boys were exhilarated; doing bad things was such fun. Vincent was the first to go across. It was fearful with all that space below, but fun. It was a good thing the board was two inches thick; a one inch one could have broke. When Vincent went through the window into the camera room it was dark. Granville was holding the light on Shaun.

Vincent watched Shaun come across. Granville had no one to hold the light for him. He stuck the light in his mouth and started across. Granville was coming across just like the other boys had, on his knees and sliding his hands ahead of him on the board. He got a sliver in his right thumb.

"Ouch!" he exclaimed, expelling the light from his mouth. The light made a twirling pattern as it fell to the bottom of the stairs. It bounced, and went out. "Holy Shit!" yelled Granville, "I can't see anything." He was about half way across and it was dark as it gets. The others were just as blind and it was quiet as a cemetery. "I ain't never seen it so dark," claimed Shaun, almost in a whisper. "Me neither," agreed Vincent. "It's a hell of a lot darker out here!" wailed Granville, with quivering lips.

Granville decided he would go back so he could retrieve the light. He started moving backward, but his fear was interfering with his equilibrium and he lost his balance and fell. Granville screamed and the boys heard a "Thud" followed by a "flump, flump" as he rolled down the stairs.

"Are you alright?" yelled Vincent, and the two boys stretched their ears, but all they heard was silence. "Don't screw around;" hollered Shaun. They listened and heard a giggle. Granville had been feeling himself, frantically, to find out if he was all right. It is hard to do in the dark.

After Granville decided he was okay, he started crawling around looking for the light. After about five minutes he found it. Granville turned it on, but nothing happened. He cursed, and jiggled the switch, but it was no good. By tapping it against his heel the light came on. Granville sighed with relief and headed back up the stairs. He remembered the board and looked for it.

"Look for the board," yelled Vincent, when he saw the light. "I found it," answered Granville. He took it to the top of the stairs and put it in place. "Are you still coming across?" questioned Shaun, "I sure as hell am," he replied, and started across. "Don't swallow the light," joked Vincent. "You are dumber than I thought," yelled Shaun, and he laughed. "He is not dumb," claimed Vincent," He just seems that way because his parents are first cousins."

"Stick your head up your ass," retorted Granville. "It is already there," blurted Shaun, and laughed.

Granville got across, and through the window. They found the projector and pulled some film out of it. They cut a strip off to experiment with. Shaun lit a match and they found that it burned quickly. They burned film until they tired of doing it. The boys made it back across the bridge and out of the theater without getting caught.

Vincent didn't see much of his sister while they lived on G. Street. He went to school with her in the morning, but she was in a lower class. After school she went her way, which was usually home, and Vincent went his way. Grace saw the handwriting on the wall. She was losing control of her son. Grace knew if she did not get him away from the urban life and back to the rural, he would be getting into trouble.

Grace had saved a few dollars and much to her surprise, Charles had sent her some money. Grace decided to return to Fort Bragg where her parents could help her. Grace told her children and Audrey was glad to go back. Vincent hated leaving his new friends, but was glad to return to his old ones and Anna. And then it dawned on him; he would be going back with a different name.

CHAPTER 5

As luck would have it, the old house they had lived in had been vacant for a long spell because of a probate problem. The owner had died and the heirs had gone to battle, but the battle was over and Vincent and his family moved in. The house still had only two bedrooms, but now Grace and Audrey were able to share a room with twin beds. Vincent now had his own bedroom for the first time in his life. Both bedrooms were on the top floor. The house had been redecorated. Sharing a room with Audrey had made it possible for Grace to live in the house without haunting memories of Charles.

Grace found work right away in a cafe at Noyo Harbor. The cafe was on the south side of the river, about half way down the narrow serpentine road that went from Highway One down to the harbor. The road ended at a fish processing plant and named "Paladinis." The fisherman who didn't sell on the other side of the river sold to this plant.

On the road between Paladinis and the cafe there were other small buildings. There was not room for anything else because there was a steep embankment alongside most of the road. Some of the buildings housed business, like a bait shop, a marine hardware store, but most of them were just cabins or storage buildings.

In one of these cabins lived a fisherman. His name was Henderson Grover, but most everyone called him "Doc." No one seemed to know why he was called that. If asked, Doc would give a shy, half a grin. Doc was hiding some bad teeth with the other half.

Doc was about an inch shy of six feet tall, but he looked shorter. He walked a little stooped and was tired looking. Doc always wore flat soled, hand made moccasins. They were the only shoes that were comfortable to him. This was because of the shape of his feet. He had a very high instep; one like you would expect to see on a Vargas Girl pin up, not on a fisherman. Doc always wore Levi jeans and a shirt with a sweatshirt under it. He covered his head with a navy type skullcap.

Doc was thirty-five years old and a bachelor. He looked older because of his posture and his hair, which was unusual. Doc's sideburns had grayed the opposite way of most men. The bottom end of his hair was black to the top of his ears and gray from there up. The top of his hair was blond and gray mixed. Doc had a big head with a handsome face. He did not have a single wrinkle on his face; it was smooth as a baby's behind. But Doc was in poor health. His diet had been poor for decades.

Doc had an electric hot plate in his cabin, but all he ever fixed was coffee, eggs, potatoes, bacon and hot cakes. Doc had a two burner stove on his boat, but only made coffee on it. The boat was forty feet long and he fished for anything he could sell. The name of the boat was "The Papoose." The boat was too big to work alone so Doc always had to have a partner. He had made a mistake by building a bigger boat than the old one. Doc had made more money with the smaller boat.

Doc was coming to the cafe where Grace worked almost every day. He had started for his stomach's sake. Doc had been plagued by indigestion for many years. His panacea had been Arm and Hammer Baking Soda. It didn't help much, but he took it anyway. The doctor had told Doc a better diet would help him.

Doc had been stung by an early love and it had turned him against the weaker sex and romance. But Grace was different. Even though Doc had found out Grace had been married twice and had two children, he could still see her innocence and lack of guile. Doc had started coming to the cafe for his stomach's sake, but he was now coming for his heart's sake. Doc was sweet on Grace, but he was awfully shy.

Doc never drank anything stronger than coffee and he didn't give a hoot about nightlife. Doc didn't even go to movies; he claimed they gave him a headache. He had migraine trouble.

Doc loved nature and was an avid sportsman. He loved to fish and hunt. Doc loved all sports, especially baseball. Doc had wanted to be a professional player, but his father had denied him; He had told him it was the work of the Devil. And that was not all, Doc had a beautiful singing voice and that was more of the Devils work.

Doc was a new kind of man for Grace. Her other men had been heavy drinkers, party animals. This newness made Doc very attractive to her. He was so new, so good, and almost too good to be real. And Doc didn't even swear. The worst word that ever came out of his mouth was "Shoot," and he had to be mad to say that. Even then he said it under his breath.

But Grace was already dating another fisherman. He was not handsome like Doc, but he did have more money. Goldy was what he was called. What kind of name is that for a grown man? And he did drink like a fish. Goldy liked to party, but he did have a beautiful home in Eureka.

Grace was ready for a change. One night Doc asked her out for a drive. She was excited about it, but her children were not. They both liked Goldy and he was a lot of fun, plus he had a lot of money, a big boat and a nice house in Eureka. But Grace didn't give a hoot about money, or a fancy house.

Doc picked Grace up in his old Plymouth coupe and drove her to the beach. They talked for a while and then he sang to her in his soft, sad voice. After that she knew she wanted to spend the rest of he life with him. In all her life no man had ever sang to her. Grace might have swooned if she hadn't been sitting down.

After Doc brought her home they sat in the car and talked. Goldy was waiting in hiding for them. He had parked his car up the road, and had waited in the dark. Goldy sneaked up to the driver's side of the car. Doc had his window down and Goldy socked him on the side of his jaw. Doc jumped out of the car and gave Goldy a thorough thrashing. What a hero. Grace never heard from Goldy again and never would have been too soon.

Going back to his old school with his new name was a day of stress for Vincent. He had concocted a story, though. At roll call he waited with trepidation for his new name to be called. It seemed like it was taking forever and he was sweating it.

"Vincent Cardoza," called the teacher. Vincent gulped and raised his hand, but nothing came out of his mouth. Vincent felt naked as eyes that knew him as Charley stared at him. His fellow students in the hallway surrounded Vincent and one of them was Anna. "Charley?" she asked with disapproval," Why did you change your name?" "I got in trouble in Eureka," answered Vincent, with a red face," I had to change my name to escape prosecution." "What kind of trouble?" asked Anna and all the other children. "I swore to my mother I would never tell anyone," replied the now mysterious Vincent. That was all he would say on the subject and had to repeat it many times. Vincent was a mystery for a while and he liked it, but it didn't last for long. The interest of children is a finite thing indeed.

Vincent still had a crush on Anna, along with many other guys, but he never really tried to get anywhere with her and it was not because he didn't want to. He knew it would be in vain. Vincent believed she was out of reach. She was so gorgeous. Anna came from a wealthy family and she still had the older, bigger boyfriend. Also, he had a Buick convertible.

Vincent had no real concept about girls. The only girl he ever knew was his sister and sometimes she was a mystery. He had not a clue as how to talk to girls and he felt inadequate around them. Vincent had a tendency to put girls on a pedestal. That was where he had put Anna; he had put her even higher, in an ivory Tower.

Vincent was especially moronic about girls he thought were nice girls. He believed they were pure as the driven snow. Vincent could not believe they had nasty thoughts like he had. He could not believe they had fantasies about having sex. Vincent had them all the time. He had even had wet dreams and wished he could have them any time he wanted. Vincent had even tried to will them.

One day Vincent ran into Anna at the movies. It was a Saturday matinee. She was sitting with some girls and he sat next to her. They whispered about this and that through the movie. Vincent felt amorous and wanted to kiss her, but had no idea how to go about it.

"What would you do if I tried something with you?" Vincent whispered to Anna, feeling supremely stupid after doing so. "Like what?" she whispered. "I don't know," he whispered, blushing, "Guess." "Put your hand up my dress," Anna whispered and giggled. She was way ahead of him, as most girls are. Vincent was flabbergasted. He gulped before he blurted. "Oh, No!" he struggled with speech," I would never do that to you!" What a disappointment that must have been for her? No girl wants to wait that long. All Vincent had on his mind was kissing her. This sudden mind bender had emptied his head and he had ended up doing nothing.

Later, Vincent wondered if she would have let him put his hand up her dress. Then he wondered what he would have done if she had let him. He wondered for quite awhile what it would be like to have his hand up Anna's dress and this kind of thinking quickly caused a swelling in his plumbing.

One weekend, Grace and Doc went to Reno and tied the nuptial knot. Doc's brother, Max, a retired naval officer, was best man. Lilly, his beautiful Hawaiian wife was also there for the ceremony.

Much to Vincent's consternation, on the next day, Doc moved in with Grace. He moved right into her bedroom and Audrey had to move out. What supreme gall. Vincent did not want this guy sleeping with his mother. He did not want to think about what he was doing besides sleeping. What a horrible picture that conjured up for him.

It was because of these kinds of thoughts that Vincent and Doc did not get along well from the start. It had not mattered to Audrey, she just accepted the change and adapted to it. Audrey did enjoy a good conspiracy, though and every time she had a chance to help Vincent conspire against Doc, she would do it.

Doc had a bottle of premium whiskey a friend had given him years ago and Doc had never broken the seal. He had saved it for a special Occasion. Vincent broke the seal with a razor blade and the cut was close to being invisible. The children drank some of it and added water to make it full again. Vincent turned this into a repeated activity. He even gave some of his friends a drink and the bottle was losing its natural hue.

Doc's friend, the one who had given him the whiskey, came for a visit and it was time to bring the bottle out. Right away the color of the bottle was noticed and Doc's face also changed color. After he inspected the seal, he yelled for Vincent. The threatening yell had sent Vincent out the back door. He walked to The Harbor Inn and spent the night with Paul. Doc gave him the silent treatment for a few weeks.

Doc didn't have an ornery bone in his body, but when Vincent would talk back to his mother, Doc would growl at him just like his dog, Snuffy Smith. Snuffy wanted to be human; he would copy Doc. When Doc would take him for a ride, Snuffy would sit up on the seat and pretend he was a man. Snuffy would watch Doc out of the corner of his eye and would copy Doc's moves. When Doc looked straight ahead, so would Snuffy. If Doc looked out the door window, so would Snuffy. If Doc would raise an eyebrow, so would Snuffy.

Snuffy was better company for Doc than most people. He never argued with Doc. Snuffy didn't always agree with Doc. For instance, if Doc would go somewhere without taking him, Snuffy would turn his back on him when he came home. Snuffy would shun him like a scorned woman. His eyes would get red with resentment. This attitude could last for hours, or end in a flash if Doc would say, "Let's go boy."

When Doc would speak to Snuffy, Snuffy would raise an eyebrow and nod his head in agreement. Snuffy was black with red spots above his eyes that looked like eyebrows. It was uncanny the way the dog understood. He could make you feel stupid. You could say something to him that you thought was reasonably intelligent and Snuffy would raise that eyebrow, curl his lip and smirk at you like you had said the dumbest thing in the world.

Snuffy copied Doc and Doc copied Snuffy. That must have been how Doc learned to growl. When something angered Doc, he would growl and a message would follow. There is no telling where Doc learned to talk, but he did not learn it from Snuffy. Vincent did not like it when Doc growled at him. After all, he was just his mother's lover; he had no jurisdiction over him. Vincent discussed this reasoning with Audrey and she totally agreed. When it came to a showdown, though, he was usually meek, but not always.

Snuffy and Doc had a model A Ford they used for hunting. It had fat tires and was a coupe with a rumble seat. Doc did the driving and Snuffy did the hunting. Snuffy had not learned to drive; he was waiting for Doc to teach him. Anyway, it was taking all of Snuffy's time to teach Doc how to hunt.

Doc had hotcakes for breakfast every morning and so did Snuffy. Snuffy loved hotcakes and he loved to save one for later. He would take one outside, and bury it. Audrey decided she would tease Snuffy. She watched out the window to see where he would bury it. She watched him bury it and then went out and dug it up. Snuffy's eyes got red with anger.

He was smart as a quiz kid though and she only got away with it twice. After that he buried the cake where he could not be seen from the window. You had to get up early in the morning to fool Snuffy Smith.

Audrey had a new girl friend and her name was Sally Blake. She was the same age as Audrey and she was a pretty girl. She had soft, green eyes and curly hair that was a light color, but not blond. She was well developed for her age. Voluptuous describes her better. Cupid pulled a double whammy and stuck an arrow in the heart of both Sally and Vincent.

Sally started staying overnight with Audrey on Friday nights. Since Vincent and Audrey now had to share a room, he had to sleep on the couch downstairs when Sally was there. One night before going up to the bedroom with Audrey, Sally whispered to Vincent that she would come back down after Audrey went to sleep.

Sally was not bashful like Vincent; she had been flirting with him from the start. He waited for her with breathless anticipation. She came barefoot and he did not hear her. In her nightgown Sally sat next to him. He was lying on the davenport.

"I told you I would come," Sally whispered. Vincent was flustered by her nearness, her perfume. "I didn't know if you would come," was all he could say, for his mind had deserted him. "I told Audrey that I like you," she told him," Do you like me?" "I do!" Vincent exclaimed, after gulping. She was moving faster than his mind.

"Do you think I'm pretty?" Sally asked, coyly. "No," he blurted and it had just rolled out of his mouth and then he was flustered, for she was speaking before he had been able to finish. "You don't think I'm pretty?" she asked with dismay. "No," Vincent blurted," I think you are beautiful." He could not believe he had been able to say it. His face burned as the blood rushed to it. Sally laughed with relief.

"That's even better," she replied," Would you like to kiss me?" No grass growing under her feet. "I would," Vincent answered with his voice going through the change. The lamp was low, but Sally could still see him blush. Vincent was clumsy, but they managed to kiss. Once their lips met the fire of passion was ignited. She put her tongue in his mouth and French kissed him.

This was a new and exciting experience for Vincent. As they got familiar with each other Vincent got bold and French kissed her. This boldness was what Sally had been after. As Vincent's passion bloomed his exploring instinct came forth. His right hand moved to her breast. Vincent was surprised; her breast was softer than he thought they would be.

Sally's gown was thin; it was almost like she was naked. He could feel the heat of her body through it. He felt her nipples; he could feel them harden as he fondled them. His loins were on fire and he did not know what to do next. She got tired of waiting.

"Would you like to put you hand inside my gown?" she asked, with feigned timidity. "I would," he replied, so flustered his hands were shaking. Her gown was loose at the shoulder and his hand went under it. Her flesh was soft and warm, her skin unbelievably smooth. She squirmed under his hot hand. "Have you ever done it before?" she asked out of the blue. She was way ahead of him. "Done what?" he asked, dumb as a stone. "Made love?" she asked and he choked and coughed. He had not expected such a question. "Well, Ahhh, no not yet," he blurted, wishing he had said something else, anything.

They had turned the lamp off, but their eyes had become accustomed to the darkness and they could see each other. Vincent could see that while he had been feeling her breast, Sally's gown had worked its way up her legs and he could see her panties. Vincent had a one-track mind; he could not concentrate on two things at once. His hand was on her breast, but his mind was further south on her torso. His hand had quit doing what it had been doing.

"What's wrong?" Sally asked, missing the stimulation. Vincent couldn't tell her he had been staring at her panties. "Oh, Ahhh, Nothing," he blustered, and then he got brave." I was looking at your legs," he lied and this gave her pleasure. Sally looked down at herself and saw that her panties were showing and this did not bother her, not in the least.

"Do you like what you see?" she asked, demurely, which she was not. "I do," Vincent replied, not knowing what else to say. "You can touch me there if you want to," Sally offered with hope. "I do," Vincent answered, with his heart in his throat and his hand on the move. Sally's thighs parted as his hand moved from her knee, up. A magnetic force moved his hand up her leg, one that had been programmed by the genetic code. Sally moaned with pleasure as he moved his hand up the inside of her thigh. He trembled with anticipation, as his hand got closer to the apex of her thighs. She was on fire with the anticipation of him touching her where he shouldn't be touching her.

As Vincent's fingers touched her where he shouldn't, his pulse was throbbing in his ears. She moaned with desire and lay back on the couch. Vincent was in the way so he got on the floor facing Sally and continued exploring. He put his fingers inside her panties and touched her. She arched her body to his fingers and he pulled her panties down some to facilitate his exploring. Vincent's hand went under her and squeezed her ample bottom. Her thighs closed on his hand,

"Are you going to do it to me?" she asked, breathlessly. "If you want me to," Vincent replied. "I do," panted Sally," I want you to." He replied and pulled her panties down the rest of the way and then off. She opened her thighs for him and he touched her. "I want to see you," Sally whispered. Some of the blood left Vincent's loins and went to his face as he stood and she pulled down his shorts. His family maker sprung out as hard as it would ever get.

"Oh, Goodness " she exclaimed as she felt him, "I hope you know how to use it." Vincent got between her thighs on his knees. He felt her thighs against his. He wasn't sure how to get it in and the sofa pillow wasn't very stable under them. Vincent fumbled some and then she helped him in. It was amazing to Vincent that her body could be so hot inside. He couldn't believe it was happening. He was actually having sex with a beautiful girl. The wonder was almost erased by the overwhelming sensation and fervency.

Sally was moaning and moving with him. She wanted him in further so she wrapped her legs around him and pulled him in. Their fervor was getting him to his orgasm quickly and then a light came on upstairs. It was difficult to stop, but they had to; they were afraid of getting caught. They dressed as fast as they could, afraid someone would come down the stairs. They waited in silence; their fear was cooling their passion and the magic of the moment was gone. They sat for a time in silence, holding hands.

"I know a boy who was awful hot," Sally whispered," And a girl who was in heat." It sounded asinine to Vincent. "Are you sorry?" he asked, wondering if she was ashamed and if she would want to do it again. "No," Sally replied," But it was a little embarrassing." "Are you ashamed?" he questioned, feeling some himself. "A little," she answered," but only because I thought we would be caught with our pants down," and she giggled. "Do you want to try again sometime?" Vincent asked. "As soon as possible," she replied, and giggled again. "Me too" answered Vincent with a sigh.

The next night the children met at the movie theater. They sat in the last row of the balcony. They saw little of the double feature. Vincent had his hand where it shouldn't be most of the show. By the time the movie was over Sally was as hot as a two-dollar pistol and Vincent might have been even hotter.

Sally took Vincent on a short cut to her house. She led him down an alley and stopped in front of a garage with a door that opened to the alley. The moon was bright. Searching her face in the moonlight, he asked why they had stopped? "It's my neighbor's garage," Sally answered, as she swung the door open," We can go in here for awhile." She pulled him into the garage. An old Buick was parked, a black one.

"I'm cold," Sally told Vincent," Let's get in the back seat for a while before I go home. After they got in the Buick they started where they had left off at the movie. While he loosed the buttons on her blouse, she was doing the same to his pants. She was faster and had him in her hand. She gave him a squeeze. "I like the way it feels," she told him and giggled. "I like the way you feel it," he answered as he moved it in her hand. "Stop that!"

she ordered, "Wait till you get it in."

It was a frenzy getting their clothes off in the car, but they finally got organized so they could do what they desired to do. They went at it furiously; they did not want to be stopped again. "OH God!" she exclaimed, through clenched teeth. She squeezed her legs around him. She sucked her breath in between closed teeth, making a hissing sound as she went into orgasm. Vincent felt like she was sucking his toes inside out as he went into his. They lay still for a while; they were getting their breath back.

"I didn't know it would feel that good," Sally whispered, a little embarrassed by her fervency. "Me neither," Vincent replied, still in her, losing his erection. He flexed. She moved her pelvis, and giggled. "Stop that" Sally pleaded. "Why?" Vincent asked, doing it again. "It feels funny," she told him and giggled. Vincent pulled out of her, limp and got out of the uncomfortable and ridiculous position. They both moved to a sitting one. It was light enough from the moonlight for them to see. She looked at his shrunken appendage and giggled.

"You shrunk," she teased and Vincent covered himself with his hand. He started to dress, "Won't it come back?" Sally asked in a teasing manner. "I guess so," he answered, a little perplexed. "Don't you want to wait and see?" "Why?" he asked. "So we can do it again," Sally replied and laughed. "Do you want to have a baby?" he asked, ruefully. The thought had never entered her empty head.

"Oh, God!" Sally exclaimed," What If I do?" "I hope you don't," Vincent answered. "But what if I do?" she asked with dismay. "I don't know," he replied, helplessly, "We are not old enough to get married." "Would you marry me if we were old enough?" she asked. "I guess so," he replied, with his brain out of gear. "You guess so!" Sally exclaimed with dismay," you guess so?" "I would. I would," he answered, hurriedly.

"Do you love me?" she asked, worriedly. "I do," Vincent, replied, after catching himself; he had almost answered, "I guess so." "I love you," Sally told him and kissed his lips. "I'm glad," Vincent answered and returned her kiss.

They finished dressing inside the car. It was awkward and they helped each other. The stimulation caused arousal on his part and she squeezed him. "You keep that thing in your pants," Sally ordered and the children finished dressing. They walked toward her house holding hands, stopping often to kiss, not wanting to get there, to separate.

They were joyful with their new intimacy, awed by it, fearful of its possible consequence. Sally had just finished her period a few days before there love making. It was a long wait before she knew if she would miss the next one. It did come late and they were relieved.

The next Friday night Sally stayed overnight with Audrey. She came down to Vincent after Audrey went to sleep. They smooched and soon

Sally was so aroused she forgot her fear of getting pregnant. But while Vincent was inside of her searching for delight she voiced her fear in a whisper and it caused him to lose his potency. "What's the matter?" she asked, as she felt him go limp. "I don't know," Vincent replied, ashamed of his impotence. He shrunk and came out of her.

It happened every time after, because he could feel her fear even if she didn't state it. It was frustrating and they started to avoid each other. Then it was embarrassing when they met and soon they stopped. Puppy love doesn't usually tolerate such stress.

CHAPTER 6

Vincent had lost his first love. He now had to find new ways to expend his energy. While consorting with Sally, he had neglected his friends, so he went back to them and they became creative in sowing a garden of trouble. David and Vincent were walking to the harbor from the Inn after visiting with Paul. They saw a couple of bikes parked under the bridge in tall grass. The boys were tired of walking. They both knew better, but they borrowed the bikes, anyway. The boys who owned the bikes saw them. Not being told of the borrowing, the boys assumed their bikes were being stolen. They yelled, but the two thieves pretended not to hear.

Doc had to drive Vincent and David all the way to Ukiah to go to court. It was summer and a hot day. Vincent had poison oak on his face and the itching was vexing him to no end. The judge gave the boys a lengthy lecture and put them on probation for a year. He warned them not to get into any more trouble during that time, and to stay away from each other.

Two weeks later the boys, Vincent, David, Richard and Jake Mcklasky were bored. Jake had an old car, a rag top convertible and the top was a rag. Jake was a few years older than the boys and he was what is called "street smart." The boys were driving around the harbor when they saw a for sale sign on a tavern. The tavern was in the flats toward the jetty. The building was round, with a flat roof. It had closed and was out of business.

The boys wondered if anything was left in the place. They decided they would return after dark and investigate. The boys drove down to the jetty and threw some rocks at the ocean. It didn't take long for them to tire of that. It wasn't like throwing rocks at windows. The rocks went "plop" in the ocean. Rocks through a window made a fine crashing sound, something one could get their teeth in.

"Get over on your side!" exclaimed Jake at Vincent. He had let

Vincent drive his car to Caspar, a wide spot in the road, south of Noyo on Highway One. The road is narrow and serpentine. Vincent was taking his half out of the middle. Right after Jake had yelled, Vincent went around a blind curve, taking his half out of the middle. Coming the other way was an old man doing the same thing. They came near to exchanging hood ornaments. The boys were on the ocean side of the road and almost went off the side of an embankment. Vincent pulled over and stopped, his heart was stuck in his throat. He laughed, excitedly, after he had regained his breath.

"God, this is such fun!" Vincent exclaimed, looking over at Jake, who was sitting next to him. He perceived by his expression that Jake thought otherwise. His face was pale. "I would like to be old when I die," complained Jake, with a sort of snarl. "Would it be alright with you if I drive?" There was a trace of contempt in his voice.

Vincent didn't answer. He just vacated the car and walked to the front of it. Jake slid over to the pilot's place. Vincent turned his back to the car, dropped his drawers and mooned the pilot. The top was down. David and Richard were in the rumble seat. "Nice ass," commented Richard and he stood for a better view.

"You are a crude individual," commented David, who also stood. "Get back in the car you moron!" exclaimed Jake and he laughed. Vincent ran over to the passenger's side and climbed in without opening the door. "Do you see that square thing with the handle on it?" asked Jake. "You mean the door?" asked Vincent. "It is a door, isn't it?" asked Jake," What do you think it is for?" "To keep me from falling out," retorted Vincent. "You got shit for brains," Jake informed Vincent. "Birds of a feather flock together," retorted Vincent. Jake raced the small, flat head V-8 then popped the clutch and peeled out. The spray of gravel and dust combined with the smell of burning rubber in their noses.

It was cloudy and cold. The top of the car was a rag and Jake never used it. He had a coat on, but the boys did not have theirs with them. Vincent suggested they drive up Simpson's Lane. It was about five miles east from the ocean. It was usually warm there and there were apple orchards. Jake drove there and up the Lane until the sun was out and it was warm, almost hot.

Jake parked next to an apple orchard. The boys went over the fence. It was nothing but old cross bar timbers of cedar. The orchard looked neglected, with ripe apples on the ground. The apples were small, but sweet. One had to watch for worms, though, for they also like ripe apples. It is not good to find half a worm in an apple you are eating.

It was warm and good in the orchard. The boys lay on a soft rug of leaves made by many seasons of leaves that had fallen to the ground obeying Newton's law. It was inevitable that the boys would start thinking and talking about sex. "Let me tell you virgins about sex." bragged Jake," I have been screwing girls ever since I discovered my prick was more than a pee-pipe."

"I am not a virgin," exclaimed Richard. "Me neither," added David, with not as much conviction. Vincent held back, he did not want to talk about Sally. He didn't even want to think about her because it still hurt. "How about you?" questioned Jake, and the other boys stared at Vincent, waiting for his answer. He tried to answer, but Jake didn't give him a chance.

"You ain't never seen a cunt in your whole life!" "That's a dammed lie!" retorted Vincent, indignantly. "What does one look like?" asked Jake, mocking. "It just looks like a cunt," answered Vincent. "See, you don't know!" exclaimed Jake and he laughed out loud and the other boys joined him. "A cunt is a cunt," explained Richard," And nothing else looks like one." "It looks like lips pointed the other way," added David and they all laughed. "And smells like tuna," added David "Ugh!" exclaimed Jake," What kind of tuna have you been eating?" The boys were quiet for a while after that demonstration of obscenity. They were all trying to think of something outrageous to say.

"I'll bet my prick is the biggest," bragged Jake, "Twice as big." "That is bullshit!" exclaimed Richard. "Want to bet?" asked Jake. "I'll bet." "How much?" asked Jake," And make it easy on yourself, for you are going to lose." "Five bucks," answered Richard, indignantly. "Put your money where your mouth is," ordered Jake. "Put your prick where your mouth is", retorted Richard. "He would have to be a contortionist to do that," suggested David. "It would be every boys dream come true," offered Vincent. After that, Jake dropped his pants and pulled it out.

"Good God Almighty!" exclaimed Richard, while the other boys just stood with their mouth agape. "You got a cock like a horse." He pulled his wallet out, and handed Jake a five-dollar bill. "Mine is bigger," claimed Richard," but it is just too much trouble to bring it out." "That is bullshit," exclaimed Jake," And what do you mean by trouble?" "I got it strapped to my leg," answered Richard. "How come?" questioned Jake; he was incredulous. "If I should get a hard-on it would rip my pants," answered Richard and then he guffawed," And if you believe that I'll tell you another one." The boys laughed until they were laughed out and then Jake got serious.

"I knew a guy who had a prick bigger than mine," Jake said, in a serious manner, "and he killed a lady with it." The boys were quiet, waiting for him to elaborate, but Jake appeared to be thinking. "How did it happen?" asked Vincent. "The guy was discussing the size of his prick with the boys at the bar and one of the ladies overheard the conversation. He claimed it was so big he couldn't find a girl who could accommodate him.

"What happened?" asked the boys in unison. "She told him she could accommodate him." "What happened?" they asked in unison. "She died," answered Jake. "Why?" asked the boys, with eyes agape. "He tore her up inside," Jake answered," He was just too big for her and she bled to death." "Ugh!" exclaimed Vincent," that's awful." "That is awful." agreed David. "Just terrible!" exclaimed Richard.

"I made it up," confessed Jake and he laughed with glee. "You miserable prick," exclaimed Vincent. "Don't call him that," said Richard," that is part of a man." "You are dog shit!" exclaimed Vincent. "A day old cunt rag," offered David. "A hundred noses of snot," commented Richard and they all laughed out of control.

The boys headed back to Noyo. It would be just about dark by the time they arrived. When they were at the harbor Jake parked the car in front of the general store. Jake was thinking it might look suspicious if he parked in front of, or even close to the tavern. The boys went into the store, which was due to close in about an hour. They bought soft drinks and some peanuts. They left the store and moseyed up the road toward the tavern. It was about an eighth of a mile and didn't take long to get there.

The tavern was a stucco building about forty feet in diameter. It had windows all the way around, but they were fewer at the rear of the building. The door to the storage room was there but was locked. They could not see well, all they had was a penlight. The boys entered the building through a window in the storage building. It was not locked.

The storage room contained two cases of mixed soft drinks. Jake opened the back door and stacked them outside against the building. When the boys went into the bar area, Vincent spotted a big cash register. He made a beeline for it and pushed the button for the cash drawer. It had one nickel in it. What a letdown. He put the nickel in his pocket. When Vincent glanced at his pocket he saw two very large bottles on a shelf under the register. He picked one up, and it was heavy. It was champagne. The other bottle was the same.

"Look what I found!" exclaimed Vincent, in a loud whisper. Jake shined the penlight right on the bottle. Vincent was holding the bottle up with both hands; it was heavy. "It's a magnum!" proclaimed Jake," It is party time." "What is a magnum?" asked David. "A magnum of what?" asked Richard. "A magnum is a giant bottle," answered Jake," And this one is full of champagne." "Two magnums," corrected Vincent, "And they are both full of champagne." "We could be drunk for a week!" exclaimed David. "Or twice as drunk for half a week," suggested Richard.

"We better get the Hell out of here," suggested Jake. He said it in a relaxed manner, as if he was use to doing such a thing." You guys wait here while I get the car and be ready." he added, "I don't want to stay long once I stop the car."

It was fun, but Vincent was wondering what would happen if they got caught. David and his self were on probation; they were not even supposed to be together. They were laughing with excitement when they heard Jake coming back. When he was back they loaded their plunder. Vincent could only carry one of the magnums at a time and Jake had stayed in the car; he was ready to escape. The boys ran to the car with their ill-gotten, gains. Two round circles of light were coming up the road toward them.

"Hurry!" yelled Jake and Vincent hurried as fast as his feet would go, his heart pounding in his ears. He tripped and almost fell. "Holy shit" Vincent exclaimed, as he handed David the magnum and entered the car, "I thought I was going to fall." "You are going to wish your ass was holy if we get caught," muttered Jake, with apprehension. He let the clutch out easy and the car moved slowly away from the tavern. The circles of light were coming straight toward them. Vincent could feel the hair on the back of his neck standing up as the lights came closer.

"What if it is a cop?" whispered Vincent, as if to keep the imagined cop from hearing him. The others were wondering the same thing, but kept quiet. And then the cars met. Like two ships in the night they passed each other. The boys heaved a sigh of relief in unison. Jake drove past the store, under the bridge and back on the highway. He headed south for Caspar and a secluded beach he was familiar with, one he could drive the car up to.

"I never pulled a job like that before," commented Vincent. Exhilarated by the escape, but a little fearful of what they had done, wondering what they might do next. "Me neither," echoed David. "Me neither," added Richard," But that is no reason to stop learning new things." "You quit learning the day you were born," scorned David. Vincent laughed. "You guys are already as smart as you are ever going to be," he added. "May your prick stay soft forever," cursed Richard to Vincent. "May your breast grow and hang to your belly button," retorted Vincent. "All shit aside," remarked Jake," I don't think any of you children would fare well in jail." He spoke scornfully. "I already don't like jail," commented Vincent," and I have never been there." "My dad was in jail," confessed Jake. "What for?" asked Vincent "Armed robbery," answered Jake. "Wow!" exclaimed Richard "How did he like it in jail?" he asked naively. "No one likes it in jail, you moron," quipped David. "Did he tell you anything about jail?" asked Vincent, seriously. "He was in prison," answered Jake," He said the food was awful and there isn't any pussy." "Oh, my God!" exclaimed Richard, "No pussy?" "None," answered Jake." Well, almost none." "What do you mean?" asked Vincent," How can you have almost none?" "Some of the guys use guys for girls," answered Jake. "How do they do that?" asked Vincent, not sure, but wanting to hear it said. "A blow job, or a poke it in the rear," answered Jake. "Yuk!" exclaimed Vincent, "Why would anyone want to do that?" "Some are forced into it," replied Jake. "I would poop on someone who poked me!" exclaimed David, disgustedly. "He would probably like that," retorted Jake. "That is revolting!" exclaimed Vincent "Some big guys make little guys give blow jobs," added Jake. "I would die before I would suck on a cock! Exclaimed Vincent. "You would not die," argued Jake," If you had a knife to your throat you would suck." Then he added," Some girls do it, you know." Vincent shook his head in the negative, not wanting to believe Jake, but the thought of girls doing it did change his thinking. "Do you know any girls who do that?" asked Vincent. "Of course I do, but I'm not telling," retorted Jake,

Jake slowed down and turned in toward the ocean and then he parked on the beach. He turned the tired engine off and the lights. The boys could hear the surf. They all bailed out of the car at the same time. The moon was shining on the surf, turning it silver where the foam was. The surf was only two hundred feet away. It was light enough for the boys to see each other.

"Anyone thirsty?" asked Jake. "Dry as a powder horn," answered Richard. "Thirsty enough to drink piss," answered David, stupidly. " Good!" exclaimed Vincent," cause I got to piss," and he started to unbutton his pants as he moved toward David. "You bring that thing out," said David, while backing up," and I'll stomp all over it."

"Pop!" went the champagne cork. Jake had opened it with the corkscrew on his jack knife. "Screw the bullshit!" exclaimed Jake," Let's drink champagne." "We don't have any cups," mentioned Vincent. "It is a big ass bottle," remarked Richard. "Just pass it around," suggested Jake," And it will get lighter." He held it up, and took a long pull. Jake passed the bottle to Richard. It was all Richard could do to get it to his mouth. He guzzled like it was soda pop.

"That is sooo goood," Richard said, "It goes down just like soda pop." He wiped his mouth. Richard said it like it was a surprise. The only thing his father ever had around the house was cheap whiskey. This was smoother than his father's whiskey. Richard handed the bottle to his brother.

"I don't see how this stuff is going to get us drunk," Richard commented. "Champagne sneaks up on you," commented Jake, who had drunk it before. He moved his finger in a circle, motioning for the bottle to get back around to him. The bottle kept going around and around and in a little while Vincent's head was doing the same.

Richard had a silly look on his silly face. David was sitting on the sand, Indian fashion and Jake was pissing at the moon. "I feel gooder than ever," commented Richard, with a moronic look". Are we going to drink the other bottle?" "Can you walk?" asked Jake. "What do I do first?" asked Richard, foolishly. "Put one foot in front of the other," answered Jake. "Like this?" asked Richard, moving his left foot in front of his right foot. "By Jove!" exclaimed Vincent," I think he's got it." "I wonder if he can do it again?" questioned David and he guffawed. David wasn't in any better shape than his brother. Richard was teetering a little as he put his right foot in front of his left. His feet were getting further apart. Richard giggled.

"Something isn't right," he reported, as he held his arms out to keep his balance. "Something isn't right in your head," ridiculed David. "His brains are in his underwear," remarked Jake, with sarcasm. "He just needs help," stated Vincent, as He went down to his knees. He pulled Richard's right foot away from his left. "Whoa!" Richard yelled, "I fear there is an enemy in my camp." "You are your own worst enemy," remarked Jake. He laughed and dropped to the sand. Jake grabbed Richard's other leg and pulled it away. Richard fell on his ass. "Dog pile!" hollered David and he jumped on top of his brother. Jake jumped on David and Vincent jumped on Jake.

"Let's pants him!" yelled Jake. David started to tickle his brother, knowing he lost his strength when tickled. Richard was giggling and protesting as the boys pulled his pants off. He looked so silly with his skinny legs and his knobby knees. "God!" exclaimed Jake," He scares me to death." "Why is that?" asked Vincent, puzzled. "Cause he gives me a hard-on," explained Jake. "He is awful pretty...Isn't he," teased Vincent. "Cuter than a pot bellied pig," added David. "I think we should remove his shorts," suggested Jake, and see what he has in there."

Richard jumped up and ran down the beach. He was knock-kneed and he was a silly sight from any direction. And he was too drunk to run, he kept falling. Richard's pursuers were also too drunk to run, almost unable to stand. And they all had the drunken giggles. Every thing was funny to them. A mountain of poop blocking the refrigerator door would have been funny.

"Hey, Dickey." yelled Jake, between giggles. Jake was lying on his stomach after falling. "Please let us catch you. Heehee. I'm sooo tired," he said and laid his head back down in the sand. "Promise you won't take my shorts off," pleaded Richard. "I promise," answered Jake. He giggled with fingers crossed. "I don't believe you," replied Richard, suspiciously. "I swear on my mother's grave," swore Jake, holding his right hand up. "But your mother isn't dead," claimed Richard, in a maudlin tone, almost ready for tears.

"That was sneaky of me, wasn't it," replied Jake and then he got on his feet. "I'm coming over to you now," Jake said and started walking to Richard. The others followed. "You promised," reminded Richard. "I promised," agreed Jake. "He promised," corroborated David. "He did," agreed Vincent and the boys were now standing over Richard, looking down at him. Jake had a wicked leer on his face. "I still think we should take his shorts off," suggested Jake. "It would be fun," agreed Vincent. "Let's do it," said David, a traitor to his brother. "But you promised," whimpered Richard. "But I lied," answered Jake, as he moved to grab Richard. As Jake grabbed Richard the boys moved in to help him.

But the scene changed from glee to pandemonium. Although Richard was a timid fellow, but was being insulted in a way he could not tolerate. Richard fought for his honor like a tiger. Richard kicked Jake in the groin and hit Vincent on the chin with his fist. After all the violence, it made him sick and he topped it off by vomiting on his brother.

They never got his shorts off. The boys went back to town to the Boys Club. They tried to play some pool, but their offensive attitude and odors caused them to be evicted. It had been a night to remember.

CHAPTER 7

Doc bought an acre a little north of Cap's place. Much of it covered with brush. The soil was black, rich and rooted. A mattock was the tool to get the job done. The family went to work. It took a week to clear enough room for a driveway and a space to live on. Doc built a wood floor and put up a sixteen by sixteen, square foot surplus army tent. He put in a wood burning stove for heat and cooking. Doc dug a hole and set up an outhouse toilet.

After school and on weekends, it was Vincent's chore to clear brush. He was paid a three dollar a week allowance. This went on for weeks and then stopped for a while because Doc had bought an abandoned logging camp. It consisted of a cook shack and some single level, barracks. The buildings were constructed of redwood, board and bat. The windows were sliding sash that opened vertically, but had no weights. Pins of metal held the windows open. The doors were of paneled pine. The doors and windows were white, but the redwood siding was never painted. The lumber was dry as a powder horn, full of splinters.

The children's summer vacation was the time to dismantle the camp. The family went to work and found out right away they had a large chore ahead of them. The redwood was dry and split easily. The family had to handle it with kid gloves and had to be careful with splinters.

Redwood splinters are just awful if they get into flesh. Often they cause infection. They got into the flesh easily and are sharp as needles. With hammers and crowbars the family dismantled the camp. They pulled thousands of nails, separated, stacked, loaded and transported the lumber to their acre. Then they unloaded it and stacked it again. It took two months.

Doc had never built a house before, but he didn't let that stop him. Cap helped him plan it and then Doc went to work with the family's participation. Doc set forms and the slab was poured. It was sixteen feet wide and thirty feet long. He put in a septic tank, a leach field and plumbed in a toilet. They framed the house, put windows and doors in, roofed it, wired it, and plumbed. The family put siding on the exterior and sheet rock on the interior, painted and moved in. The house ended up with a bedroom on each end, one bathroom, with the kitchen and living area in the middle.

When they finished they had enough lumber left to build another house. They covered the lumber and let it sit. Vincent went back to his chore of cutting brush and things went on as before. Doc and Vincent tolerated each other and that was about all. Audrey and Doc got along; she got along with everyone. Vincent spent a lot of time with the Williams family to get away from Doc. It just seemed like they rubbed each other the wrong way.

Vincent liked to be around Abigail. But she showed no interest in him and he had no interest in being rejected, so he ignored her as much as he could. It was hard after seeing her the way he had, naked as a Jaybird.

One night, while staying overnight with the Williams the brothers and Vincent decided to sneak out to the bowling alley. The boys had to go out the dormer window on the second floor. The roof had cedar shingles and was slippery from a recent rain. David went out the window first. Vincent was just getting his leg out the window when he heard a sound. It was something like when you put cardboard where the spokes of your bike wheel will flip the edge of it. David was sliding off the roof. Vincent stopped climbing out the window and listened. The noise stopped and David screamed as he slid off the roof. David was lucky, the ground turned out to be mud. "Splat" was the sound made when he landed fanny first in the mud.

Vincent went back in the window. Richard was already on his way down the stairs and Vincent followed. The lights came on and all the family was up, including Zen, who lacked a sweet nature during normal times. Zen went out the door first and all followed. David was still sitting in the mud where he had landed. He had a dazed look on his face. Zen went over to David. Zen's face was fire and brimstone.

"What in Hell do you think you are doing?" Zen yelled. The dazed look on David's face was replaced by fear; Zen was a harsh man. If angered enough, he would resort to a leather whip he had made for such occasions. David got up and inspected himself. "I'm alright," he claimed," I just wanted to sit on the roof and look at stars," he lied.

"That is a crock," retorted Zen," It is overcast and there are no stars." Zen was not a man to fool with. "You go on up to bed and I will deal with you in the morning. David didn't get much sleep. He worried all night about morning and what was in store for him. Come morning, David was so sore it was all he could do to get out of bed. By then Zen had cooled and left him alone

A few days later, David straight wired one of Zen's old cars and the boys were on their way to the harbor. On the way down the crooked road, David had a collision with a pregnant lady driver. The collision was a head on. It was lucky no one was going over five miles an hour. Vincent saw the accident coming, and he put his feet against the dash. When the cars hit the seat moved out from under him and his behind landed on a jack and a bunch of tools stored under the seat. The woman who was driving the other car had just been released from the hospital. She had to return to it by ambulance. Lucky for David she had not sustained any serious injuries. David sustained some injury to his pride and his behind from the homemade leather whip.

Vincent had a shotgun Cap had given him. It was a single shot, four ten gauge. Vincent used it for hunting quail and bats. The gun shot a small pattern. Vincent liked to hunt quail early in the morning and bats at twilight. Quail are small, but very delicious; they have a wild taste. The bats he could never hit; they just seemed to dodge the shot. They may be as blind as bats, but it doesn't seem to bother their vision.

One night after an unsuccessful attempt to kill bats, Vincent was walking home. He had the shotgun pointed toward the ground. He was thumbing the hammer, unconsciously. He had forgotten the gun was loaded. It was dark by then and when the gun went off, an orange flame came out the end of the barrel. It blew a hole in the ground in front of his foot. A person can learn something every day.

One morning Vincent went quail hunting with Richard down by the Hare Creek Bridge. Vincent had the shotgun, while Richard had a twenty-two rifle. No one in their right mind hunts quail with a rifle. They are hard enough to hit with a shotgun. The boys had no luck and decided to go for a walk on the beach before going home.

Vincent went over the cliff first and ran down to the creek. He jumped across it and walked down the beach toward the surf. Vincent thought Richard was right behind him. He was thinking about Abigail and the bathroom scene. Vincent saw the sand kick up In front of him and he heard the crack of the rifle. He looked over his shoulder and saw Richard. He was standing at the top of the cliff, laughing. After considering the trajectory of the bullet, Vincent realized that it must have just missed his head.

Vincent knew he had to teach Richard a lesson. By this time Richard was running down the cliff, laughing his head off. When Richard leaped across the creek, Vincent raised the shotgun and shot at Richard's feet. Vincent knew he was too, far away to do serious damage. Richard's feet went out from under him and he fell in the creek. The creek was cold and Richard got out of it in a hurry. He was shivering and still had hold of his rifle. Vincent ran to see if he was all right.

"What in Hell did you do that for?" asked Richard, in a huff, "Because you were laughing," answered Vincent," And what you did was not funny... you just missed my head." "I'm sorry," pleaded Richard, "I was just goofing off." "I'm sorry, too," answered Vincent, "We shouldn't be goofing off with guns." Richard's tennis shoes were full of shot, but he wasn't hurt. They were not mad at each other. It was a rare occasion when that happened.

Vincent noticed Doc was staying home often. Sometimes he would sit by the stove for hours with his head up close to it. Sometimes he wouldn't say a word. Snuffy would lie by his feet. Grace told Vincent that Doc had migraine headaches. Vincent felt sympathy for Doc, but wanted to hate him. Doc was always trying to discipline him and he didn't like him sleeping with his mother.

But Doc was a hard man to hate. He was so damned nice, and who could be so reasonable and so good. It just was not natural. The man was just not to be trusted. Doc was too, nice. Vincent watched him like a hawk, but he just never did anything that wasn't nice. What a burden for Vincent.

Fishing was getting difficult for Doc. He was not in good health. An enlarged heart kept him out of the service in W.W.2 and he smoked to many Chesterfield cigarettes. Many bachelors do not take care of themselves and Doc was one of them, or had been. No one can live on coffee, cigarettes and hot cakes. Like most woman, Grace knew she could save her man from himself. She pumped a good diet into him and he started to gain weight, but she couldn't make the headaches go away.

Doc grew tired of fishing. He had never been happy with his new boat. Doc was a loner and did not like having to have a partner. Doc made less money and worked harder. And he was missing his family. Both his brothers and his parents lived in the Valley, that foreign place, where there was no ocean and no beaches. After a few weeks in limbo, Doc decided he would take a trip to Ophir Flats to scout around. This was where his family lived. Vincent didn't want to think of a place like Ophir Flats. With a name like that, what kind of place could it be? It was stuck out in the middle of nowhere and hot. No ocean. No beach girls.

Doc was only gone for a week. When he returned he informed his new family he had bought an acre in Ophir Flats. He was going to build a house there with the lumber that was left over. No one was happy except Doc. Grace was not happy, she didn't want to leave her parents and brother, but she hid it well. Grace would go where her man went. Vincent would go, but grudgingly. Now he had another reason to dislike Doc. Audrey didn't care. Nothing bothered her.

Doc put the boat up for sale and it sold in two weeks. The property didn't move, so Doc turned it over to a realtor. Doc's younger brother, Don, borrowed a lumber truck to help with the moving of the lumber. One day he showed up with it. Vincent liked him right away, as anyone would. Don was like a friendly bear, big and easy-going. Don was always in a good mood and happy. It just wasn't normal to be in a good mood and happy all the time. One brother was too good and the other too happy.

Vincent wondered what the other brother would be like. Vincent felt relieved when he met ex-commander, Max Grover. Max was the black sheep of the family. He had been a boxer in the Navy, and was not to be fooled with. Max liked to drink, swear and tell raunchy jokes. He was not crude around the ladies; he was a perfect gentleman around them. Max was different than his brothers. It might have been because he left home early to join the navy. He might have joined to get away from his tyrant of a father.

Max wasn't quite as tall as Doc, but bigger in the body. He was barrel chested. Max had dark hair, graying at the temples. He had piercing eyes, but an easy manner. Max married a lovely Hawaiian girl. Her name was Crystal. She was slender as a reed with delicate features. Crystal was small, not over five feet and she was pregnant.

Max had married Crystal when she was very young. He married her in Hawaii where she had been born and had lived all of her life. After Max married her, he transferred Crystal from her island paradise to a wino hotel in Ophir flats. He had bought it on an earlier trip. Crystal was to help him manage it.

The hotel, an ancient Victorian wooden structure, was on the worst street in Ophir Flats. It was the Skid Row, street. Skid Row was Feather Boulevard; it ran parallel with the Feather River. A levee separated the town from the river. Taverns lined the Boulevard. There was a men's clothing store on one corner and the Grover hotel on the other. There was a grocery store and the rest of the establishments were taverns.

There was a reason for it. There were two railroads in the Flats, the Western Pacific and the Southern Pacific. There was a hobo jungle by the levee. The hobos lived in shacks made of anything they could find, such as rusted tin roofing. The hobos panhandled for enough money to buy their wine. Some of the railroad men stayed in Max's hotel, but most of the clients were people down on their luck. Max and Crystal ran the hotel in the day and lived on Snob Hill at night.

They drove a long black Buick and lived high on the hog. Max saved enough to buy another hotel at the better end of town. Vincent got the job of keeping the stairway brass clean and polished. This gave him a little spending money and some times he worked on Max's yard. Vincent stayed with Max and Crystal while Doc was building the house. Doc and Grace stayed with Don and his family. Audrey stayed with Doc's parents.

Doc's mother was a lovely lady. She had a sweet face with a matching disposition. She was gentle, with a soft voice. Her hair was long and white.

She wore it in a bun at the back of her head. "Mom" as everyone called her, was not quite five feet tall. She looked perfect in a granny rocker. Mom was old, but she had no wrinkles on her pretty face.

Pop Grover was his wife's opposite. He was always preaching but not practicing what he preached. He was a handsome old gent but one couldn't talk to him for two minutes without a sermon about the Devil and his ways. Vincent learned before Doc had married his mother, he sent his father money every month to help with bills. After the marriage Doc had stopped this charity and Pop had resented Grace because of this.

Vincent hated starting a new school. It seemed like he had done it a thousand times. He didn't know a soul and he was not a gregarious person. Vincent was more of an introvert. It was more up to strangers to do anything about making friends, which they did.

Vincent liked boxing so he signed up for the team. He only weighed a hundred and twenty pounds, but was fast, with a mean left jab. Right away he discovered he had a glass jaw. If a hook caught him he was in trouble. Knowing this, Vincent had to learn how to protect himself.

Vincent became friends with another boxer who was in a heavier weight division. The kid was a hard puncher. At first it made no difference because the kid couldn't hit Vincent. Boyd Stewart was the boy's name. Boyd couldn't hit Vincent and Vincent couldn't hurt' Boyd. It took a big guy to hurt Boyd.

Boyd was a handsome kid, in an odd sort of way. He was a few inches taller than Vincent and about twenty pounds heavier. Boyd was well built and a fine athlete. He was a good tumbler. He could stand, do a back somersault with a twist and land on his feet.

The more Vincent boxed with Boyd the better Boyd got. After awhile he got to where he could hit Vincent and Boyd could knock him out if he wanted. It didn't take Boyd long to learn that Vincent had a glass jaw.

Boyd was different looking. He had red wavy hair. It was not orange like most red heads; it was dark red. Boyd's eyebrows were full and black. He wasn't pale like most carrot tops; he was well tanned, but had a million freckles. Boyd had a boyish grin that lit up his face. Vincent and Boyd were fast friends at school but the friendship never got past school. One time Boyd was to pick him up in front of the school in the evening but Boyd never showed up. In time Vincent learned that Boyd was a bullshit artist.

Gold was the cause of Ophir Flats. The Feather River had been the vehicle for transferring gold from the Sierras to the Valley. Ophir Flats was right in the path. First the prospectors came with small operations; giant dredgers followed. The dredgers got most of the gold, but not all. When the dredgers had left they left acres upon acres of rock piles in their wake. Except for the mountains, Ophir Flats was almost surrounded by rock piles.

The site of Vincent's new home was in the start of the Sierra foothills. It was in rolling hills covered with oak trees and pines. There was also a healthy crop of poison oak and rattlesnakes. When the house was finished, it had three bedrooms. They were at the back of the house on the west side. The house had a large kitchen, living room and one bath.

An outhouse was there because there was no water to flush the toilet. Doc bought two P-38 wing tanks to haul water from a spring in the mountains. The water was cool and clean, but the whole operation was a pain in the tail feathers. The family had to heat water and take a bath in a galvanized tub.

Vincent made a new friend and his name was Mario Palucci. Vincent met Mario at the pool hall. Mario was a year older and a hundred pounds bigger than Vincent. He looked like Charles Atlas, but had done nothing to earn this body. It had been a gift from the Supreme Being. Mario had dark Italian eyes. They were big and pretty. His nose was big, but not pretty. It had got in the way of fist many times. His nose was Mario's Achilles Heel. It was prone to serious bleeding when it got in the way of a fist. This happened almost every time he got in a fight. Mario did not lack courage and he was strong as a bull. He was just slow. He could not get out of his own way.

Mario had two brothers, Frank and Aldo. Aldo was soft spoken, industrious and a good Catholic. Frank was none of these. He was lean and mean. Frank looked, acted and sounded like a Mafia brother. He was always dressed first class and seemed well heeled, but had no visible means of support. Frank never worked and lived with his parents. Frank was bad news and no one messed with him.

Frank's Achilles Heel was his stomach. He had ulcers. He was less than thirty and had already had three fourths of his stomach removed. Frank loved the nightlife but could not have alcohol and that was one of the things he wanted to do most. Sometimes Frank would try to drink, but he would suffer for days. Maybe this was why he was so mean. His bad stomach was the only thing that saved him from himself.

The Palucci brothers had been born in Sicily. They had come to America with their parents. They were young boys then. The family had settled in Schenectady, New York. They had lived there long enough to learn English and to develop an accent. Frank's was the worst. He sounded like a New York hood. The family moved to California when Mario was ten and settled in Ophir Flats, not far from the river. They had bought an old house with an olive orchard. The dilapidated house stayed that way.

Mario's father drank a lot of fermented grape juice and he was a little crazy from it. Vincent saw him chase Mario with a butcher knife. Vincent never knew for sure if he would have used it on Mario. Vincent had never seen the old man go to work, or heard about it, either. Aldo was the one who brought home the bacon. He worked as a mechanic for a new car agency in Chico, California. It was a collage town twenty miles north of Ophir Flats. Aldo drove to his job five days a week. Mario worked sometimes, but he kept the money for himself.

The brothers had a sister. She was about ten, a pretty little fluff of Italian curls. Her brothers had spoiled her rotten. The boys doted on her, except for Frank. He only loved himself. The girl always got her way. Her name was Carmen. The Palucci parents could speak no English. The brothers could speak fluent Italian; Carmen just a little. She had been born in America. Vincent could never understand what they were talking about when he was at Mario's house. The family only talked to each other in Italian. Carmen never talked to Vincent. He was never sure if she was snooty, or shy.

Mario was a bullshit artist. He had learned at an early age how to manipulate people with lies and deceit. He had little aversion to saying things that were not true. Mario was charming and so gregarious that most people had a tendency to overlook his faults. Doc told Vincent that he wouldn't trust Mario any further than he could throw him. Most of the time when Mario was not telling the truth was when he was bragging. Vincent liked to believe that Mario would not lie about anything that was important. Vincent had always been hesitant about judging.

Doc needed a well dug on the property. Mario talked Doc into letting him do it with Vincent's help. Since the boys had to do it by hand, it had to be a big well, big enough to get into the hole and dig with a pick and shovel. The ground was hard and the deeper they dug the harder it got. By the time they were in the hole over their heads the ground was too, hard to dig with a pick. Mario talked Doc into renting a jackhammer powered by internal combustion. It was cheaper than renting a compressor for an air powered one. Mario was mechanically inclined. He loved to work with anything that had power and made noise. The jackhammer made a lot of noise and it was all one could do to hang on to it.

Mario liked to show off his muscles so he took his shirt off and went at it with gusto. Mario forgot the carbon monoxide. The exhaust came right out of the side of the hammer. It was a hot summer day and there was no way for the carbon monoxide to get out of the hole. Mario was digging away at bedrock with the gas hammer when he started acting strange. Vincent was standing at the top of the well watching. Mario's face blanched and a frightened look came over it. Mario killed the hammer and started trying to get out of the well.

"Help me!" Mario yelled "Get me the hell out of here!" Vincent stuck a homemade ladder into the well and went down to help Mario. Mario was frantic; he had never felt that way before. Vincent had to calm him before he could help him. With considerable effort he managed to get Mario out of the hole. Then he was feeling a little strange himself. When Mario was out of the hole his eyes went back to their normal size.

"Holy Shit!" he exclaimed, "I felt like I was going to croak." "You could have," retorted a relieved Vincent. "If you had not killed the hammer and I had not been here to help you." "How could I have been so stupid?" asked Mario while shaking his head in dismay. "I should have known about the carbon monoxide." "You can't help it if you are stupid," answered Vincent in a sympathetic tone. "You didn't know either," retorted Mario with chagrin. "Yes I did, "Vincent stated and laughed. "Bull shit!" exclaimed Mario; he was getting angry. "Why didn't you warn me then?" "I just wanted to see if you would die," answered Vincent and then he started to laugh. "It is not funny.'" stated Mario, but his lips were pulling at the corners. Vincent laughed almost out of control.

"You should have seen yourself running around in the hole with your eyes big as saucers," cried Vincent. Then he broke down in fits of laughter. Mario tried to remain serious. He even started to make another protest, opening his mouth to do so, but he gave up. He was feeling better now and he could not hold back the mirth that was welling up in him. "You asshole." It was all Mario could say before the fit came over him.

Both the boys laughed so hard they ended up rolling on the ground. They could not stop. When they started to get control, if their eyes met they would lose it and start all over again.

"You stay there," ordered Vincent and he ran around to the other side of the house. He stayed until he thought it was safe, about five minutes. "Is it safe?" he yelled at Mario. "I think so," yelled Mario. Vincent walked to Mario and when their eyes met, they were able to control themselves.

"You got any money?" asked Mario. "About ten bucks," answered Vincent, "You got any?" "About the same... Would you rather dig a hole or drink beer?" "My hand fits a beer can better than a shovel," answered Vincent. "Mine too," agreed Mario and off they went.

That particular well never got finished; Doc filled it. After that fiasco Doc bought an ancient well driller. It was mounted on an ancient Chevrolet truck. Doc had a well location witched and he drilled a well. Doc sold the driller for more than he paid for it. The money Doc lost on the first well he made back on the second one. Perhaps it was because Doc was so good. Who knows?

CHAPTER 8

The well did not produce enough water to carry Grace's garden, flowers, bushes and fruit trees through the summer. Doc bought a two thousand gallon, galvanized, water tank. He had it delivered to the property and had it placed close to the well. He built a wooden Tower, thirty feet tall around the tank. Doc built a support for a pulley above the Tower and then he rigged the pulley. Doc ran the cable from the wench on his jeep through the pulley, back down through the tower to a cable on the tank. He winched the tank to the top of the tower. Then he built a platform under the tank and rested and secured the tank.

Vincent was awed by Doc's ability to do this kind of task. And he did it all alone. After this feat, Doc built a shop all by himself. The frame was old water pipe welded together and covered it with sheets of corrugated metal. Doc didn't want anyone to help him; he liked to work alone. Maybe Snuffy helped him a little. Anyway, Vincent grew to have respect for Doc. This respect created a new relationship with Doc.

Doc took Vincent fishing and taught him how to fly fish for trout. Doc's favorite was the Black Gnat. Vincent learned about the trout's habits and how the trout would get wise. That is, if they were lucky enough to live long. Doc showed Vincent how to tie a fly to a short line, which attached to a small willow pole. He showed how to sneak up on a trout that was in a hole in a stream. One had to sneak up or they would flee at a sound or even a shadow.

The terrain that Doc fished was usually steep, rough and brushy. Doc liked to go to places that were hard to get to, because they were not fished as often. Vincent learned to hold the pole out through the brush. Then point it at the fish while holding the fly in his fingers under tension and shoot the fly in toward the fish. Once there, tease the fish until it nibbled and jerk the line to snag the fish.

As most young people, Vincent was impatient and inconsiderate. He didn't like waiting for Doc and would just fish ahead of him. Even in the wake of frightened fish, Doc would still catch most of the fish. Vincent could never figure out how he did it.

Vincent liked to fish for trout and he liked to eat them. Doc taught him how to kill and clean them. He told Vincent that it was cruel to let the fish die slowly. He showed him how to kill the fish by pressing on the back of its head with his thumbnail.

One summer vacation, Vincent and Audrey learned how to mine for gold. Doc, his brothers and his father, had some mine claims in the Sierra Mountains. One of these claims was at Four Trees. Four Trees wasn't a town, it was just a location, a reference point. There were four large pine trees growing together.

Four Trees was about thirteen miles south of Buck's Lake. Buck's Lake was man made and twenty some miles south of Quincy, California. Quincy was on Highway Seventy and was on the route to Reno along the Feather River Canyon.

The trip to Four Trees was longer and easier via the Canyon route. Doc always took the alternate route on the Old Quincy Road. The old road to Quincy was narrow, rough and serpentine. There were many small sawmills on this route and heavy logging traffic was heavy.

In the summer when the asphalt was hot enough to fry an egg, the truck tires would work the asphalt loose. Chuckholes would appear, making the road a rough ride. It seemed the holes never got fixed. The road was awful the whole way to Plumas County and then it got worse. It was torture riding on it in a Jeep, but we took many trips on this road for hunting, fishing and gold mining.

The family had two cabins on the Four Trees claims. The upper cabin belonged to Doc and his brothers. The lower one belonged to Pop. The cabins were on a steep, ravine and one had to go down a steep gravel road to get to them. Doc said that back in the old days a model T had to traverse the hill in reverse gear.

The upper cabin had a spring about twenty yards above it. The water from it was ice cold and clear as water could be. It was piped to the cabin. The water was so good it was hard to keep from drinking too much. The water from the spring kept a food cooler on the front porch cold. The cooler had a screen and covered in burlap. Water dripped over it like a swamp cooler.

The upper cabin had two floors. Most of the beds were on the upper floor. There was a partial petition dividing the top floor. On the lower floor there was one room and the kitchen. There was a cast iron, Wedgwood cook stove in the kitchen. It was the only heater in the cabin.

Pop's cabin was down the hill about three hundred yards, it was on the other side of the mine. The mine was a small tunnel into the side of the hill. Shored with timbers of old railroad ties, the tunnel was into the hill about fifty feet.

The tunnel started at a vein of rich ore that had once been exposed and followed a trail of ore rich quartz. The family had found some small pockets of gold ore. They had dug down as far as they could. The hole had filled with water. The tunnel started in the side of the hill in the continued search for the vein. So far, the vein was not found.

A five stamp mill had been set up about fifty feet from the opening of the tunnel. A small gauge track ran from the tunnel to the mill with an ore car on it to carry the ore. An old Dodge engine had powered the mill. The engine turned a giant camshaft with five cams on it. Each cam would lift one stamp and when the cam would go by, the heavy stamp would come crashing down on the ore. This repeated action pulverized the ore. Then it would run through a sluice box. The sluice box would catch the bigger gold. (There wasn't much of that) A silver plate covered with quick silver would catch the fine gold. (There wasn't much of that, either)

It was dark in the mine, so they had to use carbide lamps to see what they were doing. The lamps attached to their hard hat. Digging in the tunnel was hard work. Sometimes, the guys would take a break by looking for gold elsewhere. Sometimes, they would dig in the open pit mine. It was dug with an ancient, steam shovel. Although old, the shovel still functioned well. But it was a slow process to move it and so it did not get moved often.

Red fir bark fired the boiler. They got the bark from fir snags, which were dead trees. Lightning killed most of them. The boiler had a voracious appetite and they spent a lot of time looking for and getting bark. The bark would usually just fall off when pulled. It often was in large chunks six to ten feet long.

When they were using the steam shovel, Vincent was in charge of keeping the fire going in the boiler. The boiler had a safety system that Vincent was not aware of. A pressure valve that released automatically when there was too much pressure. The pressure was not released all at once. When it first started to release it would make a whistling sound, much like a whistling teakettle. The whistle would build into a banshee like scream. Then it would go all the way making a blast like a steam locomotive.

Anyway, Vincent was feeding the fire eating dragon and the whistle started to blow. It was the first time that he had ever heard it and he thought something might be wrong with the boiler. Vincent had wondered what might happen if the ancient thing should decide to blow up. Vincent looked over at Doc, who was operating the iron monster and he didn't look too concerned. Doc's brother was in front of the machine; he didn't look concerned, either.

The whistle kept getting louder. Its eerie sound was making the hair on the back of Vincent's neck stand up. Vincent thought the others couldn't hear it. The shovel made a lot of noise with the tracks creaking and the bucket banging and grinding.

Doc and Don were pretending they didn't hear the screaming valve. They knew that it would scare Vincent because it had done the same thing to them. Just for fun, they wanted to see how Vincent would react. The whistle was now a banshee scream. The adrenalin in Vincent's blood was preparing him for action. But he didn't have a clue about what action to take. He just knew that the old boiler was going to blow.

Vincent hollered at Doc, but he couldn't hear him. And neither could Don. Vincent backed away from the boiler. He wanted to cover himself or get behind something. Fear took over his thinking and then the big blast came, "PSHOWWW!" It frightened Vincent to his wit's end and he dove off the shovel, landing in the soft dirt.

As soon as Vincent had landed, he looked back at the shovel to see if Doc had escaped. The iron monster was standing still. Doc and his brother were suffering from uncontrollable fits of laughter. Vincent grimaced, for he knew he had been had. Vincent was indignant and there was just no way to save his face.

"You should have seen the look on your face," jeered Doc, with tears in his eyes. He was trying to laugh out of one side of his mouth, trying to hide his bad teeth. But he lost control and showed them all as he guffawed out loud. Don was also having a convulsion. Vincent felt like a buffoon and saw through the insult and into the humor and was able to laugh at his own ignorance. Vincent never did get comfortable with the safety valve; it always made his skin crawl.

Bored with the tunnel and the pit, the crew set off on a prospecting trip. They didn't go any great distance, but stayed in about a ten-mile radius of the mine. The guys took picks, shovels, gold pans and ore sample bags with them. The plan was to visit dry creek beds, take ore samples and go to Wildcat Creek to do the panning. Audrey took charge of the ore sample bags. She was to tag them with their location to know where the ore came from.

After the ore samples were collected, Vincent and Audrey panned next to each other on Wildcat Creek. The creek was deep in a canyon in rugged terrain. Squatting at the creek's bank they panned away. They dipped the pans in the cold water, then moved them in circular motions to wash the dirt and sand away.

Vincent heard a metallic sound coming from Audrey's pan. Vincent had never heard that sound before. He knew what it was. Like the first time he had heard a rattlesnake rattle, he knew what it was. Now he knew he was hearing the sound of gold.

Vincent had stopped panning and so had the others. They had also heard the siren call of gold. Vincent had his face as close to Audrey's pan as he could get it. She was getting excited, as the sound of gold got louder. The sand got black and then Vincent saw a yellow spot appear in the sand. He held his breath, as the spot got bigger. Audrey's eyes got bigger; her mouth was agape. When the nugget was exposed it was as big as the nail on Vincent's little finger. It was a beautiful thing to behold and to touch.

The tags had come loose from the ore bags and some were lying loose in the box. The crew didn't have a clue from where the nugget came. With over twenty bags of ore the one nugget was all there was. They never found its source.

Seasons went by and Vincent put two years of his life into High School and got bored with it and he quit. He was only sixteen years old. If he had got any kind of argument from his mother, or from Doc, Vincent might have stayed in school. Doc was old fashioned, though; it was all right with him if Vincent quit. After all, Vincent might go to work and pay for some of his keep. His mother didn't argue, either. She told him that it was his life.

Mario had been a bad influence on Vincent. Mario was free; he could do anything he wanted. He could go anywhere he wanted and at any time. Mario hadn't been to school for years and he knew just about anything there was to know. Mario thought so, and maybe, so did Vincent. But, there were few jobs around for a sixteen year old with no experience.

The first summer Vincent worked in the cannery, he got a job tailing off. He caught the wet, 303 cans as they came out of the cooler. He put them on trays to dry. His hands stayed wet all day, and one could not wear gloves, for one could not catch the cans fast enough. The moisture from the cans caused the skin on Vincent's hands to get dry. His hands got so dry the skin cracked and bled. His hands would be so stiff in the morning it was all he could do to open them. But, he stuck it out and his hands calloused, and got tough.

When the season had ended, Vincent had saved enough to buy an old Chevy, a 1936, coupe. He bought it at a wrecking yard. It was a worn-out green, somewhat like British Racing Green. The old, tired car got him from here to there, for a while, that is.

The Chevy had a six-cylinder engine, with overhead valves and poured Babbitt bearings. They were not as tight as they needed to be. There were shims to take out to tighten the bearings, but it was too late for that. The crankshaft was already a little egg shaped.

Mario showed him how to tighten the bearings with some leather. He told him they would not stay tight long, but maybe long enough to trade the car. This Vincent did. He traded for a 38 Ford sedan. Vincent thought he had put one over on the used car dealer. But the clutch on the Ford started smoking before he even got home. It's impossible to put one over on a used car dealer. Not long after he had fixed the clutch, the rings went out of it and it started smoking like a freight train.

Vincent wanted the car hopped up, so he took the Ford to a mechanic who did that sort of thing. The mechanic bored the cylinders out too far and the rings never did seat right. It had a lot of power with the over sized pistons and the planed heads, but it used a lot of oil.

Vincent had dual, straight pipes put on the car so he would not lose any power in the exhaust. He plugged the heat risers so he would get a pretty sound from the backpressure. The exhaust was so loud Vincent could not resist the temptation to peel out. The car layed a strip of rubber every time it left a stop sign.

The loud exhaust system got him introduced to the Ophir Flats Police Department. The law made him remove the straight pipes and put on regular mufflers. What a drag, the Ford sounded impotent, it had been castrated.

Vincent made a new friend and his name was Mack McGee. They met at the pool hall. Soon they discovered that they were neighbors; Mack lived down the hill from Vincent. Mack had a comical face; he always wore a silly grin. Mack always looked like he had just got away with some misdeed. When Mack laughed he wouldn't go "Ha ha" like everyone else, he would go "He he." He was different, for sure.

Mack wasn't bad; he just was not responsible for his actions. He was just a little strange and his whole family was that way. It was like they had all walked out of a book like "God's Little Acre." The McGee family was from Arkansas or some foreign place like that. They were a strange family; they were almost normal. One would notice their difference with spending any time with them.

There was a time when one would know Mack's difference right away. If Mack imbibed anything that contained alcohol, his personality would instantly change. All it took was one beer. One beer and Mack became a total fool. The more Mack drank, the worse he got. He liked to drink. Sometimes he would get downright obnoxious. He would repeat himself until you wanted to nail his mouth shut. Or, he would get maudlin.

Sometimes, Mack would say foolish things that made no sense. He would do foolish things that didn't make sense. Sometimes, he would get himself into foolish situations. They were unimaginable situations to a normal person. One time Mack had gone to Los Angeles and got drunk. When Mack was drinking he had an aversion for money; he spent it like he couldn't get rid of it fast enough. On this occasion he had spent all his money, and he had ended up in jail in the drunk tank. While passed out on the floor, someone had stolen his shoes and socks.

No one can look more foolish than a man clothed with no shoes or socks. What a tragic, comical, Chaplinesque kind of image this was of Mack. A guy hung over, disheveled and hitchhiking from L.A. to Ophir Flats while bare footed in the winter.

Mack wasn't a bad looking guy. He had big, brown hound dog eyes. He had a lantern jaw. His hair was brown, straight and thin. He was gregarious and his face reflected this quality. He had a comfortable look. One was never intimidated by Mack's looks.

Mack was bigger than Vincent. He was about five ten and about one hundred and fifty pounds. Mack was long and lean. In boots and jeans, he looked a cowboy. Mack sounded like one, also. He was muscular with narrow shoulders that tapered to his neck. Mack had a good-looking body. One of the girls had remarked that he looked great from the neck down.

Mack had lied about his age to get in the Navy. His irresponsibility had earned him a dishonorable discharge. He had been grateful to get out for any reason. His foolishness had made him the butt of many practical jokes. Mack was easy going and slow to anger, but he did have a temper. When pushed too far, he could turn into a mean machine with a windmill of roundhouses.

Although Mack was still a young fellow, he had seen most of the U.S.A. via freight trains. He had told Vincent about a trip through the South with his uncle. The train had stopped at a whistle stop for water. They and some hobos had got off the train to see. They wanted to find something to eat. They had knocked on the doors of houses about a quarter of a mile from the train. Anyone that gave, gave them corn bread and beans.

They had heard the train whistle blow while they were eating their corn bread and beans under a tree. The guys ran, but the train had been moving out by the time they got to it. His uncle's legs had been longer than his. The uncle had made the train and had got on it. By the time Mack had reached the train it was moving out fast. Mack had grabbed the handle on the car and had been jerked right off of his feet. Mack had hung there like a flag, not being able to let go, or get his feet down. His uncle had pulled him the rest of the way onto the train. Vincent had had to laugh with the image of Mack hanging there like a flag. And that silly grin on his face was just too funny. It was like something from the Keystone Cops or Laurel and Hardy. Mack was funny without trying to be.

Mack had a pretty little sweetheart and her name was Betty Jane Potts. Betty was timid, blond with her body made for a bikini. It was easy to see that Mack and Betty were in love. The two of them could kiss longer than anyone Vincent had ever seen. Anyone could see that they were intimate.

Audrey made friends with two sisters, Lois and Lucy Jones. Their father owned a fruit stand in Ophir Flats, by the lower Bridge. Both sisters were cute as a bug's ear, but Vincent had a crush on Lois. Lois was smaller than Audrey. Lois and her sister only wore Levis and tight ones at that. Lois had a fine little behind.

Lois was quiet and so was Vincent. He had feelings for her, but didn't have the words or the courage to do anything. The two never got past the kissing stage because of this. Vincent talked to Audrey about it and told her how much he liked Lois.

"She likes you!" exclaimed Audrey, exasperated with him for being so square. "But you never do anything." "What do you mean?" asked Vincent, dumb as a rock. "You never try anything!" exclaimed Audrey, still exasperated about having to explain things to her older brother. "You mean she wants me to?" asked Vincent, incredulous. "Of course you dip shit, all girls want to believe they are desirable." "But she is so nice," complained Vincent, "l didn't think that she would want me to be fresh with her." "God!" exclaimed Audrey, "You are so stupid sometimes and she walked away, "No one is that nice." she told him, over her shoulder.

But Vincent just could not make himself be naughty with Lois. He was afraid of a repeat happening of his Fort Bragg romance. He was awfully unsure of his ability to perform. Vincent was awfully afraid of rejection. Vincent wanted to be intimate with Lois, but what would he do if she wouldn't let him.

When Vincent was alone with Lois his palms would sweat and he would want her so bad his loins would be on fire. But he just could not make himself get fresh with her. Vincent thought how awful it would be if he were making love to Lois and lost his erection. That was just too horrible to contemplate. It wasn't bad when they were running with the gang and there were few chances for them to be alone.

Betty Jane Potts had a friend and she started running around with the gang. Her name was Mary Ann Cunningham and she had a brother named Buck. Mary also had a little sister and they were all carrot tops. Between the three of them they must have had at least a billion freckles.

Mary was a pretty girl for a red head. She was tall and slender, almost thin. She had a regal bearing about her. She held herself erect, her back straight as a board. Mary walked carefully, slow and proud. It wasn't that she was vain; it was an unconscious thing. Maybe one of her ancestors had been royalty, maybe a Scottish Queen?

Mary's brother, Buck was similar, but not the same. He did not have such a regal walk. He had it from the waist up, but not from the waist down. Buck's feet didn't point straight ahead like Mary's, his pointed out at an angle, like a duck's. Walking like a duck robbed him of his regal bearing.

Buck was smart, though; he was always thinking, and fooling around with scientific things. He loved electronics and always had something apart, like a radio, or clock. He shared good looks with his sister, but they did not look alike, except for the red hair.

Buck had a 1936 Dodge, four door sedan. The car needed paint and every thing else. Buck was a fair mechanic, though and he managed to keep the old heap running. One day he left the car parked up on the hill by the railroad station. He was playing pool with his new friends, Vincent, Mario and Mack down at Maynard's pool hall.

Buzz, Maynard's son, was on a run of wild pinks on the snooker table. When Buzz got into position on the wild pink, there was just no telling how long the run would last. Or how many points he would rack up. Every time Buzz sunk the pink it was six points. Buzz was an expert with the cue and everyone knew it. The other players would do their best to keep him away from the pink, which is the number six ball. But if he did get on it, they would just hang up their cues and watch the show. Once Buzz got on the pink, it didn't seem like he would ever get off. And even if he did get off, he would just use a little English and get right back. Vincent had a hunch that when Buzz got off a run it was by choice. When he had got tired of it, he'd miss on purpose.

Buzz was just a young guy, twenty, or maybe less. He must have spent his childhood with a cue stick in his hand. Buzz gave you the impression that he was a smart aleck, but he wasn't. He was just an expert and most experts have an aura of superiority.

Anyway, Buck had his car parked by the railroad station. The boys had been in the pool hall for about a half hour. A guy ran into the pool hall and he was excited.

"A car is on fire!" he yelled, "It's up by the railroad station." For some reason it didn't seem real and everyone laughed and the games went on. Buck was a little slow on the draw and then his mouth dropped open. "My car is by the station!" he exclaimed and he walked fast, with his feet pointed out. The cue stick was still in his hand.

Buck walked out the door and the gang followed. They saw a big cloud of smoke coming over the buildings. After they rounded the corner they heard the sirens. They ran the rest of the way. The smoke was black, blue, brown and yellow. Buck's car was engulfed in flames. The flames were all colors; they were consuming many different materials.

"I don't believe this cried Buck, helplessly. "Holy Shit!" exclaimed Mack, "it's too late for anything." "Fuck a duck!" was Mario's worldly exclamation. "Shit house, Mickey Mouse!" was Vincent's contribution. By the time the fire was out, there was nothing left of Buck's car but a black hulk. The inside of the car was gutted. All the tires were flat. The Fire Chief was looking for the owner of the hulk. Buck started to step forward, but Mario held him back.

"Don't say anything," cautioned Mario, "or you will get stuck with the tow bill." Buck didn't step forward, he construed the bill would be more than the car was worth, as it was only junk now. In a little while the tow truck came, hooked on to Buck's car and towed it away. It was Buck's hope that he would never see it again, and he never did. It wasn't worth the trouble for the law to look for the owner.

Mario was always driving a different car. Some times he drove the family car, an old LaSalle, a thirty-six model. It looked like a gangster's car. He didn't get it often, the family was aware that Mario thought he was a champion racecar driver.

Mario was a skilled driver; he had that Italian flair for making machines do what he wanted. Perhaps it was because Mario loved machines. He was smart about machines, and he would try almost anything, just to see if it would work; but he was no Einstein. Mario had this old Buick, a thirty-five model, and it had thrown a piston rod. Mario got a bright idea. He took the piston clear out of the engine, and put a weight in its place to balance it out and thought it would run okay.

Vincent handed Mario the wrenches while Mario pulled the head, pan, and piston, with the rod. Mario made a clamp out of plumber's tape and clamped a lead weight to the crankshaft. He put the head and pan back on and put the oil back in the pan. Mario had an excited grin of anticipation as he turned the ignition on and pushed on the starter. When the car started, his expression changed to consternation. The whole car was jumping up and down. And shaking violently, Mario shut the engine off. He had a sheepish, grin. He said and shrugged "You never know unless you try."

Mario's brother, Aldo, was working one day in Chico. He was test-driving a new Plymouth for his company. He stopped at a stop sign, but the diesel truck that was behind him couldn't. Aldo saw him coming in his rear view mirror and he clutched his Saint Christopher Medal. The truck drove right up on top of the car, smashing the top flat. Aldo came out of it without a scratch. He swears the medallion saved his life. Who knows?

Aldo got some kind of settlement for the accident and he bought this gorgeous car. It was a Forty One Buick convertible. It wasn't new, but it was special. It was a two door, with a back seat. It had seventeen coats of maroon lacquer and a Carson top. It had white sidewalls and the prettiest sounding dual mufflers Vincent had ever heard. Aldo would never let Mario, or anyone else drive it.

CHAPTER 9

Vincent was getting ready for his seventeenth birthday. Audrey had already had her sixteenth. It was hot, arid and sultry in May, like every May in the landlubber's paradise of Sacramento Valley. Vincent had not yet got use to the stifling heat. It would help if it would cool off at night. But once the rock piles that surround Ophir Flats get heated up, it stays hot all night. Although it did cool off a few degrees by late evening, it didn't seem so as Vincent lay on his sweat-wet sheets.

Vincent's bedroom was at the rear of the house, as the rest of the bedrooms were. At the back of the house was a screened-in porch. It had places made for window sash, but there were no sash, just screen. In the winter the screen was covered with clear plastic, the kind with a fine wire running through it. The plastic was removed, as it was every summer, to let whatever breezes come into the house.

Vincent couldn't lie on his back, as it made him nervous, it seemed he couldn't breathe well in that position. This made it seem even hotter to him, as he was usually lying with his face in the pillow. What Vincent wouldn't give for a cool ocean breeze? Vincent lay with his face jammed into his pillow. He turned it often in search of a cool side. It always seemed cooler when turned over, but didn't stay cool long. Vincent tossed and turned. He could only lie on his stomach or left side. He couldn't lie on his right side as it made him feel like when he lay on his back. It was the same kind of feeling that he got when he was in deep water, the barber's chair, or at the dentist. Vincent knew it was some kind of claustrophobia. He couldn't remember when he had started with the problem.

Vincent wished he could trade the Feather River for the lovely, Noyo River. The Feather was all right, but it was no Noyo. The Feather River had no ocean next to it. The ocean was three hours away no matter which direction one took; three hours was the nearest ocean. That was just too far to be from the ocean.

Vincent missed the Hare Creek beach. He had gone to it almost every day. Vincent had had many dreams on that beach. He remembered lying on the warm sand, dreaming that he was lying on Anna. He pressed his body into the sand, pretending that it was Anna. Vincent got an erection thinking about her. Vincent could see her petal like lips and rosy cheeks in his mind's eye.

The last thing he needed was an erection; that was no way to cool off. He tried to think of something else, but his loins were mesmerizing him with that familiar sensation. Vincent tried to think of his drawing; he liked to draw houses with the floor plans. Vincent would like to be an architect someday. He had been drawing houses for a long time. He liked to draw modern, different houses. Vincent thought about houses, but it didn't help, his loins were his master. Vincent finally gave in to sensuality and masturbated. Then he was ashamed; he always was.

Vincent thought of his birthday, which was on the next day. He would be seventeen. Vincent would have his birthday without his family; they had gone to the mountains to escape the heat. They had wanted him to come, but he had been afraid that he might miss something. The family was going to be gone for a week and that was too long to be gone. He might miss a chance of being alone with Lois and maybe not being tongue tied with her. Who knows what might happen?

Vincent's mother had baked him his usual birthday cake. She had stocked the house with a week's supply of grub. She had bought him a gold wristwatch and Audrey had got him only a card because she was broke. Audrey hadn't wanted to go, but Grace had not wanted to leave her. They had all gone and Vincent was alone, but that was not bad.

Vincent must have gone to sleep because the next morning when he woke up it didn't feel like he had gone to sleep. He must have, he thought. One can't wake up without first going to sleep. It was still hot. Vincent had to have some coffee to wake up and had to have something to eat before he could have a cigarette. Vincent couldn't smoke on an empty stomach.

Vincent had his coffee and breakfast and sat down to have a smoke. He knew Mario would be arriving soon. They were going to take two cars, pick up everyone and go to Bidwell Bar for a day of swimming. Vincent didn't like swimming there as the water was cold as ice and the stones on the riverbed hurt his feet.

Walking around in the water was about all Vincent did. He still couldn't swim. But there was a lot of shade there from big oak trees, quaking asp and madrone trees. It was a pretty drive over the narrow, serpentine road through the foothills. Lois would be there in her tiny swimsuit.

Vincent put his cigarette out in the dried, red clay dirt. He heard

Mario coming. Vincent knew it was him because he could hear his car dragging bottom on the high spots over the dirt driveway. The seven-inch shackles on Mario's car caused it to drag bottom. Mario pulled up in a cloud of dust.

"Dust to dust and ashes to ashes," Vincent said to himself, wondering what it meant. He waved his hand around in a futile attempt to get the dust away from his nose. Vincent hated the dust. He closed his mouth; he could feel the dust in his teeth. Mario got out of his car and swaggered over to Vincent. Mario had to swagger; it was the only way he knew how to walk. It was that, or his jeans were too tight.

Mario was like a woman who had big feet, who pretended she had little ones and bought her shoes too small. Mario always bought his pants too small. They always looked like they were about to burst at the seams. Mario was wearing a white T-shirt with his jeans and tennis shoes. Vincent never wore tennis shoes; he hated them. They not only made his arches ache, they also made his feet itch. Vincent always wore engineer boots, or penny loafers. It was too hot to wear boots, so he was wearing his loafers.

Mario came toward Vincent, hunching his big shoulders, walking like an ape and making ape-like, noises. Mario had to goof off because he was a goof off.

"That's cute," commented Vincent, "It's in harmony with your I. Q." Mario kept coming at him. He put his arms around him and hugged him. Mario jumped up and down, with Vincent in his arms. "Let go of me, you big ape!" commanded Vincent. "Only if you give me a banana," answered Mario. "You already got a banana for a nose," replied Vincent, with mirth. "Are you saying that I have a yellow nose?" asked Mario, with a look of consternation. "No," answered Vincent, "it's just shaped like a banana. "All famous people have big noses," bragged Mario. "What's that got to do with you?" asked Vincent, incredulous. "I'm going to be famous someday," answered Mario, with feigned indignation. "A famous outlaw," agreed Vincent and laughed.

"Happy birthday to you", replied Mario, ready to end the exchange. He turned around and went back to his car. "Don't go away mad," said Vincent, wondering what Mario was doing, "Just go away." Mario went to the pilot's side of his car and brought out a six-pack of beer and a pint of whiskey. "Let's get a head start," suggested Mario. "I like the way you apes think," answered Vincent as he went to meet his friend.

Vincent had much affection for Mario. It was impossible to not like Mario. He was so animated, so full of fun and ideas. His mind never stood still, you could see it in his eyes. You could feel the gears turning in Mario's head. He was always in a good mood, never pessimistic. That's not saying he never got mad. He was a volcano when he got mad, but his anger never lasted long.

"I'll have the first drink," said Mario, who was not hung up on formality, "Being as I bought the bottle." He opened the bottle and put it to his mouth. Mario started to take a drink, but he stopped and his eyes got wide. He looked apologetic. "Oh, but I forgot. It's your birthday," he said, in an exaggerated tone and he handed Vincent the bottle. Mario opened a can of beer as Vincent took a pull from the bottle of whiskey. He handed Vincent the beer and he took a gulp of it to wash the whiskey down.

Vincent was grateful that he had eaten breakfast. Whiskey tasted raunchy this early in the morning. He had never had enough of it to get use to it. The whiskey felt good in his stomach, but it had not in his mouth. Mario took the bottle as Vincent handed it to him. He took a big slug of it and handed it back, but Vincent declined.

"It's too early to get drunk," said Vincent. "Your right," agreed Mario, "It's too early for you to get drunk. You might have to drive after I get drunk." Vincent knew that it was bullshit. He had never seen Mario drunk. He had seen him drink enough to get that way. But he had never seen him stagger, or look stupid, or anything to cause one to think that he was drunk. Vincent thought that it was because Mario had been drinking the family wine since he was a child. Vincent knew it helped to be big, but he had seen a lot of big guys drunk.

"Let's go do something before we pick up everyone," suggested Mario. "It's too early to get them, anyway." "What?" asked Vincent, his interest piqued; Mario always had interesting ideas. "I know where there is some copper wire," answered Mario. He had watched a P. G. and E. crew working a little ways up the Feather River Canyon. He had seen them leave a bunch of coils behind.

"What are we going to do with the wire?" asked Vincent. "Cut it up, burn it and sell it for scrap," answered Mario. "You mean steal the wire?" asked Vincent. "Nawh," answered Mario, "its just waste they leave behind."

Vincent wasn't convinced that what they were going to do was not wrong, but maybe Mario was at least half right. They always needed money for gas, booze and cigarettes. The thought caused Vincent to need one, so he stuck one in his mouth, struck a match on the leg of his Levis and lit it. Vincent wondered why he had never seen Mario smoke. He knew Mario had been in the Navy and had got out with less than an honorable discharge. Vincent believed that all sailors smoke, drank, fornicated and raised a lot of Hell.

"How come you don't smoke?" he asked Mario. "How come you do?" asked Mario in return and Vincent had to think about that, because he wasn't sure. Vincent remembered stealing his mother's cigarettes when he was young. "I don't know," answered Vincent, "I guess I just got into the habit." "Well I didn't," answered Mario, "Because it's stupid."

"What's stupid about it?" asked Vincent, who was getting indignant.

"You ain't supposed to put anything into your lungs but air," retorted Mario. "Everybody does it," answered Vincent, rationalizing. "I don't," retorted Mario. "I enjoy smoking," stated Vincent, still rationalizing. "You think you do, anyway, Mario agreed. " They help my nerves," stated Vincent. Vincent knew that he was losing, but didn't want to give in. "They are what cause you to be nervous in the first place," stated Mario. "That's bullshit!" argued Vincent, "They make me feel good." "They make you feel good after they make you feel bad," stated Mario, in a matter of fact tone. "That sounds so stupid," retorted Vincent with contempt.

"There are none so blind as those who will not see," quoted Mario. "What the hell is that supposed to mean?" asked Vincent. He was getting indignant. "It means you don't want to hear the truth," replied Mario. "What is truth?" retorted Vincent and he added, heatedly, "I can quote the Bible too."

"Think back.'" ordered Mario, "How did the first cigarette you ever smoked make you feel?" "Sick," answered Vincent, sheepishly, after hesitating with the answer. "You see," explained Mario, "You are addicted to nicotine and after a certain time without it, you start feeling nervous. When you have another cigarette it makes you feel better." Vincent could see that Mario was right, but he didn't have to like it.

"I'll quit, someday," Vincent answered, with irritation. "Let's have another beer," offered Mario, cheerfully, in an attempt to placate. "I'll buy that," agreed Vincent, grateful to change the subject. Mario got the beers, opened them and gave one to Vincent. "Skosh," toasted Mario. "Skosh," repeated Vincent and they drank. "Let's go make some moola," suggested Mario. "Love that filthy lucre," answered Vincent and the boys walked to Mario's car and got in. Mario started the car and they drove off, headed for the Feather River Canyon.

The boys went up the Eight Mile Hill and a few miles past the Rock House, a restaurant and bar that was built out of large stones. It sat in a canyon, on the left side of the road, on the way east. Mario pulled into a wide spot in the road and parked. He climbed up the embankment and Vincent followed. It was steep going and brushy. The boys reached the top of the bank and Vincent followed Mario up a steep ravine. Vincent could see where some clearing had been done and holes dug. There were poles on the ground and some coils of new, copper wire cables. The cables were about an inch in diameter.

"This stuff isn't left over," commented Vincent, a little out of breath from the climb, "It's brand new and has never been used." "They have tons of it in their warehouse," retorted Mario, "But we don't have any." "This stuff is new," complained Vincent, "It belongs to the P. G. and E." "As much of it as I can carry belongs to me," answered Mario and he picked up a coil in each hand and headed back down the hill.

Vincent hesitated for a moment and then he picked up one of the coils. The coil was much heavier than it looked and Vincent groaned from the burden, but he was not to be bested by Mario. He picked up another coil with his other hand and headed after Mario. Vincent walked fast to catch Mario, but he stubbed his toe on a root. He didn't fall, but had to run to keep from it and he got away from himself.

The weight of the coils caused Vincent's momentum to get out of control. His feet were trying to keep up with his body. It didn't take long for him to be at a dead run. Vincent almost flew past Mario. Mario's mouth was agape as he watched Vincent fly by him. Mario had been puffing from the weight of the coils and Vincent had just gone by him like the coils were nothing. Mario was flabbergasted. He didn't see Vincent go head over heels at the bottom of the hill. Vincent got up, brushing himself off, looking to see if Mario had seen him fall. Vincent saw that he could not have, so he picked up the coils and carried them the rest of the way to the car. Vincent set the coils down and waited for Mario. He did his best to look nonchalant. In just a little while Mario arrived, huffing and sweating. He looked in amazement at Vincent standing there, looking so leisurely.

"How the Hell did you do that?" asked Mario, incredulous. "Do what?" asked Vincent, feigning naivety, while stifling a guffaw, almost choking. "How did you run with that stuff?" questioned Mario, "It was all I could do to walk with it." "It's all in the wrist," answered Vincent, weakly, his mirth was sapping his strength. His face was getting contorted from the strain. The mirth was escaping in little, jerky, spasms and then it all came out. Just like when the safety valve had cut loose on the steam shovel.

"Eeeeaaaahhhaaa." Vincent laughed and then he was in a convulsion. Mario couldn't help but laugh with him, or at him, but he looked confused. He didn't have a clue what he was laughing about. Mario was only laughing because of Vincent. "Hahahahehe," laughed Mario, "What in the Hell are we laughing about?" Vincent tried to tell him but it is hard to talk whilst having a convulsion.

"I got away from myself," Vincent finally got out, between the fits and then he lost control again. Mario continued to laugh with him, whilst waiting for further elucidation. "What does that mean?" asked Mario, weakly, he was about to join Vincent in a joint, convulsions. "I couldn't catch me," answered Vincent, as well as he was able and then he was lost again. His stomach was starting to hurt, giving him some incentive to gain self-control. Vincent was hanging on to the car and so was Mario. Vincent tried to inject some pertinence into the communication.

"We better get the Hell out of here," he suggested, but even that sounded funny. While still in the throes of mirth, they put the coils of cable into the trunk and placed themselves in the car. Mario started the car and they took off. It was exhilarating to escape the place of wrongdoing and it stimulated conversation, but the mirth devil was still lurking.

"I still don't understand how you did it?" questioned Mario, "How did you run with that stuff?" "I had to!" exclaimed Vincent and he giggled. "I don't understand," answered Mario, still puzzled, "Was something chasing you?" "No," answered Vincent, "My feet were chasing my body." Mario got a gleam in his eye; he was starting to comprehend what had happened. He giggled. "You mean?" Mario asked, and he giggled some more and it evolved, along with his comprehension, into a laugh. "You mean the weight of the cable pulled you down the hill?" And about that time, Mario's memory took him back to when he had seen Vincent shoot by him like a bullet. The mental image was vivid and it clutched his funny bone. It was like a hand clutching a hand full of water. Mario's funny bone turned into water and the mirth spilled out in a flood.

Mario laughed so hard he had to pull the car over and get out of it. He went to the front of the car and Vincent to the rear. They stayed that way until they got control of themselves. The boys avoided looking at each other on the way back to Vincent's place. They were almost back before they could look at each other safely.

"Let's take the cables over to the chopping block," suggested Mario and he carried two of them over. Vincent followed with the other two. Mario took the fasteners off one of the coils and laid about a foot of it across the chopping block. He told Vincent to give it a whack with the ax. Vincent took the double bladed ax and gave the cable a good whack. "Thunk," it sounded and the piece fell to the ground. They continued until the four coils were laying in pieces on the ground.

Mario went over to the house and got the hose. He pulled it over to the work area and told Vincent to turn the water on. When Vincent had done so, Mario proceeded to wet the work area. He told Vincent he didn't want to start a fire that he couldn't put out and then he asked for some diesel fuel. When Vincent brought it to Mario he poured some on the pile of pieces of cable and set it on fire. Black smoke billowed up from it.

"I hope the fire department doesn't come," said Vincent as he watched the smoke head for the sky. "It won't burn long enough for them to get excited," claimed Mario. In a little while the cable looked black and aged. Mario hosed it down to cool it off.

"You got something we can load it in?" asked Mario. Vincent had to think for a moment. "Would a galvanized tub do?" "That ought to do it," answered Mario and Vincent went around to the back of the shop to get the tub. He watched for rattlesnakes while he was back there. There were a lot of them in the area. After the boys had loaded the tub they put it in the trunk of Mario's car. The trunk lid wouldn't close all the way and they had to tie it down.

"Let's take it to Charley's," suggested Mario. Charley Goody was the junk man. Junk, scrap metal and anything used was Charley's business. Charley was good at it; he was a natural born, pack rat and he had no competition. Charley had acres of junk and his yard was right on the main drag. It was right in the middle of town, across the street from the biggest shopping center in town.

Charley's place was an eye sore and so was Charley. Although he was prosperous, you couldn't tell by looking at him. Charley shaved once a week, whether he needed it, or not. Charley must have changed his clothes on the same day. Charley looked like he was born in the floppy hat that he always wore. You can bet he wore the first dollar he made over his heart. Charley smoked Bull Durham, he was too cheap to smoke tailor made. It would be a cold day in Hell before he ever bought a pack of cigarettes. Charley would smoke one of yours, if it offered and he would save the butt for later.

Charley was a regular Arab when it came to dickering. Mario was no slouch, but he always lost to Charley. But, the boys got twenty-two dollars for the copper and that was enough for the booze for that day. The boys left Charley's and headed directly for Olie's Little Liquor Store. It was on the same street as Charley's, three blocks away.

Both boys were happy. Life was good. Who could ask for anything more than cars, money, booze and girls? One had to keep it in that order, too. After they had restocked their booze, Mario headed for Vincent's place.

"Let's go pick up Betty Jane first," suggested Vincent. "We can get her and then go get Mack and take them to my place." Vincent smiled and added, "I'm sure they will be able to think off something to do while we pick up the rest of the crew."

Vincent was sure the two were having sex together. Having sex with Betty Jane was a pleasing thought, but Vincent never coveted. He tried not to, anyway. Mario had a different attitude. He smiled more. "I think they are screwing every chance they get." Mario commented, "And I will screw her too, if I get the chance."

Vincent looked at him out of the corner of his eye and wondered if Mario would. He wondered if he would do it while she was Mack's girl. Vincent had a suspicion that he would and he didn't like it. Vincent looked at Mario with disapproval, but Mario didn't see him.

Betty Jane lived in the Flats, the downtown, residential area, on the south side of the levee. She lived only a few blocks from the levee, in a square, white, old wooden house. It rested high off the ground, because it had a basement. The house had a stairway to the front porch. The trim on the house was gray and so was the door.

Betty Jane was waiting for the boys on the porch. She was a small girl, not even five feet tall and not even a hundred pounds. Betty Jane had a pretty build. Her legs were slender and smooth looking, the kind you would like to wash with your tongue. Betty Jane had a fine little ass and her waist was tiny. Her breast looked squeezable and her shoulders were soft.

Betty Jane's face was cute, but not pretty. She had some bad teeth, with an overlap in front. Betty Jane's hair was blond and straight. She had a timid, innocent look and she was shy, humble and innocent. Even though Vincent believed she was no longer a virgin, she still seemed innocent to him. Vincent believed she had been one before Mack had got into her. He believed that no one else would get into her while she still loved Mack. Vincent could see that she was wondering where Mack was.

"We haven't picked him up yet," he told her before she could ask, "We are on our way to get him."

Betty Jane was bright and bubbly, full of the expectation of good and looking forward to seeing Mack. Their love had given her a security that she needed, one she didn't have at home. Her father was affluent enough, but he was an alcoholic and a tyrant. His substance came from the ownership of a variety store. Things were all right when he was at the store, but when he was home the fighting was hot and heavy.

Betty Jane had two brothers and an older sister. The younger brother was a homosexual, but he didn't want it known. Although she loved him, Betty Jane had no respect for him. The sister was mean to her and the older brother had no time for her, or any interest.

Vincent got out of the car and let Betty Jane get in the middle. She had a straw bag with her and Vincent knew that her little swimsuit was in it. Betty Jane was wearing white shorts, a pink polo shirt, with pink socks and white tennis shoes. She was cute as a bug's ear.

"You will have to ride on Mack's lap when we pick him up" Vincent told her, with a wide grin. "You won't mind that, will you?" he asked, lasciviously. Betty Jane giggled, turned a little pink and cast her eyes down. "I like to ride on his lap," Betty Jane said, demurely. "Why is that?" asked Vincent. "It feels good," she answered, without thinking. "What's it?" asked Vincent, playfully, "What's it?" "Stop that" Betty Jane complained, giggled and elbowed him in the ribs. This little banter went on as they rode out to her sweetheart's house.

"If you were not Mack's girl," Vincent teased, "I would make a pass at you." She giggled and looked up at him. "I wonder what would happen?" she asked, coquettish. "You would probably succumb to my charms," Vincent answered. "What is succumbing?" Betty Jane asked, looking up at him. "Giving in to my charms," he answered roguishly. "What charms?" she questioned and giggled. "My handsome face?" he asked, wetting his eyebrows with his pinky. "That's handsome?" Betty Jane asked, looking at his face and laughing. "How about my beautiful body?" he asked, mischievously. She looked him over and sneered. "That's a body?" she questioned and playfully poked him in the ribs again.

"She really digs your body," commented Mario, bored with not being a part of the action, he liked being in the center. He gave Vincent a horselaugh. "It's too bad you don't have Vincent's face!" exclaimed Betty Jane to Mario and then she flushed at her impudence. She had always had a soft spot for Vincent.

"Oh, ho!" exclaimed Mario, "What's this we hear from fair maid, Dost her heart yearn for other pleasure?" "Oh, no!" she exclaimed, flustered at revealing herself, "I didn't mean that," and then she blustered," I just think he's pretty." Betty Jane was red in the face now and she pointed her eyes at her lap. "Stop teasing me," she pleaded Vincent tussled with her hair affectionately and put his arm around her shoulders and gave her a hug. "Come on," he consoled, "We are just playing with you." She lifted her head; she was smiling, sheepishly. "I know," she answered and about that time they descended the hill to Mack's place.

The home was a ranch style, wood house that his father had built decades ago. The house sat close to and parallel with the road. About ten acres of kinfolk lived in the property behind them. Mack lived with his parents, who were well into their years, a sister who was older and much bigger than Mack and an older brother, who had a jelly belly.

It would not be surprising to Vincent if there were a still stashed out there in the oaks and pines. Mack's relatives seemed to have an aura of that sort of thing, like they may have migrated from the Ozarks. They were strange folk; they were different and one could not put their finger on just what the difference was. Perhaps, it was just because they came from a different part of the country. But Vincent had wondered about mixed blood, a little cousin begetting, maybe?

Betty Jane went right to Mack. She was like one of the family at his house and everyone expected her to be one of the family, eventually. Mack met her at the door and picked her up off of her feet. He kissed her, soundly and carried her to the car. It wasn't hard to see that they were in love; they made no attempt to hide it.

"Yo." greeted Mack, with his happy face, a Cheshire cat, grin across his face. It didn't take much to make Mack happy, Betty Jane, a few dollars in his pocket and something to do. "Yo, ho," answered Vincent and Mario, in unison. The two lovebirds got in the car, with the girl on the boy's lap. Betty Jane looked as happy as a bug in a rug and so did Mack.

Mario backed the Ford out of the driveway and the children were off in a cloud of dust. The girl kissed the boy on his lips and ran her fingers through his hair, affectionately. His hound dog eyes were aglow with pleasure. She felt good on his lap, with her lovely bottom pressing his loins. He flexed himself and she gave him a knowing, little, grin, as she felt the gentle nudge. The two cooed at each other in an unintelligible language.

Vincent could see that all that kept them from fornication was the present company. Vincent felt his own loins stir and he didn't need that, so he tried to think of something else. Vincent was grateful that it took only a few minutes to get from Mack's place to his.

"Do you want to wait here?" Vincent asked the lovebirds, "While we go after the others?" "Uh, hu," answered Mack, with a silly grin and his girl shook her head in the affirmative. Vincent watched them in his rear view mirror, as he drove off in his car with Mario as his copilot. They wouldn't need two cars with the lovebirds staying behind. Vincent watched them run into the house. He knew what they would be doing and he was covetous. He felt that it was wrong and he pulled his eyes and his mind away. Mario had not been unconscious all this time.

"We know what they are going to be doing," he commented while rolling his eyes around, "Don't we?" He poked Vincent. "I hope he doesn't knock her up," Vincent answered, with concern, "She is too little to be pregnant. She would be all stomach." "She wouldn't be able to see her feet for months," joked Mario.

CHAPTER 10

Vincent loved the drive to Bidwell Bar. The narrow, crooked road was a gradual rise from the valley to the Bar. The road began as a trail that the gold miners had built, or maybe it had started as a deer trail. It was about five miles of country road lined with oaks, manzanita, madrones, quaking asp and pine trees. There was a little breeze, but it was enough to make the leaves on the asp quake. The colors, the blues, greens and yellows were bright, crisp and beautiful. The day was so bright it made one squint.

Buck, his sister, Mary, Lois and her sister Lucy were riding with Vincent. The lovebirds were riding with Mario. It was a quiet ride. The noisemakers were in the other car, meaning Mario and Mack. Lois was sitting in front, between Buck and Vincent, while Mary and Lucy were in the back. They all had a can of beer in their hand. The radio was on full blast and Mary and Lucy were giggling about something. It was quiet in the front seat. Buck didn't have much to say and Vincent was tongue tied with Lois.

That didn't stop Vincent from thinking; he was anticipating the pleasure of seeing Lois in her swimsuit. He had seen her in it before, but it was still new to him. He wished that she already had it on so he could look at her thighs. Vincent loved to look at the inside of her thighs; her flesh looked so silky there. He wished that he could touch her there; he even wanted to kiss her there. Vincent blushed, thinking about it.

Vincent could feel the heat from her thigh coming through his pants. He wondered what it would be like to see and feel her naked body, to make love to her. His thoughts rushed blood to his face. Vincent was grateful that Lois couldn't read his mind. Vincent hoped God couldn't read it either, but he must be able to, or he wouldn't be God.

The old road was above the Bar. There were two bridges. The original suspension bridge had got so old and rickety they had to build a new one, but even so, it was now old. The original bridge had been saved by the efforts of the Historical Society and was now used as a footbridge.

The Bar was down in a canyon, via a narrower and more crooked road. The children traversed it and parked in the shade of a grove of oaks. There were a lot of cars parked. There was some kind of a barbecue going on, one's olfactory nerves told one so.

There were redwood picnic tables, dark colored by the elements, scattered among the trees. It was about time for lunch and happy faces were being stuffed. There was a beer can in almost every adult's hand. It was getting to be a very hot day. Vincent and his crowd were shedding their garments. The boys were ogling the girls; it was the natural thing to do and it was expected of them.

The girls all looked fine in their suits. But Mary being pale would have to spend a lot of time in the shade or in the water up to her neck. If one would stay in the water for long, though, they would turn blue. The water was as cold as snow.

Vincent was watching Lois as she walked to the water. Her bottom was doing just what it was supposed to do, making her look fine. She dove right into the water, causing Vincent to cringe, knowing how cold the water was. He wondered how she could do it. Vincent watched her swim as he walked to the water. He thought that she should be reincarnated as a fish. Lois would make a fine looking fish, he thought, to himself. She would drive all the boy fish crazy. He wondered if boy fish got erections. He was sure getting one.

Vincent stuck his toe in the water; he felt his testicles shrink and his erection. A shiver went up the full length of his body as he ventured further into the water. He had to force his loins into the water and an involuntary protest escaped from his lips. He inhaled through his clenched teeth.

Vincent hated the fact that he could not swim. He felt foolish and inadequate. He also felt helpless and there did not seem to be anything that he could do about it. Vincent hated walking around in the water while the others were swimming and having fun. He swore as he stubbed his toe on a rock. Vincent had tender feet and he hated the bottom of this particular body of water. It was layered with cobblestones, worn round and smooth. It was hard to get a solid footing on them, they moved under your weight.

Vincent hated the fear more than anything. He would feel frantic if he were in too deep and his footing felt insecure. Some times he felt like a coward, especially if someone was teasing him like they were going to pull him in. It would terrorize him and he would have to act like it didn't.

Vincent would hide his fear with anger. He was slow to wrath and slow to forgive. His friends knew this, and left him alone, but, unfortunately, there were others. Vincent had ventured into the water up to his chest trying to overcome his fear. When he slipped on a cobblestone he managed to regain his footing, but a redneck had seen the fear on his face. He had been swimming under the surface and had bobbed up twenty feet from Vincent.

"Come on in," jeered the redneck, "The water is great." Vincent was startled, but felt no fear until he saw the redneck's face. He had seen that look before and it had always meant trouble. Vincent was in no position for trouble. He stood there for a moment, trying to think of something to say that might avert trouble. The redneck started toward him.

Vincent started to turn around to flee, but knew the agitator would get to him before he could get to safe ground. Vincent didn't want his back to the guy. He gritted his teeth and waited. He wanted to yell for his friends, but he didn't want them to think that he was chicken. Vincent waited with fear gripping his innards.

The redneck had reddish blond hair. A lot of them do, who knows why? He had a smart aleck look on his face, as all of them do. Vincent hated him, instantly. He knew there would be no reasoning, only adamant stupidity.

"Don't you know how to swim?" asked the redneck, with more malice than mischief. Vincent said nothing; he just watched Redneck's eyes to see when he would make his move. Redneck came face to face with him, within arms length. "I guess I had better teach you," he said, with a malicious grin on his face, "It will be fun."

Hate, caused by fear had turned Vincent's stomach into a fist. He didn't say anything. He knew words were not a sword with this kind of people. Words would be a waste of time. The redneck made a move for his arm.

"Come on fella," he jeered. Vincent had been shifting his weight and hadn't lost his balance. With a lightning fast left jab, Vincent hit the jerk on the nose, turned and headed for shore. If the redneck had been surprised Vincent had not seen it and never looked back. Mario had seen the hit. He had watched the guy move toward Vincent. Mario had been watching to see what was going to happen. Vincent's punch had come out of nowhere, almost too fast to see. The redneck was thrashing around in the water and had lost his footing because of the punch. It had hit him squarely on the end of his nose, blinding him.

The redneck was enraged by the time he had got his footing and his vision back. He swam after Vincent. Vincent was already to his ankles on his way out of the water. Vincent walked out of the water and turned to see his enemy. Redneck was out of the water to his knees. He was coming after Vincent like a raging bull after a red cape. Vincent was not going to back down, though his enemy was much bigger. He might have, had his friends not been there. He was afraid of the big redneck, to the point of nausea. But he was not going to run. Vincent took a boxer stance and stood ready.

Vincent saw the enemy slow down with a change in expression coming over his face. Out of the corner of his eye Vincent saw Mario standing just to the right of him. Mario was spread legged, ready for action, big as a barn.

"What's happening?" asked Mario, with a devilish grin, anxious, for trouble and a chance to show off in front of the girls. "This asshole wants to teach me how to swim," answered Vincent, with new confidence. "Oh, goody." answered Mario, with enthusiasm, "He can teach me too." Mario stood there with his Charles Atlas figure, the grin even wider. It was comical to see the rage melt from the face of the redneck. His nose was still bleeding.

"You want to teach me how to swim?" asked Mario. "I guess I'll pass," answered the redneck, not wanting to have a single thing to do with the hulk that was standing in front of him. He turned around, and went back to the water. "What happened?" asked Mario. "He was trying to pull me into deeper water," answered Vincent, "And you know how I am about water."

"Haw haw," laughed Mario, "But he didn't, poor redneck." "Piss on rednecks!" retorted Vincent, with vehemence. "What did you do to him?" asked Mario, as the rest of the group gathered around them. "I hit him on his nose," answered Vincent, as he hit his palm with his fist.

"You hit that big palooka?" asked Lois, after taking in a breath of wonder. She was looking at him with new interest. "Didn't he hit you back?" she asked. "He wanted to," answered Vincent and he laughed. "Why didn't he?" asked Lois, perplexed by his laughter.

"When he saw Tarzan here," Vincent answered and laughed, "He went the other way. Lucky for me," he said, with humility. "You would have mowed him down," said Mack, with conviction. "I don't know about that," answered Vincent, "He was awful big." "The bigger they are, the harder they fall," stated Mack. "If they fall," retorted Vincent, with pessimism, as the group moseyed back to where the cars were parked. They were going after more beer. Lois was hanging on to Vincent's arm.

"Why did you hit him in the first place?" Lois asked him, not having heard his explanation. She got hold of his hand and held it. There was an intimacy about her move that hadn't been there before. Vincent responded with a squeeze to her hand. He explained to her and she asked him why he didn't learn how to swim. Vincent told her that he was afraid of the water and told her why. "All the more reason to learn," she pleaded. "Someday," answered Vincent, not believing himself. Lois looked at his eyes, but said no more about it.

The adrenaline in Vincent's blood from the fight mode had left discomfort in his stomach. He had discovered that alcohol would relieve this discomfort; it was a constricted feeling. Mario handed everyone a beer and Vincent opened his and chugalugged it. It smoothed his stomach and he was quiet. Vincent was always quiet with Lois, they had no rapport; they seemed to have nothing to talk about. They had a physical attraction and that seemed to be all. Vincent was wondering why he couldn't talk to her. He knew it wasn't just her; it was hard for him to talk to any girl.

It was not that way with Mary; she was like one of the guys. Vincent couldn't figure why his head turned off when he was with a girl, especially a pretty one. For one thing, he had no idea what would interest them. Vincent yearned to be able to converse with Lois. She was a pretty, desirable girl and one has to start somewhere. It seemed to him that conversation should be the vehicle. The thought came to him that one had to build a fire before one could roast a hot dog and a little, grin showed on his face. Lois caught it.

"What's funny?" she asked, inquisitively. "Nothing," he answered, but he couldn't suppress a grin. "Come on.'" she pleaded, "Tell me. "I can't," he told her, "it's too, embarrassing." "You never tell me anything!" she retorted, angrily and then she pouted. Vincent got himself another beer. When he was sipping on it he heard Mack's foolish, intoxicated, voice.

"I'm going to jump off the bridge.'" he bragged, loud enough for God to hear him. "I hope it's a tall one, "quipped Mario. "Try to land on your head, so you won't get hurt," offered Vincent in good fun. "Screw you guys!" exclaimed Mack, as he flipped them the bird and headed for the bridge.

It was a single suspension bridge, about twenty yards, long. It had a little tollhouse on one end that was now used as a concession booth. The deck of the bridge was about four yards above the water. Some young boys were jumping from the rail. Some of them had already jumped and had returned for another go at it. They were standing in the sun shivering with goose bumps and teeth chattering. Mack climbed over the rail and jumped feet first, with the grace of a new born calf. He was holding his nose as he hit the water. In a few seconds his head broke the surface and his thin, straight hair looked even thinner as it was plastered to his head. His eyes were wide open.

"Holy shit!" he exclaimed, ending in a splutter, as his lips went back into the water. He raced back to shore like he was being chased by the Devil. He got out of the water dancing like a clown, trying to get warm. When Mack got back on the bridge, the rest of the gang was waiting for him. "Buurrrhhh!" exclaimed Mack, "That water is as cold as a whore's heart."

"And just how do you know about whores?" asked Betty Jane Potts, petulantly. "Vincent told me," answered Mack, glibly and that was rather unusual; glib was not one of Mack's traits. Betty Jane looked over at Vincent. "Don't look at me!" he exclaimed, defensively, "l don't know a thing about whores."

"I know all about whores," bragged Mario, his brown eyes, bright. "Sure you do," said Mary, not believing. "How did you learn?" asked Lois, her interest piqued. All eyes were glued on Mario. "I was a sailor!" exclaimed Mario, as if that should explain it all. "So?" asked Lois, again, "How did you learn. "A pimp took me to one on Mission Street," bragged Mario, proud as a peacock. All eyes were riveted on him now and he liked that, he was a natural born, show off. "How old were you?" asked Betty Jane, the girls were asking all the questions. "Sixteen and never been kissed," answered Mario, beaming. "Never been missed," quipped Mary. "How did you get in so young?" asked Buck. "I lied about my age," Mario answered. "Like you are lying now?" asked Mary, who had always doubted his honesty. "What did she do to you?" asked Lois, with a raised eyebrow and she giggled, "Maybe you better not tell me," she added. "She did everything.'" exclaimed Mario, lasciviously, rolling his eyes, "Around the world." "What's around the world?" asked Lois, innocently. "You don't want to know," answered Vincent, embarrassed; he had heard the answer to that.

"She licked him all over with her tongue," explained Mack, without any ceremony, "And gave him a blow job." "Oh, my God!" exclaimed Betty Jane Potts, "Do they really do that?" She shivered and then she giggled.

Vincent was watching her face and was wondering whether the shiver was from revulsion, or excitement. He just could not read her face enough to know, but would guess the latter. Vincent thought to himself, "Maybe Mack is in for a trip." Vincent looked at Lois. Her face was impassive, but he knew she was embarrassed. She was a shy girl and hid her feelings. Vincent felt like being horrid, for a reason he knew not and he stepped out of character for a moment.

"And how long is your tongue?" he asked Lois. The girl's face turned crimson, she had been thinking about the "Around the World" thing and it was like he had caught her. Everyone was looking at her, waiting for her reaction to his crude question. She was awfully embarrassed, but she was a brave little soldier and she answered defiantly. "Long enough," and everyone laughed at her pluck.

Lois was not mad at Vincent for embarrassing her: it was the most stimulating thing he had said to her since she had met him. She wished he would do more. She liked him a lot, but sometimes he bored her to tears. She knew that he thought she was too nice to do things to her, but sometimes she did not want to be nice. She wished he would cooperate, and help her to be bad.

Lois liked to believe that she wanted to stay a virgin until she married. She liked to believe that she would not go all the way with Vincent, but she would at least like to go part of the way with him. He could, at least get a little nasty with her. Lois had thought about what it would be like to go all the way with Vincent. She had even wondered how big he was. Though these thoughts and the images they had brought forth had excited her, they had also embarrassed her. She had always pushed them into a corner of her mind.

All the gang had wished Vincent a happy birthday, one by one, as they had been picked up. Lois wanted to get him alone before she did it again. She sent him after a blanket and some lotion, so they could soak up some sun together. She found a sunny spot away from the gang and waited for Vincent.

"I hope you have a happy birthday party," she told him, as he spread the blanket and she sat on it. "Thanks," he answered, feeling uncomfortable about not being able to invite her. He handed her the bottle of lotion. She opened it and started putting it on her lovely legs. Vincent wished he could do it for her.

"Why can't you have girls at the party?" she asked. "The guys just want to get drunk and crude," he answered, hoping she would believe him. His mother had not wanted girls there; she had been afraid that with girls there the party might get out of hand. Vincent had suspected she had feared an orgy. He wished it could be an orgy; he had never been to one before. Lois accepted his explanation, but he suspected she had not bought it. He could tell by the look on her face, but she asked him no more.

"Would you put some lotion on my back?" Lois asked him, "I can't reach it." She handed him the open bottle. Vincent went behind her and spread some of the lotion on his hand. He smoothed it gently on her back. Her skin felt so much different than his, smoother, softer. Her skin got oily with the lotion and felt sensuous, sending a message to Vincent's lower end.

"You have a nice back," he told her. "Is that all?" she asked, petulantly. "All of your body is nice." "Is that all?" "Lovely?" he asked. "I guess lovely is all right," she agreed.

Lois was so shy; she could not believe that she was being so forward with Vincent. She felt different with him ever since the confrontation with the redneck. Vincent didn't seem like a boy anymore. He had hit the guy on the nose and hadn't acted like a tough guy. She did not know why, but at that moment she wanted his hands on her.

"Would you put some on the back of my legs?" she asked, as she lay on her tummy on the blanket. Lois laid her head on her arm and closed her eyes. Vincent gazed at the girl's curvaceous bottom with desire. Her position on her tummy had raised it to a lovely contour. Her thighs were open just a little. Vincent started putting the oil on the girl's feet and worked his way up.

Perspiration was popping out in little beads on Vincent's forehead as he put the oily lotion on the soft flesh behind the girl's knee. His eyes were glued to her bottom while he put the lotion on the inside of her thighs, clear to the edge of her suit. How he wanted to see her bottom without the suit covering it.

Vincent was on fire with desire. He thought of a childhood lyric, "Liar, liar, pants on fire, hanging from a telephone wire." Only he wasn't lying, but his pants were on fire. It was hard not to put his hand on those beautiful mounds. And that wasn't all that was hard. Vincent's hand was so close. He held his breath as he almost touched the apex of her leg. The round mound was so inviting, so tempting.

Lois had held her breath; she had prayed he would touch her. His hand was so close to the fire. Vincent's hand was hot, making her fire hotter. Lois pleaded in her mind for him to touch her, wanting to move her body, the part she wanted him to touch, to his hand.

"What are you doing to my little sister?" asked Lucy, with mock suspicion, "What is your hand doing where it's at?" "Just putting lotion on her," answered Vincent, flustered and red faced. "The sun doesn't shine in there!" exclaimed Lucy.

Lucy had always been a smart-ass, full of mischief. Lois was red faced, also, she felt like she had been caught, even though she hadn't done anything but think. Lois was embarrassed. She realized that had she been alone with Vincent she might have gone all the way with him.

Lois jumped up, ran to the river and jumped in. "What have you got to say for yourself?" questioned Lucy, suspicious of all the embarrassment. "All I was doing was putting lotion on her." blustered Vincent, getting indignant. "Where the sun doesn't shine?" Lucy asked, with her hands on her hips. "I wasn't watching the sun," retorted Vincent, ticked off now. "I know what you were looking at!" she shot back, quickly as a snake's tongue. "I look at what I like!" snapped Vincent, defiantly.

"She does have a pretty ass, doesn't she?" The girl was laughing at him now, amused by his discomfort. She couldn't be mad at him for his obvious desire for her sister, a little jealous, maybe. "She does have a pretty ass," answered Vincent, grinning now; he had realized that she had been teasing him. "Do you like my ass?" Lucy asked, turning it to him. It was a nice ass, but not as voluptuous as her sister's. "It'll do in a pinch," he answered, making a move to do such a thing. She slapped his hand away, laughing. "You are a naughty person!" she exclaimed and wiggled herself away, heading for the river.

Vincent was getting in the mood to party. He got up and went to the car. He would have another beer and some whiskey. Vincent was going to get primed for his birthday party. The plan was to get shitfaced, drunk. His testicles were hurting from the turning on and off. He was a plug with no receptacle, a light without a socket, and a wiener without a bun.

CHAPTER 11

Mario left to go after more booze, but that was not all he was going to do. He was going after a surprise present for Vincent and the rest of the boys, a present he had not told anyone about. It was after dark and the boys were just about out of booze. They had taken the girls home, had ate the cake, played some poker and had started to get a little bored.

Mario had a cure for this and he called her "Hot pants." She was a Thermalito nympho and her specialty was the "Gang Bang." And Mario had made a date with her. Dora was the girl's name. She was kind of cute, in a crude sort of way. Dora's hair was curly, dirty and blond. She had a good body, about five feet of it and no more than a hundred pounds. Dora was eighteen years old, which is a good age, not too old and not young enough to be jail bait. Mario was thinking that she might be a good vehicle for the clap, as she got into the car.

"Are you ready for a party?" asked Mario, with a leer, pandering to her crudeness. "I'm ready to fuck all night!" she exclaimed, cheerfully. Mario's eyes opened wide and he cleared his throat. He had not expected such a direct answer. "That's nice," he answered, trying to look cool. "How many boys do you have?" she asked, in obvious anticipation. "Four of us, counting myself," answered Mario. "Oh, goody!" she exclaimed, exuberantly, "Maybe by the time I get through with all of you, one of you will be able to go again." Mario rolled his eyes around, but was unable to comment.

Vincent was not only surprised by Dora's entrance, he was aghast, speechless. He had heard of Dora's exploits and here she was, in his house, in his mother's house. What if his mother should find out? How could he hide his feelings from the guys? He could not contaminate himself with this girl. He could no more stick his dingus into this girl than he could stick his nose into a pile of cat poop.

"What a good idea," commented Vincent, after he had regained his composure. He tried not to look alarmed as he tried to motion Mario away with his eyes. The other guys had gathered around Dora; they were all aware of her hobby. Mario followed Vincent into the john. "We got to get her out of here!" proclaimed Vincent, "I do not want pecker tracks all over my mother's house."

"Let's take her for a ride," suggested Mario, not to be thwarted by trivial details. "Good idea," agreed Vincent, "The sooner the better." They whisked the softheaded nympho away from Vincent's abode. Vincent was driving his Ford with the girl between him and Mario. The rest of the boys were in the back seat with their anticipation erections.

Dora was just too crude for Vincent and he didn't think there was anything that she could do that would raise his root. At the same time that Vincent was headed up the Cherokee Road, Mario's hand was headed up the girl's leg.

The road was narrow and serpentine, mostly an incline, as far as he had planned to go. The road went up to Table Mountain and all the way to Highway Seventy. The road was rough as a cob in some places. The terrain was rocky, volcanic and scrub oak, studded. Before they had got to their destination, Dora had shed her panties, had opened Mario's fly and was squirming on his lap, with him in her.

Unbelievable sounds were coming out of Dora. When they arrived at their destination Mario ordered everyone out of the car. That is as he could while the girl was squirming on him. The boys bailed out and Mario got into the back seat with the girl to continue their fornication.

The boys stood there and watched the car rock from its internal commotion. In a little while the car stopped rocking and Mario got out. He was buttoning his fly; he was wearing a satisfied grin. He'd just got out of the car, when Dora stuck her head out the window. She looked wild and disheveled.

"Next!" the girl hollered. Vincent couldn't believe his ears. He felt pity and a little sick. There was something missing in the girl's face and her voice. He could see her clearly in the moonlight. Something was missing in her; it made her seem alien. Mack, who would fornicate with a snake if someone would hold it for him, went forth, enthusiastically.

The car jumped around again for a little while and then Mack got out with the same kind of look on his face. He was buttoning his pants. "Next!" Vincent groaned as he thought of the pecker tracks that were going to be on his back seat. He was hoping that Buck would be eager, but Buck was shy and he may have even been a virgin, and he held back. "Next!" They heard the voice again and it was not at all patient. Dora's head was stuck out the window; she was looking to see who was next. Buck's feet were glued to the street.

"You go next," pleaded Buck, to Vincent. "Don't any of you assholes want to fuck?" hollered Dora, impatiently. Vincent pushed Buck forward and he got into the car, reluctantly. There was no one left for Dora but Vincent; he was next. He stood there with consternation, loath to get in the car with her, repulsed by her but not wanting to look like a pansy to his buddies. What could he do?

"Next!" sounded the siren call. There was no escape. Vincent had to maintain his image. He got into the car. The girl stunk so bad he recoiled from her touch. She tried to unbutton his pants. She felt his spurn. "What's wrong with you?" she asked, as she continued to unbutton his pants, with eager fingers. "Nothing!" he exclaimed, defensively, but he wanted, desperately, to remove his nose from the scene. Her odor was insulting his olfactory nerves. Vincent was repelled by her and there was nothing he could do about it.

"You don't want to fuck me?" she asked, incredulously. He wanted to save his image but realized there was no way that he would be able to. Vincent bolted out of the car inhaling deep breaths of the clean night air. "I just can't get a hard on," he explained to the guys. It worked with them, but not with Dora.

"You chicken shit prick!" Dora hollered out the window. The guys laughed. The angry, girl rode in the back seat on the way back down the hill, calling Vincent names all the way. "What was wrong with you?" asked Mario, after they had dropped the girl off. "She stunk like a dead whore!" exclaimed Vincent, with disgust. "Why didn't you just hold your nose and dive in?" asked Mack, who probably loved nasty odors. "Ugh!" exclaimed Vincent, holding his nose with contempt. "You are just too pure for this world," jeered Mario. "You will never be a pussy eater," commented Mack.

After the debauchery, the boys were thirsty and ready to party. They went back to Vincent's and partied into the wee hours of the morning. The boys crashed in various places in the house; where they had either fallen asleep, or passed out.

By the time the guys left the next day, there was nothing left in the house to eat, except Hungry Jack Pancake mix and some syrup. And on top of that, they had dirtied every dish, bowl and glass in the house, not to mention the pots and pans. What hadn't fit in the sink had ended up in a laundry tub on the floor. Vincent managed to get everything cleaned up before the family got home. He was getting awfully tired of hot cakes. He might never eat them again.

Mario and the manager of the Empire Theater were friends. It was a little theater, a block away from the main theater, The State. The Empire was a one level theater, while the State was two; it had a balcony. The State ran first run movies, while Empire ran seconds.

The manager was Bob Anderson; he was about thirty. His features were flat, making him look like a pugilist. Bob's wife, Betty, was a pretty, petite blond. She worked at the theater as his girl Friday.

Mario did occasional odd jobs for Bob and for this Mario had free access to the theater and could bring a guest. Vincent was Mario's guest most of the time. One Saturday night, right after Vincent's birthday, Vincent and Mario were enjoying a free movie at the Empire Theater. They both heard a commotion in the lobby and went to see what was happening. A drunken tunnel stiff was causing the trouble. There were always a lot of tunnel stiffs in town on Saturday night. They were there to spend their big checks having a good time. They were called tunnel stiffs because they worked in tunnels. Some called them miners and that was their true nomenclature.

The miner's work was dangerous and they acted accordingly. They lived like there was no tomorrow and for a lot of them, there hadn't been. There were many accidents, some on the job and some on route, back and forth to the job. The miners made big money. They worked hard and played harder. At this time the P. O. E. Project was going full blast. It was a long-range project to obtain electrical power from the Feather River. For this end a series of dams, tunnels and powerhouses, with huge generators were placed.

A big, drunk, tunnel stiff was being obnoxious to the girl at the snack counter. The manager was temporarily out of the theater. The girl was pretty, small and blond. Mario, egomaniac that he was, jumped at the chance to impress her and to be her hero. The tunnel stiff had his back to Mario and was facing the girl at the snack counter. The miner was leaning on the counter. Mario walked up behind him and tapped him on the shoulder.

"Hey, mister!" proclaimed Mario, in a swaggering tone, his chest and ego puffed up like a mating pigeon, "I think you should leave the little lady alone." The miner spun around with eyes blazing. He was a blond guy, Nordic looking. He shoved Mario back with both hands. "Who asked you? You Guinea bastard!" exclaimed the angry miner. Mario saw red; this term was equal to calling him a black person. Mario was dark, but not that dark. He made a move to push the miner back, but before he could, the guy hit him on his nose.

"Blap," it sounded like a wooden club hitting a cantaloupe. Mario got a surprised look on his face and then the blood started gushing from his nose. He got scared. "Get me to the hospital!" Mario exclaimed. In his fear, he had forgotten the fight. The miner was also, scared and sorry; it showed on his face. He was trying to apologize. The miner said he was sorry over and over as Vincent was trying to get Mario out the door. Just about this time, Bob showed up and wanted to call an ambulance, but Mario declined, he was too scared to wait. "Vincent will take me," Mario said, in a bubbly sound through his hand, which was holding his nose.

Mario had his car parked on High Street, pointing up the hill toward the railroad station. The hospital was in the other direction. Vincent helped Mario to get to Mario's Ford and into the passenger's side. Vincent got into the pilot's side. Mario kept his face pointed toward the door in an attempt to keep the blood from the white rabbit fur glued to the dash.

"Hurry up!" commanded Mario, fearfully, "I'm bleeding to death!" His fear was contagious. "Alright!" answered Vincent, impatiently grinding the gears, trying to get the car in reverse. He wasn't going to take the time to go to the corner and turn around. He was going to cut a U-Turn in reverse and head the other way.

It was a good plan in principle, but the maneuver did not work out as planned. There was no one parked behind Vincent so he took off in reverse gear. He was not use to the necking knob that was on the steering wheel; it was a palm knob. Vincent shot onto the street with the Ford in reverse and the knob got away from him for just a second. But long enough for him to lose control and slam into the side of a car parked across the street. It caved in the pilot's door. The car was a shiny new Buick and still had the paper license in the window.

"Get the Hell out of here!" yelled Mario, hysterically, which Vincent did, without any further ado. Vincent made it to the Community Hospital without any further difficulty. He took Mario into the emergency vestibule. After the paper work was complete, Mario disappeared with the white coats.

Vincent wondered how they would treat a person who was having a heart attack. Would they take care of the paper work first? It was two hours before Vincent saw Mario again. He was pale, but was on his feet. Mario told Vincent that the doctor had had to sear the inside of his nose to stop the bleeding. He said he couldn't feel his nose; they had shot it full of Novocain.

"If I want to make it home alive," remarked Mario as they walked to the car "I had better drive." Vincent grinned sheepishly, but said nothing. "I hope no one saw you hit the car," said Mario, prayerfully, "That was hit and run, you know." "I know," answered Vincent, "I hope no one saw, too," and then he laughed. "What's funny?" asked Mario. "I'll just say that you were driving," answered Vincent and laughed again. "Ha, ha," replied Mario, but he was not laughing, "You are about as funny as a death in the family." By this time they were at Vincent's car and Vincent got out of Mario's Ford. "I'll see you tomorrow," said Vincent. "Not if I see you first," replied Mario, with a straight face and then he grinned and waved as he drove off.

One night, toward the end of the week, Vincent was sitting at the dinner table with his family. Somehow the conversation topic turned to

Jesus Christ. Vincent remembered reading an article in the last Sunday paper. It had been an article about a man who claimed to be the second coming of Christ. Vincent was telling what he could remember about the article, when Doc interrupted him.

"It wasn't in the Sunday paper," he stated with authority, with a smug look. "Yes it was!" retorted Vincent, irritated by the rude interruption and Doc's insinuating attitude. Vincent answered with certainty; he remembered there was a picture of the guy. He had had long hair and had been wearing a robe. He had looked just like the Jesus Vincent had seen in a movie recently.

"It wasn't in the paper," argued Doc, stubbornly, "I would have seen it." "Maybe you need glasses," retorted Vincent, getting aggravated. "I can see better than you can," stated Doc and this was the truth, but it didn't have anything to do with the argument. This was just a clash of wills. "Maybe your eyes were closed," answered Vincent, defiantly, "Like your mind." And this was the truth; Doc's mind was closed. He was adamant about a lot of things. You had to think like he did, or you were wrong. "I'll go find the article," said Vincent, as he started to get up. "It doesn't exist," stated Doc, with arrogance.

Audrey was appalled by Doc's arrogance; she was liberal about everything. "Are you calling Vincent a liar?" she asked, rebelliously. "No," answered Doc, "He just doesn't know what he is talking about." Vincent pushed his chair back from the table, abruptly. He was by nature, a humble, meek person, but Doc's arrogance had burned it out of him and now he was mad.

"And you don't know your ass from a hole in the ground!" stated Vincent, with a quiet fury and he turned his back from the table and walked away. "You shut up that kind of talk!" said Doc, loudly. "Go to Hell!" answered Vincent and he walked into his room and closed the door behind him.

Audrey had been behind him and not knowing, Vincent had closed the door in her face. Audrey opened the door behind him and came into his room. Vincent spun around, thinking that it was Doc. He was relieved to see that it was his sister.

"He had no right to talk to you like that," she consoled. "God!" exclaimed Vincent, with exasperation," He is so self righteous!" With a feeling of futility, Vincent started to search his room. It was the last place he could remember seeing the article. "I wish I could find it," he muttered. "He would not believe you if you did," said Audrey, with resignation. He will never admit to being wrong about anything," she stated. Knowing what his sister had said was true; Vincent stopped searching and sat down on the edge of his bed. Audrey sat next to him. He was grateful for her loyalty. "I'll get even," he said, softly, but he knew he wouldn't even try. It was not his way. Vincent would just resent it and do nothing. It had already given him indigestion.

His mother tapped softly on the door. "You had better apologize to Doc," she pleaded. "When Hell freezes over," exclaimed Vincent through the door and she left it at that, hoping that God would take care of it.

Early, one Sunday evening about a week later, the gang was having a beer bust out at the Rocky Honcutt swimming hole. It wasn't much of a swimming hole, but it was out in the boonies, where they could make all the noise they wanted. There were some oak trees by the hole and from the branch of one of the trees hung a rope. Someone had tied it there many moons ago. One could swing out over the swimming hole. Mack was swinging on it, making Tarzan sounds. He went back and forth a few times and then, about half way out, he let go. He fell, holding his nose, with arm and legs flailing. Mack hit the water feet first, with a splash. He stayed under in the murky water as long as he could. It was long enough for everyone to get concerned and then his funny face broke the surface and all laughed with relief.

Everyone was there, except Audrey. She had started her period and had been suffering from the cramps. Audrey had asked Vincent to come and get her later. Vincent, selfish as he was, had wanted to see how far he could get with Lois without his sister around. He had not said anything to his friends about it. Vincent had thought if he didn't say anything, he could just act like he had forgotten. He didn't think that she would have got over the cramps, anyway.

Vincent drank a lot of beer and had a lot of fun with Lois that day; it was the best time that they had ever had together. He might have even got into her pants had he not got so drunk. Vincent had drunk so much his tool had become just a spigot.

Audrey had waited and wondered why Vincent had not come back to get her. It mattered not, now, a sailor, whom she had met through Lucy, had showed up. Stacy Marks had come to get her in his baby blue, 1935 Ford coupe. It was a pretty little thing with its teardrop skirts and rolled, pleated upholstery.

Stacy had not been wearing his uniform; he had been wearing Levis instead. He was small, with a baby face and he looked no older than Vincent. Stacy was twenty, but he looked and acted like a teenager. Grace, thinking that Stacy was a teen, had let Audrey go out with him. Grace thought that she would be safe; God had always watched over her children.

Audrey had not said a word about Stacy being a sailor on leave. Or that there had been another sailor waiting for them at The Red Dog Saloon and that he had been a year older than Stacy. Danger excited Audrey and she had always liked to walk along the wild side. She had always said that she was going to live fast, die young and leave a beautiful memory. She had said that many times. She had been kidding, of course.

There were a lot of taverns scattered here and there, all over the valley. Most of them had a jukebox, a little dance space, food and beer. Stacy and Audrey had picked up his buddy, Duke, at The Red Dog Saloon and they had headed out into the valley. Duke had bought a case of beer to take with them.

The trio headed west on Highway 162 and landed in a tavern in Richvale. There was a lot of western music on the jukebox and that was what they wanted to hear. Audrey loved to dance and she had two sailors to dance with. She also loved to drink, but they wouldn't serve her in the tavern, so she had to go to the car for refreshments. The trio stayed there for a couple of hours, dancing to the music of Hank Williams, Ernest Tubbs and other note worthies.

The trio got itchy feet and headed further west. It was warm, the moon was full, they were thirsty and so were the mosquitoes. The sailors told salty stories. The trio laughed, drank beer and swatted mosquitoes for about twenty miles and they landed in a tavern in Butte City.

There were few taverns in Butte City, but they only needed one at a time. And they didn't need the bottle of whiskey that Duke had bought at the liquor store, either. They already were feeling no pain. They got a little wild and after Duke had tried to do a tap dance on the little cocktail table, the trio had been escorted to the swinging door and told to go home.

Just outside of town, Stacy made a sharp left turn on Highway 45 and headed south. The two drunken sailors and Audrey landed in a tavern in Colusa. They stayed until it closed at two in the morning. They were all drunk, tired and sleepy as they headed for home. Duke was in the pilot's seat and he was driving too fast. Stacy was making out with Audrey, who was sitting in the middle. She was giggling at something he had said in her ear.

Duke got on the wrong road and failed to negotiate a turn. The little Ford's wheels got into the soft shoulder and Duke lost control. The car went over an embankment. It landed upside down in an irrigation canal. The car hit the water hard and Audrey's head went through the top of the car, which was part, wood and part clothe. Audrey was dead before she could scream. Her silly wish had come true.

All three had been ejected from the car. Audrey's body floated down the canal. Stacy and Duke swam to shore. They searched in vain for Audrey. They walked five miles to a farmhouse and called the sheriff. It was hours before Audrey's body was found.

CHAPTER 12

Vincent awoke with a hangover; a nightmare woke him. He dreamed that he was a little boy and had been in a tub taking a bath. He had been playing with a little wooden boat that his grandpa had made for him. Vincent had heard a noise behind him and it had spooked him. He had twirled around to see what it was, but before he could, someone had pushed him down into the water. Vincent had been pushed down to the bottom of the tub on his back. He had struggled and tried to see who it was through the water, but soap had got into his eyes. Vincent had struggled; in frenzy he had awoke in a sweat.

Vincent looked over at his clock; it read five in the A. M. Hangovers made him too nervous to lie in bed. It was still warm. He went to the bathroom to relieve his bladder. Vincent took an Alka Seltzer to relieve his headache. He took a shower to wake his self and to wash the sweat off. While eating corn flakes, he decided he would hitch a ride up the canyon and see if he could find a job on the Power Project. It would be cheaper than driving his car and his tires were rags. Vincent finished getting dressed, had some more coffee and left the house.

Walking helped his nerves and by the time he got to the highway, about two miles, he felt better. Vincent was glad he had got away before his sister had got up; he was feeling guilty about not picking her up. He had not yet figured what to tell her. He wished he had gone back to get her. He hadn't made out with Lois, anyway. The lie had been for nothing. It hadn't really been a lie, though; he had just pretended to forget. It was still a lie in his mind, though. Sooner, or later, he would have to face her about it, but at least he had postponed it.

Vincent caught a ride with a bunch of hung over tunnel stiffs. Some of them were still drinking and one of these was the pilot. He was flying a little low, causing the odds to be in favor of them becoming statistical.

Vincent was frightened as the car careened around blind curves, but there wasn't a whole lot that he could do about it. A bottle of whiskey was being passed around and the first time it got to him, he declined. The miners didn't want to be late for work and Vincent knew that it would be futile to try to get them to stop to let him out. It was a dangerous road and Vincent wanted, desperately, to get out of the car.

The pilot passed a truck on a blind curve and Vincent's heart was in his mouth until he saw it was clear. The miners cheered the pilot when he passed the truck and it was clear. The bottle came to Vincent and this time he took a slug. The whiskey was raunchy stuff; it burned all the way down and bounced when it hit bottom; like his stomach wasn't sure what to do with it. By the time they got to their destination, Jarbo Gap, Vincent wasn't feeling well at all. He lost his corn flakes, milk and whiskey under the shade of a tall pine tree. Vincent felt awful and wished he were home in his bed.

Vincent felt something else, too, he had felt it all morning, but he couldn't put his finger on it. He felt uneasy, depressed. Maybe it was because of Audrey. Vincent was still feeling guilty about what he had done. But he knew that when he explained it to her, she would forgive him. So why did he feel so fraught with something, he knew not what?

Vincent stood there in limbo with the feeling that he was in the wrong place. He started walking toward the construction trailer where they did the hiring. Vincent stopped when he saw a bunch of workers getting off shift; they were headed for their cars. Forgetting why he was there, Vincent went over to one of the cars and asked a bewhiskered miner for a ride back to town. The big man, with a red and gray beard, kindly told him that he was welcome to ride with them.

The ride back wasn't hurried like the ride up had been, so Vincent leaned back in the seat to relax. He could not relax, he felt tense, some kind of dread. He wished the driver would go faster, but he didn't know why, he had nothing special to do when he got home except face Audrey. Maybe he just wanted to get it over with.

At least he was safe, the driver was sober and they were on the inside of the canyon now and would be most of the way down. It was a very steep canyon in some places, with sheer drops to the river, from fifty, to two hundred feet. The scenery was beautiful and he tried to absorb himself in it. Most of the walls of the canyon were perpendicular and have solid rock. There were boulders in the river, from the size of a brick, to the size of a cabin.

The bearded man dropped Vincent off at the Long Bar Road and Vincent started walking home. It was hot already and he was walking slowly; he was in no hurry. Vincent was whistling an old Hank Williams tune, "Your Cheating Heart." Vincent loved sad songs and he loved to whistle, sometimes he drove people nuts with it.

About half way home, Vincent heard a car coming behind him. He turned around, not to see who it was, he already knew; he had recognized the sound of the car. Vincent had turned to greet the people who were in it. It was his mother and Doc. He could see through the window that something was wrong and his stomach tightened.

Vincent dropped the thumb that he had stuck out; the hitchhiker's thumb. The car stopped and Vincent went to the door. His mother was sobbing quietly. He had never seen his mother like this; he knew something awful had happened. Vincent was afraid to ask what was wrong. His mother's sobbing made him cry. He was crying because she was, even though he knew not why. Vincent got into the car and started to wonder where Audrey was. A feeling of panic came over him, forcing a cry from his trembling lips.

"Oh God!" Vincent cried, "It's Audrey, isn't it?" "Audrey was killed last night," answered Doc, gravely, with a face of stone. His mother turned to him and for a moment he looked into her eyes and she looked into his. Vincent saw her anguished soul pleading with him to make it untrue.

Vincent tried desperately to deny what he had just heard and there was a feeling for a moment of unreality. Vincent turned again to look at Doc, hoping for a denial from him. "It can't be true!" Vincent exclaimed, hoping, but knowing the futility. "It's true," answered Doc, somberly, "I just identified her body."

Vincent's mother sobbed harder. Vincent was stunned. He felt like he had suddenly run out of blood. Vincent felt cold, clammy and nauseous. And then, for a moment, he was protected by numbness; it was an inability to think. But that didn't last long and he remembered. Vincent remembered that he had not gone back to get her. His mind raced, looking for an excuse, but there was none. His soul groaned with the burden. Vincent's face blanched, he felt as if he would pass out. Vincent wished he could die. His mother saw his anguish. She forgot herself and reached out to him and they were holding each other. "Poor Vincent" his mother consoled.

Guilt flooded Vincent's mind like a giant wave, pushing him down into the pit. Vincent was sobbing, uncontrollably, out loud. His heart was in anguish, condemning him. His heart was crying in silence, "I have killed her! I have killed her!" When they got home, Vincent went straight to Audrey's room; he wanted to feel her presence.

Vincent wondered if he would ever be able to tell her that he was sorry. Vincent knew he would have to wait until he died and then he didn't know if he would go where she was. Vincent looked at a picture of her on the vanity. She was wearing her Levis, tipping a can of beer, her dark eyes were laughing.

"I will never see you again," he said to her picture, "not for as long as I live; maybe not forever." Vincent lay face down on her bed and cried quietly. He was alone with his guilt. Vincent wondered if his mother knew that he was supposed to have come back to get Audrey. He prayed she didn't know. Vincent felt she didn't know.

Neither Vincent, nor his sister had been in the habit of telling their mother anything they didn't have to. Vincent figured if his mother did know she would have asked him why he had not returned. He wondered if she would ever forgive him if she found out the truth. Maybe she already knew the truth and was just being kind to him.

Vincent dragged a heavy body around, watching, waiting to see if any sign of his mother knowing would show up on her face. After awhile, he knew that if she knew, he would know. Vincent felt some relief, believing that she did not know. He prayed that she would never know; he knew that it would hurt her badly.

Vincent had a heavy cross to carry, too heavy for a boy his age. The days dragged by with condolences. Friends called, relatives called, everybody called, all saying the same thing, over and over. They were all sorry and wished there was something they could do. What could anyone do? Death was so final. What could be more final?

Audrey's body had ended up in a funeral home in Gridley, a little farming town about twenty miles south west of Ophir Flats. The funeral would be there in a few days. That was where Audrey was to be buried. Vincent never asked why, what difference would it make? Vincent thought of his sister constantly. He wanted to keep her alive in his head; that was the least he could do. He didn't want to forget the terrible thing he had done, either.

Vincent needed to punish himself someway. From now on, every time he enjoyed himself, he would feel guilty. Every time he woke up in the morning, he would feel guilty. If it had not been for his selfishness, she would still be waking up every morning. And not only that, had she not stayed to tell the fisherman where he was, he would have drowned.

The day of the funeral came too soon. Now that Audrey was gone, it was easy for them to get into the Plymouth coupe. There was only one·seat in it and Audrey use to have to sit on his lap. Vincent use to playfully complain about how heavy she was. He remembered how good her hair would smell. There was a pain in his throat as he longed to feel the weight of her on his lap and to smell her hair. Vincent's thoughts brought a sigh from the depths of him and his mother squeezed his leg gently.

The ride to the mortuary was silent. It seemed long, but it was only about twenty minutes. There were few cars there and Vincent spotted his grandparents green, Studebaker pickup. Mario's car was there and Mack had borrowed his parent's old Chevy. Vincent could see that all of his friends were there.

Vincent's grandparents had not come early like they had wanted to because Clint had taken ill and they had had a hard time getting away. Vincent's grandparents were in the family waiting room. His Aunt and Uncle from Half Moon Bay were there.

Vincent was getting sick of sympathy; it seemed to him that it only magnified the sorrow. He wished they could have had an Irish Wake and then he could have got drunk. Vincent's grandpa had dark bags under his eyes; he looked like he hadn't had any sleep for a long time. Audrey had been his favorite grandchild; she had been his favorite person, next to his own children, that is. In fact some of his children had been in second place to her.

The organ music and the smell of flowers made the atmosphere heavy and even more sorrowful. Vincent hated the music; it was like dragging heavy chains around. Ordinarily, the flowers would smell good, but now they smelled like death.

The family moved into the parlor and sat up front in the Family section. Vincent could see his grandpa out of the corner of his eye. His big head was bowed down to his chest. Cap was sobbing, quietly. Vincent's mother's eyes were dry, she was cried out, but her face was pale and drawn.

Although Vincent was with his family, somehow, he felt like an outsider, like an outcast. Perhaps it was because of the guilt he felt. He felt like he should be banished and ostracized. Vincent would be if the family knew. That was what he thought, anyway.

The minister rambled on and on. He rambled on about God's love. Vincent wondered if God loved Audrey so much why had he let her get killed. The minister rambled on about God's wisdom and of his infinite plan.

"Some God damned plan!" thought Vincent, vehemently, almost saying it; the rage was boiling within him. The minister rambled on. Vincent trembled from the vehemence of his profane thoughts of God. His face was white from guilt, frustration and rage. Vincent cried as he watched his mother's silent suffering. His grandfather's massive shoulders were shaking from his grief; he had lost his beloved "Brownie" forever.

Vincent had not thoroughly accepted his sister's death. Deep within him there was still a flicker of hope. Miracles do happen, you know. The whole thing still felt unreal to him, like a bad dream. Maybe that was what it was? Maybe he would wake up and find it had just been a nightmare.

The minister had finished and the dreaded time had come; it was time for viewing the departed. Vincent's legs felt weak and his knees, fluid, as he walked toward the flower-shrouded casket. He felt a shiver run through his whole body as he looked at his sister's mask of death. He was confused, as it did not look like her at all. Audrey's skin was too yellow; her lips were too thin.

The terrible truth hit him, the mortician had just done a bad job and it was Audrey. His soul screamed. He stumbled and almost fell on the casket. Cap caught him and held him up. It was the first time that he could remember his grandfather holding him. Vincent sank his face into the big man's chest and sobbed unintelligibly, "It's my fault; it's my fault." His grandfather hugged him and they sobbed together. It was the first time they had ever felt close.

Vincent returned to his haunted house. He was alone, now. His mother had Doc, but he had no one; his guilt had separated him from them. Vincent's sister's room sat empty, next to his, a monument to his guilt, a constant reminder of it. Vincent knew that no matter what happened to him, no matter how long he lived; he would never be able to forgive himself. He would never be able to forget, He must not ever forget.

After Vincent had finished with his crying, he felt as if he would never cry again, never have feelings again. He felt emptied out, hollow. Vincent kept his burden to himself and it ate at his soul. He became a solitary man, that terrible summer. Vincent became quiet, withdrawn, and morose. His friends tried to cheer him, but to no avail.

Vincent went places with them, that is, his body did, but his mind stayed in his prison. Vincent's eyes were open, but looking at things not visible to anyone else. Vincent stopped singing and whistling. Joy was guilt to him. This went on for several months and then, to everyone's relief, he seemed to come out of himself. Vincent started joining in; he seemed almost normal. It was only on the surface, though. Vincent was using this normalcy, this joining in as a vehicle for escape; he could not tolerate the weight of his cross.

Vincent found relief in alcohol. If he drank enough, he found escape. The more often and the more he drank, the more escape he found. Vincent became a "Good Time Charley." He was the life of every party he could find. Sometimes he drank until he would pass out. He liked to drink until he passed out; it was his escape.

There wasn't always enough booze available to get him there, though, so he was always trying to find more ways to make money. Mario was a lot of help for him, there. Mario could always find ways to make money. Italians have that in there genetic code, so do Jews; it seems so, anyway.

Mario looked older than his years. He could con a con. He could sell snowballs to Eskimos. Mario was extremely likable and charismatic, but crooked as a dog's hind leg. Everyone liked Mario, even Doc, but Doc had once made the remark, "I wouldn't trust him any further than I could throw him."

Sometimes Mario would contract an orchard. He would make a deal with a rancher to harvest for a percentage of the profit. There was never a written contract. Mario, and his friends, would harvest the fruit and sell it. Sometimes the rancher got paid his share, or less than his share.

Sometimes it would be oranges, or prunes, but usually it was olives, oil olives. Oil olives are knocked off the trees with a wood pole. Mario didn't fool with canning olives, they had to be picked by hand and it was too tedious for him. Knocking the oil olives off the trees is faster. Canvas is placed under the tree, and then the olives are knocked off and they fall on the canvas. When the corners of the canvas are lifted the olives roll to the center. The leaves are separated away and then the olives are scooped into wooden boxes. When there were enough boxes, they were loaded and hauled to the processing plant.

There were three, oil processing plants in the area, one in Thermalito, another at the south end of Ophir Flats and the last in Palermo (Little Italy) a rural community about eight miles south of Ophir Flats. The boys sold most of their olives in Palermo.

Vincent was hauling the olives there with his Ford, because the truck that Mario had been using was broke down. Vincent had a trailer hitch on the back of his car, and they were hauling the olives in a trailer. The olives just had to make it to market. If not, the boys would have no party money.

The boys had not yet ran out of money, therefore, they had not ran out of booze. One of the nice things about contracting was one could drink and work at the same time. It didn't always turn out good, though. On the last load of the day, after drinking too much, Vincent was driving too fast. The trailer started to sway and soon it got away from him. Soon, the trailer had control of the car and the olives were spilling all over Palermo Road. Due to the side racks on the trailer, they had not lost much of the load. The trailer had come close to jack knifing and there is no telling what might have happened.

Vincent got his draft card in the mail and Mario fixed it for him. Mario had discovered that the typewriter at the Empire Theater printed numbers that matched the numbers on the draft cards. Mario had used liquid ink eraser and had changed the numbers on his draft card. Mario had used his adulterated card to get booze. Now Vincent could do it and he could drink in bars and to the bars he went. Some of them didn't accept the bogus card, but most did and there were a lot of bars in Ophir Flats. There were other towns, also, Marysville, Yuba City, Chico; they were numberless. As long as Vincent had money, he could escape.

Mario conned a guy into letting him use his truck, and trailer, for a percentage of the profit. Mario contracted with a rancher to haul hay to the slaughterhouse, which was out on the Cherokee Road. Mario asked for Vincent's help and he got it. There was another helper, and his name was Bill Cauldwell. Vincent had never met him, but Mario had known him for a long time. Bill's mother was full blooded, Cherokee and Bill was a carrot top. He was about the same age as Vincent. He was jolly with a cherub face and he was prone to be pudgy.

The three of them were out in Richvale all day bucking hay. They only got one load, but it was a big one, stacked nine high. They were worn out; the bales had been heavy, over a hundred pounds apiece and they had loaded it by hand. When the boys left the field it was after two in the afternoon and they were hot and hungry; they had not had lunch. By the time they got to the slaughterhouse none of them wanted to unload until after they had got something to eat. They unhooked the trailer, and headed for Vincent's place in the truck.

They had to go up the steep gravel hill to get to his place. When they were almost to the top of the hill, Mario saw a package at the side of the road. Without thinking, Mario put his foot on the brake and pushed it in. The truck came to a stop and right after it had, the brake line broke. Mario stepped on the gas to keep the truck from rolling back, but it was in too high a gear and the truck stalled.

Mario pulled the emergency brake, but it was not connected. The Truck was rolling backward and picking up speed. Mario tried to get the truck into another gear, but could not. He guided the truck to the left side of the road, where there was a bank. He tried to slow the momentum of the truck by banking it, but the bank was too low and the rear dual wheels climbed the bank. By this time the truck was moving quite fast.

Vincent was sitting in the middle. Bill opened the door and bailed out; he was motioning for Vincent to follow. Vincent watched Bill go end over end in the gravel and that was not the thing he wanted to do. Vincent closed the door and looked at Mario. Mario was looking at him, begging him with his eyes, not to leave him. His eyes were big and his olive tan had turned to ashen white.

The road was getting closer to the window on Vincent's side and the angle of the truck was getting steeper and precarious. The bank was getting higher. At the bottom of the hill was a small house. The owner was standing at the bottom of the hill watching the careening truck that was coming directly at his house. He was praying that the truck was not going to go through it. There was a fork in the road just before it got to the house. One fork made a right turn in front of the house and the other fork went by the side of the house. In the middle of the right turn on the bank the truck was climbing sat a boulder and it was about three feet in diameter.

The truck headed straight for this boulder. By this time it was at a precarious, angle, for the bank had climbed to about four feet. The road was a blur at Vincent's window. He braced himself. Vincent knew they were going to turn over. He hoped that he would still be alive; he knew his mother could not take another funeral. Vincent was awfully frightened, but there was nothing he could do but wait.

When the rear wheels of the truck hit the boulder, the truck was air born, but it had turned sideways. The rock had diverted the truck from the house. The truck was in the air, upside, down. The top of the cab hit the road, first; it caved it in, leaving an egg shaped, knot on the top of Vincent's head. Needle sharp hay hooks were flying around in the cab and also a small toolbox. A corner of the box hit Vincent on the corner of an eyebrow.

The truck bounced and was air born again for a moment. Then it made a four point landing on its wheels, sideways, at the bottom of the hill. The truck was still on the road and it was still running. There was a big cloud of dust that had followed them down the hill.

The owner of the house ran to the truck, followed by Bill, who was limping. The dust cleared and the boys were still sitting in the truck; they were searching themselves for wounds. They we're surprised and delighted that they were still alive. They looked at each other and their eyes were wide and joy was growing with every moment. For a moment Mario loved Vincent for not leaving him, but that passed with the flooding of joy. The wound on Vincent's eyebrow was bleeding a little and his head hurt, but that was all that was wrong with him. Nothing was wrong with Mario. He was so relieved to find himself in one piece he laughed hysterically and Vincent followed.

The two were out of control by the time Bill and the owner of the house got to them. Bill's clothes were in rags; his hands were bleeding from trying to break his fall in the quartz gravel. He had lacerations on his face. He, who had left the truck, had been hurt the worst.

"Holy shit!" exclaimed Bill, "I thought you guys were goners for sure." The boys had got out of the truck; they were still searching themselves. "I thought so too," answered Vincent, "I sure as Hell did!" And then he laughed some more, and Mario was still laughing. "Oh, God!" exclaimed Mario, "I'm so glad I'm not dead!" He hugged himself and his faced beamed as he continued. "I love me so!"

"I just knew you were going to go through my house!" exclaimed the white faced, owner. "You guys would be dead," commented Bill, "Really dead!" "I wish you wouldn't use that word while referring to me," pleaded Mario. "You guys are going to have to be more careful," suggested the house owner in a serious manner.

"The brakes went out!" exclaimed Mario, in self-defense, "And it was the box." "What box?" asked Vincent. "What box?" asked Bill. "What box?" asked the house owner. "The box that I stopped for!" exclaimed Mario; "I thought there was something in it." "You stopped for a box?" asked Vincent. "For a box?" asked Bill. "Yeah!" exclaimed Mario, before the owner of the house could ask the same question, "What are you guys, a bunch of parrots?"

Mario was getting exasperated; he had realized that it had been pretty stupid. "I stopped for a God damned box!" "I wonder what was in the box we almost died for?" asked Bill. "Stop the truck on the way back up the hill," suggested Vincent, but he was laughing so hard he almost couldn't finish, "And we can check it out." "Screw you!" exclaimed Mario and then they all laughed out loud, except for the house owner; the humor of the situation had escaped him. Mario climbed back into the truck to check things out; the engine was still running. "Anyone like a ride?" asked Mario.

"Remember," commented Vincent, as he got into the truck, "You still don't have any brakes." "If I had a lick of sense," stated Bill, as he got into the truck, "I would walk the rest of the way. "Don't forget to stop for the box," suggested Vincent, with a straight face. "Screw the box!" exclaimed Mario, as he maneuvered the truck, and started back up the hill. "There's the box!" exclaimed Bill, as it came into view. "Screw the box!" exclaimed Mario. "Screw the box," agreed Vincent.

No one was at Vincent's house when they arrived. Vincent was glad he would not have to tell his mother about the accident. The boys ate lunch and went back to the slaughterhouse to unload the hay. The frame of the truck had been bent in the accident and Mario lost his deal with the owner.

CHAPTER 13

The accident had changed Vincent's thinking, on the surface anyway. It hadn't assuaged his guilt any, but it had made him glad to be alive. He knew for sure that he wanted no part of death. Something was still going on in his subconscious. He was certainly steering his course down the highway of self-destruction. Vincent continued to drink as much as he could get his hands on; he seemed to have a voracious appetite for it. The only thing that slowed him down was a periodic lack of funds.

One night, Vincent killed an almost full, half-pint of whiskey in one guzzle and this was on top of a night's drinking. Vincent passed out and it scared his friends. He blanched and they couldn't find his pulse. Vincent came to before they could get him to the hospital.

And this was not all he did that was a threat to his longevity; he loved to drive like he was in an Italian road race. Vincent usually did it when he was alone. He loved driving on gravel roads, putting his car into power slides around sharp curves.

The Feather River Canyon was his favorite place to drive; it was the most dangerous. Vincent loved to test his nerve on this road. Careening close to the sheer cliffs was exhilarating and exciting. He drove himself to frighten himself and the more it frightened him, the more he loved it. Vincent also loved the road to Bidwell Bar, but the Canyon was better, it was more dangerous, with drops of two hundred feet straight down to the river. A drop like this would most likely be lethal.

Shortly after his eighteenth birthday, Vincent made a new friend. His name was Walt Hedger. Vincent met him at the Employment Office. Walt was tall, around six feet and he was handsome, with dark eyes and dark, curly hair. Walt was rather a kook, though, with some rather unusual idiosyncrasies. Walt cleared his throat a lot and usually had to expectorate after doing so. If he were outside, this would pose no problem, other than the disgusting sound and visual display.

Walt liked to see how far he could spit. If Walt was indoors it was a different matter and in some ways, even more disgusting and crude. If there was no spittoon, and there usually wasn't, except in some bars, he would spit in his hand and wipe it on his handkerchief. If he did not have one, he would wipe it on his pants. It was a loathsome and embarrassing habit. Walt had to do it, though; it was due to some kind of phobia. He would feel like he was choking and whatever was causing it, just had to come out, no matter what.

There were some things Walt couldn't eat because of this phobia. Walt couldn't eat anything with coconut in it; it would choke him every time. He couldn't eat any kind of nuts. Walt was constantly searching his food for something that shouldn't be in it. He carried a plastic lid around. If drinking from a glass, or cup, he would cover it with the lid to keep bugs from getting into it.

Walt wore thick, horned rimmed glasses. He couldn't see much further than his nose. Even so, he thought he was the world's greatest driver. I mean, really, one can't drive any better than one can see. Walt was downright spooky to ride with. One always had the impression that he couldn't see where he was going and on top of that, he drove too fast.

One side of Walt's car had deep scratches the full length of it. It was the result of taking a corner too fast, leaving the road and taking out a section of barbed wire fence. His car, a 1936 Chrysler sedan, had a hood ornament that wasn't bolted down; the nuts were gone. Being heavy, it stayed in place most of the time, but if a hard bump were hit, the ornament would fall off. The car looked like a gangster's, with its side mounted, covered, spare tires and its long hood. It had an overdrive gear and it would go like a bat out of Hell.

One time, after hitting a hard bump, Walt slammed on the Brakes and stopped the car. Walt stuck his head out the window; he was looking for the hood ornament. He asked where it was, but the ornament had never left the hood. That should give you an idea about how well Walt could see.

Walt had a lady; she was ten years older than he was. She had four small children and they all had different fathers. She had not been married to any of them and Walt had not been one of them.

Hauling these children around had given Walt a disconcerting habit. Because he couldn't see well, he would often slam on his brakes. When Walt did so, he would throw his right arm out to keep the children from falling. Even if there were no children, he would throw his arm out and Vincent would have to duck.

Helen, Walt's lady, had a pretty face, but she had a large, body. She must have been a hundred pounds bigger than Walt. She had a sweet disposition, and took good care of Walt and her children. Helen was getting

County Welfare because of the children. She seemed to have other resources. She always had money, nice clothes, a car and a nice house to live in, which she shared with Walt. Helen always carried a roll of money in the top of her stocking.

Walt had only a few things on his mind and sex was Number One. Number Two was the mirror; he thoroughly loved to look in the mirror. Walt was always combing his pretty hair. Number Three was gambling; he loved to gamble. Walt loved to play the horses, the football pool, the baseball pool, and any kind of pool. He loved to play snooker and Eight ball. But there was a small flaw in Walt's character that got in the way of these endeavors. Walt hated to lose. Walt was what is called, "A sore loser."

Walt was a better snooker player, a better pool player and a better card player than Vincent. Sometimes Walt would lose to Vincent and this really galled him. Sometimes Vincent would get lucky and he would just beat the pants off of Walt.

"Oh God!" Walt would exclaim, "What a slop artist you are!" When Vincent would get on one of these lucky streaks, he would beat Walt over and over again. It wasn't just Vincent's luck that beat him; it was that Walt's anger would throw him off his game.

Vincent knew if he got on a lucky streak, he could keep beating Walt, if he could keep him angry. Vincent would make snide remarks. "You use to be a better player," he would say, or, "You should practice more," and his favorite was, "I'm sure glad I don't have to wear glasses." That one would get Walt burning.

Walt knew what Vincent was doing, but he just couldn't keep himself from getting mad. "Don't get mad," Vincent would say, "You know you will lose if you get mad." Then Vincent would lay the final insult on him, "And you know how you hate to lose." Walt finally got wise. When Vincent got on a lucky streak, Walt would just hang up his cue and say he was tired of playing.

Walt liked to believe that he was of superior intelligence than Vincent. When the Pacific Gas And Electric Company hired the boys, they put Walt on the brush cutting crew. They gave Vincent the job of Dam Tender at the Rock Creek Dam. Walt had to cut brush all day, while Vincent sat in an office all night. This really galled Walt.

Every half hour Vincent would have to look out the window and check the water elevation at the dam. There was a gauge on the water. Vincent would call this information to the Rock Greek Powerhouse. Basically, this was all he had to do. Once in a while, usually after a storm, he would have to go down a metal, spiral, staircase, down into the core of the dam. It was around a hundred, and twenty steps. He would have to open a valve, with a big, metal, wheel and let some of the water out of the dam.

Vincent bought used pocket books by the bag. Reading was all there was for him to do, between gauge checking. Vincent loved to read and he loved to tell Walt how many books he was reading at his office. Vincent knew Walt was working his behind off and he knew Walt hated physical labor. He knew that he abhorred getting dirty. Vincent liked to tease Walt. Walt was a bit of a snob and Vincent thought that it would be good for his character growth.

The boys were living in a P. G. and E. facility at Storrie, up the Feather River Canyon. The lodging was comfortable, in two floored, wooden buildings. The food was good, but of little variety. The bagged lunch was exactly the same every day. The sandwich was on white bread, with ham and cheese with butter instead of mayonnaise and no lettuce. Desert was always a piece of pineapple pie, always. The P .G. and E. must have had a deal with some bakery that only made pineapple pie. Pineapple pie may have been the cheapest.

The boys didn't see a whole lot of each other during the week, but they went to Ophir Flats on the weekends. Vincent tried driving back and forth from home a few times, but he kept falling asleep at the wheel. He would wake up, just in time to keep from going off the road. This was not the kind of thrill that Vincent was looking for; he liked to have some kind of control. The job only lasted a few months and Vincent was glad when it ended. He was getting tired of reading and pineapple pie.

Walt didn't smoke, and he didn't drink much either. He didn't like hangovers. He dissipated himself in another way; he was a genuine sex addict. Helen must have been one also. Walt's tongue was always hanging out and that wasn't all that was hanging; Walt was hung like a stud horse.

That summer was like every other summer, working only when one had to. It was swimming parties, booze, girls and the drive in theater. At one of these swimming parties the boys were skinny-dipping and drinking beer at Little Rocky Honcott. The moon was full and so were the boys; full of booze, that is. There were no girls involved in this adventure. All the boys were stupid drunk. Vincent and Walt were there, along with Mario, Mack and Buck.

Little Rocky Honcott was named for its rocks. The place was little, but some of its rocks were not. Some of the rocks were as big as a cabin and some of them were flat on the top.

There was a pool amidst the rocks and a creek fed the pool. In the summer the creek got down to a trickle and the pool became a little stagnant. The crawdads liked it and there were a lot of them. The boys went there because it was isolated. They could drink all they wanted and they could make all the noise they wanted.

Vincent had a brainstorm but didn't tell anyone, he just did it without anyone's notice. Vincent had the bright idea that he wanted a moon tan. He had never heard of a moon tan, but now it made sense to him, nonsense, though it was.

Vincent's thoughts were of the female form when he lied on his back on the top of a giant boulder. His pecker was standing at attention. He fell asleep, or passed out. The moon was shining down on his naked body, bathing him in a soft, borrowed light. In a few seconds, his pecker went to sleep. Mario missed Vincent first. He was the least drunk. He looked for him, but couldn't see him.

"Where the Hell is Vincent?" he asked. The others started looking, but Vincent was nowhere to be found. "He can't swim a stroke," commented Mario, uneasily. "Sinks like a rock," added Mack. "He might be under the water," suggested a morose Buck. "Look for him in the water!" ordered Walt, who was not use to drinking as much as his new friends.

Walt started wading around in a circle, hoping to find Vincent with his feet. A light bulb went on in Mario's head. He got the brilliant idea of calling for Vincent. Any idea was brilliant for boys in their condition.

"Hey Vincent!" yelled Mario, but Vincent's ears were off. "Vincent Cardozaaaaa!" he yelled again as loud as he could and then they all yelled at the same time. Vincent awoke and stood up, checking his moon tan out as he thought of it. He stretched and yawned and about that time Mack spotted him. It was a kind of holy experience for him, with the alcohol making the event dramatic. Vincent had come back from the dead.

"There he is!" Mack yelled, in wonder, pointing at him. "What in the fuck are you doing up there?" yelled Mario, in anger and relief. All eyes were upon Vincent. He giggled and covered his pecker with his hands. "What's happening?" he asked, in a booze, generated fog. "What are you doing up there?" yelled Mario. In the confusion he had forgotten to swear. "I'm getting a moon tan," answered Vincent, like it was a natural and normal thing to do. "What in the Hell is a moon tan?" asked Mario, exasperated, "We thought you had drowned your mangy ass. "How could I drown on a rock? Vincent asked, with considerably diminished I. Q. "What is a moon tan?" asked Mack, seriously and it was a kind of blessed event when he got serious. "It's a tan by proxy," answered Vincent, who was amazed by his own articulation. "Can I get one?" asked Mack, who was getting tired of talking, wanting to get prone and so were the rest of the boys. "Come on up," offered Vincent, cheerfully, "There is plenty of moon for everyone." Vincent started to lie back down, but remembered his thirst, "Bring some beer." Then he sat in a semi-lotus position and waited.

Mack climbed the rock first, packing a six-pack with him. He had an opener between his teeth; he had no pockets in his birthday suit. Mack opened two beers and gave one to Vincent. Mack sat next to Vincent; he let his legs dangle over the edge of the rock. Walt followed and then Buck, Mario came last, grudgingly.

"You guys are a bunch of loonies," Mario told them as he opened a can of beer, "You can't get a tan from the moon." "You can get sunburn from the snow." argued Vincent. "That's different!" argued Mario, "You egghead!" "It's not," reasoned Vincent, "sunlight reflecting off the snow is no different than sunlight reflecting off the moon." "You will be a corpse before you get a moon tan" argued Mario. "It is worth a try," offered a tired, Mack, as he lay on his back. "Maybe it will give us a greenish hue," suggested Walt, as he lay on his back. "Maybe we will turn into cheese," suggested Mack. "Haw haw," guffawed Mario, "You are already cheese; cock cheese." "You are just jealous," retorted Mack, "Because my cock is bigger than yours." Mario couldn't say anything to that, for the proof was hanging there. He looked down at himself sheepishly and lied on his back.

There was silence for a while, as the boys soaked up the Moon's gentle rays. The rays were meant for lovers and werewolves not for tanners. It has been said, though, that lunar rays cause lunacy. This night the lunar rays had caused a little lunacy and some inspiration. Or was it the booze?

It started with Vincent. He had been kind of a loner, but he was beginning to love being with this gang of boys. He felt affection for them all. It was the longest he had been able to run with a bunch of guys; he felt close to them. Vincent felt inspired; it must have been the lunar rays.

"The Moon Patrol," he said it to himself, quietly, while still lying on his back. Liking the sound of it, he went on, "Let's call ourselves the Moon Patrol." No one commented for a while. "The Moon Patrol," said Mario, pondering it. "The Moon Patrol?" questioned Walt. "The Moon Patrol." It was just a statement from Buck.

"Captain Moon." stated Mack, rather forcefully; he had been inspired, also. Mack had never had the pleasure of being in a gang and Vincent had always stuck up for him when others made fun of him. Mack knew that he was different, but Vincent had always accepted him. He felt affection well up in him, "Vincent is Captain Moon!" he exclaimed. All the boys felt the camaraderie.

"Captain Moon and the Moon Patrol," said Mario, mulling it jealously, but liking the sound of it. "The Moon Patrol are we," stated Vincent, poetically. "Friends forever to be." "Joined together by destiny," added Walt, dramatically. "Bound together by the bonds of beer," added Mario, in a flash of wit. "The Moon Patrol," said Buck, because he couldn't think of anything else to say. The Moon Patrol laid on the rock for a couple of hours, drinking and bull shitting and sleeping. They were soaking up the questionable benefits of lunar rays. When they went home, they felt as if they were part of something.

When winter came, none of the boys were going to school except Buck. Time weighed heavy on the boy's hands. "Idle hands are the Devils workshop," is an old saying, but still a pertinent one. The boys started cruising the High School at noon and after school. They would pick up girls, lay rubber and just make a general nuisance of themselves. Most of the time they would pick up Mary and Betty and who ever they happened to be with. Lois and her sister had drifted off in different directions.

Mary started running around with a pretty blond girl. Her name was Greta, and she had Nordic ancestors. Once Vincent had seen her; he had eyes for no one else. He was thoroughly smitten. Greta Henderson wore glasses, but they did not hide her sexy eyes. That was what Vincent thought. "Bedroom eyes," was what he called them. Her eyes were blue as the sea, and sultry. Greta always looked a little bored with things. Her voice was soft, sensuous, low and throaty.

The girl's body was something else. She was almost as tall as Vincent; she could look him straight in the eye. Greta's form was something that Vincent had a hard time not staring at. She had that kind of a fine behind that he just loved, a tempting shape it was. Greta's waist was small and her cleavage fine. She walked proud, with her back straight and her head held high.

Greta was never nervous or hurried. Vincent never saw her run. Even though she was sexy, she still seemed innocent and this made her even sexier. Greta had a peaches and cream complexion, not the kind that most California blonds have. Greta's was fair, with rosy cheeks, the kind Anna had; only no one had it quite like Anna. Greta would never get laugh wrinkles; she did not laugh often. Greta's laugh was more of a soft, giggle. It was a rare occasion that a real laugh would come out of her.

Vincent, being introduced as Captain Moon, had piqued the girl's interest. The two were paired right away. It was like some common law had gone into affect. They just started going together. It had been love at first sight for Vincent, but not for Greta, it just seemed like the practical thing to do. It was not that she didn't like Vincent, she did, but it was not love, it wasn't even infatuation. There just wasn't anyone around that she liked more. It was just the practical thing to do.

"Why do they call you Captain Moon?" she had asked. "It's just a name," he had answered. "But why?" she had asked, impatiently and after he had explained it to her, she had giggled, "A moon tan? That is so silly." "Drunks are silly," Vincent had stated. "Do you get drunk often?" she had asked. "As often as I can." "But why?" "What else is there to do?" "How do you buy it?" she had asked and he had explained about the bogus draft card. When he had shown it to her, she had eyed it covetously. "Mario has one," he had told her.

Vincent was spending a lot of time at the Henderson house. He got along well with Greta's parents and her younger sister, Linda. Linda was a new teenager; she was thirteen. Linda was petite and a pretty blond. George, the father, was a mechanic at the cannery where Vincent usually worked in the summer. The mother, Maggie, was a housewife.

George was a big man, not tall, but big around. He drank a lot of beer and it showed on him. George had a big stomach and he talked like he was out of breath. His face was round and jovial. George had a healthy glow, his skin, his color looked healthy. He was blond like his girls and he was strong as an ox.

Maggie was a big woman, not fat, just tall, with big bones. She had a sweet, pretty face, with a disposition to match. Unlike the rest of her family, Maggie had dark hair. Neither of the girls looked like her. Linda looked more like her father than Greta, but they both looked like him, facial features, that is.

The Hendersons lived about five miles east of Ophir Flats, in an area called, "Garden Ranch." It was a pretty area, out in the boonies; Oak studded, with rolling hills. It was complete, with mistletoe, Christmas berries and poison oak. The house sat in a gully below the road. It had a creek behind it and hills. It was a small house, two storied, that George had built with the help of his father, who lived on the next acre.

Mario had a different car, one that he was fixing up, customizing. It was a thirty-six Ford sedan. It was lunchtime and Mario was driving. The boys were cruising the High School. Greta was in front, between Mario and Vincent. Mary, Walt, Mack and Betty Jane were squeezed into the back seat. Walt still liked to play around, even though he did have a regular shack-up.

Mario pushed in on the clutch and put the little Ford into low gear. He was going to lay a strip of rubber; that was the plan, anyway, everybody does it. Mario got ready for it, with both hands on the wheel. Mario pumped a few drops of adrenaline into his blood. He looked out the window to see how many were watching.

It is an ego trip, you know. He revved the engine to the red line and popped the clutch. The car just sat there, nothing happened. It just sat there with the engine revving. How embarrassing. They all just sat there for a while, no one wanting to get out, too embarrassed. The girls didn't know what had happened, but Mario did.

"What happened?" asked Greta and Mary, in unison. "We broke an axle," answered Mario, wanting to cover his head with something. "Is the car broke?" asked Mary, wondering what she should do. "The car is broken," answered Mario. "We have to walk?" asked Greta, looking at Vincent. "We have to walk," he answered. "Oh no!" she exclaimed and slid down in the seat, not wanting to be seen. "Someone has to get out and push the car," suggested Mario. Kids were starting to mill around the impotent car, laughing and pointing. "Who?" asked Vincent Walt and Mack, in unison, knowing it would have to be them. "You all!" exclaimed Mario, "Push it around the corner so we can park it." "Then we can go get my car," suggested Vincent.

His vehicle was parked down by the pool hall. They all got out and pushed the Ford around the corner. The girls also pushed and some of the kids who were milling around. The girls went to the little grocery store around the corner. The boys went to get Vincent's car to pull Mario home.

Saturday night, Vincent, Mack, Walt, Greta, Mary and Betty Jane went to a dance at Robinson's Corner. Ernest Tubbs was singing there. The building had been used as a combination dance hall, skating rink. It was a large building, with hardwood floors. There was a bar at the front end of the building with gas pumps out side. The place was just about the halfway point to Marysville. It sat on the corner where the Marysville Road and Gridley Road intersect. There were always cars parked along both roads when there was an event. There were not adequate parking facilities.

The gang liked to get primed before going to a dance, so they drove around for a while drinking beer and whiskey and listening to music on the radio. When they all felt high enough they went to the dance. They were stamped on the arm when they paid their admission. It was an invisible mark that would become visible under an infrared light. It was so they could go out and return.

They danced and drank all night, making many trips to the car for booze. Vincent could drink at the bar, but the others could not. Vincent could not afford to drink at the bar, anyway, so he also depended on the stash.

They had had to park a long way from the building. Every time they went to the car for drinks, they guzzled as much as they could hold. By the time the dance was over they were all in high spirit, bombed out, shit faced drunk. The girls were not quite as bad as the boys, but none of them were sober enough to drive. Mack thought he was, though, so he drove. Mack didn't care if he had too much; anyway, it was more fun that way.

Mack didn't have a whole lot of sense when he was sober. When he was not sober, he had none. Betty Jane, who was sitting as close to Mack as his skin, was use to his foolishness. The others were squeezed into the back of the car like sardines. Involved in desire and passion the others were too busy to take notice of how he was driving.

Mack was driving too fast and when they were within five miles of home he failed to negotiate a turn and went out into a field. The car went completely out of Mack's control and into the control of centrifugal force. Mack was still in the curve he had got into when he missed the turn. A very large oak tree was coming straight at him, and he had to get into a tighter curve to miss it.

Betty Jane saw what was happening, but fear had closed her vocal chords. Before the lovers in the back seat knew what was happening, they were upside down. If the car hadn't rolled, they would have hit the tree. The car rolled over twice before it came to rest on its top. The kids in the back had stopped kissing. They were hanging on to each other; there was nothing else to hang on to. When the car came to a stop, the children were on the ceiling of the car with the seat on top of them. The windshield had shattered all over Mack and Betty, but the seat cushion had protected them from most of the glass.

Greta was the first thing that came into Vincent's mind and he asked her if she was all right. "I'm okay," she answered, "I think," she added. The next thing that Vincent thought of was fire and he tried to open the door, but it was jammed. He went to roll the window down, but the handle had been broken off. Vincent felt panic. He kicked the glass out and crawled out of the car. By the time he had got out, Mack and Betty Jane were out; their doors had not been jammed. Vincent was helping Greta out and Mack helped him. By this time Walt and Mary were out the other side; their door had not jammed. They all inspected themselves and each other and were amazed to find that no one was hurt, not even a scratch.

There was broken glass everywhere. The front wheels of the car were still spinning and that was the only sound, except for the throbbing sound of the pulse in their ears. It was eerie, standing there, watching the wheels spin. No one said a word until the wheels had stopped; they had been mesmerized by them.

"We could all be dead right now," said Vincent, somberly. "We would be if we had hit that tree, "commented Mack, contrite, "Sorry about the car." "It's all right," answered Vincent, contrite himself for having almost caused his mother to go to another funeral. He wondered why God had saved him again and why He hadn't saved Audrey. "It was just an accident," he added. Vincent looked at Greta; gratitude filled him.

"I'm so glad that you were not hurt," he told Greta, softly, with emotion she did not understand. "Me, too," she answered and giggled, not knowing what else to do. "It happened so fast," said Betty Jane, softly. "A person could die without even knowing it," commented Mary, with qualm. "I know," answered Vincent, with remorse, thinking of Audrey.

They stood there looking at the remains of Vincent's car. Vincent was looking at how close they had come to the tree. Its trunk was about three feet in diameter. He knew the tree would not have budged. Vincent remembered a tree that had been hit by a car and it had been less than a foot in diameter. Some friends of his had been in the car and they had all been killed. Only the driver had escaped with his life and he was in prison for manslaughter.

There had been five of them in the car. They had gone to San Francisco to join the Navy. They had all got drunk. On the way home on the Marysville Road, the driver had been driving too fast. He had lost control on a soft shoulder and had hit this little oak tree.

Two of the guys had been in the front, with three in the back. The car had hit the tree between the grill and the right front fender. The tree had come right through the car. It hit the front passenger between his legs, cutting his body in half, just as if done by a chain saw. The boy who had been sitting in the middle of the back seat went clear through the car and out the windshield headfirst. His body had jammed in the windshield, but his head had kept going for another thirty feet. The hood of the car had been painted red with his blood. The other boys had died from head injuries.

Vincent could see they had only missed the tree by the roll of the car. It had been so close a shiver went up his spine. He shook his head.

"Close call," he commented. "Too, close!" exclaimed Mack. "Personally," said Walt, who had yet to say a word, "I do not want to do this again." "Where are we?" asked Greta, being a practical girl. "About five miles out," answered Vincent, knowing they were just a few miles from the curves by the Wagon Wheel. "Might as well start walking," suggested Greta. They started walking to town, but didn't go more than a mile when Vincent's car passed by them being towed by a tow truck. They hollered and waved at it, but it didn't even slow down.

Vincent's car would get to town before them and it wouldn't even run. What a revolting development. The boys made obscene gestures with their fingers at the disappearing car and truck. In a short while an elderly couple picked them up in an old Chevrolet and took them all the way to Mack's house. Mack got his dad's car and took everyone home. Vincent paid the tow bill on his car and towed it home with Mario's help. The engine in his car was okay, but the rest of the car was trashed. Vincent found a black, 1940, Ford sedan, shy of an engine. Vincent bought it for a hundred dollars. The rest of the car was in cherry shape. Mario towed it to Vincent's place, where the two of them pulled the engine out of the wreck and installed it in his new acquisition. Vincent was way ahead; this car had hydraulic brakes. Life went on.

CHAPTER 14

Vincent became a regular customer of the Claim Jumper and so had Mario. The Claim Jumper was right across the street from the State Theater. It was a cocktail lounge, but it wasn't of the run of the mill, type, it was different. It was three business establishments in one. The entrepreneur of these establishments was Ned Bell. Ned was a man of boundless energy. He was bartender, barber and chef and he was master of all three. Ned had a big, booming voice that rattled the glasses when he yelled, or laughed. Ned never talked softly; he did everything with gusto.

Ned had short gray hair, with a widow's peak. He had a big, head, big, dark eyes, big, dark brows and a big mouth. Ned had big hands with fingers like bananas. He had big feet and a big body, over six feet of it. There wasn't a speck of fat on Ned.

Ned had a big heart. Ned gave credit to anyone he thought deserved it, but he had no use for four-flushers. He was a sucker for a sad story, but you didn't get a second chance if he found out you were giving him a crock.

Ned was very liberal; no one gave him trouble and got away with it. Troublemakers went out through the swinging doors, one way or another. All of Ned's regulars knew this, but sometimes he would have to straighten out strangers. Ned was a gentleman. He didn't allow foul language in his place when there was a woman present and often his wife was there.

When entering the Claim Jumper the two chair barbershop was to the right, the cafe was on the other side of it. A hallway from the bar led to the barbershop and cafe. Ned's wife, Katie, helped him run the cafe. All three establishments were part of the Claim Jumper.

The Claim Jumper was a jumping place. It had a long bar. At busy times, which were most of the time, it required two bartenders. It was a noisy, bawdy bar. It didn't hurt that the Southern Pacific Railroad Depot was just around the corner and the Western Pacific Railroad Depot was only a few blocks away. The Roundhouse was at the south of town.

Due to the proximity of the Claim Jumper, the railroad hands and tunnel stiffs frequented the place. A whole lot of them had bar tabs, but most of them were good for it. They were a hard working, hard playing honest lot and they were making Ned rich.

Ned loved being a bar tender; he drank right along with his customers. Ned also loved being a barber and a chef, but he couldn't be in three places at once. Ned had one bartender who helped him most of the time and a few who helped him at various times. Ned always hired first class bartenders, ones who loved their work, loved to please the customers and drink with them when necessary. Ned was like Humphrey Bogart; he didn't trust people who didn't drink.

Ned's regular bartender was Bob Clay and he was Vincent's favorite. Vincent never saw Bob tipsy, but he often drank right along with his customers. Bob wasn't loud like Ned, but he would talk and joke with you and he was sensitive and sympathetic. At one time Bob had been the manager of the State Theater. Bob always mixed perfect drinks; they were always perfect. He made the best Singapore Sling in the world. Moscow Mules, Bloody Marys, Stingers, Black Russians, Side Cars, Martinis; Bob made them all.

Once, when Ned's dishwasher quit him, Vincent washed dishes for him at the cafe. Vincent needed the money and Ned needed a dishwasher. It was hot that day and after Vincent had washed about a thousand dishes, he got tired and he looked it.

"Want something cold to drink?" asked Bob, through the cafe doors, the swinging kind. "Sure," answered Vincent, wiping the sweat from his brow. Bob brought Vincent what looked like a glass of ice water, but it turned out to be iced vodka. It was a big glass. Vincent got high while finishing the dishes. Vincent then went to the bar and got drunk the rest of the way. He then went home to bed, feeling no pain.

A couple of nights later, Vincent and Mario walked through the swinging doors together. Ned was tending bar and barbering at the same time. It was late and there was only a handful of customers, all of them tipsy and so was Ned. He had a guy lying on his back on the bar and Ned was giving him a shave with a straight razor. The guy was too drunk to care if his throat got cut.

"Captain Moon and the goon squad, or is it Moon Buddies, or whatever the Hell you are!" greeted Ned, loudly. Everyone had heard about the moon tan incident by now. "What can I do you out of?" Ned asked. "We brought some money with us tonight," answered Vincent, cheerfully. A lot of people were on tabs, including Vincent. "That's the best damned news I've heard in a long time," answered Ned, "You going to pay your tab?" "Hell, no.!" retorted Vincent, "I just want to buy some drinks." "I guess that's better than nothing," replied Ned holding his hands up in a gesture of futility. "Name your poison," he said, as he continued to shave the man on the bar. "Gimee a Moscow Mule," replied Vincent.

"Awww horse shit!" exclaimed Ned, waving the straight razor around like a flag, "Can't you see that I'm busy. Can't you have an ordinary drink? Here!" he exclaimed, slamming a bottle of bar whiskey down on the bar with a thud, "Have a shot of this. It'll curl your toenails and it's on the house. "I'll try anything that's free," answered Vincent. "I knew that," retorted Ned, as he poured him a full one in a shot glass. He gave him a water back to chase it, knowing he would need it. "How about you?" asked Ned of Mario? Just about that time, Vincent's drink was on the way down his throat, leaving a trail of irritated flesh. "Holy Shit!" gasped Vincent, hoarsely, holding his throat, "Did you buy that poison across the street?" He was referring to the Shell gas station that was around the corner and across the street.

"Good stuff, Ain't it?" asked Ned, with a shit eating grin spread across his face. "I think I'll have something else," commented Mario, with a look of consternation, "Make it a Burgie." "Coward!" exclaimed Ned, gruffly, but still grinning through his teeth. He got Mario a beer and opened it with his free hand and sat it in front of Mario. Ned went right back to shaving without giving Mario a glass. Mario opened his mouth to ask for a glass, but changed his mind. He picked up the bottle and put it to his mouth.

Just about the time Mario started to swallow his first swallow, a Harley Davidson came crashing through the swinging doors. The big twin bellowed out its muffler-less straight pipes as the pilot played with the throttle. The Harley pilot's name was Bart, and he was drunker than seven hundred dollars. Bart had a Cheshire Cat Grin across his handsome face, ear to ear. He was big, healthy and robust looking. Bart's face was flushed, full of pleasure. He was a railroad hand, an engineer. The glasses and bottles rattled, as the big, twin belched out its song.

The surprise got Mario's drink stuck in his throat and he expelled it across the bar. Ned looked aghast. The drunken shavee sat up. Ned's face contorted with a grimace as his mind searched for adequate words to express how he felt.

"Shut the God Damned, two wheeled, abomination of a whore off!" he hollered, with a booming voice. The pilot turned his engine off, kicked the stand down and got off his machine. "Hey, Bart," hollered Ned, to the pilot, "Why don't you take that piece of iron shit out the door and why don't you stay out there with it?"

A bigger grin went across the pilot's face. "You know you don't mean that," answered the pilot, "You know you love me like a son." "I wouldn't give my son the time of day!" retorted Ned, with a sourpuss face, "Now, why don't you tell me what you would like to punish your liver with." Bart swaggered up to the bar. He had a barrel chest, stout looking, like someone you wouldn't want to mess with. He scratched his curly hair and sighed.

"I'm just a poor, stinking wino today," he replied. Bart pushed two stools apart, put one boot on the brass rail, spit into the spittoon and lit a cigar. "I've been plastered for three days on cheap port," he said. He laid his face on his arm on the bar for just a moment and then he lifted his head. Bart continued. "I think I'm on a running drunk." He stood with his elbows on the bar and his face resting in his hands. In a moment he spoke again, "I'm not sure yet, it may take me a week to find out." "You don't have to wait to find out," offered Ned; "I can tell you now" he ended, with exasperation. "Tell me what?" asked the pilot, who was suffering from a diminished brain cell count. "You are on a running drunk!" exclaimed Ned, after putting his big face into Bart's. "Who told you?" asked Bart, amazed at Ned's perspicacity. "You told me, you idiot!" exclaimed Ned and by then he was laughing, "What in the Hell do you want to drink?" "Pour me a giant glass of cheap, port," answered Bart, "The kind with the screw on cap, Or gimee a wine bag if you have one. I wanna see if I can squirt it in my mouth like they do in the movies."

"Sheeee-it!" exclaimed the big bartender, "You are crazier than a horny flea crawling up an elephant's ass." Ned then poured a big glass full of ruby port and asked, "How in the Hell can you drink this swill?" "It has alcohol in it!" exclaimed Bart, "Don't you know? Give everyone a drink." "Ya hear that, everyone!" exclaimed Ned, exuberantly, "Bart is going to buy us all a drink."

Ned poured Vincent another shot of the raunchy whiskey without asking what he wanted and Vincent asked for more water. "What?" asked Ned, eyes big with feigned, incredulity, "Captain Moon wants water?" He slammed a glass of water in front of Vincent, "Baptize your throat with that," he told him. After Ned had given everyone in the house a drink, Ned went back to the pilot. He put both of his big hands down flat on the bar in front of him.

"Those who play must pay, Mister Rockeeefeloooor," he told him and turned his right palm, up. "How much?" asked the pilot. "Twelve dollars and fifty cents," replied Ned. "Is that all?" asked Bart, seeming to be incredulous. "That's all," answered Ned with both palms up now. "Put it on my tab," ordered the pilot, with a flourish of his hand. "You are a wheeler dealer!" exclaimed Ned, with feigned disgust. "A real wheeler dealer." Ned wrote it on the tab and went to the other end of the bar to talk to some of his other customers.

Geo Pacheco came in and sat one seat away from the pilot. Neither one of them knew each other. Vincent didn't know him either, but had seen him around. He knew he was the brother of a very pretty girl he knew, but had never been able to get close to. She had always been in love with one guy, a rodeo rider.

Bart got up and put some money in the jukebox. Ernest Tubbs started singing, "I saw a rainbow at midnight, out on the ocean blue." and the song went on. Vincent liked the song and it was one of Mario's favorites. Mario hummed along with it. Geo hated it, though, but no one knew. Geo wasn't much bigger than Vincent, a little taller. He was dark and as handsome as his sister was pretty.

When the song finished, the pilot got up and put some more change in the jukebox. The same song started playing again. Everyone laughed at Bart, except Geo. Bart repeated this action several times and everyone was getting a little tired of it, but Geo was seething.

When the song started playing again, Geo got up walked over behind Bart and hit him on the back of his head. He did this without saying a word, surprising all, including Bart, who jumped off his stool and whirled around. He was incredulous.

"What in the Hell did you do that for?" he asked Geo. "You made me mad with that song!" retorted Geo, who was still seething. "Well!" answered Bart, his face flushed with anger and moving closer to Geo, "You Pecker head! You made me mad now and that is just too bad for you!" And then the pilot was all over Geo and in just a few seconds, Geo was on the floor and it was all over. Bart walked straight over to the jukebox and played the song again. Geo got up and stumbled out the doors. Ned walked over and unplugged the jukebox.

"I think it's about time you went home," he told the pilot. "I think you are right," Bart answered, "Cause I'm tired." He finished his drink, walked over to his Hog and started to get on it. "Start it outside!" barked Ned. The pilot didn't have room enough to turn the Hog around, so Vincent gave him a hand while Mario held the doors open. They got the Harley and its pilot out the door and in a few seconds, it roared off into the night.

The shaver had finished the shave and the shaved was asleep on the bar when the boys left. All that raunchy whiskey had relaxed every nerve in Captain Moon's body, almost to the point of non-functioning. Mario was on his way, also, but he never got as drunk as Vincent. Mario coasted along when he drank; he didn't guzzle like the Captain. Mario wondered why Vincent drank like that; he had been doing it ever since his sister's death. He could see that his friend didn't drink for the fun of it; he drank to get drunk. Mario tried to take Vincent home, but Vincent would have none of that. Mario took Vincent to his car and they parted.

The next night the boys walked through the swinging doors again. The smoke was like valley fog and the joint was jumping. Ned was not behind the bar, nor in front of it. There were two unfamiliar bartenders taking orders. There were a bunch of regulars there, but Vincent didn't see any that he was friendly with, but Mario did. He was an old guy, he looked like a rancher and he smelled like one from the horse poop that was on his cowboy boots. The old guy was wearing a cowboy style; his straw hat that looked like it had been chewed by one of his horses. He was wearing dirty jeans and a dirty shirt. The guy would have to drive home; he was certainly too drunk to walk.

There were empty seats on both sides of Sam Portelo; that was how Mario introduced him. The seats were empty because Sam smelled like a goat. Vincent shook hands with Sam and was surprised. Although Sam didn't look very stout, he had a grip like a vise. Vincent had to cringe from it but hid it as well as he could. Sam waved the bartender over; he called him, "Reed." Reed was a small guy with delicate features. He wore a western type bow tie.

"What do you want, you old turkey?" asked Reed, in a friendly, familiar manner. "I want to buy my friends a drink," answered Sam. "Are they old enough?" asked Reed, smiling. I drink here all the time," proclaimed Captain Moon. "Me too," proclaimed Mario. "I believe," answered Reed, "But I gotta see some I.D," apologetically.

Both boys reached into their pockets at the same time and got their fraudulent draft cards out of their wallet. Reed looked at Vincent's first, raising his eyebrow a bit as he looked at it, and then at Vincent.

"Don't you have a driver's license?" Reed asked. "I got it wet when I went swimming," answered Vincent, trying to keep a straight face. Vincent had a hard time lying without laughing. Reed looked at the card, hesitated for a moment and asked him what he wanted to drink. "Moscow Mule," answered Vincent. After Reed had taken care of Vincent, he looked at Mario's card. He looked at Mario and Mario looked a lot older than Vincent. "I suppose you don't have a driver's license either?" "Not on me," answered Mario, "It's out in the truck." Reed scrutinized the card. He held it close to his eye.

"This card looks like you printed it yourself," commented Reed. He held it up to the light. "I did," answered Mario, holding a straight face, Vincent laughed. "Yours did too," said the bartender to Vincent and then the bartender laughed, "What are you drinking?" he asked Mario. "Jack Daniels, with a water back." "Want a refill?" Reed asked Sam. "Yo," answered Sam and Reed filled his shot glass with scotch and gave Mario his drink.

"Here's mud in your eye," as he tasted of his first drink. "Skosh," replied Sam. "Here's to you, Sam," said Vincent, as he put the Moscow Mule to his lips. His lips almost stuck to the cup. It was so cold, it hurt his throat, but it was so good. The vodka, diluted by ginger beer and lime, went down so easy. It didn't take him long to finish it and he ordered another.

"You are not one of those freeking Reds, are you?" asked Mario of Vincent. "You are always drinking Russian drinks," he added. "No," replied Vincent, "I just like vodka." He liked it because it didn't taste strong in a mix. Vincent also liked it because it didn't leave him as bad a hangover as some other drinks. And he liked the way they mixed it at the Claim Jumper.

Vincent was thinking about how it was getting so he couldn't drive by the place without stopping. He felt so comfortable that he could sit for hours. Vincent liked to watch himself in the mirror behind the bottles and the customers. He liked to read their lips and figure out what they were saying.

Vincent and Mario's eyes met in the mirror and it was a mistake, they were both still tickled about fooling the new bartender. Mario held his drink up in a toast and took a little drink of his whiskey. Some of it went up his nose and he blew it right back out. Vincent had a drink in his mouth, ready to swallow and a beginning laugh choked him, expelling his drink across the bar. Vincent jumped from the stool and made a mad dash to the latrine.

The latrine was only a few stools away. Vincent went in the door. The little room was empty and smelled odiously sweet from the mixture of urine and deodorant. Vincent relieved his bladder and his mirth at the same time. Vincent stayed in the John until he could look in the mirror without laughing and then he returned to the noise and smoke.

Vincent was feeling relaxed and cool from his drinks. He remembered that he needed to call Greta. There was a pay phone on the wall at the far end of the bar. Vincent walked to it and placed a call to her. Linda, Greta's younger sister, answered the phone.

"Hi." Vincent answered, cheerfully, "This is Vincent." "High Vincent" she purred, in a voice made sweet by a crush she had on him, one he had no knowledge of. "I like your voice," he teased," it sounds sexy." "Oh Vincent!" she wailed, "You stop teasing me." "I'm serious," he answered, "If it were not for your sister I would chase you all over the place. She got brave. "You wouldn't have to chase me very far," she answered. "What would happen if I caught you?" he asked, with a wink she couldn't see, but could sense. She giggled. "I don't know," she answered, trying not to sound demure, but failing, "That would be up to you," and then, dejectedly, "Here's my sister."

"Hi." greeted Greta, cheerfully, "Where are you?" "At the Claim Jumper," he answered, equally cheerful. "What are you doing there?" she asked, not quite so cheerful. "Drinking Moscow Mules, "he answered. "Are you coming out?" Greta asked, with a voice a little, flat, her ego being a little wounded because he hadn't been out as often as he had been coming. "In a little while," he answered, "Gotta go now." "Bye," she said and hung up after hearing him do so. Greta went to her bedroom to wait and Vincent went back to the bar to drink. Mario was having an animated conversation with Sam. Mario could not talk if his hands were tied.

"Did everything come out alright?" he asked Vincent. "Only what went in," replied Vincent. He emptied his copper cup and ordered another drink. "Fucking Communist!" jeered." Mario. "Fucking Red Neck!" retorted Vincent. Sam got off his stool, wobbly from drink. He bumped into an equally drunk tunnel stiff who was on his way to unload his bladder.

"Watch out you clumsy old bastard!" he exclaimed, as he gave the old man a shove. Sam went on his ass on the floor. The tunnel stiff turned and headed for the John. "Hey!" yelled Mario, as he went after the miner, "Wait just a God damned minute!" He touched the miner's shoulder and the miner whirled around, lightning fast and punched Mario on the nose. It happened so fast, everyone was surprised, but no one was as surprised as Mario. The miner turned back around and went on in to the latrine. The fight was over; it could have been the shortest one in history.

"Jesus!" exclaimed Vincent, "Who would have thought that drunken asshole could move so fast?" Vincent looked at Mario, who was now bleeding profusely. "Oh no!" Vincent exclaimed, "Not again." Mario's eyes were big and red; his nose was doing some serious bleeding. "Get me to the hospital," he pleaded, woefully. "Do you need an ambulance?" asked the concerned bartender. They looked at Mario and he shook his head in the negative. Mario's eyes had filled with tears and he couldn't see so well. Vincent led him to the door and to his car. "Try to get me there without an accident" pleaded Mario.

Vincent got Mario to the hospital without an incident. It was almost two hours before he was able to get finished with Mario. Twenty minutes later Vincent was parking his Ford in front of Greta's house. Greta opened the door and waited for him on the porch.

Vincent was late and he could see the pout on her face in the porch light. It didn't subtract anything from her pretty, countenance. Her cheeks were full and pink, her face aglow with the effulgence of health.

"I didn't think you were going to make it at all," she complained, with a pout, "Have you been drinking in that bar all this time?" Vincent kissed her on the pout of her lips. "Naw," he answered, "I had to take Mario to the hospital again." "What happened to him this time?" she asked, surprised. "Same thing," answered Vincent, "His big nose got in the way of a fist." "I can't believe it!" she exclaimed, incredulous, "He looks so tough." She giggled. "I wish I could have seen it," she added. "Not a pretty sight," commented Vincent. "Mario looks like he could beat anyone," she said, shaking her pretty head. "Mario is strong as a bull, but slow as a turtle," explained Vincent, "it doesn't do much good to be strong if you can't hit who you are trying to hit or can't get out of the way."

Vincent put his hands on Greta's hips and pulled her to him. As soon as they had touched he felt an erection manifesting. He wondered if she could feel it and the thought brought a rush of blood to his face. Vincent impulsively planted a kiss on her soft, full lips so she would not see his blush.

Vincent ran his hand across her back, letting his hand move down and rest on the beginning curve of her lovely rump. His erection was growing fast and it felt good to rub in against her. He feared that she would feel it and he pulled away. Having felt him, Greta's desire had heated.

"What's wrong?" asked Greta, a little coquettish. Vincent tried to read her face. He sensed she had felt his erection and the thought sent another rush of blood to his face and also to his loins, compounding his problem. "I just wanted to look at your face," he told her, trying to cover his embarrassment. "Your bedroom eyes, they turn me on," he told her, as he caressed her curves. "What do you mean?" she asked, innocently. "You excite me," he answered and blushed again over his candor, and her scrutiny.

"Why are you so shy?" Greta asked, touching the tip of his nose with her fingertip. Demurely, she asked, "Are you afraid of me?" She traced his lower lip with her fingertip. Vincent was pensive for a moment. "I guess I am," he answered. The ache for her was building. "Let's sit in the car for awhile, "he suggested," I have to leave soon. "All right," she agreed and put her hand in his and he led her to the car.

When they were seated, without any preliminary conversation, they moved into an embrace and a slow kiss. There never was much said between them. They smooched for a while and then she stuck her tongue in his mouth and it was the first time. Vincent did the same to her and it put a lot of fire in their smooching. He pressed her breast for the first time, she responded with a little moan.

The light from the moon was like a light in the car. Vincent caught himself looking down at Greta's lap. Her skirt had worked its way up, revealing a delicious portion of her thighs. Greta's legs were slightly parted, the inside of her thighs a terrible temptation. Vincent wanted to touch her there so bad his testicles were aching.

He put his hand on the outside of her thigh, running it to the edge of her panties, under her skirt. She responded with fervency in her kiss. Vincent started to put his hand on the inside of her thigh, but he chickened out. He was so shook he had to leave. He didn't want to do anything embarrassing.

"Hey, you with the bedroom eyes," Vincent whispered in Greta's ear, "I gotta go to bed." "Daddy wouldn't like it," she answered, and giggled. "I mean in my bed," he answered. "Can I come with you?" Greta asked, sweetly. "My mother wouldn't like that," he told her. "Would you like it? Greta asked. "I would love it!" Vincent answered, with enthusiasm, "But I wouldn't get any sleep."

"Oh, Vincent" she exclaimed and playfully slapped him on his shoulder, "Shame on you. What ever could you mean?" she asked in mock shock. Vincent opened his door and got out. He went to her side and opened her door and she got out of the car. Greta put her arms around Vincent and gave him a long, hard kiss, pressing her body to him. He returned the pressure and put his hand on her bottom. She responded, but them she pulled away, her face was flushed. "Good night, Vincent," she told him and turned. Greta quickly walked to the house, opened the door, waved and went in, closing the door behind her.

Vincent was left there, all turned on, not knowing how to turn off. He stood there for a moment with his testicles aching, and his member throbbing. He tried to think of anything but the inside of Greta's thighs. Vincent could not, so he got into his car and drove off. Vincent's car made a beeline straight back to the Claim Jumper, just like it had a mind of its own. Vincent's mind was on Greta and he couldn't think of two things at the same time, so his car had to drive its self. Vincent couldn't get his mind off Greta; he was still on fire.

Vincent went inside The Claim and ordered another Mule. He sat on the stool looking at the mirror, trying to get his mind on another track; his world was in his head. Vincent thought of his draft card, wondering if and when he would be drafted. Some of his friends had already gone to Korea. They were not really friends, though, just acquaintances. Some of them had already been killed.

Vincent looked at his pretty hair in the mirror and wondered what he would look like in one of those awful haircuts. What he would look like in uniform. He shuddered at the thought of being bossed around like he had seen in the movies; ordered to ones death without any recourse. And he would have to leave the Flats and Greta and the Moon Patrol.

CHAPTER 15

One Saturday morning Vincent went with Mario to sell some scrap metal. Mario had stolen it from various deserted mines in the county. Vincent wondered if Mario had ever stolen from Doc's mine, and he asked him.

"Hell!" answered Mario, grinning, "I do not know; where is his mine?" "If you don't know," answered Vincent, with a grin, "You will never find out from me." "Chicken shit!" retorted Mario. They drove back from the salvage yard after selling the goods and Mario handed Vincent a ten-dollar bill. He told Vincent it was for helping him. "Thanks," Vincent replied," I needed that." "Let's get the rest of the Moon Patrol," suggested Mario, "and the girls and let's have a swimming party out at the lower dam. "We gotta have booze," Vincent reminded him. "I thought that was understood, Captain Moon," answered Mario. "Let's go get the booze first," suggested Vincent, "So we can have a head start." "Good thinking," answered Mario and he chuckled and went on, "I like to make sure I drink the most. Haw, haw, especially when I'm buying." "I like to drink the most too," retorted Vincent, "especially when you are buying." "May your testicles shrink to your naval." answered Mario, "And may your penis retreat into your bunghole."

After Mario had bought some beer they went to the river, down by Bedrock. Mario parked in the shade of some oak trees. Vincent took an opener from the jock box and opened two cans of beer. He gave one to Mario.

"Up your bucket," he toasted Mario. "Up your ass, also," replied Mario and they clicked their cans together in jovial, camaraderie. They chugalugged the beer. Mario crushed his can with one hand and asked for another. "Thatsa gooda stuff," he kidded, "But eetsa maka me thirsty." Vincent bent his can with two hands and opened two more and they chugalugged again. "Thatsa more better." sighed Mario, rubbing his belly. "We should have got some whiskey," claimed Vincent, "Or vodka to get a buzz going." "It's too, frigging early to get drunk!" exclaimed Mario, and then he got jivey, "Captain Moon," he sang, "Wanna get drunk too soon," while bee-bopping his hips around. "I didn't know there was a proper time to get bombed," replied Vincent, "What time should I start?" "After we get the girls," answered Mario. "Let's go find the guys," suggested Vincent, "And then we can go get my car to carry the girls in." "Oh, no you don't!" exclaimed Mario, "You can't have all the girls."

First they went to Mary's. They honked the horn and she came out the door, with Buck right behind her. They both wanted to go, so they went back into the house to get their things. Vincent and Mario watched Mary's slim figure as she walked away. She walked like she had a book on her head.

"Have you ever fooled around with Mary?" queried Mario. "No!" exclaimed Vincent, surprised, he had never thought of her that way, they had always been just friends. "No," he added, "I never have." Vincent didn't know why he hadn't; she was certainly pretty enough. It was a mystery; she had always just seemed like one of the guys. The girl and her brother came back out, got into the car and they drove off.

"Let's go get Mack, first," suggested Vincent, "And then we can go get my car." "Let's get Walt after that," suggested Mary, she had a thing going for him, "I think he's cute," she added and giggled. "Walter Palter will fool with your halter," quipped Vincent, as he turned and looked at Mary, who was in the back seat with her brother. Mary stuck her tongue out at him. "I hope so." she replied, gushingly and then she blushed all over. "Don't forget," quipped Mario, "He has a common-law, shack-up." "He still isn't married," replied Mary, "And I just want to play, anyway."

When they got to Mack's, Betty Jane was there; they were both sitting on the front porch swing. She was wearing cut-off Levis and a white halter. When she found out they were going swimming she told them she had her suit on under her Levis. She said she knew she was going to go swimming with someone, somehow.

Mack was happy as a bug in a rug; he didn't care what he did as long as there was Betty Jane and booze. Mack went in the house to get his trunks and Mack's mother came out the door to see what was going on. She was a lot older than Vincent's mother; she looked haggard. Her hair was gray and curly; it looked like she had forgot to comb it. Mack's mother was nervous and kept reaching up to straighten her hair. She talked fast, with a mountain folk, accent.

"What are you young-uns doing today?" she asked. "Going swimming." "Where to?" she asked. "The Lower Dam," answered Vincent. "Ugh!" she exclaimed, "There are eels out there," she shuddered, "Don't like eels, don't like snakes, and don't like spiders!"

"There aren't as many eels as their use to be," explained Mario, he laughed and continued, "They ate each other up." Then he laughed some more. "Yeh," agreed Vincent and he was also laughing, "one ate one, and then one ate those two and then one ate those three and then one ate those four. And they kept getting bigger and bigger and now there is only one left and he is twenty feet long." They all laughed at his bullshit and then Mack came out and they left.

They all went to Vincent's next and when they got there, they all got out of the car. Grace had heard them coming and she greeted them at the back door, where everyone entered the house. No one ever used the front door; it was just there for looks. Grace was popular with all of Vincent's friends. She was always friendly and never critical. She also made the best cookies in the world. Vincent went into the house first, followed by the pretty red head.

"Mary, Mary," commented Grace, "You are such a pretty thing. When are you going to get married?" she asked. "Right after I get pregnant," answered Mary, cheerfully, with a twinkle in her eye and a hearty laugh. "Oh, my!" exclaimed Vincent's mother, while shaking her finger at the laughing girl, "You are such a naughty girl." "That's what I heard!" proclaimed Vincent, "l heard that you were a real naughty girl." "I heard that, too!" exclaimed Mario, with a serious look, "l heard, that your mother was having a lot of trouble with you." "I heard that, too," commented Mack, in his nonsensical way, with a little flourish of his arms, "heard that you were real naughty."

"Well!" answered Mary, in an artificial, huff, "it sure was not with any of you guys." "You are just kidding," offered Grace, "you know you would like to marry one of these handsome fellows." "They are not what I would call the cream of the crop!" exclaimed Mary, in mock disgust. "You could do worse," suggested Grace, seriously. "I don't know how," quipped Mary, "I would have to go to school to learn how." "Hey!" exclaimed Mario, to Mary, "You better talk nicer about us, or we will take you out in the boonies, and dump you." "I second that!" proclaimed Vincent. "I third it!" proclaimed Mack. "Me too," added Buck, a man of few words.

Vincent went into his room to put on his trunks while the gang was talking to his mother. He took his jeans off, put his suit on and then he put his jeans on over them. The beer was wearing off and Vincent needed another. He looked over at his sister's picture. He wished he had some whiskey. Vincent told himself that he would get some with the money Mario had given him. He couldn't think of a better use for it. Vincent went to the kitchen, where everyone was and put his arm around his mother.

"Got any cookies?" he asked. "Don't I always?" she asked in return, "I'll give you two apiece," she added. Vincent started to protest, wanting more, but she cut him off. "That's all you get," she told him, in a putting your foot down way. "Doc likes my cookies, too." And she went to the cookie jar.

"Your mother looks too young to have a bonehead son like you," remarked Mario, to Vincent. "She really does," agreed Mary. "She looks younger than my mother," added Betty Jane. "And Vincent is too ugly to have a mother as pretty as he has," joked the joker, Mack, "there must have been an accident, or something worse." "There could have been a switch of babies at the hospital," suggested Mario. "Maybe he was adopted," offered Buck and everyone looked at him, surprised by his non-silence. "With friends like you," retorted Vincent, "I don't need any enemies."

They all headed out the door to go to the cars. Vincent wanted some whiskey; it was on his mind as he walked to his car. No one knew which car they were going to ride in and Vincent wanted to be alone so he could go get some whiskey. Vincent suggested that he go after Walt and they would meet at Greta's.

"Where is he?" asked Mary. "Probably at the pool hall," answered Vincent. Mary had wanted to go after Walt, too, but she didn't want to go into the pool hall. It was too hot to wait in the car, so she got in Mario's car along with the rest. Vincent was grateful as he watched them drive off in a cloud of dust. He kissed his mother, and left.

Vincent headed straight for the liquor store to get him a bottle of whiskey. He liked to drink vodka better, but it tasted awful straight out of the bottle. Whiskey or brandy was about the only hard stuff that tasted good to him. In the liquor store the clerk asked him for I.D. and he handed him his draft card. The clerk accepted it with a jaundiced eye. He sold him a bottle of I. W. Harper, a premium whiskey that Vincent had first tasted at a Hole Through Party.

When the miners are digging a tunnel through a mountain and they get it dug all the way through, they throw what is called a "Hole Through Party." This one that Vincent had gone to had been held at the Municipal Auditorium. It had been a dance party with wall-to-wall people. People from all over Butte County came to celebrate. Everyone shows up for free booze. Vincent had got drunk on whiskey, served in large paper cups, filled to the brim. It had been a great party. There is nothing quite as loud and as rowdy as a bunch of drunken tunnel stiffs.

Vincent was grinning when he left the liquor store, partly because he had fooled the clerk and the rest because he had his whiskey. Vincent anticipated the smooth, but crisp taste of the whiskey. He anticipated the warm trail it would leave on the way to his stomach, the warm glow when it got there. Vincent liked the way it gave him confidence. He didn't know how it did it, he didn't care; all he knew was that he needed it.

When Vincent got in his Ford, he broke the seal on the bottle with his fingernail. He opened the bottle and put it to his nose. The smell was sharp, but he liked it, he could feel its power just smelling it. Vincent took a strong pull from the bottle, as it got into his mouth he could feel it finding its way into his blood. He left some under his tongue until it was numb. In a little while the nervous feeling that was perpetually in his stomach left and the world was a better place.

Vincent drove to the pool hall and parked in front. He walked into the smoke polluted atmosphere of the pool hall. Some familiar railroad hands were playing billiards on the front table by the entrance. Billiards is the game with the big table with no pockets; it is strictly a bank shot game. Buzz was running some pinks on the next table and keeping tally with the overhead paraphernalia.

Walt usually played snooker, but all of the snooker tables were being used. Vincent found Walt in the rear of the building playing eight ball with Joby Gates. Joby was a tall, skinny kid who worked at the cannery. He had a pretty girl friend that Vincent would like to play house with. Vincent could tell by the look on his face that Joby was losing the game. Walt looked jovial; he dearly loved to win.

"Who's winning?" asked Vincent. Joby looked up while racking the balls. Losers have to rack the balls. "I think the guy cheats." Grumbled Joby. "I don't have to cheat with you," retorted Walt, with his superior air, using a Boston kind of accent, one that he didn't get from Boston. Vincent wondered how anyone could cheat playing eight ball anyway, there was just no way, unless the opponent was blind.

"Eight ball in the corner pocket!" exclaimed Walt, with the confidence of a champion and he shot hard. The ball hurled like a bullet to the pocket. Walt had shot almost too, hard. The ball almost didn't stay in the pocket. It vibrated around in the pocket, looking like it was going to bounce back out of it. It then dropped into the pocket, rolled down through the inside of the table and into the receptacle.

"God damned slop artist!" grumbled Joby. "Pure artistry." retorted Walt, with aplomb. "Pure bullshit!" exclaimed Vincent. "What's up, Captain Moon?" asked Walt. "Beer's up!" exclaimed the Captain, "The rest of the Moon Patrol is waiting at Greta's." "I'm ready for that!" exclaimed Walt, with gusto, "Let's went." He hung up his cue, "I would have won anyway," he said to Joby, like a smart ass.

"Why did you call him Captain Moon?" asked Joby, "And what the Hell is the Moon Patrol?" Walt proceeded to give him a line of bull. "Only members of the patrol can know the answers to those questions and it cost ten dollars to join and you have to have a sponsor." "What are the benefits to belonging to this Patrol?" asked Joby. "Lots of parties and protection," answered Walt and then he laughed. "Plus," he went on, "we will teach you how to play pool." "Protection from what?" asked Joby. "People who are antagonistic, replied Walt, "or maybe someone is messing around with your girl. Things like that." "I'll think about it," answered Joby and he did look interested. "Don't wait too, long," cautioned Walt, "we are only going to take in a few select people."

"Why don't you come with us?" asked the Captain. "Naw," answered Joby, "l gotta pick up my girl." "Bring her along," suggested the Captain, with a bit of a leer. "I don't think so," answered a cautious Joby. "Let her go with us," suggested Vincent, lasciviously "and you stay here." "No way in Hell!" exclaimed Joby, adamantly.

"Let's evacuate this place," suggested the Captain. "I'll follow you anywhere," answered Walt, "as long is it leads to girls and booze." "I will not lead you astray," promised Vincent. The two walked out of the pool hall with Joby watching and wondering what he would be missing.

When the boys got into the car the Captain of the Moon Patrol was feeling pretty healthy from the booze he had already imbibed. He looked for the boys in blue and could see none. There were no cars parked in front of him. Vincent started his engine and let it warm up a little, He pushed the R. P. M's up to get the pipes to sound off. Vincent pushed the clutch in, put it in first gear, pushed the engine close to the red line and then he popped the clutch. The Ford shot forward, leaving a strip of rubber and a cloud of smoke all the way to the stop light.

The light had just turned red. Vincent jammed on his brakes, slid into the stop area and past it a little. He backed the Ford to the correct side of the intersection and waited for the light to change, looking all over for cops. Seeing none, Vincent let out a sigh of relief. When the light changed he moved forward with caution, not wanting to push his luck.

Vincent had his jug stashed in the glove box. He wanted a drink, but it was only a pint and he wasn't in the mood to share it. Vincent felt selfish, but wanted to be sure that the bottle would last him all day, so he didn't take a drink. Vincent knew Walt would not want whiskey this early, but if he knew it was there, he might say something to the others.

When they arrived at Greta's there was activity in the front yard. The gang was there with Greta and her family. George was sucking on a can of beer already. He was standing next to a giant, yellow radiator; it was one that looked like it would fit on a Caterpillar bulldozer.

Linda was wearing a pair of white shorts. She looked truly delicious; too young, but still delicious. Vincent parked at the top of the hill in front of the house. He had never driven his car in their driveway because it was always full of cars. George had an old pickup, truck and a big, old, blue Buick, about a 1948 model. One, or both of the vehicles was always in the driveway and the driveway was small.

The two boys got out of the car and walked down the hill. George had his shirt off because it was hot. He had a lot of flesh on him but it was healthy looking flesh, smooth and tan. Everyone greeted the boys. George and Maggie were always amiable. Linda was shy around Vincent, but always tried to talk to him, but she never had much to say.

George reached down and picked up the giant radiator and started to raise it to his chest. There was muscle under his fat; you could see it ripple underneath. The radiator slipped from his grasp, but he caught it with his knee. George must have had a few too many beers and he was just showing off. George lifted the radiator over his head.

"That looks easy," commented Walt. George looked at him, grinned and walked over to him with the radiator still over his head. He lowered it and handed it to Walt. "Show us how easy it is," he told Walt. Walt grabbed the radiator, but when George let go of it the weight of it surprised Walt and it showed all over his face. He tried to lift it over his head, but could get it no higher than his chest. "Show him how to do it Captain Moon!" ordered George and he let out a hearty guffaw.

Greta had already told her family the Moon story, but Vincent hadn't known. He was surprised by the title coming from George. Vincent hoped that he would be able to do what George had told him to do. He would at least die trying. Vincent took the radiator from Walt, who was glad to get rid of it. Walt was embarrassed by his lack of strength. Vincent had a time with the radiator, but he got it over his head.

"Captain Moon makes girls swoon!" hollered Mack in his singsong voice. It tickled Vincent's funny bone. He started to laugh and laughing sapped his strength. Vincent let the radiator rest on his head while he tried to regain it. Everyone was laughing now, especially George, he was having a fit. He let Vincent struggle for a while and then he helped him get the radiator off his head and back to the ground.

"Oh, God!" exclaimed George, "I wish I could have got a picture of that." Vincent still couldn't stop laughing. George had his arm over Vincent's shoulder; he was laughing so hard he was using Vincent to hold himself up. Vincent got so weak he squatted to the ground and George followed him.

Greta was looking at Vincent with a new interest. She had felt there was something special about him, but knew not what it was. He was different than the other boys she had known; he was Captain Moon. Greta watched him laugh, she watched with a new affection, but she didn't understand it. She didn't think that it was love.

George and Vincent were finally able to get up enough strength to stand up. Mario walked over and picked the radiator up like it was a toy and lifted it over his head while showing off his muscles. No one was impressed. Vincent had already done the feat and he was smaller than the rest of the guys. Mack did it next, just to see if he could. He did it with a struggle and so did Buck but with more a struggle.

Vincent was proud that he had been able to get the radiator over his head. George was way bigger than he was by at least a hundred pounds. Walt, Mack and Buck were also bigger. As for Mario, he couldn't be compared; he was just a mountain.

Greta had appreciated him; he could tell by the way she had looked at him. She came over to him, and felt his bicep and he flexed it for her. "Mmmmm!" she exclaimed, as she squeezed it. She thought about the muscle in his pants and felt horny. "I made a bunch of sandwiches," she told him, "we can't live on beer."

"We could live on love," Vincent answered impulsively. He blushed, for it had just come out of his mouth without any thought. He was always getting his foot in his mouth that way. "I don't know," claimed Greta, with a sly look on her pretty face, "I have not tried it... have you?" Vincent's face got red; he had been having a fantasy about her, a naughty one. He tried to look away. Greta broke out in a mixture of giggles and laughs.

"Oh, God, Vincent!" she blustered, "You are so adorable when you blush." She impulsively planted a kiss, a quick one on his lips. Vincent was pleased that Greta found him adorable, but he was not sure it was the way he wanted her to think about him. It didn't seem very macho, but he guessed it was preferable to not being adorable.

"You really are adorable," commented Mack, after hearing Greta's little praise. He turned to the rest of the crew, "Don't you think Captain Moon is adorable? Greta thinks he is." "Oh God, he is," chortled Mario, "just like a puppy's tummy." "Like a bucket of mud," added Walt. "Like a bucket of shit, you mean," added Buck. "I think he really is adorable," added Mary, seriously. "Really." "I think he is as adorable as my Teddy Bear," blurted Linda, impulsively and then she blushed all over. "The one that you sleep with, I bet," chortled Mario, as he rolled his eyes. The girl's face got redder and she ran into the house. Vincent felt her discomfort and it showed on his face.

"She has a crush on you, you know," Greta whispered to Vincent, "she asked me if she could have you if I ever broke up with you." Vincent was surprised and secretly, pleased. "What did you say to that?" asked Vincent. "May as well keep you in the family," answered Greta and her parents had heard enough of the conversation to know what it was about. "Yes," said Maggie, "we may as well keep you in the family." and she gave Vincent a warm, motherly smile. "God forbid!" exclaimed George and he chuckled. Vincent and Greta both laughed out loud. "The stuff is getting too deep around here for me" said Vincent and he chuckled and added, "let's go swimming." "Tally ho!" exclaimed Buck and everyone looked at him. He blushed at the attention and turned his eyes down.

"Ask Linda if she wants to go with us, "suggested Vincent to Greta. "Ask her yourself," she answered a little cool. Vincent turned and walked into the house to do so. He was surprised that Greta seemed miffed. The bedrooms and bath were upstairs. When Vincent saw that Linda was not downstairs, he called for her. Right after calling, he heard the toilet flush. For some reason he felt embarrassed; he felt like an intruder. Right after that, Linda came into the room, hardly making a sound. She was barefoot. Her face was flushed from some secret thought, or maybe it was because she had flushed the toilet at a bad time. Vincent wished he knew what it was.

The girl had a golden tan; her skin looked soft, smooth and warm, like a baby's. Linda had a lovely body and Vincent really looked at her, like it was the first time that he had seen her. Vincent looked at her long, slender, perfect legs. He wanted to touch them and he blushed at the thought. Vincent let a long, soft whistle escape between his teeth. Linda blushed, but most of it was from pleasure.

"If I were a little younger," teased Vincent, "Or you were a little older?" and he left it like that. "What?" she asked, demurely. "You know what," he answered. She was blushing, but getting bolder. "I'm almost fourteen," she told him, hopefully. "As dangerous as you look now, I would be afraid of you if you were any older," he told her and he wasn't kidding. "I bet you are not afraid of anything," she retorted. "Why don't you go swimming with us?" Vincent asked her, wanting to change the subject. "Why do you want me to go?" Linda asked, wistfully. "Because you are so pretty," answered Vincent, "and I like to look at you." "You can look at Greta," she retorted, jealously. Vincent moved closer and ran his fingers through her silky, blond hair. Her eyes were wide, blue and innocent. "I want to look at you, too," he told her. Her face was flushed and her heart was pounding. "I will go," she told him, breathlessly," I'll go put on my suit" and she turned and ran up the stairs. Vincent's eyes followed her lovely rump up the stairs. He blushed as he felt desire and he forced his eyes away from her. Vincent went back out side and joined the others.

"Is she coming?" asked Greta and Vincent nodded his head. "She went to put on her suit," he answered. "You guys are in for a treat," Greta commented, with a grin. "How so?" asked Vincent? "She has a polka-dot bikini," answered Greta. Mack overheard her and his eyes lit up with anticipation. "Swear to God?" he asked. Betty Jane shot him a look laced with venom and then she poked him in the ribs with her elbow. She grinned when he winced. "Swear to God," answered Greta, "and it fits her too well and you boys better remember that she is only thirteen.

Moon Patrol eyes were patrolling the door that Linda would be coming out of. Tongues were almost hanging out. When she finally came out the door, there was an audible sound, a sigh of disappointment from all of the boys. The pretty girl was wearing a split skirt that totally covered the bikini. Linda noticed, immediately that she had been ogled, but the looks had changed. Her eyes darted to everyone's in an attempt to read the looks.

"They are just wondering about the bikini that you have on under your skirt," explained Greta. Then she directed her conversation to the disappointed Moon Patrol. "Have patience," she advised, "sooner, or later she will have to take it off." At first Linda got rosy on every exposed part of her, and probably on the rest of her too. But Linda got spunky. "Well!" she exclaimed, "They will just have to wait, wont they?"

They all climbed into the two cars. Greta, Linda, Walt and Mary went with Vincent and the rest with Mario. Vincent had still ended up with most of the girls. He led the way and Mario followed. Vincent headed for the lower dam, which was a spillway, about five miles south of town, out in the rock piles.

The cars stayed close; there was always the chance of some kind of car trouble with the kind of cars they drove. No one had made enough money, yet, to buy a good one. The gas gauge on Mario's car, didn't always function, leaving the possibility of running out of fuel. They were all firm believers of Murphy's Law. (If anything can go wrong, it will.)

Sometimes the guys wouldn't have a spare tire and the tires that were on their cars were worn out. Sometimes they were worse than just wore out; sometimes they were rags, with a boot, or boots in them. A boot is a big patch covering a big hole in the casing of the tire, usually a blow out hole. There was always the chance of a boot rupturing and the tire going flat all of a sudden. The Moon Patrol would rather spend money on booze and girls than on tires.

As Vincent drove south on Highway Seventy he could feel the heat of Greta's thigh against his leg. It was soothing like a balm. It was good and relaxing to be with her and his friends.

They passed the Knot Hole, a tavern frequented by rednecks and noted for its Saturday night mayhem. It was on the left, sitting near the bank of a hill and on the right were willow trees, rock piles and dredger ponds. They passed the Wagon Wheel, a rustic nightclub that sat on the top of the hill; it was also on the left.

Vincent had gone to the Wagon Wheel once with Mario and his Mafia-looking, brother to see a floor show. The comedian had told a story about murdering his wife, dismembering her and flushing her down the toilet. He said that after that every time he sat on the throne he could feel her cold eyes staring up at him.

The highway was serpentine at this point and Vincent had to watch for the turn off, it was right on a curve. He spotted it and turned off onto the gravel road. It was a one-lane road; it was graded right out of the rock piles. It was winding, with many variations in elevation. Mario followed in Vincent's dust. It was a couple of miles out to the dam and the going was bumpy. The road was primarily made of cobblestones. By the time the gang had made it to the river they were all hot, tired and thirsty.

There were some large oaks about forty feet from the river and the boys parked the cars in their shade. It was hot in the cars, so they bailed out of them as fast as the laws of physics would allow.

The rock piles went to about twenty-five feet shy of the river. The rest of the way to river was a smooth concrete slope; it was a gentle one. The gang spread the blankets out on this slope; it was a perfect place to lay and get a tan. After the slope broke into the river, it broke off abruptly and went straight down into the river. The river was about five feet deep at this point; it had been dug out for the spillway.

There was an open gate in this area of the dam and the water wildly rushed through it. On the other side of the gate there was a concrete wall. And then there was the rest of the dam with the water running over it serenely. It was about a couple of hundred feet across the dam. Vincent looked out across the dam, he could see the tails of a couple of eels sticking out of the water; they had attached themselves to the dam. Who knows what they were doing, taking a nap, maybe?

The water was shallow across the dam. On the other side of the gate one could walk across it. One could get to the concrete wall on the other side of the gate without braving the cataract waters. This was accomplished by walking up the river a ways and then walking or swimming to it.

After the wall the dam had a cable strung all the way across it. It was supported by two foot high, pipes, set at about fifteen foot intervals. The river went right over the top of the dam, but it was quite safe with the cable there to hang on to.

CHAPTER 16

Mario put the ice chest with the booze in it in the shade, under one of the oaks. Greta put hers next to it. It was full of sandwiches and soda pop. "Bars open!" shouted the big Italian. Everyone was ready for beer, including Linda, but Greta wouldn't let her have any.

"Your sister is a party pooper," offered a sympathetic, Mack and he took a long pull from his beer. "Tell me about it!" exclaimed a pouting Linda. "I'm going in," said Mack. He sat his beer down and ran to the river. He ran down the concrete slope and dove straight into the rushing water, just above the cataract. All were watching, holding their breath. Even though Mack was a strong swimmer, he just barely made it across without being washed into the cataract.

After Mack was safe, Vincent was watching Linda, waiting for her to reveal herself. She had been watching Mack and his foolhardy stunt. Vincent had seen a look appear on her face and knew what she was going to do. His heart picked up a beat in anticipation, and alarm. Linda unfastened her skirt and it fell to the slope, revealing the most perfect little body that Vincent had ever seen. Linda's tan was the golden kind that some Southern California blonds have from spending their summers on the beach. Vincent couldn't help but stare at her.

Linda just stood there for a moment. Vincent gazed at her. She must have felt his stare, for she turned and their eyes met. Linda read his eyes, her face flushed and she ran down the slope. She dove into the river, right where Mack had and she made it across with ease. Vincent was in awe of her beauty and grace. He wondered how he could follow an act such as that; he couldn't swim a stroke. Vincent felt awfully inadequate. He chugalugged his beer, but it didn't help. Mack had walked further out on the dam. Linda was just standing on top of the concrete wall, looking like a goddess.

"Don't come out here!" hollered Mack, "Unless you like eels." With body English, Linda made it quite clear that she wanted nothing to do with eels. She turned around and dove back into the river. She swam upstream for about thirty feet, then turned, swam to shore and got out of the water.

Although it was hot, Vincent knew Linda would be cold after being in the icy Feather River. He picked up his towel and without a thought of Greta, went to Linda and put the towel around her shoulders. Linda was shivering and was surprised. She looked up and smiled, bashfully when she saw it was Vincent. He dried her shoulders, briskly, to warm her.

"Thanks, Vincent," she said, meekly, "Would you dry my hair too?" When he started to dry her flaxen hair his leg touched hers and he felt desire. "I never realized that you were so pretty," he told her, softly, "I wish you were a little older," he added, with frustration.

"Oh, Vincent," she pleaded, timidly, "Would you wait for me to catch up with you? I have always wanted to be your girl." Greta had told him that Linda had a crush on him, but he had not thought that she was so serious. "Does Greta know how you feel?" he asked, somewhat confused by the girls candor. "She knows!" she answered, with vehemence, "but I know her," Linda continued, "even if she didn't want you, she would not let me have you." Her fire moved Vincent. "If she doesn't want me by the time you are old enough," he told her, "I'll let you have me, if you still want me by then." "I will!" she answered, hushed, but passionately.

Vincent dried her hair and moved to give her a kiss on her cheek, but she turned her head at the last moment and the kiss caught her on her willing lips. It was so delicious; he could not pull away. It was so delicious he didn't want to and when he tried, she clung to him.

That moment when her lips had clung to his was the sweetest moment Vincent had ever experienced. It was like a magic spell; he felt suspended in beautiful feelings he had never felt before. Greta broke the spell; she called him from the blanket. She wanted him to put some lotion on her back. Vincent pulled his lips away from Linda and their eyes met. Vincent was shocked to see such passion in the eyes of a girl so young.

"I'm sorry," he told her, regretfully, "but duty calls." "I wish it were just duty," she replied, jealously. He walked back up the slope to where Greta was, but his heart was not in it. He wanted to stay with Linda, but she was just too young for him. He would just have to push those thoughts out of his head.

Greta was lying on the blanket; she was lying on her back with one knee up. She was watching Vincent come to her. Greta was admiring his lean, muscular, figure, wishing he were more aggressive with her. She knew she would give herself to him if he would just try. Greta had a fantasy of him making love to her and it brought a flush of heat to her face and to her Venus mound. Vincent was now standing over her, with his dark, good looks and his charming grin. Greta felt a flood of affection for him and handed him the lotion. She looked up at him through long lashes and gave him a little pout.

"Was that a kiss I saw?" she asked petulantly. Vincent was still a little spellbound from his encounter with Linda. He was having a little trouble with his tongue. "I was just trying to give her a little peck on her cheek," he told her clumsily, "but she turned her face." Greta was enjoying his discomfort and she teased him. "Did you enjoy it?" she asked sweetly. She could see how that had flustered him and now she was laughing. This only compounded his fluster, but he saw what she was doing and decided to play her little game. "Did Sampson love Delilah?" he answered with a question. This caught her off guard and her eyes got flinty for a moment. "Remember what happened to Sampson," she warned him and smiled. "I remember, but my strength is not in my hair."

Greta decided she would play with him a little longer. She reached up and caressed his flank with her fingertips. She was amazed at how hard the muscle was. She touched the flat of his stomach and it was as hard as a board.

"What part of your body is the strongest?" she asked, but she was thinking of only one part of his body and she could not help glancing at the bulge in his trunks. Greta felt a flash of heat as her blood rushed to get her ready. Vincent was having trouble too. He was getting horny and confused.

Vincent wasn't sure if he loved Greta; Linda had messed up his head. He wanted both of the girls, but knew he could not have Linda. Why did life have to be so complicated? Vincent knelt to his knees and started putting lotion on Greta's back. Her body was smooth, firm and warm. The contact of his oily hands on her flesh was erotic. He wished that he could remove her halter and rub the oil on her naked breasts.

Vincent put the oil on her back as far down as he could, to the edge of her suit. He gazed at the lovely swell of her bottom, which he wanted desperately to caress. Perspiration was popping out in little beads across his forehead. Greta turned and looked at his mouth. She wished they were alone; she wanted him to touch her all over. He looked at her mouth, she licked her lips and he kissed them.

Vincent could hear Mack off in the distance, he sounded as if he was in trouble. Vincent looked up and searched the water. He saw Mack a couple of hundred yards up the river, clear over on the other side. Mack was hollering, waving his arms. Vincent couldn't hear him well enough to make out what he was hollering about. Mack was floating downstream, heading for the dam.

"What's wrong with him?" asked Greta, impatient, frustrated by her lost passion. "I don't know," answered Vincent, a little relieved by his lost passion. The rest of the gang had gathered at the river's edge to watch

Mack, whose head had just gone under. He came back up, spluttering and thrashing. "Maybe he is playing games, "suggested Mario, who was an excellent swimmer, "He is always playing games." "He isn't playing games," retorted Vincent, with a frown, "One of you guys should go help him." "He can't drown," commented Walt, in a nonchalant, manner, "All he has to do is grab the cable when he gets to it." "He may not make it to the God damned cable!" answered Vincent, angrily. He no sooner got the words out of his mouth than Linda went to Mack's rescue. She dove into the icy water and swam to him. The water wasn't very deep where he was and she helped him to his feet. It was plain to see that Mack was having trouble with a cramp in his leg. Mack half danced, half hobbled to the dam with Linda's help. The two stood by the dam for a while and then walked across. When they got closer Vincent could see the pale in Mack's face, plus the anger.

"Don't you assholes know when someone is drowning?" Mack shouted angrily. Walt laughed defensively. "You have heard the story about the boy who cried wolf too many times?" asked Walt, like a smart ass," And then he laughed and that was not a good thing to do. "I got a story for you!" growled Mack and he went at Walt like a freight train, "and it's about a knuckle sandwich." Mack hit Walt with a whirlwind of haymakers and knocked him to the ground.

Walt had stopped laughing. It took both Mario and Vincent to pull Mack off Walt. In just a moment, Mack was sorry for what he had done. He was concerned about Walt's injuries, which were minor; he had a cut lip and some abrasions on his face. In a little while they were all drinking beer and laughing.

"That's the last time I'm going to laugh at you," Walt told Mack, sheepishly. "I'm not going to laugh at him, either," claimed Mario, mocking fear by rolling his eyeballs. "I'll laugh," joked Vincent, "because I can out run him." They all looked at Buck to see what he would say. "Don't look at me," pleaded Buck, defensively, "I only laugh when I'm alone." Vincent grabbed Linda around her tiny waist and pulled her to him. He had just enough booze in him to make him impulsive.

"I'm going to initiate this little beauty into the Moon Patrol!" he proclaimed and then he kissed her full on her lips. Linda took advantage of the situation by kissing him back for all she was worth. Everyone shouted his or her approval, except Greta. Her eyes were shooting daggers at her sister. "I proclaim!" proclaimed Vincent, after they had finally got disconnected, "This little beauty," and he gave the girl a hug. Vincent continued, "To be the official life guard of the Moon Patrol." Linda was beaming. "And furthermore," he went on, "she will have to officiate at all Moon Patrol swimming parties."

"Hooray for our life guard.'" shouted Mack and he toasted her with his beer. "Hooray for the new Moon!" exclaimed Mario and he toasted her with his beer. The rest of them followed suit, except Greta, who was doing her best not to sulk. Linda was so pleased she could hardly contain her self. She gave up and kissed Vincent again. Greta's face reflected her disapproval as she tugged at Vincent's arm.

"Come on, Vincent," she pleaded, "I'm going to burn if you don't finish putting lotion on me. "She gave Linda a hostile look, which was returned. Vincent, wanting to cool the situation he had created, took Greta by the hand and led her to the blanket.

Linda went back to the river. Vincent watched her out of the corner of his eye. It was such a pleasure to watch her walk; she had a natural grace. The rest of the Patrol followed her into the water. Mary couldn't swim, but she went into the water up to her knees. She was pale and had at least a million freckles. Vincent was concerned that she would burn.

"Hey, Mary," he yelled, "have one of those heroes rub some grease on you so you won't burn." "I'll do it," yelled Walt enthusiastically and went to Mary's aid. "That's a good idea," claimed Mack and he took Betty Jane out of the water and led her to a blanket. She didn't have to worry much about burning; she already had a nice tan. Betty Jane had on a bikini, also. She looked good in it, but not as good as Linda.

Vincent was putting the finishing touch on Greta's back, while having a fantasy about putting lotion on her front. She must have sensed something, for she asked him what he was thinking about. His face turned red. "I can't tell you," he blurted. She turned and looked at his face. When she saw he was blushing, it piqued her curiosity. "Come on, Vincent... tell me!" Greta pleaded. Vincent had an unusual moment of boldness.

"I was wondering what it would be like to put lotion on your front," he answered. She blushed, but it was more from pleasure than modesty. Greta didn't say anything for a moment. "Let's go for a walk up the river," she suggested. She was tired of waiting for Vincent to get aggressive. She was tired of being a virgin and she wanted Vincent to change her status. She wanted it done right away. "Bring the blanket," she told him as she got up and waited for him.

Talking about this and that and touching, they walked up the riverbank. After they had walked a couple hundred yards they came to a sandy, grassy area surrounded by oak, willow trees and brush. It was very secluded. Vincent spread the blanket and Greta laid on it halfway on her side with one knee, up. She beckoned him with her hand. Greta's eyes were liquid. Vincent saw the lust in them and it frightened him a little, but not enough to stop him. He knelt and kissed her lips. Greta's lips were soft and open; her tongue darted into his mouth. She pulled away after a long kiss.

"Vincent," she said, softly, "I think I would like it." "Like what?" asked Vincent, totally in the dark. "I would like to have you put lotion on my front." Vincent's heart did a flip, flop. Greta took off her halter and laid it on the blanket. Vincent's eyes went wide as he gazed at her beauty. Greta laid on her back with her right knee up.

"Would you put lotion on my front?" she asked and her look was a little wicked. Captain Moon's hands were shaking as he put some of the lotion in the palm of his hand. He could feel it in his loins as he smoothed it on her breasts. Vincent could feel the hot blood making his member swell. He smoothed the lotion all around the outside curves and then around the inside. Vincent smoothed it around the edge of her nipples. He watched her nipples become erect and then he put lotion on them gently with his index finger. Greta's eyes were closed and her mouth was open. Her breath was hot and heavy. Greta closed her mouth and moaned softly. Vincent kissed her nipples and ran his tongue over them. Greta pulled his face to hers and kissed him with a wild passion, exploring the inside of his mouth with her tongue.

"Oh God, Vincent!" she exclaimed, I'm on fire!" She let go of him and lied back, moving her head from side to side, moaning. Vincent continued to put the lotion on Greta, smoothing it on her belly and into her belly button. He smoothed it to the edge of her suit and she squirmed.

"Put some on my legs," Greta panted. Vincent started on her left ankle and slowly worked his way up to the inside of her thigh. Beads of perspiration were popping out on his forehead. He smoothed the lotion on the inside of her thigh to the edge of her suit almost touching her apex area. Vincent did the other leg the same way. When he came to the apex of her legs again, he lingered, gently smoothing the lotion on her silken flesh. Vincent rubbed her so close to her loins that he touched her there, ever so slightly. A gasp escaped Greta's lips and her body like a magnet elevated to meet his hand. Vincent pressed his hand on the mound between her legs. She moaned, closed her legs and squeezed his hand with her thighs.

"Oh God Vincent!" she cried, "Make me naked." Vincent pulled her suit off and Greta was naked. Her pubic hair was blond and curly. Vincent touched her there. Greta sucked in her breath between her teeth. Greta opened her thighs for him as he explored further. She opened like a blooming flower and he touched her there. And then they were both trying to get his suit off. Vincent had such an erection; they had difficulty. When they got his suit off he went on his knees in front of her and it was her turn to explore. Greta felt the shape of him with her fingers. There was a drop of clear, lubricating fluid at the orifice. Greta touched it and smeared it around. The sensation was almost too much and he shivered.

"It's slippery!" she exclaimed and she lied back down, pulling him down with her. "Put it inside of me." she pleaded, "Hurry." Vincent got between her thighs and his body found its way into hers. The fire that was inside of her and the fire in him were fused into frantic ecstasy. Their bodies became as one, fluid like, a frenzied search for more sensation.

Fortunately, and not because of knowledge or expertise on Vincent's part, Greta reached her orgasm before he did. She reached it with violent passion. She made animal like noises, wrapping her legs around him, almost squeezing the breath out of him. After she had reached her climax the sensation eased off slowly. She was still enjoying it when he reached his. Vincent felt as if his ejaculation would never end, like he would turn inside out. A groan escaped him as he was spent. They lay exhausted, both feeling his erection slip away.

"I liked it better when it was hard," she told him and she giggled. "Me too," he answered, embarrassed by his loss of virility, suddenly feeling his nakedness. "Have you ever done it before?" Greta asked. "No," Vincent lied, "But I would sure like to do it again." He moved off of her and lay by her side. He caressed her breasts and he gazed at her body. "Your body is beautiful," he told her, "I didn't know that anything could feel that good." He wondered why he had lied to her. "I know." she agreed, as she ran her fingers through the hair on his chest, "If it had felt any better I don't know if I could have stood it." "Practice makes perfect," quoted Vincent. "You mean the more we do it the better it gets?" she asked, with eyes wide. "That's the way I heard it," he answered. "Oh my God!" she exclaimed in wonder and the thought did excite her.

"Roll over." Vincent commanded. "Why? Greta asked and giggled. "I'm a bottoms man," he told her, "l like bottoms." She giggled and rolled over on her tummy. Greta's fanny had lovely curves. Vincent caressed the curves with his fingertips; he ran one finger down the inside, and she shivered. "That tickles," she told him, "But don't stop." He kissed one of her cheeks, and then the other. Vincent felt the returning of his erection. "Do you like my fanny?" she asked? "I love your fanny," he answered, while caressing it and the inside of her thigh. He let his hand rest on one cheek. "Your hand is hot," she commented.

"It isn't the only thing that's hot," Vincent told her, while putting his hand between her thighs and squeezing her mound. Greta rolled over; she saw his erection and her eyes got wide. "Oh my God!" she exclaimed, "We had better get back to the others." She reached for the bottom half of her suit. "I can't go back like this!" he complained, holding his erection. Greta looked at it and quickly started to get into her suit. He grabbed her suit before she could get it all the way on, she had it up to her knees.

"No you don't!" Vincent exclaimed and laughed. He got her suit back off of her and they wrestled for it, laughing and giggling. Vincent ended up on top of her. Greta opened her thighs for him and he went into her again. They made love slower this time and it was sweeter than the first time. They lay for a while, deliciously spent, not wanting to move. Greta was the first to speak. "Now that we have started this," she said, pensively, "How are we ever going to be able to stop?" "Why do you want to stop?" he asked.

"People are supposed to get married before they do it, aren't they?" she asked. "I don't know," answered Vincent," Is that why people get married?" They were both lost in thought for a moment. He was laying half on top of her with one leg between hers. "I think marriage is to protect the children," she stated, thoughtfully and then her eyes got wide and her mouth dropped open. "Oh my God!" Greta wailed, "What if I get pregnant?" Suddenly she became self-conscious about her nakedness. She got up and hurriedly put her suit on and Vincent did the same, for the same reason. "Do you think I'm a whore?" she asked, with her eyes cast down. "No!" he told her, with conviction, "Whores do it for money." "Do you love me?" she asked him, searching his eyes for the answer. Vincent hesitated. Yesterday he had been certain, but now he was not. He hesitated too long.

"Vincent!" she wailed, "You say it all the time." "I guess I do," he blurted, before he could think it out. "You guess?" she asked, incredulous, "You guess?" Greta glared at him, waiting. Vincent got defensive. "You have never told me that you love me," he stated firmly. She softened and lowered her eyes. "I know," she answered, "I'm sorry. I guess I'm too young to know what love is." "I guess I don't know either," he answered. "I do know one thing though," she stated sweetly. "What's that?" he asked. "I like you a lot and I love to do it with you" "Me too," he answered affectionately.

"What if I get pregnant?" she asked. "I don't know," he answered truthfully. "Would you marry me?" she asked. "I don't know," he answered, "I guess I would." "What made you unsure?" she asked and they were silent for a while; they were pensive. Greta spoke again, "Was it because I let you make love to me?" "I don't know," he answered defensively, not wanting her to go any further. The girl frowned, a look of suspicion flitted across her face. "It was something that happened today. Wasn't it?" she asked and her voice was getting icy. "It's my sister, isn't it? My little, sister!" she finished with vehemence. "Come on!" answered Vincent, defensively," She is just a little girl." Vincent knew in his heart that he was lying. He knew his feelings for Linda had adulterated his affection for Greta. He believed that if he truly loved Greta, he would not want Linda so bad.

"I'm not a virgin anymore!" wailed Greta, with tears in her eyes, "And how come it didn't hurt. It was supposed to hurt," she cried. "I don't know," answered Vincent sympathetically and then he laughed and added, "It didn't hurt me either." Greta giggled, and slapped him on the shoulder. "It's not supposed to hurt you, you big boob, she told him and giggled. Then she asked him, demurely, "Did I make love good?" "I don't have anyone to compare you with," he answered, and kissed her softly on her lips, "But if you had been any better I might have died," "What a way to go!" she exclaimed and giggled. "Amen to that!" he exclaimed and sighed.

They got up and he shook the sand from the blanket.

"We better go back to the others," suggested Vincent, "Before they start wondering about us." "Ha ha!" Greta exclaimed, with a wry look, "You can bet they are already wondering what we have been doing." She was pensive for a moment and then she asked, "You won't tell anyone, will you?" "Of course not!" he exclaimed, resenting the implication. "I don't know if I can be with them," she told him, with apprehension, "without my lost virginity showing." "Where's it going to show?" he kidded her. "On my face, you idiot!" she exclaimed, looking at him like he was a clod, "Where else?" she added. Vincent shrugged. "I don't know if I can hide my feelings, either," he told her and they were both lost in thought for a moment. Vincent wondered if Greta would tell Linda, but he dismissed it and then he got an idea.

"I know!" he exclaimed, "Let's pretend that we are having a fight. That will take the heat off of us." "That's a good idea," she agreed, enthusiastically. "What shall we fight about?" "Don't say anything," he answered, "just act mad and I'll act mad. We can think of something to be mad about later." Greta agreed. They both practiced their mad act on the way back to the others. The others took notice of their mutual hostility. No one said anything, except for Mack, who was never encumbered by social grace.

"We were about to call for an air search," Mack commented, with a know it all look on his silly face, "but we couldn't find a phone." He rolled his eyes lasciviously, "Were you chasing butterflies?" he asked. "Stuff it!" retorted Vincent and Greta gave Mack a look that should have turned him into stone. Linda eyed Vincent and Greta with suspicion. "Come and swim with me," she coaxed Vincent and he was grateful for the escape. "Good idea," he answered, "But I can't swim a stroke." "It's about time you learned," Linda answered, "Don't you think?"

As they walked to the water he told her about his near drowning when he was a boy. She was very mature about it. "I understand your fear," Linda reasoned, "but nearly drowning is all the more reason to learn how to swim." Linda was looking at his face as he answered. "I agree, but knowing that doesn't help." "You have to overcome your fear before you will be able to swim," was her reply. "Such wisdom from a thirteen year old," chided Vincent. "I'm almost fourteen!" she retorted, crisply. "What made you so wise?" he asked. "Girls mature faster than boys," Linda informed him, as a matter of fact. Vincent looked roguish as he eyed her pretty body up and down. "I believe that is a true," he stated, as he moved his eyebrows up and down imitating Groucho Marx, "I do believe that is a truth." The girl blushed, but she was pleased.

Vincent followed Linda into the water. He hated this water; it was just too cold for him. He felt his testicles shrink as the water came to his loins.

The familiar, constricted feeling came into his chest. He sometimes got the same feeling in a close space or in a situation he couldn't get out of, like being in the dentist chair, or the barber's. Vincent knew the feeling was a manifestation of his near drowning experience. He wondered if the feeling would ever go away.

"You can help yourself get over the fear," Linda told him, as if she had been reading his mind. Vincent was into the water past his stomach and that was about as far as he was going to go. "Close your eyes," she commanded, "Hold your breath, put your head under the water and keep it there as long as you can." Vincent complied and in a short time he came back out, gasping for breath. "Keep doing it," she ordered and he did.

After he had done it four times Linda told him to open his eyes while his head was under. Vincent did and he came right back up, gasping. The shock of the cold water on his eyes had caused him to inhale some of the river. After he had done it for a few times he was able to stay under for a little while with his eyes open.

"Sit down in the water and open your eyes," Linda told him," And I will join you." Vincent hesitated; he was apprehensive about not having his feet under him. "Don't be chicken!" she scolded, and he sat down, comforted by her hand on his. Vincent opened his eyes and saw Linda's outline in the water. He could not see her clearly. Linda had gone to her knees in front of him. She let go of his hand and put her hands on his shoulders. She was almost on top of him now. Linda leaned over and gave him a kiss on his lips. Vincent put his hand on the back of her head and kissed her back. Her weight caused him to lose his balance, and he fell slowly on his back. Linda fell over on top of him, but that didn't stop the kiss. They didn't stop until they were both out of breath and then they came up for air.

They both broke the surface at the same time. Linda had a wide grin on her pretty face, just like the one the cat had had right after it had swallowed the canary. Linda broke out with joyful laughing when she saw his face. He was never very good at hiding his feelings; he wore his heart on his sleeve as the old saying goes.

"You liked it too, didn't you?" she asked, with her face aglow, water dripping from it while jumping up and down in the water. She was oblivious of whether anyone was watching. "You little devil." he answered, unable to conceal his delight in Linda, "You know I did." Their eyes communicated mutual consent. And they were just getting ready to go under and try it again when a beach ball bounced off his head and into the water.

"I was just trying to get your attention," quipped the red headed girl, who had thrown the ball, "You two look awful cozy out there." Mary's white skin was turning pink. "You had better get into the shade." chided

Vincent, "And soon. "And what are you guys doing?" kidded Mary, with one eyebrow raised. "She is just trying to teach me how to swim," answered Vincent, defensively. "Oh," retorted Mary, "is that what she is trying to do?" With that said, Mary turned, and walked out of the water, and into the shade.

"People aught to mind their own bees wax," muttered Linda, a little cross, and she was shivering. Vincent looked to see what Greta was doing, and she was lying on her stomach, tanning her backside. "Let's go under one more time," he whispered," I want to kiss you again." Joy lit up the girl's face. "I want to kiss you a hundred times," she whispered in return. They went under, and found each other, bodies locked in an embrace. Their lips met, and they kissed until they could stand it no longer, and then they had to go up for air. They broke the surface of the water together. It was impossible for either of them to hide their joy.

"Do you feel like I do?" she asked, with a radiant face, looking so gorgeous with water dripping from her lovely body. "Yes, I do." he answered, happily, but his voice changed; it went to somber, "But its too soon for us." The joy vanished from the girl's face momentarily, but returned. "You do like me, though. I know you do," she answered, softly. "I more than like you." he whispered. "I could kiss you all day long."

Linda's eyes got wide, and her knees weak, she knew he felt like she did. "I wish you could." was all Linda could say, for she was shivering. Vincent led her out of the water and over to the towels. He picked up a towel and dried her hair and shoulders. Linda stopped shivering. She wanted to put her arms around him, but knew she shouldn't. He wanted to embrace her, but knew he shouldn't. "We will have to play it cool for awhile," he whispered to her," It is too soon for us." "I want to be older!" Linda wailed, "I want to be your girl." She was close to tears. "I know," answered Vincent, "I want that too, but your parents wouldn't allow it. We have to wait."

Vincent was in need of a strong drink. He used the excuse that he needed to get some cigarettes, but he also needed to get away from the girl to think. Vincent knew she was just too much temptation for him and she was just too young for him to do what he wanted to do with her. He knew that he would be unable to resist the temptation.

Vincent left the girl and walked to the car, to the passenger's side, which was facing away from the river. Vincent looked to see if anyone was watching, but there was no one. He opened the door and then the glove box. He took out his bottle and knelt to the ground. Vincent opened it and took a strong pull from it. The whiskey felt good in his stomach, he had needed it.

Vincent had been a very busy boy and it was still hard to comprehend what had happened to him. He had fallen out of love with one person and into love with another, both on the same day. Maybe he just didn't know what love was? Maybe his brains were in his pants? All kinds of thoughts were going through his head as he knelled and sipped his whiskey.

Vincent knew he still wanted Greta, but he knew it wasn't love. Vincent also knew that he wanted Linda and he believed that it was love, but he wasn't sure, how in the Hell could one be sure? What in Hell was love? Was there some kind of test? How many times could one fall in love? Does loving one-person feel different from loving another? What a mystery love was.

Only one thing seemed certain; it all seemed easier with a belly full of whiskey. Vincent took another couple of slugs and put the bottle back in the glove. He went back to the group feeling considerably better. The rest of the day they all drank beer and played together, like the children they were.

CHAPTER 17

That night in his bed, Vincent reminisced about making love to Greta. He wondered what it would be like to make love to Linda. He fantasized about it. He thought about it all the next day. Vincent thought about Linda being so young and realized that Greta was only sixteen and she could already be pregnant. They would both be relieved when she started her period.

Vincent had seen condoms before, but had never used one. Someone had told him that using one was like washing your feet with your socks on. He hadn't know what that meant and still didn't. Vincent looked for a drug store with a man behind the counter and asked for condoms with a red face.

"Do you want reservoir ends?" asked the druggist, with a poker face. Not having the slightest notion of what the druggist was talking about, Vincent answered as sophisticated as possible. "Of course!"

Later on that afternoon, Vincent and Greta were on their way to the lower dam, together, alone. They were going to go swimming, but neither liked to swim. They hadn't put on their suits yet. Greta was wearing a loose, cotton skirt, with a halter. Vincent was operating the steering wheel with one hand while stroking the inside of her thigh with the other. Her legs were slightly parted and her left hand was resting palm down on his leg. Vincent could feel the heat of her hand through his pants. They were both in anticipation of what they knew was going to happen.

"I got something for us today," Vincent told Greta secretively. "What is it?" she asked, quickly, having caught the tone of his voice. "I'll show you later," he teased. They were almost to the parking area, and Greta was pouting. "Come on, Vincent, Show me," she pleaded. He squeezed her leg, and then withdrew his hand. He needed it to park the car. Vincent parked the car, and then he kissed her while fondling her breast. He started to run his hand underneath her skirt, but she squirmed, and stopped his hand. "Show me!" she demanded and Vincent retrieved the package of condoms from the glove box and handed it to her. She looked at the package, turning it over. "What is it?" she asked, with an innocence that Vincent was not sure of. "Rubbers," he answered, nonchalantly. The girl blushed and she grinned, slyly. "Ooooh!" she exclaimed, as she opened the package, "I know what these are for." Greta took a condom out of the package and inspected it. She pointed at the reservoir.

"What's this for?" she asked and Vincent blushed. "So it won't break from getting too full," he told her, and they both were getting excited. "How do you put it on?" she asked him, innocently. "You are going to put it on me," he told her. "Ooooh," she cooed, "I get to put it on you. What are you going to teach me next?"

Greta reached over, gave his erection a squeeze and opened the car door. Greta jumped out of the car and ran. Vincent jumped out, ran around the car and after a short chase, he caught her. They were both breathless and laughing. They stopped laughing and kissed passionately wanting each other.

Vincent had to pull away so he could get the blanket out of the car. He spread it on the sandy soil. He went on his knees to smooth it. Greta was still standing, facing him. She took off her halter and Vincent moved up to her. He ran both his hands up the back of her legs and underneath the back of her panties. He caressed her bottom. Vincent put his head under her skirt and kissed the inside of her thigh, pressing her to him with his hands against her bottom.

"Oh God, Vincent!" she exclaimed, "You drive me crazy." She pulled her skirt off over her head. While she was doing this, he was pulling her panties down. She stepped out of them and he pressed his hands on her bottom, and kissed her belly button. She ran her fingers through his hair, pressing his face to her body, she moaned. Vincent stood, and they embraced in a long kiss, pressing to each other.

"The only way I can get close enough to you," whispered Vincent; "is to get inside of you." "Get inside of me!" she commanded, hotly and she went to her knees. She unbuttoned his pants, hurriedly, and she pulled them down. Vincent stepped out of them and she pulled down his shorts, freeing his erection. She examined it with her eyes and her fingers. He braced himself for the sensation.

"Give me the rubber," she ordered, excitedly. Vincent handed it to her and she examined it. "How does it go on?" she asked, and he placed it in position for her. "Roll it right on back," he told her, and she rolled it, slowly all the way. "This is fun," she told him, as she stroked his shape. Then they were down on the blanket together. Then her thighs were open, and he was between them. And then he was inside her.

"I liked it better without the rubber," she remarked, after they had exhausted each other, "your thing was hotter then." She complained further, "And I couldn't feel you come in me, either." "I know," answered Vincent, in sympathy, "But it was still awfully good. And you don't have to worry about getting pregnant, so we can do it more often." She laughed and rolled over on top of him. "Oh, goodie!" Greta exclaimed, exuberantly, "Let's do it ten times a day." Vincent groaned and pretended to expire.

This sexual activity with Greta went on for months. Going to her house was an enigma, because Linda was almost always there. Vincent wanted to stay on the good side of both of the girls; he wanted to save Linda for later, when she would be old enough. He was enjoying his sexual activity with Greta, but it was cooling because it had been purely physical. He had the feeling that Greta was looking around. Vincent wasn't looking around; he was saving Linda's affection for later. Someday she would be old enough for him and she was a beauty. Linda was the kind of girl he would want to marry, but that was in the future and this was now.

Captain Moon was feeling no pain when he left the Claim Jumper; he had been there for over three hours. It was Saturday, early in the afternoon, the day after the swimming party. Vincent had realized that he had better leave or be bombed before dark. Vincent thought he would drive around for a while and then go home and take a nap. Vincent was sleepy, but knew he couldn't take a nap right away. He knew the bed would feel like it was moving and he didn't like the spinning, sinking feeling he knew he would have. Vincent felt good, loose as a goose. He couldn't remember ever feeling better. The good old Moscow mules did it every time.

Vincent walked to his car parked in front of Charley's Chinese Restaurant, which was a half block east of the Claim. He got into his car and drove off, heading south and under the railroad under pass. Vincent thought he would drive out toward Bangor. For some reason he was in a hurry, there was no reason to be, he just was. Vincent was impatient when he had to stop for a person who was making a left turn.

Patience and youth have never been partners. When he got behind a slow driver it increased his impatience to the point of tailgating the car. When the driver of the car signaled for a right turn, the Captain jerked his steering wheel and started to pass the car on the left lane. But the car turned left. Vincent hit his brakes, but the booze had slowed his reaction time. He hit the car on its left rear fender, putting a small crease in it. Vincent got out of his car when the other driver got out of his. The driver was a white male, about thirty years old, he looked like a redneck and it made Vincent cringe. The other driver was inspecting the damage.

"We need a cop!" he exclaimed and he seemed calm, not like a redneck at all. "I'll go call for one," answered Vincent, grateful for a chance to get away from the scene. Knowing too hat his breath must have smelled like skid row on a Sunday morning. There was a liquor store across the street. Vincent ran across and into the store. He bought a bottle of coke and a roll of breath mints, opening both as he called the police on a pay phone. He ate two breath mints and went back to the scene. Vincent chugalugged the coke. He was still high, but felt he could fake it out if he didn't have to talk too much.

Vincent was aware that when you hit someone from behind it is always your fault in the eyes of the law. He traded information with the other driver. Vincent told him to get the damage fixed and send him the bill. The other driver, who was of a meek and trusting nature, was grateful. When Vincent saw the black and white approaching, his heart picked up its pace. He was most apprehensive when the officers got out of their vehicle and approached. Vincent recognized one of them; he was Rosco Smith. Rosco had given him a ticket just a week ago for laying a strip of rubber downtown. Vincent didn't know the other cop. Rosco was trying to suppress a grin, but he wasn't having much success. He enjoyed his work.

"Vincent, Vincent!" he started, cheerfully, "Do I get to give you another ticket so soon?" Rosco inspected the damage and continued talking while doing so. "How come I am so, lucky?" He scratched his head, "Are you trying to support the whole Ophir Flats Police Department?" he asked, still grinning. "I guess I was in too, much of a hurry," replied Vincent, with a sheepish, grin. Sergeant Rosco was nobody's fool; he knew that something wasn't kosher. But he liked Vincent because he had never got smart mouthed by him. "You haven't been drinking have you?" he asked with suspicion, but quietly, so the other driver wouldn't hear. It was against Vincent's nature to lie, but one has to do what one has to do. "No." Vincent answered, emphatically, "It's a little early for me."

Vincent felt the lie in his face; he knew it had flushed. Vincent knew he was a poor liar. Rosco searched his face before he spoke and then he turned to the other cop. "Vincent doesn't look like he has been drinking does he?" he asked the other cop, while shaking his head in the negative. Vincent was sweating blood and Rosco knew it. The other cop gave him the once over and he was shaking his head in the negative. Vincent was starting to get a little less tense.

"Hmmm," came from the other officer, while he rubbed his jaw, scrutinizing Vincent's face, "Hmmm, nawh, he looks okay." The other driver had been observing, but hadn't said anything; he knew he had given a bogus, signal. "Are you going to pay the damages?" Rosco asked Vincent. "Of course," he replied, and Rosco wrote him a ticket for going ten miles an hour over the speed limit. The other driver left after being excused by Rosco.

"Now, tell me what really happened?" asked Rosco, and Vincent told him. "Why didn't you say something?" asked Rosco. "There was no use," answered Vincent, "it was my fault, anyway." "You got that right!" exclaimed Rosco, "It was your fault, and don't make the same mistake again! And get a better brand of breath mints. Or better yet, don't ingest things that give you bad breath."

Vincent knew he hadn't fooled Rosco, he had just felt benevolent. Vincent knew he would not be so lucky the next time. "Thanks Rosco," replied Vincent, "I'll remember what you said." "Let's go find a crime," said Rosco, to the other cop and they got in their patrol car and left. Vincent sighed, got into his car and left. Vincent turned around and headed for home. Driving much slower this time he felt grateful for cops like Rosco; cops who would give a guy a break once in a while, there were just a few of them left.

Vincent's mother could smell the booze on him, but she did not say anything right away, she just looked her disapproval. Grace fought with herself to keep from saying anything. She remembered the old saying, "Bite your tongue," and she believed that was what she was going to have to do to keep from saying anything. Her irritation with Vincent lost her the war with her tongue.

"You don't want to be like your father do you?" she asked, with a trace of sarcasm. "I don't know," answered Vincent with equal sarcasm, "You divorced him before I knew him." Grace was silent while she was biting her tongue. With her will she let that one go by, knowing that she did not have a pertinent reply. She felt like one of the accusers of the adulterous woman whom Jesus had told, "He that is without sin among you, let him first cast a stone at her." Grace didn't say anymore.

Vincent went to his room to sleep it off. It was hot, so he stripped down to his shorts. He lay on his bed on his stomach and went right to sleep, but his sleep was fitful. Vincent dreamed. He was in a rocking chair, rocking. He wanted to stop, but the chair wouldn't stop, it kept rocking harder and harder. The chair rocked until it rocked so far forward it wouldn't rock back. It was then that he saw he had been rocking on the precipice of a bottomless pit. He was going over the edge, into the blackness. He tried to scream, but couldn't make a sound.

Vincent awoke, wet with sweat, still trying to scream. He lay for a while, wanting to go to sleep, but afraid to. Vincent raised and sat on the edge of his bed. He contemplated his naval, wondering why he had been having so many nightmares. Vincent got up, went into the bathroom and took a cold shower.

Grace heard him in the shower. She fixed him his dinner while he was showering. Doc had gone to the mountains, so it would be just her son, and herself. Grace wanted to be bright and cheerful for her son; she knew that if he got depressed, he would only drink more. She was aware that he was having a drinking problem, but she wasn't sure what was causing it. She knew that Audrey's death had hit him hard, but she thought that he should have gotten over that by now.

Grace had a tendency to blame it on the Curse of the Cardoza's. It was easier to blame history than to look for a present cause. Grace believed that Vincent had inherited the Curse. After all, his father had and his father's sister and brother and many more who had had the Cardoza blood. This bad blood had come all the way from Spain. The vehicle had been a Spanish land grant, one for a thousand acres, located on the west coast, near Goleta, California. The Cardoza family must have had the thought that they could leave the curse behind. But sailing across the ocean they had discovered that blood was thicker than salt water.

Vincent finished his shower and dressed. He went out to his mother, who was smiling and cheerful. Sometimes her cheer and optimism irritated him and this was one of those times. He loved his mother more than anyone, so he bit his tongue and forced a smile.

"Come and get it," was his mother's cheerful greeting. Vincent didn't want to eat; he wanted to drink. "Looks good, Mom," he lied, cheerfully and sat at the table. It was just unreal how happy his mother could appear to be; she was the world's greatest actress, or she was really happy. She was pretty and youthful when she was smiling. "What have you got on the ball for tonight, son?" Grace asked. "Go find Mario, I guess, hadn't planned anything," he answered, but he was still irritated from having to eat and his mother's cheer. What he wanted to say was, "Get drunk on my ass."

Vincent finished his dinner, doing his best to act grateful, while all the time wanting to escape. He held up his end of the conversation over trivia and bid his mother goodnight with a kiss on her forehead.

Vincent went back to the Claim with a serious intention to get drunk. He found Mario there and they proceeded to helping each other to reach this lofty, goal. Mario was feeling very good when he came up with the idea to go to San Francisco the following weekend and get Vincent's ashes hauled. Mario laughed with glee when Vincent asked him what that meant.

"I'm going to find you a little whore on Mission Street and she is going to show you what it means," stated Mario smugly. "Now I know what you mean," answered Vincent, trying not to look stupid. "Are you ready for it?" asked Mario. "I'm always ready for that!" exclaimed Vincent, trying to look lascivious. "Come on," kidded Mario, rolling his eyeballs around, "You never had a piece of ass in your whole life." "Like Hell I haven't!" exclaimed Vincent, with indignation. "Aww Bullshit!" exclaimed Mario, "The only thing that you ever ejaculated into was your hand. Shit! You don't even know what a cunt looks like." "Yes I do!" retorted Vincent, hotly," A cunt looks just like your mouth!" Mario was surprised by Vincent's vehemence, but then his face was swallowed by a grin. "You are right," replied Mario, laughing, "You do know. You must have seen one," and then he laughed some more, "But just one," he added, teasing. "I've seen a lot of them," retorted Vincent. "Sure you have," answered Mario, with sarcasm, "in your wet dreams." "God bless wet dreams," replied Vincent, trying to change the subject. "God bless wet dreams," agreed Mario and then they were silent for a while, concentrating on their goal of inebriation. The boys drank until the bar closed and then went home to sleep it off.

It was a slow week for Vincent and the anticipation of finding a whore in San Francisco made it even seem longer. He had cashed a check that he had got from the cannery and figured he had enough money to have a good time. Vincent was excited by the prospect of what this whore was going to look like. What she was going to do to him and he was also apprehensive.

Mario was honking his horn. Vincent went out the door, after kissing his mother goodbye. He thought to himself that it was a good thing she didn't know what he was going to do.

"Are you ready to get laid?" asked Mario, as soon as Vincent got into the car. "I've had a hard on all morning," answered Vincent, "Don't drive slowly on my account," he added. "You had a hard on all morning and you haven't masturbated yet?" kidded Mario and he started to laugh. "I'll just go ahead and do it now," stated Vincent and he proceeded to unbutton his jeans. "Whoa!" exclaimed Mario and he giggled. "I don't allow pecker tracks in my car." "Unless they are yours," retorted Vincent and he stopped unbuttoning his pants. He started to giggle, too. Giggles are reflected in giggles.

"Have you ever had a blow job?" asked Mario. "Not this week," answered Vincent, with a bored look, which he couldn't hold and he giggled some more. "I would be embarrassed," he said. "What do you do while she is doing it?" "Hang on to her ears!" exclaimed Mario, gleefully and then he was laughing out of control. He couldn't let go of the image he had of Vincent doing what he had told him to do. Vincent followed; he was thinking the same thing. They laughed until Mario could no longer drive and he pulled over, stopping the car.

Vincent rolled his window down and stuck his head out of it to keep from looking at Mario and Mario did the same. When they got under control, they took a chance and looked at each other, but neither one spoke for a few moments. Mario broke the silence. He couldn't stay silent for long; his Italian blood wouldn't allow it.

"Wouldn't it be awful to laugh yourself to death?" he asked, with a straight face. Vincent giggled and answered with difficulty. "Yeah, Haw haw, and the mortician would have to melt your face to get the laugh off of it," answered Vincent. Mario fought to control his face, but his face won and the insanity began again and they had to look away from each other.

Mario, without looking at Vincent, started driving again. Lake Ellis provided them a distraction. They had gone through a couple of stop signs and there it was. It was a small lake, at the east end of Marysville. It was man made and a haven for ducks and geese of all kinds. The lake had water lilies around its banks. The floating birds were competing for the food being offered by tourists and locals.

Mario had brought a bag of stale bread to feed the birds; his mother had fixed it for him. Mario gave some of the bread to Vincent and they proceeded to spread their bread upon the waters. The ducks and geese were tame and appreciative. They are a lot like people, some of them dignified and well mannered, but others are turkeys and pigs. Unfortunately, the pigs and the turkeys were getting most of the bread. Mario threw some bread out as far as he could; the ill-mannered birds were flocking for it. Vincent then threw some for the nice birds. It didn't take long to run out of bread and then they were back on the road again.

Mario started singing and Vincent joined him. They were singing a Hank Williams song when they stopped at the Nut Tree to use their restroom. After that they went to the snack bar and had a cold beer. They were not asked for their identification and Vincent was surprised. Mario told him that he just looked older that day.

It was late in the afternoon when they got to Fisherman's Wharf and both of the boys were starving. Mario took Vincent to an Italian restaurant he knew called "Maggio's." It was a plush place. Walking in they were surrounded by a wine colored, velvety Victorian setting.

"This place looks kind of high on the hog?" asked Vincent. "You only live once," replied Mario, "and besides that, it's on me," and he puffed up like a mating pigeon. Mario actually did puff up. Vincent never did figure out how he did it. His face would puff up with pride and his body would follow with a strut. Only an Italian could get away with it, anyone else would look ridiculous.

The hostess led them to a table with a view of the harbor. The hostess was a classy looking lady; she was tall and very slender. She had black and silver hair, which was tied in a bun at the back of her head. Her smile was quick and sophisticated, but not without warmth.

A wisp of a girl came to wait on them. Vincent's heart did a flip-flop when he saw her. It was like she came out of nowhere, like a gossamer thing, hair floating like it was in a breeze, but there was no breeze. The girl's hair was fine, curly and auburn colored, with flashes of light. Her eyes were blue as the sky, full of life.

She was smaller than Vincent's mother and delicate. Her coloring reminded him of Anna, peaches and cream, with rosy cheeks. The girl had fine, dark eyebrows, arched and came to a fine point at the ends. The girl's eyes were big, blue, warm, innocent and inviting. Vincent felt like he could float right into them. She was wearing a colorful, peasant costume, with an off the shoulder blouse. Her voice was musical and modulated.

"Can I help you boys?" She asked, as she handed them menus. "You already have," answered Vincent, who was staring at her, unable to do otherwise. "How did I do that?" she asked, modestly, looking through long lashes. "By making my eyes happy," answered Vincent, bashfully, with his face flushing. "Oh," answered the girl and the move put her full, red lips into the kissing position and then she gave him a sweet smile, fluttered her lashes and looked at Mario.

"Is your mama as pretty as you?" asked Mario. "Prettier," answered the girl. "That just can't be possible!" exclaimed Vincent and the girl gave him another warm smile. She had her pen in hand, waiting. Mario ordered stuffed peppers and Vincent ordered the same. "When in Rome, do like the Romans do," stated Vincent. "I hope you can eat like a Roman," replied Mario. The girl took their order and left.

"Mama Mia!" exclaimed Mario, "How I love the Italian girls. I'ma gonna taka her homa witha me." Vincent laughed. "I don't think she is going to give up Frisco for Ophir Flats," he told Mario. "You got that right," answered Mario, "But I could lie to her." He rolled his big brown eyes around, "Maybe I could get her pregnant before she knows what's happening," he added. "Sure you could," retorted Vincent, with a chuckle, "you could use chloroform on her." "You are such a negative thinker," criticized Mario. "I know," answered Vincent, "but I am positive about it."

The girl came back before Mario had a chance to comment. She brought some soup bowls and a basket full of sour dough, French bread. The bread had been cut part way and the aroma teased the olfactory nerves. When the girl leaned to put the basket on the table, Vincent's eyes were drawn to her cleavage. The girl was fresh and delightful and so was her cleavage. Often, part of something is more tantalizing than the whole.

Mario seemed to be locked in a single train of thought. He rolled his eyes at the girl. "Mama Mia!" he exclaimed to her, "Your Mama must be beautiful!" "My Mama is beautiful," the girl agreed, and she smiled. The girl left and an Italian boy, with tight, black pants, brought a large crockery vessel with handles on it. He placed it on the middle of the table. It contained steaming hot, minestrone soup. The boy ladled their bowls full of the aromatic liquid. He put the lid back on the vessel and left.

The boys buttered their bread and ate a bowl of soup. The soup was good. It had of all that stuff that is supposed to be in it, like beans, vegetables, pasta, onions, garlic, oregano and all that other good stuff. The last time Vincent had soup like that was at dinner at Mario's house. Mario's mother had come from the old country and so had her recipes. She could not speak a word of English, but one does not have to talk to cook. This soup tasted like she had made it.

The girl brought herself and a giant wooden bowl; it was filled with a mixed vegetable salad. She asked the boys what kind of dressing they wanted. Vincent couldn't think of the name of the kind with the little blue specks. He was so captivated by the girl; his mouth didn't want to work right. What came out of his mouth didn't sound anything like what he was trying to say. Vincent was trying to say, "I like the dressing with the blue stuff in it." But what came out of his mouth sounded like, "I like undressing," and he stopped, realizing what he had said. Vincent's face got awfully red, and his mind went blank.

"I'll just bet you do." answered the girl, in a coquettish manner, "But let's get back to your salad, would you like it dressed or undressed?" By this time Vincent had regained some of his composure, even though Mario was snickering at him. "Give me your favorite dressing," replied Vincent, "that way I can learn something about you." The pretty girl put a big, dipper of creamy, Roquefort dressing on his salad.

"That's the kind I like!" exclaimed Vincent, "Are we not birds of a feather?" he asked her and the girl laughed. "I don't know about birds," she answered and she seemed pleased with herself. "I like your taste buds, too," claimed Mario and she put a dipper of the pungent stuff on his salad. Mario wiggled his eyebrows at her and she wiggled hers back. "Eat." she told them and left.

"I would like to eat her.'" exclaimed Mario under his breath, licking his lips. "You ain't the Lone Ranger," replied Vincent, "I would like to drink her bath water. "I would like to give her a bath with my tongue," replied Mario, while rolling his eyes around. "It is God's will that it be my tongue that bathes her," retorted Vincent. "God does not think dirty like we do," stated Mario. "Do you think licking her naked body would be dirty?" Vincent asked, with a feigned, innocent look. "It is not the licking," stated Mario, sticking with his piousness, "but the fornicating that would follow that I would frown upon." "Unless it was you that was fornicating," stated Vincent, righteously. "Unless it was me," agreed Mario.

When they had finished the basket of bread the girl brought them another. When they, had finished the salad, the girl took the bowl away. In a little while the boy brought them spaghetti with sauce and meatballs. The girl brought them freshly grated Parmesan cheese and they heaped it all over their spaghetti. Vincent was getting full.

"I thought we had ordered stuffed peppers?" questioned Vincent, in a complaining, tone. "We did," answered Mario, "They will bring them after we are stuffed." They finished eating the spaghetti and by the time the peppers did get to them, Vincent was stuffed. He looked at his with disdain, playing with it with his fork. "You gotta eat it!" exclaimed Mario, "Or they will be insulted. "I don't know if I can," answered Vincent, with dismay. Right after he had said it, he cut loose with an award-winning belch. "Now I can," he said, with a sigh of relief.

After they had finished with the peppers the girl came back and asked them what kind of desert they wanted. Vincent asked what kind of ice cream she had and she read him off a list of flavors.

"I'll have some pistachio and your phone number," Vincent told, the girl. He couldn't believe he had been so impulsive; it just wasn't like him. His face got warm with her smile, but she didn't say anything and she turned to Mario. "Sounds good to me," Mario told the girl and she turned, and left.

"Looks like all you are going to get is pistachio," remarked Mario, with humorous sarcasm, "you could be a little too impulsive." "I know," answered Vincent, "but what have I got to lose, I will probably never see her again." That had been the only reason that he had been able to be so forward.

Although Vincent was handsome, he was not aware of it. There were too many things about himself he didn't like. He wasn't as big as he wanted to be. His hair was dark and he wished it were blond. Vincent wished his eyes were blue, but they were hazel. He thought his lips were fuller than they should be. Negative thinking made him unsure of himself.

After they had finished their ice cream, Mario pushed his chair back from the table. "Oh, God!" he exclaimed, "I feel so good, let's go get laid." Vincent slid deep in his chair. "Jesus Mario!" he exclaimed in a loud whisper, "They could hear you out on the wharf! And I'm too, stuffed to get into a prone position." "Haven't you ever done it standing up?" asked an incredulous, Mario.

The girl came back. She looked at the two of them and gave the bill to Mario; he had been reaching for it. She gave Vincent a piece of folded paper. He glanced at the paper as he unfolded it. Vincent was delighted and he blushed. The girl's name and phone number were written on the paper. Vincent looked at the girl and she was smiling, sweetly at him. He swallowed and looked back at the paper. "Carla Maggio." He wondered if she was related to the owner of the restaurant.

"Carla Maggio?" he asked and she read the question in his eyes. "My parents own this place," she told him and she wasn't bragging, she sounded humble. "This name and number are engraved on my heart forever," Vincent told the girl. "Forever is a long time," she answered, "don't wait too long." "I think I'm in love," said Vincent, fighting a quiver in his lip.

They got up to leave and the girl hadn't moved, she was standing close to Vincent. "Are you going to call?" she asked, wistfully. "You can be sure of that." he answered, his brain boggled by her interest. They started to leave, but Vincent remembered he hadn't told her his name. He turned around to see her starting to turn, but she was still watching him. He reached out and with his fingertip; he touched her bare arm. "My name is Vincent Cardoza," he told her. "I'll remember," she answered. "I'll call you," he promised. "I hope so," she answered and walked away. Vincent turned and looked back as he was going out the door, but she was out of sight. He sighed and continued out the door.

"Christ, Vincent!" exclaimed Mario, "That little beauty has the hots for you." "Nawh!" exclaimed Vincent, "She was just being nice." He was embarrassed, yet pleased. "Christ!" exclaimed Mario, in disgust, "I swear, your brain is cubicle, no one could be as dumb as you. What could she want with you when she could have me?" "Maybe she don't like Italians," answered Vincent.

CHAPTER 18

They were both laughing when they came out the door. Mario suggested, with enthusiasm, "Let's go down to Mission Street and find us a whore." "Holy shit!" exclaimed Vincent, "Let's wait for a while so I wont be so damned full." "It will be awhile by the time we get there and find a pimp," answered Mario. "And if we walk around too, long we will be too, tired to fuck." "You have such an attractive way of putting words together," commented Vincent, wryly. "It is a natural talent for Italians," answered Mario, thinking he had been complimented.

Mario drove to Mission Street and cruised for a while. Soon, Mario found the area with the greatest concentration of gin mills and people on the street. He found a place to park, and did so.

"Let's go find us a pimp," suggested Mario and he started to get out of the car. "What does one look like?" asked Vincent and then he realized he had exposed his ignorance again. Mario looked at him, chuckled, shook his head and got out of the car. Vincent got out and they walked up the street for a while. Mario walked into a jumping, bar and Vincent followed. They were in a different world when the swinging doors closed behind them. The smoke was like morning fog. The boys stood in their tracks for a while, surveying the scene. The place was an international settlement. There were blacks, Mexicans, Nordics, Orientals and even some Rag heads. Some were dancing to the flamenco music that was coming from the brightly lit, Wurlitzer (juke box).

They found a couple of bar stools and sat down. The old man who was sitting next to Vincent was wearing black Frisco Jeans, a dirty, striped shirt, a black leather vest with silver buttons, a black skull cap and he smelled like a goat. He was smoking a rum soaked Crook, which enhanced the goat smell.

A red, headed, hag was on the stool next to Mario. Some of her hair was red, but there were other colors. She was skinny, seedy looking; she looked like she had rode in on a broom. Ammonia like vapors was coming from her direction. She had on a short, short skirt, from which her bony legs dangled grotesquely. She was drinking boilermakers and talking to her reflection in the mirror. The old broad was smoking from a long, pearl handled cigarette holder. Her face was made up like a streetwalker. She looked like a whore, a one a magic spell had suddenly turned ancient. She looked old enough to fart dust. The bartender was middle aged and stout. He had gray hair and mustache but his eyebrows were black. He raised one of them when Vincent asked for a Moscow Mule.

"You don't look old enough to drink," commented the bartender, gruffly. "And we don't have Moscow Mules. So show me some I. D. and order another drink." Vincent complied; he got his wallet out and showed him the bogus, draft card. "Looks like you made it your self," claimed the Bartender, in a bored, tone. He lowered his eyebrow to scrutinize the card; he looked back at Vincent and raised it again. "But I guess it will do," he said and Vincent ordered a Screwdriver. The bartender looked at Mario. "I'll have a double shot of your bar whiskey," said Mario, who had other things on his mind. "You got guts!" exclaimed the bartender and he served him his drink first and then made Vincent's drink. Mario hadn't drunk from his drink, yet and he got off his stool.

"I'm going to look around," he said and wandered off. Vincent watched him wander and head for the John. When he returned, Vincent was sipping on his Screwdriver. Mario had a slug of his whiskey and his eyes got big when he swallowed it. He quickly chased it with water. "Holy Shit!" he croaked, "This crap has battery acid in it." The bartender just happened to be passing by. "Want some more?" he asked and laughed, looking pleased with his self. "Maybe next week," answered Mario.

Vincent heard the sound of trickling water and so had Mario. It was running off the Hag's stool and on to the floor. She was urinating, but seemed to be unaware. "Aww Shit!" exclaimed Mario, in disgust, "You wait here," he told Vincent, "I'm gonna go and see if I can find a pimp." Vincent watched him walk out the door and then he moved to another stool, away from the Hag.

Vincent was wondering about the whore, what he was going to do with her and what she was going to do with him. He did not have a clue as to how to act. He was worried that he might not be able to get an erection. Should he take all of his clothes off? Should he feel her up? Should he kiss her? Vincent had no idea what to do. He hoped that Mario wouldn't pick an ugly one, or a fat one. He knew he would not be able to perform if it was so.

Vincent's drink was helping with his apprehension, but he knew if he had too much he wouldn't be able to perform. Life sure got complicated, sometimes, he thought. Vincent got a shot of brandy to go with his screwdriver; it wasn't doing the job fast enough. Mario came back, he was grinning like the Cheshire cat. He had a little Filipino guy with him. "Must be a pimp," thought Vincent, to himself.

"Come on!" exclaimed Mario, gleefully, "Let's go!" and Vincent had to gulp the rest of his drinks. Mario was already leaving with the pimp, Vincent followed. The excitement and the apprehension, was making Vincent's knees feel weak. The Filipino walked fast, it was all Vincent could do to keep up. They walked down the street a block turned the corner and walked another two blocks and turned another corner. They followed him another half a block and he turned into a multi-floored apartment building. After they got into the building, they followed the pimp up two flights of stairs.

"Five bucks apiece," whispered Mario. At the second landing the pimp went straight ahead and made a right turn and went down the hall. The walls were cream colored, plaster, with a walnut wainscot, doors and trim. There were numbers on the doors. The pimp stopped at door number thirty-eight and knocked. In a short time he knocked again.

Vincent was hoping she wouldn't be there. He was wishing he wasn't where he was. His heart picked up a beat when the doorknob turned. When the door opened there was a pretty Portuguese girl standing there. She looked to be about halfway between twenty and thirty. The girl was built slender and good, an inch or so shorter than Vincent. She was wearing a silk robe that was trimmed in black velvet. The girl smiled with lips of generous proportions.

"Come in," she offered, as she backed into the room. The pimp smiled at her and left. Mario stepped into the small living room and Vincent followed. It was sparsely furnished. The girl was looking at them. "Probably wondering which one of us she is going to screw first," thought Vincent. He was sweating, but it wasn't hot. "Which one of you handsome gentlemen is first?" asked the prostitute. "I am," answered Mario, quickly and the lady of the night led Mario into a hall, out of Vincent's sight.

Vincent sat on a brown, mohair couch. He fidgeted with his collar. He could hear them in the next room; he could hear them laughing. And then he could hear the bed squeak. Vincent was getting an erection from the mental pictures his mind was conjuring. He wished he had a drink. Vincent was nervous, but at least he had an erection. He tensed when the bed stopped squeaking. In a little while Mario returned, alone. He was grinning, and he was puffed up like a toad. His eyes were animated.

"Good Fuck!" Mario exclaimed, but holding his voice down, "She will call you in a bit. I told her your name." Vincent hadn't thought of it before, Mario had already ejaculated into her and he didn't like the idea of going in after him. The thought cost him his erection.

"Oh, Vincent," she called, with sexual meaning, through the wall. Vincent was not ready for this; he would rather have gone to a firing squad, or maybe the electric chair. He felt his joystick shrink. How could he let her see the miserable thing? Vincent got up and walked down the hall. "A man's gotta do what a man's gotta do," he thought to himself, but he wished he could fly away, or jump out of a window. There was ice water in his knees. The door was open and he saw her. She was standing, wearing nothing but a black garter belt and black nylons.

"God!" thought Vincent, "She is beautiful." Her skin was dark, olive, as that color is sometimes called. She was the same color all over. Her breasts were not big, not small. They were firm, no sag. The nipples were dark. Her pubic hair was black and looked like soft fur. Her legs were long and slender; there was no flab on her. Vincent walked in and closed the door. He stared at her and she looked at him. He just stood there, confused. She put her hands on her hips and smiled.

"Well, honey boy. What would you like to do?" she asked. "I, Ahhh," blustered Vincent, who was flustered beyond any he had ever been before. He felt the blood rush to his face. Her eyes got wide. "I don't believe it!" she exclaimed, "This is your first time, isn't it?" "No, no. It's just the first time with," and then he stopped. He couldn't call her a whore.

The girl laughed out loud. "Don't be a square," she told him, "You can say it. I'm a whore and I make my living fucking. And that is what you are here for. So let's get on with it," and with that said, she started unbuttoning his pants. Vincent knew his face was red; he could feel it. He was so frightened and didn't know why. Here was with a beautiful girl taking his pants off and he had never felt more alone in his whole life. All he wanted to do was flee, but he was trapped. His chest felt constricted, like someone was standing on it.

Vincent was sweating, profusely. He knew that he was hyperventilating and he tried to calm himself. He took his shirt off while she was helping him to get his pants off. It was light in the room and soon he was naked. Vincent felt awfully exposed; his member was hanging, limp. Vincent felt like she was staring at it.

"Can we turn the lights down?" he asked, meekly. "Whatever turns you on, honey," the girl answered, while she was turning most of the lights out. That was better, he didn't feel quite so exposed, but did feel awfully impotent. He knew that he would never get it up, not in this room, not with this woman.

"Come," she beckoned to him and she was now stretched out on her bed, looking very alluring, indeed, but she looked like a black widow to Vincent. He would just have soon got into bed with King Kong. Vincent obeyed, his body did, anyway, but his mind was frozen. The adrenalin was there to make him run and it was making him feel dizzy.

Vincent just couldn't get himself to kiss the woman; he felt no affection for her. "What a square I am," he thought to himself. He did get up enough courage to explore her breast, but that was all he could get up.

"Can't get it up, huh?" she asked, sympathetically, "Here, let me try," and she rolled over on her side, facing Vincent. She started playing with his loose member in an attempt to stir some lust into it, but to no avail, it was dead as a doornail. There was almost no sensation in his member, almost like it had been frozen, or stuck with a shot of Novocain. "It doesn't look like it is going to work for you today," the girl said with sympathy "Maybe next time?" "I'm sorry," answered Vincent, contritely, "I must have had too much to drank." "That will do it every time," she stated, with sympathy.

Vincent felt great relief as he got back into his clothes, but he was in such a hurry to get away from the girl he forgot to pay her. She must have been confused also. She must have thought he had paid the pimp, for she never made any claim. Vincent thought about it when he got out of her room, but then he thought that Mario had probably paid her. It seemed to him Mario had said that it was going to be his treat. Vincent faked a satisfied look as he went back into the room with Mario. The girl was still in the bedroom.

"Good stuff, huh?" asked Mario. "Best I ever got into," Vincent lied, as debonair as he could, "Let's get out of here." "Are you sure you had enough?" asked Mario, with a straight face. "She turned me inside, out," replied Vincent, "I won't be able to get it up again for a week." "Let's go home," suggested Mario, "I seen enough of this town for awhile." "We can get there in time to get drunk," replied Vincent. "I like the way you think," answered Mario and he walked out the door, with Vincent right behind him.

On the way back across the Golden Gate Bridge, Vincent remembered he had not paid the girl and he asked Mario if he had. Mario was aghast. "I didn't pay her for you!" he answered, in an accusing manner, he was incredulous, "You mean you didn't pay her?" he asked and his eyes were big. "Didn't you say that it was going to be on you?" asked Vincent, defensively, feeling low enough to crawl under a snakes belly.

"Shit!" exclaimed Mario, "Shit!" He shook his head with disdain, he was seething and silent for a while and Vincent said nothing. In a little while Mario cooled off. He shook his head. "I did say that," confessed Mario, "When I first invited you, but I forgot." They were both silent for a while. Then Mario went on, "We wont be able to go back there again," said Mario, sadly, "Not even on the same street." They were quiet for a long time. Mario couldn't stay quiet for long; his Italian blood couldn't tolerate it.

"Maybe we can find us a black whore out on Blueberry Hill," suggested Mario. Blueberry Hill was another name that was used for the areas on the south side of town. There the black's had their taverns, "On the wrong side of the tracks," one might be inclined to say. "I don't know about that," replied Vincent, sounding prudish.

"Flowers is all different colors," stated Mario, sounding pious and full of wisdom, "But they is still flowers." "You mean pussy is pussy," retorted Vincent, who liked to condense other people's utterances. "It all looks the same in the dark," uttered Mario, with authority. "Not if you have seen it before it gets dark," retorted Vincent. "It all feels the same, anyway," said Mario, with less conviction.

"Let me get this straight," argued Vincent. "You would just as soon screw an ugly old fat broad as you would some lovely California beach bunny?" "I wouldn't put it that way," argued Mario. "You said it was all the same," retorted Vincent. "I guess I was a little hasty," replied Mario, "I guess I meant anything is better than jacking off." "Not to me," answered Vincent, with conviction. "Says the King of Jack offs," retorted Mario. "Better than Queen of suck offs," answered Vincent and he laughed. "Screw you!" exclaimed Mario and he gave Vincent the bird. "May all your wet dreams go dry!" cursed Vincent. "May your wife have fat legs!" " May yours be a Lesbian!" "May your children have another father!" "May your children be mine."

CHAPTER 19

It was evening and there wasn't much left of summer. The cannery season had ended and Vincent didn't work enough to save any money or to qualify for unemployment insurance. Money was scarce. The Moon Patrol was doing every thing it could to supplement the supply that it did have. The Captain and part of the Patrol, was making use of their siphon hose. Vincent didn't like the idea of stealing. He had stolen before, but had always felt guilty about it. But it was exciting and the Moon Patrol was broke and bored.

Vincent, Mario, Walt and Mack were in Vincent's Ford. The siphon hose and the five-gallon cans were in the trunk. It wasn't real late, but it was a weeknight and almost everyone in Ophir Plats was in bed asleep, or trying to sleep, or whatever else one does in bed.

The streets are rolled up early in Ophir Flats. Vincent drove to the south side of town, a poor side of town, where there were a lot of poor blacks and whites. It was not a part of town where they should be stealing gas, or anything. The thought that most of the people who lived in that part of town were poor had never entered their minds. It just seemed like a safer place to steal. It didn't seem like the cops spent much time there patrolling.

Vincent spotted an old Dodge sedan. It was parked in the shadow of a tree, away from the streetlight. There was no sidewalk and the car was parked parallel with the street. It was in front of a house that was set back from the street, at least fifty feet. It was ideal.

Vincent drove around the block. The objective was parked in the middle of the block. Vincent came around the corner. He turned off his lights when he got close enough to the Dodge to do so. Vincent shut his engine off and coasted in behind the car, and parked. The boys all got out of the Ford.

It was warm and quiet, except for the love songs of the crickets. The moon was bathing the night with a soft light. A street light up the street had little affect on it. Captain Moon opened the trunk; he removed the can and the hose. He shut the trunk, quietly. Mack offered his expertise.

"Here." he said, a little too, loud and he grabbed the hose, "Let me show you guys how it is done. I'm a pro at this." "Shhhh," cautioned the Captain, "It wouldn't be prudent to wake the owner."

Mack examined the hose by sticking his finger in the end of it; it was very small. "Holy shit!" Mack exclaimed and then put his hand over his mouth, realizing he had spoken too loud. He whispered, "This thing is long enough, but is no bigger than a pencil on the inside." "Who gives a rat's ass!" exclaimed an impatient, Mario, "Let's get it done before we end up in the sheriff's motel, he has only one flavor of bread and water."

"I hate bread and water!" exclaimed Walt, "They could at least give a guy some peanut butter to go with it." "If brains were a role of pennies," scoffed Mario, "You would have a penny." Walt didn't retaliate; he hadn't forgotten his scuffle with Mack. He just grinned, sheepishly. Mario went on, "I can't believe I'm out here doing this with you morons," he complained.

Mack stuck the end of the hose into the tank of the Dodge. He blew on it as he put it in and stopped when he felt the resistance of the gasoline. Mack started sucking on the hose and at first he couldn't get the gas to flow. After a lot of sucking, the gas came all at once. Mack spit and sputtered as the gas came into his month, unexpected. The gas went up his nose and he dropped the hose. The gas ran out on the ground. Mack cursed with a string of cuss words that would make a sailor blush.

"Did anyone write that down?" asked Mario, laughing, "That just had to be a prize winning, curse." "And loud enough to wake the dead" cautioned the Captain as he picked up the hose and put it in the can taking notice of how minute the flow of gas was. "I could piss faster than this gas is running." he complained. Mario came and looked, after pulling the hose out enough to see, "Shit house, Mickey Mouse!" exclaimed Mario, "it will take a fricking hour for the can to fill." "We ought to go for a walk, or something," suggested Walt, "in case the cops come" and right after he said it, a cop car pulled up across the street and parked. Mario's eyes got big as saucers.

"We are royally screwed now," whispered Mario, with fear. "Just act like this is a normal thing to do," whispered Vincent. The Moon Patrollers swallowed, gulped and tried to look casual as two officers walked across the street and over to the boys. One of the cops was big and hard looking, but he was grinning. The other cop was small and he was not friendly looking. They were sheriff's deputies.

"Are you boys having trouble?" the big one asked, still grinning. "No trouble," answered Mario, with an alter boy look on his face. "No trouble," added Walt, looking like a Watchtower pusher. "We are just siphoning gas," explained Mack, helpfully. The smaller, unfriendly looking deputy looked at Vincent and asked, wryly. "And what is your rendition of this fairy tale?" Vincent was always calm under pressure. He would get nervous when it was all over with. Vincent pointed at Mack and explained, "His car has gas in it, but it won't run. We are siphoning gas out of his car to put in mine, which will run, but is about out of gas." Vincent rubbed his head and added, "But it is going to take awhile." "Why is that?" asked the curious, deputy. "The hose is too small, replied Vincent "We will just have to stand here and wait." He rubbed his head again and went on," I wonder how many times we will be investigated before we get the can full? The deputy smiled at the suppositional, predicament. "Just show me your Drivers license," ordered the deputy, "And your registration, then I can radio in and no one else will bother you."

Captain Moon could hardly contain his glee as he complied with the deputy's request. The other deputy was still grinning as the report was called in. After that, the big one spoke, "Okay," he said, jovially, "You guys try to be quiet so you don't disturb anyone's peace." He gestured at the other deputy, "Let's go look for trouble," he said to him and they left. When the deputies had left, Vincent looked at Mario's face; his eyes were about to bug out of his head. His mouth was agape.

"Holy Shit!" Mario exclaimed, as quietly as he could while filled with amazement and exhilaration, "Let's get the Hell out of here before they come back." The other Patrollers were in agreement, but not the Captain. "No," he said, "Let's fill the can first." "You gotta be crazy." retorted Mario. His feet were itching to leave the scene. "Why would they come back?" asked the Captain, "They have already called in, so the other cops won't bother us. Let's wait for the gas." "You forgot one important detail, Captain Moon," reminded Mario. "What's that?" asked a dubious, Vincent. "If the people we are stealing gas from should hear us, and call the law," explained Mario and he hesitated. "So?" questioned the Captain, impatiently. "The cops have your license number, phone number and your address," replied Mario. The Captain gulped and whispered, with feeling, "The Hell with the gas!" he exclaimed, "Let's get the Hell out of here!" And they did with an adrenalin, accelerated pace.

About a week later, some of the Patrol, along with a non-member, was pulling the same stunt. "As a dog returned to his vomit, so a fool to his folly." (Proverbs 26:11) By this time greed had raised its hydra head and three five-gallon cans were in the trunk of Vincent's car. The non-member was Carl Smith, a new friend of the Patrollers; he was seventeen and had been raised in Juvenile Halls and reform schools.

Carl's mother was a whore. They lived together in a dilapidated, two storied Victorian that had been turned into apartments. It sat at the top of the hill, amongst a grove of pine and oaks, almost hidden, across from the

Southern pacific Railroad depot. It looked haunted.

Carl was about Vincent's size, but bigger in the hips and shoulders. He was pale; he looked like he had been raised on bread and water. Once he told Vincent that his mother had told him that when he was a baby she had put whiskey in his formula to keep him quiet while she was servicing customers. She was a pretty woman, but she was pale and didn't look healthy. Both Carl and his mother looked like a couple of Count Dracula's creations.

It was Carl's plan to make a career out of crime. Nothing interested him unless it was illegal. His heroes were Capone and the likes of him. Carl was familiar with crime and the police. The most important thing he had ever learned was you are not a criminal unless you get caught. Carl had injected his greed into the Patrol.

The boys not only had three cans, now, they had a bigger hose. They had stolen gas from a dump truck, which had been parked next to a garage on Canyon Highlands Drive. And from a Buick parked by the levee, near the Municipal Auditorium, from a Packard parked near the Chinese Temple and from a Plymouth parked in the south side of town.

All three cans were full to the top and Vincent headed for Palermo via the old Bagget Road. The Bagget Road crossed the railroad tracks and then went on and dead-ended at the Palermo Road. Vincent went to the top of the hill, but didn't cross the tracks. He pulled off the road to the right and parked on a knoll, under a grove of oaks. The moon was shining bright and it was a quiet place, a good place to transfer some of the stolen gas to Vincent's gas tank, which was nearly empty.

The boys sat in the car for a while, bull shitting. Vincent started to light a cigarette, but Mario commented that it smelled gassy in the car. Vincent didn't light the match, but got out of the car instead and opened the trunk. The smell of gas was strong. He thought they must have spilled some when they put it in the trunk. Vincent took one of the cans out, along with a funnel and started putting the gas into his tank. While Vincent was pouring the gas, Mack came over next to him and started to light a cigarette. Vincent had both hands busy with the gas.

"Holy shit!" Vincent exclaimed. Mario heard him and caught Mack's hand before he could strike the match. "Holy Shit!" exclaimed Vincent, to Mack, "Are you fond of explosions?" "No," answered Mack, sheepishly, "Not if I am going to be in them." About that same time, a black car from the County Sheriff's Department drove up and parked under a tree close to them, about twenty feet away.

"Oh, God!" exclaimed Mario, in a hushed lament, "My mother always told me she should have drowned me." After saying this, he dropped to his knees and hands. He crawled down the side of the knoll, into the darkness. "Up the creek without a scooter!" exclaimed Mack, with a silly grin on his face, the one he used for all occasions. "Without a paddle," corrected Captain Moon. "What do I need a paddle for with a scooter?" asked a confused Mack. "Try not to think about it," answered the apprehensive Vincent.

A deputy got out of the car; he was alone, walking toward them, carrying a long flashlight, which he hadn't turned on. The deputy was young and trim, he didn't have a big belly like they do in the movies. He wasn't quite six feet tall and he was fair, with a blond mustache that matched his hair, which was cropped, short.

"Got trouble?" he asked when he got close to them. "We ran out of gas," explained the Captain, "But we had some in a can in the trunk and we just finished putting it in the tank." "Why do you carry gas in the trunk?" asked the deputy, he looked suspicious, "It can be dangerous, you know." "My gas gauge doesn't work," answered Vincent. "When did you buy the gas?" asked the deputy. "Yesterday," answered Vincent, without thinking. "It smells pretty gassy around here," commented the deputy, as he turned his flashlight on and flashed it on the trunk of the car. "You have a gas leak," the deputy said and Vincent saw the gas dripping from the rear of the car; he cringed, as the truth got closer. "Open the trunk," demanded the deputy. Vincent's stomach felt like he had swallowed a brick and his heart was in his throat. He opened the trunk. The deputy looked at the cans and looked at the boys with an "I knew it" look on his face. He moved the cans around, looking for the leak. The deputy found it in the bottom of one of the cans and the can was still about half full.

"This can would be empty if you had bought the gas yesterday," claimed the deputy. The Captain's blood ran cold. "You boys didn't buy this gas," stated the deputy, with conviction, "You stole it." The Captain's knees turned to water. They were caught. He was mute. What would his mother think of him? The deputy looked around, his voice was cold.

"There was another guy here," he claimed, "Where did he go?" "What you see is what you get," blurted Vincent. He hadn't meant for it to sound impudent, but that was the way it sounded to the deputy. "You are in deep trouble if you hide him!" exclaimed the deputy. He was mad, he had not had a good look at Mario and he was not particularly fond of impudence. The deputy took the older boys to the County Jail and Carl to the Juvenile Hall, where he was right at home.

Vincent was aghast when the judge sentenced him to thirty days in the County Jail. The judge had decided that he had been the leader of the adventure and those who play must pay. Carl got two weeks in Juvenile Hall and Mack got two weeks in the County Jail. Mario got nothing. He never got caught and Vincent knew he was doing the extra time because of Mario. And because he was the leader of a gang called, "The Moon Patrol." Vincent knew not where the police had obtained that information; he was getting famous.

The jail was full, but the drunk tank was not and that was where they put Vincent and Mack. Vincent's mother had cried and Doc had not been happy at all. He was much too pure for such happenings. Doc had tried to retrieve some of the gas for Vincent, but he had been stopped. The law hadn't thought that he should have the gas just because he was doing time for it. The law isn't always fair, not by everyone's standards.

The Drunk Tank was a one-room cell. It was about twenty-five feet, square. There was one toilet and a shower at the south, end, around a corner, with no door. It was at least fifteen feet to the ceiling. The windows, four of them, were tall and narrow. They were two feet shy of the ceiling, but started six feet above the floor. Vincent could only see sky through the windows unless he stood on the garbage can. Vincent would slide it under the window he wanted to look out and stand on it. Others did the same.

There were no beds in the Tank. There was a narrow metal bench that was bolted to the wall. It went around the perimeter of three cell walls. There were no pillows, nor blankets. It was hot and there was no air conditioning. Vincent was getting a good idea of what society thought of its drunks.

Two meals a day was all they got to eat, unless someone brought them something. Ancient, diluted coffee was the only beverage, served twice a day, rain or shine. Breakfast was usually lumpy oatmeal and two pieces of soggy toast. Sometimes they would get a boiled egg in its shell, along with the mush and Vincent would save the egg for lunch, because there was no lunch.

Dinner was not much better than breakfast. The cook had learned countless ways to fix cabbage, hamburger, pasta, potatoes and leftovers. Vincent's appetite was good; he ate every thing that was given to him. He did have trouble with his digestion. He would have traded his soul for some alcohol.

Vincent had no idea that he was already addicted to alcohol. He had no major withdrawal problems, but did feel lousy and nervous. He felt tired all the time, he felt like he needed a drink. This feeling went on for about a week. Before it started to subside he started to feel stronger, but he couldn't seem to get his stomach under control.

One doctor, some years ago, had told him he had a nervous stomach and he would just have to learn to live with it. Vincent had learned to live with it; he had found his panacea, alcohol; it was the elixir of life. But he had to do without it in jail. Captain Moon promised himself that he would never let himself get into a position where he would have to do without. Not ever again.

Many strange, souls entered the Tank while Vincent and Mack were incarcerated. Some of the guys had just got drunk and into trouble. But some were bonafide winos and alcoholics who had been separated from their God, alcohol. It was the god of dreams, nightmares, hallucinations and death.

There was one wino Vincent would not soon forget; he came in on the fifth day. This man had entered the Tank in an acute state of alcoholism. Vincent had never seen a face that shade of purple. The parts of the man's eyes that were supposed to be white had been yellow. His teeth had been chattering and his flesh had been quivering. He had looked to be in his late fifties. His clothes had been old, filthy and smelling of human excrement. This alcoholic had been suffering with delirium tremens. He had begged the guards for a shot of paraldehyde and the guard had got philosophical with him.

"One drink is too many," he had said, piously, "And a thousand is not enough for you, you stinking wino!" The guard had said, with sarcasm. Vincent had felt sympathy for the Wino and intense dislike for the guard. Every thing the guard had said was true, but it was in vain coming from him because he had no charity and his uttering did no one any good. They were just vexations of spirit. It was like telling a vampire he had no need of blood.

Soon, a head guard had come with a gift for the wino. His eyes had lit up when he saw the paper cup; he had been through this before. The cup had been tiny; it couldn't have held more than an ounce.

"Paraldehyde?" the wino had asked, with joyful expectation, with hands shaking, reaching for the cup. "Paraldehyde," the sympathetic guard had answered. The wino's tragic face had cracked with a toothy grin. His hands had been shaking so bad the guard had had to help him get the cup to his mouth, where he had emptied it with one gulp. After the wino had swallowed the colorless elixir, a long sigh had escaped from his lips. In an instant his tortured face had relaxed, the shaking had left his limbs and the quiver had gone out of his flesh.

"Did you see that?" Vincent had asked his partner in crime, after being amazed by the wino's transformation. "Yeah," the unamazed Mack had answered, "I have seen it before. I have an uncle who is like that, he is an alcoholic." Vincent had thought to his self, "Why was this Magical power given to this liquid? Why did God give alcohol the power to destroy a man? A certain amount of it could make one feel good, but too much could kill." It hadn't made any sense to him at all. After the paraldehyde had given the wino the illusion of health, he had told his story.

"I know I look older, but I am thirty five years old. I have been a little hard on myself. I went to law school, but ran with a fast crowd. I drank too much and flunked out. My childhood sweetheart, the one I was going to marry, dumped me and married one of my law school chums, one who graduated."

Vincent remembered that tears had come to the wino's eyes. When he had started talking about his sweetheart he had nodded off and had fallen asleep. Vincent had wondered what his sweetheart would think if she could see him now. He had asked Mack that and Mack had said that his own mother would not recognize him; he was not long for this world. Vincent was talking about it again with Mack. One has to talk about something in jail; there are not many things to do.

"I will never let booze do that to me!" stated Vincent, with emotion. "It has already started to," replied Mack, in a serious, tone, one not used by him very often. "What in the Hell do you mean by that?" retorted Vincent, defensively. "It already has a hold on you." answered Mack "That's bullshit!" exclaimed Vincent, getting indignant. "Didn't you need a drink when you first came here?" asked Mack, "It was all you talked about." "Didn't you want a drink when we first came in?" asked Vincent. "Wouldn't you like to have one now?" "Sure." answered Mack, "But I never need a drink." "Come on" retorted Vincent, agitated over the truth. "You drink as much as I do." "That may be true," replied Mack, "but I drink for fun, or because there isn't anything else to do, or because everyone else is doing it. You drink like you are driven to it by a crew of devils!"

Vincent stopped arguing. He was quiet, introspective. He could say no more. In his heart he knew what Mack had said was true, but he did not know what to do about it. Vincent looked over at the wino; he was asleep on the bench. Vincent felt trepidation, "Is that to be my fate?" he asked himself, silently.

Word of mouth told the boys that the wino had broken into a cocktail lounge, one the A.B.C. had shut down for some reason. He had stayed plastered in there for seven days. A cop, who had been patrolling the area had heard him and had investigated and had caught him. He hadn't eaten for the seven days.

On the seventh day of Vincent's incarceration, on a sunny afternoon, Vincent heard a pebble hit one of the front windows. He pushed the garbage can under the window and climbed on it and looked. Just below the window, on the sidewalk, stood Mario, Greta, Linda, Mary, Buck and Carl. They were all wearing broad grins.

"Hello, Jail Bird." They all greeted in unison, "Anything we can do?" "Yeah." answered Vincent, joyful to see his friends and especially for Linda. "You can break our ass out of here." Mack jumped up on the can with him and Mario put his finger to his own lips. "Shhhush," he hushed, "You are just trying to get us in there with you." "You guys can go home," kidded Mack, "Just send the girls in." Carl put his arm around Greta and she smiled at him.

"I'm going to take care of Greta for you," Carl told Vincent. "That's awfully white of you," replied Vincent. He had no problem with that, for his thoughts were of Linda. Linda was looking at Vincent and he was looking at her. There was a message in the looks.

"Thirty days is a long time," said Greta and she gave Carl a coquettish look. "Tell me about it," replied Vincent, ruefully, "But some of that time has already been spent." Vincent had read that look and knew what it meant. Greta had opened her thighs for Carl, but he didn't care about that; he was not rueful about that. It was Linda, she looked woeful behind her grin.

It would be twenty-three more days before he could touch Linda. Before he could see her without looking through bars. And that wasn't all; Vincent wasn't very pleased with himself. "What could she be thinking of me?" he wondered," What was her parents thinking of me?" Vincent knew he should stay away from Linda until she was older. He was aware of what little ammunition he had for fighting the war with temptation, but he also knew he would not be able to stay away from her.

Vincent knew that by the time he got out of jail he would no longer have a physical relationship with Greta. That would compound the temptation with Linda. He was ready for the break with Greta. He was beginning to feel that sex without love was the same as masturbation, using another's body instead of one's hand. At least a hand couldn't get anyone pregnant.

"Could you float me a loan?" Carl asked Vincent; he was being a smart ass and Vincent laughed at his audacity. He thought to his self, "I'm going to loan you money to spend on my girl. Fat chance." But he remembered that she wasn't his girl any more. "Sure," replied Vincent, "I'll call my banker and he will forward the funds you need." They all had a belly laugh from that one, and then Vincent thought he would play along with their cute game. "Mario!" he ordered, "You keep Carl away from Greta." "I'll kill him if he looks at her!" promised Mario. "Buck!" commanded Vincent, "You keep Mario away from Greta." "I'll kill him if he looks at her," Buck promised, "But who is going to keep me away from her?" "I will!" exclaimed Greta and they all gave Buck a horselaugh.

CHAPTER 20

It was night and Vincent was prone, flat on his back on the hard metal bench. He was trying to sleep, but it was eluding him. He had been in the Tank for one day over two weeks and Mack had gone home. Vincent was trying hard to go to sleep, but his thoughts would not let him. He was lonely. There were people in the cell with him, but they were strangers and most of them were not the kind of strangers you would meet on any ordinary day. Most of the strangers one meets in jail are self-indulgent strangers and most of them to the extreme. That was what got most of them in jail, one way, or another. A thief is just as self indulgent as a drunk and so is a wife beater, or a man who will not pay his child support. Most of Vincent's cellmates were just drunks. After all, he was in the Drunk Tank.

Vincent would have loved to have a drink. "A Moscow Mule' would sure go good right now," he thought, but there was no use in thinking about that. Thoughts of Greta and Linda drew his mind away from booze. He remembered what Greta's naked body looked like, what it was like to make love to her. Vincent wondered what Linda would look like naked, with her lovely hair spread out on a pillow, with her thighs open for him. He had already seen most of her body, all except what was covered by her little bikini. Linda's body had been beautiful and he knew she would be beautiful, naked.

The image of her, naked, laying on her back on pink sheets with her golden hair spread out on a pillow, caused a lust in him that made it an awful temptation to masturbate. But he was afraid one of his cellmates would catch him, so he resisted.

One of the prisoners was snoring quite loud. Vincent wondered which one it was and while he was wondering, one of them cut loose a cabbage fart. The methane gas carried the aroma to Vincent's nostrils, causing them to flair for a second. The aroma amalgamated naturally with the other stinks of bodies, urine, excrement, vomit and stale booze. Vincent wondered why God had created anything, or anyone. The world was such a stinking mess. What was the purpose of it all? Life, with inevitable death seemed so senseless. He remembered something he had read, "Where moth and rust doth corrupt." That was all of it he could remember and had no idea what it meant. It must have been in the Bible or that little book his grandmother use to read all the time. His Grandmother had been a Christian Scientist, one of those odd balls who don't go to doctors or take medicine.

Vincent had thought a lot about death since his sister had been killed. He thought a lot about life after death. He was terribly afraid of death and he so wanted life after death to be true. Vincent wanted so badly to see Audrey again, to see her face again, and to be able to tell her how sorry he was. But Vincent could not see how a person could live after their body had died, after it had rotted away in the ground, after there was nothing left but bones. He remembered the story of Lazarus and how Jesus had raised him from the dead after he had laid in his grave for four days and had already begun to stink.

"Sure," Vincent thought to himself, "Jesus could do it. He was the Son of God. But what good did it do? Lazarus just had to die all over again. Vincent could see no master plan in living and dying. "One little accident," he thought, "In a second I could be dead." A chill ran through him. The thought of oblivion frightened Vincent, terribly; he had difficulty comprehending it. Vincent tried to imagine what it would be like to not exist and he could not. Vincent shuddered. "If Audrey had not been there," he thought, "I would have drowned. I would be dead right now, at this very moment." Vincent wondered more about life after death. "What if it is true, will I see Audrey the moment I die, or will I have to search for her? Will she have aged, or will she remain the age she had died? Will I go directly to Heaven, or will I have to lay in the grave until Gabriel blows his horn?"

These kinds of thoughts confused Vincent and he tried to think of something else. His thought went to God and procreation. It seemed to Vincent that God could have thought of a more practical way to procreate. He believed the whole sex thing was both crude and obscene. Vincent couldn't understand why birth had to be painful and even dangerous.

"God had some really bad ideas," he thought, "But what could one do but play his silly game?" Vincent wondered why God hadn't just continued to make adults, like he had done with Adam and Eve; he hadn't needed babies then? Having no answers to anything, Vincent gave up and went to sleep.

All good things must come to an end and so it goes for bad things. Vincent's days as a jailbird went by slow, but they did go by. And when the days had gone, he knew that something else had gone; his relationship with

Greta had gone. But he had known that when she had come to the jail that first time and only time. Vincent had known then that she was sharing her loins with Carl. So Vincent was free, in more ways than one and he was grateful. He was tired of the relationship, anyway. There had been no meaning to it; it had all been physical and it had been used up before he had gone to jail.

Vincent had been so sure that it was love and now he was certain that he had never been in love with her. He had been infatuated, for sure, but it had been one hundred percent physical. Now Vincent wondered if there was anything he could be certain of, besides death and taxes. He was certain that he would die someday, maybe soon. Vincent decided he had better take whatever he could get, whenever he could get it.

Vincent still had to go to Greta's place to visit with Linda and still liked to visit with George and Maggie; they had agreed to keep him in the family. They had not condemned him for his mistake with the law, "Boys will be boys," they had said. They had told Linda she was too young to date Vincent, but it was certainly all right for her to have him over. And agreed she could go swimming with the gang.

Vincent was visiting with Linda one day when Greta wasn't there. This was an occasion for both of them, because every time Vincent had come to see Linda, Greta had been there. Even though Greta did not want Vincent for a steady diet, she was jealous of her sister's relationship with him. Greta still wanted him physically, but he had insisted on a monogamous relationship and she suspected he wanted none at all.

Linda was kind of breathless. "Let's go for a walk," she suggested, timidly. "I have a favorite spot I want to show you" "Sure," answered Vincent, "if your mother will let us." "She will," answered Linda and her face flushed, "I already asked her." "You little devil." answered Vincent, delighted by her candor, he was grinning.

Linda was wearing her white shorts and she was fresh, sweet and lovely. Her lack of guile was charming. Linda was just a wonderful little person to be with. Vincent did not feel aggressive with her, he didn't feel nervous with her; he just felt good with her.

They left the house and walked up the driveway to the road. It was a wonderful day to be alive. They both felt good, almost giddy, from the anticipation of good. They walked north, up the narrow, serpentine road. The road was lined with oaks and willows, some of them were weeping. There were bushes with bright red berries, not the kind a person could eat.

The two were holding hands as they walked. This beautiful girl led Vincent up a path, away from the road. He could not take his eyes off her; every place on her was pleasing to his eyes. The path led them to a meadow. There was a grove of willows, with a soft rug of clover under them. Linda pulled on his hand and they ran to the grove and sat in the clover.

The sun filtered down through the willow branches. The trees were in a circle, with the sun coming down through them. It gave a feeling of a domed ceiling, like some kind of natural cathedral. It was such a beautiful place, making the moment so precious; neither of them could say anything for a moment. Vincent had the feeling God had made the place just for them. Linda ended the reverie.

"I come here to dream," Linda told Vincent, shyly. "What do you dream about?" asked Vincent; he had a sweet anticipation he did not understand. Linda lowered her eyes, and her cheeks flushed. "Mostly about you," she answered, so softly he almost couldn't hear. Vincent felt like he would burst with joy. He knew he must be careful with her, though, because she was so young, she had just had her fourteenth birthday and she was so vulnerable.

Vincent went to her on his hands and knees. Linda's eyes were still down. He planted a kiss on her forehead. She raised her eyes and he jumped up. He ran to the biggest tree in the grove, took out his pocketknife and started to carve on the trunk. Linda came, timidly, to see what he was doing. Vincent carved the outline of a heart, with his name at the top, inside of the heart. Then he carved an arrow through the heart. He could feel her warm breath on the back of his neck as he carved her name below the arrow. He felt her fingers in his hair, her joy in her fingers.

"Oh, God!" she exclaimed, breathlessly, "Do you mean it?" asked the tremulous, girl. He turned, and looked into her eyes, they were wide and her lips were parted. "I can't help myself" Vincent answered, his heart was full, "I do love you, but we mustn't tell anyone." Linda could not contain herself; she went into his arms with her face buried in his chest. "I love you, too.'" she said, softly, "I always have, ever since I was a little girl." "You still are a little girl," he answered, while stroking her golden hair. "I am not a little girl!" she exclaimed, defiantly, pressing herself harder to him and then kissing him on his mouth, ardently. Her ardor lit his passion and their lips were locked. He felt her in his loins and he broke away.

"No! He exclaimed, breathlessly, "I guess you are not," and she went back into his arms, kissing him, passionately. Vincent got an erection right away and he had to protect her. He broke away and ran to another tree; he started to carve on it. Linda followed him.

"Why did you run?" she asked. He did not know what to tell her, so he told the truth. "I have to protect you," he told her. "From what?" she asked, incredulous from innocence. "From me," he answered, while carving another heart, cooling himself. Linda watched Vincent with mixed emotions, as she now understood. It was terribly frustrating, having a woman's feelings in a fourteen-year old body. They were feelings she did not thoroughly understand. Her mind and body were ready for love, but the time was not.

Linda would have given up her virginity for Vincent, but only for him. Before Vincent, the idea of sex had been crude to her, even revolting, but not now, not with him. Vincent was beautiful to her. Looking at him melted her heart, and filled her with joy. Touching him compounded these feelings, adding a new one, a warm hunger in her. She knew what it was and she knew what she wanted to do. The feeling was new and exciting. The thought of making love with Vincent held no fear for her.

Linda had to break the doldrums, so she pinched him on the rear and ran, giggling like the schoolgirl she was. "You little vixen!" he shouted, "I'm going to get you for that." "I hope so!" she shouted with glee. Vincent chased her and she ran in a circle, not wanting to leave her favorite place.

Vincent was running out of breath, but she was running strong. Linda decided she had better let him catch her, so she pretended to trip and he caught her by the ankle. They went down together in the clover. They held each other, laughing, out of breath and then they were kissing, but it was just sweet and innocent. This was only for a few moments and then came desire. Their kissing became passionate, hungry. His hands wanted to explore her lovely body, but he held them at bay. She wanted him to touch her where he should not; her senses were aflame. They pressed their bodies together. Vincent knew if he didn't stop, he wouldn't be able to, so he stopped.

"We have to stop." he groaned. She moaned, her body didn't want to stop, but her mind told her that she should. She relaxed and laid in his arms." I love you," she told him, softly, "And I will be a woman soon, will you wait for me?" "I will wait," he promised her. "I love you and I will wait." The two sweethearts walked hand in hand, back to the house, talking about the future, cooling their passion.

Not having Greta for a sexual partner was hard on Vincent; she had been such a lusty one. He knew it would be years before he could make love to Linda. He didn't know if he could do without it for years. He guessed he would just have to masturbate.

Vincent visited Linda as often as he could, but it was sweet torture for both of them. And it was uncomfortable for them when Greta was there; she did her best to make it uncomfortable. It became such a hassle for Vincent; he finally had to tell Linda that he wouldn't be out so often, to her dismay.

Uncle Sam intervened in Vincent's enigma with Linda. The intervention made his bogus draft card real to him. He had never been overly concerned about being drafted. He thought that due to all his physical problems, he would not pass the physical. Vincent had been having a terrible time with his health. He was smoking three packs of Lucky Strikes every day, lighting one off of another. He was as nervous as a cat on a hot tin roof. Part of his anatomy had to be moving at all times, a hand, foot, or both. Vincent even had to rub his feet together, like a cricket, to get to sleep at night.

Sometimes, when Vincent was extremely nervous, he would have heart palpitations. He could always tell when a spell was coming on. His heart would skip a beat and then the beats would increase in speed until his heart would feel like it was going to beat its way right out of his chest. Then the beats would gradually slow down to normal. It always scared the Hell out of him.

Vincent was becoming a regular hypochondriac. He was certain there was something wrong with his heart. He would catch himself feeling his own pulse, either at his wrist, or neck. "God! What a pansy I'm becoming," he would say to himself. Vincent would worry about his heart stopping and then he realized there was nothing he could do if it did stop. It always would frighten him when he thought that way and he would light another cigarette, or have another drink, or both.

Much to Vincent's surprise and consternation, he did pass the Army Physical. After passing, he did believe that a person would have to be near death to not pass it. After passing the physical, they gave him thirty days to get to Fort Ord and basic training.

Vincent spent all of the time he could with Linda. He saw her every day, despite the hassle with Greta. When it came time to leave Linda, with a quiver in her lips, she told him she would wait for him forever and then the tears came. He told her when basic training was finished he would get a pass and he would come to see her. Of course there were tears in his mother's eyes, but there was a smile on Doc's face, it was under the skin, but Vincent saw it.

Vincent's greatest fear was Korea. He was just certain if he made it to Korea, he would never come back alive. Many of the boys from Ophir Flats had died there already and some that he knew in Fort Bragg. He was already having a big enough problem with the fear of death and now it was compounded.

Almost the very first negative thing they did to Vincent at Fort Ord was cut off his pretty hair. It was cut even, though, short all over. At least no one would be able to grab him by his hair. Vincent hadn't known that his head was so knobby. He hated to look at himself in the mirror. At least he didn't have to comb it. He didn't have the time to comb it, anyway.

None of the clothes that he was issued fit him; they were all too big. Vincent thought he looked like Charley Chaplin's tramp in them. He had lost weight and even his own clothes fit him like a tent, but he wouldn't be wearing them for a while. With the haircut he had, he wouldn't look good in anything, anyway. His ego was at an all time low; he felt awfully insignificant.

Army chow tore up his stomach, especially the C-Rations, which they had at least once a week and sometimes twice. These were rations that had been designed for combat. They were extra rich for the extra energy needed for troops who were in combat. They didn't give Vincent extra energy; they gave him extra gas and heartburn. Lately, it seemed like everything he ate did this to him.

Basic training was an awful ordeal for Vincent. He had no stamina and because of the dampness and changeable climate of the Monterey Peninsula, he was constantly suffering from a cold, the flu or an earache. Vincent went to the dispensary, often. The doctors there seemed faceless, anonymous. It seemed like they were not real doctors, but trainees of some kind. It seemed as if their panacea for every ill known to man was the A. P. C. Pill. Vincent soon discovered that these pills were nothing but a combination of aspirin, caffeine and some other ingredient he was not certain of. If you had an earache, you got two A. P. C. Pills. If you had a stomach problem, or a backache, colic, ingrown nails, probably even dandruff, you got A. P. C. Pills.

Vincent went on sick call because his nose was stuffed so bad it was all he could do to breathe, his lungs were also congested. The faceless, doctor, he was wearing a mask, told Vincent he probably had a cold. He prescribed the usual medication. He told the doctor about the palpitations, which he told everyone he saw in hope of finding a cause. The doctor informed him it was nothing but his nerves and the condition would pass as soon as he got used to military life. The doctor also suggested it would help if he would quit smoking.

That was the most absurd thing Vincent had ever heard. Cigarettes calmed him; he would go nuts without them. And get used to military life? That would be right after Hell freezes over. He hated military life with a passion. All them assholes ordering him around, telling him what time to get up, what time to go to bed, what time to eat, what time to shit and probably what time to die. "Screw the Army," was his motto.

Vincent was amazed when the faceless doctor gave him an appointment with a nose and throat specialist at the base hospital. Private Vincent was not aware that the specialist was a Major and was also one of the faceless doctors he had been seeing at the dispensary. After a thorough examination, the Major informed Vincent that he was suffering from a sinus infection. He also informed him he had abnormally small Eustachian tubes, the tubes that equalize atmospheric pressure on the eardrums.

It seemed like Vincent always had to learn things the hard way. He kidded with the Major, he said, "That moron at the dispensary told me that all I had was a cold." The Major had a mask on, but Vincent could see his face go livid under it. He took the mask off, and there was a feeling of trepidation for Vincent as he recognized the Major.

"I am one of those morons who work at the dispensary!" exclaimed the irate Major. Vincent could have sworn he saw steam coming out of the Majors ears. "I'm sorry, Sir" apologized Vincent, profusely, "I thought they were all trainees down there." It would have been better if he had said nothing; he had only compounded the insult. Vincent said nothing more and neither did the Major, who was seething.

Vincent was always having trouble with officers. He could tolerate the lower ranks, for he seemed to be one of them, but officers, they were the faceless authority. They were like cops to him. They were worse than cops, for they had more authority over you than cops. It was hard for Vincent to get use to the discipline. He had never had much of it at home, but he was of a meek nature, and tried to do what he was told. Vincent had always been basically good because it was his nature and not because he had to be. When Vincent was a little boy it was a rare thing for him to get into trouble, even at school, he had always been non-aggressive.

It wasn't always Vincent's fault when he got into a scrape with an officer, like the time with the lazy eye. Vincent's right eye had always been lazy; it was because the eye was near sighted and astigmatic. When the lazy eye got tired, it stopped looking. One doctor had told him, "No brain in its right mind would want to look through an eye like that."

As a result of this lazy eye sometimes shutting off, there were times when Vincent had poor peripheral vision on his starboard side. One time he was walking on the base, headed for the P. X. to drink some beer. He was walking across an intersection. Vincent turned his head to the left to look at something and an officer stepped off the curb, coming toward Vincent, to the right of him. Vincent did not see that he was an officer. He was just a blur to Vincent.

"Halt, soldier!" exclaimed the officer, from behind Vincent, Vincent heard and he halted. He turned and faced the officer; he was a First Lieutenant. The sun was in Vincent's eyes and he stared at the officer for a moment, confused. "Don't you salute officers?" asked the officer, curtly. "I do when I recognize one," answered Vincent, without thinking. The officer was plainly, indignant. "Well!" exclaimed the officer, "Don't you recognize me as an officer?" Vincent's face flushed. He kicked his heels together and saluted, smartly. His salute was returned. When the officer dropped his salute, Vincent started to drop his. "Hold it there!" commanded the officer and Vincent complied. The officer walked around him, looking him over. "Why did you not know I was an officer?" he asked. "Because you were to the right of me," answered Vincent, still stiff, at attention, "Sir." he added. The officer gave him a frosty look. "What has that got to do with anything?" asked the officer, incredulously. "My right eye is lazy," explained Vincent. The officer's countenance softened a little. "What does than mean?" he asked, and Vincent explained. "You mean to tell me?" asked the officer, even more incredulous, "that some of the time you can't see with your right eye?" "That is correct," answered Vincent, still at attention. "At ease, soldier," ordered the officer and Vincent let his salute drop, but he certainly was not at ease. The officer had about half a grin on his face now. "What in the Hell are you doing in the Army?" he asked. "I don't know," answered Vincent, "I was drafted." The officer smiled. "The next time I see you coming," he said, good naturedly, "I'll try to stay on your port side." "Thank you Sir," replied Vincent. "Carry on, soldier," said the officer and Vincent saluted him, the officer returned it and they walked away from each other. Vincent never saw him again.

Vincent hated the Army more each passing day. He hated the confinement, being a number; it was all he was to the Army. If he went to Korea and was killed, that would be all the Army would lose, a faceless number. There was nothing about the Army that he liked. He didn't like getting up before the chickens and he especially abhorred every hour of his day being scheduled by someone else.

Vincent did not want to go to Korea; he was scared to death of it. He knew guys from the Flats who had gone there and had not come back. Dan Durham was one of them. Dan had been a big kid, always in trouble. He had been the one who had told Mario about the guns. The guns had been stolen from a sporting goods store in Marysville; a city twenty-six miles West of the Flats. Butch Costa had been selling the guns.

Dan had told Mario and had arranged a meeting with Costa. Vincent had gone with Mario. They had met out in the boonies at about twilight. Costa had wanted more for the forty-five caliber, automatic pistol than Mario had wanted and Costa wouldn't dicker. Mario had declined from the purchase. As they were driving away from the meeting, Mario had looked in the rear view mirror and had seen Costa raise the pistol.

"Duck!" Mario had commanded," He is going to shoot." Vincent had ducked and had heard the explosion go off in the chamber of the pistol and the "thunk" sound when the lead had put a hole in the trunk of Mario's car and then another explosion and another "thunk."

Dan had been a hero in Korea. His unit had been separated from his platoon and had been ambushed. Dan had been packing a B. A. R. (Browning Automatic Rifle); it was a machine gun. Dan had told his guys to go get help while he held the enemy off. When his men had returned with help, they had found Dan with a large hole in the front of his head, and the back of his head had been missing in action.

Vincent and his platoon had spent days and days practicing with their M1 rifles without firing them. The first day they fired them Vincent had trouble. The noise of the rifle on his starboard side had caused pain in his ear. The pain had ruined his aim, causing him to flunk with his score. They had finally sent him to the hospital to find out what was wrong and had discovered he had a perforated eardrum. The noise had irritated the scar tissue in his invalid eardrum. An abscess had caused the perforation in his youth.

Vincent had been dismissed from the rifle range and any shooting. This action had ruined his Army career, which he would not have pursued, anyway, but it had saved him from Korea. Vincent would stay a private for his whole tour of duty; to make rank he had to qualify on the rifle range. Vincent was grateful. It had been only a few days since his nightmare. He had dreamed he was in Korea and had been walking across a railroad trestle. The jungle had been below; he could see it between the ties at his feet. An M1 Rifle had been cradled in his arms. Nine pounds they weigh, a great rifle, but too damned heavy. It had been ready to fire, with one in the chamber and a full clip.

There had been no noise but the birds. He had felt the bullet hit him and then he had heard the crack of the rifle. Vincent had felt the hot lead hit his anus, tear its way through his bowels, chest, throat and exit out the top of his head. He had felt the fountain of blood spurting out the hole in his head, flooding his face and eyes. He had run, blindly off the trestle into space and oblivion. A few weeks later Vincent received orders to go to Cook's School in San Francisco, at the Presidio.

CHAPTER 21

The Presidio was so different from Fort Ord. Although the buildings had floors like the barracks at Fort Ord, they were built of brick, rather than lumber. The terrain at Fort Ord had been basically flat, almost treeless, while The Presidio was resting on beautiful rolling hills. It was full of cared for, landscaped trees, bushes and flora. The solid brick dormitory was warm and comfortable. Vincent's bunk was on the third floor, by a window. Out the window was a beautiful view and it seemed like most of the time the sun was shining.

Cook's School was not like Basic Training at all. Basic Training had not only been a learning time, it had been a conditioning. On warm days at Fort Ord, classes were held in hot, stuffy classrooms. During inclement weather classes were held outside on the bleachers. These classes on the bleachers had helped keep Vincent's colds on a regular basis. The hot, stuffy classes had always made Vincent sleepy and he couldn't keep himself from dozing off. Standard procedure had been to put those who fell asleep during class on K. P. (Kitchen Police.) Vincent had pulled K. P. almost every time he had had class in a hot room.

It wasn't just the atmosphere in the room that had made Vincent sleepy; it was the boredom. It was a rare occasion when the instructor had been animated by enthusiasm. Classes were started early in the morning at Cook's School and was finished in the afternoon. Vincent's pass was open and he could go anywhere he wanted after class. Vincent had his Ford parked on the base, just behind the dormitory, and he always had booze in the trunk.

Vincent was missing Linda. He had only seen her for a short while, just before school had started. She had left on a vacation with her family. Vincent thought about her all the time, but he had found Carla's phone number in his wallet. It was behind Linda's picture. Vincent remembered the lovely girl he had met at the Italian restaurant, whom he had neglected to call. Now he had her phone number and wanted to call her, but he felt guilty about it because of Linda. But Vincent was lonely and he couldn't see Linda and he kept remembering, what Carla looked like.

It was Friday night and temptation had become too much for him. He worked up the courage squelched the guilt and called her. A woman with a gentle voice and soft Italian accent answered. When he told her who he was and asked for Carla, she informed him she was Carla's mother. She told him that Carla was on her way out the door and she would try to catch her. In a few minutes a breathless Carla answered the phone. Carla's voice was sweet just like he had remembered.

"Vincent Cardoza?" she asked, she remembered him, but had given up on him a long time ago. "I remember you," she said, a little petulant, "But why didn't you call? I waited for you to call." Carla's candor delighted him, but he couldn't tell her the truth. He couldn't tell her that he had been in love, or that he had been in jail. "I was afraid you were just being nice to me when you gave me your phone number," he answered, humbly, "And I'm deathly afraid of rejection. I just procrastinated until now; I hope I'm not too late?"

"But, Vincent" she complained, "Do you think I would give a stranger my phone number just to be nice?" She paused to catch her breath and her wits. "A girl just wouldn't do that." she informed him, "Not in San Francisco!" "I know." pleaded Vincent, "It was just stupid. But please forgive me and let me see you." He was sincere, already loving her voice. "I want to see you too," she replied, candidly, "But I have a date and was headed out the door." She hesitated for a moment while her mind raced, "We could have lunch tomorrow," she suggested, thinking it would be nice to get acquainted in the day time; night time was different. "I would like that," answered Vincent, gratefully, "But how will I find you?" he asked, with a trace of qualm. Vincent was still nervous about driving in the City. She heard the qualm and knew he was a stranger. Carla had lived in the City all of her life; she would show him around.

"Why don't I pick you up?" she asked and he told her he was stationed at Presidio. "Close to Lombard and Ruger?" she asked. "Not far at all," he answered. "I'll see you there at one" she told him, "I have to go now." "Wait!" he exclaimed, frantic she would hang up, "How will I know it's you? "Look for a white XK120," she answered, "Bye." and she hung up the phone.

"That's a Jaguar," he told the dead phone. Vincent held on to the phone for a while, like he was waiting for her to pick it back up and talk to him, like if he hung it up, she wouldn't be able to. "I'll see you tomorrow," he told the phone, wistfully and hung it up. "But what will I do tonight?" he asked himself. "I'll see what Capp is doing," he told himself.

One of the guys he schooled with had been in his platoon at Fort Ord; they had started cook school together. His name was Jack Capp, but everyone called him Capp. They had become pals; at least they were drinking pals. Capp did love his booze. Capp was considerably bigger than Vincent. Capp was tall and raw boned. He was big, but not meaty; he just had big bones. A hole in an eardrum had got Vincent to Cook School, but a trick knee had got Capp there. He would be coming down the stairs and his knee would go out on him and he would fall the rest of the way. Running was the same risk for him; he never knew when it was going to happen.

Capp had a booming voice and a booming laugh. He had straight, blond hair that hung on his forehead and a jovial smile that split his pock marked face. Capp had a profane mouth and a heart of gold. He was stout as a bull, except for his knee, which always seemed to be causing him a minor injury. It was amazing that his injuries were always minor; falling down stairs is dangerous.

It was like his knee had a mind of its own and was out to get him. You would think his knee would have sense enough to know that anything that happened to Capp happened to it. Capp always had a bruise on him somewhere and the knee was even more misbehaved when he was drinking and Capp was doing that whenever he was off duty.

Having nothing to do until lunch the next day, Vincent went looking for Capp. Vincent also liked to drink and he especially liked to drink with Capp. With him it was never a dull moment. Vincent heard him first, he was singing in the shower. He found him alone; the rest of the troops had skedaddled. No one hung around after duty on Friday for fear of being put on the duty roster for the weekend. Vincent had risked it to find Capp.

Capp didn't give a hoot about the duty roster, he just took things as they came; he was inexorable. That's not saying he didn't get mad; he did and often, but it never upset him, it was like water on a duck's back, trouble that is. Capp liked opera and that was what he was singing. That was what it sounded like to Vincent. It was not recognizable, only Capp knew what he was singing. It was loud.

Vincent had told Capp about Captain Moon and that was what Capp always called him, but sometimes he would shorten it to just Moon. Vincent sat on Capp's bed, the one underneath, that is, for Capp had an upper bunk. Vincent waited for him, not wanting to disturb his joy, he could not sing like that every day. In just a little while Capp appeared clad in a towel.

"Captain Moon!" he exclaimed, surprised that he was still on base, "Why are you still here?" He had told Capp that he was going to call Carla. "I have a date for tomorrow," replied Vincent, "But nothing for tonight." "I'm glad to hear that!" exclaimed Capp, enthusiastically, "Cause I want to get drunk and I need your help." "You don't need my help to get drunk," answered Vincent, with feigned skepticism. "Yes I do." argued Capp, "I can drink more when I'm with you." "How is that?" asked Vincent, "Cause you can hold a tank full," answered Capp, "And I try to beat you." "Well, shit!" exclaimed Vincent, "Let's go have a contest." "You are on, Captain Moon."

Capp dropped his towel to put on his shorts; he was hung like a stud horse. "You should put a saddle on that thing," suggested the envious Vincent, wryly. All men are envious when they see a phallus bigger than their own. "I would rather put it to work," answered Capp, with a look of lechery. "You could use it for a jack," suggested Vincent. "How's that?" Capp asked. "Just stick it under the car and get a hard-on," answered Vincent, and then he laughed, then they both laughed, raucously.

Vincent was wearing Levis, so Capp put on his. He put on a red shirt and his cowboy boots. "Let's go," he said. "Where's your coat?" asked Vincent. Capp was from southern California and he always forgot his coat. "It's warm," he argued. "It is now," answered Vincent, "But it won't stay that way." "You don't look like my mother?" Capp said it like a question. "Just take one and leave it in the car, suggested Vincent, "So you wont be wanting mine." "I couldn't wear your tiny coat," teased Capp and he laughed, "I wore a bigger coat when I was ten." "And you had a bigger mouth when you were five," retorted Vincent, laughing. "And a bigger cock when I was four," replied Capp and they both roared. They had been doing all this yakking on the way to Vincent's car; Capp didn't have one.

"It's time we stopped this foolishness," said Vincent, when they got to the car, "And have a drink." He opened the trunk and grabbed a couple of beers. "Would you like a warm beer, or a warm beer?" he asked Capp. "I would rather have a warm beer," answered Capp, capriciously and Vincent handed him one. They both got in the car and sat there until they had finished their beer, which didn't take long.

"Where to?" asked Vincent. "The Robin Hood Club," answered Capp. "Where is that? "Can't tell you, have to show you," answered Capp, while pointing in the direction for him to go. Vincent followed Capp's finger all the way to the club. Vincent didn't know where he was, nor could he find his way again without Capp. Vincent was like that, he had no sense of direction; he would have made a terrible Boy Scout.

Vincent had never paid a cover charge before and he grumbled about it all the way to the bar. He would rather have spent his money on drinks at a less expensive place. "It's worth it," promised Capp, "You just be patient." "I hate it when you talk like that." grumbled Vincent, "You sound just like my mother." "I hope, for her sake," replied Capp, "That I don't look like her."

It was early, and the place wasn't packed yet. Vincent wanted to take a table while one was still available, but Capp insisted on sitting at the bar. "Why do we have to sit at the bar?" asked Vincent, impatiently. "Have patience, Captain Moon," replied Capp, "You will know and very soon."

Capp liked to rhyme things. "Poets," replied Captain Moon, "Are never appreciated until they are dead." "I can wait," answered Capp, he had a quick, wit. "I hope providence can," answered the Captain.

"Hey, Moon?" questioned Capp, "What are you drinking tonight?" He wasn't like Vincent, Capp never changed his drink; he always drank bourbon and water. Capp was always curious about Vincent's drink; he was forever changing it. Vincent's mouth was dry as a powder horn; he needed something cold, sweet and frosty. Something different than a Moscow Mule and something he could chugalug to quench his thirst.

"I'm gonna have a Vodka Collins," Vincent told Capp; he liked the tangy lime flavor.

The bar was extra wide, made out of thick, laminated oak. The floor on the bartender's side had been raised with a rack to facilitate serving. Vincent wondered why the bar was so wide. The stools were plush, but Vincent preferred to stand. He put his foot on the shiny brass rail. Capp sat on the stool next to him.

"My big feet are used up," Capp said. "And you want your ass to match," commented Vincent, and right after he had said it, the bartender came. He was wide, like the bar and he had no neck. There was just a gradual slope from his ears to his massive shoulders. He had a pencil line mustache with eyebrows to match. His eyes looked hard, but his voice was like a woman's. The bartender looked like an escaped mutant from a Ray Bradbury tale.

"What can I do for you boys?" asked the mutant; he sounded like he wanted to do something more intimate than just serve them drinks. "Vodka Collins," answered the Captain. No Neck looked at him with a flat face. "I know you are probably old enough to get drafted," replied No Neck, "But are you old enough to drink?" Vincent handed No Neck his draft card. No Neck looked at it, raising his plucked looking eyebrows. Raising them plowed furrows across his fat brow. "Don't you have a driver's license?" he asked. "I lost it coming west," answered Vincent, sounding like he had made the trip in a covered wagon. "Where did you come from?" asked the bartender, he was not from California, he looked like he might have come from the Moon. "The foothills of the Sierras," answered Vincent. "A regular Marco Polo," jeered No Neck and he turned to Capp. He looked at Capp's pock marked face and looked back at Vincent and stated, "If he is old enough, I know you are," he told Capp. "Bourbon with a water back," ordered Capp. "That's the one I make best," replied No Neck, as he left to make the drinks. "How come the bar is so wide?" asked Vincent. "You will find out soon," answered Capp.

The place was filling up; the bar was full and the tables were almost that way. Moon had sat on his stool to keep it from being taken. The bar was long, with a bartender taking care of each end. Three girls were taking care of the tables. The girls, pretty ones, were just old enough to be there. They were wearing matching jumpers; the skirts were very short. The jumpers were black, and the blouses red. Under the skirts were peek-a-boo, red panties. Eyeballs followed the girls anticipating a peek.

A combo came out to the music platform, near the far end of the bar. They started playing some music, some popular stuff. Moon was working on his second drink; the first had gone down like soda pop. Capp had got rid of his also; he couldn't let Moon get ahead of him. Couples started to dance on the small floor in front of the combo. After several dances the combo took a break. When they returned they started playing that familiar burlesque tune which is played for strippers.

"Clear the bar!" hollered both bartenders. The customers moved their drinks back and the boys did the same. There were steps at the other end of the bar which the boys couldn't see from where they were and to them it looked like this gorgeous, voluptuous female rose up like some heavenly body and stood for a moment on the other end of the bar. The music stopped for a moment to just a soft drum roll. Her shimmering, lavender gown clung to her voluptuous body like it had been sprayed on. The music started with a slow, romantic tempo. This star of the show started a sensual dance down the bar, coming toward the boys. It was a good way to give a guy a stiff neck and other parts of his anatomy.

The girl had long blond hair to the middle of her back. Her face was heart shaped; her lips were full and sensual. Her movements were graceful and in harmony with the music. She danced a pass down the bar and back to the other end.

"Take it off!" hollered one of the lustful patrons and then others hollered, including Captain Moon and Capp. The shimmering gown slipped off of her like magic and underneath was a black laced, slip; it was thin enough to see through. The beauty kept her heels on and made another pass, back and forth.

"More!" someone hollered and then the rest. The music changed back to the original burlesque music and the girl was dancing another pass, losing her slip along the way. She was down to black lace, panties now. Her dance was getting more lustful, her gyrations more suggestive. Watching her from this angle was a particularly, erotic pleasure. By the time the girl got back to the other end she was down to a teeny bikini-like suit, full of sparkle.

The girl made another pass. By the time she was above Vincent and Capp, she was down to a teeny patch over her pubic area with tassels on her nipples. While she was doing her thing above them it was an exciting view of her gyrating loins. "Bet she could screw you to death!" exclaimed Capp. "God!" exclaimed Vincent, "What a way to die!"

The show was over now and all the guys were turned on. For the guys who didn't have girls, there was nothing left to do but drink and that was what Vincent and Capp did. For some reason the Captain didn't switch drinks; he stayed with the Vodka Collins, only God knows how many, at least twenty. God must have driven the car back to Presidio.

Capp got sicker than seasick; he didn't know which end to puke from. He got the dry heaves and kept falling out of his bunk, which was an upper one. Capp made a loud thud every time he fell. Vincent couldn't sleep because of it, so he took Capp's mattress and put it on the floor where Capp did not have so far to fall. Capp, with all his groaning, sounded like he was going to die, but he didn't. He was okay the next morning, except for a little headache. Vincent, whose metabolism was not as stout as Capp's, felt worse. There had been just too, much citrus acid in the drinks he had, not to mention the vodka.

When he looked in the mirror, his face complained to him, there were trails of dried acid running from the corners of his mouth to his jaw. Vincent stuck his tongue out; it was covered with what looked like a white fungus. His face was a similar color and the white of his eyes was pink. "Pink always goes well with white," he told himself, "With any luck at all I will be dead by noon," he lamented and then he remembered Carla. "Oh, shit!" he exclaimed, "I have to get well in a hurry."

It was only six in the morning, but Vincent couldn't sleep well when he was hung over, he was always nervous, with his stomach tied in knots. He had learned that the only cure for his disease was a little hair from the dog that had bit him. He felt dehydrated, out of blood and in need of a fix.

Vincent showered, shaved, dressed and left. He knew he would not be able to eat anything until after he had been primed. It was cold and he was shivering. Vincent went to his car and drank a cool beer. It wasn't cold and it tasted awful, but he got it down. It felt like it was going to come up, but he held it down with will power. Although it warmed his stomach it made him shiver even more.

"Have to have some brandy," he told himself, "And fast," as his heart was doing little flip, flops. He drove to a liquor store he knew was open early. That was the first thing he did in a strange town; find out where the early morning bars and liquor stores were located. Vincent bought three half pints of Christian Brothers Brandy. He put two of them in the glove and opened one. He broke the seal with his teeth while he was driving. He drank a few snorts while driving to Baker Beach, which wasn't far from Presidio.

The beach was foggy and deserted, except for some gulls. Vincent walked along the beach, hung over, lonely and forlorn, wishing he was back at the Flats, wanting to see Linda, knowing his weakness. Vincent chastised himself for being so weak, but then he rationalized that no male could be expected to wait so long. Of course, he wasn't deliberately planning on being untrue to Linda; it was just that he was so lonely.

The brandy was doing its job, but it was making him feel sleepy. He jogged for a while to make the cold air move across his face. This helped and Vincent decided he better find a café and get breakfast, but his alcohol direction finder zeroed in on a bar first. He almost drove past it, but he caught the open door out of the corner of his eye. He would have breakfast later. A cold one sounded too good. A frosty Sidecar would fix his stomach, maybe two of them.

Vincent drove around the block and parked in front of The "No Name Club". The club was in an apartment area, with a Deli on the corner. It was light inside from the open shades and windows, an attempt to get rid of some of last night's smells, of which some were still there. They were not offensive to the Captain; in fact, they were comforting for some reason. He was comfortable in a bar; it gave him a feeling of security. Vincent pulled out a stool and sat on it, looked at his reflection in the mirror and sighed.

The bartender was of ruddy complexion; he looked like his blood had been adulterated by alcohol. His hair was sandy and his face jovial, but he was quiet; he just stood in front of Vincent and grinned, waiting patiently for his order.

"A real Bloody Mary," ordered Vincent, "With everything in it." "You got it," replied the jovial bartender and he went to do his work. The bartender returned in a few minutes with a tall Bloody Mary. It looked like a salad growing out of a glass of blood.

"Enjoy," said the bartender. Vincent did, but he could only drink one and the charm was gone; it just was not potent enough. Vincent remembered that he had originally wanted a Sidecar, they had more kick; he ordered one. Captain Moon was starting to feel a little better; the alcohol was numbing the sharp edges of his nerve endings. He looked at his reflection in the mirror and cautioned himself, reminding himself that he still had to meet Carla. He smiled at himself.

There were only two other patrons in the bar, an older man and woman; they were whispering to each other. They were both drinking Boilermakers, a good way to get drunk in a hurry. Vincent wondered how many they had drunk. He tipped his drink to his image and sipped. He sipped until he had finished four of them and he decided he had better quit before he couldn't. Vincent knew he should have had something to eat before drinking. He wasn't hungry and the alcohol had numbed the part of his brain that would have told him so. Vincent knew, though, that he had better eat something, anyway.

He asked Smiley for directions to a café and left. At the cafe, Vincent ordered scrambled eggs, sausage and hash browns. He couldn't eat it all; his eyes had been bigger than his stomach. It had shrunk from the frozen Sidecars. After eating, he got so sleepy he could barely keep his eyes open.

Vincent couldn't return to the barracks for fear of being nabbed for duty and he couldn't take the chance of missing Carla. Vincent hoped she hadn't changed. He hoped she hadn't got fat. "What if she has got fat?" he thought to himself. She wouldn't have told him, she wouldn't have told him over the phone, "I got fat since I last saw you, so if you don't like fat girls, don't come." It wasn't that he didn't like fat girls; it was he couldn't get romantic with one. Fat turned him off.

The Captain decided he would go back to the beach and take a nap in the car. He would sleep sitting up so he would not mess his hair. He drove back to the beach, parked, turned some music on the radio and quickly dozed off. Vincent slept for a couple of hours; it was almost noon when he awoke. The buzz was gone; leaving an out of sorts feeling and for Captain Moon there was one cure for every thing. He took a pull from the brandy bottle, leaving some of the brandy to dwell under his tongue. He let the rest of it trickle down his throat and into his stomach, leaving a trail of illusionary warmth and comfort. His tongue numbed, pleasantly.

Vincent started the car, and drove back to the Presidio. He parked behind his barracks in the usual place. Vincent needed to empty his bladder and change, so he took a chance and went in to the barrack. There were a few stragglers hanging around, so he felt reasonably safe from being drafted into some kind of duty. He emptied himself, washed his face and changed his shirt. It was about time for him to leave, so he lit a cigarette and started his walk to the rendezvous. He thought about Carla on the way and then he thought about Linda. He loved Linda, but he still wanted to see Carla.

CHAPTER 22

Vincent was nervous, what could he say to her? How should he act? Vincent had a half pint in his coat pocket, but he didn't want to foul his breath, not any worse than it already was, not until he saw what kind of girl she was. He had only seen her once and that seemed like forever ago. He paced back and forth, puffing on a cigarette.

Vincent stopped and listened. He heard the Jaguar before he saw it. "Huurooom," it went as she shifted gears. "Huurooom," and then he saw the front of the Jag as it came around the corner into view. The top was down and Carla's auburn hair was blowing in the wind. The Jaguar was beautiful, but he forgot all about it when he saw her face. Carla stopped the car at the curb, next to him and he got a good look at her face. The wind had accented her lovely coloring. Her cheeks were rosy, her eyes bright and blue as the sky. She was so lovely it tied his tongue.

A thought popped into Vincent's head, "What is she doing with me? She could have anyone she wants." Vincent knew he was staring, but he just couldn't get his brain into gear. He would swear her eyes were laughing at his discomfort. The only time Vincent had seen Carla she had been working and she had looked different, now she looked sophisticated. Carla looked like she belonged in a Jaguar or a Rolls. Her clothes were expensive looking, yet she looked casual. She had on a blue leather jacket that brought out the blue of her eyes, a white blouse and Navy blue skirt.

"I hope you are Vincent," she said and laughed, "and if you are, I hope you are going to get in." "I'm trying to get in," he answered, while fumbling with the door, feeling like his fingers were all thumbs, "And I am Vincent Cardoza," he told her when he finally got the door open, " And I hope you are Carla and even if you are not, I'm going to go with you, anyway."

Vincent got in and sat on the leather seat. He wasn't far from her, as the car was not very wide, no wasted space. He was close enough to her to smell her. Although he wasn't familiar with her smell, he knew that it was expensive; it was a fragrance he could get use to. His eyes were drawn to her knees; her skirt had scrunched up from driving, enough for a good peek. Carla's legs were bare. She needed nothing on them; they looked silky and smooth.

"Do I pass?" Carla asked and their eyes met. She was not embarrassed by his scrutiny of her. "You pass," he replied, "But I'm sorry I stared at you." "I'm not." she told him and "Huurooom" went the car, as it zoomed off in the wind. He watched her legs as she shifted gears, her lithe body moved well. "Where are we going?" he asked, to make conversation. "To a favorite place of mine," she told him, cheerfully, for she felt an anticipation of good. The feeling she had had for this man the very first time she had met him was still there. He wasn't tall and he wasn't that handsome, but he had something that made her heart flutter. She hoped it wasn't just physical attraction, although she knew that was part of it. Carla could see the sensuality in those dark, greenish eyes.

"Where is this favorite place?" Vincent asked, watching her lips, watching for them to move. Her lips were full and moved in such a tantalizing way. Vincent had the desire to reach out and touch them with his fingertip, to feel them as they moved. "Sausalito," she answered, with her lips forming a little pucker to get the first syllable out. Her tongue moistened her lips when she had finished. Her mouth entranced Vincent; her teeth were white, like little jewels. He smiled and nodded his approval of Sausalito, he had heard good things about it, but had never been there.

It felt great to be riding in this beautiful car with this gorgeous girl. Vincent savored the feeling like a tasty treat in his mouth, feasting on her with his eyes, all of his senses seeming new. Carla turned on the radio and he eyed her profile as they crossed the Golden Gate Bridge. He shivered from the cold wind that was blowing across the bridge. Vincent needed a shot of brandy, but resisted the temptation.

Vincent gazed at Carla's lips, they were moving. She seemed to be singing along with the music coming from the radio, but he couldn't hear her for the noise of the Jaguar, the traffic and the wind. He fantasized touching her mouth with his; he wondered what her tongue would feel like in his mouth. The thought sent a shiver of delight through, him and a hot flash of desire. Carla drove off the highway and down the winding road into downtown Sausalito. She drove around looking for a place to park, but everyone else was doing the same thing; it was the weekend and Sausalito is a favorite place of tourist.

"This is hopeless." she complained, "I'll park in Daddy's place." Vincent raised his eyebrow, "Daddy has his own special parking place in Sausalito," he thought, silently. The girl drove down into the harbor area and parked in a place marked "Private Parking." She killed the engine and told him, "He parks here when he goes to his boat." She noticed his questioning, look, "Daddy," she added. "Does he come here often?" asked Vincent, not sure of what else to say. "Not as often as he would like." she answered in a sad tone.

"He use to bring me here a lot when I was young; he took me sailing. He taught me how, but now he has no time, he is awfully busy." "Do you still go sailing?" asked Vincent. He loved boats, but had never been on a sailboat, only commercial fishing boats and skiffs. Vincent had rode the ferry from Frisco to Oakland many times when he was a boy, but that shouldn't even be considered, for they were more like a barge than anything else. "Whenever I get the chance," she answered, pleased with his interest. "Do you sail your father's boat?" Vincent asked. "Oh, no!" she exclaimed, "It's too, big for me. Sometime we sail it together, but haven't done it for a long time," she told him, wistfully.

"How big is his boat?" Vincent asked, picturing a hundred-footer; he was wondering just how loaded this guy was. "It's a fifty two foot Cheoy Lee," she answered and he digested that for a few seconds; that was a little more than half of what he had pictured. "What do you sail?" he asked, as she started to get out of the car. "I have my own boat." she answered, happily, "Daddy got it for me on my eighteenth birthday. "Of course," Vincent thought to himself. "Why would I not know that? They were both out of the car and she started to walk away from it.

"I'm starved." she proclaimed, "Let's go eat." "Aren't you going to put the top up?" he asked, thinking maybe she had forgotten. The area is patrolled," she assured him, "And anyone could get into it with a razor, anyway," she added.

Carla had a good walk, some girls don't you know. Some of them take big paces, like a farmer measuring a field. Others walk with their toes pointed out, like a duck, with their tail end waddling behind. Some walk with their toes pointed in, pigeon toed. Carla walked well; everything moved like it was supposed to.

Vincent felt comfortable with Carla and this was unusual for him, especially with a girl he didn't know. He was uncomfortable around most girls he did know. Vincent wondered if it had anything to do with astrology. He was a Taurus; he wondered what her sign was. He couldn't just come out and ask her, or could he?

"How long have you had your own boat?" he asked her, with a guileless look. "It's been a year," she told him, without thinking. Then she saw through his innocence and she grinned, "You tricked me, didn't you and now you know my age." "You surprised me," he kidded, "I thought you were close to sixteen." She giggled. "Sure you did," she answered.

Vincent still didn't know what month she was born, so he thought he would try a different approach. "I'm a Taurus," he stated, hoping she would reciprocate. "Are you bullheaded?" she asked, playfully. "No, I'm not," he answered, too, quickly. "Well, maybe a little" he added humbly. "I'm a Crab," she announced, playfully, "Didn't you notice how I walked sideways," and she laughed, and did a little, side step away from him. He immediately moved with her and was beside her again. "You can't get away from me that easily," he kidded her and she put her arm through his. "Who said I wanted to?" she replied and they walked arm in arm, feeling comfortable with each other.

"Here it is," she told him, and she steered him across a ramp, to a restaurant; it had been built on pilings, over the waters of the bay. The exterior of the building was covered with vertical, cedar siding, board and batten that had weathered to silver, gray. The interior was a good deal plusher than its rustic exterior. It had been finished in natural oak and bright Portuguese tile. They sat at a table with a Bay view. Vincent was glad she had chosen to sit inside, rather than on the deck, for he was chilled to the bone.

It was time for Captain Moon to have a drink, no matter what anybody thought, he needed it to maintain his harmony. When the waitress asked if they wanted anything from the bar, he looked at Carla, not only to see if she wanted anything, but also to read her expression. She shook her head in the negative. Vincent sensed that she would have no objection about him having anything, but he was going to order something, anyway, so it made no difference. He ordered a vodka martini, a dry one. It would be one hundred percent booze and would not be too hard on his breath. Carla changed her mind and ordered a Shirley Temple, which contains no alcohol. He wondered if she was a teetotaler.

"Tell me about yourself? Carla asked, after the waitress had left. "I'm just a poor, soldier boy from Ophir Flats," he told her, woefully, with a sigh and added," A lonely soldier boy." She shook her head, stifling a laugh. "That's the saddest story I ever heard." she told him, equally, woeful, "You should put it to music." "I can do that," he answered, for he liked to fool around with words and tunes; in his head, that is. Vincent started with it: "I'm just a poor soldier boy from Ophir Flats and every one is calling me the Sad Sack. I'm wearing khaki trousers and a short hair cut, walking twenty miles a day, no blisters on my butt." The waitress interrupted him by delivering their drinks and he stopped to take a drink. Carla was smiling in appreciation.

"That was pretty good!" she exclaimed, quietly and she gave him a little round of applause. "Awe shucks!" he exclaimed, with exaggerated humility, "Twernt nothing." A pretty girl at the adjacent table gave Vincent a sly grin. Her Gorilla gave Vincent a cold glance and Carla looked through the girl like she was transparent.

"What other talents do you have?" asked Carla, with an eyebrow raised, expectantly. "I'm a good kisser," he bragged, but was embarrassed after saying it. "Who told you that?" she asked, delighted by his apparent modesty. "A hundred beautiful virgins," he told her, casually. "Did you help them stay that way?" she asked, skeptical. "Beautiful, or virgins?" he asked. "Forget I asked," she retorted, "I don't want to know."

Carla had a serene beauty, an aura of tranquility, but she wasn't all that tranquil. It was just that she had been out with so many nerds and had been praying for her soul mate to appear. Then out of the blue comes Vincent, the first man she had felt good with, comfortable with and she didn't know a thing about him. Except, he was from Ophir Flats, wherever that is, he is in the Army and he makes her heart flutter.

"The crab salad is good," suggested Carla. She noticed he was having a hard time with the menu, but not knowing that he was suffering from a bit of a hangover. "Sounds good," replied Vincent, "but I'm not very good with raw things. No enzymes, I guess." "The crab omelet is good, too," she offered, trying to be helpful. "I think I could handle that," replied Vincent, gratefully, not liking weighty decisions when he wasn't all there. He sipped on his martini, wanting to chugalug it. Chugalugging a martini would be a sure sign of some kind of compulsive indulgence, though. It could even be considered crude.

Carla informed Vincent she wanted the crab salad and some ice tea, and he gave the waitress the order. He had the crab omelet. They talked some more trivia while waiting for their order. Vincent was watching Carla's hands while she was talking. She had long slender fingers and although she was wearing some rings, none of them looked like they had encumbered her with any kind of commitment. The skin on her fingers looked smooth, almost translucent.

Carla was using her hands expressively, like most Italians do, her gestures fluid and graceful. Her nails were not extra long, but looked manicured, painted a pinkish color, which complimented her coloring. Carla's lips were done in the same color. Her lips looked extremely kissable, with enticing curves that beckoned his with every move, causing him to purse his, and lick them.

Carla's eyes were so blue and so clear, they glistened like they were on the verge of tears and they were so alive, so animated. She captivated Vincent; her hand and lip movements charmed him. He wasn't hearing all she was saying, but seeing and feeling the movements. The waitress finally brought their order and it broke the mesmerism. Vincent smiled at Carla and she returned it.

"I'm glad you are back," she told him and he looked surprised. "Where did I go?" he asked, confused. "I don't know," she answered, "But I asked you two times why you are in the Army and you never answered."

Vincent looked down at his plate while blushing. "I'm sorry." he blurted, "I was watching your lips and hands and didn't hear you." Vincent was too honest sometimes and impulsive and now it was her turn to blush, which she did wonderfully, looking even more radiant. She had just stuck a dainty piece of salad in her mouth and was chewing it. Carla looked at him, questioning.

"Don't you like my lips?" she asked, almost sure what he said had meant he did. "I love your lips.'" he gushed and his blush got deeper. Vincent groped for more words to explain, but he could only say what he meant, "They are so kissable." Her blush got deeper, some of it from modesty, but most from pleasure. Carla loved his honesty; she knew she could believe what he said. She didn't know what else to say, she wasn't quite ready to tell him that she loved his lips also. Carla changed the subject.

"Why are you in the Army?" she asked, smiling broadly, unable to suppress her pleasure in what he had said. "I was drafted," he told her, "I am not in by choice." "Will you have to go to Korea?" she asked, worried. She had not thought too much about Korea, not having any brothers. It just popped into her head, now it seemed personal. She did not like any war, but it seemed like there always was one. "I hope not." he answered, seriously, "The thought of someone shooting at me scares me to death!" "How long will you be at Presidio?" she asked. "Only about six more weeks," he told her," Until I finish with Cook's School." "A cook?" she questioned, as she was thinking, "That should keep you away from the shooting, shouldn't it?" "I hope so," he replied and added, "They sent me to cook school because of a perforated ear drum." And then he told her about not being able to qualify on the rifle range, about having to stay a private for his whole tour of duty. "That doesn't seem fair," she told him, "But sometimes bad is good... that hole in your ear might save your life."

They talked and talked, enjoying each other to joyfulness and it seemed like lunch was over too, soon. Carla's hand was flat on the table, fooling with her napkin. Vincent reached out and put his hand over hers. It was the first time he had touched this heavenly creature. Carla's hand turned and was in his. Her hand was soft and warm, her touch pure joy, like he had touched something forbidden.

"How much time do we have today?" he asked, hopefully. "Time enough to show you my Pelican," she answered, with a wide grin. "You have a pelican?" he asked and added, "Of course you do. Why didn't I know that? You look like the sort of person who would have a pelican." He waited for her to elaborate, but when she didn't, he asked, "And where do you keep your Pelican? "I just leave her tied up," she answered. Vincent put a tip on the table for the waitress and they both got up from the table. "Is she in a yard?" Vincent asked, wondering about the wisdom of leaving a large bird tied up. He remembered seeing one in Half Moon Bay when he was a kid. It had been caught in an oil slick. He had tried to clean it but it had died.

"Oh, no!" Carla exclaimed and laughed a delightful little laugh, almost a giggle, "I leave her in the water." Vincent paid the bill and they walked out the door together. They talked as they walked back to the car and he wondered about the pelican that was tied up in the water.

"How long have you had this pelican?" Vincent asked. "A years or so," she answered, "Daddy gave her to me." "How old is your bird?" he asked, feeling foolish for some reason and she got a look of surprise on he face. Oh. No!" Carla exclaimed," she is not a bird; she is a boat. She was built in 1948 and then she broke out in a giggle. "I've been had!" he exclaimed, "The Pelican is your sail boat." "Oh, duh," she answered, and giggled some more, "I'm sorry I pulled your leg; but it was fun," she added.

"That's all right," he replied and laughed at himself, "But I will get even." "Oh, oh," she said, "That sounds like a threat." "That's right," he retorted and they were to the car as he finished his sentence. "The Pelican is in Tiburon," Carla told him, as she got into the driver's side, "it's not very far," she told him, as he sat on the leather seat. She started the car.

"Are you ready?" she asked, as she pushed in the clutch and put the Jag in gear. "I'm ready," he answered and she backed out of the space, and took off with the sleek Jaguar singing its song through every gear change. When through the gears, it purred a modulated little roar. Vincent loved the song and wanted to drive the car.

"I read about these cars," stated Vincent," They are supposed to clock a hundred and thirty two point six miles an hour, stock." She looked at him, and shook her head. "I don't know about that," she answered, "I have never had it over eighty." "At least you know you can," he retorted, watching her legs every time she shifted gears, her skirt moving up a little every time. He was thinking that even her legs looked kissable. His thoughts got hot and he pulled his eyes away from her legs and it wasn't easy to do.

Carla drove to Tiburon and to the harbor. She parked the Jaguar in a parking lot. Vincent felt like he was in high society and he liked the feeling; he felt right in place. Vincent loved sport cars and yachts, but had never been exposed to them, only vicariously, through movies and magazines. But he knew that this was his element. Vincent felt like pinching himself to make sure he wasn't dreaming.

This absolutely gorgeous girl was leading him to her yacht; could this be true? And then they were standing beside a sloop with the name "Pelican" painted across her stern. She had a wide beam and wasn't very long, no more than twenty five feet. She was a little squatty looking. Vincent would have bet that was how she got her name and Carla must have read his thoughts.

"She is squatty looking," she told him, "And that is how she got her name. She reminded me of a pelican. But she is a great little ship, easy to sail, lots of room below, comfortable and safe; not very fast, but safe." Carla took off her shoes and he did the same. "Regular shoes leave black marks on the deck," she informed him, as they boarded the Pelican. Carla unlocked the hatch, opened it and entered the boat by climbing down the little ladder. Vincent followed her.

It was fairly light in the boat with the hatch open and the light coming in the portholes. Carla gave him a tour of the Pelican, which didn't take long. Vincent was impressed by the room she had in her. There was a separate stateroom forward, a head with a little shower, a refrigerator, sink, stove and a combination eating and navigational area that contained a brass, gimbaled compass.

Vincent eyed the polished compass, enjoying the functional beauty of it. It had been suspended on gimbals so it would always be in a level position. He fondled its form as Carla sat at the table and then he sat next to her. All the interior of the boat was varnished, wood.

"It's a hunky dory little ship," commented Vincent, with appreciation, "She looks like she has everything." "She does," replied Carla, looking at him with new interest, "And she even has a diesel engine. But where did you pick up a nautical term like hunky dory?" "I came from a long line of commercial fishermen," he answered and then he told her about Cap, and his uncles.

The Pelican's subtle motion was soothing, it was making Vincent's eyes heavy and Carla noticed. She asked him if he wanted a soda, telling him she didn't have anything stronger. Vincent told her he would and was thinking he could use it to chase a drink of brandy, but he didn't tell her, wondering if he should bring the brandy out. He watched her move as she went after the sodas; he knew he wanted to spend a lot of time watching her move. When she came back with the sodas he took the half pint out of his pocket.

"Would you like a little nip to warm your tummy?" he asked Carla and she looked surprised. "What is it?" she asked, as she reached for it to inspect it. "It is brandy," Vincent told her, "I like it when I'm cold." "That's Daddy's favorite," Carla told him, "And I like it too," she told him. Vincent finished opening it and handed it to her. She took a dainty little swig from the bottle. Vincent laughed, but it was more like a giggle. "Don't drown yourself!" Vincent exclaimed in jest and she laughed.

Carla's eyes had a light of their own. She had one hand on her Coke bottle, and her other beautiful hand was resting on the table, just inches from his. Carla was thinking of how comfortable she was with Vincent, even though he did arouse her like no other man had.

Vincent was getting a stiff neck from turning to look at Carla and was trying to think of a graceful way to move. He finally gave up and just moved across from her. Vincent could no longer resist her hand and reached out; he put his hand over hers. Carla smiled without saying anything. He inspected her fingers in a caressing manner. It was arousing for both of them. Their eyes met and for a moment she was afraid of herself.

"Would you like to go sailing for awhile?" she asked him, a little, breathlessly, needing an escape. "I would love to." he answered, grateful, not wanting to make any wrong moves with her. "I'm not dressed for it, though," she informed him, "I'll have to change to some pants." Carla stood, went into the stateroom and closed the door. In a little while she came out wearing faded jeans, a turtle neck sweater and white sneakers. Vincent admired her with a once over.

"You would look good in a gunny sack," he told her. "I'm pleased that you think so," she answered, modestly, "And now we have to get underway, sailor." "But I'm not a sailor," he retorted, pretending to complain, "I'm a soldier." "You are a sailor today, soldier," she told him, in a commanding way. "Aye, aye, Captain," replied Vincent, obediently.

"What would ye have me to do?" he asked. Carla laughed, but put on a straight face. "You can turn us loose from our mooring when the time is right," ordered Carla. "Whatever that means?" questioned Vincent. "Untie our ropes, ye landlubber!" exclaimed the prettiest Captain there ever was. "But wait until I get old Betsy cranked up," she added and went to the controls. Old Betsy had been already to go, she had just been waiting for someone to push her button. Some girls are like that.

"Topside!" ordered the pretty captain, after the engine had started. Vincent followed Carla out, admiring her stern all the way up the ladder. "Do you have anymore sneakers on board, Captain Bligh?" asked Vincent, he hated going without shoes. "Some of Daddy's are here," answered Carla and she laughed and added, "But you could take up residence in them." "I guess I'll just have to be brave," answered Vincent, "And lean on my little bottle," Vincent took the brandy out and took a swig from it. He offered it to her, but she declined.

"Put that away, sailor!" she commanded, but then she had to laugh. She straightened her face after and added, "Or walk the plank." "Where is the plank?" asked Vincent in jest, "I would rather walk the plank." "Free us from our moorings, ye land lubber!" commanded the girl captain, her auburn hair wild in the wind.

"God!" thought Vincent, "She is so, beautiful." And she was beautiful with her hair blowing in the wind, her body moving in graceful motions with the boat and nature and moving Vincent's heart.

Vincent jumped off the Pelican and freed her from her moorings. He jumped back on her and they were off. When Carla got the boat clear of the dock and the other boats, she gave Vincent the wheel while she set the sails.

Vincent admired her agility and her seamanship. There wasn't much else he could do, but get in her way. After Carla got the boat going, then she was able to talk. Vincent asked her if she could navigate.

"Daddy taught me how to use the sextant," she answered, "And I have some radio equipment. But I never leave the Bay." "Why not?" Vincent asked. "No reason to," she told him, "Everything is here." "Someone told me," commented Vincent, "that if you could sail San Francisco Bay in any of its weather, you could sail almost anywhere." "I think that is probably true," she answered, "The weather out here can get pretty awful.

"Will you teach me how to sail while I am here?" he asked. "I will certainly try," she answered, "But we won't have much time for it today. I have to go to work tonight and tomorrow I will be busy. We could do some next weekend." "I'll just watch you today," he suggested. "I'll let you get away with it just this once," she replied, happily. Carla was happy. She hadn't been this happy for as long as she could remember. She knew she would be close to Vincent; she just knew it.

They sailed for a couple of hours and then they had to come about and headed for shore. When they got back in their mooring and down below, she changed her clothes. Vincent took his bottle to the dregs and there hadn't been much of it left. A half pint isn't much booze for Captain Moon. Vincent wanted to kiss Carla and he was thinking about it when she came out, but he didn't want to push her. He did have a low tolerance for temptation, though. He was a straightforward kind of person, though, no guile, whatever.

"Can I kiss you now?" he asked, a little clumsily, he put his hand on her shoulder. "I was hoping that you would," she told him and her lips were soft, so soft. Her lips were yielding, her kiss the sweetest and he was gentle. Her closeness made him feel giddy and he pulled away from her, gently. "When can I see you again?" he asked, in a husky whisper. "Come to the restaurant tomorrow night at nine," she told him, with lips that were not yet satisfied. Carla kissed him again, one for the road.

END OF PART ONE

CHAPTER 23

It was Sunday morning and Private Cardoza had a whole day and part of the night before he could see Carla. This lovely creature, this girl he could not get off his mind, this dream he saw when awake, or asleep. Vincent could hardly contain himself. How could he get through the whole day and part of the night? Anticipation was burning a hole in his heart.

It was a wonderful, San Francisco day, a gusto day, with a gusty breeze and a bright, cheerful sun. Vincent felt half good, which was a few notches above normal for him and he could always make himself feel better. It was in the wee hours of the morning, but Vincent was already to go. He left the Presidio in a hurry; nothing was going to keep him away from Carla, at least not some unforeseen, duty.

Carla was still in bed, her perfect body prone, between rose colored sheets. Her head, covered with glorious auburn curls, was resting on a large, down filled, silk covered pillow; the same color as her sheets. Carla's gown which was almost nothing was also silk; and so too, her matching panties. Both the gown and panties were pink, but the gown had a rose colored ribbon around its off the shoulder, neck.

Carla felt wonderful. She felt alive, gloriously alive. The silk felt sensuous against her skin. She made a feline like, stretch and thought of Vincent. Carla remembered his eyes, clearly, dark, greenish, brooding, laughing, flirting and sensuous, they were. She remembered his long lashes, lashes that curled up on the ends. Carla had to use eye make-up to make her lashes longer, but he didn't need it. Her perfect eyebrows looked like they had been plucked to a perfect point. Give a girl break.

Unconsciously, she touched her breast with her fingers. It brought a rush of blood to her face and to her loins; she had fantasized that it was Vincent who had touched her. Then she didn't know what to do with her hands, for every time she touched herself, the same thing happened. Carla

225

wondered what she would feel like if he really had touched her. She gave in to her fantasy and caressed her body with her fingers, pretending they were his.

It was hypnotic as her fingers traced over her breast, fondling her nipples. Carla closed her eyes as sensuality took over her senses. She squirmed as desire filled her. Her hand went down across her belly and touched her pubic area. Carla groaned as she squeezed her thighs together, compounding her sexual excitement.

Carla jumped out of her bed and went to the window, looking out, trying to control her thoughts. She felt so sensual; it was hard to distract her self. Carla continued to look out her window, which was on the second floor of her family's Victorian mansion. She looked out over Land's End and the ocean. The sky was clear enough to see China, but the horizon got in the way. Carla concentrated on the horizon and the scope of her view helped to cool her a little. She turned and walked toward the shower, losing her apparel along the way, leaving a trail of pink on the thick, oyster white, shag.

Carla had to walk through her dressing room to get to her shower. She stopped and looked at her reflection in the full length, mirror. She was aware that she was pretty, but she was self-conscious about looking at her naked self, especially while she had Vincent on her mind. It was almost as If he could see her through her eyes. Carla continued to look at herself, feeling naughty about it.

"Such a prude you are," she told herself and made herself take a closer look. She examined her breast and her flat tummy, wishing that she had a tan all over. The sharp contrast between the pale of her breast and pubic area to the rest of her was noticed. Carla sucked in her tummy and let it out; deciding it was okay. She turned to look at her fanny, inspecting it for droop and there wasn't any.

"Vincent will like me," she commented to herself and then she blushed and hurried away from the mirror. She was embarrassed that she had already contemplated Vincent seeing her naked when she barely knew him. Carla was still a virgin. She believed it was important that she save herself for her wedding night. She was a good Catholic and she wanted a big, Catholic wedding. Her parents could afford it and she wanted it. So far, she had not even come close to losing her virginity; no one had turned her on that much, until now. Carla was not sure she would be able to say no to Vincent. She would have to be careful with him.

Vincent was nervous, with that "Ants in the pants" feeling. He decided he would like to sit in a nice bar somewhere and have a few shots of blackberry brandy to sweeten his stomach. But then he decided he would rather sit in a skid row bar. For some perverse reason, Vincent always felt comfortable in a skid row bar, especially early in the morning, as they were the only ones open. It had not yet reached the eight hundred hour. Vincent knew he could find one of these dives on Mission Street. He drank a warm beer in his car and then he drove there. It didn't take long for him to find the joint he was looking for, it was like he had a built in homing device. Vincent parked, walked across the street and walked through the swinging doors.

They all smelled the same, these places, like stale beer and yesterday. Yesterday could not be washed or disinfected away. Yesterday was here to stay. Vincent guessed that was why one always thought in reverse in one of these places. No one thinks of tomorrow in yesterday's place, yesterday's time warp.

The bartender was female and she was a tough looking, broad. She looked like a construction worker, or a logger. The smoke was thick and she was playing razzle-dazzle with a guy. He looked three sheets to the wind. She left her game in limbo to wait on Vincent. He ordered blackberry brandy; she got it for him and went back to her game.

The joint was busy but it was a quiet crowd. Most of them were just trying to get well and most of them were probably thinking about yesterday. Not Vincent, though, he was thinking about the future, mainly, tonight. He wondered what would happen. He had kissed her and she, definitely, had kissed him back with lips that had been soft, sweet and yielding. Vincent thought about Linda for a moment. He did love her, but she was a girl and Carla is a woman. "What an exciting woman she is," he told himself, under his breath. Vincent was aware that Carla was high class; she was not like any girl he had ever known. He was going to have to treat her different.

He thought about the half pint. He would not be able to pull that routine regularly, yet he never knew when he would need to. Vincent thought of a flask. If he could find a pretty one it would seem more refined. Maybe he could find one at a pawnshop. When he ordered another drink he asked about a pawnshop. He was told there was one three blocks up the street, on the others side. He was told that it would be open in an hour.

Vincent was grateful his mother had been sending him a few dollars. She knew his pay from the Army was not enough. He knew he spent too much on booze, but he had kept his cost down by buying most of it at cut-rate stores. Vincent tried not to spend too much in bars. Vincent thought that if he could find a flask, he could buy his brandy in the big bottle and funnel it into the flask. He could keep the big bottle in the trunk of his car. He knew he could save money that way, if he didn't drink it too fast.

Vincent had a few more shots of the sweet brandy and then he walked to the pawnshop. He found several flask and one had a pretty silver cover. Vincent bought it and then he went to a liquor store, where he bought a quart of Christian Brothers Brandy. It wasn't high priced, but it was good stuff. He also found a small funnel and bought it.

Vincent decided to go to Golden Gate Park, where the first thing he did was fill his silver flask. Then he took a big swig from the bottle before putting the cap back on. After that he went to the aquarium and the zoo. His favorites were the gators, snakes, big cats, apes and the monkeys. Being early Sunday morning, the park was not crowded, but there were a few early birds.

Vincent drove around for a while, doing some girl watching. A windy day in San Francisco is great for that if you like to watch girls fighting to keep their skirts down and some of them don't even try. It is said that some of the prettiest legs in the world live in San Francisco, where climbing the steep hills keeps them trim. And that isn't all that makes it a special place, for variety is there, all kinds of girls, all colors, shapes and size.

Vincent was in a holiday spirit. He was dressed casual; he didn't have many different things to wear. Levis were his usual fare and that was what he was wearing, along with a yellow polo shirt and a brown, leather jacket just in case it got cold. Vincent was wearing his penny loafers and his flask was in his coat pocket. It would be the last thing that he would forget. Vincent spotted some kite fliers with a large dragon kite in the sky and it was way up there. He parked the car so he could watch. He stood under a tree, which had large, shiny leaves. It had flowers that smelled sweet and they were white.

Vincent pulled out his silver flask and opened it, holding it in a possessive manner, enjoying his ownership. He was that way with his things, not really wanting to share them. He held the opened flask under his nose, savoring the pungent aroma. It was startling at first whiff. Vincent took a sip and let it run under his tongue, where he held it and enjoyed the numbing sensation. He could feel the affect of the alcohol being absorbed by his flesh, adulterating his blood stream.

Vincent let the brandy trickle down his throat without swallowing. After, he enjoyed its warm trail to his stomach. He took a big pull from the flask and swallowed it. Vincent truly enjoyed his spirits and didn't know if he could do without. He did not want to find out. There was only one kind of booze he didn't like and that was Scotch. It tasted like rotten wood and it gave him instant heartburn. But the rest of the spirits, he loved them all. One might even say that he worshiped them. Many people do, one might even call it idolatry.

The fliers of the dragon kite were oriental and they knew what they were doing. The kite was getting smaller and smaller; looking like it was going to find its way to Heaven. One of the groups was a teenage girl. She was lovely, delicate looking, with fine legs and a fine behind. She was great to watch from the waist, down, but she was almost flat breasted. She had long, raven hair and a doll like, face. "Too, bad about the chest," Vincent told himself.

Vincent got hungry for a hot dog, so he drove to look for a stand. He found one on wheels and bought two dogs with everything on them. Vincent was glad he had the brandy with him; he would not have been able to eat them without it. They would have been uncomfortable in his stomach. He gobbled them down, chasing them with the brandy.

Vincent was grateful he had made it through basic training. During that period, all he had been able to get to drink of the alcohol variety had been beer. It had not had sufficient punch to suit Captain Moon. One would have to drink a barrel of it to get a buzz on.

During the basic training period, Vincent had been introduced to C-Ration cigarettes. These cigarettes were free. Although they were national brands, they had had a lot of shelf time and smoked dry and hot. Although everyone got these cigarettes for free, there were many moochers. One could borrow cigarettes from friends, but they had to be good friends. Everyone had got into the habit of putting C-Ration smokes in one pocket and good ones in the other. Moochers got the C-Rations. Habitual moochers got jaded after awhile and would not accept the C-Rations, they would just move on to the next victim.

Vincent had a lot of time to kill. He got tired of wandering around in the park, so he went back to the Zoo. He wanted to watch the monkeys some more. They looked like malformed, ugly, dirty little people. They ran around like chickens with their heads cut off, chasing each other, scratching at fleas. Vincent watched the monkeys for a while and then he walked around the zoo. Vincent got tired and got it into his head that he would like to sit in a dark lounge, sip on some Martinis and listen to some soft music. He drove to the Cliff House area, found a cocktail lounge, parked and went in. The lounge was not as dark as he wanted, but it was a bar and he could always close his eyes if he wanted to be in the dark.

At first he was going to find a booth, but changed his mind, wanting to keep himself company, he could do it in the bar mirror. Vincent found a lonesome stool and bellied up to the bar. He looked at his reflection in the bar mirror and was comfortable. He liked to drink with his reflection; it gave him a feeling of security. He was comfortable with himself; he never intimidated himself. The bartender walked up to Vincent; he looked like a bartender, with his black, bow tie and his maroon vest. He also sounded like one.

"What's your pleasure?" he asked, amiably, his mustache twitching, just like David Niven's. "A very dry Martini," replied Vincent "A good choice," commented the bartender and he quickly put one together with finesse, making his job look like an art. Quite a few hours and quite a few Martinis later, Captain Moon was a mellow, fellow. He decided he had better get the Hell to somewhere else while he could still navigate. He got up and walked out, grateful that he wasn't staggering. One would not know by looking at him that he had been drinking for hours, but his breath would probably ignite if a flame came close. Captain Moon was feeling no pain. He wasn't feeling much of anything, but good. But he was no fool, He knew he had to play it cool, or he could ruin his date with Carla and he was not about to do that.

Captain Moon didn't get stupid drunk, not usually. Vincent got happy drunk, unless he were to start out depressed and then he would just get more depressed. That does not mean he never did stupid things when he was drunk. For instance, like standing up while riding the roller coaster, which he had done and had came close to falling off. Vincent did like to do dangerous things when he was drunk. He didn't go looking for them, but did them impulsively. If a situation were to present itself, so be it. One time he raced a train to the crossing, and it had been a close race. It had been much too, close. If it had been any closer he would have had to change his pants. One race with a train had been more than enough.

Vincent still had a few hours to burn before he could see Carla. He walked down the hill toward the beach to let the cold ocean breeze clear his head. After he felt refreshed, he walked to a restaurant, where he ate a cheeseburger, and some fries, which helped to soak up the Martinis. When he had finished, he walked back to the car and drove it to the beach. He walked the beach anticipating Carla until it was time to go.

Vincent drove to Fisherman's Wharf and parked the car in a parking lot. He walked to Maggio's. He was about a half hour early, so he went into the lounge and sat at the bar. He had the bartender get him a bottle of Miller High Life beer, which he nursed while waiting for Carla. He was seated next to the place where the waitress picked up her orders. When the waitress came, Vincent asked her to tell Carla he was waiting for her. He nursed his beer while his anticipation grew. He thought of Carla, of her blue, eyes, lavish curies, of her slender, body, and of her kiss. He wanted to kiss her again and as soon as possible.

Vincent was lost in thought, when he suddenly realized that he was looking at Carla's reflection in the mirror. This vision of loveliness was coming toward him. Her lips were turned up at the corners with a smile, lips that had been created for smiling, laughing, and kissing. Vincent turned and she was standing in front of him, she was still smiling.

"I'm glad that you are punctual, she told him, "I'm glad you didn't make me wait like you did the first time. "I'll always regret that" he replied, sincerely, as Carla's face was a mirror of her thoughts, no guile there. "Well," she answered, followed by a musical laugh, "Maybe we can make up for it." Vincent was delighted with her candor and the way she looked. Carla was wearing a black cocktail dress of some soft looking material that went just below her knees. There was black lace above the bodice, at the cuff of the half-sleeves and around the hem. She wore a strand of pearls around her lovely neck.

Vincent had the urge to smell her neck, for he knew that was where the delicious aroma of her perfume was coming from; an area most compelling, like all of her areas. Pearl earrings were hanging from her pretty ear lobes, on dainty gold chains. Vincent wondered what her ear lobes tasted like. Carla was wearing high heels, but Vincent was still taller. Vincent realized he was still sitting on the stool. He felt foolish while getting off of it and grateful that he was still inches taller. Vincent looked her over. He started a low, wolf whistle, but didn't finish it.

"That is some uniform!" he exclaimed, "Is that what you wear to work?" "Of course," she replied, "I'm the hostess." "Of course you are" he retorted, "I knew that." "I'm glad you came," she told him and he knew that she meant it. "I hope you are as glad as I am," he answered and she smiled. "I'm gladder," she replied, still smiling. "No." he argued, "I'm gladdest." "Are we having our first quarrel?" she asked, laughing lightly. "I hope so," he answered, hopefully. "But, why?" she asked, wondering what he was up to. "Cause then we can kiss and make up," he replied. "Oh, you are a sly one," she told him.

"Can we go somewhere else?" he asked, hopefully. "It's a nice night," she answered, "We could go for a little drive for a starter. "In your car, I hope," answered Vincent, "I do not want you to even see mine." "The kind of car you drive makes no difference to me," she told him and he knew that it was true. She turned and started to walk away, "Follow me," she told him. "I would follow you anywhere," he told her and followed. "You better wear a coat," he told her, "It is cold outside."

Following Carla was a pleasant thing to do, for her movements were both graceful and enticing. Vincent was graceful, but when he was following her, he felt like he had two left feet. Vincent followed her out the rear of the lounge, down a hall, to an office. The office was small, but plush.

"This is mine," she told him, with an Italian flourish, but she wasn't bragging, she said it like she was grateful for it. "It is my home away from home," she added. Carla slid one of the closet doors open, which was a full length, mirror. She took out a coat, one of at least a dozen. Vincent helped her put it on. Her nearness and her perfume were heady, causing a stir, which he feared might be perpetual whenever he was close to her. The coat was soft black leather. The collar, cuffs and around the hem, was black fur, the soft looking kind you want to stroke. Vincent thought she looked like a movie star. She was facing him now; she had her hands by her side.

"Do I look alright?" she asked and Vincent shook his head. "You got to be kidding me!" he exclaimed, "Are you sure you want to be seen with me?" he asked. Carla laughed and pulled on his arm. "Come on," she said, "Let's go get my car," and she led him to the exit and to a private parking area at the rear of the building. Vincent spotted Carla's Jaguar and eyed it, maybe a little enviously. The lighting was bright and Carla saw his look.

"Thou shalt not covet thy neighbors car." she kidded him. "I wish I was!" he exclaimed and she didn't know what he had meant. "You wish you were what?" she asked "Your neighbor, he answered and she smiled, pleased. "How sweet you are," she told him, and he wanted to say, "I know," but he stopped himself and just in time. It had been on the tip of his tongue. He was grateful he hadn't said it. "Where is your car?" Carla asked him and when he told her, she suggested he go get it and pull it in to her space when she pulled out. He was embarrassed for her to see his car, but he went and got it anyway and did what she had suggested. He walked over to the Jaguar and got in.

"I need some air," she told him, "Let's go for a drive with the wind in our hair." The top was already down, so there was nothing to do but go. "Let's go to Half Moon Bay," she suggested, "it's a nice drive." "I know," replied Vincent, "I use to live there when I was a little boy. I do have an Aunt, and uncle who still live there." "Do you want to go by and see them?" she asked, hoping he didn't. "It would be too, late for them," he answered.

Vincent was glad she was driving. In the day light, with the help of maps, he could find his way around, but at night, forget It. Somehow they ended up going by the Presidio, down Fulton to the beach and then they started down the coast. It was a lovely ride in the Jaguar, watching Carla's hair blowing in the wind, listening to the music on the radio and the roar of the dual, overhead cam engine.

Vincent was just about to turn blue, though, by the time they got where they were going. Vincent wasn't very well insulated for the cold. He was in dire need of a shot of brandy. He hadn't brought his flask out, he had been afraid of spilling it in the car. When she parked at the beach, he pulled out his silver, flask, and offered it to her. "This will thaw out your toes," he told her and she took it gratefully. "It is cold!" she exclaimed, through chattering teeth. "Maybe we should put the top up," she added and then she took a dainty pull from the flask. Carla took another before she handed it back.

"Where did you get the pretty flask?" she asked and then she felt the brandy hit her stomach. "Mmmm, that feels so good." Carla told him. By that time the flask was at his lips and the brandy was feeling good on its way to his stomach. "I bought it yesterday at a pawn shop," he answered, "But I'll bet your dad drinks better booze." He then felt stupid for saying booze. "Daddy loves French cognac," she replied, "But this is good and it makes me feel warm." "It is all an illusion," commented Vincent, "But who cares?" "It is making me hungry," she told him, "And I want to dance." "I like the way you think," he replied, "But where do we go?" "We have friends who own a restaurant here," she told him. "But we have to hurry to get there before they close," and with that said, she started the car and peeled out. "It is just down the road a ways," Carla told him.

The road was curvy and went down by the harbor. Carla pulled into the driveway of the restaurant. It was on the other side of the road from the ocean. It was an old, handsome building, with many French windows, a painter's nightmare. It had one floor, and was white, with a green trim. The paint was weathered, with the green showing oxidation, giving it a look of weathered copper. The place looked expensive and Vincent was worried about the tab. Carla seemed to be reading his thoughts.

"Ernie won't let us pay," she told Vincent," And we never let him pay when he comes to our place." They walked into the restaurant and the place was fairly dark, but Ernie spotted Carla right away. Ernie was about the same size as Vincent and he was handsome, in a dark, Portuguese way. He came straight for Carla, with his arms out, his face cracked open with a grin, with one eyebrow raised, the other drooping with a lazy eye.

"Carla, Carla!" Ernie exclaimed, as he came rushing to her, "My beautiful Carla," and then he had her in a bear hug. He looked to be about fifty, with a smidgen of gray hair at his temples. Vincent could see that Carla was just as glad to see him. "Where have you been, my little chickadee?" he asked, stepping back and kissing her hand. "I'm still working for Daddy," she told him and then she introduced Vincent.

"You are such a lucky guy," Ernie told Vincent, "I wish I was you." "We just met, Uncle Ernie." pleaded Carla, with a flushed face, she had always called him that ever since she was old enough to talk. "That don't mean anything," claimed Uncle Ernie, "I can see how you feel. Carla's face flushed again, for she hadn't known that her feelings were showing. "Vincent is in the Army" Carla told him, in an effort to change the subject, "Learning to be a cook." Ernie got a sly grin on his face and looked at Carla, squeezing her shoulders with his hands. "And I'll bet he is cooking already," he said and wiggled his eyebrows, compounding Carla's blush. Vincent was also getting a little red in the face. "Stop that!" exclaimed Carla, "You wicked old devil!" And then Carla laughed and so did Ernie. "Come," said Ernie, "I have a cozy table for you," and he led them to it and lit the candle. "Whatever you want is on the house," he told them with a generous gesture of his hand. He seated Carla and threw her a kiss as he left, "I'll come back," he told them.

"You seem to inspire affection," commented Vincent. "I have known Uncle Ernie all of my life," replied Carla. "You haven't known me all your life," retorted Vincent and she looked at him through long lashes, knowing what he had meant, but not sure of what to say. She was feeling affection, too and a little impetuous.

"Let's dance a little before we eat," Carla suggested, she was feeling the low, soft music that was coming from somewhere. There was no band.

They got up and walked to the small dance floor and started dancing to what sounded like the Glen Miller Band. It was easy and they fitted together like peas in a pod, their bodies feeling each other, getting use to each other and after a while, wanting each other.

There were two other couples dancing. Vincent and Carla were dancing alone, oblivious of the others, acutely aware of each other. When the music stopped, they kept dancing, but a little slower. When they finally stopped, they just stood in each other's arms, lost in each other. The spell was broken by a woman's laughter and Carla blushed. She hadn't known Vincent long enough to feel this way. They separated and strolled back to their table, both deep in thought.

"You children look like you were made for each other," commented Ernie, seeming like he had appeared out of thin air. "You are just a hopeless romantic," retorted Carla. "Thank God for that." replied Ernie, making a cross on his chest, like a good Catholic. He took their order and got himself out of the way again. Carla had the Chef's Salad and Vincent had prawns. The couple had a quiet meal, saying very little, feeling a little self-conscious. They lost that feeling after a few more dances and somehow, they ended up at the Pelican.

CHAPTER 24

Carla and Vincent took off their shoes and held them in their hands as they boarded the good ship, Pelican. It was well after midnight, but they were both reluctant to say goodnight, and they wanted to talk more. It was too, cold to sit in the car and neither one wanted any company; they had gone to the Pelican. It was cold in the boat, so Carla lit the oil heater and they huddled around it until they had warmed up. Carla left on the heater and lit the stove.

"Want some tea?" Carla asked. "Sounds good to me," answered Vincent, planning to lace it with some brandy. It was warmer now and they moved to the table and sat facing each other. They talked for a while of nothing until the teakettle whistled and Carla got up and made the tea.

"Sugar?" she asked. "Two teaspoons," he answered and she brought it to the table and sat back down. Vincent brought out his flask. He laced her tea with brandy after she had agreed with a nod. "And some for Captain Moon," said Vincent, as he laced his tea. He had said it without thinking; it had just come out of his mouth. She laughed, more of a giggle, not knowing why. "Who Is Captain Moon?" she asked, her curiosity piqued. "He is me," answered Vincent, wishing he had not mentioned his alter ego, but now he had to go ahead and explain it to her. When he had finished the silly story, she giggled. "I knew there was something different about you!" she exclaimed and laughed because of the mental pictures she was having. Her hand went to his and then their hands were holding intimately. They both felt the heat and she squirmed. They locked eyes and conversation ceased. Carla's lips parted.

Vincent rose from his seat halfway, leaned over the table and kissed her on her mouth. Her mouth was soft and open. The kiss swept them into passion. She wanted to stop herself, but couldn't. She told herself she would stop in a moment, as her body rose from the seat by a power of its own. In a moment they were standing with their bodies pressed together, trying to get closer, lost in a passion. Finally they had to break to catch their breath, their lips reluctant to part. She took a deep breath and buried her face in his chest, embarrassed with her self.

"I have never felt like this before!" exclaimed Carla, "What must you think of me?" "I think you are the most beautiful girl in the world." he answered, in a whisper, as his lips caressed her ear lobe. "And I have never felt this way before either." He ran his fingers through her curls and then he buried his face in the luxury of them. He breathed in her fragrance and then he was kissing her neck, wanting her so badly he felt weak in the knees.

Carla wanted to be a virgin on her wedding night; she just had to be. She had always feared that if she were not, her marriage would be a flop. But somehow their bodies ended up on the bunk. She was halfway under him, with his right leg between hers. They were lost in passion as he caressed her breast.

"Oh, God, Vincent!" she moaned, "I'm a virgin." She stopped to get her breath and then went on. "And I have to be one on my wedding night," she told him breathlessly. Vincent could feel her heart pounding like a hammer. He knew she was afraid. He stopped for a moment and put his face in her breast. He could smell her perfume and her body. His leg was still between hers, his erection pressing against her leg.

Vincent moved to pull away, but then his right hand was on her hip, almost on her lovely behind. Vincent could not stop himself. His hand moved and he was caressing the lovely mounds of her behind. While he was caressing, her dress was working its way up her hips. His hand moved under her dress. Vincent felt the silk of her panties. His hand moved along the edge of her panties and then went under the edge, touching her flesh. Carla squirmed and moaned as he caressed her bare bottom, running his fingers between her cheeks. It tickled her and a shudder went through her body.

Vincent moved his leg from between hers and put his hand on the inside of her thigh. Her flesh was unbelievably smooth and warm. He caressed her there and her thighs opened for him. His hand moved up and was almost touching her most intimate place. She moaned, softly.

"If you touch me there I will not be able to stay a virgin," she whispered in a voice reflecting the struggle with herself. Vincent tried to stop his hand from going any further, but he had never been able to discipline himself successfully. Vincent's hand moved on to her mound, where she was soft, warm and open. She was crying softly, but her body was responding to his search. His hand went inside her panties, and he touched her where he should not. She moaned and moved her body to his hand.

Somewhere in Vincent's subconscious, Vincent's lust for her had been subordinated by his sympathy and his sympathy had softened his erection. Not wanting her to know of his plight, he forced his hand away. He embraced her and kissed her hair. Vincent held her in his arms and Carla snuggled to him, ashamed to say anything. Finally, she asked him why he had stopped. He kissed the tears on her cheeks. "I couldn't hurt you. You told me you wanted to be a virgin on your wedding night and you were crying."

"I'm sorry; "Carla wailed, "But I do want my wedding night to be special," and she was crying again. "You must think I'm an awful fool." "I don't think that at all," he consoled and then they were silent for a while, while she clung to him. He broke the silence, softly. "I hope I will be the one you share your wedding night with," he whispered, with his lips on her ear, tasting her. "I hope so too." she replied, impulsively and turned his head, and kissed his lips. She sighed and they were silent for a moment.

"Oh, Vincent!" she exclaimed, "I think you just proposed to me." "And I think you just accepted?" he answered, with a questioning look. "I did!" she answered in wonder, "And I hardly know you." They pondered this magic for a moment. "I do know that I'm in love with you," Carla told him and hesitated for a moment. She continued, "I think it was love at first sight. When I first met you; do you think that is possible?" Vincent felt ashamed. He knew that if it had not been for his impotence, he would not have been able to stop himself from taking advantage of her passion. And here he was, letting her believe that it was his goodness that had saved her. He was totally ignorant of the fact that it had been his sympathy and goodness that had caused his impotence in the first place.

"I believe in love at first sight," he told her and kissed her face all over, passionately. Then their lips connected and they were lost in passion again. They kissed until Vincent could stand it no longer. "Oh, sweetheart." he moaned, "We just have to get out of here. I just don't know how long I can resist you." "I know exactly how long I can resist you," answered Carla, softly, with her lips on his throat, "Just until my next heart beat."

Vincent gently separated himself from her. She looked down, and saw that her dress was up to her waist. She blushed and Vincent saw it. He put his hand on the inside of her thigh and caressed her there. "You have the prettiest legs I have ever seen," he told her, "It's going to be hard waiting to see the rest of you." He pulled her dress down and stood up, pulling her up into his arms. They stood that way for a long time, reluctant to separate.

"We have to go," he finally told her. "I know," she answered, "But I wish we were both going to the same place." "I know," he answered. They left the Pelican and walked to the Jaguar. "I'm too, dreamy to drive," she told him, while they stood in front of the car in each other's arms, "Would you drive us?" she asked. "I don't know if I can take my eyes off of you," he answered, "But I will try."

Carla gave Vincent the keys and they got into the car. Vincent started the engine. He could feel the power with his body, but it wasn't as exciting as he had anticipated. Any excitement would be mild after the excitement Carla had caused him and was still causing. He wondered if he would ever lose his erection, now that it had returned. She put her hand on his thigh and he knew that he would not lose it while he was still with Carla.

The remaining weeks of school were dwindling. Vincent knew he would have to return to Fort Ord for assignment when it was over. He had no idea where the assignment would take him. He saw Carla almost every night and his wanting her was at the desperate stage. She was all that he could think about.

The lovers tried to think of places to go and things to do that would keep them from having too much petting time. The two went to a lot of places up and down the coast, as far south as Pismo Beach. They had wonderful times traveling in the Jaguar. It was especially nice when the weather was nice enough to have the top down. Sometimes Vincent would drive and he loved driving the Jaguar. But he loved it more when Carla drove, for then he could watch her. He loved to watch her hair blowing in the wind; the way she would sweep it out of her face with a feminine movement of her hand.

It gave Vincent exquisite pleasure to watch her face when she talked. The way her lips went up at the corners when she smiled, the way she threw her head back when she laughed out loud. Vincent's eyes followed her body when she shifted gears, the way her legs moved when she pushed in on the clutch; the way her skirt would move up, exposing her lovely knees and sometimes a delicious peek at the inside of her thigh. Sometimes, when that happened, he would have to touch her there.

Every movement that Carla made was seductive to Vincent, even though they were not intentionally meant to be so. Every moment that he spent with her, Vincent wanted her and it seemed like no matter what they did, they would end up at the Pelican, where they wanted to make love, but had not.

One Saturday night, a week before the end of Vincent's Cooking class, he had dinner with Carla and her parents. Carla had been an only child, which was unusual for an Italian family. Carla's mother, for medical reasons, had beer unable to bare any more children. Carla's mother, Rosa, was being her usual, jovial self.

Rosa was a big woman, in body and heart. She had a beautiful, infectious smile that lit up her face and the room that she was in. Sometime she spoke in Italian to her family and Vincent could not understand, but it sounded pretty to him. He was use to it, for Mario's family had done the same thing.

Carla's father, Tony Maggio, was totally different than his wife. She was earthy, like a peasant, while he had the bearing of an aristocrat. Tony was always in a tailored suit. His back was straight as a plank. He had silver hair, with a mustache to match, but it didn't detract from his youthful, vigorous, countenance.

Tony's face was stern but there was a twinkle in his eyes that sometimes exposed his second nature. When it came to business, Tony was one hundred percent, business. When it came to play, he was one hundred percent, play. There was no half way for him. He loved his wine and loved it even more when it had been distilled, aged into his favorite spirits, cognac. The older it was, the better Tony liked it and he could afford the old.

Tony had inherited a shipping line from his father. It had been close to ruin, but he had built it back to a successful line. He was still President of the Board, but the line almost ran itself. Tony liked the restaurant business and that was the only reason he was in it, he didn't need the money.

Carla didn't work because she had to; she worked because she wanted to and because her father had told her that work builds character. She was planning on going to college, but had yet to decide what her career was going to be. Now there was Vincent and he was filling her mind.

Vincent had met Carla's parents at a previous dinner, so the atmosphere was relaxed and congenial. After they had all filled on delicious food and wine, they moved to the living room for after dinner brandy. The conversation moved to Korea and Communism. Mr. Maggio was a fervent, anti-Communist; he was all for stringing them all up by their toes and worse things.

They talked some about sailing. Tony talked about some of the trips they had made to Moro Bay, The Puget Sound, Mazatlan and landfall in Paradise, Hawaii. It was Interesting for Vincent, for Carla had been teaching him how to sail. He learned how to tack against the wind, how to operate the winches, where the gunwale was, which was port and starboard.

Vincent had been fantasizing sailing trips with Carla. Vincent was good with mechanical things. He had been able to help Carla with some of the problems on the Pelican. Vincent had not had much experience with diesel engines. But he did know the difference between a gas engine and a diesel and had been able to help with the minor engine problems.

They talked until they were ready to go. Carla and Vincent went for their usual ride and ended up, as usual, at the Pelican. They had spent a lot of hours on the Pelican, sweet tortured nights of wanting and not having. They were again, starting the passion that can melt fortitude. They were standing and had just finished a long, slow, kiss, which passion had made their legs fluid. They sat on the edge of the forward bunk, which was curved to the shape of the hull. The Pelican was moving a little, a soothing motion. They were both silent for a few moments. Carla was wearing a peasant type outfit, with a white, off the shoulder blouse and a full, brightly patterned, skirt. Her feet and legs were bare. Vincent was wearing jeans, a polo shirt and his feet were bare.

"We just have to get married!" exclaimed Vincent, with a soft, intensity. His hands were making a gesture of frustration. "I love you!" he exclaimed, with passion, "I just have to see you. I just have to make love to you." He was kissing her throat, then the cleavage of her breast. She ran her fingers through his hair and then she pulled his face up and smothered it with passionate, kisses. "Oh, God!" she exclaimed, "I want you too, but Mamma will want a big, church wedding and that could take months." Carla concluded with a sigh.

Vincent was burning with desire, he spoke low, but intense. "I have to leave in a week," he told her, "And I don't know when I will see you again. I don't know how I can stand it." A long sigh escaped from him. "I know!" Carla wailed and then their lips were together. They lay together on the bunk, their bodies pressing together, desperately trying to be one. His hand went under her blouse and he caressed her breast.

"I just have to look at you." Vincent told her as he raised her blouse. She raised her arms and he pulled the blouse off over her head. He could see her eyes in the dim light. They were open wide, desire shining in them. The desire had melted her resistance.

"I hope you like me," she whispered, as she reached back and unsnapped her bra. He removed it the rest of the way, his eyes absorbing her. He caressed her breast with his eyes and then with his fingertips and then with his lips. His tongue tasted her nipples and a shiver of delight went through her. Vincent kissed her down to her belly and he tasted her navel with his tongue. Carla started pulling his shirt off and he helped her. She ran her fingers through the hair on his chest. She pulled him down on her, his bare chest against her bare breast. They kissed hungrily.

"I have to see the rest of you." he panted. Her skirt was elastic at the top. He pulled it down, and off of her. Her slip came off with it revealing her long lovely legs and her panties. "Do you like me?" she asked, meekly, as he touched the inside of her thigh. You are beautiful," he told her, as he caressed the inside of her thigh. "I want to see you," she told him and he stripped to his shorts. She caressed his leg and then he was laying next to her again, halfway on her, with his leg between hers. Their lips met again and their bellies, with perspiration where their flesh touched.

And then he was exploring again. He explored her with his eyes and fingertips. His fingers went along the top of her panties, down the inside of her thighs, to her knees. Her leg was raised as he caressed the underside of her knee and then the underside of her thigh. Vincent ran his fingertip along the lower edge of her panties, across the front and then his hand was resting on her mound. She was soft and he pressed her there. Carla moaned and put her hand over his, helping his pressing her there.

Vincent moved his hand to the top of her panties, lifted the edge and moved his hand inside. His hand moved down until he was touching her pubic hair and then he was touching her intimate place. She moved her body to his fingers. He got on his knees and pulled her panties down and off. He gazed at her naked body.

"I want you to roll over," he told her and gently helped her. "Why?" she asked, as she rolled over and the voluptuous curves of her behind were revealed. "So I can see what you look like on this side," he answered, while running his fingers down the small of her back and then over her cheeks, exploring the cleavage. "Do you like my back side?" she asked "I love all your sides," he answered and then his lips were on her behind, kissing her curves. The closeness of her intimate places filled Vincent with a lust he had never experienced. He rolled her back over and then he was kissing the inside of her thighs. Carla was almost overcome with excitement over what he was doing.

"Oh, God, Vincent!" she moaned and she was breathing rapidly, "What are you doing to me?" And then his tongue was in her. Carla could not contain herself and was writhing with excitement. Her fingers were in his hair and she couldn't help but press his face to her. She could not stand the excitement any longer.

"Let me see what you look like." she pleaded and she wasn't meek anymore. As he got up off of his knees, Carla pulled his shorts down. She touched him, felt the shape of him and his hardness. "Touch me with it," she pleaded and laid back, her thighs open. Vincent took his shorts the rest of the way off and then he was between her thighs with his touching hers. He touched her secret place with his hardness, teasing her, moving and touching.

"Oh, God!" she wailed, "I can't wait any longer!" She squeezed him. "Put it into me!" she pleaded and he entered her slowly, savoring the first hot feeling. Her body rose to meet his as he penetrated further. When he had penetrated as far as he could, their bodies strained to get him further. They both moaned with pleasure. When he reversed his motion, she gasped with intensified pleasure.

Their bodies were fused with passion. They became as one, moving together, searching for the delights of each other, the excitement building. And then every sensation in their bodies compounded, concentrated and then exploded into orgasm. They both moaned and gasped with the almost unbearable pleasure. She kept on going, slower, for her orgasm lasted longer.

The lovers lay together, passion and energy drained to the dregs, unable to move, or say anything. Vincent broke the silence. "Are you sorry?" he asked. "Oh, no!" she exclaimed, passionately and kissed him all over his face, "I'll never be sorry about anything I do with you." "Are you sure?" he asked, not convinced, knowing how bad she had wanted to be a virgin on her wedding night and now it could never happen. "It was too, wonderful to be wrong," she assured him, but her mood changed and she was pensive for a moment. "But I don't know what God thinks about it" she said, thoughtfully.

"Do you think He was watching us?" asked Vincent, thinking he was being cute, but she was aghast and her eyes got wide as she thought about it. "Oh, God!" she exclaimed, "What an awful thought," but she giggled, "You are horrible," she told him. "I know," he answered, "And the more you get to know me the worse I get." "I had better go to confession right away," she told him. "And you had better go too," "It would take too, long for me to confess," he told Carla and she gave up on that subject and they talked about other things. They talked about getting married. They even talked about having children. Eventually the subject got around to when to get married.

Vincent wasn't desperate about getting married now. He did want to marry her; he just wasn't desperate about it now. Vincent had been desperate before, when he believed he would have to wait until they were married before they could make love. But he had made love to her and it had been wonderful and now he didn't have to wait.

Vincent wondered if he was a cad for thinking that way. He acted desperate so he wouldn't hurt her feelings. They talked more about marriage and decided they would wait until he knew what his next assignment was before they made any plans. They also decided not to say anything to her parents until they had a plan.

Vincent graduated and learned his new assignment was to be back at Fort Ord. Carla was pleased about this, for he would be only a couple of hours away from her by Jaguar and she would be able to see him often. "It could have been worse," she had told him, "They could have sent you to Alaska."

They had another two nights of passion on the Pelican and then it was time to go. They would talk more about the wedding the next time they saw each other. He would write and phone and she would write and phone. He would miss her and she would miss him. He loved her and she loved him. A tearful kiss goodbye and Vincent went off to a different kind of war.

CHAPTER 25

Although Vincent was assigned to the Sixth Military Police Company, he was not an M. P. He was just a cook assigned to that unit. He did wear their braid, though, which made him look like one of them. Vincent also had the privilege of the M.P. Club. It was an on-base cocktail lounge for Military Police Personnel. The Club was adjacent to Vincent's barrack and to the Stockade, which was a prison for military personnel. Vincent was now a cook for that prison. His kitchen served two chow lines, one for Military Police, the other for the prisoners. A wall separated the two dining rooms. The lower part was wall and the upper part was wire screen.

Most of the prisoners were black or Mexican. The kitchen had prisoners for K.P. duty (kitchen police). When translated that means; dish washers, floor cleaners, grease trap cleaners, waiters, garbage engineers and potato peelers. Most of the cooks Vincent worked with were black or Mexican, but Vincent had no prejudice and he got along with all of them. Vincent had never had any prejudice, for he had never been exposed to racial problems.

A large percentage of the prisoners who were in the Stockade were there for going A. W. O. L. (Absent without leave.) Most of the prisoners were "Short timers," there for hours, days, weeks, or months. But some were "Long Timers", in for years. No matter what length of time was spent in the Stockade, it was all "Bad Time", time that didn't count. In other words, if a soldier had a four-year tour of duty left to do and was put in the Stockade for four years; he would still have four years of duty left to do. This "Bad Time" thing caused most of the prisoners to behave badly.

One of the major rules for personnel who worked in the Stockade was not to patronize with the prisoners. This was not hard to abide by with the prisoners who stayed behind the wire, who never came into the kitchen. But it was hard with the prisoners who did, who worked in the kitchen every day, who swapped stories and bummed cigarettes.

Vincent had never been an intimidating person, he was even less now. He had no rank, he wasn't big and his health was getting worse all the time. Of course he had rank over the prisoners, but he never used it. Vincent never ordered anyone to do anything. If he needed something done he would just ask a prisoner and if the prisoner didn't want to help, he would just ask another.

Vincent soon made friends with all the prisoners, and the other cooks. Vincent worked with prisoner every day and after awhile he didn't think of them as prisoners at all. He was on a first name basis with all of them. Vincent knew their wife's and children's names and what the prisoners were going to do when they got out of the Army.

Manuel was a cook. He was Mexican, with black hair, flashing black eyes and black mustache. He was small and slender, even more slender than Vincent. Manuel did every thing fast, darting around like a shrew. He talked fast with an accent. He was a P. F. C. He had rank over Vincent, every one did.

Manuel was always laughing. He was always trying to get Vincent to go to Watsonville to get him laid. He told Vincent there were hundreds of pretty Mexican girls there who would love to get into his pants. Vincent told him he would some day, but Vincent was not really interested. All he could think about was his Italian beauty and his fading health. Vincent could not understand why he was feeling so awful. Sometimes he felt so nervous he thought the particles he was made of would just fly apart and he would be scattered in the wind. His stomach always bothered him no matter what he ate and he always had heartburn.

The doctors could find nothing wrong with him, other than the fact that he was run down, nervous and smoked too much. Vincent just had to have his cigarettes. It was asking too, much to give them up. If Vincent wasn't a hypochondriac, he was close to it. Vincent was always worried about his heart. He was still having the palpitations. He gave up coffee, but it was hard. Getting up at four in the morning without coffee was close to being uncivilized. He just couldn't drink it anymore as it wired him something awful. Vincent tried all kinds of over the counter drugs for his nerves and stomach. He tried Seltzers, he liked the bubbles, but they just didn't work. They just didn't do what the advertisement said they would. Vincent could find only one relief and that was at the M. P. Club.

Vincent couldn't keep booze in the barrack. His only storage was his footlocker and it was subject to inspection at all times. Sergeant Spreker had his own room. Vincent knew he had a bottle stashed in his locker, but rank has its privilege and rank would never do Vincent any good. Vincent had brandy in his car but couldn't park it on the base. That left only two places to get alcohol on base, The M. P. Club and the P. X. (Post Exchange.) At the P. X. one could get nothing stronger than three-two, beer. Vincent drank brandy and bourbon at the M. P. Club.

Vincent couldn't get a drink in the morning and that was when he needed it the most. It was the only medicine he had. It was his panacea for all ills the flesh is heir to. Vincent had an awful time every morning trying to wake up without coffee. His nerves were raw to the quick, his legs made out of rubber and his stomach feeling like it had caved in, its sides rubbing together.

Vincent could never eat breakfast. All he could do was drink hot water and smoke cigarettes. After he started work, he could only do that at break time. Sometimes he felt as if he would pass out before break time, but he never did. Vincent just kept putting one foot in front of the other, hating every minute of it. Every day was a struggle, with the only hope of relief, the M. P. Club.

One night after his shift, Vincent was sitting in the Club getting well. He was moving a double shot glass of brandy around in circles in the wet rings it was leaving on the bar. He was looking at the bottles, glasses and their reflection in the mirror. Diverse sizes, shapes and colors of bottles full of diverse kinds of booze that all did the same thing; diverse sizes and shapes of glasses that all did the same thing. Vincent was listening to the sweet sounds of Rosemary Clooney coming from the brightly lit Wurlitzer. She was singing one of his favorites, "Tenderly."

Vincent sat looking at the faces in the mirror, among which was his own. The mirror was like the ones in many other bars, except for one thing. The faces in it were all male. There were not many female personnel in the M. P. Co. and it was a rare occasion when one of them came into the Club. But that was all right with Vincent. He only came to the club for one reason and that was to get well.

Vincent had not made friends with any of the M. P. personnel and the other cooks hardly ever came into the club. Holyoak, a Mormon and a cook, didn't drink. He never came into the Club; he was too pure for such frivolous degeneracy. He even wore special, one-piece underwear to help maintain his purity. Holyoak did seem to be pure. He never swore or did anything bad. Vincent wondered how in the world he ever had any fun. But he must have, Holyoak was always smiling, quick to laugh, always happy. It was like he had a secret that kept him that way.

Vincent didn't mind drinking alone, most of the time he preferred it. Being alone was the only way Vincent could relax, it was just the way he was. Alcohol helped Vincent to relax around people, but it didn't do the whole job unless he got thoroughly, bombed. This night Vincent sat and got relaxed, he just kept getting more relaxed. He was so relaxed by midnight it was all he could do to get off the stool and make it back to his bunk. Not many hours later, as Ernest Hemingway said in the title of one of his books, "The Sun Also Rises." And the sun did rise and it did shine and bright. Vincent did rise, but he didn't shine, nor was he very bright. He felt much worse than he had on the previous morning.

Sometimes getting relaxed is not healthy and Vincent did not look healthy at all. He might have made a healthy looking corps, but he was not a healthy looking living person. He wanted to ask the Sergeant for a drink, but knew it would be fruitless, so he suffered. Vincent couldn't even smoke; that just made him feel worse. He knew that if he felt any worse he would be dead.

Vincent went to the mess hall and went to work. He got dizzy and went outside to get some air. He felt weak, so he sat on a bench. He had heard it before, but now he knew what it meant; "With any luck at all I'll be dead by noon." He had heard a guy say that in a bar and that was just the way that he felt, maybe even worse. About halfway to noon, which had seemed like forever, Vincent noticed that some of the kitchen police were acting a little peculiar, acting silly, some of them and moving aimlessly.

Vincent's olfactory nerves started picking up on a pungent odor that made him suspicious. He couldn't identify the odor, but he believed it to be from some form of fermentation. Vincent's suspicion was being confirmed by the progressive exuberance of the kitchen police. After some investigation by the kitchen staff it was discovered that the K.P. had been making their own booze. They had saved some gallon sized, pickle jars, and were fermenting apples, potatoes and raisins in a ventilator shaft that ran across the ceiling. Vincent tasted enough of the concoction to make him feel better for a little while and it didn't taste half bad.

Vincent just couldn't help making friends with Sergeant Stark, a prisoner who had lived in Marysville before getting into the Army. Marysville is only twenty-six miles west of the Flats and was one of Vincent's old stomping grounds. Stark was an easygoing guy, he spoke softly with an Arkansas accent. Stark and Vincent became friendly while talking about their mutual areas. Stark had gone A. W. O. L. many times to visit his mother who lived in Marysville.

The tranny had gone out of Vincent's Ford, and he had bought a forty-seven, Pontiac off a Monterey, used car lot. The car had been well used and had only cost him a hundred dollars. Vincent had planned to drive the car until he could fix his Ford and then sell the Pontiac. He knew he could make a profit from it.

Vincent told Stark about it and Stark wanted the car, he was getting released from the Stockade in two weeks and needed a car. Stark offered Vincent a hundred and seventy five dollars for the car. Without thinking about it enough, Vincent sold it to him, forgetting about the rule against patronizing with prisoners. Vincent had cleared seventy-five dollars overnight, which was more than he made for a whole month in the Army.

Although Stark was a trustee and could go anywhere on base, he could not go off base. Somehow, while doing janitorial work in the Company Commander's office, Stark managed to steal a blank pass and filled it out himself. He drove the Pontiac off base with the pass and drove it straight to Marysville where he had been caught many times before.

The dingbat just could not wait. In his hurry to escape, Stark had left the papers to the Pontiac in his footlocker. The Military police had found them while searching for Stark. Vincent had signed the papers over to Stark, for it had been a cash deal. At about midnight the M. P. s stormed in and rousted Vincent out of his bunk. They only gave him enough time to jump into his whites and it was cold enough to freeze the balls off of a brass monkey. They stuck Vincent in a holding cell, which was no bigger than a phone booth. It wasn't big enough for him to lie down. There was a wooden bench to sit on, the floor was concrete and there was no heat.

Vincent sat shivering until eight the next morning. After he had told his story to the higher authority, he was reprimanded and his pass was revoked for two weeks. Vincent was a hero with the prisoners for a while. For a long time prisoners were asking him to sell them a car. In just a little while Stark was back on duty, but he had lost his trustee status. He also had gained new, bad time.

Carla was upset about not being able to see him for two weeks and she was even more upset the next time she saw him. Vincent had been losing weight and his dissipation had put him in a weakened condition. His night in the holding tank had given him a cold and the cold had progressed to walking pneumonia. His coloring was not good, either.

The two sat in a restaurant in Monterey. Carla's face was beautiful, but stressed with worry. Vincent's face was pale and gaunt. He was too tired and sick to smile. Vincent tried, but he felt more like crying.

"What is happening to you?" Carla asked, woefully. "I don't know," answered Vincent, his voiced strained, almost a whisper. Carla made him promise to find out. The next morning he did and he was admitted to the base hospital. The doctor told him he had pneumonia.

Vincent couldn't seem to get well. In fact, he seemed to get worse every day. He was not aware, but along with the pneumonia, he was also going through withdrawal from alcohol. Vincent wished he could get a drink, but was not aware that his body needed one. He was hungry all the time, but had difficulty eating. Vincent's stomach felt like it had shrunk into a fist. He was suffering from alcohol; induced colitis and his nerves were at the breaking point.

After thirty days in the hospital Vincent feared that he would die if he did not get out. He was down to a hundred and fifteen pounds and not improving. They did not know what to do except keep him in the hospital. Vincent convinced them to release him, which they did, reluctantly.

Vincent had it in his head that the stress of cooking, especially in the Stockade, was the root of his physical problems. He told this to the next doctor he saw and the doctor was inclined to agree with him. Vincent's release from the hospital had preceded him and by the time he got back to his Company he was already on the duty roster for the next morning.

Vincent had his same old job back. He went directly to his commander and told him he had not recuperated yet and would not be able to cook anymore because of the stress it caused him. The commander called the doctor and he evidently confirmed what Vincent had told him, for he was taken off the duty roster. Vincent was told to wait for his new assignment. He was given his pass, but no duty. He was in limbo. Vincent had written Carla every day while he was in the hospital. He hadn't called her to let her know of his release, he knew she would want to see him right away. He was just dying to see her, but he still felt too ill.

Vincent's nerves were getting better. He had not had a drink for a month, but was having a hard time with his stomach and the palpitations. They frightened him something awful. The doctors had not yet isolated the cause. They had told him it was just his nerves; he would just have to learn to live with it. Vincent did not believe the doctors. He was certain he had some bad thing wrong with his heart and that he was on the brink of death. One evening he got the idea that the cigarettes were triggering the palpitations and he quit smoking. It was easy for him to quit; the fear had made it easy.

Vincent also went back to his favorite panacea. He thought he would try some brandy for medicinal purposes, to see if it would make him feel better and it did. Some things never change. The brandy only made him feel better while he was drinking it and he couldn't drink all of the time. Vincent wished that he could.

It was almost a week before Vincent called Carla and told her he was out of the hospital. Three hours later they were sitting in a cocktail lounge in Monterey having a drink together. He had met her there, wanting to get off the base. Vincent had been in the lounge almost an hour before she got there. Vincent had been sipping his brandy and was as straight as he could be, considering his fragile, health. The brandy had put some color in his face, but it would be gone by morning. Vincent had been watching the door, but his heart still did a flip-flop when Carla walked through it.

Vincent wondered if she looked like that when she got up in the morning. He knew she hadn't had much time to get ready, but here she was, looking like a movie star. How could this lovely girl be in love with him? Vincent couldn't understand, but was grateful that she was.

He was so glad to see Carla he felt giddy. He was afraid his emotion would get the best of him. Vincent didn't want to be maudlin. He was afraid to talk while not having dominion of himself.

Carla walked straight to him and he was proud as a peacock as eyes followed her. She was wearing a blue outfit, skirt, and blouse, with a matching jacket. The soft blue of the outfit worked magic with the blue of her eyes. She tried not to have a worried look on her face, but it was there. Carla was thinking how frail Vincent looked. For a moment she had no words as she held his gaunt face in her hands, but her kiss was worth a thousand words, gentle and sweet. Vincent couldn't talk. He wanted to cry, but that was not a manly thing to do, so he just cried inside.

"How's my soldier boy?" she finally asked. "I've been better," he told her, ruefully, "And I'm afraid I will never be a soldier." "I wish I could take you home with me and take care of you," she answered. Then she brightened a little, "Mama could fill you with pasta and goodies." "I could go for that," agreed Vincent, "Army chow is going to kill me." "You don't look like you eat at all," she scolded. "I had to go on a liquid diet," he told her with a wry grin and he took a drink and not a sip. The brandy was starting to do its job. Carla wasn't smiling and on her face was a frown, just a little one.

"When was the last time you ate anything?" Carla asked. "Yesterday, I guess," he answered. "Can't you remember?" she asked, ruefully. "Can I get you anything?" he asked her, for the bartender was standing in front of them, waiting. Vincent ordered another drink for himself. Carla told the bartender she would have the same as Vincent. The bartender poured their drinks and left right after being paid.

"I think you should eat something," she suggested, trying not to sound preachy, but she felt preachy, so that was the way it sounded. But Vincent was not to be disgruntled. His troubled thoughts had been sufficiently adulterated by alcohol, enough for his alter ego to come forth. Captain Moon flagged the bartender down and ordered a couple of bags of peanuts. He gave one of them to Carla. She had to smile at his cuteness and realized she would have to use another approach,

"That wasn't what I had in mind," she scolded, "I have not had dinner yet." The Captain looked at his watch. "You poor darling.'" he jested, "You must be starving." And then he was inspired. "Let's go have some sub gum foo yong," he suggested, he could always eat Chinese food. "What in the world is that?" Carla asked, having never heard of it. "Chinese scrambled eggs," he told her, "With some kind of meat in it and a fancy sauce and I think whatever happens to be in the kitchen." Then Vincent remembered a Chinese place he used to eat at in Marysville until the place got cited for using cat meat. "It could even have cat meat in it," he added and then explained.

"Couldn't we just go to a nice Italian restaurant?" Carla asked, with some apprehension. "They don't have sub gum at Italian restaurants," he informed her. "Of course they don't," she answered, "I knew that." And

Captain Moon polished off his drink, smartly. "Let's go find us a Chinese cook," Vincent told her, as he got off his stool, feeling much better than he had when he sat down. It was like he had gone into remission. It was the wonder drug. Vincent couldn't see how anyone could do without it; he knew that he couldn't.

Carla was looking at Vincent with curiosity. She had just realized she had not seen a cigarette in his hand since she had got there. She wanted to say something, but she also wanted to wait to see how long he was going to go without.

"What's wrong?" asked the Captain, picking up on her look. Carla wiped the look off her face and put on an "I don't know what you mean." look. "What do you mean?" Carla asked. "You were making me feel like a goldfish," he answered. "I was staring?" she asked, innocently. "You were staring," he confirmed. Carla could not think of an excuse, so she told him the truth. "I was wondering how long you were going to go without a cigarette," she told him. "For the rest of my life," he answered, "I hope." She was joyous, for she hated the smell of the vile things. She had not told him that for fear of embarrassing him. "I'm so glad!" she exclaimed, happily, "How long has it been?" About a week," answered the Captain, "But I still have not stopped wanting them, especially when I'm drinking."

Carla had her arm through his as they walked out the door. "Let's take your car," he suggested, "Mine is a bucket of bolts compared to yours," he added. "This way," she told him, as she pulled him in the opposite direction he was going. "You can drive, too," he suggested" I would rather look at you than the street," he told her with a bit of a leer. "What part of me do you want to look at?" she asked him, innocently. "I would like to start with your legs," he told her. "And then what?" she asked. "Places others don't get to see," he answered, licking his lips, lasciviously. They got into her car, with her at the wheel.

"Where are we going?" she asked. "I don't know," he answered, "Just drive around until we find a place." While she brought the Jaguar to life, he turned on the map light. "What's that for?" she asked. "So I can look at your legs," he told her and she pulled at her dress, modestly. "You embarrass me," she told him, shyly. "Do you want me to look at some other woman's legs?" he asked. "You better not!" she scolded and she pulled her skirt up to her thigh. "That's better," he told her, as he caressed the inside of her thigh. She tried to close her legs, but couldn't while driving.

"Stop that!" she exclaimed, as she stopped his hand with hers, "I can't drive with your hand up my dress." "Why is that?" he asked. "Could you drive with my hand in your pants?" she asked. "To the nearest motel," he told her and laughed. Reluctantly, he removed his hand from her leg. "I'll be good for now," he told her, "But I don't know for how long." "I know you can't behave for very long," she told him, "And I don't want you to, I don't want you to be too good." "You don't have a thing to worry about," said Captain Moon, who was getting thirsty. The Captain searched the street for a Chinese restaurant. After about fifteen minutes Carla spotted one and she headed for the parking lot.

"Let's get some food in you to soak up the brandy," suggested Carla, in a motherly tone. "I hope they have Sake in here," said the Captain, in an answer to her motherly tone, not being in the mood for a mother. "Maybe you have had enough," she suggested, more like a friend than a mother. "Enough is a relative term," he answered, "Enough for what?" he asked. Carla saw that she was spitting against the wind and gave it up.

They went into the restaurant and the hostess, who was a pretty oriental, seated them in a booth. It was curtained and private. The place had a very oriental atmosphere, with lots of bamboo, silk and statues. When the hostess left, Captain Moon whispered to Carla and not as quietly as she would have liked him to.

"Confucius say," and he was talking with an oriental accent, "Woman who fly airplane upside down have crack-up." Carla giggled, "You are awful," she scolded. "I have been told," he said and referring to the hostess, "That their crack runs horizontally when they are standing up, that is, but I have never seen one." "Shhhhus," whispered Carla, getting embarrassed, "They might hear you." And just then the waitress walked in and she was an oriental girl, pretty and delicate. She was wearing a snug fitting, silk gown, split to show her slender legs.

"Is it true what they say," Captain Moon was asking the girl and he saw the aghast look coming to Carla's face. Then he went on, "About Oriental girls?" Carla's face was red from apprehension. "What do they say?" asked the girl, innocently. Captain Moon didn't answer for as long as he could get away with it, trying to build Carla's apprehension and then he answered with a grin. "They say they never have to shave their legs." Carla's face started to relax.

"That's not true," answered the girl without guile, "I have to shave mine all the time. The girls lovely legs showed through the split in her gown and the Captain looked at them with admiration. "And a splendid job you do," he told the girl. The girl gave him a flirty smile, took their order and left with the Captain's eyes in pursuit.

"I'm glad they have Sake," commented the Captain, to Carla, who was giving him the jaundiced eye over his interest in the waitress. "You seem glad about her legs, also," retorted Carla, wryly. "I can't help looking at legs," he told her, "But I would rather look at yours." "I would rather you did," she answered and then the waitress came back with their Sake. She gave the Captain a wink and told him to enjoy. She smiled sweetly at Carla and left. Carla looked right through her.

Captain Moon was eating with gusto; he hadn't had a good meal for days. His little ceramic Sake cup kept getting empty, though. He had to fill it four times by the time they had finished their dinner. She had drunk one cup, plus her tea.

"You don't like Sake?" he asked. "Not as well as you," she answered, a little petulantly. "Perchance I heard a barb?" he asked, with an eyebrow raised. "I'm sorry," she told him, "I'm just worried about you." The soldier's mood changed to depression. "I'm worried about me too," Vincent told his girl and he thought about morning. He knew what he was going to feel like in the morning and there was nothing he could do about it. All of his mornings were the same. He was afraid it was going to be this way the rest of his life. Some times he wished that he would not wake up.

"I wonder what it is like to die?" Vincent asked, without thinking. He had a haunted look on his face as Audrey came in to his mind. "Audrey knows," he said to the shadows in his head. "Who Is Audrey?" asked the worried girl, frightened by this dark side of him, "She was my sister," he told her. "Was your sister?" she asked, confused. "She was killed," he told her, and then he explained to her how it had happened. "You can't blame yourself," she pleaded, "It was just an awful accident." "But I do," he answered, in quiet desperation, wanting to pound his fist on the table.

"Come on, Vincent," she suggested, as she rose from her seat, "Let's go get some air." He got up and followed her; he stumbled a little at first. He paid the bill and they walked out into the night and the brisk, ocean air. "Let's go for a walk on the beach," he suggested; he had always liked to take his troubles to the ocean and it seemed like a place of beginnings and endings. "I would like that," she answered. "Run me by my car, first," he told her. He wanted to get a bottle of brandy from the trunk. She started to ask him why, but changed her mind as she already knew the answer. They walked to her car and she drove him to his. He got his jug and she drove to the beach.

The moon had a soft, eerie glow as it filtered through a light fog. The couple walked down the beach without saying any thing for a while. Vincent was imbibing while Carla was biting her lip, wanting to say something, but knowing her words would be wasted. He finally broke the silence.

"I don't know how to get well," he told his girl. "They offered you no advice at the hospital?" Carla asked, suspecting she already knew what his problem was. Her uncle Jason had been drinking himself to death for years. She hoped that Vincent would not turn out like him; this must not happen. Carla loved Vincent and she just had to ask him, she had to see his reaction. She had to do something. "Maybe you are an alcoholic?" Carla asked. "I'm too young to be an alcoholic," he answered, incredulous. "I don't think there is any age limitation to it," she told him. "Maybe I am," he agreed, "It runs in my family and there is nothing I can do about it." He took a strong pull from his jug. "You could quit drinking," she suggested, hopefully. "I can't," Vincent told her, "Not now, I would go crazy. I'll quit when I get out of the Army." "I hope you will stay alive for me," she whimpered, in anguish.

"Let's go back to the car and get warm," suggested the Captain, who was getting chilled to the bone, he was starting to shiver. They got back into the car and the top was up. It was cold, but not cold enough to make anyone shiver, but he was shivering. Vincent drank some more and it made him feel better, but it did not stop the shivering.

Carla drove to a motel and got Vincent into bed. She used her naked body to warm him, but it did not stop his trembling. It was the first time he had ever had the trembles. They lasted for hours, until he fell asleep, exhausted. The next morning Vincent started with a little hair off the dog. Carla left him, reluctantly, disturbed by him, worried about their future together. One week later Vincent had his new orders. He had to be at Fort Richardson, Alaska. He had a thirty-day leave and then he had to catch a ship at Tacoma, Washington.

CHAPTER 26

Vincent had his gear in his car and if he never saw Fort Ord again it would be too soon. He still had not called Carla to tell her of his new assignment. He still felt awful and was hoping to feel better before calling her. Vincent had to leave Fort Ord immediately. He was not going to spend any of his leave time there. When he finally did call Carla, she told him her parents had gone on a trip on the yacht while the restaurant was being renovated.

"Why didn't you go with them?" he asked, without thinking, his mind was not functioning at full capacity. Alcohol does kill brain cells. "You know why!" she exclaimed, a little exasperated, "I had to know if you were all right." Vincent didn't tell her about the transfer, he didn't want to tell her over the phone. Vincent told her he was on a thirty day leave and was on his way to visit his mother, but wanted to see her first. "Come to the house," she told him with anticipation, "I can hardly wait to see you. And we will have the house all to our selves."

When Vincent arrived at the circle drive in front of the house it was brightly lit. Carla kept the Jaguar garaged at night, so the driveway was empty. Vincent was parking his bucket of bolts when Carla came out the door. She wasn't good at hiding her feelings, so she didn't try. She tried to contain herself, but could not. Carla ran to Vincent, but stopped short of him. It was a good thing that she had, for she would have bowled him over in the condition he was in. That was what had stopped her, the condition he was in. Vincent even looked worse than the last time she saw him. The brandy was no longer coloring his face.

Some of the joy went out of her face and she wailed, "Oh, Vincent!" and then she was in his arms, embracing him, smothering his face with kisses, tears flooding her eyes. "I love you so much!" she cried, "If anything happened to you I would just die." Vincent was touched by her display of love and concern. He was overcome by it, plus his physical weakness, and his frustration. Vincent could not speak for a moment. His tears mixed with hers as they kissed.

"I'm so glad that you love me," he told her, as he held her adoring face in his hands, "And you know that I love you, you must know?" he said It like a question. "I know," she said softly, "I know." She backed her face away from his. Her eyes were luminous. "I know that you love me," she said and then she embraced him. She felt a tremble go through the full length of him. He felt dizzy, and could not stop his trembling. His teeth chattered and his heart did a couple of flip-flops.

"I need a drink of your father's brandy," Vincent told Carla, weakly as she helped him into the house. She led him to the den. It was a man's room, with natural woods and leather furniture. A fire was burning in the huge stone hearth. Carla helped him to lie down on a leather sofa; she put a pillow under his head.

Vincent's head was swimming, his face was pale. He lay on his back and asked Carla to put a pillow under his feet; he needed to get the blood back into his head. Carla was frightened; she quickly put a pillow under his feet and got him some brandy. Vincent raised his head to take a drink and saw her fear.

"I'll be alright," he assured her, "The brandy will help in a minute." "But what's wrong?" Carla wailed. Vincent was still dizzy. He sat up and put his head between his knees. "I don't know," Vincent answered and asked her for a cold rag for his face. Carla ran to the bathroom and wet a washcloth with cold water. She brought it back to him, along with a towel. Carla gently wiped his face with it and as soon as it touched his face, a cold shiver went through him and he trembled. "Someone just walked over my grave," he said, in an attempt at jest. Vincent was like that, he tried to find humor in the darkest times.

Vincent tried to drink some brandy. He had to hold the glass with both hands because of the trembling. "A blanket," he stuttered, "I'm so, cold." Carla ran to the linen closet and by this time she was crying. She brought a quilt back and covered him with it. She went on her knees and burled her face in his chest. "I'm so, cold." Vincent told her again, "Lay on top of me." Carla got under the quilt and laid her little body on top of him. In a few moments he could feel her heat coming through his clothes. "You are a hot little number," Vincent teased, "I wish I could spend the rest of my life in bed with you."

It amazed Vincent that he could get an erection feeling the way he did. He needed to get some more brandy in him, though, so he asked her to let him up. He told her he needed some more brandy and she got up and poured him some. She sat on her knees, watching him like a mother. Vincent sat up and drank the glass of brandy. The large charge made him feel better and he asked for more and she poured it. Vincent took a sip of his refill and stood up, but he sat right back down again, for he felt weak and dizzy. Beads of perspiration popped out on his forehead from the effort.

"Vincent, you are scaring me, let me call our family physician. Please!" Vincent shook his head in the negative. "I'm alright," he argued, "it's just a spell left over from my hospital stay and it will pass." "When was the last time you ate anything?" she asked, searching for another link to his illness, needing a way she could help him. "I ate at the base before I left," he answered, "And I'm not hungry."

Vincent did not want to eat any thing, knowing it would negate the affect of the brandy. "I think you should go to bed for awhile," she told him. "Only if it is your bed and you are in it," he answered, "And you have to be naked." She raised her eyes, momentarily, for her bedroom was on the second floor, she was wondering if he could make it. He saw her look and he raised his eyes. "I know where your bed is," he told her; she had told him of her view from it. "Am I invited?" he asked. Carla blushed and he knew that he was.

Carla watched him with a worried look, like a mother with her sick child. Vincent was familiar with that look; he had seen it on his mother's face a million times. "I'll nurse this brandy for awhile," he told her, "And then I'll see if I can make it to your bed." He grinned, "I'm not going to let an invitation like that go by. The girl blushed again.

"Maybe you should go to bed by yourself," she suggested, "Something other than sleep might not be good for you." "You naughty girl." he scolded, "Do you mean to tell me you would take advantage of me in my weakened state?" Carla answered, quickly "Yes," I would. Vincent asked," What if your parents come home?" "They won't be home," she answered, in a matter of fact, tone.

Vincent was starting to feel a little better, but was worried. He had never felt this bad before. Vincent wondered if he would experience this kind of spell again. He knew it was the brandy that was making him feel better, but also knew he couldn't drink forever. "The Sun Also Rises" he reminded himself.

Carla was sitting next to him, the worried look was still on her face. Vincent took her hand in his and gave it a weak squeeze. He smiled with pale lips. "I'm ready to climb the stairs now," he told her and he picked up the bottle of brandy, "But I'm taking this with me, for medicinal purpose." Carla's worried look turned to something closer to a frown.

"Maybe you shouldn't drink anymore," she offered, but not wanting to be a nag, she added, "Until you find out what is wrong with you." Vincent had to tell her something. "I'm just not over the affects of the pneumonia yet," he replied," And I'm not happy with my new assignment."

He let that one hang until she started to open her mouth to reply and then he went on, "I'm sorry," he told her, "I should have told you right away." "What?" she asked, before he could get it all out. "They are sending me to Alaska for a year," he told her, and Carla's worried look turned to one of horror, she was aghast.

"Oh, God No!" she wailed, "Are they trying to kill you? You are in no condition to go anywhere!" "They had to do something with me," he told her. Then he tried to explain; "When I got out of the hospital they wanted me to go back to my old job, but I told them I couldn't. I told them I couldn't cook at all, that the stress was causing me to have a nervous condition. It is a wonder they didn't order me to do it. The doctor must have corroborated my story."

Carla was speechless with incredulity for a moment and Vincent was cold again. He noticed the fire needed to be stirred, so he got up to do it. He got up too, fast and got dizzy. He reeled, tried to catch himself, but failed. Vincent fell forward and hit his forehead on the sharp corner of the stone hearth. It knocked him out and put a two-inch gash in his forehead. A fountain of blood gushed from the gash. Carla tried to stop the blood with her hand, but only got blood all over her self in the attempt. She took the wet cloth, and pressed it to the wound, which had already started to swell. Just then Vincent became conscious and he saw the blood on Carla.

"Oh my God!" he cried and Vincent remembered his fall, "I got blood all over you!" Carla was crying from fright while trying to laugh at the same time, from relief. The girl regained her composure. "Don't worry about the blood," she consoled him, as she pulled the cloth away from the wound to inspect it. "It will wash off." Carla quickly pressed the cloth back down, blood was still bubbling out. "This is going to need stitches," she informed Vincent. "It will be alright," Vincent assured her. He pressed the cloth so she wouldn't have to and Carla let go of it.

"It is not alright," she argued, "You need stitches or you are going to have a big scar." "Would you still love me if I had a scar?" he asked her, as he got into a sitting position to survey the mess he had made." Of course I would," she told him, "But maybe not as much." "Aha!" he exclaimed, "I knew it all along." "Knew what?" she asked. "It was just my pretty face you wanted," he answered, with mock indignation. "That's not true," she told him in a coquettish manner. "There were other parts of you I wanted." "Did you get any of the parts you wanted?" he asked, grinning with pale lips. "Uhu," she answered and giggled, "I sure did." "Did you find a favorite part?" he asked, teasing and she did a genuine blush this time, but she kept right on, "I sure did," she answered, "I surely did." "Can I guess what it is?" he asked and grinned. "Probably so." she replied and started a continuous giggle. "Can you give me a clue?" he asked. "Is it bigger than a shoe box?" She was laughing now. "Not quite," she answered, as best as she could.

Vincent got pale again. He took a drink. She pulled the cloth away and the blood was still oozing.

"You have to get stitches in this," she told him again. In the morning," he replied, casually. "Tonight!" she retorted, "Or you will bleed all over my bed. Carla started to help him up. "I will take you to the hospital, and get your head sewed back together," she told him. "I will call and let them know we are on our way." Vincent looked at the blood on her dress.

"You had better change your dress" he suggested, "Or they are going to think I assaulted you." Carla looked down at her dress. "My, God" she exclaimed, "You are right," and then she helped him to the couch. "I'll go change," she told him, "While you rest." "Put your dress a in cold water with vinegar in it before my blood gets dry," he told her. "That's a good idea," she answered, as she left the room.

As soon as Carla had left, Vincent got up and poured himself a drink. He wished he had brought his flask with him, but had left it in the car. Vincent looked at the blood on the floor, grateful he had not got any on the expensive looking Persian rug; which was only a few feet away. He sat back down and nursed his drink. It was good stuff, quality brandy.

Vincent did his old move of letting the brandy run under his tongue, to leave it there until his tongue was numb. When it was numb, he let it run down his throat. Yes, it was quality brandy. Everything in the house was quality, including Carla. The only thing in the house that was not quality was his self. Vincent wondered if all this might be too good for him, if Carla was too good for him. He did believe that Carla was too good for him, but maybe, he thought, if he were surrounded by quality it would rub off on him. He had always believed that he was meant to have the good life, to have quality things. He just didn't believe that he was quality. In fact, he had always felt a little inferior. He was sure that he lacked courage and character, but had always tried to hide it, even from himself.

Vincent ran his fingers across the soft leather of the sofa. It felt smooth, sensuous to his fingertips. He loved the smell of leather, it was a comfortable smell. He looked at the expensively bound books on the shelves on both sides of the fireplace and at the thick Persian rugs. Vincent knew that some of the furniture was close to a hundred years old, some of it maybe more. He also noticed the oak sideboard with the marble top, the Tiffany lamp with the glass shade of muted green, the French desk with designs made of many sizes and shapes of wood veneer and its top which was in leather.

There was an inkwell on top of the desk. It was unusual. Vincent got up to look at it and picked it up. The well was about a four-inch cube. It was heavy, made of brass. It had a filigreed frame, a solid domed lid, which was hinged and engraved. Behind the filigree was muted green glass, much the same as the lampshade.

Vincent opened the lid. The well was empty and clean. Vincent was curious. He knew about these things for his mother had always been an antique buff. Grace couldn't afford to own them, but she could afford to want them. She must have drug Vincent through a thousand antique stores. Vincent turned the ink well over and on the bottom was the engraving, "Tiffany, New York." Vincent thought to his self, "This one room is worth more than my mother's whole house."

Vincent wished his mother could live in such luxury, but he knew it would not mean much to her and mean nothing to Doc. He would sit on the leather sofa with his pliers in his back pocket and soon there would be a hole in the sofa. Doc wouldn't care he would wipe his greasy hands on his mother's towels. It would not take Doc long to ruin this room.

"I should talk", Vincent said to his self, "I just got blood all over everything. At least Doc doesn't drink. Doc was the only husband his mother had who didn't drink. Doc did smoke, though. Vincent felt like he had drunk himself sober, he just hated that. He didn't have the slightest buzz on, he just felt tired, tired to the marrow in his bones. What he was drinking was not doing him any good. Vincent knew he would feel awful when the sun came up. He dismissed the thought with a careless wave of his hand. Carla came back into the room. She had changed into a gray skirt, black sweater and black suede, pumps.

"Let's go, Captain Moon." she said, trying to be cheerful, "They will be waiting for us." Vincent tried to stall. He hated hospitals; they smelled like ether to him. Ether had made him awfully sick the first time he had had his tonsils out. He had vomited so much he thought he would turn inside, out. And all his suffering had been in vain. The surgeon had missed a small piece of the organ and the rest of it had grown back.

"Don't you think we should clean up the blood before we leave," Vincent suggested, an obvious procrastination attempt to put his trip to the hospital to a later time. It can wait," Carla told him, firmly, "Let's go," and they went. Vincent held the cloth to his head on the way and for a while the two were quiet. Carla broke the silence.

"A whole year," she said, in a somber voice, "What am I going to do without you for a whole year?" "I wish we were married," he answered, matching her mood. "I wish we were, too," she answered, "But how would that help?" "I wouldn't have to worry about you falling in love with someone else," he answered. "I will never love anyone else!" she exclaimed through tears. "Don't cry." Vincent pleaded and they were both quiet for a while.

"Let's elope," Vincent suggested, right out of the blue, "Now is the perfect time, with your parents gone." Carla was so surprised she almost let go of the wheel. Like all Italians, she had a need to express herself with her hands. "Oh, Vincent!" she exclaimed with joy, "I want to." but then she looked dejected, "But it would break my Mama's heart. I'm her only child and she wants a big church wedding,"

"Don't tell her," offered Vincent. "What do you mean?" she asked. "We go to Reno and get married secretly," he replied, "And have a church wedding when I get back from Alaska." Vincent could see from the look on her face that her mind was racing, weighing "We would have to get a blood test," she stated excitedly, "And a license." "Call your doctor and see if we can get a blood test while we are at the hospital getting me sewed. We can get a license in Reno." he was feeling really seedy, but it didn't dampen his spirit. "Sam will do it for us," claimed Carla, "He is our doctor; he brought me into the world."

Vincent was still holding the cloth to his head when they went into the waiting room of the emergency wing. Carla took him to the sign in window where he answered questions and filled out papers. Carla told him she would talk to Sam while he was getting squared away. In a while she came back with a big grin on her pretty face.

"He is doing it," she whispered in Vincent's ear. "Doing what?" teased Vincent. Carla was excited and filled to bursting with affection for him. Her only release was in touching him. She put her fingers in his hair and fooled with it. Carla whispered in his ear and tickled it. "I love you," she whispered, kissing his neck. "Sam is setting it up for us," she told Vincent, "I'm going to marry you before you can get away from me." She was effervescent and he was excited, but it was having a bad affect on him. The extra adrenaline was compounding his health problems.

Vincent's ears started to ring and his face blanched. Vincent felt a dizzy spell coming on, just like the ones he use to have when he was a kid, the ones that seeing his own blood had caused. He moaned and started to get up, but his head was swimming and he went to his knees. Vincent tried to get back up, but fainted. He felt Carla's arms go around him before he went out.

When Vincent awoke he found himself in bed. He knew instantly that he was in a hospital bed; no other bed is as hard and uncomfortable. It was like a person was being punished for being sick. He was flat on his back and he hated that position, for it seemed hard for him to breathe while in it. The first emotion he felt was fear, he had always been afraid of hospitals. Vincent remembered fainting. The second emotion he felt was relief, he spotted Carla sitting beside his bed. He was grateful for her, for nothing is worse than being afraid and alone at the same time. Carla was smiling through her worry.

"What happened?" Vincent asked. "You fainted," Carla answered, kissing him on the cheek. "You have been out for almost an hour." She pressed the button for the nurse. Feel your forehead," Carla told Vincent.

He felt it and looked surprised. "Sam put the stitches in while you were out," she told him. "Did he say why I had passed out?" asked Vincent, still a little bewildered. "He thinks you are suffering from nervous exhaustion," Carla told him, "and you might have a slight concussion." "I don't want to stay here," complained Vincent, "I just got out of the hospital." Vincent didn't want to stay. He needed a drink. He was afraid of what would happen if he did not get one; afraid he would start the trembles again. He now believed that was why he had felt so bad in the Base Hospital.

A big man came into the room. He was wearing traditional whites of a doctor. He looked to be in his mid-fifties. His hair and mustache were salt and pepper gray. His eyes were a startling, pale blue. The man was well over six feet tall and was bristling with vitality. Vincent wished that he felt like the doctor looked.

"This is Sam," said Carla, "He already knows who you are." "How are you feeling?" asked Sam, as he held Vincent's wrist to check his pulse "Close to death," answered Vincent, "or at least, very old, very tired." "Hmmm," answered Sam, watching his watch, "Feeling a little old? Well it's no wonder. It looks like you have been burning the candle from both ends." Sam looked thoughtful. "You certainly do have a pulse," he commented, "A little too much pulse," he said and grinned. Sam buzzed for the nurse. "I want to get some blood from you," he said, with a sly, grin, "Some for me to find out what is going on in you and some for Carla, so she can marry you." The nurse came in and went to work on Vincent. "Get some blood from Carla while you are at it," Sam told the nurse and he turned to Carla, winked and added, "I hope you are going to let this guy get well before you go on the honeymoon." Carla blushed, modestly. When the nurse was finished with Vincent, Sam probed his chest with the stethoscope, thumping Vincent's chest and back with his fingers.

"How much do you smoke?" Sam asked him. "I use to smoke three packs a day," Vincent answered, "But I quit." "Don't ever start again," ordered the doctor. "I can't," replied Vincent, "They make me feel strange." "Good!" retorted Sam and he listened some more. "Have you ever had pneumonia?" he asked. "I just got out of the hospital from it," replied Vincent. "Your chest sounds like they let you out too soon." commented Sam. "I need to get out of here," said Vincent, trying to keep the desperation out of his voice, "I'm on a thirty day leave." "And you don't want to spend it in here," agreed Sam, "But we do need to do something about your condition and we can't without knowing what is wrong." How long?" asked Vincent and his lip quivered with dread. "Tomorrow morning," answered Sam. Vincent felt panic and Carla saw it. "Please stay." pleaded Carla. Vincent did not want to stay, but he couldn't put Carla through any more. He had already got blood all over her and had frightened her, considerably. He resigned himself to do it for her and was just too, tired to argue about it. Vincent agreed to stay, much to Carla's relief.

Vincent felt as if he was going to have a nervous collapse. He asked Sam if he could have something for it and Sam told him the nurse would give him a mild sedative that would enable him to sleep. In a short while an oriental nurse came in and gave Vincent a shot in his lower cheek, the one that followed him around. He fell asleep while talking to Carla and when he awoke she was gone. Vincent was lonely and felt awful. He hated hospitals; there was no way that anyone could feel good in one. Being in one was almost like being in jail.

Vincent's bladder felt like it was going to burst. He got up to relieve it. When he stood he felt dizzy. His innards were on fire and he felt nausea. Vincent made it to the toilet and sat on it, being careful not to get his cloak, which was open in the rear, inside the bowl. He hated these cloaks that let ones behind be exposed. Vincent's bowels were burning. Everything in them had turned into hot, liquid. He had the runs and every time he thought he was finished, he wasn't. He would no sooner get back into bed and he would have to get back up again. After a few hours of this, the sedative wore off. Vincent felt hollow. He felt like an old snag would have felt if it had had any feelings.

A snag is a tree lightning had struck and killed. After years of death the inside had rotted out leaving nothing but a hollow shell. Vincent had heard lightning strike some of the trees and one not far from their cabin in the mountains. It had made a cracking roar, like an explosion and the whole cabin had shook like a giant had picked it up and shook it, trying to shake the people out of it. Vincent hadn't slept that whole night. He had expected the lightning to hit the tin roof, ricochet from it and hit the old iron bed he had been laying on. A person can tell when the lightning has hit close. It is close when there is little time between the flash of light and the clap of thunder. Vincent had always been afraid of it, afraid to touch a light switch or a faucet, take a bath, or even sit on the toilet.

Vincent was cold, but was perspiring like a race- horse. He started to shiver, so he rang for a nurse. She brought him an extra blanket and covered him with it. It didn't do him much good, for he was soaking wet. Vincent wished he could have some brandy and he thought of the brandy that was in his car. He knew that if the car were near, he would leave the hospital and go to it.

Vincent didn't get well enough to get Carla to Reno. He did stay with her for a while, while she nursed him. The blood test had shown high alcohol content and traces of sugar. Sam told Vincent he would have to slow down, or risk diabetes and some other horrid things that Sam explained, graphically. Vincent decided he would try to quit and he never had another drop while he was staying with Carla.

It was a happy time for the lovers, even with his frail health, days of gentle love, concern and patience. Although they were disappointed about Reno, Carla decided the subterfuge was not God's will. Vincent didn't care a whole lot about God's will, but he agreed; it was the easy thing to do. Vincent did manage to make it back to the Flats. Neither his mother's love nor her cooking could heal him. His friends could not cheer him. Not even the Moon Patrol; not even Linda.

CHAPTER 27

At last they were going to leave Tacoma, Washington, where Vincent had been waiting two weeks for a ship to Alaska. The rain had been continuous since he had arrived. He had never seen such rain in all his life. It was like God had turned on a billion hoses and then had forgotten them. And that was not all, it had been cold. Vincent had not been warm since he had arrived. Vincent knew his health was part of the problem, but the weather on the Sound was most of it. God had surely forsaken this place. He would never understand why the area was so populated. And the Base, Fort Lewis, it must have been built on a rock pile. Vincent had spent many hours picking up rocks. There was rocks and gravel everywhere.

"Idle hands are the Devils workshop." The Army goes by this motto religiously. There was nothing at Fort Lewis, nothing pertinent, that is, for the soldiers in waiting to do. The Army hates to see soldiers enjoying themselves, especially in a casual manner, so they dream up trivial things for them to do. The most popular of these dreams is called "Policing the area." That sounds like a job for a cop.

In Army language "policing the area" means picking up trash and cigarette butts. At Fort Lewis it means picking up rocks. Since Fort Lewis was built on a rock pile, at least it looks that way, how does one police rocks from a rock pile? One picks them up and puts them in a pile. When there are too, many piles, one simply moves the piles around. Isn't that ingenious? Our defense has never been in more capable hands.

At last Vincent was standing on the deck of a troop ship, along with hundreds of other dogfaces and some of the sailors who were running the ship. The water of the Sound was calm and the movement of the ship was almost imperceptible. Orders came over the loud speaker that now was the time to take the Dramamine. If one thought it was needed; after one got sick, it was too, late.

Everyone had been issued the pills, but Vincent had only seen a few take them. He hadn't taken any. He had been on a lot of boats, and he had never been seasick. Vincent had never been on a ship before, though. It must have been that no one wanted to be seen taking the pills. Everyone wanted to be a hero. The guys proved how tough they were, they just went ahead and got sick. Now that takes guts, and I mean that literally. Some of the heroes were puking their guts out before the ship had left the dock, before the ship had moved, before the anchor had been pulled.

The Army seemed to be getting even with Vincent for refusing to be a cook. They gave him a bunk that was as far forward and as far down as one could get on the starboard side of the ship. The bunk was curved to conform to the bow of the ship. Sleeping on the bunk was like sleeping on an elevator that goes up and down, constantly. To make it worse, the bunk moved in other ways that no elevator has ever moved. To make it worse, there was a heat register just above his head that blew hot air on him.

Vincent didn't feel well at all. He wasn't well when he got on the ship and all the motion and commotion had only compounded other infirmities. The motion of the ship was not his biggest problem; it was the other troops, the ones who were sick. Vincent had never seen green people before; they were the same color as their vomit. The smell was awful.

The decks, steps and companionways were slippery with vomit. It was all over the bathrooms and on the stools. It was in the mess hall and the mess hall was a mess. The visual affect of all this, plus the assault on the olfactory nerves had kept Vincent on the constant verge of nausea. It was only with will power that he kept himself from vomiting. He knew that if he ever started, he would not be able to stop.

Things had really gotten bad two days out when they ran into a storm. Even the sailors were sick. Vincent believed he was the only person on the ship who was not puking. He wasn't sure about the captain, though, he had never seen him. The Captain probably ate in his own private mess hall.

Vincent never missed a meal, even though he never felt good enough to eat. He knew he had to keep something in his stomach, but he refrained from imbibing liquids. Vincent also stayed away from the P.X. as much as possible, for it was there where the sick ones would congregate when they got hungry. The cabin where the movies were shown was far forward and on the starboard side of the ship. It had the same elevator motion as his bunk, which caused a great deal of evening nausea. Vincent stayed away from there. He had already seen most of the movies anyway.

One night it was so hot from the heat vent blowing on him above his head, Vincent couldn't sleep. He took his blankets and his pillow up on deck and slept under an asphalt mixer that was strapped to the deck. It was also a passenger.

Vincent wondered how seasickness could be so awful without being fatal. He had never seen such sick, helpless men. He had seen one trooper lying on his back, puking straight up, with it running back over his face. He could have choked to death had he not been turned over. Vincent was amazed that no one had fallen overboard. Many of the men were spending much of the time lying over the rail.

The storm lasted almost to Seward, Alaska, where they made landfall. It was truly wonderful to get off of the ship, but the land they landed on was in no way inspiring. It was cold, white, slippery, bleak and almost dark. Vincent couldn't tell what the weather was doing, but it seemed to him to be frozen fog. It wasn't pretty in Seward; it was just white and bleak. Vincent was disappointed, the place seemed dismal to him. The country was barren, with hardly any trees and the ones that were there were scrubby.

There was a train waiting for them, an empty one and it wasn't first class, it wasn't even third class. As a matter of fact it had no class at all. What it did have was a lot of broken windows. It was thirty below zero outside, so it must have been thirty below inside the train.

All the dogfaces were carrying their tightly stuffed, duffle bags. Vincent's was probably heavier than he was. They had to get on the front of the train and carry their duffle bag through to the rear of the train, there were no porters. Vincent didn't count the cars, but by the time he got to his seat he was about to collapse from exhaustion.

It was an old train and one of the many windows that were broken was next to him. Vincent just knew he was turning blue. He was so cold he knew that if he tried to piss it would freeze on his liquid elimination orifice. He knew the train was not going over thirty miles an hour. It would take forever to get where they were going, and he was not quite sure he would survive the journey.

The first moose Vincent saw surprised him and even delighted him, but after awhile a lot of them got to be old hat. They also became a nuisance. They would get on the track and the train would have to stop. The animals were so tame they would have to be chased off the track. They were just like cows with big horns. Once the moose had been chased off the track the train would slowly work its way back up to its break neck, speed.

There was a bus waiting for them in Anchorage; it took the weary soldiers to Fort Richardson. It was just a few miles further. The terrain getting there was flat, but the spot the bus parked on was on a slope, which was covered with ice. Vincent got off the bus and when he threw his duffel bag over his shoulder, he lost his footing and fell. He slid on his fanny all the way down the slope. Vincent had already seen all of Alaska that he wanted to see.

The barracks were nice. They were multiple floored, reinforced concrete and built to be earthquake proof. Vincent's bunk was on the top floor with a northern exposure. On a clear day he could see Mount McKinley, which was some miles further north. It's the highest mountain in North America.

Freddy Scianelli was on the bunk next to Vincent; on the top bunk. Freddy was a big Italian, with black curly hair. He had big, dark, humorous eyes and a florid complexion. Freddy was not what you would call fat, but he had a belly that jiggled when he laughed. His belly jiggled often, for Freddy was a happy kind of guy. He was shy and introvert, though and he didn't open up to every one, but he did to Vincent.

Freddy was an Army cook and had been a cook before the Army got him. A cook was just what he wanted to be and that was just one of the things that Freddy was happy about. Vincent didn't want to be a cook, but that was what the Army wanted him to be; that was what they had trained him to be. They were not happy with him when he told them his story. They put him on hold until they could corroborate his story. The brass found out he had been telling the truth. He was given the duty of light custodial janitor of the basement offices in the Headquarters Building. Vincent had always been a good organizer. The janitor duty was supposed to be an all night one, but Vincent organized it down to three hours.

The custodial position was a night one and was supposed to be a full shift. Vincent was relieved of all day duty, including reveille. What a racket Vincent had fallen into. He went to bed just a little later than the rest of the guys. He didn't have to get up in the morning until he wanted to and the day was his. Vincent didn't even have to wear his uniform. He wore Levis, sheep lined boots and a leather flight jacket, which was also sheep lined and he wore long Johns.

The other guys thought Vincent was sleeping in so he could go to work at night. What they didn't know wouldn't hurt them. Vincent couldn't go to his job until after six in the evening and he would usually be finished by nine. Then Vincent would go to town. He couldn't go to bed too early, someone could get suspicious. Vincent would stay in town until he thought it was safe. Sometimes he would bar hop in town until the bars were all closed.

Vincent tried hard not to drink. He thought he was trying anyway, but it was impossible in Alaska. There just wasn't anything else to do. Vincent was lonely and homesick. He vowed he would kiss the street in the Flats if he ever got back there again. Vincent missed Carla something awful. He went to bed every night with an erection from thinking about her and she was not the only one he was thinking about. He knew that Linda was growing up and he wasn't there to watch. He loved her, but Carla was a woman and Linda was still a girl. Vincent didn't know what things would be like if Linda was a woman, or what it would be like when she turned into one. Which one would he love the most? He knew he couldn't have both of them.

Vincent found a cocktail lounge downtown, close to the movie theater. The biggest martini he had ever seen was made there. One of them before the movie would give him a buzz that would last all the way through the movie. It was the only time Vincent felt half way good, when he had a buzz on. He couldn't stay that way, though, for he had a job to do. Vincent couldn't afford to anyway.

Vincent hardly ever drank with the other guys. They just never seemed to go to town together, except in the daytime or on weekends. Freddy's home was in Fairbanks and he went home every chance he got. Freddy always had a bottle of peppermint schnapps in his locker. He would often share it with Vincent when there was no one else around. Vincent shared his brandy with Freddy on the same basis. The lockers were not often inspected and when they were there was always advance notice.

Mailey, the blond kid on the other side of Vincent, was a pussy hound and he always went searching alone. Mailey was always coming in with a sore dick. It seemed like he was trying to wear it out. Tokuda, a dogface of Japanese heritage, didn't drink, not seriously. He might have one beer if he was coaxed. He was born and raised in Hawaii, he had lived there all of his life. Tokuda always seemed to be in harmony with himself, his neighbor and his environment. He had that easygoing attitude a lot of people from Hawaii have. Tokuda always had a grin on his handsome face. Vincent thought he was handsome for a Japanese person. He looked very healthy and solid. He was about the same height as Vincent, but he was bigger, barrel chested. He looked like he could be a formidable foe if angered, but Tokuda never got mad at anyone, or anything. It just wasn't normal.

Tokuda had a calming affect on Vincent and they became friends. They spent a lot of time together and talked about many things. There was a lot of time to kill in Alaska and talking was about the only thing that was free. Vincent tried to find his friend's secret. He seemed to have one. There was something that caused him to be calm, and serene. Vincent asked him about his philosophy, but there didn't seem to be anything that had been written in stone. Live and let live was about what it amounted to. Tokuda would not discuss religion, he said it confused him.

Vincent went to the doctors in Alaska, but they could find nothing wrong with him. He was beginning to think he was a hypochondriac. He started spending a lot of time at the Post Library. He read everything he could find about psychiatry and psychology. What he read did not dissolve the heartburn, relax the knot in his stomach, nor quench his thirst.

Alcohol was the only thing that made Vincent feel good, but it also made him feel bad. What an enigma was the Curse of The Cardozas. Vincent was beginning to believe the curse was his fate and there was nothing he could do about it. Vincent wondered if God could cure him, but he didn't know how to ask. God hadn't saved Audrey, so why would he bother with him. Why even bother to ask.

Time passed slowly, but it did pass. Two letters a week came from Carla. Vincent answered then as soon as he had read them. A letter a week came from his mother and he answered them right away. Between the letter writing, the library, his job, and his drinking, most of his time was used up. He read a book about metaphysics; it was written by a woman, a thing he did not often do. It wasn't that he was prejudice, or anything like that, he just liked books written by men better. This authors name was Mary Baker Eddy. Although he did not understand much that was in the book, it had made him think more about God. In this book she claimed matter to be but a false concept, illusion. This was a little far out for Vincent, his mind wasn't ready for that. He was totally caught up in the physical, and the sensual. Vincent did believe in God, though. He believed He was in another dimension, one you had to die to get into and he wasn't ready for that.

Vincent didn't have much trouble with the cold weather; it was a different kind of cold. It didn't bother him as long as he was moving. One time he had to go on a field inspection, which took place on a frozen lake. The troops had to stand at attention in front of their pup tents until the inspection was over, which took a considerable length of time. Vincent felt short of breath; he was so cold. When he got back to the barrack he looked in the mirror and his lips were blue. Blue is not a good color for lips,

Vincent got along with most of the troops, even the ornery ones, and there were some of them. There were some Eskimo troops who were born and raised in the area. Most of them were like children, somewhat like native Hawaiians, fun loving and slow to wrath. But some of them had their blood adulterated with Russian blood. Some of them were ornery, especially if their blood had been adulterated again with alcohol. Some of these breeds had flat faces, with black, opaque eyes.

Once, while Vincent was having a movement in the latrine, in one of the stalls, he felt like he was being watched. But how could that be, the door was closed. He looked up, and there was one of the flat faces staring down at him. He had been hanging there, quiet as a snake, watching.

Vincent developed a voracious appetite for reading, but only gained confusion from it. Vincent had only come to one concrete conclusion; it was his mother's fault he was the way he was. He knew he was selfish and self indulgent, but his mother had indulged him, had spoiled him and that was a fact. And she had been the one who had doctored him for every conceivable illness before he had even got it. She had been the one who had given him nine thousand enemas. How he had hated having that hose shoved up his rear.

Vincent needed something, but knew not what it was; he didn't have a clue. He knew there was something missing in his character. He didn't even feel like a man, he felt like a lost child. Vincent felt like he was pretending to be a man. Maybe it was because he never had a real father to relate to, to teach him how to be a man. He felt worthless and he could not understand what Carla saw in him. How could he marry her in the state he was in? How could he do such a thing to her? How could he support her? He knew nothing, he was nobody. He was Captain Moon and that was all. That was all the rank he would ever have. Carla was too good for the likes of him and that was for sure.

Vincent was clutching at straws when he started going to Christian Science services on Sundays in the base chapel. The minister was also a practitioner, who heals with prayer and so was his wife. Vincent even had dinner a few times at the minister's house. His wife was a good cook. Vincent learned a lot about God from these good people. They were comforting saying things like, "God is love." But he didn't believe that all these far out metaphysical ideas were going to help with his immediate physical problems.

When Vincent's night job ran out he was in limbo for a few days while waiting for them to find him a new job. His luck held and he fell right into another cushy one. He didn't have as much freedom, but it was a cushy job. Vincent went to work on the maintenance crew of the only military golf course in the area. During good weather it was the crew's duty to take care of the grounds and run the clubhouse. It sold beer and packaged snacks.

Most of the time the weather was inclement and they sat in the clubhouse drinking beer and playing cards. They made extra cash by finding lost golf ball, selling them back to the officers. Most of the players were officers. They lost a lot of balls, for woods surrounded the course. One tee was shot over a cliff with a canyon between it and the fairway. The canyon had a hearty appetite for golf balls.

When winter had ended, and the ice had melted, Anchorage became mud and mosquitoes. The streets were mud. All the cars that were parked on the street were covered with mud on the side of the car that was facing the street. The mosquitoes must have grown while hibernating all winter. If a few of them had brains enough to get together on a project they would have been able to pack a soldier off into the woods to suck out all his blood. The mosquitoes seemed to love the repellent that was issued.

At least the sun was out and it was warm, sometimes hot. Vincent had got pretty tired of looking at white, nothing but white. Now all the small trees had turned from green to a bright, yellow and the sky was blue almost all the time. After awhile the mud turned into dirt, but the mosquitoes never changed, they just stayed thirsty.

Vincent never went anywhere while he was in Alaska. He had wanted to go to Nome, Fairbanks and Ketchikan, but he just never felt good enough to go. He was tired, and the only place he wanted to go was home. That even had priority over Carla. Vincent needed to be somewhere where he could just do nothing. A place he wouldn't have to think about anything and where he wouldn't have to please anyone.

There was one thing Vincent had managed to do while he was in Alaska, he had managed to stay sober. Although he had imbibed the whole time, he hadn't got drunk a single time. Perhaps it was because he hadn't had any drinking partners. It may have been his fear of his mortality that had slowed him down.

The time for Vincent to head south finally rolled around. He was not at all sad about leaving the land of the midnight sun. There was just nothing there that he wanted. After the Brass had relieved him of duty, it was sitting and waiting for an available plane. And it was not much of a plane with only two engines.

Ten soldiers, including Vincent, caught the plane at the Air Force Base not far from Anchorage. It was storming when they got on the plane. Vincent was grateful he didn't have to return to California the same way he had left Washington to go to Alaska. After they had made it to their flight altitude, lightning danced across the planes fragile wings. It was a bumpy ride. Vincent was not used to flying and there was no booze on the plane. He was a nervous wreck by the time they landed in Monterey.

A bus took the tired soldiers to Fort Ord where some of them, including Vincent, would muster out of the Army. It took three weeks to get through the red tape and most of the time was spent just waiting. Vincent mustered out with three hundred dollars in his pocket, plus twenty-six weeks of unemployment benefits. His prayers had finally been answered. He was out of the Army. Vincent was a civilian again. Hallelujah!

CHAPTER 28

Carla was coming to get him. Vincent had stored his Ford at the Flats while he was in Alaska. He had told Carla he would take a bus, but she would not hear of it. She had been breathless on the phone and excited about seeing him. They had not touched each other for almost two years. Vincent hadn't told her he was leaving Alaska. They both had expected him to muster out in November, on about the fourth. The date had been moved to the end of October. When Vincent had first found this out he had subordinated his desire to tell Carla the good news wishing to surprise her. Before leaving Alaska he had written a letter telling her he was going on a bivouac near Fairbanks. He would be there for a week and maybe more. He would be unable to communicate with her while he was there. Vincent had put his hanky over his mouth and had pretended to be a clerk while talking to her on the phone.

"This is Western Union," he had said, "With a message from Vincent Cardoza to Miss Carla Maggio. Are you Miss Maggio?" "Yes," she had replied, excitedly. "The message reads," he had told her, "Dearest Carla. Stop. They have relieved me of all duty. Stop. I am at Fort Ord waiting for you. Stop. Come and get me. Stop." He had paused while Carla waited for more.

"Is that all?" she had asked, impatiently. "No," he had replied and had taken the hanky from his mouth, "You are beautiful, and I want to make love to you." "Oh, God!" she had exclaimed, "Is it really you? Are you really back? She had been so excited. "I am back!" he had exclaimed, "And I want to touch you as soon as possible."

Carla had been happy and a little peeved at the same time. She had been peeved that he had pulled such a despicable trick (that had been her very words). Her joy had dissolved her fit of peeve, which hadn't been too concrete, anyway.

"I want to come and get you right now." she had told him. "I could take a bus," he had suggested, "But it will take forever to get there." "I will see you faster if I come and get you," she had answered. "I'll wait for you by the wharf in Monterey," he had told her, "And I hope you will bring hungry lips." "Mmmm," she had answered, "And I do have them." "Hang up the phone and get here!" he had ordered and she had hung up like it was a sweet pain.

Vincent was waiting for Carla on the wharf. He had left the base, unable to stay on it a minute longer. Vincent just had to feel like a civilian again and he couldn't do it on the Base. Vincent was wearing Levis, boots and a leather jacket. He looked like a genuine civilian again. He laughed; it felt so good to be free. Blustery wind was in his face, giving his hair a carefree look. He was drinking a can of beer, eating a hot dog. He could eat almost anything if he washed it down with booze. Vincent felt almost good. The caffeine and nicotine were out of his system. He was still nervous, but nothing like before. He had gained about ten pounds and looked healthier. Vincent had kept doing his exercising no matter how bad he had felt and he was as hard as a rock.

It wasn't noon yet and although the sun was shining, it was cold. Vincent was glad he had his jacket on. He had always been cold blooded, had always had a hard time keeping warm. Vincent took a drink of his cold beer and it made him shiver. It felt warm in his tummy. Vincent saw Carla coming and his heart jumped into his throat. He could not hold back his joy. His hot dog and beer fell to his feet. Vincent ran to Carla, but it was all he could do to see her through the moisture in his eyes. She saw him and came running at the same time. She had felt the same mind flooding joy. They ran right into each other's arms. They embraced, jumping up and down, dancing to the music of their hearts. They laughed, but couldn't talk; their joy had locked their tongues. They kissed each other's face, lips hungry for the taste of each other. They stepped back, looking at each other, still unable to speak. They rushed back into each other's arms. People were staring at them, but they were oblivious. Carla was the first to be able to speak.

"Vincent Cardoza!" she exclaimed, her voice tremulous with emotion, "Don't you ever, ever leave me again!" "May God strike me dead if I do," answered Vincent. She put her fingers over his lips "Shhushh," she whispered, "You don't have to go that far." They were still holding on to each other, it just felt too good to let go. The two held each other tight. Vincent let go and held her face in his hands. He gently kissed her lips, wanting her in a sweet and gentle way.

"I wish we were on the Pelican," he whispered, softly. "We can be there in a few hours," she answered, feeling the same need. "I will make love to you with my eyes until we get there," he told her, passionately. "Will you promise to make love with something else when we get there?" Carla asked, with a flushed, face, embarrassed by her own naughtiness. "You naughty girl," Vincent answered, "You are so good when you are bad. And I promise to do anything you like." "Anything?" she asked, wickedly. "Anything," he answered, rolling his eyes, lasciviously.

The Jaguar's top was up, so they both took their coats off before getting in. Carla was wearing a pink, cashmere sweater. It revealed the lovely curves of her breast. With a gray, soft looking skirt with pleats, she was delightful to look at. After she had sat down and her skirt had slipped back, revealing her lovely knees, Carla looked even more delightful. Vincent devoured her with his eyes. He watched her every move.

Vincent looked for changes in Carla, but there were none, except she was more beautiful than he had remembered. All of her was beautiful. Her hair was beautiful. He realized that every strand of it was precious; every part of her was precious to him. Passion flooded him as he suddenly wanted to kiss all of her, every part of her. Carla looked and saw the passion in his eyes, and returned it as he put his hand on her knee and then caressed the inside of her thigh.

The drive to the Pelican was not a hurried one. They knew what was waiting for them, and they savored the anticipation. Soon, as the time just seemed to have melted away, they were in the Pelican. Nothing had changed. The hunk was waiting for them, an altar of love. They stood by it and gazed into each other's eyes as he gently removed her clothing, savoring every touch, every move and every sight. When she was standing naked she helped him remove his clothes. There was no haste; time was standing still for them. Then he was standing naked, facing her with his member at attention. Then they were embracing and then they were on the bunk.

"I'm going to kiss you all over," Vincent informed her, with passion. "Oh, God!" Carla exclaimed, "I hope I can stand it." Vincent pulled her hair away from her neck, kissing it just below the hairline. He rolled her over and kissed her shoulders and her back, following her spine to the gentle curves of her lovely behind. Vincent kissed it all over while gently caressing the inside of her thigh. Her thighs opened and a low moan escaped from her parted lips.

Vincent kissed her legs all the way to her feet and then turned her over.

They lay together in an embrace, with his leg between hers. He kissed her neck and breast while exploring with his fingertips, tracing the outline of her body. Vincent kissed her belly down to her pubic hair. He kissed her knees and the inside of her thighs, kissing his way up. She knew what he was doing, for he had done it before. Carla pulled her legs up and then his tongue was in her. She moaned with lust and pleasure, and when she could stand it no longer, Carla pleaded.

"Oh, God, Vincent, I'm going to die If you don't do it to me right away!" And he rose up between her thighs and put himself and his burning passion inside of her. They consumed each other until there was nothing left but sighs and his pretending to sigh; he had had a hard time and was trying to hide it. At the time of his orgasm his heart had done a flip-flop. His stomach had drawn into a knot and he had been left feeling short of breath. He tensed up and she felt it. Vincent felt strange, just like he was going through withdrawal, just like he needed a drink.

"What's wrong?" Carla asked, sounding like she was afraid she had done something wrong. Vincent pretended to have a cramp in his foot. He rolled over, off of her and pulled his foot up and rubbed it. "Just a cramp," he answered. "My body isn't use to such deliciously, violent activity," and then a little, strained giggle escaped from his tight lips. Vincent felt awful, but didn't want her to know. Vincent didn't want her to know that making love to her had made him ill. How could he tell her that? He forced himself to relax and lay back down, but felt like heading for the nearest bar. Carla snuggled to him.

"Are you alright now?" she asked, not too concerned, believing his ruse about the cramp. They lay together kissing each other's face. She sighed and said, "When you make love to me the world just disappears." "Me too," replied Vincent, as she kissed his chest. "I love you," she told him, "And so does my body. It takes control of me when you touch it." "I know," replied Vincent, straining to sound normal, "Your body drives me crazy. I have dreamed of making love to you for months. Now I have and now I know I will never get enough of you." "Me, too," Carla told him, "I want you every time I get close to you."

"Maybe we shouldn't get married," Vincent teased. "Why not?" Carla asked with a worried look. "We might love each other to death," Vincent answered and chuckled. She giggled. "What a way to go," Carla answered, while he was feeling a dire need for a drink. "Is there any brandy on board?" he asked, trying to sound casual. "I think there is," she answered, solicitously, knowing the hard time he had had with his health, "I'll get you some." She got up, and walked naked to the cabinet in the galley. She got a bottle, poured some in a cup and brought it to him. Vincent sipped on it and put some under his tongue. Right away the knot started to leave his stomach.

"You look good in your birthday suit," he told Carla. He was trying to cover his distress with a little humor; a distress the brandy had started to dissolve. Vincent had been trying to stay off the hard stuff, not wanting to get on a running drunk. They were just too hard to get off of. He was thinking to himself, "Now I'm really screwed, I can't make love without a booze chaser. What a choice, alcohol, or celibacy?" Vincent knew he had to get away from Carla; at least long enough to find out what was wrong. He certainly could not marry her without knowing. He felt Carla staring at him.

"What's wrong?" Carla asked, "You look pale." "I do?" he asked, trying to look surprised, "I guess I have not recuperated yet from the Alaska trip." Carla's breast was a temptation to him even when he was ill and he reached and fondled her. "You could get into trouble doing that," Carla cautioned, pulling his hand away, kissing it. "And you don't look like you could handle any trouble right now." He knew this was his opportunity to tell her what he had to do.

"I have to go home and see my mother," Vincent told her, "I feel terribly used up, I need to rest, and I feel like I could sleep forever." She didn't argue, she could plainly see his distress. "I want to drive you there," she told him, "I want to meet your mother." "I was hoping for that," he answered, "My mother will love you." "I hope so," replied Carla, with a trace of qualm. "I know she will," Vincent assured, confidently, "For you are a lovable person. Vincent was feeling amorous, with an erection in progress. He kissed her breast, on her nipple.

"Stop that!" Carla ordered, with an exaggerated firmness. "I can't help myself," Vincent told her, taking her hand and putting it on his erection, "See what you do to me." "Are you sure?" she cautioned and she shivered with delight as his fingers ran through her pubic hair, her foreboding melting with desire. Carla didn't let go of his erection either, she fondled it. "I do see," she told him with lust.

In a moment they were making love again, slower this time and when Vincent had his orgasm, there was no problem. It felt like he would turn inside out, his orgasm seemed like it would never stop and he moaned through it. "God!" he panted, "I didn't think I would ever stop." I know," She replied, "It was wonderful. Are you alright?" "Yes," he answered, relieved, "Except I have lost my erection." "Thank God!" she exclaimed, without thinking. "Do you think God gives and takes erections?" asked Vincent, sanctimoniously.

The look that came on Carla's face tickled him so he had to give up his straight face as a surge of giggles took over him. Her face went from aghast to grin in a split second. "You are truly awful." Carla informed him, between giggles. "God made me that way," Vincent answered, defensively. "He most certainly did not!" retorted Carla, a little shocked. "Who can we blame then?" asked Vincent, still having a problem with the giggles. He took a drink of brandy. "We can blame Eve for eating the apple," she replied. "It was probably Adam's cock," he told her and laughed so hard he had to get up and sit on the edge of the bunk. He had a catch in his side. Carla pushed him the rest of the way off the bunk with her feet. Vincent sat on the floor, giggling. Carla sat on the edge of the bunk and ran her toe through his hair.

"How did a good Catholic girl fall in love with a raunchy guy like Captain Moon?" she asked, affectionately. "Just luck," Vincent answered, fatefully. "I don't know if it be good or bad, for you, that is." "It was good," she told him, "I have never been this happy." "I wonder if I can keep you that way?" he asked, a bit doubtful. "Why do you wonder about that?" Carla asked, surprised. "Because I don't have anything," Vincent answered, "And I do not know anything. I don't know how I'm going to support you. "Daddy can help you," Carla gently assured him, "He has many connections."

"I'm just a country boy from Ophir Flats," stated Vincent "What can I do?" "Don't sell yourself short," she scolded, "You can do anything you put your mind to." "I'm not so sure about that," Vincent answered, meekly, "All I have ever done is work at the cannery and odd jobs. And where would we live?" "Where do you want to live?" Carla asked. "We can't live in the Flats," he told her, "There is nothing there and it is too damned hot." "Why can't we live here?" she asked, "On the Pelican?" he asked and laughed, knowing she had meant San Francisco. Carla started to answer and he cut in. "Oh, you mean in your father's house?" "Of course not, you silly goose," she answered, "Daddy would find us a place," "What are we going to pay rent with?" Vincent asked, "I have three hundred dollars mustering out pay and that is it." "I have some savings," she told him, hopefully, "And Daddy has some properties.

Vincent hesitated to answer, wondering why this didn't bother him. Her parents and Carla had money. Knowing that he would have to accept their help. Shouldn't he have some pride? "Why doesn't this bother me?" he asked himself. He wondered why it wasn't going to bother him.

"Lucky for us," Vincent finally answered, seriously. "Don't worry so," Carla answered, mistaking his tone for worry, "We will both work and we will pay back every penny they loan to us." "Do we have to?" Vincent complained and then laughed. "That's my Captain Moon," she replied and kissed him.

Vincent's mind went on another trail of foreboding. He thought of the curse, and how it was dogging him. If something couldn't be done about sex making him sick without booze he would be in deep trouble. Vincent knew he was addicted and he knew addiction was progressive if he imbibed at all. What an enigma this was. "I guess I could become a priest," he thought to himself, dejectedly.

"What is wrong?" asked Carla, sensing his mood. "I feel so impotent without an erection," he answered and laughed. "That's because you are," Carla told him and giggled, "You wouldn't want to have one all the time, would you?" she asked. "Oh yes I would," he answered, lasciviously, licking his lips. "You want to have a whole house full of kids?" she asked. "I will buy condoms by the case," he replied. "Ugh!" Carla exclaimed, "How unromantic," she said and she joined him on the floor and kissed him. Carla was on her knees.

"You had better get dressed," he warned her," I can feel a big one coming on." "Stay away from me!" she exclaimed, as she got on her feet, "You are a bona fide sex fiend." While Carla was trying to put her panties on, he was kissing her behind. She was giggling so hard it was hard for her to dress. "Stop that you beast!" she exclaimed, "Or I will have to call the Shore Patrol." "Come on," he pleaded, still trying to pull her panties down, "You are safe," he assured her, "I am clear out of sperm." "Down boy!" she ordered, "I am never going to believe that," and she put the rest of her clothes on. "I feel rejected," he told her, woefully. "After two orgasms?" Carla questioned, "Be brave and have faith in future activity," she assured him.

Vincent had another drink of brandy and it tasted better. Vincent was worried about what was causing his problem and the worry was making him thirsty. Then he worried about being thirsty. He wanted to get away from Carla but didn't want to appear anxious about it. He was trying to think of what to say to her.

"When do you want me to take you to Ophir Flats?" she asked, she was anxious to meet his mother. What perfect timing he thought, he hoped she was not reading his mind. "We can go now, or we can rock the Pelican until morning, and go then," he answered and leered. "We better go now," she answered, looking at him askance, one eyebrow raised, "Before you kill yourself." "Perhaps you are right," he said, "But I would consider dying in that manner. "You would," she answered and laughed. "You horny devil."

"I wonder what time it is?" asked Vincent, trying to see his watch. It was getting dark in the boat, which only had portholes for windows. Carla turned a lamp on. "It's about five," she answered, "How long a trip is it?" she asked. "About three hours in my car," he told her, "But it should be less in yours." "It will be late by the time we get there," Carla informed him, "Maybe you should rest and go in the morning." "You mean sleep alone?" he asked with remorse. "Yes," she answered, "You need a recharge." "I would rather plug into you," he answered with regret. "I went for months without you but it didn't make me any stronger." "I don't want to leave you," she informed him, "But you are the one who said you needed a rest." "It is true," Vincent agreed, "And maybe my mother's cooking, and my old M. D. could whip me back into shape." While he was talking fatigue was settling in on him like a mist, with his eyes getting heavy.

"Why don't you take a little nap while I go call my parents," Carla suggested, "And we can go have some dinner, later." Vincent got back on the bunk without any hesitation and lay on his back. "Hurry back," he said, and went to sleep while she was kissing him goodbye. While he slept Carla wrote a note. It said she was going to get some things so they could spend the night on the Pelican and for the trip to the Flats. Then she called her mother and told her what she was going to do.

It was two hours before Carla got back to Vincent and he was still asleep. She watched him as he slept. He looked so peaceful, but she knew he wasn't. Carla felt helpless, unable to help him. Carla desperately wanted to. With anguish she wished her priest could perform an exorcism on him, but she knew it would not help. Vincent's devils were not from the Devil, but from his own mind.

Vincent had told her about his sister. He had told her of the Curse of Cardoza. Carla was aware that he might always feel guilty about his sister's death. She was afraid of the Curse, for she was a bit superstitious, like some Catholics and there was the heredity factor. She prayed to her God that her love would save him; it was all she had. As Carla watched him sleep her heart told her she would love Vincent until her last breath, no matter what. Carla watched; a sentinel of love.

Vincent awoke with a start; he was wide-awake. His mouth was as dry as a powder horn. He swallowed and there was not enough spit to make it all the way down. Depression hit him like cold water in the face as he realized the Curse had icy fingers on his entrails. How could this be? He hadn't had that much brandy. He saw Carla's lovely face, full of love, watching him. She was like an angel with the lamp light gently on her face. Captain Moon put on his mask of normalcy and reached for the brandy.

CHAPTER 29

The Claim Jumper had been like a giant magnet ever since Vincent had returned. Carla had got along so well with Grace and Doc, she was reluctant to leave. Doc was acting like a child around Carla; she had charmed him right out of his good sense.

Vincent had an awful hangover from all the brandy he had imbibed; he had faked normalcy as well as he could. Vincent's wanting Carla to leave had nothing to do with his love for her. Vincent had just wanted to be by himself for a while on familiar turf. He hadn't really wanted to get rid of her; he had just wanted to get away from her temporarily.

The Ford started up just like it had been running yesterday and it felt good to have its steering wheel in his hands. Vincent's feet had been itching to find the Moon Patrol. He had resisted going anywhere, knowing full well, had he found them while Carla was still around, he would have stood a good chance of getting into trouble with her. And that wasn't all that Vincent had wanted to do. An urge to see Linda had been gnawing at him. He had been feeling guilty about that. Vincent had to see her though, he just had to. He just had to see what she looked like, how the years had changed her.

Carla had stayed for a couple of days and now she was gone, but the hangover was not gone. The only thing that had saved him from much suffering was the bottle of brandy he had left in the Ford so long ago. It seemed like years, but was not. Vincent was missing Carla already and a half hour after she had gone he was walking through the swinging doors of the Claim Jumper. It was in the middle of the afternoon. It was hot, and Vincent wanted an ice cold, Moscow Mule. Ted's big face was behind the bar. He looked at Vincent for a second and then his face broke out in a shit eating grin.

"Well kiss my ass!" Ted bellowed, "If it ain't Captain Moon." "In the flesh," answered Vincent. He saw John Brannigan out of the corner of his eye, he was belly up to the bar, two seats to the right of Vincent. He hadn't seen much of John since High School, they had been friends then.

John was about Vincent's height, but about twenty pounds bigger. John was handsome, in a dark sort of way, different looking. There was Indian blood in him from his mother; his father was Irish. John had inherited his mother's dark skin, hair and eyes and his father's build and temperament. John moved over towards Vincent.

"Captain Moon?" John asked Vincent, incredulously. "Haw, Haw," laughed Ned, in his booming voice, "He likes to run around naked in the moon light, Haw, haw." "Where the Hell have you been?" John asked. "Alaska," answered Vincent, "In the Army. I just got out." "Welcome home!" exclaimed Ned, enthusiastically and he handed Vincent his big hand. Vincent's was swallowed in it. "I'm buying you a drink," Ned stated. "I'll drink to that," answered Vincent. "Name your poison," said Ned. "For months I have been dreaming about one of your Moscow Mules," answered Vincent. "Aha!" exclaimed Ned, his eyes aglow, "I got you addicted to them, didn't I?" "You got that right, answered Vincent. Ned already had the frozen copper cup out and a bottle of ginger beer opened. In so many seconds the frozen drink was in Vincent's hand and his lip was sticking to the brim. He swallowed. He wiggled his body, like he was feeling the drink thrill his body.

"God, Dam!" Vincent exclaimed, "That is so good!" He drank the rest down and slid the cup back to Ned. "Old Ned ain't lost his touch," bragged Ned, with his booming voice. "Thank God for that," answered Vincent, as Ned put another one together for him. "Come on Vincent!" exclaimed Brannigan, "What is this Captain Moon bullshit? he asked, with one of his big eyebrows raised on his broad forehead, he must have worn at least a size ten hat. He had a cynical look on his face. He was a cynical person. Brannigan only trusted animals, he was a nature lover.

Vincent told him the story and he guffawed and retorted something in Spanish, he was always doing that. It was like he wanted to be part Spanish instead of Indian. "Speak American," said Vincent, "So I'll know what you are saying." "Maybe you better not know," kidded Brannigan and then he chortled. Vincent didn't answer, he was thinking about the vodka, knowing full well that he should not be drinking it. He should be drinking beer and not even that. Vincent sipped his new drink, planning on beer for the next one. He wanted to see if he could get the Moon Patrol together without getting soused.

"I have to make some calls," Vincent told Brannigan, as he got off his stool. "Male or female?" asked his friend. "Both." answered Vincent on his way to the phone. He heard raucous voices coming from the far end of the bar. He was walking toward it; it was the area where the phone was. Vincent passed One Arm Frank on the way. Frank greeted him with a red, friendly face, tipped his whiskey at him, but didn't speak.

A couple of tunnel stiffs sitting in the corner were the source of the raucous sounds Vincent had been hearing. They were verbalizing rather loudly. Vincent knew they were tunnel stiffs because of their loudness. After spending a week in the tunnels, with the drilling and the blasting, the men were temporarily hard of hearing. After years it would be a permanent condition.

Vincent recognized the miners. One of them was Dink and the other one was The Greek; that was what he was called. The Greek was a big handsome man with black curly hair. He was easy going and he was slow to wrath. Dink was small, but well built. He was a foot or more, shorter than the Greek. He had short, sandy hair. Dink's face was perfectly symmetrical. Dink was telling the Greek about the meanest snake in the world, the one with two heads, one at each end of its body. Dink was telling the story with a poker face and the Greek looked incredulous.

"Come on!" retorted the Greek, "If it has a head at both ends, how does it poop?" Dink was laughing and trying to answer simultaneously. Dink giggled and then he answered, "He can't poop."

The Greek was kind of slow, so Dink let it soak in for a few seconds and then he continued, "He can't poop. That's what makes him so God damned mean!" Dink stopped laughing and the two men looked at each other. The Greek looked serious. "He can't shit?" asked the Greek. He asked like a little kid who was having a hard time believing what he had just been told. His brain cells had got a little spongy from too much booze. And then like a light had turned on in his head, comprehension flashed across his face as he had realized that it was funny. "He can't shit!" The Greek exclaimed and then he chuckled and then he belly laughed. Then they both roared out loud and so did the rest of the patrons, of which there were not many. Vincent exchanged greetings with the miners and then he picked up the phone. He called the big Italian first and Mario answered the phone.

"Dug any wells lately?" Vincent asked. "Captain Moon?" Mario asked. "It should be private Moon," Vincent answered. "Where the Hell are you?" asked Mario. "The Claim Jumper," answered Vincent, where else? "I'm on my way," answered Mario. "Wait a minute," asked Vincent, "Would you call the rest of the Patrol for me?" "Will do," answered Mario, "Save some booze for me." After Mario had hung up the phone Vincent had an urge to call Linda; he had retained her number in his memory. He called with the hope her sister would not answer.

"Hello?" answered Linda's questioning innocent voice. Vincent just answered, saying no more, wondering if she would recognize his voice. Linda didn't answer for what seemed like the longest time. Vincent was just getting ready to say more. "Vincent?" she asked, ever so softly, "Is that you?" He could feel her excitement. "It is I," he answered, loving her voice, remembering how he had felt about her, feeling it again. Vincent wondered how he was going to tell her about Carla. There was no reason to tell her right away, he would wait for the right time.

"Why did you stop writing to me?" she asked in anguish. He hadn't written to her for a long time, he hadn't known what to say to her. Vincent had thought she would be better off if she forgot him. He still didn't know what to say to her, so he fabricated. "You were so, young," he answered, "I wanted you to have a chance to be sure about your feelings." It sounded lame to him. Vincent hoped it didn't sound the same to her. "My feelings are never going to change!" she told him with emotion, "I thought you knew that." "You were so, young," he repeated, "And you still are. You are only sixteen now." "My heart doesn't know how old I am," Linda pleaded, sounding like she was ready for tears.

"I have missed you something awful Vincent told her, trying to avoid the tears, "I want to see you If you still want to see me?" "Oh, I do, Vincent" she answered, sounding like she wanted to come through the wire. "Can you come out for a little while tonight?" Vincent asked, "Will your mother let you go with me?" "I'm going with you no matter what!" she told him, fiercely. "I'll be out about eight," Vincent told her. "Where are you?" she asked, "I hear music." "I'm at The Claim Jumper." "Who is with you?" "John Brannigan, but you don't know him." "I love you," she told him, meekly. "I love you too," Vincent answered, without hesitation. It was the truth. It was so true that Vincent didn't know if he could tell her about Carla. He didn't know if he could tell Carla about her. What an awful fix to be in.

"I can't wait to see you again," Linda told him with a tremulous voice. "Me too," answered Vincent, "I'll see you later." "Okay," Linda answered, but neither one wanted to hang up. They both hesitated. "Are you going to hang up?" Vincent asked. "I can't," she answered, "You will have to." "Let's both do it at the same time," he suggested. "How will we do that?" she asked. "Let's kiss over the phone." "How?" she asked. "Parse your lovely lips," Vincent told her, "And pretend we are kissing and I will do the same. And be a little noisy about it, and then hang up." "Okay," she agreed. "Do it now," Vincent told her, and they both did. Vincent hesitated before hanging up and so did Linda. He hung up first, knowing he would have to.

Vincent was remembering Linda's face, wondering if she had changed; a teenager can change a lot in two years. Vincent was walking back to his stool when Mario walked in. They both spotted each other. The big Italian headed for Vincent with a grin that was swallowing his face. Mario was so glad to see Vincent, and he felt shy about it, but his gregariousness took over.

"Captain Moon!" Mario greeted and stuck out his big hand. "You big ape," greeted Vincent, as he grabbed Mario's hand, pulled him to him and hugged him. Mario was embarrassed, but hugged him back. "You been keeping that nose out of Fist City?" asked Vincent. "Most of the time," answered Mario, while reaching for his nose, caressing it like it was precious. "Any more Moons coming?" asked Vincent. "Mack, and Walt," answered Mario, "Buck joined the Air force."

The two Moons walked back to Vincent's stool and his drink. Vincent introduced Mario to Brannigan, but they both had seen each other around. Mario bought Vincent another drink and ordered a beer for himself. "Are we going to get drunk together like we use to?" asked Mario. "Maybe later," answered Vincent," I'm going to see Linda at eight and have to stay sober until after that." "Ah ha!" exclaimed Mario, while rolling his eyes lasciviously. "Have you seen her lately?" asked Vincent. "I see her once in awhile," Mario answered, "She went to a swimming party with us about a month ago." "Does she have a boy friend?" asked Vincent, worried, but trying not to look so. "She is still waiting for you. Mama Mia, you are lucky!" "She looks good?" asked Vincent. "More than anyone has a right to," answered Mario.

Just about that time Mack came through the swinging doors. His whimsical face was split with a shit-eating grin. A straw hat was sitting on his odd shaped head. Mack's head was narrow at the temples, like a duck's. He looked like he had just walked out of The Ozark Mountains.

"Captain Moon," greeted Mack, in his singsong voice, "And Looootenant Moon, I presume." "Hello, Private Moon," greeted Mario, getting even for the low rank he had been given. They all shook hands and Mack gave Vincent a bear hug. Mack had missed Vincent more than any of them. Vincent had always treated him better than anyone. "You ought to drink a case of beer every day," Mack told Vincent, "it would put some fat on you." He patted Vincent on the tummy, giggling in his silly way. "You should, too, you bag of bones," retorted Vincent, as Mack didn't have an ounce of fat on him, either. "I will if you are buying," quipped Mack. "Me, too!" exclaimed Mario, "Can I get in on this?" asked Brannigan. "Dutch treat from now on," answered the Captain. Just then Walt Hedger walked through the doors and the whole thing started over again. The boys reminisced, kicked a few dead dogs and drank. It didn't take any time at all for eight o'clock to roll around and took Vincent another twenty minutes to pull himself away from his friends. He told them he would return by eleven or so.

Captain Moon felt better than he should when he parked on the road above the Henderson residence. He hoped Greta would not be there, he only wanted to see Linda. Vincent popped a breath mint into his mouth, got out of the car and walked down the hill. Linda came out the door before he got down the hill; he could see her clearly in the porch light.

Vincent knew Linda was sixteen, but she looked eighteen. Linda looked so shy. She was so lovely, her figure had rounded out; she was not a little girl anymore. It seemed like such a long time since they had seen each other; Vincent knew that was why she looked so shy. He felt a little uncomfortable himself, but she was so, lovely and he was remembering her sweet kisses. Vincent walked almost up to her and stopped about a yard, or so from her. He looked her up and down and gave her a wide, grin.

"Are you Linda," he asked, pulling her leg, and she was aware that he was. "The cute little girl who use to live here?" "Uh, huh." Linda answered. "I knew you would be beautiful." "Stop that!" she gushed, modestly. "Are you going to let me hug you and squeeze you and kiss you?" he asked. Linda got brave and ran toward him. "You had better," she told him as she ran into his open arms. They kissed and all the old feelings came back, compounded by her maturity. She felt so, soft, so, good in his arms. Her lips were soft, so yearning. Vincent's knees felt weak, his heart was pounding. He swept her off her feet and twirled around with her in his arms. Linda was equally excited, covering his face with kisses, and tears of joy, laughing and crying at the same time.

How could he possibly give her up? There was no way he could tell her about Carla. He knew he couldn't tell Carla, either. He loved her too. But Linda was in his arms. Neither of them wanted to let go of the other. Linda was unreservedly, joyous, while Vincent felt joyous and guilty at the same time. Vincent's mixed emotions caused his love for her to feel illicit, making it seem even more exciting. Finally, Vincent pulled away.

"We can't stay out here all night," he told her, "What would your parents think?" "Let's go in," she answered, breathlessly, her face flushed by her emotions. "They will be glad to see you," and she grabbed his arm and pulled him in the door. "Is Greta here?" Vincent asked, praying that she wasn't. "She lives in Hayward now," Linda answered, "She is going to college there." Vincent didn't say anything. "Did you want to see her?" asked Linda. "I came to see you," he answered and by that time they were in the living room and Maggie was giving him a hug. After she had finished, George was shaking his hand. They were both glad to see him and they jabbered about this and that.

Linda had already had consent to go out with Vincent. She hadn't had the chance to tell him and so he was still wondering if she could. Vincent didn't remark about it, he just waited. Getting impatient, he finally looked at her and asked with his eyes and some body language. Linda smiled, reading him.

"Are you ready to go?" she asked and Vincent was. They left after saying goodbye to her parents. Vincent was thinking how good things had gone as he was walking this lovely creature to his car. It hadn't got totally dark yet and the moon was providing some romantic light. They were holding hands as they walked up the driveway. Her parents had let her go on the condition she would be home by eleven.

"Let's go to our place for just a little while," suggested Linda, hopefully. Vincent was parked on the wrong side of the road. The car pointed in the right direction to go there, so all he had to do was drive a couple hundred feet and park again. They ran hand in hand to there place. The Moon was filtering its light through the trees, and it was so quiet, so serene; it was almost unreal.

"I wonder what Count Dracula is doing tonight?" asked Vincent and the girl moved into his arms. He hugged her and she buried her face in his chest. "I missed you so, much." she told him, softly, woefully, "I was afraid I would never see you again." "I'm sorry," he answered with sympathy "I would never hurt you on purpose."

Vincent ran his fingers through her hair and then he tipped her head up and kissed her on her sweet, open lips, lips that fit his perfectly. Linda's lips were so, entrancing. Vincent traced the outline of them with the tip of his tongue. It stirred her passion and she did the same to him. Then her tongue was searching the inside of his mouth. Linda was so, excited and her ardor was stirring his passion to the red zone. He had to put the brakes on someway. She was still only sixteen, no matter how much of a woman she was, physically. Vincent picked the girl up off her feet and twirled her around until he was getting dizzy and she was laughing. Vincent put her down, grabbed her hand and pulled her to the tree he had carved their names on.

"It is still there," she told him, breathlessly, "I look at it every day." Vincent was moved by her faithfulness. He swooped her up in his arms and carried her around the center of their place, kissing her face and eager lips. "My woman child," he whispered to her, "How long would you wait for me?" "Forever and forever!" she answered, ardently. Vincent, dizzy from the twirling, kneeled and laid the girl down on the soft clover bed. He almost fell on her. They went into an embrace and a kiss they couldn't pull away from until they were both out of breath. Vincent's desire was burning. He desperately wanted to explore her lovely body, but he knew if he touched any of her intimate places he would not be able to stop himself.

"I love you," Linda whispered, fervently," I love you so much I feel like I'm on fire." "Me, too," answered Vincent, "But we have to get out of here," and he started to pull away from her to get up, but she pulled him back. "No, no!" she pleaded, wanting him, "Why do we have to go?" "I'm afraid I will not be able to stop myself," he told the girl. "What if I don't want you to stop?" she asked him, bravely and what a temptation it was for him. Every fiber of his being wanted her, but she was just too young. Vincent had to stop himself, but she was kissing him again. The hot blood was pumping; the swelling straining at his clothing. He jumped to his feet and pulled her up. Linda got up, reluctantly, pouting. They stood, facing each other, their bodies touching. She whispered to him. "You could do anything you want to me, you know."

"I want to make love to you," Vincent told her. "But I'm too young," she finished for him, "And when will I be old enough for you?" she asked, petulant. "Two more years," he told her, feeling as if he had said the impossible. "And just how old were you?" she asked, frustrated and defiant. Vincent was flustered, not knowing how to answer. "What do you mean?" He asked to give himself some time to think. "How old were you the first time you made love?" Linda asked, still defiant. Vincent was a little embarrassed by her forwardness, even though he had just told her he wanted to make love to her. "About fourteen," he answered, knowing he had talked himself into a corner as soon as he had opened his mouth. "See!" she exclaimed, defensively. "It's alright for you to do it, but not alright for me. And I'm older than you were." "But it wasn't alright!" Vincent retorted and now he was on the defensive and he was explaining without a whole lot of conviction. "We were not supposed to do it," he told Linda and it sounded so lame, he thought.

"But you did it anyway," she argued, "So how come I have to stay a virgin, but you didn't have to?" "You can get pregnant," he retorted, "But I can't." "How old was she?" Linda asked, changing her course. "About thirteen," Vincent answered, sheepishly. "Well, golly!" she exclaimed, childishly, "I wish it had been me. "Did she get pregnant?" Linda asked, after a second of thought. "No," he answered, "But." "See!" she retorted, before he had been able to finish. "But she could have!" he exclaimed, "And we were so, afraid." "Did you ever do it again with her?" she asked, a little more calmly. "No," he answered, "We were too, afraid and then we got ashamed about it and then we broke up." "I see," she said, softly, sympathetically, relating to the situation.

"And it is different with us," Vincent explained with affection. "I'm an adult and I'm supposed to protect you from me. "But I don't want to be protected from you," Linda told him, playfully, fondling his behind, which was a new activity for her. Before Vincent could catch himself, he was petting her behind. It felt so good his hand stayed there after he had stopped fondling. He wanted so much to do more.

Linda pulled his head down and her lips found his. Her lips were pleading and then urgent. Vincent was urgent. He had to do something, for his senses were reeling with passion. He pulled his lips away from hers, bent over and picked her up, with her torso hanging over his shoulder. He patted her fanny and carried her out of their (almost) Garden of Eden.

"It's not safe in here," Vincent told Linda on the way out. He laughed to relieve the stress, "You are too dangerous." "Put me down, you bully!" she ordered, playfully and she giggled. "I wish I was taking you to my cave," he answered and it was the truth. "What would you do to me there?" she asked, coquettishly. "Play with you, I guess," he answered. "What if I was eighteen?" Linda asked. "I would play with you I guess." "You lie!" Linda exclaimed playfully

"Yes I do, yes I do," Vincent answered and laughed.

Then they were at the car. Vincent put the girl on her feet and then he took her in his arms, playfully, unable to let go of her. "I love you, my woman child," he told her. "I love you too, my man child." she answered, sweetly and he leaned back on his car, with her weight against him and they kissed a soft, slow one. "You taste so good," he told Linda, licking her lips, gently, "Good enough to eat." he told her, not meaning anything suggestive. Then he thought about what he had done with Carla. Then he was thinking about it with Linda; there was a naughty picture going through his head. "So do you," Linda answered, tasting his lips with her tongue and then putting it in his mouth. Vincent did the same to her. He kissed her throat, inhaling the scent from her breast, which was so delicious he wanted, desperately, to take her clothes off, to see her body, to feel it, to feel the inside of her.

Vincent's legs were tired, so he turned around and sat Linda down on his fender; he was standing between her knees. He leaned over to kiss her, not thinking about being between her legs. When Linda reached out to put her hands around his neck to kiss him, she pulled on his neck and when she did, her pretty bottom slipped on the fender and slid into him. Her thighs automatically opened to accommodate him. This position made both of their kisses more fervent.

Vincent was between her thighs and both them were on fire. He was thinking of her virgin mound, how sweet it would be, while she was just feeling his pressure, surrendering to her passion. The girl put her legs around him and squeezed him to her. The only thing that stood between them and intimate uniting was their clothing. If it had disappeared, he would not have been able to stop himself. And then they heard the car coming. It cooled them and they separated, quickly getting into the car. They sat for a few minutes after the car had passed, thinking about their last kiss, both knowing, had they been somewhere different, something would have happened.

"I guess it was a good thing we left our secret place," Linda commented, demurely, softly. "We will have to be more careful." Vincent cautioned, his palms and forehead wet with perspiration, "I don't know how much temptation I can take." "I can't take any," she told, meekly, "Not with you." "We better go do something," Vincent told her, "We could go to a movie," he suggested. "We could go to the Drive In," she suggested, hopefully. "The Passion Pitt?" I don't know if that's such a good idea," he answered, with a raised eyebrow.

"My clothes are already messed up from rolling around in the clover and fooling around on your fender." Linda told Vincent, haughtily and then she giggled like a schoolgirl, which she was. "You make us sound pretty naughty," Vincent answered and chuckled. "We could have been," she said with regret. "Let's go to the Drive In," he said and started the car.

The Passion Pit was already full, almost to capacity. It was Saturday night. They had to park almost in the last row, which they didn't care, not even a little. Vincent had already seen both of the movies; he had already seen almost all movies. He had seen them on the base for a quarter. Linda hadn't seen either one, but she was only slightly interested. Linda had other things on her mind, amorous things. Linda scooted against him as soon as he got parked and rested her hand on his thigh. Vincent was tempted to put his hand on her thigh, but resisted and put his hand over hers. He felt it would be a safer place to put it. They talked about trivia and things while the movie got into progress. It was a light, fluffy comedy with Doris Day and Rock Hudson. The sweet hearts talked about the future, college and that sort of thing.

"What are you going to do?" Linda asked, "Are you going to live here?" "I have to go back to the Bay Area, "Vincent answered, "That is where the money is." He couldn't tell her about Carla. He thought to himself about Carla. He hadn't been thinking about her at all. Vincent thought about what a louse he was being. What was he going to do? He couldn't give up either one of them. He didn't know if things would work out with Carla. He didn't know if he could stand city life. He would just have to play it by ear.

Linda was stroking his arm with her free hand, pulling at the fine hair unconsciously. A romantic scene was in progress on the giant screen "I wish we were doing that," Linda commented, dreamily. Vincent was thinking the same thing and couldn't resist. He turned and put his arm around her, putting his face to her neck, by her ear, inhaling her sweet fragrance. Vincent kissed her pretty ear lobe. It was so, sweet, so, soft, with her lovely hair in his face. Affection flooded his senses. She moaned with an innocent yearning, turning her lips to his, incredibly soft lips, moist, luscious, delightful lips.

They were in each other's arms now, squeezing, kissing and wanting. Vincent tried, but just couldn't stop himself from caressing her. The girl was so, desirable and so wonderfully put together. Her breast was firm and her breathing was deep as he fondled her. "I wanted you to do that," she whispered, her voice was tremulous. "I dreamed about it" Linda told Vincent while he was wishing she were not wearing a bra. He was wrestling himself at the same time, feeling guilty, worried about how far he might go with her, knowing how low his resistance to temptation was. "I shouldn't be doing this," he told her, unable to stop himself.

"I want you to," she told him, wanting him to do everything, worried about when she would see him again. "I don't know when I will see you again," she told him as she undid her bra. Vincent felt the stress go out of it and his hand went under it. He sucked in his breath as he felt her form, the lower side of her breast, so rounded, so perfect. Her nipples were extended as he traced them with his fingertips. He lifted her blouse and kissed her breast, putting his lips to her nipples, kissing them, sucking them like a baby. Linda was moaning, panting, and kissing his hair, wanting him, new to such passion. His hand was on her thigh, under her skirt; he had to stop.

CHAPTER 30

Vincent had stopped, but not without considerable effort. His hand had been caressing the soft, silky flesh on the inside of her thigh, almost to her most intimate place. Linda had squirmed and had moved herself to his hand in an effort to touch her to him, wanting him to touch her there. His hand had almost reached her virgin mound; he had felt it in his mind but had stopped himself and had pulled away from her. It had been the hardest thing he had ever done, but he could not bring him self to make love to her and then leave her to marry Carla. And now he had to think of what to say to her.

"I'm starving," Vincent told Linda, breathlessly, "I am going to the snack bar." He got out of the car. He had such an erection it was uncomfortable walking. He wished he could go somewhere to relieve himself of the sexual tension. He made it to the snack bar to get some drinks and popcorn. By the time he made it back to the car some of the tension had left him and she had partially composed herself. During there passion she had ended up on the passenger's side of the seat. That was where Linda was sitting on his return. She was quiet as they munched their snack.

"It's getting lonely over here," Vincent complained, after awhile, "Are you sure you want me?" she asked, self-consciously. "I want you too, much!" he retorted with emotion," That is the trouble." he motioned for her to come to him and she moved over to him, obediently. "Is this close enough?" she asked, like she was asking for adult approval. "That's close enough," he answered, still frustrated, "We have to play it cool for the rest of the night."

"Why?" she asked, disappointed, "Why can't we neck, every body else is doing it." "It's too, dangerous for us" he retorted, with frustration. "Why is that?" she asked, not to be put off. "I get too, hot," he told her, not being able to think of anything else, "And so do you." "I'm not afraid," she told him, defiantly. "Well I am," he retorted. "Afraid you will do it to me?" she asked like a schoolgirl. "Yes," he answered, thinking the sparring had ended.

"I'm not afraid," Linda told him and Vincent sighed, but didn't answer. "I'm not afraid for you to make love to me. I want you to." "It's against the law," he told her, not knowing what else to say, excited by her candor. "There are laws to protect little girls like you from bad guys like me," Vincent told her, wondering why he had called himself a bad guy. "I wouldn't tell on you," she told him, seriously. "Do you think I would? And you know I'm not a little girl anymore." "That's not the point," he argued, "I know it would be wrong to take advantage of your love, and innocence." "Well, I don't want to be innocent anymore!" she exclaimed, vehemently. "Well I want you to stay innocent until I marry you," he blurted, just as vehemently and then he realized what he had said. Vincent thought to himself, "Now you have done it, you moron."

"Are you going to marry me?" she asked, excitedly, "When?" "I don't know," he answered, confused, not knowing how to fix what he had said, "I haven't asked you yet." "When are you going to ask me?" Linda asked, expectantly. "I don't know," he answered, stalling for thinking time, "When you are older." "It makes no difference to me," she answered, "I have already said yes in my heart." Vincent groaned inwardly, wishing he could have two wives.

Maybe if I don't marry either of them, I can have both of them, he thought, after he had taken her home and was on his way back to the Claim. But he knew that wouldn't work either, he believed he would lose both of them that way. He would have to stall his marriage to Carla someway, until he could make up his mind.

The Claim was full of smoke and drunks by the time he got back to it, and Vincent was powerfully thirsty.

"Well it's about time!" the boys complained after they had spotted him. Dick Justice and his pretty sweetheart, Regina, had joined the group, everyone called him "Spider," but no one knew why. Spider and Vincent had gone to Print Shop together in High School. Spider had been the class clown. Booze turned Spider's vocabulary into colorful profanity. One of his stories was in progress and there were numerous four-letter words.

"I will start over for you," he told Vincent. "Reggie and I went to the movies," he pointed to his girl, "I asked her if she wanted anything from the snack bar." Reggie was waving her hand and shaking her head in the negative. It was apparent she did not want the story told, but Spider went on. "She said she didn't want anything. I asked her if she was sure and she said she was. I got a Coke and a box of popcorn and we went up to the lodges and sat down."

Spider was a good storyteller; he had good timing, like a regular comedian, one of those monologue artists. He was a funny guy when he was drunk, gregarious as all get out. But when he was sober he was a regular hermit, self-conscious, introverted.

"Reggie started eating my popcorn," he went on like he was getting aggravated; Reggie giggled and turned her head away. "I told her I would go get her some, but she said she only wanted a little of mine, but she kept putting her paws in my popcorn box, pulling out big handfuls." Spider got this big grin on his face and looked at Reggie. Reggie looked at him and giggled, she never laughed. "I got this idea," said Spider, "And I went ahead with it. When the box was almost empty, I opened the bottom and emptied it. I unzipped my pants and pulled out a boner; it had got that way from thinking about what I was going to do. I put the empty box down over my boner and waited." Reggie slapped his shoulder and turned her head the other way. "When she reached into the box to get a handful of pop-corn, she got a handful of boner instead. Reggie let out a screech that could have been heard across the street."

Everyone just roared, except Spider, who just stood there with his foot on the rail and a smug look on his face. "And that's not all," he continued, and then he laughed until he was in control again, "She wouldn't let go of it." Reggie got up and hurried into the ladies room while everyone lost control. "What did she do with it?" asked someone, "How long did she hang on to it?" asked another and this kind of banter went on until they had worn it out.

Dan McGee was sitting on one of the stools close by. He was a sandy haired, Irishman. He was a bartender when he was not on the front side of the bar. Dan was shit-faced drunk and there were six highballs sitting in front of him.

"What are all the soldiers for?" asked Vincent. "They give me a feeling of security," answered the too happy Irishman. "I can understand that," answered Vincent and he was being truthful. After that the boys settled down and proceeded to get seriously drunk. By closing time they were all sloshed and none of them were ready to give it up.

"Let's go to Cadillac Flats, "suggested Mack. The place was an area outside the city limits, at the south end of town. Much of the black community lived in that area, and they had their cafes and nightclubs there. Although they stopped the sale of booze at two A. M., they kept their establishments open for dancing, eating, gambling, and whatever else they could get away with. The cars became the bars; everyone had booze in their car.

Reggie took Spider home and the rest of the group went to Cadillac Flats. They hit the Cotton Club first. Between the dark and the smoke, it was hard to see at first. The place was packed and the dance floor was full. Fats Domino was singing "Blueberry Hill" via the Wurlitzer. Most of the dancers were black and some of them had no partner; they were just doing their own thing.

"Let's get some chili before we drink anymore," suggested Mario, who didn't like to drink on an empty stomach. His brother had lost a large part of his stomach for doing just that. Everyone was willing, for they had the best chili in the world at the Cotton Club. It was made with pork instead of beef, seasoned just right, thick and it was hot. They all agreed, except Captain Moon. He knew that eating would kill his buzz and he had drunk all night to get it. Mario convinced him they would just drink some more buzz when they were finished eating and Vincent agreed, reluctantly. While he was eating his chili his buzz got away, just like he knew it would.

Vincent went to the latrine first, to get away from the others and then he went out to the parking lot to find some more buzz maker. He knew there was part of a bottle of brandy in the trunk of his car, but there was not much left. There was beer in Mario's car, but he wanted none of that; it would just make him feel full.

Vincent went to his car, drank the rest of the brandy, and then he went looking for a source. He knew it would be easier to find someone who was willing to share if he was alone. His head felt cold and he went back to his car to get his hat. His hat was one of those straw ones like Sinatra wears, one of the dark, narrow brimmed ones with a light colored, wide band. Vincent wore it sometimes in San Francisco, to keep the pigeon shit out of his hair. After he had put his hat on, Vincent spotted some Fly Boys; they were passing a jug around. He recognized one of them, his name was Les. Vincent walked over and asked him what he was doing at home. Les had joined up when he was seventeen and had ended up in Korea.

"Just on leave," he answered, "Come and drink with us." "Don't mind if I do," answered Captain Moon. "What are you drinking?" he asked and Les handed him the jug with his delicate hand. Everything about Les was delicate, including his voice. "Thunderbird," he answered, softly and then he giggled in a feminine sort of way. Thunderbird is an aperitif wine, twenty percent alcohol by volume. It was easy to drink, it went down easy, a little too easy. It went down easy enough to cause one to think it had little power, which was not so at all. Neutral grain spirits had been added to it to bring it up to twenty percent, to give it more punch.

The Captain wiped the orifice of the bottle with his palm, an automatic futile sanitary attempt, and took a big pull from the jug. It was the first time he had tasted Thunderbird. It was sweet, tasted good and went down easy, like a soft drink. "That's alright," The Captain commented, with appreciation, as the wine warmed his innards. "Yeah," replied one of the Fly Boys, "And its cheap crap, too." Les made introductions, but they were forgotten almost as soon as they were made.

A pretty black girl sashayed over to the group. She was about the

Captain's age and was just about as tall. The girl had delicate features for one of her race and her skin was lighter than most. She was very sexy looking.

"Hey, Frankie," she called to the Captain and he turned to see if she was addressing someone behind him. "I'm talking to you," she told him, with her finger pointed at him. She had slender fingers, adorned with rings. Vincent realized then, that it was the hat, she was calling him Frankie because of the hat. "Yes," he answered, as he gave her a slow, once over, admiring her tight, orchid colored skirt and her tight, white Angora wool sweater. The girl stood with her feet apart, her hands on her shapely hips. She smiled, revealing perfect, beautiful white teeth.

"You wanna play games with me?" she asked Vincent, brazenly, leaving Captain Moon agape for a second, not being used to being propositioned so boldly. When he realized she was a hooker, he wondered what she would be like and he appraised her. Vincent had never made it with a black girl before, and the thought was intriguing. He would bet she could screw one to death. "How much?" he asked, wondering what her naked breast was like. Was she a lighter color where she was covered? Vincent was getting erect thinking about it. The girl moved her hip in an erotic way and pointed her finger at him. He felt horny as Hell, "Twenty bucks for you, Frankie," she told him, "Cause you is so cute." Vincent would have loved to make it with her, but he was on a tight budget, and did not want to run out of booze money before finding another source.

"What's my credit worth?" Vincent asked her playfully. "Plenty of nothing," she answered playfully. She laughed, looked at the Fly Boys, and asked, "How about you guys?" and one of them obliged her. "I like to play games," he told her, "Where do we play?" "I live across the street," she informed him as she pointed to a small house with a dip in its green, tarpaper roof. The Fly Boy took out his wallet, extracted a twenty from it, and handed his wallet to Les.

"You keep my wallet until I get back," he told Les. "Let's go," he told the girl. She wanted to call him a dirty name for his little show of mistrust, but she needed the money. She showed him a mouthful of teeth, took him by the arm and led him to her house of commerce,

The boys passed the jug around and told some raunchy tales. The Captain decided he should check up on the Patrollers. He told Les what he wanted to do and he was pleased that the other Patrollers were there, for they were also his friends. A short, stocky airman went with them, his name was Gil. He had a fish face that went with his name, he even had bulgy eyes like some fish do and he had no neck. At least it looked that way because of the muscles that sloped from his head to the end of his shoulders.

They were all just about bombed all the way. Fish Face was having a hard time walking to the Cotton Club. Actually, he was just having a hard time walking. His mind wanted to go one-way, and his feet another. Les was staggering a little, but he had always held his booze well, even though he was small and delicate. He looked like a fifteen year old kid, with his flat top haircut. Les always got asked for his I.D.

When the boys got into the Cotton Club, Captain Moon spotted Mack dancing with a fat, black broad, who must have been over fifty and poorly maintained. She was badly, ugly. Her face was something that should never have happened, and her body should have been left behind, in fact, a large part of her body was behind her. When Mack was drunk he was a poor judge of feminine beauty. He would screw a snake if someone would hold it for him.

Mario came over to the Captain, he looked sober, but he wasn't. He could drink a lot; he had been drinking wine since he was a little kid, just like the rest of his family, just like Italians do. Wine had driven his father to insanity, and then to death. The Captain could remember seeing him chase Mario around the kitchen while wielding a butcher knife and enraged over something Mario had done.

"We got to get Mack out of here," Said Mario, "He is putting the make on every broad in here." "I believe you are right," agreed the Captain, "He would put the make on a female cadaver." "And go all the way with her," agreed Mario, and he continued after watching Mack for a few seconds. "He has already got some of these guys pissed by making passes at their broads. We better get him to a different place so he can start all over again." The Captain agreed, and so did Les. Fish Face didn't comprehend much of anything; he was loose as a goose.

The dance floor was crowded; they had to look every once in a while to keep track of Mack. They found him and he was still dancing furiously with the same ugly broad. Brannigan was dancing too. It looked like he was dancing some kind of Indian war dance. He had absolutely no rhythm; he was just dancing with himself. Who else would want to dance with him?

The music got into the Captain's feet and he started dancing with himself. Mario watched him for a few minutes, and then he started. He mumbled to himself about doing what the Romans do. Walt was dancing with a pretty black girl, who did not look old enough to be there. She was sticking to Walt like hot glue. Les and Fish Face had gone to relieve their bladders and were coming back when the music stopped. They joined with Mario and the Captain to gather around Mack. Walt was still busy with the girl and Brannigan had gone outside. Mario and the Captain got hold of Mack and led him off the dance floor.

"We have to get you out of here," the Captain told him, as he motioned for him to look at the biggest, meanest looking black in the place. "That guy is after your ass, and your blood," he told him. Mack gets this unhinged look on his face, even more unhinged than was normal for him.

Mack starts pounding his chest, making noises like Tarzan. "I'll murder the bastard!" he yells, and everyone in the place was looking at him like he was from outer space.

The Captain and Mario knew words would be futile. Mario stepped behind Mack and grabbed him under his arms, lifting him off his feet. The Captain got him by his feet and they carried him, struggling, and yelling, all the way out of the Cotton Club. When they got him out the door, and stood him on his feet, Mack came out swinging, but he was too drunk to hit anyone. Mario and the Captain danced around him, keeping out of his reach. They continued until Mack was out of breath. Mack finally got tired and stopped. He just stood there, tongue hanging out, trying to catch his breath.

"What you need is a drink," the Captain told him. "By God you got that right!" exclaimed Mack, instantly. "I'll go get the Thunderbird," offered Les, "We have another gallon of it," he said and ran after it. Mack sat on the ground, Indian fashion, and lit himself a cigarette. He inhaled a drag from it and let it out slowly. He got this look on his face, like he was in a trance. Mack's face was angelic, looking; he looked like a lost child. The Captain knew what was coming next; he had seen that look many times before. He knew the words that were forming behind Mack's lips before they came out.

"A-www Shit!" exclaimed the Captain, and then Mack was singing his song. "Ohhhhhhhhh, I thought one day I would have some fun and learn how flying aero planes was done." "Awe Shit!" exclaimed Mario and Mack sang on. Mario had been through this before, also, but Mack kept right on singing; he was oblivious to everything when in this state. Nothing could stop him from singing his song, maybe death? It was an Okie sounding, song, a many versed song and Mack knew all of them. It was suspect that he made some new ones as he sang.

The Captain covered his ears in a futile attempt to stop the awful sounds that were assaulting them. There are some things that one can't stop, or change. He sat down with Mack, and the rest followed. They passed the jug around. Mack would stop long enough to take a snort and then go right back to his song with his maddening, sing-songy, voice. It went on and on and on. After what seemed forever, Les suggested they go to The Black Dahlia, a joint just up the street. The Captain decided he would take his car, for they were all too drunk to walk. The place was only a couple of blocks away; short blocks. Mario went to find Walt, after the Captain had suggested it. He did not want the party to be too scattered, in case of any trouble

Walt and the girl he was with, walked over and the rest of them got in the Captain's car, including Fish Face, and they drove to the other club. The parking lot was full, near capacity, but a place was found. They primed themselves before going in, some on beer, and some on Thunderbird. The Captain had the latter.

They walked into the place single file, with the Captain in the lead. Mario was next, followed by Les, Fish Face, with Mack trailing, still singing his song. The place was thickly dark with nicotine smog and was full of blacks, just like it was supposed to be. There were only a few whites. Some of the patrols started dancing, some were just milling around. Some were eating and some were gambling at the tables playing poker. No one paid any attention to them when they walked in.

Mack was the last one in and he was having a problem. When he was drinking his brain went into slow motion, or suspended animation. He was suffering from a delayed reaction. Mack was just starting to get real mad at the black guy in the Cotton Club who had been the cause of him being separated from his black beauty. Mack had stopped singing and the Captain was watching Mack's face. It was going through a strange metamorphosis. It was changing from dreamy-singy to red faced, swelling, and yelling. Mack's mouth came open. Captain Moon knew something awful was going to come out of it and he held his breath. Mack's eyes closed, his face swelled from vehemence as the pressure built on his vocal cords. And then it all came out like a clap of thunder; a bolt of lightning to put to sunder the noise, and joviality of the atmosphere of the Black Dahlia.

"All of you black bastards are chicken shit!" "Oh, my God!" exclaimed the Captain, after he had sucked in his breath. All vocal cords had muted, with the only noise coming from the Wurlitzer. Mario's big Italian eyes got bigger as his olive tan, blanched. "Holy Shit!" was all he could manage. The Wurlitzer ran dry, and there was deadly silence. The Captain wanted to get out while they were still in the time warp. The hair on the back of his neck was rising as he grabbed Mack, pulling him to the exit. Mario raced past him, and out, with Les, and Fish Face on his heels. Walt and the girl had gone back to the car to neck, or whatever. And then the Devil awoke, and there was pandemonium.

All of the blacks in the house tried to get at them at the same time and it was the only thing that saved them. They created a bottleneck of bodies, momentarily blocking the exit. The Captain, and Mack got to the car last, and the rest of them were in it by that time, including Brannigan, who had been outside taking a piss. The black girl who had been with Walt had ran from the car, not wanting to associate with those who were about to die.

The Captain could hear the crazed mob yelling, and screaming as he tried to start the car. He cringed, for he felt as if they were right on top of him. He was afraid to look to see how close they were. Vincent was sure he would mess his pants if the car didn't start right away.

"Go, go, go!" shouted Mario, hysterically, trying to laugh and scream at the same time. Right after that the car started, but it had to be backed up before it could go forward. The mob of blacks was almost upon them. The Captain jammed the tranny into reverse and jammed the accelerator. The car shot back faster than he had anticipated and he caved in the door of a yellow, Cadillac convertible.

By that time some of the mob was just about close enough to touch the car. Vincent got the car out of reverse, and into first. He put the pedal to the metal and the car shot forward, with black fist pounding on the windows. His tires were spinning, throwing dust and gravel all over the mob.

The Captain knew he had to make tracks. He knew the black deputy who patrolled Cadillac Flats would be hot on their trail. Out of the corner of his eye he had seen the deputy running for his vehicle. Vincent was also sure he would radio for assistance. The Captain headed for the Garden Ranch area trying to think above the din of voices and excitement that was the atmosphere of his car. With severely diminished thinking capacity, He was trying to come up with a strategy that would save them from the long arm of the law. Vincent got a bright idea (he thought). If he turned around and drove back the way he had come they would be overlooked. The law thinking they were just another on coming car.

Vincent spotted a house that sat back off the road. The lights were on in the house. He wondered about it, for he was aware that it was in the wee hours of the morning. There was a large area in front of the house where he could turn the car around. He pulled in to turn around, but discovered to his amazement, and consternation, he was going way too, fast. He slammed his foot on the brake, but his wheels just slid in the gravel and he had no control of the car. The car slid into a ditch, bottoming out on the oil pan, with the front wheels in the ditch.

"Wonderful!" commented Mario, with sarcasm, as they surveyed the situation. The Captain's anesthetized brain decided he should go to the house, and call a wrecker. He had a one-track mind, and now he was worried about the car being stuck, instead of thinking about the law being after them. He walked to the house with his troops following. When he got to the house, and onto the veranda, he could see that the front door was ajar.

Vincent rang the doorbell but no one answered. The door had a window in it, and he could see there was a phone on the wall, opposite the door. He rang the bell a few more times with the same result. Vincent had noticed there was no car in the driveway, and assumed they must have gone somewhere. He rang the bell again, and when no one came, he stepped into the house; he was just going to use the phone. The two airmen followed him in. The rest of the crew stood on the veranda.

The Captain called a wrecker, and unknown to him, while he was doing it, the Fly Boys were wandering through the house. Les stole a ring and watch from a jewelry box he had found on a dresser. At the same time the Captain hung up the phone, Mario came rushing in from the veranda, his face was blanched, and his eyes wide. The group followed him in.

"The cops are coming!" exclaimed Mario, "And I'm out of here!" he added, on his way to the back door, with Brannigan. Walt was on his heels. "Go for it," answered the Captain, wishing he could do the same, but knowing his car was a witness against him. He pulled the curtain and looked out the window. "Holy Shit!" he exclaimed, "It is cop city out there!"

The black deputy was there, along with his partner. Another Sheriff Department vehicle was there, a city patrol car, plus a Highway Patrol car. They were all milling around his car. "Looking for us," whispered the Captain, and he giggled, sounding inane in relation to the situation. A white, pot bellied deputy headed for the door. "Holy Shit!" exclaimed the Captain, under his breath and he giggled again. It was some twist in his thinking, alcohol induced, that was causing him to giggle. It was the only way he had to relieve the stress of the situation. The rest of the guys wanted to run, but it was too, late.

For a moment the Captain felt like he was in a Laurel, and Hardy movie or one of the Keystone Cops was banging on the door. But a real, pot bellied, deputy was banging on the door. The Captain giggled again, tried to straighten out his face, failed miserably, and opened the door.

The deputy not only had a big belly, he had a big red face and he was breathing heavy, like his belly was in the way. He stared at the Captain for a long time. It was like he was having a hard time formulating the words he wanted to say and then he spoke, with a suspicion born from intuition.

"Do you know where the guys are who belong to that car parked out front?" he asked, politely. Captain Moon was doing a superb job of suppressing a giggle. As he craned his neck to look out the window, Vincent tried to look like a concerned citizen. He pointed at the black deputy and his partner. Pot Belly turned to look. "Those guys," said the Captain, "Belong to that car," and he pointed to their car. The deputy's face got redder as his suspicion grew firmer. The Captain continued with his inane dissertation. "And those guys," and he pointed at the Highway Patrolman, and his partner, "Belong in that car," and he pointed at their car. He went on, "And those guys," but the red faced deputy interrupted him.

"Do you live here?" asked the deputy, with suspicion, one eyebrow raised. Captain Moon grinned sheepishly; he looked up, hoping to find the answer written on the ceiling. "I'm living," he answered, "And I'm here." He was still grinning the same way, he couldn't wipe it off. The veins in the deputy's neck, and forehead were swelling. "But you don't live here, do you?" he asked again, pointing at the floor, reasonably certain, now, that he did not. "But I am living here," argued the Captain, "This is where I am."

"What's the address here?" shot back the deputy. "I don't own the place," answered the Captain, "I'm just visiting." "Who are you visiting?" asked the deputy, who was getting more irate. "The people who live here," he answered, and just about then the black deputy who had been doing the patrolling came inside. He looked at the Captain suspiciously for a moment, and then recognition registered across his face.

"That's him!" The deputy exclaimed, excitedly, "That's the driver, I saw him get in the car!" "I knew it!" growled Pot Belly, with satisfaction, and relish. "Can I call my mother to come, and take me home?" asked Captain Moon, and then he giggled. "I'm taking you to your new home," retorted the deputy, with a broad grin across his face, "I'm taking you to your new home.

CHAPTER 31

It was summer and Vincent was riding in a sheriff's car; they wouldn't let him drive his own. It was hot and he was sick with alcoholism and fear. He was afraid if he didn't quit drinking he would die and if he did quit he would die. He was also afraid he was losing Carla. Vincent knew he had to do something, and he was doing it. Carla had wanted him to go to a private hospital to dry out, but they had already tried that. Vincent was remembering the horror of it on the drive from San Francisco to Auburn, on his way to Dewitt, the State Mental Hospital.

It had been three years ago. He had been on a long drinking spell and had ended up in the emergency ward of San Francisco General. He had vomited blood, and quite a bit of it; he had ruptured a blood vessel in his stomach. Violent retching had caused it. Vincent stopped remembering long enough to remember how nervous he was. He wasn't certain what was in store for him. The bartender had told him they would give him drugs to help through the withdrawal period. Vincent was afraid of drugs, especially after what had happened to him three years ago. After they had stopped the bleeding they had given him a shot, and a reaction had followed, a bad reaction.

Vincent was wishing he had not started this trip. He was getting awfully nervous, needing a drink, terribly. He had primed himself, but they had cautioned him that they would turn him away if he were intoxicated. Vincent had been careful not to get that way, but now was wishing he hadn't listened. Now the priming he had done was wearing off. The weakness was setting in, and his stomach was turning into a fist. But he was stuck, now. He had turned himself in, signed the papers and was trapped for thirty days.

Vincent was remembering again that awful reaction, how bad he had felt, how he had feared death. And their looks of fear had compounded his.

305

They had thought he was going to croak, too. They had tried to give him another shot to counteract the first one, but he had refused, vehemently, gritting his teeth, and suffering it out. On top of that they had given him Antibuse without telling him, or Carla.

Vincent had conned Carla into sneaking him in a torpedo of port. He had choked and had turned black after the first swallow. They had feared they were going to lose him again. Vincent had lain there with Carla holding his hand. He had recited the Twenty Third Psalm, it was the one his mother would have recited and the only one he had memorized. Vincent had been just about certain he was going to die. Sometimes he wished he had. If he was going to die an alcoholic, why drag it out?

Why was all this bad stuff happening to him, anyway? He had tried. It had been awful trying to decide what to do about Carla, and Linda. He still loved both of them, and now he could never have Linda, for he had married Carla. Getting back into the same drunk tank had pushed him toward Carla. He had come to the conclusion that there was no way he could stay in Ophir Flats, and stop drinking, not as long as the Moon Patrol was there. After a month in the drunk tank he had said a tearful goodbye to Linda, and his mother, and had headed back to the City by the Bay. Even if the Moon Patrol had not been there, the ghost of Audrey was.

Vincent tried to figure out how he had got into this mess after being so good. He hadn't had a drink for a long time, but the work in real estate had made him so nervous. His face would hurt from all that smiling, and his ear would hurt from pressing the phone against it. God! How he hated it. He knew now that he was never meant to be a salesman. He liked staying clean all day, but oh how he had learned to hate that office.

It was a pretty drive to Auburn, especially after they were in the hills. Vincent wasn't seeing any beauty; there was none in his consciousness. All that he could see, or feel, was the pit his mind was digging for him. He knew how bad he was going to feel. Vincent could only hope their drugs were going to help him.

And what was going to help him when he got out? He knew he would still have a need for something. What was going to help him with his nerves? What was going to get him through the day, to tolerate the people, their moods, all that paper work, all them damned phone calls, all the damned regulations, and all the new ones they would always have to learn? Some times he wished to God Carla's father had not helped him to get into Real Estate.

"Almost there," reported the deputy, cheerfully and Vincent felt like kicking him. Vincent said nothing. No booze for thirty days; that was nothing to be cheerful about. He would bet a hundred dollars the deputy was going to have a high ball just as soon as he got off work.

Vincent had gone three years without a drink, and he had made a lot of money. Tony, Carla's father, had helped him. Tony knew everyone. He had helped him with a giant landfill project, with the procurement of land for it. Tony had helped him with a lot of other industrial property, and had helped him to buy a dilapidated mansion for Carla, which they were still in the process of renovating.

Even after two sons had been born he could still not forget Linda. Vincent had called her for a while, but it had only made it harder, and the calls had been too emotional. He had thought it would be better for her if he just let her forget him. He would never be able to forget her, he knew that.

Vincent still hadn't figured out why Reed had turned out to be so blond. Reed was his first-born. His eyebrows were so light you had to be close to him to see them and he was growing like a weed; he was going to be a big one. They had used the regular Catholic birth control method, but it had not worked. And just a year and a half after Reed, Mark had been born. He had been smaller and quieter.

They had driven to the Dewitt Hospital in Auburn, California and Vincent felt near panic. It was a mental hospital and he was going there to dry out. He wouldn't be able to get out for thirty days; it was just like going to jail again. Vincent was feeling very weak, and shaky; his innards were on fire. He got signed in and his pasty face got him to his bunk. Withdrawal was closing in on him, consuming his senses. They told him that after today he would have to stay off his bunk during the day.

Vincent felt more ill as his detoxification progressed. On the second day they wouldn't let him lay on his bunk, so he sat on the latrine stool instead. He had to anyway, for he had dysentery, and weakness. He felt as if his life was going to drain out of his anus. He would no sooner get finished and the urge would hit him again. When he wasn't sitting on the throne, he was standing by it, waiting for the urge.

And there were not any drugs, none. There was nothing for his nerves, nothing for his weakness, nothing for his insomnia, nothing; Cold Turkey. They were giving him some chalky stuff for his acid stomach, and some pink liquid for his diarrhea. But that was no help at all with the withdrawal symptoms. It didn't even seem to help the acid stomach, or the diarrhea.

The nervousness and weakness were the worst. Vincent felt tired, and weak enough to die; to just drop dead. He was even to the point, sometimes, where death would seem preferable, but his fear was greater. All he wanted to do was lay on his bunk, but they wouldn't let him, so he walked the halls, and sat whenever he could. It seemed like there were miles of halls to walk. Most of the huge complex consisted of many rectangular buildings connected by hallways. They were more like covered, windowed, walkways. Vincent had been told there were more than two thousand patients. Only two psychiatrists serviced them and some psychologists, too.

There were three meals a day, but they were not good, not even as good as ordinary hospital food. The food was not even as good as the worst restaurant food. Vincent couldn't ingest all that was on the menu. The food he could ingest only compounded his digestive difficulties. Somehow the staff had learned to cook cabbage in diverse ways. Almost all the meals had some cabbage, or hamburger, pasta, tomato sauce, or all the latter.

The fat in the hamburger caused his gall bladder to attack him. The tomato sauce gave him heartburn. The cabbage gave him methane gas. It gave everyone gas. Sometimes the air was thick enough to cut into squares. Vincent's withdrawal symptoms seemed to compound every physical malady he had ever had. His panacea for all these maladies had been alcohol, which he now could not get.

There were a lot of strange people in the hospital, people with diverse infirmities. There were a lot of nuts for two bona fide shrinks. As far as Vincent was concerned, judging from his personal observation of shrinks, this was truly the blind leading the blind.

There was a young fellow; his name was Timothy, who just happened to be from the Flats. He was about Vincent's age, maybe a year younger. He was getting shock treatment. Although Timothy was silly as a goon, and somewhat immature, Vincent could see no reason for giving him this kind of therapy. But Vincent hadn't known what he was like before the treatment, so he had no way to judge. Timothy was a mama's boy, and he could hardly wait to get home so she could tell him what to do.

Red Barstow was a happy, red headed drunk. He was happy when he was locked up, that is. He was afraid of living on the Outside; he was afraid of freedom. Red had good reason to be. He knew he could not quit drinking, and no one was going to change his mind about that. Red knew if he was free, he would drink himself to death, and he was scared to death of death. Red fared well in the institution, but after a time, they would have to turn him loose. When he could no longer tolerate freedom and its responsibilities, he would go on a drunk knowing his relatives would have him committed.

John Smith, and that was his real name, was an engineer. He had a way above average I. Q. and he was arrogant about it. He claimed he was not an alcoholic. He said he was just there for a rest. John did admit he drank too much, but it was because he was depressed. He said he would be all right as soon as he could get out of this miserable place. It had been his wife's idea for him to come, and she was the one who should be locked up.

James Long was a handsome man, but he was a gimp; he had a clubfoot. He also had marital problems, but the problems were all in his head. His wife was very pretty. Because of his clubfoot, James was a green-eyed monster. He was jealous beyond reason, frightened of losing his wife to a normal footed man. His only escape from his foot was the bottle.

Laura Sinclair was a dark haired beauty, but her beauty had already started to harden, and she had not yet reached thirty. She was sophisticated and haughty. Her being there was just a mistake, one she was going to rectify and soon, with the help of her attorney.

After a week Vincent was allowed visitors, and Carla came to see him on the first day. He was still weak and gaunt, but he was so glad to see her. She was beautiful, and forever optimistic, but he was not so sure about their future. Vincent tried to hide his insecurity from her, but he was pessimistic. He knew himself better and knew how weak he was. He also knew he was building up a terrible thirst.

After another week had gone by he had the opportunity of occupational therapy. He chose the paint crew. He thought it would be better than roaming the halls. An older, white haired gent was running the crew and his name was Casey. He was an Irish and he had a twinkle in his eye like most of them do. He was kindly and didn't overwork anyone. He was in no hurry, he wasn't going anywhere. The work was easy, and it was outside. They only used rollers with extension handles, and paintbrushes. Vincent liked the work, liked it better than selling real estate. He thought about doing something like it when he got out. Maybe if he could find something without stress. He would not be so nervous, and maybe not so thirsty. The weeks were going by slow, but the paint crew was helping to pass the time. It was helping him to get his strength back.

One day, during his last week at the hospital, Vincent was walking down one of the long hallways and looking out the windows. Vincent saw a sight he had never seen before, one he would never want to see again. The hair rose on the back of his neck. It was like he had discovered some aliens from another planet. These people were certainly different from any species he had ever seen, or believed possible. There were a lot of them, and they all looked alike. They had odd shaped heads, and vacant expression. Most of them were bald and had no eyebrows. They were marching in rows, going somewhere, or nowhere, looking like rows of monsters.

What in Heaven's name could be wrong with them, he wondered. Vincent felt an overwhelming surge of sympathy for them, the sight almost incomprehensible. Emotion welled up in him, and spilled from his tear ducts. He asked himself how God could let something like this happen. It was times like this that he questioned God's existence, but knew some kind of God had to exist. One cannot have an affect without cause. But what kind of God would let this kind of thing happen? Maybe God had no control over it.

Sometimes creation seemed a senseless thing to Vincent, and this was one of those times. What was the point in being born, and then to die or to be born like one of these creatures. A shiver went through him as he pulled his eyes away from the horror. Frankenstein was a happy fairy tale compared to this. He moved down the hall as fast as he could; he felt as if something was chasing him.

Carla had come to see him every weekend, and she had called him every day. Vincent had written letters to his mother and Carla had mailed them for him from San Francisco. Vincent didn't want his mother to know the truth. With Carla's visits, some of her optimism had rubbed off on him. At the time for his release Vincent was terribly thirsty. The day of his release he was determined he would not drink. He was not going to end up with a wet brain or swollen liver he would have to carry in a sidecar. He was going to play it straight for his family's sake.

It was a fine sunny day when Carla came to get him. Vincent rode away in the same Jaguar they had ridden on their first date. Carla did not look much different than she had then, maybe even more beautiful. She had always looked gorgeous; he could not remember her not looking that way. Even in the morning she looked that way. He had always desired her in the morning, with her eyes sleepy and her hair tussled.

"You are staring at me," she told him, but she was pleased that he was. "I know," he answered, "Just like the first time you gave me a ride." Her body was still trim, a little more voluptuous than she had been then. "What are you thinking about?" she asked, as he gave her the once over. "The same thing I was then," he answered, with a roguish grin, remembering and wanting the old trysting times. "Can we visit the Pelican?" he asked, and she blushed, for she had been thinking the same thought. "What were you thinking on that first ride?" she asked, not answering his question. "Taking your clothes off," he answered. "On our very first ride?" she asked, as if it were incomprehensible. "During and after the first five minutes," he told her. "Well," she said, coquettishly, "You already know what it is like now." "It is always the first time with you," he told her. "Let's go to the Pelican," she suggested, like he hadn't asked.

"Sounds right to me," he answered. "Are you well enough?" "Good as new," he lied; his desire stronger than his common sense.

They made the rest of the trip in anticipation, looking at each other, talking, laughing, and being romantic. By the time they got to the Pelican they were primed for love. It had been without foreplay, for thinking had taken its place. Foreplay was not necessary, but Vincent was a romantic, and he enjoyed it almost as much as the copulation. Vincent never hurried because of this pleasure. He loved to see the heights of passion he could tantalize Carla. She was moaning and pleading by the time he gave her, her reward; her body a passion furnace. But Vincent had forgotten his dilemma. During orgasm his heart did a flip-flop and his stomach turned into that all familiar fists.

How could he have forgotten? Had he expected a cure from thirty days of abstaining? It must have been wishful thinking. If only he could stop before orgasm. But that would drive him crazy. Well, he was going to go crazy, anyway. He was right back in the same old boat. And Vincent was dying for a drink, and couldn't have one. And he was still hiding his problem from Carla. This time would be different; he would go to a new doctor, and he would tell him the truth.

Vincent couldn't understand why he had never done anything about the problem. He had just done his best to stay away from Carla. He remembered how the roles had reversed. He had been the seducer at first. There had never been a problem with sex as long as he was drinking, as long as he hadn't drunk too much. It was when he was trying not to drink that he had the problem.

During the three years he had been dry, he had used every excuse in the book to keep from having sex. His job kept him away, he was, tired, didn't feel good, etc. During his dry spell she had had to chase him, wanting it more than he had. Vincent had not told her what was wrong; he had felt ashamed about it. He wasn't much of a man if he couldn't make love to his wife without getting ill. He had thought it was something the M. D. wouldn't be able to fix, anyway. They had not been able to fix any of his other problems.

Vincent went to a heart specialist this time; he knew it had to be his heart. Darius Crabtree was the doctor's name and he seemed to know what he was talking about. He couldn't find a thing wrong with Vincent's heart, but he told him that didn't rule out the possibility of something being wrong. The doctor did some more tests, but without finding anything. He told Vincent he wished he could monitor his heart while he was having an orgasm, and then he laughed. They joked about the idea for a while.

"How about right after an orgasm?" asked Vincent. "I'll take you right in, and we will see if we can find anything," answered Darius. He told Vincent that mornings would be the best time, anytime after nine." "I'll be here, "promised Vincent. The very next morning Vincent surprised Carla by waking her, and then seducing her. She was pleased, but surprised when he jumped out of bed right after his orgasm. He fled from her, muttering something about something he had forgot to do. Vincent dressed, and rushed to the doctor. It was a miracle he got there alive and without a ticket. He felt awful, and looked that way, having forgotten to comb his hair, he had run his hand through it. And the rushing and the testing had all been in vain, the test had discovered nothing.

"You will just have to adjust." the doctor told him. "But it could be something psychosomatic," suggested Darius. "What does that mean?" asked Vincent, impatiently. "Your problem could have a mental cause," answered the doctor. "What do I do about that?" asked Vincent, hopefully. "I can get you an appointment with a psychiatrist I know," answered

Darius, "She is a friend of mine." "A lady shrink?" asked Vincent, skeptical. "She is good," answered Darius, "And you can talk to her like you would your mother." My mother would be cheaper." "Your mother could be part of your problem." "Okay," agreed Vincent, willing to try anything. The appointment was made.

Vincent made a dozen trips to the lady shrink, but they were not fruitful. He didn't think so, anyway. He may as well have visited his mother. It sure as Hell would have been cheaper. It seemed to him the lady had asked him the same questions at every session; she was like a broken record. The inkblots were fun, though. At the last session she had told him he had a strong love and attachment for a possessive mother. It was quite possible this attachment was making him feel guilty when he had sex. This was all taking place in his mind, of course. That was the last time he saw the shrink. The whole idea was preposterous, ridiculous, stupid and disgusting. To think he could be thinking of his mother while having sex. Absurd!

It wasn't long and Vincent was right back in the same old routine. He was trying to be like everyone else, trying to be a good husband, father and a good salesman. He was all these things, but he was not like everyone else. Vincent felt like he was Captain Moon in disguise. He felt like he was being an actor, like he was learning his lines every morning, going through the motions. His face was still getting sore from all the smiling. It is hard to smile when one wants to frown. It puts a lot of stress on the face. And it is hard to laugh when you feel like crying.

Vincent ran himself ragged trying to stay away from the office. There were twenty people there, and he knew them all, but felt like a stranger every time he walked in. It was easier for him to talk to a stranger than to go to the office. The office seemed like a group of strangers, like a crowd. He could talk to people, one, or two at a time, but he abhorred crowds. Four or more was a crowd to Vincent. He always felt insecure in a crowd; he would even get confused.

Vincent had a one, track mind, and if too many were talking at the same time he could get confused. It even confused him to talk on the phone while someone was talking at the desk next to him. He could even forget whom he was talking to. Vincent must have been a good actor, though, for he was making a lot of money. He became the top Lister in the office. He studied diligently, and passed the test to get his broker's license. Carla was so, proud of him, everyone was proud of him, including himself. Vincent was exhausted. No one knew it but him. He was a regular turtle when something was bothering him, he would just retreat into his shell.

Vincent made it through another three years like this. He made love to his wife like he was supposed to, laying after with his stomach in a fist, and his nerves on edge. He had been a good father to his boys; there were three of them now. Their last attempt to have a girl was named Wade.

Vincent was ready to open his own office, but he needed a rest. His nerves were raw, and he needed to get away from every thing, including his family. He just had to go somewhere where he could be alone, where he couldn't hear the blasted phone. And the boys made him nervous. He loved them, but they got on his frayed nerves, he needed a break from them, too.

Vincent decided he would take a vacation. He would go to Fort Bragg; he hadn't been there since he was a kid. Carla agreed with him, and she was perfectly happy right where she was. Carla had no desire to visit a burg like Fort Bragg, where everyone probably smelt like fish. Vincent packed his luxurious leather luggage and put it in the trunk of his nearly new, Studebaker Golden Hawk that he had bought last year. It was black, with gold trim. He kissed his family goodbye, and headed north. The plan was to eat lunch at Bodega Bay, one of his favorite places. Vincent loved little remote places of solitude. Some quirk in his nature made him feel less lonely in such places.

Driving past Tomales Bay he remembered his mother had gone to High School there. She had also told him she had almost drowned there. A skiff she had been in with her brothers had capsized, and she had been caught under the skiff. Her older brother had saved her.

Vincent hadn't seen his mother for a couple of years. He was going to have to do that one of these days. He had called her, and written regularly, but hadn't been able to get away from the office. He would have to see her soon. Theirs had been a close relationship, too close for that matter, and it had been hard for him to cut the cord. Vincent still wasn't certain he had done it.

Vincent loved Highway One, and its rugged coast, its changeless beauty. It only seemed to change on weekends and holidays. It got crowded then. Vincent envied the mariners. When they got tired of people they could just sail away.

At Bodega Vincent went into a restaurant built on piling. He remembered that Charley had been a pile driver in-between diving jobs and fishing. Vincent hadn't thought of him for a long time. He had heard that Charley had died in his suit of a heart attack, somewhere in the South Pacific. He had died before they were able to get him out of his suit. What an awful way to die, thought Vincent, with a shudder. Poor Charley, he had been a slave to temptation, much like himself. He could never do what Charley had done, though. But he had forgiven Charley, so the Hell with that.

The waitress was slim and pretty. Vincent flirted with her with his eyes and she flirted back. He ordered a turkey club. A person next to him was drinking a beer and the aroma caught him by surprise; it teased his olfactory. Vincent had a sudden urge to have one himself and before he could think better of it, he had ordered one. He regretted doing so, but the waitress had already left for it. He didn't have to drink it, though. The girl brought his order, and the beer had been opened. She asked if he wanted a glass, and he declined.

Vincent looked at the beer as he ate his sandwich. He drank some water. He had eaten half of his sandwich before he picked up the beer. He stuck the opening of the bottle under his nose, and took a whiff of it, and sat it back down. He looked at it some more as he ate. Vincent felt suddenly elated. He was free, all by himself; who was going to know? And how could one beer with his lunch hurt him? He put the beer to his nose again and took another whiff. The beer being at such a close proximity to his mouth was too, much temptation not to taste and that was what he did. After tasting the beer Vincent could not resist the temptation to drink it. He couldn't remember anything tasting as good. He savored it and the comfortable feeling in his stomach. The second one tasted good, also, but not as good as the first.

Vincent left the cafe feeling good, and he felt safe. Two beers couldn't hurt him. As he was driving north, and he hadn't gone far, the beer was making him sleepy. He pulled over at the first accessible beach. The sun was out. It was almost warm, but not warm enough to put on his suit. Vincent put a blanket down on the sand and laid on his back on it. He felt good, and euphoria took him over, and he fell asleep.

About an hour later, a fly taking a stroll on his eyebrow awoke him. He swatted at it, and missed, cursing. Somehow the fly had anticipated the swat. The fly seemed to have affection for him, and kept coming back. The feeling was not mutual, though. Actually, Vincent wanted to kill the fly. Vincent got up, cursed the fly and fled. Vincent and his Studebaker headed north.

The beer had worn off, and so had the euphoria, leaving a dry spot under his tongue and an open door to nostalgia. His thoughts went to the beautiful girl he had left behind. Not his wife, whom he should have been thinking about, but the girl he had left behind. She would not be a girl now, and it had been years since he had seen her.

"Eight years!" Vincent exclaimed to himself, "My, God! It has been eight years. Oh, Jesus!" he lamented, it was all coming back to him, the hurt from trying to forget her, but never having succeeded. Vincent did some addition in his head. "Twenty four, she is," he told himself. He wondered if she was still in the Flats. Better not go there, better not open old wounds. Tears were running down his face, and the pain of regret was stuck in his throat.

CHAPTER 32

Vincent had a vague, uneasy feeling. The beer had worn off, leaving him this feeling. It was a physical feeling, something like hunger, only he felt it all over, not just in his stomach. He should have recognized the feeling, but he stopped at a country store, and bought a six-pack of beer to drink along the way. The first one tasted good, but the second one, not so good. The third beer tasted skunky. By the time Vincent got to Fort Bragg it was time for dinner and he was out of beer. He paid for a motel, took a shower, shaved, and changed clothes. Vincent was tired, and just wanted to have a nice dinner, and relax. He drove around for a while, just to jog his memory. The town looked the same as it did when he left as a teenager. "Thank God for things that never change," he told himself.

Vincent went to a restaurant that was on the ground floor of The Redwood Inn. It was a historical, wooden structure that was in the middle of the downtown area. The interior was done in natural redwood. It was plush, warm and cozy. Vincent was tired of beer; he ordered a glass of white wine to go with his prime rib. His glass got empty before his plate, so he had to have a refill. Vincent had another to get his plate empty. He knew it was too, late now, so he had another for the road.

Vincent felt helpless, now, and depressed. Why had he been such a fool? He knew he would be caught between a rock and a hard place in the morning. Physically, he hadn't felt this good since he had gone on the wagon. He tried to con himself into thinking everything would be all right. He could not assuage the sinking feeling, knowing that in the morning he would feel like warmed over, death.

Vincent had forgotten how bitterly cold it could get in Fort Bragg. He hugged himself as he went out into the night, trying to keep the cold out. He was thinking he had already screwed up, and may as well have a bottle of brandy to keep him warm. It wouldn't make him feel any worse than he was already destined to feel, he rationalized.

Vincent remembered a girl friend of Anna's. Her parents had owned a market, and the girl had worked there. He tried to remember her name; it was Columbo, or something like that. He went looking for the market, and found it. It hadn't changed, it still looked like it needed a paint job. And it was "Columbo's Market." Vincent went in, and there was a woman at the counter waiting on another woman, at the cash register. Vincent looked her over and was amazed at how much she still looked like the girl she had been. She looked like she could be her own mother. He wondered if she would remember him, he had grown a mustache.

Vincent stood behind the customer, and stared at the Columbo woman. She looked at him, but there was no sign of recognition. The customer left, and the woman was looking at him. The liquor display was right behind her. They were alone in the store. She asked if she could help. He told her he wanted a pint of brandy. All she had was Christian Brothers, and that was what he got. When Vincent paid her, he told her he remembered her, but couldn't remember her name. He searched his head, trying to remember. Who knows why people do that?

"It Is Sicilia," the girl informed him, "Where do you remember me from?" she asked, while studying his face. "We went to school together," he told her, "You ran around with Josephine." There was still no recognition. "Vincent is my name," he told her, but nothing showed on her face. "Use to be Charley," he added, and a light showed in her eyes, and she grinned. "Charley!" She exclaimed. "I remember now, you were the little guy who had a crush on Josephine." "Guilty as charged," answered Vincent, "God!" Sicilia exclaimed, "That was forever ago." "You got that right," he answered, "How is Josephine?" Vincent asked. "Same as always," she answered, sounding envious, "One romantic difficulty after another." "I would have killed for a kiss from that girl," Vincent confessed. "You, and everyone else," she told him, enviously, again. "But why didn't you tell her?" She liked you, you know." "I was too, shy," he explained. And she was going with an older guy." "I remember, now," Sicilia told him, "And she married him; she divorced him a few years later. They didn't last long." "I wanted to look up Paul while I was here," Vincent told her, hoping she would know where to find him. She got an odd look on her face.

"You didn't know?" she asked. Why do people ask that when the answer is obvious? "Know what?" he asked, seeing the dread on her face, feeling it himself. "He was killed years ago," she answered. "How?" he asked, aghast, "How did it happen?" "Paul was driving a butane delivery truck, and had been filling a customer's tank," Sicilia explained, "And the hose had broken. The butane had flooded over him. He had dropped the handle, and it had struck the bumper, causing a spark. He was burned to death.

Vincent shuddered as he got a mental picture of Paul trying to escape from the flame. He must have screamed in terror, knowing he was being killed. God! He thought, what an awful way to die. Vincent couldn't say anything; he just looked at Sicilia and shook his head, his tongue mute, his face blanched. He felt ill and Sicilia asked him if he was all right. Vincent's heart felt out of rhythm for a moment and he didn't answer until it had returned to normal. "I'll be alright," he assured her, "It was such a shock." "You look like you need a drink," she told him. "I do," he answered, holding up his package. "No!" she exclaimed, "I mean you look like you need one right now," and she pulled on his arm. She guided him behind the counter, and through a curtained doorway. It was a small room. There was a roll top desk, an adjustable chair, and a small sofa. There was a bottle of liquor on the desk. "Have a drink of this," she told him as she handed him the bottle and a glass.

Vincent trembled. The glass rattled against the bottle as he poured himself a drink. He gulped the drink down, and felt it going to work, calming him as it entered his blood stream. She pointed to the sofa, and he sat down. The bell rang and she went back into the store. Vincent wondered if he should ask about anyone else; more bad news he didn't need. She came back.

"What about the Williams brothers?" Vincent asked with apprehension. "The last time I heard, David was a big shot with a big construction company," she told him, "But I don't know about his brother." She poured him another drink, it was brandy. He took a sip this time. "What about the handsome guy?" Vincent asked, he couldn't remember his name, "The one with the curly hair. He was bigger and better looking than everyone else." Sicilia giggled, and then she laughed. Vincent was grateful; he could sure as Hell use a laugh.

"He got fat, and bald," she told him, and laughed some more. Vincent laughed with her; all news wasn't bad.

Vincent wondered about Sally, his first love, what had happened to her. "What about Sally Blake?" Vincent asked. Sicilia had to think, and then she remembered. "That pretty one you use to go with?" she asked, but did not wait for an answer, "She got married and had four kids." "Is she still pretty?" he asked. "She got fat too," answered Sicilia. "Did Anna get fat?" he asked with apprehension. "No," she answered, envious again, "She still looks like a movie star. Would you like to see her?" she asked, and the idea excited him, but it also frightened him. Vincent did not want another one to fall in love with; two was enough. "If I stay long enough," Vincent answered. "Come back tomorrow If you do," she told him, and he got up. He told her he had better let her go back to work, thanked her for her help, and told her he would try to see her again tomorrow. They said goodbye, and he left.

By the time Vincent got back to the motel he was shivering. It had not been far enough for the heater in the car to get going. He went into his room, and opened the bottle. Vincent didn't want a glass, he liked to drink out of the bottle; it seemed like the natural thing to do. He took a few good snorts to warm him, and went to bed, troubled. Vincent knew he was going to have a hard time in the morning.

Vincent sat the bottle on the nightstand, and tried to go to sleep, but his eyelids seemed to have springs in them that kept them opening. He started thinking about Linda, wondering what he had missed, knowing it had been a great love. He was depressed, knowing he was already in trouble, wondering if he would be able to pull himself out of it, afraid of bleeding again. What if he should die without ever seeing her again? He was not going to let that happen. He was going to go to the Flats and find her.

Vincent went to sleep, but slept fitfully, waking every few hours, and having a sip to go back to sleep. Before daylight had come he was getting a little claustrophobic, needing to get out of the room. He noticed that he didn't feel too bad, but he remembered he had been nursing the bottle all night. He did feel strung out, though.

He took a shower to wake himself and dressed. Vincent turned on the faucet in the sink, and let it run until the water got hot. He put some brandy in a glass, and run some hot water into it, making himself a sort of toddy for the body, a warmer-upper. He drank his drink and left the motel to look for a liquor store. He wasn't out but didn't want to wait until he was. Alcoholics need security too. Vincent drove all over town looking for one that was open, but to no avail.

Vincent did find a cafe open, though, at the north end of town; it had a beer sign in the window. There were only two parking places; he pulled into one of them. Vincent climbed out of the Hawk and went in. The cafe was busy, full of loggers and fishermen. Some were eating their breakfast, and others were drinking it; he could tell by the number of tomato beers being drunk. He didn't feel very good, but at least he wasn't alone in that state of discomfort.

Vincent sat at the counter, and ordered a tomato beer from a burly waitress. She looked like a part time logger. The beer tasted awful, and he wasn't sure if it would stay down. He put a little salt in it hoping it would help, and sometimes it does. His stomach was empty, and he knew he should eat something, but he was suffering from alcohol induced, colic, and he felt like a balloon.

Vincent felt like the world's biggest fool, knowing he had a good life, knowing he could be screwing it up with self-indulgence. Somehow he knew he would never be happy. In part it was because of his weakness, and partly because he was never satisfied with anything. And after all, what can one do to change ones self? He didn't know. One can make resolutions, work at it, and drift right back to the old ways. If one can't resist temptation, what can one do about it? Jesus Christ was able to resist temptation, but his mother was a virgin, and his father was God. That was some advantage.

Vincent felt embarrassed about asking where he might find a bar that was open, but he subordinated this feeling to his need, and asked. The waitress told him there was one open at Noyo Harbor, and he took off for it. It was just a few miles south. It doesn't take an alcoholic long to find a bar. There is an invisible beam that guides one there; the source of it is the devil himself. The Devil certainly knows how to make the wrong path, and then lead one down it. It is a good thing we have him to blame everything on. And the Devil likes it; he likes to be responsible.

Others had followed the beam, and Vincent was not alone. There were always alcoholics around to keep alcoholics company. "Birds of a feather, flock together," as the old saying goes. Vincent thought it would be good to have some minerals with his drink, so he ordered a Bloody Mary. At least he could get some food value from the celery stalk. It would keep his electrical system functioning, as long as something else didn't quit.

The bartender was short, and squatty. His hair was thin and silver, slicked back over his round head. There was a large space between his bulbous nose and his sensual lips. A thin mustache was in this space; it looked like it had been penciled in. His face looked like it had never seen the sun. He was fat and jovial; he jiggled when he walked and giggled when he talked.

"Would you like something to eat in it?" asked the bartender, of his Bloody Mary, and then he giggled like a woman. "Whatever is supposed to be there," answered Vincent. The bartender built his drink, and brought it to him. It looked like a garden growing out of a glass of blood. Vincent took a swallow, and started chewing on part of the garden. He started drinking it slow, but his body needed a jolt, so he drank it down and ordered another. "Must have been good," commented the bartender.

There was only one woman in this crew of early morning drinkers, and she looked like a fisher woman. She was wearing bibbed overalls and rubber boots. She had a drawing pad, and a pencil. She was sketching a fisherman who was staring into his drink. He was sitting next to her, but was oblivious that she was sketching him. His drink was his world. Captain Moon asked Pale Face about her. He told him she was indeed, a fisher woman, and she was also a fine artist.

The bartender told Vincent that the woman lived in a barge on the Noyo River. He told him she had a green thumb and had potted plants all over the barge. Her name was Thelma; he didn't know her last name, no one did. The Captain, wanting to see her sketch, told Pale Face to set her up a drink, on him. He did, promptly, pointing at the Captain. She raised her glass, after getting the drink and beckoned him.

The Captain picked up his liquid breakfast and went to her. Thelma's face was secretive, not revealing of her age. She could have been fifty, or seventy. Her face was sweet, and mischievous, almost pretty. Her hair was curly, long and of an indeterminate color, and in disarray. Thelma thanked him with a voice that was resonant, but a little course from too, much whiskey. The elements had turned her face into a road map of fine lines. The laugh lines were deep as she asked him if she could sketch his face.

"It is not a run of the mill face," she told him. "Make it look good," he told her, as he looked at the sketch she had just finished. It looked just like the guy who still had his face in the glass. The picture was a profile of his face, and the glass. She couldn't leave his glass out of the picture, for his face was almost in it. She tore the picture off the pad, and started on his.

"What do you want me to do?" Vincent asked. "Drink," she told him, "Or whatever else you do in a bar." "I'll drink," he retorted, "I know how to do that." She sketched quickly. "Are you trying to get well?" she asked, "Or happy?" "Both," he answered, and finished off his drink. Pale Face saw him, and jiggled over to him. "Another?" he asked. "Make it a double of your best cognac," he ordered, needing something with more punch, "And give the lady a drink. She is working for me." He said it in a playful manner, but she took it some other way.

"No I'm not!" she retorted, "I work for God!" "What do you mean?" Vincent asked, hoping he had not offended her in some way he didn't understand. "I'm doing pictures of His children so He wont forget who they are." "That's rather strange," commented the Captain. "I'm rather strange," she retorted, and then she laughed, a rather pretty laugh, not like one he would have expected from her. He studied her face with a closer inspection, and realized that she had once been a very pretty woman, maybe even beautiful.

"What's your name?" he asked her, hoping she would tell him her last name, wondering if it would link her to someone he knew. "Moss," she answered. "Thelma Moss?" Vincent asked. "How'd you know?" she asked back. "Pale Face," he answered, pointing at him. "If you already knew, why did you ask?" she asked, a little testy. "I wanted to know your last name," he answered. "What for?" she asked, still testy, "Are you writing a book?" "So I could watch for your name in the art galleries," he kidded. "I'm glad I have my rubber boots on," she kidded back, "Cause the stuff is getting deep in here."

Thelma wiped her boot off on the brass rail, like there was something messy on it. "What's your name?" she asked. "Captain Moon," he answered, with a grin, and Moss looked him up, and down. "You don't look like a Captain to me," she told him, "You the Captain of what?" "Captain of The Moon Patrol!" he exclaimed, like she should have known. "How in the world did you get a handle like that?" asked the crusty fisher woman and the Captain told her his story.

While Vincent was telling his story they both had a good laugh. When he had finished she bought him a drink and told the story to Pale Face, who then told it to his patrons. Now this wasn't the typical fish story, but it was the kind fishermen and drunks getting well do like to hear. And one bullshit story begets others. Soon, there was a regular party going on, and everyone was getting too well. Part of the party, including Moss, and the Captain ended up on the fisher woman's barge. Some of the guys ended up on the floor, but the Captain ended up on a bunk all by himself; he was anesthetized. The next morning when he awoke, he hadn't the slightest idea where he was, or how he had got there.

Vincent arose from the bunk, cautiously. His brain felt like it was outside his skull, just hanging there, pulsating, swelling, like a huge aneurysm. His mouth felt and tasted like it had been stuffed with used Kotex, and his stomach was a four-alarm fire. He needed a drink; he needed a lot of drinks.

Vincent groaned as he viewed the panorama of chaos that was in the barge. He felt an intense need for instant drink and retreat. He did not want to communicate with any of the strangers who were lying about. He searched for, and found the hatch, opened it, and escaped to the deck. It was very cold, and he shivered. Vincent looked around to orient himself. He tried to remember where he had parked the car, but his brain was not in gear. He looked at his watch, it read a little after six. At least he knew it was morning, the morning after. They were all the same. At least they all felt the same.

Vincent stumbled off the barge. The deck was slightly convex, wet and slippery. He almost fell as he stepped from the deck to the landing. He walked up the wooden landing and stepped off to solid ground. He felt as if he were on the opposite side of the river from where his car was. He walked up the hill, remembering the little cafe where his mother had worked, where she had met Doc, where he had played his first pinball machine. The building was still there, but the cafe was not. Vincent was almost across the bridge before he spotted his car. With a sigh of relief he continued across. Now he remembered the bar, and Pale Pace. Vincent looked like something the cat had dragged in when he walked into the bar, not having had time to look at his reflection. His bladder was floating, so he went into the can first.

When Vincent saw his reflection in the mirror, he felt disgust, and remorse. It was a good thing he had a comb in his pocket, his hair looked like he had slept standing on his head. He needed a shave, and he looked like the Lost Weekend. He would have a few drinks to get well, and then he would go back to the motel to clean up, and maybe catch some sleep. He felt awfully tired and could not seem to get warm. He was a shiver waiting to happen.

Pale Face shook his head and smiled, sympathetically. "You guys really tied one on last night," he commented, and the Captain nodded carefully. "You got that right," he answered, "And now I need your help." "I got the cure," answered Pale Pace, "You just name it." "Cognac," answered the Captain, "In large doses." "Three fingers in a tub, coming up," answered Pale Pace, cheerfully, while he poured a double. The Captain drank it straight down, and signaled for another. He sipped on it, and sipped down a couple more. Then he bought a bottle to go.

Vincent drove back to the motel, showered, and went back to bed. He awoke several hours later feeling strung out. Vincent decided he had better head down the road. He was going to find Linda before it was too, late. He knew he was on a treadmill going nowhere, and didn't know how to get off. He would try to pace himself until he could find her, and after that, he didn't know. He would worry about that later. He had a few belts for the road, and checked out of the motel.

Vincent decided he would take Highway Twenty through the mountains to Willits and then go over by the lakes. He got in the Hawk, and headed out. The road was narrow, and crooked; he liked them that way. A big bore, V-8, powered the Hawk. It had dual, glass packed mufflers. Vincent loved the rumble they made when he powered down. He loved powerful cars.

Some day he wanted to own an Aston Martin, his dream car. Brute force was what it had. He loved to power around curves, but his reflexes were not up to par. He was driving much too fast for his condition. And at this altitude, he was in very steep country. Vincent went into a curve too, fast, and started to slide. He tried to correct the slide by turning into it' but failed when he tried to power out of it; he had over powered. He had lost control of the Hawk, and there was nothing left to do but put on the brakes. The Hawk careened toward the edge, and came to a stop just short of going over.

The Captain was exhilarated by that time, and needed a drink. Vincent had a couple of belts, and got out of the car. The road was deserted and quiet. He walked to the edge, and looked down. It had to be over a hundred feet, and at the bottom laid the rusted carcass of a dead car; a silent witness of one who had not been so lucky. The Captain took another drink of his medicine. He felt elated by his immortality, got back into the Hawk, and moved it back from the precipice. He had another belt, and headed up the road, driving much slower.

By the time Vincent got to Willits he was thirsty for a beer, and he was hungry, at least he thought he was. He knew if he didn't eat right away he would lose the hunger and then it would be too late to eat. He stopped at the first cafe with a beer sign, and went in. Vincent had a cheeseburger, and washed it down with beer. He had four beers before he felt like leaving. Vincent got back on the road and took 101 south, but took it too far and ended up in Napa, which was way out of his way. He got lost there, and stopped at a beer joint to solicit direction and to wet his whistle.

It was a beer and wine bar specializing in ice cold, draft beer. The place was jumping, but Vincent managed to find a stool at the bar. The guy who was sitting next to him was loud and quite drunk. He looked like a person who was in that condition regularly. He looked to be around forty, and another drinker was calling him "Ray."

Ray was dressed nice, and he was clean shaved. His hair was thin, straight, gray and slicked back, close to his head. Ray was hard to understand, booze had caused a bad connection between his mouth and brain. The Captain deduced from the man's jabbering that he was the proprietor of the joint and his wife was tending the bar. She did not look happy about it or him. She looked harried. Her voice was course; his was more like a woman's than hers.

Ray had an insane sounding laugh; it was high pitched. It sounded like the one Richard Widmark used when he pushed the old lady down the stairs in her wheel chair in an old movie. Ray looked like he was waiting for his wife to do something. She made a motion for him to watch the bar while she went to the lady's room. As soon she had gone, Ray leaned over the bar, opened the cash register and grabbed a hand full of green. With an insane giggle, he sat back down on his stool. When his wife came back he said something to her and then left with a couple of guys. The Captain shook his head and drank his beer. He felt sorry for the harried woman who had made such a bad choice of husbands. And then he remembered that he wasn't the greatest of husband, either.

Vincent drank beer until he felt like a balloon; moderation was just not in his program. He asked the lady behind the bar for directions to the Flats, and then he left. He got in his car and drove east; he would be going through Winters and Woodland. He would need to make many stops to relieve his bladder as beer did that to him. He had enough brandy to get him home. The Flats was still home to him, he guessed that it always would be.

CHAPTER 33

Captain Moon felt elated as he drove into the Flats; he was home again. It had been such a long time. It didn't look much different as he drove in. He went down the street to drive by the pool hall and the Empire Theater, but they were both gone. The buildings were still there, but some other business was in them. The Shell station across the street was gone, building and all. It was now just a parking lot. Vincent drove around the corner to see about the Claim Jumper and it was gone; it was now The Flats Saloon. A beer and wine sign had replaced the cocktail sign.

Oh how the Captain hated change. Carla was always changing things. Just when he was getting use to his chair being in a certain place, she would change the room, and move his chair. He could not make her understand how important it was. Carla thought it was silly, everyone likes change. Vincent's mother had always found the best place for the furniture and then had left it that way. There was a kind of security in that.

The interior of the bar hadn't changed much, except there were no longer doorways that connected the barbershop to the cafe. They were both gone, zapped. And the patrons were not familiar (only three of them) and neither was the bartender, who wasn't smiling. Bartenders should try to smile; drunks need all the help they can get.

"What happened to the Claim Jumper?" the Captain asked the stodgy, gray haired, bartender. He didn't look like any fun at all. "Ned got cancer and died," answered the bartender, in a matter of fact tone, "And his old lady sold the place to me." That wasn't much of a conversation opener. What could he say to that? He would miss old Ned, he was a good head.

Vincent thought he better call someone, and he still had the numbers in his head, but they could have been changed after all this time. Vincent called Mario's old number first, and as luck would have it, he happened to be there. Mario was surprised to hear from him.

"I feared you had kicked the bucket," said Mario, a bit disgruntled, "Or fell off the face of the Earth." "Nothing that easy," answered the Captain. "Where you at?" asked Mario, with his careless use of the English language. "An adulteration of the Claim Jumper," answered the Captain. "First time I heard it called that," replied Mario, and he laughed about it. "You always had a way with words." "Where can I get a decent drink?" asked the Captain. "Molly's," answered Mario, "It's in Miner's Alley. I'll see you over there."

Vincent was familiar with the Alley. It was a historical place, and the alley was short, so he would not have difficulty finding Molly's. Vincent didn't move the car; he walked to the Alley, found Molly's and walked through the doors. He was surprised to see Spider tending the bar. He was serving and chatting with a group of young broads. They were flirting with him, which he was obviously enjoying, plus reciprocating. Spider did a double take when he saw the Captain. He glanced at him, and then looked back at the girls. When recognition seeped in, he looked back with a jerk of his head.

"Cardoza!" exclaimed Spider, "Where the fuck did you come from?" He was still using his favorite expletive, noticed the Captain. Spider covered his mouth after using such a naughty word in the presence of ladies. The girls giggled modestly, but they were use to the word. Spider walked over to him. "The City," answered the Captain," I just got into town, thirsty." "You were always thirsty," commented Spider, with a boyish grin, "What'll you have?" "Ten Moscow Mules would get me started," answered the Captain. "Number one coming up," answered Spider, and as he turned, the big Italian walked in.

Mario had picked up some weight and didn't seem as animated as before; he seemed reserved. They shook hands with exuberance and affection, but reserved, not a hundred percent. Time had adulterated their feelings. Most of the reservation was from Mario, though, the Captain's being a reflection of his.

John Brannigan walked through the doors. He hadn't changed much; he was still as brown as an Indian. His hair was still as black as coal, and his eyes the same color. He was sporting a handlebar mustache and was wearing a black, western hat, with a wide brim, and flat crown. He was in a shirt, jeans, and boots. Had he been wearing a six shooter strapped to his leg, he could have passed for Black Bart, or some other equally infamous, desperado. John hadn't spotted the Captain. He bellied up to the bar with one foot on the brass rail.

"Stinking half breed!" muttered the Captain, just loud enough for Brannigan to hear. Brannigan slowly turned his head, and looked at the Captain. There was menace in those black eyes and arched, satanic looking, brows. John didn't say a word, and then there was recognition. "Gringo bastard!" muttered Brannigan, right after grumbling something unintelligible in Spanish. He put on a half grin, and sauntered over to the Captain. It appeared John had already had a snoot full, but he could hold a lot more. The Captain had never known one with such a capacity.

"A drink for Captain Moon," John told Spider and then they were talking old times. John informed Vincent that he had also married. He told him the girl had only been sixteen at the time and the Captain called him a "Dirty Old Man." John told him he was raising her the way he wanted her to be. John was drinking straight shots of one hundred fifty one proof Puerto Rican rum, with a water back. The Captain was familiar with it; he had drunk it with John in the past. The drink was so strong; it had always made Vincent's throat feel raw.

Vincent continued to drink his Mules. John had just sipped the top off a too full shot glass of the powerful, and volatile liquor, which was a dark amber color, about the same color as wild mountain honey. John lit a match and lit a blue flame across the top of his demon rum. He brought it to his mouth and gulped it down, not spilling a drop. He gasped and wiped his mouth with his sleeve.

"Jesus H. Christ!" exclaimed the Captain, "You are going to blow yourself up one of these days." "No I won't," answered John with a grin, "I'll just fart a blue flame." "Have you got fire insurance on your mustache?" asked Spider. "Nawh," answered John, "If It burns off I'll just grow another one."

Mario gave him a disdainful look out of the corner of his eye, he had never been fond of John and the feeling had always been mutual with John. It was probably because John was some times too outspoken. John had always said exactly what was on his mind. If you didn't like it, it was just tough.

"It's party time,'" exclaimed John, after he had gulped down another rum. The Captain was in a different frame of mind; he didn't want to party. He wanted to find Linda while he was still able. He had to find her before he got too drunk. He asked the guys if they had seen her. John had not, but Mario had. He shook his head and looked serious. "I know you want to see her," he said, solemnly, "But maybe you shouldn't." The Captain knew what he meant; knew full well he had hurt her. But she had been so young. She must have got over it by now. Vincent was not going to listen; he was going to see her. He just had to. It was an obsession now.

"I have to see her!" he pleaded with his old friend, not wanting to hear any more in the negative. Vincent felt cold, even though it was warm. He felt a chill go through him, a foreboding feeling. He got a double shot to ward it off. "Why don't you leave her alone," suggested Mario, "You broke her heart, you know. Isn't once enough?" The Captain bowed his head. "I have to see her!" It was all he could think of to say.

"She went out with a lot of guys trying to get over you." castigated Mario, and the Captained groaned inwardly. "Did she get over me?" he asked, hoping she had and hoping she had not. "I don't think she ever did," answered Mario, "But she sure as Hell tried!" he added, with disdain. "What do you mean?" asked the Captain, with apprehension. "After she got old enough," answered Mario, "She went out with so many guys people were calling her a tramp." "I want to see her!" insisted the Captain, with passion. Vincent wanted to see her more now; emotions were swelling in his chest. What had he done to her? What could he do now? He didn't want to hurt her anymore, but he was hurting too. Vincent thought he would be unable to face life if he didn't see her. He was always selfish enough to put himself first.

"Does she still live with her parents?" he asked, feeling a little foolish after thinking she was probably living with some gorilla. "Her parents are gone," answered Mario, "Went back to the Bay Area. Linda has an apartment." "Do you know her number?" "Yes," answered Mario, but didn't say anymore, and there was no communication for a moment as the Captain waited for more. "Are you going to give it to me?" he finally asked. "Yes," answered Mario, reluctantly, and he gave it to him.

The Captain went to the phone. He dialed the number, and it rang eight times. His heart was getting an empty ache. Linda answered after the tenth ring, just when he was getting ready to hang up, he was already moving the phone from his ear. Vincent's heart did a flip-flop when he heard her voice. Her voice was different, but he knew it was Linda. She sounded out of breath, as if she had run to the phone. Maybe she had been in the shower, he was thinking, and he had an image of her standing with a towel around her. He put his handkerchief over his mouth to muffle his voice.

"The Moon Patrol is at Molly's having a reunion," he told her, "And we need a lifeguard." It set her back for a moment, for it had been awhile since she had heard about the Moon Patrol. "Who is this?" she asked with anticipation, and maybe a little suspicion. She had just been thinking of Vincent. "This is the Captain speaking," he answered, after taking the handkerchief away from his mouth. He tried to see her face in his mind, wondering what her expression was. Audibly, Linda drew in her breath. "Oh my God!" she exclaimed, excitedly, "I was just thinking about you. I can't believe I'm talking to you." "What were you thinking?" he asked and felt like kicking himself for asking. There was a pause before she answered. "About what a rat you were," she answered, but in a joking manner. For a moment he could not answered, not being able to think of what to say. "I know," Vincent finally answered. "You promised you would wait for me," Linda scolded. "I was away a long time," he told her, feeling like a lame duck, "And I had problems. I thought you would be better off without me." He felt stupid after saying it, not knowing how to explain, not wanting to reveal the truth.

"You think breaking my heart was good for me?" she asked, emotionally, almost in tears. "I want to see you.'" Vincent pleaded, praying that she would. Linda hesitated before she answered. "I want to see you, too," she answered, "I have wanted for years." "Want me to come to your place?" "I'll come down there." "I'll be waiting for you," he answered, regretting his choice of words as soon as they had left his mouth. "Where have I heard that before?" she asked, and he heard the click as Linda hung up the phone.

Vincent was nervous as he waited for her. He asked Mario how she looked. "She is a knock out!" he exclaimed, "No one has the right to look that good." John agreed with a low whistle, and Spider wiggled his eyebrows, imitating Groucho Marx. Mario raised his glass in tribute. "May God turn all ugly girls into her image," he toasted. "And may all those girls fall in love with me," toasted John. "After they have all slept with me," toasted Spider. The Captain kept his toast to himself, and just raised his glass in agreement. They all drank their drinks to the dregs, and a little while and a few more drinks Linda walked through the doors. She didn't hesitate; she walked straight to the Captain, and stopped within a foot of him. They stood facing each other.

The last time Vincent had seen Linda she was just a girl turning into a woman. Linda, the woman, took his breath away. She was almost as tall as he was. Her glorious, honey blond hair was clear to the middle of her back. She was wearing white shorts with a pink halter. Her legs were long, slender, tan and perfectly, perfect. Her tan was golden brown. Her waist was small, and her breast just right for the rest of her. Vincent couldn't see her back side, but he knew it had to be as good as her front. Her heart shaped face was lovely; her look was not demure, or innocent. She was bright eyed, bushy tailed, ready, willing and able. The Captain just stood entranced, his mouth agape. Linda tossed her head back, laughing softly.

"Do you want to shake hands?" She asked, impudently and he regained his composure. He didn't say anything, he just took her in his arms, and their lips found each other. All the feelings he had had for her, compounded by her woman's aura, came forth. Her innocence was gone, but the sweetness was still there, that incredible sweetness; it melted his backbone, and his knees. Neither one wanted to stop, but they had to breathe. They pulled their lips apart to breathe, but clung to each other.

"I'm so glad you didn't want to shake hands." she told him, breathlessly, her face flushed with excitement. "Me, too," answered the Captain, weak in the knees, needing to sit. Their friends were applauding the kiss, while other eyes were trying to get a better look at Linda. One wise ass was wondering out loud what it was the Captain had. "He has her," answered Mario, under his breath, with disdain.

The Captain was wondering why he loved this girl so much, so much it made him want to forget he was married; enough to make him wish he was not. He wished he could go back in time to marry her, to see what it would be like. He wondered what it would be like to make love to her. Desire welled up in him; he pulled her closer and kissed her again. While they were holding each other someone punched in some slow music, and they started dancing. The two had never danced together. They were natural, their bodies fitting together like peas in a pod. Their rhythm blending, making them like one. They were both wishing they were in a horizontal position, dancing to a different drummer. Linda lost her nonchalant attitude.

"I tried to forget you," Linda whispered softly in his ear, "But I never could." "I know," he answered, "I know." It sounded like he had gone through the same misery, but it was all he could say. It was all he could commit without fabricating. Although he had never forgotten her, that wonderful, sweet, tender feeling had escaped from him. He hadn't had that feeling long enough. Time and his love for Carla had caused the feeling to sink into his subconscious. But now, the feeling was back, overwhelming him, its sweetness blotting out the world, filling his senses. His mind tasted her sweetness, savoring it. His body felt her sweetness, desire consumed him. The music stopped, and they stood, their bodies communicating for a while before they joined the others.

Mario had called Mac, and when he came through the doors a round of drinks was bought by John, and then Walt walked in. No one had called him; he had just walked in to see if there was any action. Mac was surprised, and glad to see the Captain. He did not seem to be his same happy go lucky self, but he was glad to see the Captain and gave him a bear hug. Walt's hair was still perfect, without a single hair out of place. But he was still worried about it, for he was constantly inspecting it in the mirror. The Captain never was quite sure whether Walt was insecure or just in love with himself, like Narcissus, who fell in love with his own reflection in the pool. Walt wasn't selfish, or arrogant, though. Maybe he was just self-conscious. The Captain could understand that, for he was that way himself.

The music started again, and Walt pulled Linda out on the floor. He was a good dancer, much better than the Captain, more relaxed on the floor. He was also taller than the Captain, and the two made a handsome couple, but her eyes never left Vincent. It was as if she was afraid if she lost sight of him he would disappear. But there was no chance of that; he was watching her just as close, perhaps with the same fear. Vincent was watching her every move, all which were graceful and seductive to him. Watching her was disturbing to him, though. He did not want to be unfaithful to Carla, but he knew himself. He knew by Linda's looks, by her body talk and by his own feelings, that he would be making love to her before this night was over. It was inevitable. He knew he would not be able to stop himself, and he wasn't even sure that he wanted to.

While Vincent was watching Linda, Mac was telling him of his woes. He had lost Betty Jane. She had married a soldier and was lost to him forever. This was a surprise to the Captain, for he had always thought they were natural mates and would always be together. Betty Jane had got tired of waiting for him to get his act together. Mac drank too much and she had wanted someone who would take care of her. And on top of that, she had given birth to Mac's baby while being married to this other guy. Mack was in a maudlin mood, and Vincent tried to console him, and although he was genuinely sympathetic, this was not what he really wanted to do. What he really wanted to do was solve his own problem, which was how to get Linda out of Molly's, by herself, just him, and her, alone.

At last he was dancing with her again. Someone had played a slow and easy Glen Miller tune. They were dancing as close as they could get without shedding their clothes. He could feel the heat of her body coming through their clothing. He thought about her golden brown skin, what it would feel like without the clothing between them. He kissed her lovely neck.

"I wish I had waited for you," he whispered in her ear. "We can pretend that you did," she answered, and kissed his lips with passion. This message went straight to his loins. It did not make him forget Carla, though, and he felt like a rat. He could not help himself, Linda was too close and he wanted her. "How are we going to get out of here?" he whispered in her pretty ear, which he then fondled with his tongue, and she did the very same thing to him. Their sexual excitement was climbing, along with the anticipation of what was sure to come. "I'll leave first," she suggested, "And then I'll come back, pretending my car wont start." "Do you think they will fall for that?" he asked. "I don't know," she answered, "And I don't care."

They all had a few more drinks and a few more laughs, then Linda made her excuse, and left. In just a while she came back, feigning car trouble. Vincent offered to take her home. She gratefully accepted, but they were unable to get away without John buying another round of drinks. They tried not to drink in a hurry, but they both knew they were fooling no one. They all promised to meet at Bedrock at noon the next day. Linda and the Captain left.

The lovers were excited with the secret of what they both knew they were going to do. He led her to the Hawk, and she whistled at it before getting into it. After he got into the car they could contain themselves no longer. They came together for a passionate embrace, their bodies burning with desire. Her hunger for him was desperate, she had wanted him since she was just a girl. "Hurry!" Linda pleaded, "Take me somewhere." "I don't have a motel, yet," Vincent replied. "Go to my place," she told him, not wasting any words, and she told him where it was.

Linda's apartment was on Bird Street, on the lower end of town, on the second floor. When they went through the front door she led him straight to her bedroom. They stood facing each other for a moment, almost timid now that they were alone. He put his hands on her bare shoulders. "You were the loveliest girl I ever saw when you were a teenager." he told her as he traced his finger across her shoulder, up her lovely neck to her chin, and then to her lips. "Now you are the most beautiful woman I have ever seen." "You are beautiful, too," she told him, looking at his face with adoration, "And I have loved you since I was a little girl." Vincent put his hand behind her neck, and pulled her closer. "You drove me wild when you were a little girl," he told her, and he kissed her hand, putting her finger in his mouth, tasting her. "Your body was perfect then. I always wanted to see you without any clothes on," he told her, "But you were too, young." "I'm not too, young now," she informed him, as she took off her halter; she had no bra on under it, and then she dropped her shorts, and stepped out of them. Her beauty was breathtaking. Linda started to remove her panties.

"Wait," Vincent told her, "Let me do that," and she waited. He kneeled, and put his hands on her behind. He moved his hands around to feel the shape of her. Vincent pulled her panties down, and kissed her thigh. Linda stepped out of them, and he put his hands on her bare behind, caressing it, and he kissed her naval. She shivered as he ran his hands up her back, and kissed her between her breasts. Then he was kissing her breast, tasting her nipples.

Linda was on fire, and could not contain herself. She had her hands clasped to the back of his neck, smothering his face with kisses. And then she was on him, with her legs around him, squeezing him. Vincent carried her that way to the bed and they fell on it, with him on top. They kissed, and moaned. Then they were both frantically trying to get his clothes off, with him working on his upper garments, while she worked at his lowers.

Vincent was on his knees between Linda's thighs, with a fierce erection as she pulled his shorts down. She fondled him ardently, and he did the same to her, and then he was in her. "Oh, God!" she moaned, as he penetrated her, "I have always wanted this," "Me, too," he groaned, as he penetrated as far as he could. Vincent was so excited, he was afraid he would climax before Linda ever got started. Vincent tried to hold himself back by thinking of something else. Linda was even more excited than he was, she was moaning, and writhing with stored passion, pulling his seed right out of him. Vincent knew when Linda was at her peak, for she put her legs around him, and squeezed until he could hold back his seed no longer. He could hear her suck air between her teeth as they reached their highest rapture. The two laid breathless in each other's arms, spent to the dregs from ecstasy. Neither spoke for a while, afraid of breaking the magic spell.

"Oh, Vincent," she spoke, softly, "I knew it would be like this with you. I knew it would be wonderful." "It was wonderful," replied Vincent, who was now sober and in need of a drink. "If it had been any more wonderful I would have died in your arms." "I would die," she told him, "if I thought I could never make love to you again." She hugged him fiercely. "I can't let you get away from me again!" she exclaimed. He groaned inwardly, knowing he would have to leave her again, not wanting to, but having to. He was still married to Carla and he still loved her, and he had a family, another life.

Vincent lamented silently to himself, wondering how he was going to say goodbye again. He wished he could be cloned then he could give each of the women one of his personalities and trade off now and then. First things first, though, right now he needed a drink and he still had a bottle in the car. He started to rise, but she held on to him. "Where are you going?" Linda asked, she was disturbed. "I need a drink," he told her, honestly, "and I have a bottle in the car."

"There's beer in the refrigerator," she told him, as he finished getting up. "Not strong enough," he told her. "You got a cute ass," she told him, as he put his clothes on. "You have a gorgeous ass," he replied. "Thank you." Linda answered. "You are most welcome," Vincent replied, as he went out of the room, and then out of the apartment.

Vincent couldn't wait to go back in to have a drink, so he sat in the car and had a few belts. He sat until his stomach felt better. He wondered why the orgasm had bothered his stomach, as it usually didn't while he was drinking. He wondered if he was going to get to where he couldn't make love at all. That would surely be Hell on earth. After his stomach was feeling better he went back to the apartment, taking his jug with him. He was going to offer Linda a drink, but she had fallen asleep. He stood and looked at her. She was on her back with her lovely hair spread out on the pillow. She looked peaceful, so beautiful. "Oh, God," he whispered to himself, "How beautiful you are."

Linda lay half covered with the sheet, one breast bare and one leg exposed. Carefully, so he wouldn't wake her, he pulled the sheet off of her, leaving her naked. He explored her body with his eyes until the lust returned and then he went into the bathroom to shower off the sweat. He took off his clothes, opened the glass door, stepped in and started to bathe.

Vincent truly felt rotten about cheating on Carla, but he knew he couldn't help it. That was just the way he was and nothing short of death was going to change that. He was just a slave to his genitals. He knew his conscience would bother him, but he knew it would be for just a little while. The shower door opened and Linda stepped in.

"Can I wash your back?" she asked. "If I can do yours." he answered. She soaped his back, and then his behind. He turned, and put his back to the water to rinse, and he put his arms around her. He soaped her back. They were face-to-face, bodies touching. He soaped her behind, savoring her voluptuousness. He put her back to the water and lathered her breast, making sure he didn't miss any areas. He was enjoying the slippery sensuousness and getting totally aroused. He washed her tummy, playing with her belly button. "Wash everything," she told him, wickedly, and he did. Linda took the soap, lathered his chest, and then his belly, playing with his button.

"Wash everything," he told her. "I wouldn't miss it for anything," she told him, and she giggled as she put his member in her hand, lathering it. "My goodness!" she exclaimed, as if in awe, "It's awfully, hard." "You make it that way," he told her. "And just how do I do that?" she asked, coquettish, still lathering, giving him a little squeeze. "By being so damned beautiful," he told her, "So beautiful I can't wait to get inside you, and it has to be hard to do that." "Is it hard enough now?" she asked, giving it another squeeze. "Yes, it is," he answered, and laughed, "But it wont stay that way if you don't stop playing with it." "You are going to have to put it someplace where I can't get hold of it," she told him, and giggled. "And where might that be, you little devil?" he asked. "You know," she told him, as she took his hand and put it where she meant, "Put it inside of me." Their passion was too urgent to take the time to turn the water off, or to dry off. They rushed out of the shower, to the bed, and on it,

"Hurry!" she pleaded, as he positioned himself between her open thighs, and then he was inside of her. "Oh, God!" she moaned, "You feel so good." "Me, too," he moaned, searching inside of her, searching for he knew not what, something that always seemed just out of reach. Linda was searching frantically for the same something. When they were finished, spent joyfully, they laid in each other's arms. "We were made for each other." she commented, with languish. "I know," he answered, wistfully, "I know."

Vincent stayed with Linda for two weeks, unable to leave her, loving her more deeply every day. They never made the meeting with the Moon Patrol at Bedrock. He only saw his mother once for a few hours. The rest of the time the lovers spent together, selfishly consuming each other. Even after he told her he was married, she did not want to let him go, but the time for him to go finally came. "I will love you forever!" Linda told him through her tears. "I will love you forever!" he told her through his tears, "But I don't know what to do."

CHAPTER 34

For five years Vincent tried to divide himself; he was trying to hold his marriage together, but being unable to let go of Linda. He would resist the temptation to call her as long as he could, and then give in and call her, stirring the ashes of pain, rekindling the flame. He went to see Linda as often as he could, using visits to his mother as a vehicle for his adultery.

Vincent never completely got off the running drunk he had got on five years ago when he had first made love to Linda. He had managed to taper off, but had been drinking regularly, building his tolerance, needing a little more every day to maintain. The alcohol had turned into his food. His body was forgetting how to metabolize anything else. It was getting hard for Vincent to go more than a couple of hours without at least a sip of brandy; therefore he was stashing it everywhere. He had it stashed in different places on the grounds of his home, in the garage, closets, in the trunk of his car and at the office. He carried a flask whenever he wore a coat, which was most of the time, for he was as cold blooded as a snake.

Vincent gave up his brandy and was drinking vodka, for it was not as easy to detect on the breath. Vincent wasn't fooling Carla, though. She knew what was going on, but she knew it would be fruitless to nag at him; it might even make things worse. Carla was aware of his drinking, but not of his adultery. She believed his lack of lust was due to his working too hard and his drinking. She was aware he was plagued with insomnia. She knew he was having nightmares, for they would awake her in the middle of the night. She didn't know he was also having strange kinds of nightmares during the day.

Sometimes after Vincent had not slept most of the night, due to nightmares, he would try to nap during the day. He would see cartoons in color on the back of his eyelids when he closed them. They were not of Bugs Bunny, either, they were awful, constantly changing creatures doing awful things to each other. As soon as he would open his eyes they would go away. As soon as he closed them they would return. And he didn't have to be asleep for this to happen. All he had to be was be tired and strung out.

Carla didn't know what to do for him, so she prayed. Vincent's peculiar disposition was alienating him from Reed, his first son, who was now twelve years old. And the other boys were not immune, either. His mood changes were making it difficult for everyone who had a relationship with him, including his associates at the office. His mood could change in an instant from joy to depression; it wasn't very often that he expressed any joy. Vincent would have to be tipsy for that.

When Vincent was tipsy enough to be artificially happy, he would make promises to the boys, and then forget about them. Reed was beginning to look at him askance. Carla was able to make up for it a little with the younger boys, but not with Reed; he could be quite unforgiving at times. Carla would talk to Vincent about it and he would try to make up for it, but he was caught up in his curse. Vincent didn't know what to do about it, either. He had to drink in order to function, but wasn't functioning very well. He could only try to balance himself, but he was losing his balance.

It was late on a Saturday night and Vincent had imbibed way too much; he was too drunk to go home. He just didn't feel well enough to face Carla. He didn't feel well enough to do anything. In fact, he felt awful, and the booze just wasn't doing him any good. Vincent was so tired he wished he could go to sleep and never wake up. He bought a quart of vodka and went to the Pelican, where Carla found him two days later. He was unconscious and white as a ghost. He looked like he was dying. It frightened Carla something awful. She called an ambulance.

Vincent came out of his hibernation lost in a mist; the same kind that arose from the ground in the Adam Dream. It obscured reality from all who do not want to see it, and from most who do. When Vincent first awoke he didn't know where he was. He didn't know if it was morning, night, or what day, or month, or year it was. He did know who he was, but he could not have signed his name to save his life. He was certain about one thing, though, he needed a drink.

Vincent felt awful, and he needed a drink worse than he had ever needed one. He remembered the bottle he had set beside the bunk, and he tried to reach for it. The light was very bright, something wasn't right. Vincent knew he was on the Pelican, but something was wrong. He reached for the bottle again, but he was weak and something was holding him. He pulled to get free and the I. V. tubes that were hooked to him pulled out, along with the wires that connected him to the monitor. He thrashed around trying to find the bottle and fell off the bed. While crawling around on the floor looking for the bottle, he knocked the stand over that was holding the I. V. bottles. The whole thing came crashing to the floor. Vincent had shed his robe and was crawling, naked, looking for his booze. A male nurse came rushing in to see what had happened and was mortified by the ludicrous sight.

"Awe Shit!" he exclaimed when he saw the mess; the blood on the bed and the floor from the vein that had had the I.V. in it, and the naked man on his hands and knees. He grabbed Vincent. Vincent thought he was being attacked; someone was trying to keep him from his bottle. He called the attacker a crude name and tried to hit him. The attacker called for help, and two other nurses came, one of them was a woman, but she could have passed for a man. They subdued him after much effort and managed to put him in a straight jacket.

Vincent fought the straight jacket with all that was in him, but it was too much for him; he couldn't get free. He felt like he was sinking into deep, dark, water. He tried to get hold of something to hang on to, to keep from sinking, but he couldn't get his hands free. Vincent screamed in terror, and passed out. Only minutes later he awakened, but his eyes were still closed, and the violent, animated cartoons were on the inside of his eyelids.

Vincent had destroyed thousands of brain cells with the alcohol, and at first he didn't have the sense to open his eyes to get rid of the cartoons. He watched with morbid fascination as his imagination created horrid pictures. Animals of no earthly origin were killing each other and giant insects and people. But none of it looked real, they were just cartoons. Vincent got enough brain cells functioning to open his eyes. He was trembling and cold, but was sweating profusely. His stomach hurt, and his nerves were screaming. He now had enough active brain cells to realize he was in a hospital bed. Vincent moved his eyes around, not ready to risk moving his body. He spotted the I. V. connection, and he sighed helplessly. A nurse came to him, she was black and pretty.

"How are you feeling?" she asked, with a pretty southern drawl. Vincent's thinking ability was fettered by his loss of brain cells and it was a struggle to put together a simple sentence. "Not very good," he answered, weakly. "That's understandable," she told him, "You haven't been very good to yourself." "Where am I?" he asked. "You are in a private room at San Francisco General." "How long?" he asked. "Three days," she told him. "But I thought I just got here!" he exclaimed. "Only part of you been here, Honey," she told him, "The rest of you been somewhere else." She smiled and added, "I hope you are going to stay with us for awhile this time."

The girl started to leave, and Vincent pleaded with her to get him something for his ravaged nerves. She assured him the doctor would see him in a little while, and he would get something then, and then the nurse left. Vincent wanted to sleep until that happened so he closed his eyes, but the cartoons came back. He was too tired to hold his eyes open, so he watched them and drifted off to sleep.

Vincent awoke with Doctor Sam checking his pulse.

"Do you want to die?" asked the doctor and the question took Vincent by surprise and he had to think about it. "I don't think so," he answered, confused. "But you are not sure?" asked Sam and at this time Vincent wasn't sure of anything. "It might be easier to die," he answered and Sam didn't hesitate. "Death will not be easy for you." he told Vincent in deadly earnest, "Not in the way you are going about it." Sam took an instrument and looked into Vincent's eyes. "It could take years of suffering to die this way," he told Vincent, "And you could go insane, first." Vincent didn't know what to say. "I don't know what to do," Vincent finally answered. "There is no easy way," Sam told him, "But the stuff you are drinking is poison. So treat it like poison." He took a glass from the sink and held it up like it was a drink. "Imagine a skull and cross bones on it before you drink it," he told him, "It is poison and it will kill you."

Vincent was watching the corpuscles in the capillaries in his eyes. Sam had left, leaving him the comforting knowledge that a nurse would soon be giving him a shot for his nerves. After the shot he felt better for a couple of hours, and then he was right back where he started, ready to climb the walls.

That first day he was unable to ingest solid food, only some juice and it hurt his throat; it was raw from drinking straight vodka. He was a Taurus and according to his natal horoscope, his weak spot was his throat. He had been to church a number of times and had always had trouble singing the hymns. The low and high notes were usually out of his range and hurt his throat trying to reach them.

Carla had come to see Vincent right away. After they had got him ready for his stay he had been suffering so that she had been unable to stay more than a half hour. It had hurt her so to see him that way. He had looked like warmed over-death and had been incoherent, maudlin and begging her to get him out of the hospital.

Vincent saw them coming with his first tray of solid food. He was not hungry, but his mind was functioning enough to know he had to eat if he was going to stay alive for Carla and the boys. The thought crossed his mind that they might be better off if he didn't stay alive. When his bowl of cream of wheat was uncovered he was horrified. He couldn't tell what it was, for it was covered with worms. They were crawling and wiggling all over whatever it was in the bowl. The worms were different colors, some white like noodles; others were green, or blue or red.

Vincent made an awful face and the nurse asked him what was wrong. When he told her about the worms she was surprised and investigated. When she found no worms she knew he was hallucinating. "There are no worms," she told him, "You are having a hallucination.

338

Vincent was incredulous and argued with her at first, and even wanted a second opinion. When he heard one, he realized they had no motive to lie to him. He also knew he had to eat to stay alive.

The worms were thinner than spaghetti, more like oriental noodles. They were crawling all over each other and it was hard to get them on the spoon. When Vincent got the spoon full he put it in his mouth before they could fall off. He could feel them crawling around as he chewed them. When he tried to swallow, he gagged and retched. He reached for his plastic puke pan and he tried to puke. All that came out was what was in his mouth, for his stomach was empty.

Vincent waited for his stomach to settle. Vincent had an iron will when it came to suffering. The awful suffering he had experienced in his youth, suffering caused by earaches, had forged it. He tried to eat again and this time some of it stayed down. He could feel the worms crawling around in his stomach. Vincent shuddered and ate some more. He ate as much as he could and then he lay there with the worms crawling in his stomach. It was such a weird, frightening feeling; he felt like he would go crazy, like he was coming apart at the seams. Vincent felt like screaming, but he sobbed instead. He sobbed a helpless sob until he was exhausted and fell asleep.

People walking by his bed woke him. There was a door by the head of his bed where people were coming through. They were coming through in single file, walking past his bed. The people were viewing him, like he was in a casket, already dead. They seemed pleased about his death and were commenting to each other about it. He pulled his sheet up over his head and waited for a few moments and then he pulled the sheet down. The people were still filing past him, viewing him.

Vincent buzzed for the nurse and when she finally came after what seemed like part of eternity. He told her to shut the damned door and get rid of the people so he could get some sleep. The nurse was surprised and then sympathetic. She told him there were no door and no people, that he was having another hallucination. She assured him it would pass. Nevertheless, he watched the people to see if he knew any of them, but they all turned out to be strangers. They kept coming until he fell asleep. When he awoke they were gone, and so was the door.

Carla came to see Vincent that evening; she was pale and weary. He felt sympathy for her. He wished for her sake he had not married her. He knew he was making life a Hell for her; he knew he could never make her happy, never make anyone happy. He knew he would never win his battle with alcoholism, not with his temptation resistance quotient of zero. Carla kissed him softly, like he was fragile, and he was. Her eyes were red from weeping. Even her hair looked tired. She looked like a wilted flower. She started to sit in the chair, but Vincent, wanting her closer, motioned for her to sit on the bed beside him and she complied. Vincent opened his arms to her and she went into them. She was weeping softly, with her face buried in his chest.

"What am I doing wrong!" she wailed, in a whisper. "Nothing," he answered, feeling quite worthless, "It isn't you; it is me. I just can't stop myself. It's a family curse." "It's not a curse," she tried to assure him, "It is a disease and you can beat it, but you need help." "No one can help me" he argued, dejectedly, "I have already tried everything." "You need therapy," she told him. "If you mean a shrink, I have tried that too." "You just had the wrong one," she argued. "Maybe so," he agreed, wanting to end the discussion, wanting to please her.

That night, while Vincent was watching the television, Carla's face appeared on the screen. The television started filling with water, and Carla was struggling to get out of it. She was screaming in terror as the water rose to her mouth and then it covered her face. Bubbles were coming out of her mouth and her curls were floating. Carla pounded on the glass, frantically. Vincent jumped out of bed, pulling everything loose. Vincent tried to rescue her. He climbed on a chair and tried to break the glass on the screen with his fist. They came before he could save her. He tried to explain to them, but they just wouldn't listen. Vincent cried while he watched Carla drown. He couldn't save her for they had put him back in the straight jacket. Oh how he hated them. He cried himself to sleep.

Vincent was surprised and joyous to see Carla the next day. He was sure she had drowned; he had seen it with his own eyes. He laughed joyously and a little hysterically when he saw her. Carla was surprised by his joy. "I'm so glad you are alive." he told her excitedly, as he held his arms out to her. "Of course I'm alive!" she exclaimed, incredulous, "Why wouldn't I be?" "I saw you drown in the television," he argued. "How could I get into the television?" she asked him, as if he was a child. "I don't know," he answered, defensively, "But I saw you there." "It was just an illusion," she assured him, gently. "I'm so, glad!" Vincent exclaimed, and sighed with relief. "Everything will be alright," she assured him. "I suppose that is true," he agreed, with very little conviction.

Two weeks later Vincent was released from the hospital as an outpatient. His blood pressure was still high, needing to be monitored periodically. He had a minor infection in his urinary tract that had to be watched. Carla made him an appointment with the favorite shrink of her social circle, Doctor Favius Smith. Vincent wondered why a doctor with such a common last name would have a first name like Favius. He thought that his mother knew he was going to be a shrink so she gave him a screwy first name. That way he would stand out in the yellow section of the phone directory.

Favius was tall, handsome and dapper. His hair was black, but gray at the temples. He didn't say much, for mind reading took up his time. He

340

seemed to know what one was going to say before it was said. He would often answer your thoughts before they were verbalized. It was kind of weird. Vincent had the feeling that he could just sit there saying nothing and Favius would be able to carry on the conversation between them all by him self.

After months of one on one sessions and group therapy, Favius came to a prognosis that Vincent was suffering from a guilt complex. It was compounded by an inferiority complex and a sexual identity problem caused by the absence of his father and possessiveness of his mother. This was all wonderful to know. "But so what?" thought Vincent, indignantly. He didn't say that, but he didn't need to, for Favius had already read his incredulous look. He told him he had to learn to assert himself, to be more aggressive, to take charge of his life.

"But what about my alcoholism?" asked Vincent, not happy with the prognosis. "Alcoholism is a disease of which there is no known cure," Favius instructed him. "And you getting this disease was caused in part by an inherited weakness and the other part by over indulgence by you." The doctor noted the look of disdain on Vincent's face. He knew it would be there. It was also a look of fear, a need for escape. Alcoholics just hate to have the truth told to them; it cuts off their escape from self.

"But," started Vincent, but the doctor cut him off at the pass. "You can't blame anyone, anything, or any situation for your self indulgence," said Favius, with conviction. "For this action offers you an artificial, escape which you will accept every time." Favius stopped talking, waiting just long enough for an argument to start to form on Vincent's face, and then he started again, before Vincent could verbalize. "This escape is only a revolving door which will always bring you right back to your folly. Every time you try to escape this way your problem will get worse."

Vincent reluctantly tried to digest all of this, but he failed to see how this knowledge Favius had equipped him with was going to help him with his problem. His frustration was reflected on his face.

"What in the Hell can I do?" he asked, close to anger. "You must never, ever, take another drink of alcohol in any form," answered a solemn Favius. "Time will never cure you of this disease. You will have it as long as you live." "That's a long time," answered an equally solemn Vincent.

"Remember the old slogan," suggested Favius" One drink is too many and a thousand not enough. Five years from now, or ten, you might get the idea you can handle it, but it wont be true. It will always handle you." "What do I do about my nerves?" asked Vincent, like a man who had been condemned. "I can't prescribe drugs for you," answered the doctor, "You would just get hooked on them." "What can I do?" asked the helpless Vincent. "You have to learn to cope with it yourself," instructed Favius. "No one can do it for you. Find things you like to do. Try not to get too tired, or angry. Stay in group therapy so you will have an avenue to vent your frustration. Go on a vacation with your family."

This was not good news to Vincent. This was no solution to his problem; this was just an extension of it. He had never been able to help himself and now was no different. Was he supposed to wish his nerves away? People made him nervous, should he become a hermit? He had a people career, should he dump that and become an artist? How about a beach bum? How about a Guru? This was all too, much for him. He left the doctors office frustrated and depressed. What he needed was a drink. Vincent's mind tasted it, feeling it sooth his nerves, but he couldn't have one, he could never have one. Never was too long to even comprehend. He was going to have to demonstrate the old Alcoholics Anonymous Slogan: "One day at a time."

Carla had wanted to drive him to his appointment with Favius. Vincent had insisted on driving himself and he was glad he had, for he needed to be alone. He had a hard time driving, though, his nerves were shattered. An unexpected noise was like an electrical shock going through him. He was just a physical and mental wreck. The slightest physical effort caused his pulse to pound in his ears.

Vincent drove to Lands End and down to Baker Beach. He parked in the shelter of a grove of trees. It was foggy, like his mind. Vincent thought of his life, what a mess it was, what a mess he was. He wished he had the courage to kill himself. It would be so easy. All he would have to do is run a hose from his exhaust pipe into the car window, and just sit there with the engine running. In a little while he would be asleep, and then he would be dead. No more nerves, no more troubles, no more anything.

Vincent imagined the funeral. Carla, his mother and Linda would be dressed in black, with black veils covering their grief stricken face. The boys would be dressed in black, with sorrowful faces. The Moon Patrol would be there, with Mario reading the eulogy. His colleagues would be there with a profusion of fragrant flowers. It was too much for Vincent. Emotion filled his tear ducts and his chest. He sobbed uncontrollably. When Vincent had finished with his sobbing he didn't know what to do. He couldn't go home, even though he knew Carla would be waiting for him. He was exhausted and sleepy. He wished he could pull a Rip Van Winkle and sleep for twenty years.

Vincent remembered Favius had told him he could never have a drink", so twenty years would not be long enough. Things would still be the same when he awoke. He decided he would go to the Pelican and take a nap. As he drove over the Golden Gate, which was really orange, he thought about the many people who had jumped off the bridge. He understood how they had felt before doing it. He thought of what an agony of fear it must have been right after they had let go of the bridge and their last chance to live. Vincent wondered how many had changed their mind on the way down. He shuddered as he imagined the horror of it.

Vincent knew that carbon monoxide had a similar horror. He had read that before it puts one to sleep it renders one paralyzed, leaving one conscious for a spell. One being able to change ones mind but unable to do anything about it. He shuddered again at the thought. He thought there must be a better way. Vincent knew he would never have the courage to shoot himself, not sober, anyway. Vincent made up his mind. When he could stand life no longer he would go on one last drunk and shoot himself. He would have to shoot himself in the head, of course, but that would make such a mess and leave him ugly. He couldn't do that to Carla. She would probably be the one who would have to identify him.

Vincent finally got to his refuge, the Pelican. He loved the boat and he especially loved sleeping on her. The bunk was firm and the gentle motion of the boat was soothing. When he got in the cabin he laid on the bunk and covered himself with a wool blanket Carla had bought him one Christmas. He closed his eyes, but sleep would not come right away, only memories. He could not escape his gloom and he cried himself to sleep.

Vincent awoke a few hours later needing a drink. He always woke needing a drink. Vincent got up and made himself a cup of hot herb tea. The hot liquid felt good going down his throat and spilling into his stomach, but it did not relieve his nerves. His body tingled, and he was short of breath. He had to struggle to keep from hyperventilating. He was weak, and colitis was making him feel like he was swelling like a balloon. He belched to relieve it, but the relief was only momentary. His heart did a flip-flop, and he felt even weaker. He decided he had better go home before Carla had an all-points bulletin out on him.

It was a pale, gaunt Vincent who walked into the foyer of the mansion on the hill where Carla was waiting for him. They were alone, for it was late and the boys had already retired to their rooms. Carla was sitting on the stairs. She had been on her way up them when she had heard his car in the driveway. She had been waiting for him for hours, afraid that he might have succumbed to his need for a drink. The nose knows, though, and it told her he had not. Vincent walked to the stairs and sat beside her. He felt guilt for the harried look on her face. He patted her shoulder and kissed her forehead.

Where in the world have you been all this time?" she asked, softly, "I have been worried sick about you." "The Pelican," he answered, penitent. "Why did you go there?" she asked, somewhat impatient after waiting so long. "I was too upset to go home." he answered, woefully. "What were you upset about?" she asked, and her tone had turned sympathetic. "Favius told me there was nothing medical that could be done for me. He told me I had to handle my nerves myself." "He can't even give you a tranquilizer?" she asked, incredulous. "He told me I would just get addicted to it," he told Carla, not wanting to believe it was true, always looking for an escape. "Don't you think that is true?" she asked, but it was more like a statement. "With my luck," he answered, dejectedly, "It probably is." "We will have to handle it," she answered, with feigned optimism "I hope so," he answered, without hope.

CHAPTER 35

It was summer and Vincent was forty years old. He had regained much of his health by abstaining, and with the help of his new panacea, Valium. He had been taking it for three years and it had helped him to get his family on a more solid footing, and his business. Although it was causing him some problems, it was better than fighting the need to drink. When he awoke in the mornings he felt a little hung-over, but that feeling would leave after he had taken the Valium.

Vincent had been extremely nervous at the office one day and one of his associates had introduced him to this wonder drug. It had worked like a miracle. The associate's pills had been the ten-milligram size, or something that sounded like that. They were the strongest obtainable, anyway. It had settled his nerves just like a drink. Valium was the answer to his prayers, a panacea to take the place of alcohol. His associate had been getting the wonderful pills from an oriental doctor named Chu and now Vincent was getting his from Chu.

Vincent had been given a prescription for the strongest, but after taking them for a while an alarm had gone off in his head telling him they were too strong. They were making him feel too good. And they had affected his judgment of distance. One day, while window-shopping, he had banged his head on the window, not realizing how close it had been. Vincent had learned from his experience with alcohol that what goes up must come back down. The next time he went to Chu he asked for a weaker prescription and Chu gave him the fives.

Vincent never took more than the prescription called for. He didn't take less, either. He was too uncomfortable when he did. He was starting to get an uneasy feeling; it was a vague thing. His subconscious knew he was heading for trouble, but he was unwilling to face it. Vincent was feeling depressed when he awoke in the morning and also an hour before it was time to take his next pill. The depression left after he took his pill, but he was still left with the vague, uneasy feeling.

One day Vincent realized that the uneasy feeling was a manifestation of fear. Although he knew a stronger dose would make him feel better, he was afraid to take one. He knew, now, that he was hooked. He was hooked, just like he had been on alcohol, just like Favius had told him it would happen. Vincent didn't know how bad he was hooked, though; he didn't know how bad the withdrawal would be. And he was even more afraid of what he would withdraw to.

One Saturday morning Vincent overslept. It was unusual for him to do so, for he had a built in alarm and it was his stomach. Six hours after going asleep, his stomach would awaken him. He would feel like he was starving and his stomach would churn into an angry fist without immediate attention. But this morning he had overslept two hours. Carla had let him, knowing how tired he had been.

When Vincent got to the medicine cabinet, his hands were shaking. He felt exactly like he was having a hangover. His fingers slipped while opening the container and the whole open container of Valium fell into the gaping mouth of the toilet bowl. While he was in shock, and horror, the pills were dissolving in the water. Frantically, he tried to retrieve some of them, but failed.

Vincent was by nature a practical person, and after he had pulled himself together, somewhat, he decided this would be a good time to see if he could get off of the Valium. Maybe there was some less addictive drug he could try. His prescription renewal date had run out, anyway, and he wouldn't be able to get it filled until Monday, so he had no choice.

It was plainly visible to his family and especially to Carla, that Vincent was having a problem. When he told Carla what had happened, she advised him to take it easy, rest and not exert himself or get excited. That was easy for her to say; she had never been addicted to anything in her life. The worst she has ever suffered had been in childbirth, and that had been easy for her. Carla was disgustingly healthy. Vincent wasn't feeling healthy at all. He was remembering it had taken him a full year to regain his health after that last drunk.

The first two months had been Hell; the slightest noise could make him jump right out of his skin. He had been frail the whole year. His power of recuperation was diminishing with the passing years. After six months he had tried to go back to the office, but it had been too much for him. It had taken him a year to get back to the office and then it had been for part time, at first.

Vincent made it through Saturday, and through the night, but without any sleep. Sunday morning was Hell. It was worse than alcohol withdrawal. He tried to get hold of the associate who had introduced him to Valium, but he was out of town for the weekend. Vincent felt so awful and he only had one way to go, but he was afraid of it. He could drink until he could get more Valium. He didn't want to do it, but he had no choice; he just couldn't stand feeling the way he did. He would just have to be careful.

Vincent felt like his backbone was like a guitar string strung too, tight and ready to snap. His neck muscles felt as if they had been twisted like the rubber band that runs the prop on a model airplane that had been prepared for flight. His whole body ached as if he was coming down with the flue. He felt like the world had grown larger, making the gravitational pull on him greater, and he was so tired. He felt like he could sleep forever, but when he tried, sleep wouldn't come.

Vincent just had to get out of the house, he was going nuts. He had to find a quiet bar somewhere, one where no one knew him. That shouldn't be too hard to do, there were a lot of bars in Frisco. Vincent told Carla that he had to be alone for a while. He was going to the beach, or maybe the Pelican. Carla understood and he left.

Vincent decided he had better not have anything stronger than beer. He was nervous and didn't want to drive far, so he went to the nearest place, which was down by Cliff House. It was a tourist trap, and he didn't think he would run into anyone he knew.

The Budweiser tasted wonderful; forbidden fruit always does. It felt good to do something he wasn't supposed to, like a kid who gets a chance to run around naked. It felt good to be getting away with something, like a thief in the night. Vincent kept his eye on the door, watching for someone to come in that he knew. He drank the beer quickly, not wanting it to lose its delicious flavor. He drank another, but decided he would wait at least an hour before having another. It was one of the daft formulas he had tried to keep from getting hooked; an hour between drinks. But he had already broken the formula.

The beer had relieved some of his tension, making him even sleepier. Vincent bought a six-pack and drove to the Pelican where sleep was sweet. He slept for three hours and woke feeling better, but still thirsty. He had another beer, but drank it slowly. It still tasted good, so he felt safe. If it started to taste bad he would know he had drank too much. It was another of his daft formulas. Vincent nursed the beer until evening and decided he should go home.

As he left the Pelican he wondered what he would do if he couldn't get off the Valium? He knew that if he went back on the booze it would be a disaster. He couldn't worry about that now, though. He still had to get through the night and the next morning. His breath was an immediate concern and he was out of booze. He should have one more drink, one for the road. He was already feeling the need.

Vincent was still worried about someone he knew seeing him,

someone who might report it to Carla, but his need was greater than his caution. He went into a posh lounge off the main drag. He walked past a black guy who had two gorgeous white girls who were hanging all over him. They were having a gay old time, laughing and petting him and he wasn't pushing them away. All three were dressed like high society. The girls were real classy lookers and Vincent was envious. He was thinking that if the guy could keep those two happy, he was a better man than most, better than he was.

By the time the bartender got to him, Vincent decided to have a vodka martini. He thought it would help to get the beer off his breath. And then he watched the trio in the mirror, they were already loaded, and feeling no pain. In a little while they left, arm in arm, probably headed for an orgy of delights of the flesh. It made Vincent feel horny thinking about it as he watched the girl's behinds as they made their exit.

Vincent thought about sex for a while as he fingered the martini glass and sipped his drink, loving the way it felt in his stomach. He wondered why everything he liked was bad for him. He knew that a big percentage of the pleasure of sex was the anticipation and the sensual pleasure before the orgasm. Sure, the orgasm was great, but over so quickly. And when it was over, he had always been disappointed; always hoping the next one would be better. If sex was the ultimate human pleasure, life was certainly going to be somewhat of a drag. There just had to be more to life than that.

Thinking of sex caused him to think of Linda; she had been his most exciting sexual experience. She had been so exciting it had been hard for him to control his orgasm. And even with her he had had to have booze. Without it the orgasm would leave him feeling awful. He should have been a priest.

After Vincent had finished the martini he was reluctant to go home, to be intimidated by Carla's goodness; he hated that. He always felt guilty around her, especially when he was nervous, in need of a drink. Vincent knew the Hell he had put Carla through. He knew that she was aware that he was walking a tightrope. Vincent knew that Carla was dreading and expecting him to fall. He always felt guilty, for he knew that sooner or later, he would fall.

Vincent's martini was gone again, and he was still reluctant to go home. He was just starting to feel better. There was no place in the world where he felt as comfortable as he did in a bar. He laughed to himself as he was thinking he should buy a bar and move right in. He could put a camp cot in the storage room. He would be able to mix himself a drink on one side of the bar and drink it on the other side. And he could put all his drinks on the tab; free drinks for life. A short life it would be; he was sure about that.

Vincent's father had only made it to sixty-two. Vincent use to think that was pretty old, but not now, that was not really that far away. His father had only lived a few houses from his favorite watering hole and had fallen over dead walking from it back to his house after a night of reveling. The coroner had reported that he had been dead before hitting the ground. Vincent thought there couldn't be too many better ways to die. And Charley had only made it to forty-two. He had died in his diving suit, down in the ocean. He had died before they could get him out of his suit. He had partied the night before the dive. A good time Charley was what he had always been and his heart had not been able to stand all the good times.

Aunt Lydia, his father's sister, didn't even make it to fifty; she had petrified her liver in alcohol. And she had not had the luck of dying all of a sudden. She had died slowly; with suffering and with the knowledge she was dying. Lydia knew the Grim Reaper was coming for her and she didn't want to go with him. She cried to her last moment of life.

Vincent had another martini and tried to get his mind off the morbid subject. Linda popped back into his head and he wished she hadn't married that gorilla of a truck driver. How could she have married such a big nerd? And he was a jock strap on top of that; a couch potato. All he did was sit with his face in the tube, watching football, or basketball, or bowling, or any kind of game that might come on. The deepest thought the guy ever had been the score.

Vincent was concerned about his mother, also. She had been ailing for quite awhile and they had yet to find what was wrong with her. He wondered if her illness had anything to do with the resentment she had been feeling toward Doc. In the early part of their marriage she hadn't minded his running around, for she had usually gone with him. But this had gone on for years and she had got tired of it.

How could anyone want to fish, hunt, and mine for gold all of the time? His mother didn't want to be roughing it all of the time. Just once he could have taken her on a vacation where she wanted to go. And how she had wanted to move back to the coast; how she had hated the valley, the heat, the bugs and mosquitoes.

Doc was not a sentimental person. He had never bought her pretty things, never bought her gifts for her birthday, for their anniversary, even for Christmas. He could not afford such foolishness. He always had the money for a new Jeep, though, or guns and fishing equipment; they were the necessities of life. Most of the clothes Grace wore she had made herself, or were second hand, or some her sister had sent her from the Goodwill Store in Oakland. Grace had tried to save Doc's money in any way she could, but he had always taken everything she did for granted. She was his wife and it was her duty to do such things. His only duty was to keep a roof over her head and furnish her with the bare necessities of life.

His mother had even gone so far as to divorce Doc. He had kept the home and had paid her for her share. She had not wanted the house, and had moved to Oregon, to the town where her sister was living. She had bought a mobile home and was living in it when Doc had begged her to come back to him. He had been ill and in need of a nurse. The Great White Hunter had chosen her, and she had run to him. His mother had always had a foolish heart. She had nursed Doc back to health and now it was his turn, and he didn't want to stay home.

The last martini was getting to him and he knew he was not going to be able to hide it from Carla, but he would try to fake it, anyway; he didn't know what else to do. Vincent thought he better have one more for the road, though. He had one more drink, and then worried about what he would do if he needed a drink in the middle of the night, or in the morning. He bought a half pint of vodka and took it with him; it was an easy size to hide.

Vincent was almost home when he chickened out. He just could not face Carla, and her intimidating, goodness. He wished he had married a slut; it would have made things easier. He drove back across the bridge to the Pelican, where he sipped on the vodka until it was gone. He found another bar and had another martini, one to give him the courage to face Carla.

It was after ten and he knew Carla would be worried sick about him. He cursed himself for being such a coward. It would have been easier if he had gone home when he had first started to. The vodka had turned him into Captain Moon. He was grateful for that. Had it not, he would not have had the courage to call at all. He went to the pay phone and dialed the number. Carla answered right away; she had been waiting by the phone.

"Vincent?" she asked, in a worried, nervous voice, before he had a chance to say anything, "Is that you?" "Yes, Honey, it's me," he answered, sheepishly. He always called her that when he knew he was in trouble. "Are you alright?" she asked, with apprehension. He could see her face in her voice, could see the quiver in her lips. "Not exactly," he answered. She could tell by his voice, but she had to ask him, anyway. "Have you been drinking?" "Yes," he answered. "I knew this was going to happen!" she wailed, and then she was crying. "Oh, Vincent, why?" she wailed. Vincent felt helpless, knowing no way to ease her pain. For a moment he was at a loss for words. How could he explain it to her? She had never been hooked on anything. Only a fish knows how a fish feels out of water.

"I'm sorry," he lamented, softly, in despair, "I just could not help it." "I know," she answered, after a few moments of silence, and there was a different tone in her voice. "I have to see you," she told him and her voice was calm, now, "Where are you?" "Sausalito," he answered. "I'll meet you at the Pelican," she told him. "Alright," he answered and he heard the phone click as Carla put the phone down.

Vincent was apprehensive; there was something different in her voice, like resolution. Vincent guzzled a couple of quick ones and left the bar. He stopped at a liquor store and bought a bottle to boost his courage. He knew he was going to need it.

When Vincent got to the Pelican he took off his shoes and boarded her. He poured himself a drink, and with dread he waited for Carla. He felt sorry for her and felt remorse. He wished he had not been born with the curse. He knew his life was never going to mean a thing. He had made a lot of money and had spent a lot and it didn't mean a damned thing. He recalled a verse he had once read in the Bible: "All is vanity, and vexation of spirit." Vanity had to be a form of selfishness, he thought; he certainly was vexed, and hexed. "Vain also means worthless," he told himself, "And I am certainly that."

It seemed like a long time, but it wasn't long enough. He felt Carla board the boat before he heard anything. He heard her open the hatch, and then she was standing in front of him. Carla had to tell him while she had the courage.

"We have to separate," she told him, calmly, "I can't watch you kill yourself. I love you too much. It hurts too much!" Her calm broke and she was crying, and so was Vincent. He had expected something like this, but he was still surprised, and hurt. "I know," he answered, it was all he could say, "I'm sorry."

Vincent didn't want to hurt her anymore and he knew he would if he should talk her out of her resolution. He was thinking that someday he might beat this thing and then he would try to get her back. Carla came to him and held his face in her hands. Through her tears she kissed him. "I love you." she told him, between sobs, "I hope someday you will overcome this problem. I will always love you no matter what." They embraced each other as if it were for the last time. They kissed as if it were for the last time. "I will always love you" Vincent told her as she backed away from him; her hands were hanging by her side. She tried to gesture with them, but failed to express what she wanted and she dropped them back to her side, nervously.

"Goodbye." she told him, forlornly. "Goodbye, sweetheart," he answered, his voice breaking. Carla stood for a moment, afraid to turn, afraid to let go, afraid he would go off the deep end and never come back. She had to risk it though, she had tried everything else. Carla turned, and she disappeared through the hatch. Captain Moon just stood there in the vacuum of his pain, but there was a sense of relief. He was tired of trying to be somebody he was not, tired of fighting the urge to drink, tired of being afraid to drink. Maybe he was born to be a drunk. Maybe he belonged on Skid Row with the rest of the drunks; who made him better than them? And what the Hell difference did it make, anyway? He could get run over by a truck, or die of a heart attack. His insurance was paid up. "To Hell with it!" he exclaimed, and poured himself a big one.

The Captain drank his drink, and looked around in the Pelican. He thought of the first time he had been there with Carla. His mind was flooded with beautiful memories. He cried out loud, "Oh, God! Why am I doing this?" His anguish was unbearable. He jumped up and hurried out of the Pelican and off of her. He had to get away. He ran all the way to his car and had his foot on the clutch before he realized he didn't have his shoes on. Vincent didn't want to think, so he hurried back to put his shoes on. All he wanted to do was go somewhere where there was noise and booze. He was dressed well enough, so he wanted to go to some nice place.

The cat was already out of the bag and it didn't matter who saw him. He finished with his shoes, combed his hair and left. Vincent hurried to his car and drove to town. He parked close to what looked like a busy cocktail lounge. He went in and sat at the bar on the first empty stool he saw. Men occupied the stools on both sides of him. Both men had their back to him. They were talking to other patrons. The bartender was busy, but he was in no hurry. He was casual like his bright Hawaiian shirt. He looked like he might hurry if a mad dog was after him, or if he had the dysentery.

The best place in the world to be when one is lonely is belly up to the bar. One could at least look at ones self in the magic mirror. Bar mirrors almost always made one look better. The more one drank, the better one looked. And so goes for the other faces in the mirror. Women tend to look better the more one drank. Captain Moon surveyed the mirror. He felt like he was being observed. He looked in the direction the feeling was coming from. He saw her eyes move down, but she hadn't moved her head. It was a very pretty head. She had very dark hair, big eyes, but she was too far away in the dim light to see their color. She didn't look up.

The bartender twitched his little black mustache and asked for the Captain's order. He looked and sounded just like a bartender, with his bow tie and his armband. The Captain wondered what the armband was for; someday he was going to ask. He ordered a Singapore Sling and the bartender twitched his mustache again. He grinned and commented, "That's one of my favorite." It must have been, for he seemed to enjoy making it. A lovely one it was, tall, frosty, red and delicious.

The drink tasted too good and it didn't take him long to drink it. He ordered another right away and the seasoned bartender cautioned him, with good humor "Careful Governor." The Captain was aware that the drink was potent; he had drunk many of them. He sipped the next one while he tried to catch the eye of the beauty in the magic mirror. She was getting better looking all the time. He caught her eye just before she looked down, but she still looked down.

"She has played this game before," he told himself, but so had he, and he did love playing it. The Captain stared at her, but she looked into her drink. He continued to watch her and after awhile it was plain to see she was alone. She would look up, and then down. She did it so quickly, it was almost imperceptible. He decided he would reverse the silly game. He stared into his drink and waited. He could feel her looking at him, but he continued to stare at his drink.

Vincent played with her for a while, sometimes looking around the bar at everyone but her. And then he glanced at her, quickly, dropping his eyes as soon as he had seen hers. He did this for a few times and then he didn't drop his eyes, but continued to look at her. She looked back this time, smiled. This was progress, and he smiled back. This was a little frightening for the Captain; he hadn't played these games for a long time.

Vincent wondered if he should try. He really didn't want to spend the night alone, and she was such a pretty one. And she was giving him the come on. She was subtle about it, but he was certain that she was inviting him, but what if she should reject him? How embarrassing that would be. He could always go to a different bar. Vincent got another drink and sauntered her way, trying to look casual, and confident. There was an empty stool beside her, but he didn't sit right away.

"Are you alone?" he asked, and his voice sounded okay to him. He felt strangely, adolescent. "I was," she answered, her voice was soft, innocent and she was so young. "She sounds just like a nun," he told himself, silently, feeling a little like a dirty old man. Her eyes were almost big enough to fall into and they were an unusual pale blue. Her tone of voice told him he had ended her solitude. He sat next to her and offered to buy her a drink and she accepted.

The girl was younger than he had thought from across the bar, not more than twenty-five. She was thin, but very feminine, like Audrey Hepburn. She smelled delicious. Her face was classic, high cheekbones, fine eyebrows, long lashes, slender nose, lovely lips and a Mediterranean tan. Her skin looked as smooth as a baby's behind.

"Why is a pretty girl like you all alone?" he asked, not knowing what else to ask. She was timid, sounding like a schoolgirl. "Why is a pretty man like you all alone?" she asked back. Vincent grinned; he had never thought of himself as pretty. "I asked you first," Vincent answered. "Fair is fair," she acknowledged, "I left my husband." "My wife just kicked me out," he told the girl, and she was just a girl to him; she seemed so young. That made her even more desirable, for she seemed taboo.

"Is it usually the wife who leaves?" he asked the girl. "I don't think so," she answered, "My father ran off with another woman," "Are you going to get drunk?" he asked. "I'm going to try." "Can I join you?" "You already have," she replied. "Let's really get serious about getting drunk, "he suggested, "But first let's dance." "I agree to both of your proposals," she answered and he led her to the dance floor. Something slow and easy was coming out of the music machine, and the two fitted well together. They danced well together, warming to each other.

"I know this may seem irrelevant," said Vincent, "But my name is Captain Moon," She laughed a musical little laugh. "Isn't that a rather unusual name?" she asked. "I guess it is if you don't know anyone by that name." he answered, "But now you do." "Can I just call you Captain?" she asked, and then she giggled, "Or Moony?" she asked. "Whatever pleases you," he answered. "Nellie is me," she told him. "I like that name," he told her, "I think I will call you that."

They danced until the music ended generating some sexual tension, getting tuned to each other. They went back to the bar, had a few more drinks, and then they were dancing again. Their dancing became more intimate, more seductive. After a while no more seduction was necessary. They both had drunk more than enough, and they were both ready for progress.

"Where are you living?" he asked her softly in her ear; tasting her ear lobe. "I'm staying with my sister, Kathy." "Is she as pretty as you?" asked the Captain. "Prettier," she answered. "Prettier!" exclaimed the Captain, as if it was not even possible. "When do I get to meet her? He asked in jest. "Right after my death," she answered in jest, and he laughed while wishing he had a room to invite her to.

Vincent thought of the Pelican, but felt a cringe of conscience. "It's Carla's," he told his conscience, silently, "And the first place we made love." After a few more drinks, and much arousal, Vincent's conscience abated enough for him to reconsider the Pelican as a temporary trysting place.

"Would you like to come to my yacht for a drink?" he asked, and then laughed, for it had sounded so absurd, almost as bad as "Would you like to see my etchings?" The girl also laughed. "You are kidding me?" she asked, "Or are you?" she added, after seeing his expression. "I really do have a yacht," he assured her, "Not a very big one, but it is a yacht, and it's not very far from here." She looked at him with those big, doe eyes.

"For a drink?" she questioned, and then she gave him a little sophisticated grin, "Why not?" she answered with a question, "Why not go to your yacht?" "I can't think of a single reason," he answered, and he raised his glass, "Bottoms up," he said, and killed his drink. "Bottoms up," she added, and killed her drink "Let's go to your yacht," she added, as she dismounted her stool.

Neither of them was suffering from any form of morality, or conscience by the time they got to the Pelican. They had stopped and bought a jug and had drank out of it before even getting there. The Captain did remember to remove his shoes and as he did, she followed suit. As it was cold in the belly of the Pelican, the Captain lit the heater while the big-eyed girl inspected the Pelican.

"I like your yacht," Nellie commented, "It's cozy in here," and after she said it she sat on the bunk. "How do you like my bunk?" Vincent asked. "I don't know," she answered, "But I'll try it," and she lay on her back, and then turned on her side, facing him. Her elbow was up and she was resting her head in her hand. Her dress had slipped up enough to reveal the top of her black nylons and the ends of her garter belt. Nellie was very, slender, fetching; her legs were long, and smooth looking. Vincent wanted to touch them to see if they felt like they looked. Vincent walked over to her, bent down, and kissed her on her full, moist lips. Nellie had wet them with her tongue while he was coming to her. Her tongue darted between his lips, into his mouth. His hand was on her hip, and then on her bare thigh, just above her stocking. She rolled over on her back, and then his hand was on the inside of her thigh.

"Your hand is hot," she commented, in a husky whisper. "I'm hot," Vincent answered, as he moved his hand and fondled her breast. He unbuttoned the front of her dress and she sat up, unsnapped her bra, and took it off while her dress fell to her waist. Her breasts were small and firm. Her skin was olive and smooth like her face. Her long, dark hair lay on her shoulders as she laid back.

Vincent kissed her breast; she ran her fingers through his hair. Vincent undid her stockings from her garter belt and slowly removed her stockings. He enjoyed this; her legs were very lovely and the action very erotic. He caressed the inside of her thighs, slowly to her loins and then he was caressing her there. Nellie moaned with pleasure with her eyes closed, her lips parted, and her breath hot. He took the rest of her clothes off and removed his own. When she felt his body over her, she opened her thighs for him. He went between them, and then he was in her.

The fire that was in him had intensified the sensors in his loins, but had dulled his others. Vincent didn't feel, or hear Carla stepping on the deck, or opening the hatch, or entering the belly of the Pelican.

CHAPTER 36

Vincent was trying to forget the hurt look that had been on Carla's face when she had caught him on the rise on the very bed where he had first made love to her. He remembered how the hurt look had turned to ice and she had turned and had left without saying a word. He had lost his erection and had not wanted to get it back, believing firmly that he should have been castrated for doing what he had been caught doing. Nellie had been sympathetic and he had taken her home.

Vincent had called Carla the next morning to apologize. He had tried to explain to her that he had been drunk and lonely. She had told him, coldly, that had he not been drunk, he would not have been lonely. Carla had turned his excuse into vapor. He had told her he was sorry, and she had hung up on him. He doubted if she would ever forgive him; maybe after Hell freezes over.

Vincent had gone to his doctor, got a new prescription for Valium and had had it filled. He drove to the Flats and called his mother. He had hired a manager for his office and had wanted to get out of San Francisco for a while. He thought he should see if he could help his mother who was now alone. Doc still had his shop on the property, but had moved his personal things to the cabin in the mountains. He only came down on weekends, and when he did, he stayed in his camping trailer, which was parked next to the shop.

When Vincent offered to move the mobile home to a park, which was what the divorce required, his mother was pleased and grateful. She was fine that he wanted to take care of her, but she asked him if he was sure he could handle it. Vincent knew the County furnished her a woman to come in and help her for six hours a day. Not much would be required of him except to be there for her when she needed him, and to be a companion. The one problem was she smoked continuously and he had become allergic to the smoke. She promised she would go to her room when she wanted to smoke.

Vincent kept his mother in a motel until he could get the mobile home moved to a park. While it was being set up in the park the man he had hired to do the job discovered the park didn't have the required amount of amperage for an electric powered mobile like his mother's. The park manager had stated that they had. For his mother's sake, Vincent didn't resort to litigation. He decided, with the help of the set up man, that the quickest solution would be to convert the home to natural gas. Within a few days this was done and they moved in.

Vincent joined the local Board of Realtors and attempted to bring some normalcy to the situation. His good intentions were doomed from the very beginning. The stress of her separation from Doc had caused Grace to smoke one cigarette after another. She couldn't remember to go to her room to smoke and if she had she would have been in her room all the time. Her fingers were yellow from it and so was the ceiling. The smoke made Vincent ill, so he was the one who ended up staying in his room. Then Grace complained all the time about being left alone.

The woman who was helping his mother had drove Doc nuts with her diarrhea of the mouth and now she was doing the same to Vincent. Mrs. Bagley, this awful woman, this redneck woman was driving him nuts. It was all Vincent could do to tolerate her. She was a gross, stupid woman. Nothing she ever said was said with any prior thought.

One time Vincent's laundry got mixed with his mother's and Mrs. Bagley told him he should change his shorts more often. He had been having an intestinal problem, and had not expected it to become common knowledge, nor the subject of conversation. He made certain that the laundry never got mixed again and every day his contempt for Mrs. Big Mouth increased.

Vincent started feeling hung-over every morning. He had a glass of water sitting on his bed stand, and the first thing he would do when he awoke would be to take a Valium and wash it down with the water. Then he would lie there and wait for the bad feeling to leave. He would lie in bed as long as his stomach would allow, knowing the sweet, sickening smell of cigarette smoke was waiting for him on the other side of his door. Hunger would make him get up, and go out to have some breakfast. He would have to fix and eat quickly in order to get it done before the smoke had his stomach in such a shape as he couldn't eat at all. Usually he would fix hot cereal for his mother and himself. He would fix coffee for her, but he couldn't drink it. His mother was the most lucid in the morning before she had taken her drugs. It was the only time they did much talking. Big mouth showed up at ten, and from noon on it was the Soaps.

The mobile home park sat just off the banks of the Feather River on graded rock piles that had been the aftermath of the gold dredging days. The front side of the park was next to the highway; one side next to the river and the other sides by the game reserve. After Mrs. Mouth would show up, Vincent would go for a walk in the game reserve, where his only source of fresh air was located. It felt good to breathe it and he got into the habit of jogging to make himself breathe more of it.

One morning he got the bright idea that it would be nice to have a dog to jog with. He went to the pound, where he saved a dog's life. The dog was such a ragamuffin he named him that. In no time this name was shortened to "Rags." The dog was about three months old; he had long, gold, flaxen hair that hung over his face. He was almost a strawberry blond. He was very timid, as if he had not experienced much affection. He weighed about twenty pounds.

Vincent decided he would deal mainly with unimproved properties. This would give him a lot of driving and walking to do and he could take Rags with him. He purchased a Dodge Van, with a pop-top, a stove, bed, sink and refrigerator. It was a great vehicle for Rags; it had windows all the way around and he could bark at things to his heart's content. Bagley always went home at five, so when Vincent went anywhere, which was every day, he would make sure to be back by then. Bagley didn't work on weekends, so he would have to stay home most of that time.

Vincent was building a tolerance for the Valium and it was doing him less good all the time. It was no longer making him feel good; it was just keeping him from feeling too bad. He was aware that if he took more of it, it would make him feel good again, but he knew it would be fruitless, for he would just have to take more and more. Vincent knew he had the tiger by the tall again, and he didn't know how to let go.

Vincent knew he needed help, but he knew not what kind. He knew he had made a mistake with his mother; he wasn't spending any more time with her than Doc had. When he was at home with her, he was in his room most of the time, for she would not give up even one cigarette for him. His nerves were shot from her yoyo existence from one emergency to another. A year after they had moved the mobile home she had a blockage of the bowel, and she had been flown by air ambulance to Sacramento for emergency surgery.

Vincent thought his problems were part physical and part mental, but he wasn't sure about anything. No doctor had been able to find a tangible, physical disorder. He decided he would go to a mental health clinic. When he went there he was referred to a shrink in Chico, John Whitney. After a few sessions the doctor decided he was suffering from manic depression. He couldn't give him any medication for it; he had to get him off the Valium first. The strength of the Valium was cut in half, to be substituted at a later date with another less addictive drug. Vincent was able to tolerate the cut but he felt like the living dead. His body ached all the time and so did his head. Insomnia robbed him of any peace, and small noises were like bombs, causing him the non-ending jitters; his stomach was in ruins.

Vincent bought Rolaids in the large economy size and felt a little worse every day. He survived the switch to another drug, but he was hanging on by the skin of his teeth. He was walking a tightrope; his spine strung taught. And then the shrink decreased the new drug and he felt even worse. He had saved the remains of his Valium prescription for an emergency, but he didn't want to give up this soon.

And then the doctor told him it was time to switch to the anti-depressant drug. He told him to take two before going to bed and two when he woke in the morning. Vincent's fear of drugs cautioned him into taking just one pill before going to bed that night. He wasn't concerned; he did have the Valium for backup. When he awoke the next day he felt very near death. He felt as if he had lost a lot of blood during the night; he felt cold and stiff, like a corpse. He knew he was in serious trouble; he had never felt more strung out in his life. Vincent felt as if his molecules were drifting away from each other; he felt on the edge of oblivion.

It was only six A. M. He couldn't call the doctor and he couldn't tolerate the condition he was in. He took a Valium and waited to see what would happen. In a matter of seconds he began to feel strange, and it frightened him. It was the same kind of feeling he use to get when he was a kid, when he would bleed, like he was getting ready to faint. Vincent rushed to the toilet and stuck his finger down his throat. He gagged, but nothing came out. He repeated the action until some white and yellow goop came out and then he felt dizzy. Vincent went to the faucet and splashed some cold water on his face until the dizzy feeling left him.

Vincent was grateful his mother hadn't heard him. She was in the room next to him; she was a sound sleeper due to her sleeping pill. Vincent sat on the stool and waited to see what his body was going to tell him. The Valium had forsaken him, leaving him with one last hope, and he turned to it like a moth turns to light.

Vincent's hands were shaking as he dressed, but he knew a drink would fix that; a drink would save him. He prayed to God it would not make him sick. He didn't know what he would do if that should happen. Vincent left the mobile home quiet as a mouse. He started the car, eased it out of the driveway and out of the park. He headed for his favorite skid row bar; he hadn't been there for years. It would be open at this time of the morning.

Vincent almost felt comfortable, even though he felt awful. He was familiar with this; this was something he knew how to do. It was weird; he felt a kind of joy as he walked into the smoke filled dive. It was like coming home, almost the same kind of feeling he had when he came home from the service. The joint was busy with derelicts drinking their breakfast and telling their stories, each one believing their story to be unique. The place stunk from the night before, but the odor was not repugnant to Vincent. The smoke bothered him, though, but a drink would soon fix that.

Vincent didn't see a soul he was familiar with, but that was okay; he was only interested in one thing and he ordered it from the burly bartender. Vincent gulped the double shot of brandy and chased it with a gulp of water. He waited fearfully to see if he was going to be sick, but the brandy left a trail of warm comfort down his throat and into his innards, anesthetizing the raw nerve endings that had been screaming at him. He wiped his brow and sighed with relief.

"It worked?" asked the bartender with a knowing grin. Bartenders can spot a sick drunk a mile away, especially bartenders who have been down that same road, which most of them have. Vincent grinned, sheepishly. "You got that right!" Vincent exclaimed, "And I hope there is more where that came from." "All you want," replied the bartender, as he poured him another. Vincent sipped and savored this one, as if it were the nectar of the Gods. "To Hell with Valium!" cursed Vincent to himself, after the fourth double. "The Hell with shrinks."

Four doubles into the empty stomach of a sick man who hasn't had any for a while is a pretty good jolt. The Captain was feeling much better now. He had not had enough, though, not enough to kill his memory. And he knew that he had opened Pandora's Box again, but it was too late now. "The Hell with It," he told himself and raised his glass to his reflection in the magic mirror.

Four hours later the Captain argued himself into leaving his source. He walked to the middle of the block to a liquor store and bought a quart of brandy. He walked back to the Hawk, started it and drove off. The Hawk was getting old, but still ran strong. It had a Packard V-8 engine that could make it burn rubber for a city block. The car Vincent wanted was an Aston Martin, but he didn't want to spend that much money, not until he got back on his feet and making money again.

Vincent drove past the mobile home park and turned into the game reserve. He drove to his favorite spot and parked. He cracked the seal on his bottle and had a healthy pull and relaxed. He remembered that after all these years he still had his flask in the trunk, along with the little funnel. He got out of the car, opened the trunk, and retrieved the flask and the funnel. Vincent proceeded to fill the flask. After filling it, he put the bottle and the funnel back in the trunk and closed it.

Vincent put the flask in his pocket and started to walk. He walked toward the river while wondering why they had turned the place into a game reserve. He had never seen any game here, with the exception of some squirrels, rats, birds, snakes and lizards. As he got to the first bend in the road, where it ran parallel with the river, he saw a huge rattlesnake. He walked to within six feet of it and observed. The snake was at least four feet long and as big around as the Captain's wrist. The snake was just lying across the road, right out in the sun.

The road was gravel and it was hot, it seemed like the snake should melt. The snake hadn't seen, or heard the Captain. Vincent felt, somehow, that it was his duty to kill the snake. If a person were to be bit by a snake of its size, a person would be in serious trouble. He didn't want to kill it, but he looked for a rock, anyway. Vincent didn't like to kill anything. The snake was just taking a nap, not bothering anyone. It wasn't the snake's fault he was poison, and everyone was afraid of him. The Captain wasn't afraid of the snake; he had seen many of them. He felt sorry for it. Vincent wasn't being very quiet while looking for a rock and the reptile heard him. It didn't bother to make that spine-chilling rattle, it just slithered off into the grass, over the bank and into the brush. A person is not supposed to kill animals in a game reserve, anyway and a snake that size probably has a mate.

Vincent walked down the bank to the river. There wasn't much left of it now, the dam had reduced it to a wide creek. And it wasn't even a good, creek, for it was moving very slow. And in this particular spot in the river and in many others, the river could be traversed without getting knees wet. It was that shallow. It had green fuzz all over the surface. It was stuff that had come off the oak trees that lined its banks.

A couple of mud hens were swimming around aimlessly. Vincent watched; he was wishing he were one of them, covetous of their freedom. There were no alcoholic ducks, no neurotic ducks. Ducks were just ducks and no one ever expected more from them. He would trade places with them anytime. Let them go back to the mobile home and face his mother.

Vincent felt guilty about wanting to escape from his mother. She had never wanted to escape from him; she had always been there for him. She had always sacrificed for him. But she was a better person than he was; she certainly had much more courage. His mother's only failing that he could see was her lack of wisdom for choosing a mate. The first two had been drunks and the last one had deserted her in her hour of need. It was too late now; she would never have another chance.

Vincent knew that his mother would have to die to escape her misery; there was just no other way. He didn't want to think of her death, but it was her only escape and his too. He felt guilty for thinking that way. Vincent knew her dying would be hard. She would cling to life desperately, still hoping that Doc would love her again. He knew she would never give up on that. Vincent suddenly felt such pity for her that a muffled sob welled up and out of him, and then he was sobbing out loud. There was only one relief in the world for him and he pulled out his flask. It didn't save him; he still had to go back to his mother. Vincent didn't know what he was going to tell her. She would know he had been drinking. He had never been able to fool her. He couldn't just stay away. He had another drink while he thought things over. Vincent decided he would just go and tell her the truth. After all, it was his only excuse. He would tell her that the shrink had given him a bad prescription. That would adulterate some of his blame; he could live with that idea. Anyway, he didn't have a whole lot of choices,

Vincent missed Carla, his sons, and Linda. He wondered if he would ever see Linda again. What a romance they could have had if he had not married Carla. He might never see her again; never make love to her again. He groaned, audibly, and tried to pull his thoughts away from her. Why was he torturing himself so? Why couldn't he just stay in reality and forget the what-ifs? Chances are if he had married Linda, he would be wondering what it would have been like to marry Carla. Vincent decided he didn't want to see either of them until he had straightened himself out and that might not ever happen. He knew that nothing would help him while he was boozing. He knew nothing would help him until he was free of any chemical dependency, but knew not how he was going to get free.

Vincent walked back toward his car as slow as he could with his flask in his hand, thinking and drinking. His mother was already going to know he had been drinking, so what did it matter? One was as bad as fifty to her, so why not have fifty? Vincent wondered about his old buddies in the Moon Patrol; what had happened to them? Were they all alive? He hadn't called any of them, and he didn't want to, not yet. He knew they would only compound his thirst. What he needed was solitude and he wasn't going to get any of that where he was going.

Big Mouth and his mother had been waiting for him. The Captain knew his mother had confided her fear to her hired help. Big Mouth was wearing one of those "shame on you" looks on her face, and his mother had a hound dog look on hers.

"Where in the world have you been, Son?" asked his mom, looking like she would burst into tears, "I have been worried sick" about you." He told her his story, and she bought it, but not without reservations. "I hope you are not going to get on one of your long ones." she lamented. "I'll be alright," he assured her, "I'll just have to go back on the Valium until I can find another solution." "You can borrow some of mine until you get your own," she suggested. She would much rather he was taking it instead of alcohol. He told her he still had a few left.

The smoke was getting to him, so he told his mother he was tired and was going to take a nap. Bagley gave him a look that was meant to tell him he was not fooling her. Rags wagged his tail to let him know that anything he did was okay with him. Vincent went into his room and Rags followed. Vincent closed the door. The walls were thin and Vincent heard Bagley laugh. He deduced that it was probably at him. How he despised that woman. He despised her crudeness, her ignorance, her prying, and her incessant, trivial chatter. Her mouth just never stopped and nothing worthy of listening to ever came out of it.

Vincent wanted desperately to go to sleep; it was his only escape from Bagley's voice. Vincent lied down and tried to sleep, but he could not, not while he could still hear her voice. He got up, put a Rachmaninoff recording on his stereo and turned up the volume until he could no longer hear his nemesis. Rags raised his ears, and then they flopped, and he lay by the bed. Vincent pulled his flask out of his pocket and cursed under his breath; he had forgotten to refill it. It was still about half full, so there was no immediate cause for alarm. He took a couple of drinks and lay down for a nap.

The need for a drink woke him several hours later. He was lying on his back, a position he seldom felt comfortable in. He rolled over on his right side and contemplated about what he was going to do. It all seemed so hopeless. He knew he was hooked on the brandy already and he knew he lacked the fortitude to quit. Vincent also knew it would do no good to go back on Valium. He had come to a dead end; he had nothing to turn to. He had been to doctors, psychiatrist and even a mental institution. Where else was there to go? He had even tried Alcoholics Anonymous. What else was there to do? Was drinking or the life of a hermit or death his only alternatives?

The Captain's mind was not functioning properly. It had been put under too much stress and its functioning had been depressed and altered by alcohol. He got it into his mindless brain that he wanted a pistol. It came right out of the blue. He had owned a Ruger Blackhawk, single action, 41 Magnum Revolver. What a fine pistol it had been with its long barreled accuracy. What power; it had been awesome. A gunslingers holster had come with it, the kind you strap to your leg for the purpose of negotiating a fast draw. Vincent and the boys had loved the pistol, but Carla had not. She had always been afraid of guns.

Vincent decided he wanted an automatic, one small and flat, easy to conceal. The Ruger had been heavy and bulky; one would have had a hard time concealing it. Vincent knew there would be a waiting period if he bought one from a dealer. He might be able to buy one from an individual and evade the waiting period, but right now he just wanted to look. Vincent got up and he and Rags left the sanctum. He told his mother he was going for a ride. Bagley gave him a look of scorn and he called her a vile name under his breath. His mother gave him a jaundiced look, started to make a remark and then changed her mind.

"Be careful," she cautioned him and Vincent went to the bathroom, combed his hair and he and Rags left. When he closed the door behind him he felt elated, like he had escaped. He knew it was only temporary, though, but he was still grateful. Vincent's thought went back to the pistol. The thought came to him that if he ever did get it into his head to do himself in, he would like to have a gun big enough to do the job without the chance of leaving him alive and mentally retarded. He would not want to wake up with an awful headache, an awful mess, and people asking him stupid questions.

After considerable looking around he decided he didn't want anything smaller than a thirty-two caliber. He found an automatic of that caliber, Italian made, and a cheapie at that. He paid for it and left the store. The waiting period would give him some time to straighten his self out, or to get worse.

Vincent had emptied his flask on the way to town, and now he was ready for some other kind of drink, something more exotic than a straight shot. And he was not in the mood for Skid Row, either. He parked the van a block away from Miner's Alley and walked toward it, wondering if Mollie's Place was still there. It was. Vincent walked in, and there was Spider; he was on the wrong side of the bar. He was drinking instead of bar tending. He looked wasted. The Captain knew what was wrong with Spider.

"It takes one to spot one" the old saying goes. His malady was written on his face, and his body. He was still a handsome guy, but he was losing it, getting dissipated looking. His head was still big, but his body was shrinking. His nose was getting bigger, with little veins showing, and his face was puffy. Spider had a glass filled with a clear liquid and it was vodka, which had always been his drink. He looked at the Captain and smiled his boyish grin.

"Slumming again?" he asked. "You can call it that if you like," answered the Captain as he offered his hand in friendship. His friend took it with a still firm grip, almost too firm. Spider had big hands and the Captain winced "How long has it been this time?" "Too long," answered the Captain, noticing the slight jaundiced look of his friend's eyeballs. He asked his friend what he had been doing and he told him he had been drawing his unemployment insurance and drinking.

The Captain asked Spider how his mother was.

"She is healthier than I," he answered, "She will probably have to bury me." Spider suggested they go somewhere and play some pool and the Captain agreed. Spider suggested they go on his motorcycle, but the Captain was reluctant, but agreed after considerable persuasion. The two went to a redneck bar in Thermalito and played several games, but they both got bored with that and beer. They ended up in a cocktail lounge at Lake Madrone. Spider got drunk on vodka and the Captain on brandy.

Lake Madrone is a small, man-made lake in the mountains, about twenty miles north east of the Flats. The road to the lake is narrow and serpentine, lined with timber of pine, oak, madrone and fir. On the way back down the mountain Spider took a curve too fast and flopped the cycle. They were both too drunk and too lucky to get hurt. After checking things over and their selves, some adjustment was made on the handlebars and they were on their merry way. The rest of the way down the mountain was made without any further mishaps.

After that the Captain and Spider started running around together just about every day and the Captain never drew a sober breath and neither did Spider. The Captain had to drink constantly to keep up with the demonic growth of his tolerance. His mother kept silent; her eyes and mood communicated her disapproval profoundly.

The waiting period passed and Vincent picked up his pistol. The two birds of a feather started target practicing with it. They went every afternoon to a place on the Cherokee Road. It was another narrow, crooked mountain road, the one that goes to Table Mountain, a flat top mountain of black volcanic rock. The place was in a gully, about five miles out of Thermalito. Others had been using the place for the same purpose for years. There were cans galore that had been shot full of holes.

Neither of the guys could hit the broad side of a barn. It was a wonder they didn't shoot themselves or each other in their condition. They didn't seem to get any better at it, either, but it was a lot of fun making all that noise. No one could have shot straight with that pistol anyway; it was a piece of junk. This one jammed and did everything it was not supposed to do. Vincent had tried to get it fixed, but no one had been able to figure out what made it jam.

CHAPTER 37

Even though the Captain was over indulging, he was still trying to be a dutiful son. He was managing to get home close to five every afternoon, and he was still doing most of the shopping. Bagley helped with some of it, not with him, of course. She would pickup things on the way over. He tried his best to be civil with her for his mother's sake, but it was very hard. The only way he could accomplish this was to stay away as much as possible, and only speak to her when it was absolutely necessary.

Vincent had almost stopped eating; he was almost on a liquid diet. He was getting so much sugar from the booze that it was killing his appetite and his sweet tooth. He could hardly tolerate sweets. He had to give up his normal breakfast of hot cereal, toast and jam, and go to more palatable things, such as omelets, sausage, hash browns and such. Warmed over pizza wasn't bad, either.

Vincent didn't often get sloppy drunk, he just tried to maintain himself. It was hard for him to get drunk; he had built such a tolerance. He was going through a fifth of brandy every day, and sometimes into two, and that was not including the drinks he had in bars. It was too bad he still had plenty of money and would not soon run out. At this rate he was going to run out of health before he ran out of money.

The Captain liked nice clothes; he was getting tired of the ones he had. During normal times he hardly ever wore his clothes out, or his shoes. He had quite an ensemble, but now he was doing things that were hard on them, such as spilling food and booze on them. Some of these articles he had worn so long he just didn't want to bother taking them to the cleaners. He would just put them in a box and when the box was full, he would put it under the mobile home. This was not a good practice, but he was not aware at the time, he was not aware of it at all. At this time Vincent was only aware of immediate needs and mostly his own. Although he had planned on taking the clothes to the Salvation Army, he had had them cleaned. Procrastination had defeated his purpose. There were quite a few boxes under there now, and instead of spreading them around, he had stacked them. Some of the boxes were touching the bottom of the mobile home.

One hot day on the way to the shooting range, Spider got sick. They were in the van and Vincent was driving. Spider was clutching his chest and trying to belch. He was trying to belch the gas he thought was causing his pain. His face was contorted and pale. Spider asked the Captain to stop the van so he could get out. The Captain remembered his friend's father had died of a heart attach when he was only about forty years old.

Vincent was frightened for Spider and he pulled off the road as soon as he could. Spider got out of the van and started walking in circles in front of it. The Captain got out and watched, helplessly. Spider was still trying to belch the pain away; he was white as a ghost and looked like he was about to pass out. He dropped to his knees and tried to belch some more. Then he gagged and vomited,

"What the Hell is wrong?" asked Vincent, as he went to him, and kneeled by his side, scared out of his wits. "I don't know," answered Spider, in a raspy voice, "I feel like I might croak." He stayed on his knees for a few moments, still belching and then he stood. The color came back to his face. Spider reached into his pocket and pulled out a cigarette. The Captain was aghast, hardly able to believe his eyes.

"What in the fuck are you doing?" he asked, incredulously, as Spider stuck it in his mouth. Laughing, he pulled it back out. "I just gotta have another cigarette," he sang in that ageless tune, "I just gotta have another cigarette." He lit the cigarette, inhaled a big drag, exhaled and sighed a sigh of relief. Vincent had to resist the urge to hit him as he waited to see if he was going to be all right. Spider started to get into the van with the cigarette. "Finish the cigarette first." ordered the Captain, "I do not want that vile smell in my van," "You use to smoke." argued Spider, belligerently. "Use to are the key words here," retorted Vincent, "Smoking is for fools." "Are you calling me a fool?" asked Spider, still, pissed. "Wasn't lighting the cigarette foolish?" asked Vincent, exasperated.

Spider grinned, sheepishly, put the cigarette out with his foot and got into the van. He opened the door of the propane-powered refrigerator and pulled out his bottle of vodka. By this time the Captain was in the van. Spider had a slug of vodka and handed the bottle to the van pilot. Vincent took a drink, started the van and headed for the shooting range.

The next morning Spider's brother called Vincent and informed him that Spider was in the hospital; he had had a heart attack. It had happened at three that morning and he had survived, but was in critical condition. The Captain offered his sympathy and asked to be called as soon as he could have visitors. After four days Spider was released from intensive care, and went to the ward.

Vincent went to visit Spider on the first day of his release from intensive care. He looked gaunt, but he was in good spirit. He looked tired, but his color was good. Vincent was thinking he had the constitution of a horse. They shot the bull for a little while and then Spider started looking through his drawer. He was looking for something and the Vincent knew what it was.

"What are you looking for?" Vincent asked in disbelief, already knowing, not wanting to believe. Just about that time his friend found what he had been looking for. He put a cigarette in his mouth and then he took it back out. "I just gotta have another cigarette," he sang, and then he put it back in his mouth and lit his lighter. "Don't do that!" ordered Vincent with dismay. Spider lit the cigarette, and inhaled from it deeply. "Oh, God!" exclaimed Spider, "It feels so good."

Spider had a Cheshire cat grin on his face, but right after he said it his expression turned to one of pain. It was in his eyes, and his face blanched. He clutched his chest and the Captain pushed the panic button. When the nurse didn't come instantly, he ran to the hall and hollered for a nurse. In a few minutes the Spider was back in I. C. U. and he was there for three more days. He didn't smoke when he got out, not right away, that is.

A month later Spider was riding his motorcycle and jogging around the football field every day. He was not smoking and he was not drinking. Spider told Vincent he was going to make a trip to Oregon to see his ex-wife. Vincent tried to talk him out of it, knowing what would probably happen, because Spider was still in love with her. Vincent knew Spider would exhaust himself with sex. Nothing makes an alcoholic as thirsty as exhaustion. Spider went anyway and when he returned he was drinking and smoking. In a month he was drinking a quart of vodka a day, plus whatever he was drinking in the bars.

His doctor wanted to do a bypass operation on his heart, but they had to have him sober to do it and back into some kind of shape. After awhile it didn't look like this was ever going to happen. The doctor decided if he didn't do the operation Spider would die. They went ahead with it and he came through the operation with flying colors. He looked like someone had taken a chain saw to his chest. In a little while Spider was jogging again, not drinking, nor smoking, getting strong as a mule again,

Spider just could not stand it though. He was an introvert; he just could not socialize without booze and he could not tolerate being lonely. He was a people person and there was just no joy without socializing. He went back to his old ways, but he didn't get much older. In two months Spider was dead. He had died in the hospital after his liver had quit on him. He hadn't lived much longer than his father.

It just didn't seem possible that Spider was dead; he had seemed so indestructible. The very large funeral corroborated the fact he was indeed, dead. Vincent had never seen so many people at a funeral. Spider had had many friends, yet he had died from being lonely. What a damned tragedy, Vincent was thinking. He wondered if Spider's friends had known how lonely he had been. They must have known, for he had. He wondered if combined effort of all those friends could have saved him. He didn't believe they could have. No matter how many friends he had, he had still had himself for an enemy and the enemy within can be the most fearsome and deadly. A short eulogy and Spider was put in the ground and he would never be a Lazarus.

Vincent wondered if he would be next; he couldn't quit, either. Also, he had some trouble with his heart and his father had dropped dead from too much booze. It is strange how the fear of drinking ones self to death causes an alcoholic to drink even more. This was what he was doing and he knew he was getting in deep water. He was seeing things that were not there again.

This was what Vincent thought was happening when the rats came. First he heard noises in the walls and then he saw them, but he only saw them at night. He didn't say anything about them; he thought they might be something like pink elephants. And he was having illusions all right; the colored cartoons had re-turned. The rats turned out to be real. One night one ran across his chest and it had felt like a cat. He knew it had been a very big rat. One had run across his mother, also, and he knew she was not having illusions. Rags had been barking. Vincent knew the rats were real.

Vincent bought some traps and poison and the war was on, and the rats were winning. He killed rats every night with traps, and they were dying in the walls from the poison. He felt they were multiplying faster than he could kill them. The mobile home was starting to stink from the dead rats that had died in the walls, and their excrement. If his brain had not been so pickled he would have looked for the source of the rats, but he didn't, he just kept killing them. He was going crazy with hate for them. It was getting so he enjoyed killing them, an evil joy.

One night he heard a rat rummaging in the cabinet under the sink. He got a flashlight and a French knife, a big one. He tiptoed to the sink, jerked the cabinet door open, and flashed the light into the cabinet. A huge rat looked up at him; the light had blinded him. Before the rat could move, Vincent stabbed it with the knife with such force that the knife went clear through the rat and impaled it to the floor. The rat, impaled to the floor, with the knife clear through it, let out a scream, a banshee like death squeal that could have started the resurrection of the dead. The Captain laughed with an insane glee. He laughed to the rats dying squeal.

Vincent's mother had slept through the whole incident. The next morning he awoke alert enough to wonder how the rats were getting into the mobile home. Although he was sick and weak he managed to go outside to investigate. He discovered the rats had climbed the boxes and had eaten a hole in the composition floor, making a tunnel into the mobile. After moving the boxes he put a patch over the hole. When he told his mother about it, she was glad it was over. It wasn't though; there were live rats and dead ones still in the walls.

The Captain was getting weaker all the time. The battle with the rats and the bottle was taking its toll. He couldn't see how things could get worse, but knew from experience that they could and they would. About a week later, after there seemed to be no more rats, an awful odor awakened him in the morning. It was worse than the odor of the rats and it smelled of human origin. With a lot of effort he got out of bed and followed his nose. He followed it to the bathroom and the door was ajar. He opened the door and what should have been a nightmare was real.

There was human excrement everywhere. It was smeared on the walls, all over the toilet, the washbasin, on the mirrors, and cabinets. He could see that his mother had tried to clean the mess but had only smeared it. Vincent fought nausea as he followed the trail into his mother's room. She was laying across her bed in her own mess. She was sobbing her heart out, sick and ashamed of herself. She was so tired of living; so out of love. She had lost all joy. She had stopped calling him Son and was now calling him by his first name. She had been calling him that ever since he had started drinking again. He had deserted her. He had escaped into his bottle and he had been her last hope. Vincent tried to console her, but to no avail; she would not be consoled.

Vincent called Bagley to come in early to help him clean up his mother so he could get her to the hospital. After this was done the Captain's guilt knew no bounds. He had tried to be good to his mother, but had only made things worse for her. She looked bad to him when he left her at the hospital, and he feared she might not come home this time. He was all alone now in the big mobile home; just him, what was left of the rats and his illusions.

As depression engulfed the Captain; he drank even more. The more he drank, the more depressed he got. He got just about as drunk as he had ever been and passed out. He dreamed he tried to shoot himself in the head, but his pistol had jammed. His stomach awoke him a few hours later; it was hurting him, and he rolled over. He hit his head on something hard. He reached to see what it was. It was his pistol. As he examined it he saw that the chamber was partly open with a bullet jammed in it. To his horror, he realized the dream had not been a dream. Vincent wasn't sure whether he was glad the gun had jammed, though. He was glad for his mother's sake; he still had to try to take care of her.

Vincent cleaned up and went to see his mother the next day. She begged him to take her home. He had to tell her the doctor wouldn't release her as he still had some test he had to do. She looked awful; she was losing herself fast. The next day she even looked worse. She had given up hope and said she did not care if she died. The day after that she looked like a remnant of the Holocaust. She had lost her dentures, and where her mouth use to be there was a hole, a round hole with hardly any lips. Vincent couldn't sleep that night; he knew she would die.

Early the next morning the phone ringing awoke him and his heart jumped, even though he had been expecting it. It was five in the morning, and his mother had died. The only mother he ever had was dead. He would never see her alive again. If only he had been strong enough to be good for her. He thanked the doctor and hung up the phone. He would never have a better excuse to get drunk. But now he didn't need an excuse; he had no one to use it on.

Vincent's stomach was bothering him more every day, but he stayed drunk anyway. He stayed drunk for as long as he could, and then he had to take care of the funeral arrangements. He knew his mother had wanted to be cremated. She had wanted her ashes shipped to Oregon to her sister, who was going to sprinkle them on the ocean. All that was left to do was to arrange the memorial and notify next of kin and friends.

Vincent called Carla and she was there the next day. She was appalled by his appearance, but did not castigate him, aware of the trouble he had been through with his mother. She had known this thing with his mother had been a bad idea from the start and had tried to warn him. Now she was going to have to bite her lip, and not say: "I told you so."

Vincent was in such pain he could no longer drink. It was all he could do to make it to the memorial. Doc was there and some of his relatives. Carla and their sons were there, but none of his mother's relatives, or his friends. It was not much of a memorial for a good woman who had never hurt anyone on purpose, who had devoted her life to her family. She had been totally unselfish, totally void of guile, or greed. She had been gentle, loving, considerate and faithful.

Vincent couldn't help but wonder what her life had meant. She could have had a lot more fun out of life if she had thought of herself once in awhile. She could have married Goldie instead of Doc; Goldie was a fun-loving guy and he remembered his mother had had fun with him. Doc had stolen her heart, and her heart had led her astray again for the third time. Three strikes and she was out, so much for listening to your heart. Vincent hoped there would be some kind of reward for her in heaven; there sure as Hell had not been any for her on earth. All she had got out of life had been sorrow, pain and desertion.

Vincent was hurting awfully by the time the service was over. He felt as if his liver had swollen. He unbuttoned the top button of his pants to make room for it. It was all he could do to make it to the car. Carla and the boys had to take him directly to the hospital.

"His abdomen is extended, and hard." commented the doctor, with alarm, "I want X-rays right now!" They took him to X-ray and in awhile he was told his bladder was badly swollen and would have to be drained immediately. By this time Vincent was dressed in a gown that was open at the back, exposing his buttocks to anyone who might want to look. He wondered why a person would worry about a thing like that at a time like this.

Vincent was wheeled to another room. His penis was washed with an antiseptic and the orifice was lubricated with a transparent jell. The doctor took an orange colored hose from a plastic bag; it looked to be over a foot long, and about as big around as a pencil. "I have to insert this into your penis," the doctor informed him, "And push it up into your bladder." "Holy shit!" exclaimed Vincent, eyes wide with trepidation. Vincent's thighs closed. The doctor grinned. "It won't hurt," he assured him, still grinning, "Not much, anyway." "Bull shit!" Vincent exclaimed, silently, as the doctor started to insert the lubricated tube into his rod. Vincent stiffened.

"There is a valve that opens to your bladder," the doctor informed him. "When the tube touches it, and is pushed through it, you will feel a burning sensation, much like it feels when you have to urinate." He pushed it in a little further and Vincent felt the burning sensation. When it went on through the valve he felt like he was urinating. It felt good; the relief was wonderful. He could feel the pain running right out the end of his rod. "Feels good, don't it?" asked the doctor, with a big grin. "You got that right," answered a grateful Vincent, and he heard the doctor tell one of the attendants that they could not let the urine out too fast without the risk of the patient going into shock.

Vincent wished he had not heard; he was very susceptible to suggestion. After awhile the doctor put a clamp on the hose to cut off the flow. He opened it again after a while, and repeated the process until his bladder was empty. "This must be a record!" exclaimed the doctor, after measuring the amount of urine, "I didn't know a bladder could hold that much."

The pain had run out and was gone. What he needed now was a stiff drink, but he knew that would not be possible. He felt like he would pass out and he asked the doctor for Valium. "Have you taken it before?" asked the physician. "Fives," answered Vincent, "Can you handle a needle?" asked the physician, "It will get to you faster." "Stick it to me," answered Vincent, and in a little while a nurse gave him an injection.

In a little while Vincent felt like a new man. But Vincent knew it was an illusion, and the euphoria would be gone as soon as the Valium had worn off. He also was aware what Valium addiction was like; he had been down that lonesome road. He still didn't know what he was going to do, though, but he was going to have to do something.

Later, the doctor told him and Carla that his bladder had been stretched to the point of bursting. Had he waited one more day, he would probably be dead. He was told it was not certain how long it would take for his bladder to shrink back to normal. He was told that with the stretching, the bladder had lost the strength to empty itself, and it would not be able to until it had shrunk back to normal. And that was not all of the bad news. Alcohol had destroyed some of the nerve endings that operated the valve. It was not certain how long it would take to heal enough to function properly.

Fear was engulfing Vincent. He didn't know why, but the first thought that popped into his head was about sex. What would he do if he couldn't get an erection? What a stupid thing to think about. Maybe he was crazy; at least a little warped. He wondered if he was addicted to orgasm; he had heard of such a thing. He must have masturbated a million times since that first time in the bathtub. He knew that lust was not good for him, but how could one oppose instinct?

The doctor gave Vincent a choice. He could catheter himself (stick the hose up himself) or they could leave one in him and connect it to a bag that he would wear strapped to his thigh. Without the bag he would have to catheter himself three times a day; with a new hose each time. Vincent chose the bag. It would be too, hard to stick the hose up there so often. He was not aware of how much trouble the bag was going to be.

The bag wasn't very big when it was empty. When it was full it made a bulge in his pants; it was uncomfortable. It was uncomfortable all of the time; it had to bend at a sharp curve right after the orifice. It was a good thing he couldn't get an erection. He wondered how long he was going to be impotent. An erection wouldn't do him any good with that hose stuck in him, anyway. And that wasn't all the bad news about the catheter; it had a little balloon on the end of it. After the end of the tube had passed through the valve, the balloon was inflated. This kept the catheter from falling out. It took a special tool to let the air out of the balloon and the doctor had the tool.

There was a plastic drain plug at the bottom of the bag. Sometimes, due to poor engineering, or a kind of devil, the plug would come out, and Vincent would be drenched. The plug didn't care if there was a witness. There was two ways he could tell if the bag was getting full by its weight, or pressure. He wasn't always in a handy place to empty it. No matter how it came about, if the bag spilled, it was the same as pissing his pants.

Vincent's sons were sympathetic, but they were cool to him. The alcoholism had all but killed their respect. They would not understand unless they were to walk in his shoes. He had prayed that they would not, but knew they probably would. Vincent didn't know very many who drank, who didn't drink more than they should. He couldn't understand why the children of alcoholics almost always drank and usually too much.

It was hard for Vincent to believe, but it had been three years since he had left his home to take care of his mother. His sons had all grown up, the oldest being twenty-four, and the youngest nineteen. Where had all those years gone? He hardly knew his sons. Wade, the youngest, was the tallest, and the only slender one. He had dark, curly hair and large, green eyes spaced wide, with pretty eyebrows. Wade was good-natured, impulsive and usually had a wide grin on his handsome face.

Wade was still plagued with one of the problems of his youth; he still had a hard time separating truth from fantasy. He still showed some affection for Vincent. Reed, the oldest, had quit college and had freed himself from all responsibility. His hair was to his shoulders; he wore a scrounge beard and mustache. His heroes were Harley pilots, and a variety of malcontents. He smoked pot, snuffed powder up his nose and sold these elements whenever possible. His luck was holding and he had not yet been arrested, nor had he become seriously addicted to anything. Reed had a volatile temper and was prone to violence when provoked. He did not get along with his father, or his brothers, only his mother, as long as she didn't try to tell him what to do.

Mark was still in college with forestry as his major. Being in the mountains was all he cared about. He had learned this love for the mountains and nature from Doc. He wasn't as tall as his brothers, but was bigger in body. He also wore a beard. He was quiet and never laughed out loud. A smirk or grin was about all that ever came out of him. He resented his father's alcoholism the most and had not much to say to him.

Carla and the sons had left and Vincent was alone. His heart cried for the years he had wasted. There was no way of getting them back. He had alienated his wife and his sons. His mother had died and he had even managed to alienate her before her death. Vincent loathed himself. What could he do to change himself? He did not have a clue. He knew he would have to get his health back before he could do anything, if that was even possible. He knew he would have to get rid of the mobile and get the Hell out of the Flats.

Vincent wanted to look for Linda, but not while he was wearing a bag on his leg. His memories of her made his heartache, but he didn't even know if she was still married. And what difference did it make, for he was still married. He thought that he must be loony to be thinking about two women when he couldn't even get an erection.

The mobile was a God-awful mess. Vincent went to work to clean it up. He had to go very slow, for he had little energy. The slightest exertion would make him pant and perspire. It took him a whole day just to clean his room. The space under his bed and the closet was stuffed with empty brandy bottles. He found five full ones under the sink in the cabinet in the hall. He also found the bodies of more dead rats and pounds of their excrement.

Two weeks later Vincent got sick. He didn't know if it was the flue, or a virus he had picked up from the rats. For two weeks it was all he could do to get out of bed. The Valium had not been doing him any good. He had felt just as bad with it as without, so he stopped taking it. By the time he got over the virus, or whatever it had been, he was over the Valium addiction. He felt like an invalid, but at least he was free.

Vincent wasn't free of the bag yet and it was time for an inspection. The doctor had to take a peek at the inside of his bladder to see if everything was all right. Vincent didn't have a clue as to how it would be done, maybe with an X-ray. No such luck though, the method was much more mechanical.

Vincent looked at the stainless steel tool of torture with horror. It looked as big around as his little finger and looked over a foot long; it looked like a weapon and that was also the way it felt. When the doctor told Vincent it might hurt a little, he knew he was in trouble. It didn't hurt going in. It was after they got in and tried to look through it at various angles that it hurt. The pain was making him sick and then they were finished. They were only finished with that part of it, though. The next test was to fill his bladder full of water to see if it had shrunk back to normal size.

"Let me know when you feel like you have to urinate so bad you can't hold it anymore," said the technician. He pumped water into Vincent's bladder by a reverse process, through a hose stuck up his tool. It was like taking an un-piss. Vincent let the technician know when he had reached that sensation and he turned the water off. The technician pulled the hose out and had Vincent urinate into a special container. It was a measuring device; it measured the velocity of his flow. Vincent was told to strain, and force as much out as he could. Then he was X-rayed again. His bladder had not emptied enough. Curses! He would have to wear the bag for another week and then go through the whole process again.

Later that same day, Vincent got an erection while sitting on the stool. It was the first one he'd had in a long time and it felt good to have. It felt super sensitive and he couldn't resist stroking it. Vincent couldn't stop himself from ejaculating. Most of the semen came out around the hose, but some went in and plugged it. Vincent didn't notice the plugging until he felt like he needed to urinate, but nothing was going into the bag. Because of the balloon there was no way he could get the hose out to unplug it. He thought of unhooking the hose at the bag end and blowing it back through, but was afraid he would get infected.

How embarrassing this could be. Would the doctor know how the hose had got plugged? Anyway, he went to the doctor and got hooked to a new hose and bag. In a few weeks Vincent got rid of the bag, and sold the mobile home. He put the Hawk in storage. Now all he had to do was figure out what to do with the rest of his life.

CHAPTER 38

Vincent spent his forty seventh birthday on the road. He was near Bodega Bay; he was alone in the van with Rags. It was morning, with soft looking, fluffy clouds in a sky of azure blue. Gusty breezes were making the ocean choppy with white caps. The beach was empty and so was his stomach. He had not had his breakfast and this was the time he needed to do his meditation. Vincent had bought a pocket book about transcendental meditation. He was trying to learn how to use it with the hope it would help him with his nervous condition. In a short while he had learned how to do it and right away he had felt some benefit.

Sometimes it was hard for him to meditate. It needed to be done on an empty stomach, before breakfast and before dinner, both times for twenty minutes. It was hardest for him in the morning, after going all night without eating. He was always starving in the morning; it was always hungering that woke him. Sometimes he would just have to wait and do it before lunch.

Sometimes there were negative aspects, some of which had been alarming. Sometimes after he had reached a point where his natural functions, such as his pulse, would slow down. If something should startle him, he would feel awful for a few minutes. For a few seconds he would feel like he had no pulse and he would gasp for his breath. It had always frightened him, but had not happened often enough to make him want to stop. He had felt that the benefit would eventually outweigh the transitory discomfort.

Vincent had a folding chair in the van and the top was popped in the open position, letting the breezes come into the van. The morning chill was still in the air and he was wearing a coat. He was sitting in the chair, meditating. Random thoughts were coming to him and he was pushing them away with the mantra. The tale of the three little pigs came into his head and he pushed it away, but it kept returning.

Vincent's meditation was ruined by hunger and he had to give it up. He fed the dog and made himself some breakfast. While eating Vincent thought of the three little pigs. The two foolish ones had built their house with flimsy materials and the wolf had blown their house down. The wise pig had built his house out of brick and the wolf had been unable to blow it down. He wondered if the tale had been inspired by a similar story in the Bible, where one had built his house on the sand and the other on a rock.

All that Vincent had left of his mother were some pictures, books and memories. He had given her romance novels away, but had saved a rabbit eared Bible. It was bound in maroon leather, Science and Health, a Bible Concordance and a Roget's Thesaurus. Vincent knew these books had belonged to his grandmother and he treasured them. When he was a youth, he had thought these books had some kind of magical quality, but now he knew different. They had not saved his grandparents, or his mother.

Both of Vincent's grand parents had been devout Christian Scientist, but it had not saved either one of them. But he had to be fair. Medical science doesn't heal everyone, either. But it could have healed his grandmother. The autopsy had shown that she had died from the infection from a ruptured spleen. Medical science could have healed her if she had gone to it soon enough. The malady had taken a year of agony to kill her, and she had died in his mother's arms.

Vincent still believed there was truth in the Bible; he just didn't believe all of it. He didn't know how to separate the chaff from the wheat. There was no way he was going to believe that Sampson killed two thousand armed Roman soldiers with the jaw bone of an ass. He was never going to believe the world was repopulated from the life on Noah's Ark.

With the transcendental meditation Vincent was grabbing at straws. He knew he had to save himself, but didn't know how. He didn't even know why. He had lost the people he loved the most. He couldn't function with alcohol and couldn't without it, either. He had killed so many brain cells he still couldn't concentrate. His health was poor and he had no energy at all. He had no resistance to cold, or heat and was not metabolizing his food properly. He had to eat constantly and never stopped suffering from indigestion.

Vincent's nerves were still shot and there was nothing that could be done. Vincent didn't know why, but he felt optimistic. Maybe it was because he was free. He didn't have to go to work; he didn't have to be anywhere; he didn't have to do anything, or please anyone. It was too late for that. Maybe he had just inherited some of his mother's optimistic genes; she had always been that way, except at the last.

Vincent grew tired of thinking; he decided a walk on the beach would be therapeutic. The beach was deserted except for some gulls, and then he saw a squirrel in the rocks. It reminded him of the rats. What strange, crafty, and durable animals they were. They had eaten a five-pound box of Epsom salts, a big box of laundry detergent and a bar of soap that had been sitting on the kitchen sink. It must have been the fat in the soap that they had been after, but what kind of nutrition could be found in Epsom salts? Vincent had a lot of questions, but few answers.

Vincent loved the roar of the breakers and enjoyed the ocean smells as he walked along behind Rags. The dog was far ahead by now. He tried to run to catch up with him, but the dog turned, laughed at him and ran off ahead. Vincent pooped out in a hurry and sat down in the sand. Rags turned around when he saw Vincent sitting. He came running back to him with his tongue hanging out, wanting affection and trying in his doggy way to express gratitude for the morning run. Rags rolled over and Vincent rubbed his tummy for him. In a short while Rags was bounding down the beach again, yapping at the surf.

As Vincent got up and walked back toward the van, his thoughts went to his father. He hadn't really known him. He knew what he looked like, knew he had been an alcoholic. He knew he had been married five times, and he knew that he had dropped dead. His mother had told him that when he drank he got mean. He wondered if drinking had caused his father as much misery as it had caused him. At least he had been able to forgive his father. Vincent prayed that he would be forgiven, also.

A surge of grief went through him for his mother, followed with gratitude. He knew that she had always put him first before herself. He felt guilt and remorse, for he had always put himself first. Although he had tried to help her, he had not been strong enough to overcome his selfishness. He knew that crying over his mistakes was not going to help; it would take something more active than remorse.

Vincent stared at the horizon. He had never traveled much, except for his trip to Alaska. He wished he had a sailing schooner, one he could live on. He could just sail away whenever he felt like it. It sounded idyllic, but he knew there had to be a catch to it, there always was. He didn't know if he could tolerate the constant motion, or the cold that comes off the ocean. He would charter a boat and find out before he'd ever buy one,

Vincent thought of Audrey. With the thought of her came the thought of death and he wished his mind could sail away. He wondered what she was doing right then, was she thinking of him? Because of her and his mother, he could not, or would not accept death as a reality. He had to believe that he would someday see Audrey and his mother again.

Vincent wished to Christ he could have a drink. Jesus drank wine, so why in Hell couldn't he? It couldn't be evil to drink wine, or Jesus would not have drunk it. He realized there was no evil in wine, only in self-indulgence. He knew how destructive alcohol was to him, so why did he want to drink it? Was it some kind of self-hypnosis, or aggressive mental suggestion?

Vincent wanted to meditate before lunch, so he put Rags on a line and let him stay outside while he got in the van. In a little while the dog settled down in the shade, under the van and Vincent sat for his meditation. As he meditated, he moved into a new plateau. A feeling of peace came over him and it seemed as if the inside of his head filled with a white light. A message in block letters went across his vision, much like one would see on a computer screen. "IT IS IN THE TOWER," the message read. Then the message was gone; that was all of it. Vincent tried to hang on to the light, but the effort caused it to leave.

It had startled, and awed him. He wondered what it meant. Vincent tried to think of Towers. The only ones he could think of were the Tower of London, Tower of Babel and the Eiffel Tower. None of these Towers stimulated his imagination but the Tower of Babel, and he decided he would do some research on it. First he looked in the Bible. There wasn't enough information to satisfy him, so he looked in his Bible dictionary. The Tower had been started by a king centuries before King Nebuchadnezzar, but was finished during his reign. After his death, other kings tried to demolish it, but it proved to be too massive. According to the Bible, the Tower had been built in an attempt to reach Heaven.

"There are no shortcuts to Heaven!" exclaimed Vincent, surprising himself with such a profound thought. He read on, and found more enlightenment. One of the kings had turned the site of the attempted demolition into a quarry where the public could go to get bricks. It took centuries, but today there is nothing left of the Tower of Babel but a massive hole where the foundation use to be.

Vincent remembered the message, "IT IS IN THE TOWER." He still didn't have a clue as to what was in the Tower. The more he thought about it, the less sense he could get out of it, so he dropped the research and tried not to think about it, but it kept nagging him. The next day, during meditation, he went through the white light thing again but there was no bold print this time, but a thought that sounded like a voice. "The truth is in the Tower." He thought it must have been his subconscious mind that had been talking to him, but he still didn't know the answer to his puzzle.

While driving north again, the thought of the three little pigs popped into his head again. He realized that the story of the pigs and the story in the Bible about the man who had built his house on the sand were similar but had a major difference. While the story about the pigs had been about the materials they had built their house with, the story in the Bible had been about the foundation.

Vincent realized that the message about the Tower was a simple one, but profound. The Tower was but a symbol of the structure of his life. The

Tower of Babel had been built on a foundation of sand, the assumption that it could be used to reach Heaven. The Tower of his life had been built on a foundation of self-indulgence, self-will, and fear, the list seemed endless.

Vincent knew that he would have to demolish his Tower one false brick at a time, until there was nothing left of it. He would then have to rebuild his Tower on a solid foundation, using the right materials. He would have to start now; he was not getting any younger. Perhaps he would be able to salvage some of his Tower, perhaps not. He knew that selfishness was his worst brick. He wondered how he was ever going to be able to change himself.

Was it true that one can't teach an old dog, new tricks? It seemed to him there were just too many things wrong with him; he had already been programmed. Maybe it was just too late? He thought it might be easier if he could just resign himself to that thought. Vincent realized he would have to find out every thing that was wrong about his Tower before he could build another. Self-examination is a loathsome task, and it was also a lot of work. Fatigue was closing his mind, so he pulled it away from the work. He pulled over and camped for the rest of the day and night.

The next morning, after a fruitless meditation, Vincent put some oats on for breakfast. He was careful about it; he liked it to be flaky, not mushy. The trick is to use the old fashioned kind, not to let it boil more than five minutes, and not stir it while cooking.

He wished he could have toast, or muffins, but there were no twelve-volt toasters that he knew about. He made some toast in the frying pan. It was better than no toast, but not much better. After breakfast Vincent decided he had better hit the road. It was still a long way to Oregon and his aunt's place.

Vincent wanted to see his Aunt Fay, and the place where she had spread his mother's ashes on the waters. He was in no hurry, though; he was not on any schedule. He would stop every time he wanted to. He still had to go through Fort Bragg, Eureka, The Redwood Forest and Crescent City before he even got out of California.

The sun was shining, and he wished his blood were as free as he was. It felt like it was running sluggish through his veins and arteries. Vincent knew that his liver had been left with some scar tissue, but the doctor had been amazed that it was in as good a shape as it was. He had been warned, though, he might not be so lucky if there was a next time. He might be dead, instead. Or if alcohol should damage the nerves in his bladder valve anymore, he could be wearing the bladder bag to his grave. And even worse, he might not have another erection. That would be the worst fate of all.

As Vincent traveled, he pondered concepts of foundation. If the

Tower was the symbol of the structure of his life, what had been its foundation? He realized he had always blamed everything on heredity and circumstance. He was an alcoholic because it was in his genetic code. He was weak and selfish because his mother was possessive, and over indulged him. Was this the foundation of his Tower? Was he a product of his genetic code and his environment, with no control?

It was no wonder his Tower was in such a shambles. Cop-out, negative thinking had been the foundation of it. Vincent tried to stop thinking of it; he couldn't see how he was going to get the strength, or the inspiration to turn his life around. What he needed now was rest, relaxation, and a little fun wouldn't hurt. But how does one have fun without booze?

Rags was sitting on the other seat; he was looking out the window. His mouth was open, with his tongue hanging out. He had a silly grin on his face, and his tail was trying to wag its self, moving just a little. He was happy, and he had fun. He had nothing but the fur on his back, and whatever food, shelter, and attention that was given to him. He could have fun doing almost any thing. If he got bored he would just go to sleep. Vincent reached, and patted his dog on the head. Rags gave him a grateful look of affection.

Was gratitude one of his missing bricks? He asked himself this, but tried to reject the idea; it made him uncomfortable. Vincent had always tried to avoid things that made him that way. Was courage another one of his missing bricks? How many damned missing bricks did he have? He did not want to think of himself as a coward. He would rather think of himself as timid, but that wasn't very macho either.

Vincent remembered his first day at school in Fort Bragg, when the little Mexican had cleaned his plow. He had been bigger than the kid, but so afraid he had been unable to defend himself. He had even cried right in front of everyone. He had been grateful Josephine had not been a witness to his humiliation. When he had returned to Fort Bragg a few years later, after living in Eureka, he had challenged the Mexican to a re-match. He had been bigger and the kid had declined. He wondered now what would have happened had he not declined. He had done a lot of bluffing in his time and had been very lucky.

Vincent remembered the time he had snapped Louis on his bare butt with a wet towel in the locker room. Louis' German temper had flared, and he had come after Vincent with both fist swinging. He had tried to hold his arms, for he had not wanted to fight his friend. Finally he had let go of him and had told him to go ahead and hit him if it would make him feel better, and Louis had stopped. He hadn't been afraid that time. He reasoned that affection must have taken priority over the fear. He remembered like it was yesterday. He hadn't wanted to hurt Louis, and he had told him so. He had even pleaded with him and they had remained friends.

Vincent remembered the second message, "The truth is in the Tower." He wondered if the Tower being the symbol of the structure of his life was all of the truth in the message. "What is truth?" he asked himself and he remembered that Pontius Pilate had asked that same question. Jesus had said, "Ye shall know the truth and the truth shall make you free." Vincent wondered why his mind was acting like a boomerang and kept going back to the truth. He wondered why he was remembering all these words that were in the Bible. He wasn't what he would call a religious person. Maybe the fear of death had driven his mind in that direction.

It seemed to Vincent that what is truth is the same as what is real. What could seem more unreal than billions of people riding on an earthen ball through space, in an orbit around the sun, traveling at the speed of 66,600 miles per hour? And the Sun doesn't really rise in east and go down in the west, but it sure as Hell looks like it does. And when he was dreaming it felt as real as when he was awake. How could he be certain that he was not dreaming right now? Scientist say that matter is not solid but is spinning molecules made up of spinning atoms. It doesn't feel that way, nor look that way.

Vincent remembered the illusions during delirium tremens. They had sure seemed real. Where had they come from? He had read about a bird that lived only on the coast of Scotland. Some scientist had taken a mother bird of this species off her nest. They had put her in a cage she could not see out of, put her on a plane, and had flown her to Boston. They tagged her and turned her loose. In a short time she had flown straight back to her nest. She had never been off the coast of Scotland. How had she found her way back? Had it been something in her genetic code? Had she been guided by some higher intelligence? Was it God? That didn't make any sense, though. If God had guided the bird home safely, why hadn't he guided Audrey home safely? Could that stupid bird and the occupants of her nest have been more important to God than his sister?

The mysteries of life were making Vincent's head hurt. He tried to think of other things. He tried to image the way he would like things to be. He found it hard to do while driving, and dangerous. He pulled over and parked next to a beach just north of Point Arena. He made himself a cup of tea, tied Rags outside, got comfortable and went back to imaging. He imaged he was living with everyone he loved. He was married to both Carla and Linda. His mother was there, his sister, and so was the Moon Patrol. They were all living in a giant house on the beach. They had horses, and were riding them on the beach. They had all the booze they wanted and no one could get sick, hurt, or die.

Vincent daydreamed like this for a little while. Then he realized that if things could always be the way he wanted, he would probably get bored to tears. If this was true, then how could a person ever be truly happy? If we are not happy when having everything we wanted and were not happy when we didn't, when could we be happy?

Vincent drove on to Fort Bragg, picked up some provisions and left. He didn't want to see anyone. He didn't want to talk. He didn't have anything good to talk about, and when he was lonely, people only made it worse. And he was sure as Hell lonely. He would give every cent he had for a kiss from the sweet lips of Linda, or from Carla. He felt a twinge of guilt for that after thought.

"What fools we mortals be!" he exclaimed to himself, and he wondered what Linda was doing at the very moment. Was she making love to her husband? What a horrible thought. He got an image of them in the act and he struggled to push it out, but his thought returned like a boomerang. He wondered if she loved her husband as much as she had loved him. That just could not be. His ego could not accept that idea. If it was true, then what was true love? Could we all love someone else just as much, or even more?

Vincent wondered if there were any definite answers to anything. Was everything relative and irrelevant? Was every thing as fleeting as an orgasm? Is anything we do important? Would it make any difference if he lived to be a hundred or died tomorrow? What if he had drowned and his sister was still alive instead of him? His sons would have a different father, or maybe they would not have been born at all, or maybe they would have been girls. What difference would it have made? The world would not even have noticed.

Vincent was getting tired, but he pushed on; he wanted to spend the night in the Redwood Park. He stopped at Garberville to get a hamburger. He was tired of his own cooking. He got a cheeseburger with everything on it. He knew it would give him indigestion, but he ate it anyway. It was good, but he wished he could have a beer to wash it down. He thought Garberville was a pretty place, but too far from the ocean to live there.

Vincent returned to the van, and pushed on. He drove slowly; it was a pretty drive through the giant trees. They were so awesome they made him forget his troubles for a little while. That was something he surely needed. He found a place to park in a grove of the majestic trees and he parked for the night. He was exhausted, not wanting to think, so he turned on the radio. It was getting cold so he got into his sleeping bag and got comfortable. He shut his eyes and tried to sleep. Thoughts flooded his head, chasing away the sleep and the peace it could bring.

Vincent had thoughts of his sister. He remembered how pretty she had been. He cringed as he remembered how close he had come to sexual activity with her. And how they had spent so much time alone in the apartment. They had both been inquisitive about sex, and they had always been so open with each other. Vincent had told her he wished he had a girl to learn how to do it with. Audrey had reminded him that she was a girl. They had tried, but he had been unable to get it up for her. He had been grateful later. A kid he had known in Fort Bragg had got his sister pregnant. How awful that would be.

Vincent remembered the time he had found a feminine pad under Audrey's bed; how he had been ignorant of such things. He had held it up in front of her, had asked her what it was. Audrey had been so embarrassed her face had turned scarlet. Then she had got mad over his snooping. Then she had giggled. Between giggles she had informed him of what it was and it had been his turn to be embarrassed.

The bed in the van had two thick pads for mattresses. Sliding one out from underneath the upper one could make two beds. Since he had had the van, no one had used the other bed. It was very comfortable with the two pads on one bed. Vincent was about tired enough to go to sleep standing up. It is possible to do; he remembered doing it in the Army. He had been waiting in line for something at 0500 hours, after a night long, G. I. Party. This is what it is called when the troops scrub the barrack down with soap and water with a G. I. brush, which is just a scrub brush. Vincent remembered the wooden floors in the barrack at Fort Ord; he remembered how numerous G. I. Parties had warped them.

While traveling down Memory Lane, Vincent fell asleep. He awoke the next morning feeling normal, which is right next to awful. His mouth tasted like bad breath, and his gut felt raw. It was cold, so he made himself a cup of fake coffee. Its aroma was a little like coffee, but that was as close to coffee as it got. But it was hot and would help to relax his stomach.

Vincent stepped outside with his dog and was awed by the morning beauty of the Redwood Forest. The sun was trying to get into the shadows through the tops of the giant trees. It came in brilliant shafts of light, seeming to be magnified by the shadows. It was like a natural cathedral; he felt as if he was standing on holy ground. At that moment he had no doubt in his mind that God was real.

Vincent tied Rags and went in to meditate. The white light brought him temporary peace. He had an urge to read in the New Testament; he opened the book at random. His eyes found some words by the carpenter's son. "Neither shall they say, Lo here or lo there for behold the kingdom of God is within you." These words rolled around in his head until they found a slot to fall into. "Of course!" Vincent exclaimed to himself, "The kingdom of God would have to be Heaven and Jesus was explaining that Heaven is not a place. Vincent realized that his thoughts were still about the Tower. Its builders had thought that Heaven was a place, and believed they could get there by material means. And that had been its false foundation.

Vincent had always wondered about Heaven. He wondered what one would do when one got there. Heaven had to be different, or it wouldn't be

Heaven. Was everyone in Heaven good and nice, with no danger there? He had heard there was no marriage there. Did that mean there was no sex? No danger and no sex? Wouldn't that get boring? Being bored for eternity would not be Heaven. It would be Hell. It seemed like he had a profound enigma going here. Heaven could be Hell if it was too heavenly.

Some more troubling thoughts followed. If one died as an infant, would one be an infant in Heaven? If one died old and ugly, would one be old and ugly for eternity? He did not like that thought. And then his thoughts went back to sex. Could there be romance without sex? He was not sure of that, although he had always enjoyed the smooching and the foreplay as much as the consummation. The consummation always seemed like a form of suffering to him. He was a romantic and if there was going to be no romance in Heaven he did not want to go there.

Vincent realized his thoughts were getting away from him. The carpenter's son had made it quite clear that Heaven was not a place. What was it then? Could it be just a belief? How about a state of consciousness? That could be considered to be within one. Was it Nirvana? He hoped not, he did not want to lose his individuality. That thought was mind-boggling.

Vincent realized he was going to have to get a better idea of what life was all about before he would be able to rebuild his Tower. The right concept of life would be its foundation. "Hell," he thought, "I haven't dismantled the damned Tower yet." Vincent knew he still had to face all of the wrong in his thinking before he could change. He was beginning to think all of his concepts were wrong. If he were wrong about every thing, that would mean he would almost have to turn into someone else. Born again? Vincent did not want to be born again. He did not want to ever be a kid again, or a teen, not even twenty-one. The growing part was just too damned hard. He might settle for thirty-five, that wasn't a bad age. But he would rather cash in his chips than to have to grow up again. Going to sleep forever wouldn't be so bad if you didn't know you were not going to wake up.

Too much thinking was making Vincent's head hurt; it was time to hit the road. He went out and untied Rags. He laughed at the dog's indecisiveness. There were just too many trees. He darted around like a chicken with its head cut off, and then he chose one for an honoring. He had a grin on his hairy face as he did so. The tree didn't care; it would still be there long after the dog had turned to dust,

Vincent had breakfast, and headed for Crescent City. It had been a long time since he had been there. When he got there he could see no change. It was still clean, neat, with rows of clean, neat, white houses, with a splash of bright colors here and there. Even the harbor was still neat and clean. There were rows of boats of various size and color, but most of them were also white, with a splash of bright colors here and there.

Vincent talked to an old fisherman, who wore a skullcap; it almost covered one eye. He informed Vincent that the Rogue was still a working boat, and at this time it was out to sea. Vincent wanted to see the old boat, but there was no way of knowing when it would return.

Vincent was only about thirty miles from the Oregon border, so he pointed the van north, and took off. After he crossed the border it would only be a little ways to Brookings where his aunt lived. She was a wisp of a lady with a throaty voice. Her hair was short, curly and snow white. She usually had an artist brush in her hand and a dab of paint on her cheek. Her name was Fay.

When his aunt met him at the door she giggled when she recognized him. Her giggle sounded the same as her mother's, and both brother's. She welcomed Vincent in, and planted an affectionate kiss on his lips. She and his mother were the only kin who ever had the habit of doing so. She was his mother's sister. They both cried when they talked about his mother. When he asked her to take him to the spot where she had spread her ashes she agreed. She fixed them some lunch and she tried to get him to take some vitamins. She had all kinds of them; she could almost start a store. She seemed to be addicted to them, if that is possible.

"You are so thin!" Fay exclaimed, as she offered him the vitamins. "So are you," he retorted, with a negative shake of his head. He had been down that road before, and vitamins had done him no good at all. It didn't look like they were doing her any good, either. She smoked one cigarette after another. He could not understand why anyone would take all those vitamins, and then cancel the benefit by smoking. It made no sense.

When they had finished with lunch, Vincent drove her down to the harbor. She no longer had a car. Fay had driven bus for the city of Oakland for thirty years, and that had been enough driving to last her for life. She had given her car to her youngest son.

The ocean was smooth as glass. After she had told him the spot was not far out, he decided to rent a skiff instead of a launch. The skiff had oarlocks, and oars. They got in the skiff and rowed away, with him doing the rowing. It had been a long time since he had rowed, but it still felt like the natural thing to do. She told him the direction, and he went. After about a half hour had passed, she waved her arms.

"This is it," she told him. "How do you know?" he asked, looking around, wondering. "By our alignment," she answered, without any further explanation. Vincent stopped rowing and bowed his head. He tried to remember his mother as she had been before her illness, but it was hard, for her ill image was too strong. He cried as he tried to push this stronger image from his head, and then he thought of the Twenty Third Psalm. It had been his mother's favorite, and he had heard it so many times it had been etched in his memory for life. With a shaky voice Vincent started to recite the soothing Psalm, and his aunt followed. Although Vincent hadn't looked up, he could tell she had also been crying.

As Vincent recited, the ill image of his mother disappeared, and was replaced by her healthy one. At that moment, Vincent had an intuitive feeling that this was the true image of his mother, the one God was seeing. The thought startled him, for it had come out of left field, and he didn't understand. He had come to the conclusion, though, that God loved his mother and it made him feel better. He rowed back to shore with the feeling that his mother would always be safe.

CHAPTER 39

After two months of bumming along the beaches of Oregon with Rags, Vincent was feeling better and had even gained some weight. Wanting to look good again, he had bought a pair of ten pound dumbbells and had started exercising. He had always been proud of his muscles, but inactivity and dissipation had shrunk them. Now he was doing pushups, sit-ups, working with the dumbbells, and jogging on the beach.

Vincent's mind was coming back to him; and along with it, his creative urge. He started having inspirations that turned into poetry. Some times these inspirations would come while he was driving, and by the time he got somewhere to write them, he had forgotten them. He bought a small tape recorder to save them.

Little melodies started to come to him, and soon he had little songs he was singing to himself. This was great therapy.

Vincent bought a guitar with an instruction book. In a short time he had learned a few chords. He was amazing himself by playing, and singing his own songs. Rags was not always happy about it; sometimes he would howl like a hound. Either the dog had no taste for music, or it hurt his ears. Sometimes Vincent regretted the dog couldn't talk, but most of the time he was glad he could not. He was missing conversation, though.

Vincent was in Astoria, the last city on the northern tip of the Oregon coast. Vincent liked Astoria best of all the Oregon Cities he had visited. It was like a miniature Frisco, with its steep winding streets, and Victorian buildings. It did look a little ramshackle, like the economy had been going in the wrong direction. Being a realtor, he noticed such things.

When Vincent decided he wanted to be somewhere else, he usually headed there with his foot in the carburetor. He had grown tired of sight seeing, and he was lonely. He wanted to see Carla, even for just a little while, but he knew not if she wanted to see him. He was in no hurry to see his sons. He could wait until they had stopped waiting, and expecting him to fall off the wagon. He did not need people who looked down their nose at him.

Vincent drove straight through Oregon, only stopping to relieve himself, sleep, eat, or get fuel. He couldn't drive the van over sixty, for its suspension would not allow it. Around corners it was like driving a pregnant elephant. He drove to Patrick's Point State Park, and camped.

The next morning he put Rags on a leash, and took him for a walk. He saw a couple of young deer walking in the mist. Neither of them had horns. Vincent expected Rags to bark, but he didn't. The deer would walk a few steps, and stop, eyes wide and ears stretched, alert for danger. It was such a lovely sight it put a lump in his throat.

"Why couldn't life be like this all the time?" he asked Rags, knowing full well he would soon get bored with it. Life just couldn't be simple and beautiful all the time. Some person would just have to screw it up; it was human nature to do so. Vincent watched the deer until they blended with the mist, and he saw them no more. He was grateful he had been such a poor hunter. Rags looked like he had something to say but had no words to say it with so he wagged his tail instead.

Back on the road again, Vincent was wondering if Carla would want to see him. He wondered if she was seeing other men; if she had slept with any of them. He hoped she hadn't, but he didn't want her to stop living, but he hated the thought of her making love to someone else. Carla might find someone she loved more than him, and then he would lose her forever. That was a wretched thought. Forever is such a long time.

Vincent wanted desperately to see Linda, also. He felt the same way about her. What was the cure for this divided love? Maybe there was no cure. Vincent might have already lost both of them, and a cure would make no difference. What would either one of them want with a man they could not be intimate with. He knew he would have to give up sex to stay dry, unless he found a miracle cure. Sure, right after it snows in Hell.

Vincent knew he would never be able to find another woman, not without booze. Without booze he couldn't do anything with one if he found one. Even if he could function, he would not be able to make a pass at a strange woman without the aid of the demon. He would be so nervous he would trip over his tongue. What if he made a pass at a strange woman, without the aid of booze, and she reciprocated. What would he do then? The thought was fraught with fear; the fear of not being able to function sexually had always been the nemesis of his romantic ventures. Cursed with booze and cursed without it. Without it, sex hurt him, and with too much booze, he would die. He could never tell if he had had too much, until he had had too much.

Vincent did not want to think of such things this day; he felt too good for that. He felt better than he had for a long time. He also felt like the brother goose must have felt; it felt good to be heading south. Vincent had a definite urge to go south. He didn't know how far, maybe all the way to San Diego. His mother had told him that the weather there was nicer than anywhere she had ever been. San Diego sounded good; it was about as far south as he could go and still be in California.

Vincent drove to Sausalito, stopping only to eat, go to the John, and nap. He still had a key to the Pelican tucked away in his wallet. He just knew Carla would not have sold it. He hoped she had not; he wanted to spend the night on the boat, a night with fond memories. Tears came to Vincent's eyes as he remembered the first time he had made love to Carla on the Pelican; how it had moved with them like it had been a part of their tryst.

Vincent wished he could go back in time and fix things. Vincent knew not how he could fix things, even if he could go back. One doctor had told him there was nothing physically wrong with him, that his sexual problem was psychosomatic, all in his head. He also knew that without booze he would not have been able to function socially. He never would have married; would have not had children. What could he have done different?

Vincent drove to the harbor, parked and walked to the Pelican. The old girl hadn't changed, although she did look like she could use a little tender love, and care. Some of her varnish was looking dull, and her white paint could be a little whiter. She sure looked inviting, though. It had been a long time since he had sailed her. Vincent took off his shoes, and boarded her. She moved gently under his feet, supporting him, but not holding him. He felt as if time had stood still, no past, no future, just him, the Pelican, the Bay, and the stars, billions of them.

Vincent wondered what God had been thinking about while creating. Had He planned it, or done it at random? Had he made the moon and stars to light the night? If so, why had he made the night? And why was Mars bigger than Earth. Why was it not populated by some kind of creatures? Oh to be like God, to be able to cause things to be like you want. What would it be like if Carla and Linda was one person? He tried to put them that way in his mind, but could not. It would be better if he could just be in two places at the same time.

Vincent was tired to the bone. He undressed, climbed on the bunk, and went to sleep while thinking about the first time he had used it. He slept like a baby, and awoke at dawn. As it was cold, he lit the heater, and snuggled to it. He wanted to take the Pelican for a sail, but didn't have adequate clothes. He was more sensitive to the cold now. Nothing could make him feel worse than getting too cold.

Vincent's stomach was sending him signals, and after a search he found there was nothing on board to eat. He got dressed, walked to a restaurant after locking Rags in the van, and had breakfast. He felt so good he just had to see Carla. He wondered if she had forgiven him for his adultery. It was too early; he went back to the van, got his dog and returned to the Pelican.

Vincent decided he would see if the old diesel would start. He could smell the fuel as he cranked her over. In a few revolutions the old girl took off, sounding like a thrashing machine. Vincent didn't want to fool with sails, just wanted to go for a spin. He loosed the Pelican from her mooring, and backed the old girl out of her port. The Bay was calm as he cruised.

"This is truly the good life," he told himself, vocally. He wondered why he had ever thought sitting in a bar was better. He realized, though, that he hadn't really sat in bars because he thought it was better; he had sat there because he had thought it was the only thing to do. He had been addicted so young; he had thought it was the only way to live. By the time Vincent returned, moored, and dillydallied it was late enough to call Carla. It was not without trepidation that he waited for her to answer the phone. The feeling left when her voice sounded genuinely glad to hear from him.

"Where are you?" Carla asked. When he told her, "Come and see me," she answered, warmly. It seemed awkward talking on the phone, so he told her he would be right over. He made sure the Pelican was secure, and he and the dog went back to the van. Vincent drove to the mansion. It had been awhile since he had been there, but nothing seemed to have changed. Carla had heard him drive in, and she had come out the back door.

"My being away must have been good for her," he told himself, under his breath, for she did look lovely. She still had not dressed, and was wearing a frilly robe, very feminine. He got out of the van, and walked toward her feeling extremely inadequate. "You look wonderful," he told Carla, not yet all the way to her. Vincent stopped, not sure how far to go, or what to do, but she opened her arms and he went into them. He kissed her cheek, but their lips found the way, and they stayed together for a long time. It had been a long time. Carla blushed when she pulled away, breathless as she spoke.

"What have you done to yourself?" she asked, seeming to be in wonder. The last time she had seen him he had looked like warmed over death. It had always amazed her how he could almost cross the threshold of death, and come back looking as good as new. Even after all the years together she was still not aware that he always looked better than he felt. She still was not aware of his sexual problem; he had never told her.

"What do you mean?" he questioned. Carla searched for words. "You look so well, so young." "I've been a beach bum," Vincent told her, "Walking on the beach, eating crunchy granola, drinking herbal tea and apple juice." "It has been good for you," Carla commented, and Rags started to bark. Vincent had forgotten him. "I have a dog," he told Carla, turning to the van. "I can hear that," she answered, and laughed. "Let him out," she told him, "If its safe," she added. "He only bites chickens," Vincent told her, laughing, remembering how Rags had killed a chicken, one owned by a neighbor of a friend he had been visiting. It had surprised him, for the dog had always been so timid, non-aggressive. He had had to pay for the chicken. Rags bounded out of the van as the door was opened. He went straight to Carla, sniffing her ankles. He wiggled, and whined as she petted him, and then made a mad dash to the foliage looking for a place to relieve himself, squirting a little here and there.

"Where did you boys stay last night?" asked Carla, as she watched the dog. "He looks like he hasn't gone for a week." "We stayed on the Pelican," he answered," After Rags had irrigated the landing." "It doesn't get much use anymore," she told him, with melancholy. "The boys use it once in awhile when they get together" "When was the last time that happened?" "A couple weeks ago," she answered, "And I went with them that time," "Don't you usually?" Vincent asked. "They usually have girl friends," Carla answered. "Are they still mad at me?" he asked. "No," she answered, wistfully. "Do they drink?" "Too damned much!" Carla exclaimed, vehemently, giving him the evil eye for a second, "All of them." "The arrogance of youth," he commented, thinking they had not learned a thing from his problem, nor from any of their other ancestors,

"Let's go for a swim," she suggested cheerfully, wanting to change the topic. She already had her suit on underneath her robe. She was in the habit of going for a swim in the morning when the weather was nice. She took off her robe and draped it over her arm. Vincent's eyes got wide as he stared at her lovely figure. "Talk about me!" Vincent exclaimed "What?" she asked, blushing, pleased by his stare. "You still look like you looked twenty years ago," he retorted, "You must not have many female friends." Vincent wanted to tell her he hoped she didn't have any male friends, but was afraid to. Her body was entrancing him, and his loins were pleading. It had been a long time since he had made love to her, but he resisted this feeling. He knew he must tell her the truth,

"I have been eating crunchy granola, and drinking apple juice," she told him in jest, as she pulled on his arm and led him to the pool area. "It's too damned cold!" he complained. "Don't be such a sissy," Carla scolded, "The pool is heated." "I don't have a suit," he complained, weakly. "Yes you have," she retorted, "You left several of them here. They are in our bedroom, in your drawer." She pointed up in the direction of their room, "Go," she ordered, and added, "Please?"

Vincent liked the sound of "Our bedroom, and "Your drawer." Carla was treating him as if he had never left, as if he had never committed adultery. Vincent did what she wanted, and in a little while he was back at the pool. Carla was already in, she was beckoning to him, and he went in.

He tried his best to avoid body contact, but failed due to the fun they were having. The exhilaration and the warmth of the water were erotic. It was stimulating him to erection. Vincent knew it would show in his suit. Then their loins were touching as they kissed while in the water. The kiss was full of longing, sweet as anything could be. Vincent knew she could feel him. They pulled away, but holding on.

"That felt good!" Carla told him, passionately. Vincent didn't know whether she had meant the kiss, or the other. He didn't want to get out of the water until he had cooled. "Yes, it did," he agreed, "It has been a long time." She had felt his resistance, and didn't move back into his arms. She had felt his erection, but his message seemed mixed. Vincent wanted to kiss her again. He resisted as long as he could, and then he moved back to her, and kissed her again.

"Come," she said, after they had finished the kiss, "Let's get out of the pool." They got out together, and she led him to the towels. Carla shivered as she handed him one. "Would you dry my back?" she asked. "I'll dry any part of you," Vincent answered, without a thought. "That could be fun," she answered, and he dried her back and shoulders. The lovely curves of her behind were terribly tempting. He tried to resist, but could not. He dried her there, savoring the shape of her, remembering what that part of her looked like.

"Let's go upstairs," she whispered, not knowing why she had whispered. She was feeling like her feelings were illicit, making it even more exciting. Carla held his hand and he followed. He wanted to tell her of his problem; it was time that he did. If he had told her years ago, it might have helped. He must tell her before it happened.

Before he knew it they were in the bedroom. She took off her suit and started to help him with his. Vincent was almost in a panic. He didn't want to throw cold water on such a lovely happening, but he had to tell her. He stopped Carla from pulling his suit down. He wanted her something awful, but his fear of that bad feeling after orgasm stopped him.

"I have to tell you something," he pleaded. "What's wrong?" she asked, disturbed by his attitude. She suddenly felt vulnerable and climbed under the sheets to cover her nakedness. "What is it?" she asked again. "It's not you," he assured her, "I should have told you years ago." He sat on the edge of the bed, and told her his plight. Carla was aghast. "Why didn't you tell me?" she pleaded, and then she was sobbing between trying to talk.

"All these years of suffering and you couldn't tell me? Why couldn't you? Did you think I would not love you?" "I was afraid," he pleaded, and he felt like he was going to join her in the sobbing. "Afraid of what?" Carla asked. "I don't know," he answered. Then the weight of it all came down on him and he was crying like a baby. "I just couldn't face it. I thought I would find a cure, but they could never find anything wrong with me." "What shall we do?" she asked, woefully. "I don't know," he answered, "All I know is that I love you. "I have never loved anyone but you," she told him, and then they were in each other's arms, consoling, passion drained by misery.

"I have always feared it was my heart," he told her, after they had regained their composure. Carla exclaimed, "You have a heart like a bull! Booze would have killed you long ago if you hadn't!" "It does get out of rhythm sometimes," he told her, defensively. "We can't give up." she pleaded, "There has to be a way to solve this." "I have tried everything I can think of," he told her with a heavy heart. "I want you to come home to me." Carla pleaded, "And we will solve this together." "I don't know if I can." Vincent told her. "What do you mean?" she asked. "I don't know if I can live with you without passion," he answered, dejectedly, "It would be torture." "Don't you think living without you all these years has been torture, worried sick about you?" Carla asked.

Vincent had no answer for that, realizing he was being selfish again, that worst brick again. "You are right," he answered, apologetically, "I'm just being selfish again, one of the bricks in my Tower." "I don't understand," she answered, looking perplexed. Vincent did his best at explaining the Tower. "This is a lot to digest at one time," she told him. "I hope there isn't more?" "That's all for today" Vincent answered, "But I'm sure of one thing." "What's that?" she asked, with tears, in her eyes. "We can't sleep in the same bed together," he answered, and for some reason it struck both their funny bones, and they laughed together. What a relief it was. "There are many beds in this house," she told him, "And you can have anyone of them, except mine." Vincent held little hope for the survival of this kind of relationship, but he had to try.

CHAPTER 40

At least Carla had forgiven him and she still loved him, but living together had proved to be impossible. They had managed for a year, but much of it had been torture. Vincent knew if they stayed together, the Captain would return.

"Oh, Vincent!" Carla had wailed, wishing that he were wrong, but knowing he was right when he had told her of his fear. "I will always love you, and will wait as long as it takes," Carla had vowed. "I'm not sure that you should," Vincent had told her. He felt remorse for already taking up most of her life; "You have waited for me most of your life already." he had told her. "It is my life!" she had scolded, "I don't deserve you," he had told her, and he had been sincere. "I know," she had answered, but she had been kidding, or had she?

Wanting a larger vehicle with better kitchen facilities, toilet, and shower, Vincent had purchased one and was back on the road again, heading south. He still had hope that he would someday be able to rebuild his Tower, and in the process, regain sexual health. If only he could do it in time to save his marriage. He thanked God for leading him to Carla on that silly day in San Francisco. He was awed by her total forgiveness and love for him. He was resolved to make himself worthy.

Vincent wanted to stay on Highway One as long as possible. It was his plan to go all the way to San Diego, taking his time doing it, and stopping at every town he liked the looks of. He wanted to search, study, and ponder until he had put all the pieces of his puzzle together.

Vincent found his new vehicle a joy to travel in. It was like a little studio apartment with wheels. It even had colored television and stereo. It had everything except a lot of room. It was big enough for him, and Rags, though. It was plush and pretty. It smelled good; it had that new smell.

They didn't get far the first day. Vincent spent a little time in Half

Moon trying to jog some memories of his childhood. He remembered one of the houses he had lived in as a boy. He looked for it, and found it. He was surprised that it was a lot smaller than he remembered. He remembered riding a bike for the first time. It had been in front of that little old house with the phony log siding. He had kissed his first girl behind that same house.

Vincent remembered calling Charley a "Dirty black nigger" in that same house. And how his mother had saved him from certain bodily harm. He remembered Charley, early in the mornings, going from the bedroom to the bathroom with nothing on but his undershirt. His bare ass sticking out with the undershirt pulled down to cover his whatchamacallit. He remembered Pepino, his little Italian friend with the bad heart, and his older brother, who had kicked him in the ear.

Pepino's father had let his ill son drive the car to help make up for his illness. He wondered if Pepino was still alive, and then he did not want to know. After Vincent had dug up enough memories, he paid his aunt and uncle a visit. Then he headed for Santa Cruz, where he decided to spend the rest of the day and night.

Vincent parked his rig and told Rags he would return, but the dog protested anyway. He was barking as Vincent left for a walk down the boardwalk. He had a hot dog while watching the pretty girls in their tiny swimsuits. There were so many pretty girls in the world; he wondered how many times a guy could fall in love? He guessed the number would be infinite if the circumstance prevailed. He wondered if there might be some more permanent kind of love.

Vincent knew the dog would have things he needed to do, so he walked back to the rig. He put the happy mutt on a leash, took a paper bag, and pooper-scooper, and took the dog for a walk. Rags happily irrigated every tire he came close to, and did the other thing in the street. Vincent scooped it up, and put it in the first trash receptacle he came to. Rags talked to him all the way back to the rig; he did that when he was happy about something. He would raise his head and look like he was trying to talk, but what came out was a mixture of growl and howl. Vincent always growled back so he would know he had been understood.

After growing sleepy, Vincent took a nap. When he awoke he was hungry, so he fixed himself some dinner, and fed the dog. After he had cleaned his mess, he sat down to study. He opened the concordance to the Bible, and looked up the word "Love." Vincent found that there were many references. He could see this was going to take much time and thinking. Thinking was all right, though, for it was one of the things he did like to do, and the older he got, the better he liked it.

Vincent learned that in some places in the Bible where the word "charity" was used it had the same meaning as "love." He realized that his concept of love was quite shallow. He realized it might take a long time to find that perfect love, the one that cast out fear. Vincent studied for a couple of hours, and got tired. He gave up, and took Rags for a night walk on the beach. He started thinking of Carla and got horny. He wondered what part sensuality had in the scheme of things. He wondered if his own sensuality might be some of the dry rot in the frame of his Tower. Was lust something to be given into or fought? "The seed of a righteous man remaineth in him." He had read that in the Bible. He wondered if that meant one had to give up sex to be righteous. If that was the case, it looked like he was going to be righteous, in that sense, anyway. He realized he had no idea what the Bible meant by righteous, anyway; one more thing to investigate. Vincent went to bed with that thought.

When Vincent awoke it was dawn, his favorite time of day. He felt fresh, vigorous, and hungry. He took Rags for a walk, did his exercising, had breakfast, fed the dog, and headed south to Monterey. His memories of Fort Ord returned as he returned. Most of them were bad. That first Army haircut would never be forgotten. Or the thousands of trays he had washed. And he would not soon forget the potato peeling, or the grease traps. He wouldn't forget the C-Rations that had filled his innards with hot, gurgling fluids and gasses.

Vincent drove around town, walked on the famous wharf, and went to the market for provisions, and headed south. As he drove by Big Sur, he remembered the beach party his M. P. Company had thrown there. He and the rest of the cooks had prepared the food and it's serving. The M. P. Club had served the booze. All had got drunk and he had made his early morning shift without his head ever touching his pillow.

The road was serpentine and rough. The scenery was rugged, and beautiful. Vincent parked at every place that took his fancy, and walked the dog. He didn't get very far that day. The bluff was high where he parked for the night; he could hear the surf pounding against the rocks far below. It was dusk when he got out of the R. V. and he could still see the ocean. He knew it must have looked the same a thousand years ago. He hoped they would always leave this road the same. The ocean didn't seem to change, but the road could. The sun would suck the oceans waters up, but it would return, in one way, or another. The oceans seeming infinity had always had a soothing affect on him.

Vincent decided to meditate. He was calm and it didn't take long to reach the white light. He had no revelation, but had an urge to open his Bible at random. It opened at Acts, chapter nine and he read the story about Saul being changed into Paul. Saul had been a persecutor of Christians and God had forgiven him and had turned him into Paul, a great leader of Christians. He decided that if God could forgive Saul for all the awful things he had done, He could also forgive Vincent Cardoza.

Vincent realized that searching for the truth was not going to be easy; the truth was not what one always wanted to find. Before his search, he had always been able to blame his mother and the genetic code for his faults. Now it was looking more and more like his faults were his own fault. He recalled the actor, William Bendix, who used to say on his T.V. show, "What a revolting development this is." Vincent laughed and remembered how the actor could act equally as well a bad guy or good one.

It seemed to Vincent that a great portion of his problems was wrapped in his underwear. He would have to learn the difference between love, and lust. He knew that one could love without lust. He thought that when love and lust were mixed together, it was being "in love." Most of the time infatuation seemed like love. There did not seem to be any sure way of knowing the difference, only time seemed to tell. Maybe this was the reasoning behind long engagements. It might have been a good idea for Carla.

Vincent decided he should start a list of his faults so he could keep track of them, and work at getting rid of them. He feared his list might turn into a book. His faults were the weak spots in his Tower. He thought if he could pull out the weakest spots, the rest of the Tower might fall by its own weight. There he was, looking for short cuts again. The first word he wrote on his list was "SELFISH," and he spelled it in capital letters. Vincent knew he had always been selfish. This selfishness had helped to get his sister killed. He realized that being introverted and self-conscious was a form of selfishness, and something to be overcome. He felt guilty for having always put his own needs before his family's. If only he had had the courage to suffer more.

"Whoa!" he told himself, "I can't blame myself for all of it." He remembered that a weakness for addiction did travel in the genetic code, and his mother had spoiled him. And it was the way he had been raised that had caused him to be introverted. His fault was in not doing something about it after he had realized he was an alcoholic. He should have told Carla about his sexual problem years ago; it could have saved them both from much heartache.

"But I did try!" he argued with himself, remembering all the suffering he had gone through in the attempts to free himself from addiction. "One drink is too many, and a thousand is not enough," he told himself. There was no way he could deny that he was responsible for all those times he had taken that first drink.

Vincent argued with himself that his temptation resistance quotient of zero had been programmed into him. So far no one had told him how to program it out. He thought if he could figure that out and learn how to utilize it, his name could become a household word. He thought he had better go to another word; he could spend forever on this one. He knew he had to make changes in himself, and he knew it would take courage to do so. He also was aware that he did not have a surplus of courage. Somehow he would have to get this fact into his second word.

What could he write down for lack of courage? Vincent was loath to write: "Cowardice." He reasoned that being afraid did not make him a coward. He had always shied away from challenge, competition and problems. He knew he was non-aggressive. Did this make him a coward? He thought not, and wrote the word, "Meekness" on his list.

Surely, this is weakness, he thought, but then he remembered what Jesus had said in his Sermon on the Mount. "Blessed are the meek, for they shall inherit the earth." Vincent was cynical about it and said to himself, "Six feet of it." He looked up the word in his concordance, and got a different picture of it. It reads: "Gentle, kind, not easily provoked, ready to yield than cause trouble; but not used in the Bible in the bad sense of tamely submissive, and servile." He could buy this; but this did not seem like weakness, and he knew that what he had was.

Vincent removed the word from his list with some liquid that was made for that purpose, and thought he had better change to pencil. He laughed, and with a pencil he wrote down the word "Chicken." He liked to think of himself as meek. That is in this new sense of the word, but he did not know if he was so because it was his nature, or because he was afraid of being hurt. He rationalized that a person would be a fool to not be afraid of being hurt. He realized that the bad sense of meek (submissive, and servile) described what he had been, better. He erased "Chicken" and replaced it with the word "Submissive." He really was submissive. He had to be honest with his list or it would be worthless.

That was just about enough thinking for a while. His ego was taking a terrible beating. Vincent got defensive. After all, he wasn't the only selfish person in the world, nor the only submissive one. He reasoned if there were more submissive people there would be less war. And there were basic reasons for human selfishness. All the goods in the world were limited and not divided equally. Therefore, if one wanted something, one might have to get it before someone else had. Also, a person's time on earth was limited, and one had to do what one wanted to do before running out of it." Enough." He told his self, and put his books away.

On the way to Morro Bay his thoughts returned to his youth in Half Moon Bay. He was remembering the school bus incident. He laughed, remembering the potato he had stuck in the exhaust pipe before boarding it. The bus had started running awful, and it had taken some time for the driver to find the potato. They had been late for school. He chuckled, and told himself, "You were such a good little boy." Thinking of the word "Good," Red Skelton popped into his head, that part he had played, "The Mean Little Kid." How he would think of something naughty to do, and then say to himself, "If I dood it, I get into trouble." His face would reflect thinking, just for a few seconds, and then he would get a wicked look on his face, and say, "I dood it." He would then dood it, and get into trouble, always.

"That's me," Vincent told himself, and then he remembered a phrase he had read in the Bible. He looked it up in the concordance, and it read: "For the good that I would I do not, but the evil which I would not, that I do." That old saying fit him like the skin on a frankfurter. He knew that he had usually had good intentions, but his low resistance to temptation had often thwarted them. And then he remembered the saying," The road to Hell was paved with good intentions." "The spirit is willing, but the flesh is weak," was another saying that said it all.

Vincent wondered if there wasn't some way he could build a resistance to temptation. He was starting a little late in life to re-build his character. He knew he had to find some solid place to start. He hoped that he was more than just a creature of embryo, fertilized by ejaculation, ejected into a world of chance, and inevitable death.

Vincent laughed as he thought of how Bible history would have been different if Joseph had been like him, especially so, when his Egyptian master's wife had invited him to lie with her. He would have resisted the temptation, but lust would have won. It was a very good thing that Joseph had not been like him. Joseph's life had been different than his, though. All the bad things that had happened to Joseph, had always led to good. Maybe the bad things that had happened to him would also eventually lead to good. But he shouldn't forget that it had been Joseph's love for God that had led him to good. It was like some other words he had read in the Bible: "And we know that all things work together for good to them that love God."

Vincent couldn't say that he loved God, though. He wanted to, but didn't know how. How could he love someone he didn't know, couldn't see; couldn't even feel? The thought caused him to think about something he had read about matter; that it was nothing but invisible atoms, spinning in formation. If one could believe that, it would take only a step to believe that the substance of matter was mind.

This line of thinking was getting over his head. He reached into his tape tray, and pulled out his favorite Rachmaninoff tape, and put it in the player. Its dramatic sounds began to sooth the confusion of his thinking. For just a while he would like to enjoy life instead of trying to analyze it. The dramatic sounds of Rachmaninoff made him lonely. He was lonely for Carla, and her soft, warm body. He was lonely for Linda, and the love that might have been.

Vincent remembered something he had read: "The saddest thing of tongue, or pen, to know the things that might have been," He was lonely for the Moon Patrol, and yesterdays, He was suddenly so lonely for yesterdays it made his heart hurt. He could not stop the tears, for he knew that he would always be lonely. He had been all his life, and he could see nothing in the future that was going to change that. Vincent had to find a place to stop, for his eyes were full of tears, and it was hard for him to see where he was going. He found a wide spot on the other side of a hairpin curve, and he pulled over, and parked. He turned the engine off, the tape off, and wiped his eyes. He opened the door, and stepped out into an ocean breeze. Rags followed.

It was a chilling moment for Vincent, for he wanted a drink; he wanted one so bad he could taste it, could even smell it. He sniffed at the odor as if it was really there. He felt the gnawing need for it in his stomach. He was grateful he did not have any alcohol with him. He did not know if he could resist its siren call. With despair, he believed he could be both the dog, and the fool in the old Proverb: "As a dog returneth to his vomit, so a fool to his folly."

"Oh, God!" Vincent cried in anguish, "I don't want to be Captain Moon!" He had tried everything that he knew of to rid himself of this awful need. He had tried drugs, and that had been catastrophic. He had tried hospitals, sanitariums, doctors, psychiatrist, tapering off, cold turkey, Alcoholics Anonymous, and abstinence. He had never been able to stay on the wagon, and he would have to stay on it forever. He realized with a cold certainty that he had only two choices left; death or God.

Vincent didn't want to die; he was afraid to. There were still many things he wanted to do. Somewhat hopelessly, he told himself he had better look for God. He wanted to pray, but did not know how, and was pessimistic about asking God for help. He couldn't see why God would choose to help him when there were so many he had not helped. Surely most of the Jews who had been slaughtered in the Holocaust must have been praying.

Vincent wanted desperately to turn around, and go back to the comfort of Carla, but knew it would be in vain until he had solved his problem. Vincent was afraid he would continue to hurt her, to drink again, and lose her forever. He couldn't risk that, for he loved her, but he guessed he didn't love her enough, for if he did, it would keep him from drinking. This kind of thinking was hard, and he wanted escape from it.

Vincent turned on the radio after getting back in the van with the dog, and dialed in some rock, and roll, and headed south. Vincent wasn't going south just to find himself; he was also looking for nicer weather. He was tired of the cold of the north coast, and the heat of the valley. He wanted a place where he could enjoy the sun, not swelter in it, and he loved the beach and ocean. San Diego should be a great place. His mother had told him it never got too hot, or cold there. He realized it had been over fifty years since his mother had been there. Some drastic changes must have taken place. He was sure the weather hadn't changed, but the population must have changed, considerably.

Vincent thought about the Tower as he drove on to Morro Bay. He was sure that the truth he was looking for was in the Tower. He reasoned that the Tower was built with error, false thinking, un-truth, which boils down to a lie. But that meant that the truth was in the lie. He reasoned that this was true, for one couldn't have a lie without having a truth to lie about. Although it was confusing, it made sense. Vincent remembered that Jesus had said: "Ye shall know the truth, and the truth shall make you free."

It came to Vincent that his need to drink must be a lie, and he needed to find the truth that the lie was about. His stomach was hurting, and he wished he could have a beer. He could not see how one beer could hurt him, but he knew he was trying to fool himself. He decided he would tell himself the truth. "One is too many," he told himself," And a thousand not enough." He knew that this was the truth, but it certainly was not freeing him from the craving for a drink. He knew that time was not going to heal him, he was sure of that.

How could he be sure that what was printed about Jesus was the truth? And he didn't want to be a Jesus freak. He could hardly stand Bible thumpers. T. V. Evangelist sounded as phony as three dollar bills to him, all that emotional crap. Normal people don't talk like that. Vincent hoped they did not talk like that in Heaven. He might consider the other place if they did. It was probably a one-way ticket to one place, or the other, though.

When he got to Morro Bay, Vincent was hungry for Spanish food, and he was tired of his own cooking. There probably is not a town in California that does not have a Mexican restaurant, and he soon found one. He loved chicken enchiladas, but there was only two things he could wash Mexican food down with, and that was beer, or water. Many drinking persons are against drinking water. "It will rust your pipes," they say.

Vincent was one of these persons. With half a notion that God was going to help him because of his recent revelations, he ordered a beer, just to wash the enchiladas down, of course. The beer tasted unbelievably good and he drank it slow. He didn't order another; oddly he felt afraid of it and he knew this fear was healthy. The beer turned the nerves off in his stomach; he was able to eat the enchiladas with savor.

The waitress had a lovely body and Vincent left her a large tip to compensate for his staring. He left the restaurant with a full stomach, and half an erection. He went to a market to get some things to nibble on; beer had always fired his nibbling appetite. He bought a six-pack of beer so he could have one if he wanted. When he got back to the R. V. he wanted one, but he wanted to see if he was going to have any withdraw from the first one before he had another.

Vincent waited an hour before he had another, and by this time he had moved his rig to a spot by the beach. The beer did not taste as good as the first, and took him a long time to drink. He knew not to have another; he knew when it did not taste good, his body didn't want it. That was his belief.

Vincent had wanted to study, but even that small amount of alcohol had turned his thinking machine off and his memory on. He started thinking of his sexual experiences and got horny. He took a cold shower, but all it did was make him cold. He took Rags for a jog on the beach, and jogged until he was too tired to have an erection. He went to bed, and as soon as he got comfortable, the erection returned. He hoped it would give him a pleasant dream. He fell asleep with that hope.

When Vincent awoke at daylight, he still had an erection, but he hadn't had a pleasant dream. He wasn't horny, either, he was hard because his bladder was as full as it could get. After he had emptied it, he lost his erection. He was grateful. He was getting too old to masturbate, and it would hurt him the same way as sex, anyway.

Vincent dressed, and took his dog for a walk. Rags, still not use to the ocean, barked at the surf, and gulls. When they got back, Vincent sat down to meditate; he needed to do it before he got too hungry. Although his stomach was growling at him, he tried anyway.

Vincent was a little tense, for he hadn't slept well. He thought it was because of going to bed too soon after the beer. His mouth was dry as a powder horn, and that was also because of the beer. He didn't think he would be able to meditate, but after a little while he got into it, but he was unable to reach the white light. He was disappointed. He needed a message that would steer him in the right direction. He felt like a sailboat that had lost its rudder.

Vincent spent the rest of the day driving, parking, eating, walking, and thinking. The weather was as good as he had ever seen. By the time he got to Santa Barbara he was too tired to do much sight seeing, and had a minor headache. The alternator was over charging, and he could smell the battery acid boiling. There was a brownish haze in the sky he thought was causing his eyes to burn. It was either that, or the battery acid. Vincent stopped a lady pedestrian, and asked her if it was smog. She was indignant about it and told him that Santa Barbara does not have smog, and walked off in a huff.

Vincent went to a market, bought a bottle of distilled water, and filled his battery, which must have been almost empty. He would have to find why this was happening. Santa Barbara was crowded so he drove on toward Ventura. He drove almost there and parked by the beach at a place named "Rincon." The highway there was not many feet above sea level. It had been lined with very large boulders. They had been placed there to protect the highway and shore from erosion. Some of the boulders were as big as a small car. Vincent wondered where they had come from.

One had to pay to park there overnight. There were envelopes, and a receptacle provided to do so. He paid the fee, and took Rags for a walk. The dog tried to catch a squirrel, one of many that lived in the rocks. Vincent wondered what they lived on, and what they drank. He knew they couldn't drink the seawater, and he couldn't see any other. He scolded the dog, and Rags ignored him. He was an American dog, and had the right of his pursuit of happiness. The squirrel was in no danger of being caught, and Vincent enjoyed the comedy of the dog's frustration, so he let him have his way.

The sunset was so beautiful Vincent forgot to meditate. The edges of the surf turned silver as they licked at the beach. The sunset's brilliant hues changed constantly as the sun went past the horizon; gone until tomorrow. The hues stayed in the sky for a little while, and then they were gone, leaving a feeling of awe in their wake. Vincent wondered how anyone could deny the existence of the Creator while watching a sunset.

Vincent camped on the Rincon for two weeks. Every day was beautiful, but facilities were few, especially on weekends. The area was flooded with tourists. During these times, if he left his space, it might not be there when he returned, and he might not be able to find another spot. Sometimes he had spent the night in the parking lot of an all night restaurant.

Vincent had decided he was not going to go any further south; this was it. He knew that the further south he went, the worse the traffic would get. And he liked the area, with two small cities, Ventura, and Oxnard. Also, nearby were the picturesque towns like Ojai, and Santa Paula. Santa Barbara was only twenty-six miles with its culture and entertainment.

Vincent was getting tired of the hassle of parking. He wanted a phone, and a place to get his mail. He was told at the Post Office that he could get his mail General Delivery for only thirty days. He was also told he could not rent a box without having a residence. He told them that if he had a residence he would not need a box. He was told that rules were rules and resisted the urge to tell them to stick their rules where there was no daylight.

Vincent spent a week looking in the newspaper for a place to rent. He gave up, and sought the aid of an agency. They found him a small, tidy beach house in the Pierpont Keys. It had only one bedroom, but that was all he needed. The place cost more than two houses would in the Flats. The houses on the Keys were close together. There was a small house on one side of him, and a larger one on the other. The beach was his back yard.

Four children, and their parents occupied the large house. Three of the children were sisters. The other one was their brother. The girls were all pretty blonds, and they all had California tans. Their age ranged from ten to thirteen. The boy was about eight, and he was an unholy terror. He got Vincent into trouble the very first day.

The three youngest children had been running toward his rig. Knowing what they were going to do, he had yelled at them to stop. He had seen the girls hesitate, and had known they were going to stop, but he had known the boy was not. Not wanting the boy on top of his rig, he had made a run at him to stop him. The boy had been as fast as a greased pig, and had made it half way up the ladder on the back of the rig before Vincent had got to him. The boy had struggled to get on up the ladder and Vincent had squeezed his arm in an effort to stop him. The boy had pretended to be hurt. Vincent had been mad at him for not stopping. He had known he had not hurt the boy, not badly, anyway, not as bad as he had wanted to. When the boy had screamed at him that he had hurt him, Vincent had scolded him. Then the sisters were mad at him for picking on their brother.

"Why didn't you stop us?" they had asked. "I knew you were going to stop." he had told them, "And you did. I knew he was not, and he didn't." That had convinced the sisters, but not the boy. He had hated Vincent from that day on.

The mother was also a blond, and she was pretty, not yet thirty. Her name was Sheila, but was called Shelly. She was of Nordic lineage, and her skin was golden tan like her daughters. The boy had the same pretty skin, but his hair was darker, too dark to be called blond, but not dark enough to be brown. The youngest girl's name was Saundra, she was a little tomboy. The next girl was Rachel; she was almost twelve, slender and pretty as a flower. Her hair was long and blond, but darker than her mother's, or her sister's. It was an unusual color, amber, with traces of red.

Pamela, the oldest girl, had light blond hair like her mother. She was thirteen and voluptuous, but she had an innocent look, and she was sweet natured. Marcus, the father, was of light complexion but his hair was black. He was of German and Mexican lineage. He had a boyish face, which would probably always make him look younger than his wife. The family's last name was Kruger.

The girls were in, and out of Vincent's place like a bunch of squirrels, borrowing sugar, flour, pepper, eggs, and such. Often they would bring something back, like a piece of cake Shelly had made from some flour she had borrowed. The boy did not come over. He gave Vincent evil looks whenever he had the chance. Vincent didn't mind the girls, he welcomed them. They filled some of the lonely time. They were like a breath of fresh air to him. It didn't take him long to get fond of them, for they were all pretty, and he had missed having girls around him since his sister's death.

It was obvious right away to Vincent that both parents favored Pamela and Philip. It was clear why Philip was; he had a speech impediment. He stuttered, and sometimes it was all he could do to get the words out. Pamela, being the oldest, had more privileges and everyone in the family thought she was the prettiest, including Rachel. It was plain to see that Rachel was growing up in the shadow of Pamela, and she was feeling sorely deprived. It looked like she was being treated like the Ugly Duckling. Rachel was rebellious over this treatment and other things. As a result, she was in trouble most of the time.

Vincent had always felt like a black sheep, and his heart went out in sympathy to Rachel right away. She was tugging at his heartstrings; there was something compelling about her. Unconsciously, at first, he started to favor Rachel, and she responded right away. She desperately needed to be favored by someone. She started to visit him often, and she developed the habit of closing his blinds, and locking the door to keep the rest of the kids from barging in on her.

Rachel was a precocious child. She loved to tease Vincent. She was a woman-child, sometimes acting younger than her years other times older, almost like a woman. The first time he had noticed this he had just finished shampooing his hair, and she had come for a visit. He had just finished toweling his hair, and had been sitting at his desk. While he had been writing something, she had come up behind him. She had put her pretty face right into his hair, and had smelled it. She had messed it with her fingers.

"Mmmmm, your hair smells so good." she had told him, and it had been such a feminine thing, such a womanly thing. It had surprised him, even shocked him, for he had not yet realized just how feminine she was. It had even sent a message to his loins that he had not expected, or wanted. It had embarrassed him and he had not been prepared for it. He had not been use to being around girls.

"You like me better than the rest! Don't you?" she had exclaimed. She had been so charming; it had left him tongue tied for a moment. Then he knew that it was the truth, and he had been more embarrassed that she had known, making him even more uncomfortable. "I can't answer a question like that!" he had pleaded and a knowing grin had come on her angelic face. "You don't have to," she had replied, "I already know that you do," and then she had laughed, and ran out the door.

Rachel was a wisp of a girl; she couldn't have weighed more than ninety pounds, soaking wet, and Rachel was not yet five feet tall. Her eyes were a light, golden brown, with a hint of green. They reflected the mischief that was in her and her love for fun, which she did not have much of. Her lovely blond hair hung to the middle of her back. To Vincent her face was entrancing to, with its perfect profile. Her nose, though not petite, was of perfect shape and proportion for her lovely oval face. Her lips were like a flower; her chin was strong. She was a manipulative girl. It didn't take her long to have Vincent wrapped around her little finger.

CHAPTER 41

Vincent's little bungalow sat back further from the street than the Kruger's house. He had to walk past the girl's bedroom to get to his place. When Rachel was in trouble, which was most of the time, she was usually confined to this room. When she was confined to the room and alone, she would coax him over to the window, and tell him her tale of woe. Vincent was getting awfully fond of the girl, and it upset him to see her in trouble so often. He started to carry bubble gum and candy in his pocket, and he would take them to her whenever he got the chance.

Vincent knew that both of her parents had awful tempers; he had heard them yelling at each other and the children. They used the foulest language he had ever heard in a family quarrel. Shelly called Marcus four letter words that would cause a drunken sailor to blush.

"I ought to strap a mattress to her back, and put her to work!" he had heard Marcus yelling at Shelly, referring to Rachel. Vincent had been shocked, and angry; he knew Rachel had heard him. He had said it for her ear. There were many times Vincent would have liked to mash his face. Marcus was too big for him by at least fifty pounds and over twenty years younger. And Marcus was mean and ruthless. Vincent also knew that any confrontation with either parent would only make things worse for Rachel and also jeopardize his relationship with her.

Both of her parents were nice to talk to as long as you were in agreement with them. But there seemed to be a thread of paranoia running through the whole family, including Rachel. One had to be careful what one said to any of them; just the slightest thing would put them on the defensive.

"What do you mean by that?" or, "Why do you ask that?" or, "Why do you want to know?" would be their most common answer to almost any question. They would ask on the defensive, as if you had been thinking

413

something derogatory about them. He felt like he was walking on eggs when he was with them.

Marcus was mechanically inclined and was always interested and helpful when Vincent was trying to fix something. Even though Vincent could afford to take his vehicle to a garage, he still liked to fix the things that he was able to; he still liked to tinker. Marcus also liked to tinker, and just about every weekend he would be doing it on his own vehicle, a Chevy window van. He had a great set of tools, and claimed he had not bought any of them, but had brought them home from various jobs.

Vincent learned right away that it was not good to get Rachel's mother mad at him; her anger was like the wrath of God. He had walked by the window and had heard Shelly scold Rachel. Vincent could tell that Rachel had been caught with some of the gum and candy he had given her, for she had been in trouble again.

"Please don't blame Vincent!" he had heard Rachel plead, "I made him do it." That had been a surprise to him; he had not realized she had been manipulating him. A girl not yet twelve had been manipulating him. He did not know why this girl pulled at his heart so. He hadn't known how hard until Rachel had been grounded from seeing him for two weeks. Shelly had scolded him, also, but not too hard. She had scolded him hard enough for him to feel the potential of her wrath, though. Shelly knew her daughter, knew he had been manipulated. "Don't make Rachel your life!" she had warned.

It was a long two weeks and Vincent realized that in just a couple of months Rachel had become very much a part of his life; an important part. Vincent missed the girl something awful. He tried to rationalize it was because he was just lonely, but knew it was more than that. He saw her in the yard, but she was not allowed to talk to him. He could see by her expression that she was also suffering. He wanted to hug her so; it wrenched his heart every time he saw her. His little house became a prison without her presence. He spent hours walking on the beach, trying to sort out his feelings for this girl with the face of an angel.

Time passed, as always, and Rachel was coming to see him again just like nothing had happened. But now, Shelly had a weapon, and she used it. She knew that Rachel would rather be at his place than anywhere. Every time Rachel did something Shelly didn't like, Rachel would be grounded from seeing Vincent. Rachel did her best to stay out of trouble, but with parents like she had, it was impossible to do it all the time. Even in a normal family it is impossible for a twelve year old to stay out of trouble all the time.

They still managed to spend hours together, though. It was as if she had been a part of his life that had been missing and now was there. He began to feel like a part of him was gone, when she was gone. Vincent knew this was not good for him, but he was helpless to do anything. He was also having a strong paternal feeling for her. He felt responsible for her welfare, fearful that her parents seeming lack of affection for her could damage her psyche. He did his best to make this up for her.

Rachel had a poker face and she liked to fool Vincent with it. She liked to fool him by telling him things that were not true. He would never know they were not until she had told him. She would not tell him until she had made him uncomfortable. Once she had told him that her parents had found a place to move to and would be moving right away. She had waited until she had seen that he was upset and then laughed and told him she had made it up. Then there was the time she had told him her mother was going to make her go away and live with her grandmother in Ohio. She never failed to fool him.

Rachel did not like for things to change; routine seemed to be a kind of security for her. The only kind of soda she would drink was Dr. Pepper. If he bought her anything else, she wouldn't drink it. Although she would eat a few other candy bars, the one she wanted him to buy all the time was Butterfinger. She also liked things with strawberries in them. But forget any other kind of berries, and forget raisins, she would pick them out, or spit them out in disgust.

And she was only interested in one boy at a time. There was this boy she liked, but he had not taken much notice of her. He was skinny, and looked unhealthy; his complexion was sickly. He was a month younger than Rachel and was already smoking cigarettes. He was a crude boy; he used crude language, and gestures. Vincent could not for the life of him see what the attraction was, but he was the one she wanted.

Jonah was the boy's name. Sometimes he would come to Vincent's place looking for Rachel; they were just at the acquaintance stage. Rachel's sisters were either too young or too old for him, and so were the rest of the girls on the block. He would talk to Vincent when Rachel was not there. Vincent told him that Rachel would be a fox one day, but Jonah just laughed, believing he was being kidded.

Vincent had a full-length mirror on one of his doors. Rachel liked to do her hair in front of it, for the one at her house got pretty crowded and Vincent had a hair dryer that she liked to use. She also liked to use his hair spray, and lots of it. One day she brought her sister's makeup with her. She did her hair and made up her face, using eye shadow, and such. Vincent loved to watch her every move; she was so graceful and feminine. He wanted so much to hug her, but she was reserved, so untouchable. He was afraid she would misconstrue his intent, and run away. When Rachel had finished, she looked like a little movie star. To Vincent she was beautiful, not like a woman, but as a girl is beautiful. Vincent could see, though, that she would grow up to be a beautiful woman.

There was a knock at the door and when Vincent opened it, there stood Jonah. Rachel had turned to see who it was, and Jonah saw her. Vincent had stepped back to let him in and he saw Jonah's mouth drop open. He just stood there with his mouth open, and his eyes wide. He was absolutely dumbfounded by Rachel's beauty. His face flushed, and he could not say a word. Rachel's flushed, also, for she knew what was happening, though it had surprised her. Vincent had to laugh.

"I told you she was going to be a fox!" exclaimed Vincent. Cupid's arrow had struck Jonah. "She isn't going to be a fox!" exclaimed Jonah, "She already is!" Jonah had finally seen Rachel and he was truly smitten. It had been so perfect. Vincent wished he could have got it on film. Jonah was looking at her with new eyes and she was basking in his attention. The two were oblivious of Vincent as they went out his door.

Not long after this awakening, Rachel ran over Jonah's bike with Vincent's motor home. It had all started with Rachel sitting in the driver's seat, and starting the engine. She was soon bored with this, and had talked Vincent into letting her drive it back and forth a few feet at the curb. Jonah's bike was lying on the lawn, and Vincent was sitting halfway on the engine compartment, with his foot close to the brake. Rachel pressed on the gas too hard. The rig shot forward, surprising her. At the same time she turned the wheel, and the rig jumped the curb, and was on the lawn, heading straight for Jonah's bike.

Rachel was barefoot, and Vincent was afraid he would hurt her, as she had her foot on the brake. She was not pushing on it hard enough to stop, and by the time he had got her to move her foot, they had run over Jonah's bike. Right after it had happened, Jonah came around the corner of the house, and saw the motor home parked on his bike. Vincent backed off his bike and inspected the damage. The front wheel and forks were mangled. Rachel didn't know whether to laugh or cry, and was doing a little of both. Jonah was a perfect gentleman about it. He understood about women drivers; his father had told him all about them. Vincent put the bike in his rig and took it to a bike shop, and had it fixed.

Vincent still let Rachel drive the rig back and forth, even though his better judgment was against it. He had not yet developed the ability to refuse Rachel anything. Pamela and Saundra were in the rig with them this time, fooling around. Rachel was at the wheel, with Vincent next to her on the same seat. They were all in a laughing fit over something Rachel had said, and the driver's door was open. Vincent was wrestling Rachel for the keys, when someone pushed them. They both fell out the door, off balance, backward.

To Vincent it was like it was happening in slow motion. It was at this time that he realized he loved Rachel as if she had been his own daughter. Vincent forgot about his own fall, and tried desperately to get under Rachel to break her fall. He was totally out of balance, and control. He was falling backward, and so was Rachel, right beside him. He could see the fear on her face. The back of her head was headed straight for the pavement. Vincent was certain she would be hurt badly. He tried to get his hand under her head, but failed, and the back of her head hit the pavement, and bounced with a sickening thud.

A look of pain flashed across her face, and for a second it looked like she was going to cry, but her face changed, and she laughed instead. Vincent wanted to cry, he was so relieved. He couldn't remember how he had landed; he had been so absorbed in her fall. He checked himself over while she was up, giggling. Vincent was in awe of her hard head; it was a wonder she had not been knocked out.

It was sobering, this feeling of love he had for Rachel; he had never experienced it before. He loved his boys, but this was different. Vincent had never loved a girl this way, not since he was a boy, not since his sister. He loved this girl more like a daughter, but he couldn't be sure, for he had never had a daughter.

There was more to it than that, though; but he did not understand his feelings. Rachel was exciting to him, she even aroused him, and not that he lusted for her, for she was just a child. It was a physical attraction, a something his body controlled, rather than himself. She excited him, and it made him feel young to be around her. Rachel was never a temptation for him; she just made him feel alive. She was a mystery to him, constantly changing her mood, enthralling him with her femininity. Nothing gave him more pleasure than watching her.

Vincent loved to buy Rachel little gifts. He would have bought her big ones, but knew her mother would not allow it. Rachel's ears had been pierced and she liked dangling earrings, so he bought her inexpensive ones. He bought her a gold ring for her birthday, though. Rachel also liked perfume, but only one kind, the kind her mother used, which was "Jontue." So this was what he always bought her. One day he tried to find a new kind for her, and got about half sick testing different ones. He bought one he thought she would like. She took one whiff of it and wrinkled her pretty nose in disapproval. It was the last time he tried to find her a new perfume.

Vincent was in some kind of trouble with Shelly most of the time. The other children were jealous of his favoritism for Rachel, and it did cause some sibling rivalry. Vincent was aware of this, but believed it was fair. Especially considering the favoritism the parents had shown for the boy and Pamela. Just leaving Rachel and the youngest daughter out in the cold. Although Vincent was fond of Rachel's sisters, he was unable to love them.

Vincent bought all of them Christmas and birthday gifts, even Philip, even though he knew Philip hated him. He always helped Rachel with her homework; he would not help the others. If he had, he would not have had the time to do anything else.

Shelly knew Rachel could get Vincent to do almost anything she wanted; she knew Rachel took advantage of this power. One day Shelly came over to talk to Vincent about it. Shelly was a pretty girl. Vincent thought of her as a girl, for she had not yet reached thirty. She was still a girl to him, no matter how many times she had been a mother. She still had a pretty shape even after having four children. That was an accomplishment, he thought. He had seen a lot of lovely girls let their figure go to Hell after getting married, even some who had not had children.

Shelly was a sweet and loving person, but as volatile as a bottle of nitro. She could be sweet as honey and turn into a shrew in a second. Vincent had heard her explode many times; he was scared to death of being on the receiving end of one of them. Vincent knew she had been unhappy with him, so when she came, he was apprehensive. Shelly was calm when she told him he was not helping her when he spoiled Rachel while she was trying to punish her. Vincent did not know what to say, for he had no excuse, other than not being able to refuse Rachel.

"She can turn me into silly putty." he pleaded, and Shelly laughed. "I know that," she told him. "But you are going to have to try," Vincent told her that he would try, but with not much conviction. He watched her walk away. She had a nice walk; she had once been a model.

The months went by and Vincent loved Rachel more every day. He was doing exactly what her mother had warned him not to do, he was making her his life. He was becoming obsessed with her. He planned every thing he did around her. He would not let anything interfere with his being with her. Although he was communicating with Carla, it was not as often as he should. He knew this was not good for him, knew he should be working at something to keep him occupied, but he was obsessed.

Vincent didn't realize that the worst brick in his Tower, selfishness, was still jammed in there tight. Vincent was being selfish with Rachel. Possessive is selfish. He was also being so with her parents, putting his needs ahead of theirs. He rationalized it, though, he was doing it all for Rachel. He didn't realize he was helping and hurting her at the same time. He was helping by reinforcing her self-esteem, but hurting by making her dependent. This is what a possessive person does. He should have recognized this, for this was what his mother had done to him.

Rachel had a girl friend who lived across the street; she was a year or so younger than Rachel. The girl had an older brother and sister. The girls name was Jody. Although Vincent was not aware, the girl's mother did not like him. She had never met him, but had seen him from across the street. She had judged him by his actions with Rachel and by the kind of men she was use to, men she had met in saloons, some who had paid for her favors. She took it for granted that Vincent was a dirty old man, and preached to

Rachel against him. Rachel must have believed her.

Rachel had written him a note, which had been instigated by the witch across the street. She had not made up her mind to give it to him. When she came over with Jody, she had the note tucked in her hand, and was being secretive about it. She was giggling, nervously about it with Jody. The girls were being playful about it, and possibly, Rachel might not have given the note to him. Vincent, not knowing what was going on, thought they were just playing with him, and he, playfully, tried to get the note away from her. They wrestled for it, all in good fun, he thought, and got it away from her. She tried to stop him from reading it, but in vain. When he came to the place in the note where she had written she hated him, his jaw dropped slack and his heart did a flip-flop.

"Why?" he asked in astonishment, and he could see the distress on Rachel's face. She was caught with no escape. She had not planned it this way. The distress was on her face for only a moment, and then it turned to rage. Vincent discovered that she was just as volatile as her mother. She stamped her foot angrily. "I'm never coming over here again!" she yelled, and she stormed out the door, with Jody at her heels. Vincent was crushed. He was not prepared for this kind of hurt. He just stood there with the adrenaline causing his pulse to pound in his ears. His stomach tightened to a fist, and his belt felt like it was tight around his chest. He had not a clue as to what had caused this explosion. Vincent could not comprehend what he could have done, or said. The whole thing was just incomprehensible. He was so totally, flabbergasted.

At no time since his last binge had Vincent felt such a need for a drink. There seemed to be no escape from the distress that was overwhelming him. The walls were closing in on him and he had to get out of the building. He tried to compose himself so he could walk out the door; he wanted to run. He walked out with the hope he would not see anyone, for he knew he would not be able to talk. No one was visible and he made it to his rig, feeling like he was being chased.

Vincent got into his rig, and hurriedly got it started. He was almost in a panic to get off that street and he did not lose that feeling until he had. He headed straight for the beach. When he got to his favorite spot, a large flat rock on the Rincon, he parked. He took a beer out of the fridge, and opened it. He tried not to drink it fast, but he was in need of relief and he drank it fast.

Vincent had forgotten all about Rags, but the dog had not forgotten him, and had jumped in the rig right under Vincent's feet. Vincent threw the empty beer can into the trash, and took Rags for a walk on the beach. He had his head in his thoughts, and didn't see this huge Doberman coming at Rags like a freight train. When he heard its owner yelling, he looked up and saw the beast. The vicious looking creature was almost upon them.

Vincent had his shorts on, and was barefoot. He didn't know how he was going to protect himself, or Rags. Suddenly the Doberman did a somersault and landed thrashing on his back. Vincent could see then that the dog had been on a long rope; one that had been secured by a metal post. He breathed a sigh of relief, for he had been just about ready for an accident in his pants,

This fright brought Vincent back to reality, and he went to work at trying to handle his anxiety over Rachel. He could not think of a thing he had done, or said that could have caused such alienation. He realized that running away was not going to solve anything, and he went back to his place. When he got back in he discovered that Rachel had returned all his gifts.

After this, when Vincent saw Rachel, she would not speak to him, or even look at him. He realized how much he really loved her and needed her. He could not stop thinking of the problem, and could see no solution. It was on his mind when he awoke in the morning, and when he tried to sleep at night. He had a knot in his stomach that would not leave. The stress built up in him, and he could not get rid of it,

After a week of this, Vincent was almost convinced that he should leave, for the stress was driving him crazy. He was afraid he would go on a binge to relieve it. He was also afraid that if he left, he would never see Rachel again, and that thought put a fear in him he had never experienced. It was a sobering thought when he realized he was going through a sort of withdrawal again. Vincent had used Rachel to fill a void in him, and now he was addicted to her. He had traded one kind of crutch for another.

Shelly finally came over and told him what had happened, how Jody's mother had preached against him. She had made Rachel suspicious, and afraid of him. Shelly told him that Jody's mother was a whore, and had no business judging anyone. She told him she had told Rachel the same. The next morning he heard Rachel knock at the door. His stomach told him it was her. A load of adrenaline made his pulse thump in his ears. When he opened the door Rachel was standing there. She was demure, looking down at her feet. She looked up, and told him, woefully, that she was sorry. These were the sweetest words Vincent had ever heard. He stepped aside to let her in. She hesitated for a moment, looking at his face, like she was trying to read him to see if he really wanted her to come in. He smiled, and she came in. He had to resist the urge to hug her, and it was almost irresistible.

Vincent didn't ask her to explain; he was too grateful for her just being there, and he was afraid he might say the wrong thing. He just told her he was happy they could be friends again. And they were friends again, but the relationship had changed. The neighbor had planted the seed of suspicion, and fear was in Vincent's heart. He was always afraid he would say, or do the wrong thing. He was afraid to be with her and afraid to be without her.

It was like when he was on a binge, afraid to drink, and afraid not to.

Vincent had to be careful what he said to Rachel and how he said it. She was always on the defensive. Often, innocent things he said to her were taken as criticism, which was all derogatory to Rachel. Vincent learned that Marcus had been an abused child. Even though she lived in the same city, he would not visit his mother, or even talk to her on the phone. He would not allow his children to visit her, either. Vincent learned that Marcus had a drug problem; he was now on a methadone program. He also learned that Shelly was a pot smoker, and had been one since she was fifteen years old. Both parents had a can of beer in their hand most of the time.

One morning, after the children had gone to school, Shelly told Vincent that Rachel had become a young lady. At first he just stared at Shelly, for he had not realized her meaning. When he did, he was embarrassed that she had told him, and didn't understand why she had. He tried to hide his feelings, and succeeded by talking to her like it was a common subject. He thought if the mother wasn't embarrassed by the subject, neither would Rachel. Vincent bought Rachel a bottle of her favorite perfume, and had it gift-wrapped, He gave it to her that evening.

"What's this for?" Rachel asked, pleased, for she loved to get gifts. "Just a little gift to help you get through your change," Vincent answered. At first she didn't comprehend what he meant, but then her face changed, and she was aghast. "Oh my God!" she exclaimed, embarrassed, and disgruntled, "She tells you everything." Vincent told her she should not be embarrassed by a natural function of her body. Rachel was only uncomfortable for a moment and then it vanished from her face like it had never been there.

Vincent tried to get close to Rachel's parents, but it was a hard thing. The generation gap is always hard to bridge. It is also hard for a person living alone to socialize with a married couple. Vincent had told them he was separated from his wife. They had him over for dinner on some holidays, and he had always felt comfortable during the meal. But after the meal he had always felt in the way, and had left as soon as he could do so without looking anxious about it.

Marcus was a hard case. On the surface he appeared to be friendly and even gregarious at times, but underneath he was a bomb waiting to be detonated. Unlike Shelly, he was a controlled bomb. When Shelly exploded, she was out of control, ranting, raving, and screaming profanity. Marcus was calm, cold and calculating when his bomb went off. Shelly liked to hurt with her mouth, while Marcus liked to hurt with his fist.

Vincent wanted nothing physical to do with Marcus. He knew he could only hurt Marcus with a weapon. In court, he, himself, would come out as the villain. He also knew that either one of Rachel's parents could stop him from seeing her in a second, for any reason, true, or false. He was walking a tightrope, and his nerves were getting frayed. Rachel was coming to his house every morning to do her hair and makeup. Vincent loved to watch her.

"You are staring at me," Rachel would say. Vincent would plead guilty, knowing she didn't mind. He was sure she liked it, and it was evident her self-image was getting better. It took her a long time to do her hair, though she was never satisfied with it. It had to be perfect, and she could never seem to get it that way.

"Is it all right?" she asked. "Looks good to me," he answered, but he could see she suspected his integrity. She combed and fussed with it until she was almost out of time. "Do I look alright now?" she asked, almost at the last minute she could leave without being late for school. "I think you look beautiful," he answered, and he really did think it was true. "I'm not beautiful!" she exclaimed, almost in a huff, like he was giving her a snow job. The next day his answer was different. "Almost beautiful," he answered and Rachel acted insulted. "Almost beautiful?" she asked, in a huff. "I thought you didn't like to be called beautiful," he answered. "I don't think I am." she complained. "Well, beauty is in the eye of the beholder," "What does that mean?" "If the one looking at you thinks you are beautiful, you are. And I think you are." "You are the only one," she answered, demure, "I'll bet Jonah thinks you are," Vincent told her, teasing, and she blushed prettily, and looked at her feet. "He does not," she argued, hoping she was wrong. "I saw that look on his face that first time you put makeup on for him," he teased. "I didn't put it on for him!" she argued, but she broke out in a giggle and ran out the door. She was going to be late for school for sure.

CHAPTER 42

A year went by in a hurry. The older Vincent got, the faster they went. Rachel's body was changing, but her face hadn't changed much. Her body was changing to the form of a woman's. It was plain to see she would have a lovely figure just like her mother. Vincent had taken dozens of pictures of her; talking her into different poses, nothing risqué, or anything like that. Most of them were different profiles of her face. He liked to take pictures of her in the mirror so he would have two images of her in one picture. Her face captivated Vincent. He would never live long enough to see too much of her face.

Jonah was jealous of Vincent because of all the time Rachel spent with him. He told the boy he had no reason to be jealous. Sometimes he would find himself being jealous of Jonah, but he would shrug it off. Vincent still wondered about it, though. He wanted her to have boy friends because it was the normal thing for her to do. But he still found himself envious of her feelings for Jonah. He thought it was probably normal for him to feel that way, but never having any daughters of his own, he wasn't sure. He didn't have anyone he could ask. He didn't want to ask Carla, but he didn't know why he didn't want to ask her.

Vincent hadn't told Carla about Rachel, yet, and he wondered why he hadn't. It was because an acquaintance had told him to be careful with Rachel; that he could get into a lot of trouble with her, even if he had not done anything. He suspected that Carla would think the same way, and he also knew that it was true.

Vincent wondered if he hadn't been guided to Rachel by something other than chance. Maybe God had arranged it? Had he been guided like that mother bird had been guided from Boston back to her nest. It certainly was true that Rachel needed him, and he needed her. He was beginning to believe it was the Tower. Rachel was going to help him with the Tower.

Vincent could feel the war going on inside himself. Rachel had already hurt him once, and he was sure she'd do it again. Sometimes he wanted to run like Hell. He couldn't, though, his fear of losing her was greater than his fear of the pain she might cause him, and probably would. His relationship with Rachel was purging him, he was sure of that. He realized that for the first time in his life he loved someone more than he did himself, which was not a good point for his character. That must be it, though, what else could it be? He always put her before himself, and he had never done that before. There was only so much he could do for her, though, and this was frustrating; he wanted to do everything for her.

Vincent even wanted to be responsible for Rachel. He loved his own children, but had never wanted the responsibility. He had accepted it as a duty. It would give him pleasure to be responsible for her. Why was that? Was he being possessive? Was that why he wanted to be responsible? He didn't seem to know the answer. Maybe he didn't want to know?

Vincent had gone home to see Carla a half dozen times in the last year and they had communicated constantly by mail and phone. He believed the physical separation was necessary for both of their welfare. There were times when the need to see her became a compulsion, and this was one of those times. Vincent thought he could kill two birds with one stone by seeing an old drinking buddy of his, who lived in Sausalito. This friend was a dealer for classic cars and Vincent had wanted an old Aston Martin for a long time, one like James Bond drove in some of the movies.

It had always been hard for Vincent to leave Rachel; he was always afraid she would need him for something while he was gone. He had given her a key to his house so she could get in when he was not there. She had a voracious appetite, so he kept things in the fridge for her. She also liked to use his phone. Her parents wouldn't let her use their phone. Rachel also liked to do her homework at his place, away from the other children; and with his help when he was there. Maybe that was why she was petulant every time he left. Rachel never acted like she had missed him, but he always had the feeling she had. Maybe it was just wishful thinking?

Vincent checked around about the different ways to travel north without taking the motor home, and he chose the train. He would have to board it in Oxnard in the morning, and in six hours it would have him in San Jose, where Carla could pick him up. He could take the train all the way, but from San Jose it took on the pace of a turtle. He called Carla, and told her he was coming. She was excited as always. It was a mystery to him why she loved him.

Vincent told her that he thought he was making progress with the Tower, but he couldn't tell her about Rachel over the phone. He certainly couldn't tell her that Rachel was the first person he had ever loved more than himself. He didn't know how he was going to explain to her how

Rachel was helping him. Maybe he shouldn't even try?

Vincent told Rachel he was going, and when he would return. He asked her if she would take care of Rags, and she was glad to do it; she knew she would be rewarded. He gave her the San Francisco phone number and asked her to call him in the middle of the week. Vincent told her he would be gone before she got there in the morning, for he had to catch the train early.

Vincent wanted to give her a hug, but sensed she still did not trust him enough for that. In a sense this was good, he thought a certain amount of fear was healthy for a girl and especially for one as pretty as Rachel. He was grateful her mother had taught her to be leery of men, and then he remembered that it hadn't been her mother who had taught her that fear. He hoped she would some day lose her fear and trust him. He knew he would be the last person on earth who would hurt her. He went to bed missing her already. He said a prayer for her, as he did every night.

Early the next morning, a cab took him and his luggage to the depot and in just a little while he was on the train. As the train rolled slowly past Ventura, he thought it stupid that the train did not stop there, as Ventura was the County Seat. It seemed he had moved into another backward town. Vincent had bought a newspaper at the depot; he sat down to read it as soon as he had found his seat. He got comfortable by the window and opened the paper, he tried to read but the sound of the iron wheels crossing the sections of rail made him feel sleepy. He had pictures of Rachel in the inside pocket of his sport coat. He folded the paper and took the pictures out.

Vincent separated the pictures and gazed at the one of her with the double profile of her face in the mirror. Her head was held high, with her chin up, revealing the lovely neck and golden hair past her shoulders. He was suddenly filled to bursting with love for her, with a lump in his throat and eyes glazed with moisture. It took him by surprise, and for a moment he was embarrassed and he looked to see if anyone had been watching him. This sudden feeling of overwhelming love made him wonder what love really was. Where did it come from? And what was its cause. Why was it joyous sometimes and misery another. He knew that Rachel liked him, but wondered if she would ever love him.

Vincent had always been a thinker, but he was becoming a deep thinker. He was thinking that a consciousness of love could not come from organized matter; he was thinking of brain. He was thinking that the brain was just a piece of meat, organized meat, blood and tissue. He believed that no matter how these elements were organized they could not produce consciousness. It had to come from a higher source than matter. He couldn't believe that consciousness could be chemical, nor could he believe that love could be.

Vincent had read in the Bible that God was Love. If this was so, then He must be the one who puts love in our hearts. If this is true, why does love cause us to suffer so? Why did it seem like many people loved the wrong people? His mother had loved three men, and they all had been wrong for her. One would think that God could have let her have one out of three. It seemed to him, in the physical realm, everything was in a divided state; love and hate; sweet and bitter; hot and cold; joy and sorrow; high and low; sick and healthy; alive and dead. The list is endless, a conspiracy against harmony.

Vincent looked out the window at the rolling hills. He was somewhere north of Gaviota Pass. It was a different kind of mountains than the ones he had grown up around, the Sierras, but it was pretty country, more gentle, and flowing. The beauty made his mind go blank for awhile and then he remembered the favorite excuse of a mischievous fictional character, "The Devil made me do it" Vincent wondered if there really was a Devil.

According to what he had read in the Bible, the Devil was a fallen angel named Lucifer. God had booted him out of Heaven for being a bad boy. It all sounded rather silly to Vincent. The Devil seemed mythological to him, like Zeus, or Apollo. He could not believe that Satan was a real entity. He could not believe that every word in the Bible was historical fact. He believed that much of it was metaphorical, symbolic.

Vincent could not believe that God, who was supposed to be the only power, would create another entity with the evil power to be used against his creation, and Himself. That would be a kingdom divided against its self. That would be pandemonium. It would be ludicrous. Vincent thought that if the Bible, especially the Old Testament, was taken totally, literally, it would be a most enigmatical book.

Vincent grew tired of thinking. He gazed at Rachel's picture and fell asleep with her lovely image on his mind. A bladder alarm awoke him an hour later and he got up to answer the call. After he had finished he realized he was hungry and went after a sandwich. While he was eating a turkey club, Rachel returned to his thoughts. Vincent knew it was obsession, but he had no explanation. Maybe he thought of her constantly because it gave him pleasure. .

Vincent tried to think of something different by looking out the window. The mountain scenery had been replaced by the monotonous, two-dimensional landscapes of the valley. He was grateful he no longer lived in the valley. His thoughts went back to Rachel and realized that a great deal of his thoughts of her did not give him pleasure. He knew she was a continual source of pain, but he also was aware that basically it was his own insecurity that was the true source. He loved Rachel, but had no true knowledge of her feelings. He could be just a form of escape from her parents.

Vincent had not the experience with a young lady with which to guide him with his relationship with Rachel. He constantly caught himself expecting her to think like an adult. When she didn't, sometimes his feelings would get hurt, or his ego. Often, after this had happened, he would get his foot in his mouth and say something he would regret as soon as the words had crossed his lips. He would kick himself the rest of the day.

Vincent even had silly fantasies about her. One time, after one of her visits, he fantasized about being her age, about kissing her sweet, flower like, lips, which seemed to be in a perpetual pucker. He laughed at himself, remembering the fantasy, but he knew that if he were her age he would be crazy about her. But he realized that this was the very thing that made him safe with her. He would never be the same age as her, never be young enough. He would always be too old to be anything but a friend.

It was comforting to know that he could love her as much as he wanted, or could, without ever being burdened by desire. He was sure that no matter how lovely she became, he would never have this burden with her. Vincent had had enough of that kind of burden. Vincent now believed that sex, and gravity was the main burdens of the physical realm. To be totally free one had to be free from both of them. Old age would free him from one of them, and death from the other.

The knowledge that lust had led him around by the nose for most of his life was doing little for his own self-image, but he realized he had to face his shortcomings before he could purge himself of them. He had to have remorse, but he couldn't wallow in it. He knew he had to purify his thinking. He had to resist sensual thinking whenever he was around Rachel and even when he was just thinking about her. He had to gain her confidence so he would be able to help her with her own blossoming sexuality. He could at least keep his own atmosphere clean for her. He knew that self-indulgence was a speedy vehicle, which could turn ones backbone into jelly. He would have to be some kind of honest role model for her.

A knot of fear would come into his stomach at the thought of losing Rachel, "What ifs," would pop into his head; what if she moved away? What ifs are endless. This was just another affect she had on him; she made him childish and foolish. He would tell himself to act his age, but he didn't want to do that, he was too old to do that. In fact he had been thinking about getting some Grecian Formula to get rid of the gray in his hair. Vincent laughed at himself when an old saying popped into his head, "There's no fool, like an old fool." He thought there were worse things to be than an old fool, like being an old drunk.

Vincent had been doing well with his drinking, a beer now, and then, but nothing stronger. Vincent would rather be caught dead than caught drunk by Rachel. He knew she had little respect for drunks. He knew he would stay sober while she was around, but wasn't sure what he would do if he lost her. He knew Captain Moon was waiting for the right time. After finishing the sandwich, Vincent left the club car, and returned to his seat. Not wanting to talk to any of the passengers, he closed his eyes; he wanted to do some more thinking.

He yawned, stretched and thought about love again. He had thought there must be many kinds of love, but now he believed it only varied in intensity. He believed that desire had nothing to do with love, for he knew one could love without desire, and could desire without love. Vincent believed that love, laced with desire, was being in love, a little trick of Mother Nature to keep the female of the species pregnant. He also knew that being infatuated could easily be confused with being in love, and only time could help one tell the difference.

"Love is strange," Vincent told himself under his breath. He remembered the old song as it had been done by Mickey and Sylvia. He remembered some of it and hummed it to himself. He came to the conclusion that desire placed a heavy burden on love. He decided that love without desire was a more stable relationship, and would, in all probability, be the more durable. What a joy it was just to love someone without wanting. It wasn't altogether true, though, he did want Rachel to love him. If he could just know that she did. What he wouldn't give to know that.

Vincent fell asleep, and awoke as the train was pulling into San Jose. Carla was waiting for him, and they ran to greet each other, just as they always had. After embracing, and kissing, they chatted as she walked him and his luggage to the car. They chatted about the boys, the gays in San Francisco, and how hard it was getting to live there. She was still driving that same old Jag, the same one they had gone on their first date in. It was a classic now and still looked as good as it had then.

Vincent watched her legs as she shifted gears, just as he had then, and got aroused the same as he had then. Carla had always had that affect on him, and always would. Wanting her and knowing he couldn't have her was terribly frustrating and he knew he would not be able to stay long. He stared at her lovely face, and she caught him.

"What?" she asked, and he was strangely embarrassed by his thoughts. "Just remembering the first time I rode in your car," he answered in a melancholy tone, wishing he didn't love her so, wishing she didn't love him. How much easier it would make things, but still torture to think of losing her. He could see her eyes water, as if she had been reading his thoughts.

"I still love you," she told him, wistfully, as if to remind him she was still waiting for him. "Me too," he answered trying to hide the anguish being around her caused him. He tried to think of more to say, but his mind left him mute. "What have you been doing about the Tower?" Carla asked and he told her about his studies, and self-examinations, fencing around his experience with Rachel, waiting for the right moment.

When they got to the mansion and inside, its spaciousness impressed him in a negative way; it caused him to think of her being alone there, and he felt anguish over it. He groped for words to express himself.

"My place is much smaller," he told Carla, fencing, trying to think of a way to bring up the subject of her living there alone, "And it is right on the beach." "I should visit you sometime," she suggested, and he was alarmed for a moment, not sure why. "I could sleep on the couch," he answered. "I promise not to molest you!" she exclaimed, and then laughed. It relieved some of the tension and he snickered.

"You were always such a good sport," Vincent told her flatly, and she laughed. He put his arm around her and they embraced. "It's so good to hold you." he told her, sighing after. "I've missed you awfully," she cried, "When will it end?" Not knowing how to answer, he was in anguish for a moment, but he heard some soft music coming from the stereo in the living room. He led her in that direction as he tried to assure her. "Maybe when my health returns all the way," he answered, and when they were in the living room, he started to dance with her. Carla kicked off her pumps, and he did the same with his loafers. They danced, and it was sweet as they held each other. They danced until the record ended, and then they stood holding each other,

"Oh my sweet Carla," he moaned, "When I can't have you, I want you even more." "Knowing this is such a sweet, pain" she replied, "And we had better stop this." She moved out of the embrace, but she took hold of his hand, still wanting his touch. Have you had dinner?" she asked, needing to change the mood. "I had a bite on the train, but I am hungry." "Let's go to the restaurant," she suggested. Both Carla's parents had retired, and they had given it to her. She had continued to manage it to keep herself busy. It had been her salvation.

"Can't stay away from that place, can you?" It has always been my second home," she replied gratefully. "Born with a silver spoon in your mouth," he spoofed. "And how well it fit in yours," she retorted, and they both laughed. "And how good it is!" he exclaimed, knowing full well he would probably be as poor as a church mouse had it not been for her and her family.

At Maggio's they were treated as royalty, getting the best table in the house. Not much had changed, but for a few new faces. The View of the boats and gulls was relaxing, but the stress of being with Carla had turned Vincent's stomach into a chamber of gastric horror, and he ordered sparingly.

"Stomach still bothering you?" she asked. "As always," he answered. "Does it bother you when you are away from me? Carla asked, and he couldn't answer truthfully. He didn't know, for he had exchanged the stress of her for the stress of Rachel. "When I'm away from you, I miss you and worry about you, and my stomach doesn't know the difference," he answered. "You should have been a monk," she suggested, wryly. "A monkey would have been better," he answered and they both laughed. He was thinking to himself that he would have made a good monkey, and he had made a monkey of himself many times. Being a monkey could be fun, except for the fleas, and he probably would be addicted to bananas, but how bad could that be?

"If you were a monkey," Carla remarked and laughed, "Your mustache wouldn't show." "And I wouldn't have to wear pants." "I'll bet you would like that," she stated and giggled. "And girl monkeys don't wear them, either," he answered. "You dirty old monkey!" she exclaimed, "You would be nasty no matter what kind of animal you were." "I wish I could be nasty," he replied and the mood was changed. There was a vacuum for a moment and Vincent decided he would tell her about Rachel, and how she was helping him. When he showed her Rachel's picture a look of concern came on Carla's face.

"She is a very pretty girl!" Carla exclaimed, and she tactfully tried to warn him of the danger. He tried to assure her there was none, but feared he was not successful. He even sensed a little reservation on her part, of trusting him with the girl. This seemed to be a universal feeling; it seemed that everyone he had confided in had a little of it. It was like a dirty old man, hysteria. It seemed as if the general public believed that the older a man got the more lustful and out of control he got. It seemed to Vincent it was the general public that was dirty minded. Maybe that was it? They were dirty minded so they expected everyone to be so. It seemed as if a man and a girl couldn't be friends without everyone thinking there was hanky panky going on.

Vincent knew though, that if he had a daughter he would be suspicious of everyone, including some women. Sex was such a burden for mankind, he thought. Why had God made it so? He had not needed it to create the first humans so why had He needed it for the rest? And on top of that, Adam and Eve must have been created as adults or who would have taken care of them? He couldn't see God giving them a bottle, or changing diapers. Vincent tried to explain some of his metaphysical beliefs to Carla, but she was impatient. It was all too vague and transcendental for her. She was a good Catholic.

"Why can't you just accept things the way they are and let the priest do the rest?" she complained. "That doesn't work for me," he retorted. "Why?" Carla asked. "I don't believe that the way things seem to be is the way they are," he answered, and she was incredulous, but said no more, knowing it would be fruitless. "Do you think you will ever be able to come home to stay?" she asked, woefully. "Of course," he answered, with sincere conviction, "There has to be a way." "I hope it will be soon!" Carla exclaimed," This is driving me out of my mind." "I'm sorry," he answered, searching for other words to comfort her with, failing. "If I find a cure for the sexual problem," he reminded her, "I still have to be sure Captain Moon will not return." "Oh how I pray he will not!" she exclaimed.

The sexual thing was like a stonewall between them and as much as he loved her, he wanted to escape the torture of being with her. And he missed Rachel. When he was with Carla he missed Rachel, and when he was with her he missed Carla. What an enigma he was in. If it was not for the sexual thing, he would have to choose between them. He knew that any sane adult would choose his wife over a neighbor's daughter, but he was not sure that he was sane, for it would be a hard choice for him.

But Rachel felt like his daughter to him, and he felt responsible for her. It would be different if she had responsible parents, but her parents were a disaster waiting to happen. At this time he would have to choose Rachel; he could not leave Rachel in such a happenstance situation. For all he knew, she could even be in physical danger. Her sister had shown him some bruises Marcus had caused her to have on her arms. Vincent could only hope his fear of jail would keep Marcus from hurting Rachel.

There was this constant conflict between Rachel and her father. It seemed as if they hated each other. Rachel had told Vincent that she hated her father, but she didn't seem to know why, except for the way he treated her. Vincent could see that she did not want to hate him. If he were criticized by anyone, she would defend him, staunchly. Vincent had learned early not to make derogatory remarks about any of Rachel's family, or even her friends.

And there was the Tower. Rachel was helping him tear it down and she was the only one who could. He knew that without the Tower's demolition and rebuilding, he would be dead. He would be dead if he got back on the bottle. Captain Moon was so close to him, as close as his shadow, lurking, and thirsty. Carla was strong; she could do without him for a while longer. Rachel was just a little girl; he didn't know how much she could stand.

Vincent could not tell all this to Carla, for he did not want to argue with her, and he understood her side of it. She was lonely, but at this time he could not solve that problem. He hadn't been able to solve problems for years; he had run from them, or had drowned them out. He no longer had the insulation of alcohol, and he had nowhere to run. He had to learn how to stand fast, and solve his problems. He prayed that Carla would wait for him. There was no other way.

Rachel called at the appointed time. Vincent answered the phone right away, and she was a little cool. He surmised the neighbor had been talking to her again, and he had to suppress his alarm. They talked small talk, and then she asked him if he was coming home when he had said he was, and he assured her he was. He tried to talk more small talk, but she was cool and not receptive. She told him she had to go home, and they said goodbye.

After hanging up the phone, he had to suppress the urge to get in his vehicle and head south, but he remembered he had no vehicle. He hadn't seen his friend, or even called. He would have to do that right away. Too many things to do and the boys were coming home to see him, Carla had called them, and they would arrive on the following day. It had been a long time since they had all been together.

They also had to see her aging parents again. They had paid them one little visit, and Vincent had noticed that her father's back was still as straight as a board, and he still hadn't lost that air of genteel, mischief. He was still active in business, still making that green stuff. And Mama was still Mama, a little heavier.

Vincent was not able to find the Aston Martin he wanted, not for the money he wanted to pay. He was appalled by the prices. He hadn't bought a car for years, and he was shocked. He was well off, but not rich, not that rich. He knew, with some dismay, that no matter how well off he was, he would never be able to be extravagant. It was just not in his programming to be so. He was not tight; he was just conservative, careful. Even Captain Moon had been so. He thought that was rather remarkable, for he had known many people who were quite frivolous with their money while imbibing.

Vincent thought it was odd he was thinking of Captain Moon almost as if he was a different person, or personality, like a Mister Hyde, rather that a drunk himself. Maybe it was easier that way. He could blame the chemical and the other personality. He knew that kind of thinking was not going to have any kind of healing result. He also knew alcoholism was an affect, and just staying dry was not going to cure the cause.

What he really needed was to be born again, to start all over again. Maybe he could get a communist to brain wash him? His brain really could use a good cleaning. That still would not heal that awful thing that was in his genetic code. But he could always be safe from that as long as he didn't drink. And here he was drinking beer again. Why was he always tempting the Devil?

That night they had dinner at Maggio's, with Carla's parents. They were a little cool to him, for they had never approved of his treatment of Carla, but were still gracious and hid their feelings as well as they could. They also were aware that he had been trying, and they respected him for that. The old man still drank that lovely old cognac, though and Vincent could smell it across the table, and his mouth watered.

Vincent was going to have to prepare himself for his sons; he wasn't sure how to act. Had they forgiven him? Carla tried to assure him they had.

Maybe they would never be sure of him, he thought. He had fallen off the wagon so many times. And if he wasn't sure himself, how could they be? Maybe when he was sure they would be. Only time would tell. He would do his best.

Mark showed up first in a four-wheel drive, Dodge Power Wagon. He lived in Quincy, where he was working as a forest ranger. He gave Vincent a bear hug, one of the ribs crushing kind. And Mark was like a bear, big as a barn, with curly hair all over his head, and face. He looked like the mountain man that he was. He even called Vincent Dad. What a great day this was turning out to be. The one who had been the most critical of him had forgiven him.

Reed showed up next in his van. He was living in Napa, where his home office was. He was an interstate truck driver. He was taller than Mark, but not as big. He was big, but not square like Mark, not as solid. Reed was more gregarious, more talkative, more of a social animal. His free spirit had made him less judgmental, less critical. He also gave Vincent a hug and handshake. They hugged each other together, and wondered if Wade was going to make it.

The guys told stories of their escapades while Carla listened, and tried to look impressed. She had heard most of them before. Reed commented about how much booze he had put away in his life, but he laughed when he said he had never seen anyone who could put away as much booze as his Old Man. Mark told Reed that he was going to have to stop growing, that he was growing right through his hair. Reed's hair was getting a little thin on top. Before any retaliation could take place Wade showed up bearing two six packs of beer, which were being opened right away. Vincent didn't take one, not that he didn't want one; he didn't want to worry Carla.

Wade was taller than his brothers, but he was slim. He was more hyper, not slow and easy like his brothers. He had darker hair, curly, with a broad forehead, and full eyebrows. He was more affectionate and not shy about showing it. He called Vincent "Pops." He gave Vincent a warm embrace. What more could a dad ask for; he had all of his sons together.

It didn't take the boys long to go through the beer, so Mark went after more. While he was gone the topic of conversation turned to the Pelican, and it was decided they should all go for a sail. When Mark returned, Carla and Vincent got in the Jaguar, and headed for Sausalito. The boys and the beer followed in Reed's van. The boys all had open containers of beer in the van. Vincent didn't say anything, knowing it would be fruitless.

Contemplating a sail, Vincent had brought his sneakers with him. The boys hadn't, but they had all left old ones on board, and so had Carla. No one had brought ice for the beer, but it wouldn't last long enough to get warm. The wind that was blowing across the Bay would keep anything from getting warm. Vincent put on the first old jacket he could find, for he was cold already, and he couldn't have any alcohol to warm him.

Carla was also cold, so she put on a kettle of water on the stove for tea. The boys freed the Pelican from her mooring, and pushed her away from the dock. Reed started the old girl's engine while the others got the gear ready. In just a little while the sails were set, and full of wind. The Pelican didn't have any fancy rigging; some things had to be done manually.

Their mother had taught her sons well and it was a good thing; the wind didn't fool around on the San Francisco Bay. On the first tack, a gust heeled the Pelican way over on her port side and the boys laughed with glee as the old girl groaned, and gave herself to the wind. No one could suppress that free joy. Carla and Vincent gave into it, yelling just as loud as the boys. What better way could an earthling find to blend with, and use the elements? It doesn't get much better than this.

They made a trip around Alcatraz, which means the Island of the Pelicans; It had been a federal prison from 1931-1963. They had gone around Pelican Island in a Pelican. Reed had joked about what an awful place it would have been to be locked away in, knowing all those lovely San Francisco girls were so close.

As all good things must come to an end, so the sailing and the reunion. The boys left the same day, with two of them feeling better than they should. A reluctant Carla took Vincent to the train.

CHAPTER 43

Vincent got home a day later than he had told Rachel he would. She had stayed overnight with a friend, and he had been unable to see her. When he saw her the next day, she was pouting. She had that look that always unhinged him, a sultry look, and one that denied her youth.

"You didn't get back when you said you would!" Rachel scolded, her flower like lips, pursed in a pout. Vincent tried to explain to her how he had got tied up with his family; how he couldn't find the vehicle he had wanted, and how he had had to ride the train back. Reproach was still on her lovely face, which the summer sun had turned to a rich golden tan, the prettiest color he had ever seen on a face.

Rachel was wearing shorts and halter. She was the same pretty color all over. Her legs looked like a dancer's. Rachel's coloring radiated vibrant health, a magnet to the touch. Vincent loved to touch the things he loved. He resisted the urge to touch her, for Rachel was not in a receptive mood, she was very cool. Sometimes Vincent could not help himself, and he would have to caress her shimmering hair, or touch her cheek, or arm. It was not just a sensual thing, it was adoration. Touching Rachel brought every cell in his body to life. He adored her from the top of her head to the tip of her toe. Vincent loved Rachel's hands, which were big for a girl of her size. Her fingers were long, and slender. She had big paws was the way she put it; her grandpa had told her so. She wore a size eight ring, and her mother only wore a six. Her ring finger was the same size as Vincent's little finger, but his fingers were short and stubby. Her fingers were beautiful; everything about her was so to him.

Although Rachel looked like an angel, she was not. Had she been, he probably would not have loved her so much. This combination of angelic beauty and mischief was one of her biggest attractions to him. She could be a most charming little devil, "A little rascal," was his affectionate term.

In a little while they were back in their old routine of her visiting him before and after school. She would also visit in the evening when her mama would let her. Mama was what she always called Shelly, and she loved her Mama intensely. She closed her mind to all her mother's faults. Rachel had said once, though, that her parents were different. It was different when she was mad at her mother. She would call her names, or say she hated her, but this was just her temper talking. If someone else had said something bad about her mother while she was having one of these tantrums, she would immediately change her tune and defend her Mama. Rachel could call her mama anything but no one else could, except for her father, maybe.

Things were never the same as they were before the hate letter; Rachel stayed aloof. She was an affectionate girl. She showed it to everyone but him. He knew she had affection for him, or she would not have spent so much time with him, but she just could not show it to him. The only place Rachel was friendly with Vincent was in his house. Outside, she was cold, some times shunning him. If she were with her friends on the street she would not even look at him. Rachel would deny it if he confronted her with it; she just hadn't seen him.

Gradually, Vincent learned what was causing this attitude. After school one day, Rachel told him one of the boys at the bus stop had accused her of sleeping with an old man. She was upset for he had accused her in front of the other kids, out loud. There was nothing in the world that she could tolerate less than embarrassment. Vincent was also embarrassed. The whole thing was just inconceivably, awful. His heart went out to her, but he knew not what to do about it. Right after that her brother came over. Rachel had locked the door just like always. Her brother was being a brat, banging on the door, trying to get it open. Rachel got mad, and yelled at him through the door.

"Are you guys pumping away in there?" her brother yelled through the door and Vincent was aghast. He looked at Rachel, and her face was like a wax mask, void of expression. He knew what was hidden, though, she was too embarrassed to say, or do, anything. She never said a word, and her brother left. She acted as if nothing had happened. The next night her boy friend Jonah came over, Rachel had just got there. Jonah knocked at the door and Vincent opened it. When Jonah saw Rachel, he asked her to come out. When she told him to wait a minute, he got mad, for he was jealous of Vincent.

"Go ahead and stay with the old bastard!" he yelled, and in a reflex action, Vincent started to go after him with mayhem in his heart. A negative look from Rachel stopped him in his tracks. He knew he couldn't do anything to the kid, anyway, although he would have loved to wring his scrawny neck. He could not for the life of him see what she saw in this crude kid. One time he had heard Jonah knocking at Rachel's back door.

He had been with several other boys. He had got impatient with her for not coming at once.

"Come out here right now!" he had yelled, "I want to fuck you!" Those were his exact words, and Rachel had come out, saying nothing. The little jerk could do no wrong. Jonah called her crude names when he was mad at her. He usually called her a cunt at these times, which was often. Love is truly blind.

Rachel continued to visit Vincent in spite of these problems. She had more courage than most of the adults he knew. Most adults, especially a woman, would avoid like the plague, a man who caused negative gossip about her. He wondered why Rachel didn't avoid him altogether. Vincent was fairly certain it wasn't just the things he did for her that brought her to him. No reasonable person would put up with that kind of harassment, not just for that, though she did not show him any visible affection. This loyalty should have shown him it was there, but he still had nagging doubts about her sincerity. They were really doubts about his self.

"Why would she love someone like me?" he had asked himself many times. She had told him that she liked him. "Like and love are the same to me," Rachel had told Vincent more than once. "I don't even love my father," she had told him. Had Vincent been a woman, it would have been okay for her to love him. Being a man, though, he was too old for her to love. Love for a man had to be romantic, or not at all, unless it was a relative. Anything else seemed unnatural to her. "God!" he exclaimed to himself, "What a curse it is to be a man." Vincent had never heard of a woman being called "A dirty old woman," He wondered what a sex change would cost, and then he laughed at his own silliness.

The days turned to weeks and the weeks to months, and he grew to love Rachel even more. He never would have believed he could love her more and he wondered how much more he could. He wondered if there was some connection between love and stress. It seemed the more stress she caused him the more he loved her. He was miserable with her, and more so without her.

There were times Vincent wanted to move away from Rachel to escape the stress, but knew he could never do it. He was constantly afraid he would say, or do something that would make her, or her parents, mad at him. When she was mad at him, she punished him by staying away. She would ignore him for days, even weeks. She did have a cruel streak in her; she must have got it from her father. One could see that he enjoyed his cruelty.

Vincent was certain, though, that he had been led to Rachel by a higher power. He was sure that, somehow, his relationship with her was going to help him with the Tower. He smiled when he remembered part of a Bible verse: "and a little child shall lead them." Rachel was a child and she was leading him, but he knew not, where.

Rachel's parents would not let Vincent give Rachel money, so he created little jobs he needed her to do for him, chores he had always done for himself. Vincent gave her the job of keeping his house clean, but he always helped her. Once a week she did it and it was fun for him. It didn't seem to be fun for her, though. She raised her eyebrow when he told her it was fun for him. She looked at him like he wasn't operating at full capacity.

Vincent gave Rachel the job of giving Rags a bath once a week. He helped her with that, also, and it was even more fun. He was the only one who thought so, though. Rachel didn't think so, and neither did Rags. It seemed to be the ultimate insult to him. He was always joyous when it was over, though, and he would jump around, yap, and shake water all over the place.

Doing anything with Rachel was joy to Vincent; she was his fountain of youth. He always tried his best to see the good in her, and to rationalize the evil he saw. Her father had called her "The bad seed." Vincent believed that if there was any evil in her, it got there via the genetic code. Vincent didn't know why, but he believed his love for her could somehow liberate her from the evil that was in her. Evil, to Vincent, was anything that wasn't good, not some affect caused by the Devil. He could never believe in the Devil as an entity.

Rachel had always had trouble at school, not with her grades so much, but with her attitude. Her defensive attitude had sent her on many trips to the Principals office, and hours of staying after school. It had also got her into counseling. Right after her thirteenth birthday her attitude got even worse. She became belligerent with everyone, including Vincent. It was clear that she was emotionally upset over something, but no one knew what.

This went on for a few weeks, and then Vincent got a call from her school. Shelly had given them his number to call in case there was an emergency. Rachel had been kicked out of school, and they wanted someone to come and get her. When he got to the school, Rachel was belligerent, and would not go with him; she treated him as if he was a stranger. They were finally able to get hold of one of her aunts, and she came and got her.

Shelly paid him a visit the next day and she was mad. He was grateful to find out he was not the cause. She was going to get a lawyer, and sue the school. The councilor had told Rachel something that was not supposed to have been told to her. It was privileged information; it was something that had happened to Rachel when she was very young, so young she had forgotten.

Rachel had been old enough to talk, and she had told a neighbor, and the neighbor had reported it. Her father had abused Rachel, although not sexually, and had gone to jail for it. Rachel had forgotten, but Marcus had not. Instead of blaming himself for going to jail, he had blamed Rachel. She had been his scrape goat ever since. Now Rachel knew why she hated her father, and she hated him even more. It was very difficult for her to live in the same house with him. One could physically feel the tension between them.

Rachel got back to school, but she started spending a lot more time with the witch across the street, and her daughter. She still brought her homework to him, but the rest of the time she spent across the street, or with Jonah. She couldn't get along with him, either. She was mad at him more than she was glad. Vincent knew the witch was feeding Rachel poison about him and he was grateful, even joyous, when the witch and her family moved away to Fresno. At this time he was not aware that the move would make things even worse.

Rachel came back to him for a while, but she was just using him. She would run over to get something to eat, or drink and then she would leave. Or she would come over to borrow money, and then leave right away. She still brought her homework, but left as soon as it was done.

Rachel was corresponding with the witch, and her daughter. Soon they were making plans for Rachel to spend her summer with them. Vincent dreaded this, for he knew she would be preached a daily dose of poison against him. The witch had also made a condition for this vacation: Rachel was not to communicate with him while she was there.

Vincent was not capable of hate, had he been, he would have hated Maggie, the witch. She had never met him, she had only seen him from across the street, yet she hated him, and was assassinating his character. She was driving a wedge between him and the person he wanted most to love him. He wished he could hate her, but he could not, for he knew her persecution of him was motivated by fear for Rachel's safety. Vincent could resent her actions, though, and he did. This resentment was a constant irritation in his stomach, and caused him to eat antacid tablets like they were candy mints. He could not put this resentment out of his mind.

Vincent remembered an incident that had happened just before the witch had moved away. Rachel had been wearing shorts, and halter. She and Jody had got into some shaving cream, the kind that comes in a pressured can. They had sprayed the stuff all over each other. They had both looked like a couple of short cakes with whipped cream. Both girls had run over to Vincent's house. Both girls were laughing their fool heads off.

Rachel had gone to the sink to clean herself off and Vincent had followed to help her. While washing Rachel's shoulders, Vincent had noticed Jody had looked like she didn't like him doing it. She had even tried to interfere, but he had not let her. Vincent had been surprised by her attitude. Then he had wondered why he had been surprised, for why wouldn't the witch have also poisoned her daughter's mind.

Vincent dreaded the day Rachel would go away to live with people who hated him, who would preach to her that he was a dirty old man. He knew Rachel would not argue, for she was not yet sure that he was not. Maggie had told her that even though he had not yet tried anything with her, eventually, he would. Also there was the fact that Maggie was Rachel's only escape from her father.

Vincent bought a going away gift for Rachel, a matching gold necklace, and bracelet. He wanted her to have something nice to remember him by. He had planned to give it to her on the day she left. When the witch came to get Rachel, they stayed with friends across the street. Rachel went over there, and called Vincent. She told him they were going to leave in the morning. He told her he had a gift for her, and would give it to her when she came over to say goodbye. Rachel told him she had had a fight with her mother, and she had forbid her to come across the street. He told her he would call her mother, and fix it so she could come. He was sure that Rachel had lied, and that it had nothing to do with her mother.

Rachel asked him what the gift was, and he told her she would have to come over to find out. Rachel told him she might be able to come over later, and she hung up the phone. Vincent knew her curiosity would get the best of her, and she would call back. Rachel called back just about every hour. She wore him down, and talked him into letting Jody come after the gift. She promised she would try to come later. She called later, and thanked him for the gift, but she told him she could not come to see him. He told her if she cared anything about him she would come and say goodbye to him.

"I don't care about you!" she exclaimed with anger, and she hung up on him. The next morning she left without a word; Vincent was crushed. Her rejection had pulled the rug right out from under him, and he was alone again. Vincent needed a drink in the worst way, not the beer he had been drinking in moderation, but something with a jolt. He knew what would happen if he did, though, and it might ruin his chance of ever getting back together with Carla. He knew he must continue with his work on the Tower; it was his only chance.

Vincent remembered reading an advertisement. It was about an organization called: "United Metaphysical Research." It was a group of people who researched all aspects of religions that used metaphysics for healing, and for solving problems of daily living. Maybe they would be able to help him with the Tower. Vincent called and made an appointment for the next day. And then he went back to his problem. He would not be able to see, or hear from Rachel for all summer, and by the time the witch got through with her, she might never want to see him.

The appointment was a long ways away, and he still was in anguish, his stomach was a cold fist. He had to have a beer to calm him. He could handle beer. He drove Rags to the store, bought a six-pack of beer, and drove to the Rincon where he walked the beach, drank beer until it tasted bad, and then he drank some more. The cold fist in his stomach was gone, but he was even more depressed. Vincent made it to the appointment with a hangover. It was not the worst kind, but enough to make him irritable and impatient.

Vincent talked to two men, Rob Snow, and Sterling Marshal. Rob was young, about twenty-five. He was tall, with a small frame. He was always smiling, or getting ready to. Sterling was older, and more serious. Vincent told them about the Tower, and Rachel. Vincent could see the concern about his relationship with Rachel on Sterling's face, but not on Rob's. They told him they would do some research on metaphysical building, and get back to him with some literature that might help him. He gave them his phone number and address.

In an attempt to escape the depression that was consuming him he drank beer all day and night. That night he had a nightmare. He dreamed he was drunk, in rags, and filthy. He was at the Salvation Army seeking shelter and clothes. Carla, Linda, and Rachel were soldiers there, looking at him with loathing. He ran from them into the ocean. Vincent awoke trembling, and in need of a drink. Vincent was cold and could not get warm. He wished he could have some brandy to warm him. When he looked at the clock to see if the time would allow him to get to a bar, or liquor store, he realized he was thinking like Captain Moon. For a moment he worried about it, but his need struck him like an impulse, and the clock was with him; the bars would be open.

As Vincent sat in the worst dive he could find, sipping raunchy bar whiskey, he thought of Carla, and how he had ruined her life. He knew he had the tiger by the tail again. He could not imagine how he could possibly build another life with the only body he would ever have and with this mind of his, the one with the temptation resistant quotient of zero? How could he ever be able to trust himself? If he could have one wish in his life it would be to be someone else. Vincent was truly tired of being himself. But he only had Captain Moon.

Vincent wished he had the Hawk. He was afraid of driving the motor home while he was drinking, afraid he would hit something, for the rear view mirrors stuck out on both sides. He decided he would catch a bus to the Flats, pick up the Hawk, and see if he could find Linda. Vincent felt guilty about Carla still waiting for him. He wanted to call her to tell her he was drunk again, but there was not enough booze in the world to give him the courage to do so.

Vincent had to wait an hour for a bus. He had taken a full flask with him, but by the time he had arrived at the Flats it was empty and so was he.

It was too early in the morning to pick up the Hawk so he decided he would go to a bar, have some drinks, have breakfast and then get his car out of storage. Vincent caught a cab to the nearest open bar. Vincent drank for two hours before he went for breakfast.

At the cafe Vincent saw Mario feeding his face. He almost didn't recognize him, for his Charles Atlas physique had been buried in Pasta. His hair was gray and his face bloated. One could almost feel the high blood pressure pumping away in his veins. Mario looked like he was nervous, fidgety.

Mario was sitting in a booth with another man, a stranger to the Captain. He was younger, but resembled Mario; the Captain thought he was probably one of his sons. He caught Mario's eye with a wave. Mario didn't recognize him at first; Vincent had to stare before he did. When he recognized him his eyes lit up, and he waved him over.

Mario rose to shake hands with him and he had not lost his powerful grip. The power was still there, it was just padded. Mario introduced the Captain to his son, Pete, he was just one of four. They talked about old times and laughed, but the old Moon Patrol camaraderie was gone. After talk ran dry, the Captain suggested they meet later and tip a few for old times, but Mario had quit that sort of thing.

Vincent asked Mario about Linda, and he told him that she had been divorced, but he had not seen her for a long time. He said she should be in the phone book under the name of Carson. After they had parted with no plans for a future meeting, he decided he would try to find Mack. He knew Mack would be around somewhere, he would be buried in this old ghost town. At a phone booth at the far end of the cafe, Vincent found Mack's number and called. After four rings, a male voice answered. It was Mack; no one else had a voice like that.

"I haven't heard a voice like that for a long time," quipped the Captain. "That makes two of us," retorted Mack," Who in the Hell are you?" "One of your old drinking buddies," replied Vincent. "I've had a million of them," replied Mack," Which one were you?" "I like to howl at the moon." "Captain Moon!" exclaimed Mack, incredulously. "The same one," Vincent answered, and Mack told him to get over to his place pronto. Mack gave him the address, which was in Thermalito. The Captain told him he would be right over.

Thermalito was a hot place in the summer; that was how it got the name. There was not much topsoil, only a few inches to hardpan in places. For that reason there were not many trees except olive and palms; olives grow almost anywhere. Where Mack lived was north east of town, just across the river. He was still renting. He lived with his wife, Mary, and their only child, Julia, who was about the same age as Wade. Mack came to the door as the Captain drove on to the property.

The house sat on the back of the property; it was about two lots deep. Vincent could still see that it was Mack, though. As he came closer he could see that the years had left their mark. Mack looked badly worn, but he still had that Cheshire Cat grin on his face. He still had a bear hug for him, and it was returned with affection.

Mack was alone, the wife, and daughter had gone shopping. The Captain offered him a drink and that was something Mack never refused. Vincent walked back and got a bottle of cognac that had been sitting in the trunk of the Hawk for years. The Captain had retrieved the Hawk right after leaving the cafe. Mack liked the hard stuff, and this was quality cognac. He smacked his lips in appreciation.

"You always had good taste," Mack commented," In booze and women." "Have you seen Linda?" asked the Captain, not being able to wait any longer. "I know where she works," answered Mack, with enthusiasm," She is my favorite kind of person." "How do you mean that?" "Linda is a bartender!" exclaimed Mack, cheerfully.

CHAPTER 44

They parked on the golf course parking lot and walked into the lounge. Mack had told the Captain that Linda had been working there for several years. Time had been kind to her countenance. She was still a lovely woman, but something was missing, he had felt it as soon as he saw her. Or was it something else? It was a feeling he hadn't felt when he saw her. He was awfully glad to see her, but where was the excitement? Where was the magic? Where had it gone? Maybe it was because he hadn't seen her for such a long time; maybe the magic would show up later.

Linda was taken aback when he walked through the door. There he was, handsome as all get out, distinguished looking, with that gray hair, and such a tan. Here was the man she had waited for all of her life. Why didn't she feel different? Why didn't she feel more? She had come around the bar, and he was hugging her. Why did her knees not go weak? Why did her heart not pound? She was joyful to see him, but it was more like he was an old friend. Where was that old magic?

Linda was terribly frustrated, for she wanted that old feeling; she needed it. She had waited all of her life for that damned feeling. Emotion welded up in her, grief for lost love. Vincent had felt her emotion, he had mistaken it for passion. He felt guilt, and remorse for not having any. Both were embarrassed by their lack of passion, both thinking the other still had it.

"It's so good to see you, Vincent!" Linda exclaimed, trying to feel more. "Me too!" Vincent exclaimed, feeling foolish. They stepped back, and when they looked into each other's eyes, they both read the truth. They were relieved. This knowledge freed their natural, unburdened affection and they went back into each other's arms like old friends, hugging with enthusiasm.

There was deep hurting in both of them, though. They tried to drown it out with camaraderie and booze. They did a pretty good job of it, with the three of them getting smashed. When closing time came and the patrons had left, they closed the bar with them inside. For old times, they danced and drank the night away. They both got horny while dancing, both wondering if the magic would come back with sex. Mack got drunk out of his skull and they took him home at three A.M. From his house they went to hers, which was in Canyon Highlands, on the other side of the river.

Linda's house, a left over from her divorce, was on the side of a hill, with a panoramic view of the valley. Neither of them was looking for a view, though. They were looking for a place to get prone. Laughing and giggling, they undressed each other, leaving a trail of clothes to her bedroom. They made love with wanton passion, but it was all physical, and in a sort of camaraderie.

"Oh God, that was so good!" she exclaimed, after she had gone through her orgasm, moaning, and groaning." I hope you will be around for awhile." "Almost too, good." groaned the Captain," I feel like I need to be blown back out, like a rubber glove that had been turned wrong side out." "You want a blow job so soon?" she asked, incredulous, kidding him. "Can I have a rain check?" he asked, seriously. "It's only good for thirty days," she replied. "I'll be ready before then," he assured her, laughing. "I certainly hope so," she replied, and nothing more was said for a little while as they rested in their thoughts. Then Vincent asked Linda if she had a boy friend.

"Of course I do!" she replied, haughtily," But I would rather sleep with you," and she laughed. "Go to sleep," he told her, cheerfully," before I get horny again." "All I get is propositions," she complained. "Go to sleep. I'll try," she told him," But you had "better be here when I wake up." "I'll be here." He promised.

Linda went to sleep right away and Vincent arose to get a drink. He had drifted into the blues while trying to go to sleep. Although they had been wonderful in bed, with the magic gone he knew the physical would become ordinary and dutiful after awhile. Vincent had another drink and realized he had nothing left. He had lost Rachel; he had now lost Linda. He would certainly lose Carla. In fact, he should let her go. He should tell her to get a divorce, for there was just no hope because he would lose even himself before he was through. He wondered how long it would take, and how much he would have to suffer. He was doing no rational thinking.

Vincent stayed with Linda for a week, keeping her company at the lounge. He felt his health was deteriorating and he was going into depression. He knew he had to leave her before he became ill, which he knew was going to happen and he did not want her to see him that way. Linda had shown concern for him, recognizing his problem, one she saw in her patrons every day. She had tried to slow him down. When he told her he had to leave, she told him not to be a stranger.

Vincent knew he had to return home to get his dog out of the kennel, but he wanted to visit John first. He hadn't seen him for years. They had communicated by mail and phone, but it had been years since a visit. Vincent knew John was a boat person, knew he had been building a fair sized sailing catamaran for years. John had been a stake puncher for years. That is a grade setter for land moving and road building.

All had to be perfect for John and that was one of the reasons he had not finished the boat. Another reason was that John was an alcoholic. Building the boat was therapy for him. John had started the boat not long after his divorce. He had lived in a barn while building the first hull. He had moved to a boat yard in Menlo Park to build the second hull. He had built the rest of the superstructure and had attached the two hulls to it, but he had never finished it.

Vincent knew John had married again, an old sweetheart he had met in the islands, a Philippine girl. The Captain had never met her, and he was anxious to see what kind of a woman would put up with John's hard head. This hard head had been forged by his mistrust of the human animal. John trusted other animals for it was not hard for him to figure them out. He knew what he was, so he trusted himself. He had an above average I. Q. He was painfully careful about everything he did, and expected you to do the same, even though he couldn't trust you to do it.

At times this idiosyncrasy caused John to appear arrogant to some and did not always make him popular. John had always been able to drink Vincent under the table. He would not have been able to keep up with him on a long drunk, but quart for quart, he had been able to stay on his feet longer. And John could go without the next day, and he had always been able to make it to work the next day. There was no two ways about it; John was just tougher than he was.

On his way to Menlo Park, Vincent stopped at the Nut Tree to empty his bladder. Thirsty for a cold beer, he stopped at the little beer and cheese place inside, and had a cold one, along with a chunk of Monterey Jack and some crackers. He munched, drank and thought. Vincent remembered some things about Rachel, how she use to like for him to pick her up by her ankles. He remembered her trouble with her manual dexterity and her slight speech impediment. These problems had been caused by her premature birth. It had also caused one eye to be lazy, and the lid would, droop when she was extra tired.

After they had first become friends, they had often been playful with each other. She would tease him, unmercifully, and the first time he had picked her up by her ankles, it had surprised her, and then it had delighted her. After that she would sometimes ask him to do it. At that time she had only weighed about ninety pounds.

Before Rachel had outgrown her speech impediment, when she was ready to go home, she would say, " I go home now." After he had known her for just a little while, she would ask him if he had a girl friend. When he had told her he had none, she would say, "I be your girl," and then she would giggle, and add, " Just kidding." She had done that quite a few times, but after her mother had told her he was much too old for her, she had stopped.

Vincent had often wished he could cheat time and be a boy for her. What a sweet fantasy it had been; he had thought about what it would have been like to give Rachel her first kiss. Thinking of her had brought tears to his eyes. He cursed and jerked his thoughts away; it took physical effort. He shook his head, pushed himself away from the table, and left his beer unfinished. He hurried back to the Hawk and the hard stuff.

Vincent had hoped that John would still have the same address as before and knew he had as soon as he saw the old Chevy Suburban sitting on the driveway. John had roamed all over the country in that old thing. Vincent patted it on the fender as he walked by. Vincent could see that John hadn't changed much when he opened the door, except some excess weight had rounded off his corners. His beard was gray, but his hair and eyebrows were still black as the ace of spades. He had half a grin on his rugged face.

"My, my!" he exclaimed, "Look what the cat must have drug in!" He stuck out his hand. "Is it Vincent Cardoza? "It is Captain Moon today and I'm on a toot." He had his bottle in his hand, opened. "I need a partner," he told John, and took a swig. He handed the bottle to John, but he declined "I gave it up," John told him. This was a surprise to the Captain, for he remembered how much John had loved the spirits. "And it's too early, anyway," John added "It's never too early to have your spirits spirited!" exclaimed the Captain, and he took another swig.

Vincent was not what one would call drunk; he was just getting to the maintenance stage, just one step ahead of the Devil. He thought he was keeping ahead, anyway, but the Devil already had him. When one turns to the Devil for comfort, one always receives Hell. The Captain was well on his way to Hell on earth and he was no stranger to it. He had been there before, many times. One would think that once would be enough.

Almost everyone has heard a person suffering from a hangover say they would never do it again, but almost all of them do. If one does it enough, one can become an alcoholic. John was one, but he was abstaining, which is the only treatment for the disease. There is no cure. This doesn't mean that John didn't want to drink, though, for he was always thirsty, one drink away from disaster. Although John had drunk prodigious amounts, he had never had any physical problems from it. The Captain had always been envious of this physical strength of John's that he did not have. They had gone on many binges together, and he had watched John get up the next morning, and go to work without a hangover while he laid in torment. It just was not fair.

Vincent met John's wife a little after midnight. She was a head nurse, working the swing shift in a local hospital. She was small, and pretty. Her hair was black as coal with traces of silver. Her eyes were as dark as her hair, flashing with humor, and good will. She had a slight oriental accent. It was plain to see that she was John's salvation; she was taking good care of him, as much as he would let her. She was gregarious, and rolled out the red carpet for the Captain. She was a fabulous cook, which whetted even the Captains stifled appetite. John had been a lot more fun when he was drunk, so the Captain didn't stay long. Drunks like to be with drunks just like birds like to be with birds.

Two days after the visit, Vincent was back on the road, heading south. He was in dread of getting there, knowing no matter where he went Hell would be there waiting for him. He wished he had not got on this trip, but it was too late for that. Being in no hurry to get home, Vincent took a detour to Santa Cruz. He wanted to go to the boardwalk to fool around. It was about lunchtime when he arrived. He decided he would drink his lunch, he wanted something exotic, like a Singapore sling; he hadn't had one for years. He felt like he could drink a washtub full of them. He wondered why things that tasted so good were bad for you. He never could figure that one out; it was like God had a conspiracy against him.

Vincent went into the first cocktail lounge he could find. He drank a tall, red one. It was so good he drank it right down and ordered another. He sipped it and tried to relax. In a little while the first sling he had chugalugged was giving him a nice buzz. He maintained it by sipping. He sat in a chemical euphoria for hours. The booze, mirrors, music, bottles, and glasses had created this euphoria.

"The place of magic, music and mirrors," Vincent told himself, in a moment of inspiration. He thought the words should be in a song, so he made up a verse in his head, along with a little tune. "I have escaped from the place of tears, to the place of magic, music and mirrors." He sung to himself, quietly.

Vincent mentally patted himself on the back, thinking it was pretty good. He told himself he should get drunk more often. He had another sip, and sung some more words under his breath," The Devil is in my glass, and I can't let him pass, The Devil is in my glass, and he wipes out the past." It was true, he thought, the right bar could be a magic place, if one was in the right mood, which he was. And he was going to get shit-faced if he didn't get out of there.

Vincent had not paid any attention to the bartender, nor the patrons; he had been in a world of his own. He looked around and could see he was sitting with tourists. None of them was pretty, so he arose, and walked out.

He was steady, but felt like he had to think about his motion to control it. He knew that part of his brain was anesthetized, which part he was not sure, but he was in control.

A walk on the boardwalk would clear his head. The walk did clear his head, and got his blood moving. It had all settled in his rear and feet while sitting on the stool at the bar. The ocean breeze that he loved was there and lots of little bikinis. Some were good to look at and some were not. He looked at the ones that were and it made him horny. Vincent was too tired for that sort of adventure so he headed for a motel and some sleep.

The next morning Vincent awoke hung-over. He hated this kind of morning, but knew they would all be the same. Get a drink, get dressed, get more to drink, a routine not hard to follow, for one had to. To deviate from it was unthinkable, now. Vincent sat on the edge of the bed and had a swig of cognac. It went down the wrong way and almost came back up. He had to concentrate to keep it down. Vincent washed the next one down with water, and it was all right. He felt it sooth his innards and knew he was all right for a while; as long as he did not run out of booze. He would not let that happen. He still had plenty of money, and credit cards. He showered, shaved, and left.

Vincent got hungry as soon as he was behind the wheel, so he headed for some fast food. On the way, he thought a picker-upper would be a good idea, something gentle, like a sidecar. He could only get one at a cocktail lounge, so he went in search of one. It was early, but he found one, he always managed that.

A sidecar was a civilized way to start the day. Smooth and easy, it beat the hell out of orange juice. It was made with brandy, orange flavored liqueur, and lemon juice, whipped in crushed ice. It was too cold to drink in a hurry. It was what he should drink all the time, something he couldn't drink fast. After he drank four, he realized he was no longer hungry. His stomach was frozen, anesthetized. He felt very good. He wanted to stay sober enough to drive, so he left the lounge.

Back on the road again, he headed for Monterey. When he got there, he didn't stay long. He took in the waterfront and made a pit stop at a cocktail lounge, but he was tired and depressed. He wanted to get home, but the closer he came, the more depressed he became. Vincent wondered what in the hell he was going to do when he got there. Everywhere he looked would be where Rachel used to be, where he wanted her to be.

At San Luis Obispo Vincent traded highway One for 101; he wanted to get the driving over. He was tired of running, he just wanted to sleep, and do some serious drinking. He knew he would not be able to tolerate things any other way. Vincent wanted to drink instead of think. Maybe he would be able to sleep better when he was back in his own bed; he had always had trouble in a strange one.

Vincent had never been a good traveler; strange food and strange beds had never agreed with him. He was just a creature of habit. He could stand a strange woman, though, but it was too late for that. And it would not be long before his pecker would be paralyzed, anyway. And what could be more depressing than a paralyzed pecker. He laughed at that;" The big double P," he told himself," Paralyzed Pecker" He giggled at that.

In a little while Vincent saw the Seaward exit coming into view. He was grateful, for he knew he would be home in a few minutes. When he was in his house he remembered that Rags was at the kennel. He missed him, but would not be able to get him until morning. He knew Rags would be glad to see him, for he was the only one who always was. He went into his room, undressed, and went to bed. He was weary to the bone, but he had ingested lots of alcohols since he had left, and now he was a puppet, with the god of alcohol pulling his strings; a relentless god he is. This god would do anything to perpetuate his illusion of power.

This god had been working on the line of communication between the Captain's mind, and his nerve endings. First, with the liquid from fermentation, alcohol, he had made these nerve endings feel warm, and comfortable. At the same time, with this vehicle of corruption, he was aggravating these same endings, making them sore without his knowledge, for he had anesthetized them. As soon as the anesthetic wore off, the soreness would be felt and the only relief would be more of the anesthetic, which had caused the soreness in the first place.

If the Devil was real, this must be his favorite entertainment, this enslavement. There is nothing the Devil enjoys more than torment, and his favorite enticement is the pleasure of the physical senses. Temptation is his very favorite game, and he is so very good at it. Torment was keeping the Captain from restful sleep. He would no sooner get to sleep, when the nerve endings in his innards would awaken, wanting more anesthetic. He would awaken, drink some more and put his innards at peace. This medication was also aggravating the nerve endings in the machinery of his mind causing malfunction in his thinking process.

The cartoons had returned. He had known they would come back, but he hadn't expected it so soon. It is difficult to sleep while horrid cartoons are happening on the inside of your eyelids. When Vincent did get to sleep, even with the cartoons, he had nightmares. In one of these dreams someone had poured gasoline on him while he was sleeping. He had awakened in the dream with the fumes, and the sound of a striking match. He had screamed, and awakened in a cold sweat. His life was a nightmare, awake, or asleep.

Morning came again, it always does, whether he wanted it to, or not. He groaned under his breath, "The Sun Also Rises." He awoke to the glare of the southern California sun. Vincent remembered the main character in the Hemingway novel, the title of which he had just muttered. Jake Barns had been impotent due to a war wound. The Captain was thinking that this could be an advantage, but he wondered what it would be like to never have an erection, or orgasm. He was already familiar with temporary impotence. He remembered the bag with the tube in his member, and dreaded it happening again,

First things first, though, and that was a drink. He did not need to get up for it, for the bottle was on the stand by the bed. He took a big pull and swallowed. For a second it was all right, but it bounced; he had to jump out of bed to make a beeline for the John. He vomited in the toilet with the dry heaves until he felt blue in the face and then it was over. He knew he would have to be careful, or the sickness would return. He had to have a drink, though; he would have to chase it with water until it stayed down, Vincent got a glass, put some ice in it, and by this time his hands were trembling. He put some water in the glass, and took a pull from the bottle. He was apprehensive as he waited to see what would happen.

Vincent sighed with relief as he felt the warm glow spread through his innards. He fixed another drink, and sipped it while trying to think of what to do with the morning. He felt there was something he needed to do; he sipped some more. With a start, he remembered his dog was still at the kennel. He went in to shower and get ready; he took his drink with him, and sat it on the lid of the toilet tank. When he was finished with his shower and dressing, he primed himself, and went after his dog.

Vincent hadn't seen any of his neighbors, yet and he was not looking forward to it. He knew Shelly would be mad at him as soon as she found out that he was on a drunk. She knew he was an alcoholic, for he had told her so one time when she had offered him a beer. He had declined, telling her he only drank his own beer. She had told him he shouldn't drink at all if he was an alcoholic. Every time she had seen him drinking a beer after that, she had looked at him with disdain. She knew what addiction was, for she had been a pot smoker since she was a teen; she also used pills, uppers, and downers. Her husband was on the methadone treatment.

Rags wiggled his self out of joint; he pissed on the floor; that was his way of expressing his joy. Being a dog is so simple, thought the Captain, why couldn't he have been one? Why couldn't everyone be? Wouldn't the world be a better place? Who would be the pooper-scooper, though? Who would care? He giggled at his silliness. Rags sat on the car seat like a little man; either he thought he was one, or tried to pretend. The Captain offered him a drink, but Rags closed his mouth, stopped smiling and turned his head the other way in disgust.

"Some drinking buddy you are!" exclaimed the Captain, and Rags looked back at him, apologetically; he hung his head in shame. "Its alright," soothed the Captain," I'll drink your share." Rags knew he had been forgiven; he smiled, and went back to his pretending. The Captain pushed hard on the gas pedal, throwing the dog off balance, and as the dog struggled to regain his balance, the Captain let up on the gas. Rags almost fell off the seat this time, and the Captain laughed at him. Rags gave him a dirty look and turned the other way, trying his best to look dignified. The Captain patted him on the head and was rewarded with a grateful wag, all was forgiven.

Vincent took the dog to the beach for a run. Vincent couldn't run very long, for he lacked the energy, but the dog had plenty; he ran ahead until he was almost out of sight. The Captain hid behind a big rock, and waited. He had his bottle with him, so he had a drink. In a little while he peaked around the rock to see what Rags was doing; he could see he was searching for him. Vincent stayed behind the rock, and the dog went past him with his nose in the sand. The mutt looked up, and right at him, but didn't see him, for he remained still.

Although the dog did not see him, his nose had caught something, and he was moving it up, and down, trying to read it. With his nose on the trail, the dog started to work his way over to him. His tail started to wag, and he looked up. He had a serious look on his face while he was searching, staring at the Captain, but not seeing him. The Captain got up and ran straight at Rags, yelling like a banshee. Rags was startled, but he had caught Vincent's scent. He grinned and wiggled as the Captain ran toward him and jumped over him. Rags whined, and squirmed with delight, urinating in the sand.

CHAPTER 45

Vincent saw Shelly the next day. He was sick and it was showing. He was on his way out in search of a cure, one that tasted good enough to go down without coming back up.

"You look like warmed over shit!" she exclaimed to him, sarcastically. Shelly had a colorful vocabulary, especially when she was angry over something. She was angry about his drinking, knowing it was hurting him; taking his good looks away. "What do you mean?" Vincent asked stupidly, hurt and indignant, knowing what she meant, he had looked in the mirror. "You are drunk!" she exclaimed," And you look fucking awful!" Vincent felt naked, vulnerable, ashamed, and helpless, wanting to flee from her scorn. "I'm sorry!" he wailed, "I can't help it." he pleaded and he tried to walk by her, but she stepped in his path. "That's a crock of shit!" she retorted, scornfully," Do you want to look like this when Rachel comes home?" Vincent was aghast; he was not prepared for this. "Rachel is coming home?" Vincent asked, and his heart was doing flip-flops. "Of course she is!" Shelly exclaimed, just about out of patience," I'm not going to let her live with that whore."

"When is she coming home?" he asked, fearfully. "I'm not sure, but soon," she answered, "And you had better straighten yourself out." "What difference does it make?" he groaned," She don't care about me." Shelly looked at him with exasperation. "You are a darn fool if you believe that!" she exclaimed and put her hands on he hips, "Why in Hell do you think she has spent so much time with you?" "I don't know," he answered, stupidly, his mind usurped by his need for a drink. "You have shit for brains if you don't know that she loves you!" Vincent's mind was blank; he just stood there, waiting for her to finish so he could go get a drink. "Straighten your ass up!" she commanded, vehemently, and she turned on her heels, and left. He could hear her call him derogatory names under her breath.

Vincent would have sworn he saw smoke coming out of her ears. He was scared to death of that woman; he would rather fight her husband than her. He quickly walked to the Hawk and he got in. He reached under the seat, and pulled out his bottle. He took the cap off. He started to take a drink but his nose stopped him; the odor of the cognac had turned his stomach. Vincent replaced the cap, started his vehicle, and left.

During Vincent's search for an appealing cocktail lounge, he thought of Rachel returning home. It appalled him to think of her seeing him like he was, but it was just too late. There was nothing he could do about it. He couldn't get off the booze; he knew that. He would just have to be gone when she got home, one way, or another. Vincent continued his search for an appealing lounge. He couldn't go to a dive; he knew the odor would be too much for his delicate condition. In most dives the floor doesn't get cleaned very well from the night before. Booze that had been spilled on the floor smelled better when it was still in the bottle. He found an appealing lounge east of Main Street. He parked and went in.

The bartender was a woman, one who looked like she had spent a large portion of the morning with her makeup with some degree of success. But makeup couldn't fix the large appendage that was in the center of her face. It could have been a good nose had it been on a large man. Her body was not nearly big enough for her nose, but at least it was a nice body. When she looked at him, though, her gregarious, smile hid her nose and she was strangely attractive. Her voice was throaty and sexy when she asked him what he would like. Vincent asked for a Moscow Mule; it seemed an eternity since he had drank one.

There was only three other patrons; they all looked like they were just trying to get well. They were all men. It was apparent none of them were together; they all had an empty stool between them. They were all staring at their drinks, fingering their glasses. It was a form of idolatry, and the Captain was guilty of it himself. He had spent many hours at the altar of booze, believing in its power to make him well.

"What fools we mortals be," Vincent muttered to himself as he fingered his drink, waiting for it to perform its miracle. He would wait in vain, for the good feeling had gone; in its wake was a feeling of impending doom. The booze was helping to calm his nerves, but was dissipating him at the same time. He drank a couple more mules before deciding they were not strong enough, and he switched to a double martini, a very dry one. After he took a swallow, he held some under his tongue until it numbed it. He swallowed, savoring the taste. He wondered how someone had come up with such a sophisticated combination. He ate the green olive, wondering how the person had dreamed up how to make an olive edible. Vincent remembered tasting a raw olive when he was a kid, how he had spitted it out; bitter as gall it had been.

Vincent finished his drink and ordered another. At least he was getting something to eat, he thought. Ten martinis would be ten olives. The way he felt, though, ten would put him on the floor. The thought reminded him of the story about the drunk who was lying on his back on the floor, thinking he was standing, while everyone else was lying down.

"Everything is relative," he told himself, laughing. He thought how boring life must be after walking on the moon. Or when one is rich, bought everything that was wanted, done all that was wanted, and had been everywhere one had wanted to go. He would still like to try it, though. But he had noticed possessions had meant less to him since he had started his search into the metaphysical.

Vincent cursed his luck. If only he could have found peace with Rachel he might have been able to finish with the Tower, but he knew he would not. In his drunk and depressed state he could not see how he could face life without her, and he could not see how he could get past this binge. He knew he was being foolish, but he could not help himself. He got up to go to the John, realizing he had been going more than usual. He felt like his bladder would float away, but when he urinated, only a small amount came out, leaving him a feeling that he still needed to go. He wondered if he was already in trouble as he walked back to his stool.

After six martinis and six olives, he decided he had better leave while he was still able to drive. He did not want to be stopped by a cop. He had been in jail before and there was no booze there. The thought of no booze was a frightful one; he knew he would go through withdrawal without it. He thanked God he wasn't going to run out, and then he cursed himself for being blasphemous. Vincent decided God could not do anything to him, anyway, for he was already in Hell. He ordered another drink, one for the road, the last one. As he drank, he wondered if God had created the fermentation process, the source of all booze.

Vincent wondered if Mary Baker Eddy could be right about her idea of all creation being mental. He tried to comprehend the idea, but his brain cells were floating in a sea of booze. He had thought about it before, and it had almost made sense to him. He could not see through God's eyes, though, for he was having a Hell of a time seeing through his own. He pushed his thoughts back to the martini.

Vincent couldn't stop his thoughts, and he thought how nice it would be to live in a city with streets paved with gold; to not have to worry about pain, sickness, or death; to not have to worry about hunger, bad weather, war, pestilence, or bad breath. He giggled about the bad breath. He giggled some more when he thought about not having to worry about farting, or going to the John.

This kind of thinking was putting him in a better mood; he finished his drink, and ordered another. Vincent thought about Heaven again. He thought there must be no matter there, for wherever there is matter there is danger. If there was no matter there couldn't be any bodies, no female ones, no kind. That just couldn't be true, he thought, there must be different kinds of bodies; heavenly bodies.

Vincent giggled when he wondered what it would be like to feel up a heavenly body, one wearing a gossamer gown. He wondered what could be under the gown; there couldn't be a pussy there. What would a pussy be doing in Heaven? The thought tickled him so he spewed a mouthful of his drink on the bar. Vincent couldn't get the thought of feeling up a heavenly body out of his mind. He wondered what he would be feeling for if he knew nothing was there. He guessed he would just be doing it out of habit.

Vincent was in such stitches he could hardly breathe. When he got himself under control, he thought some more; how he had taken his feeler-upper habit to Heaven with nothing there to feel up. He would have to imagine that a heavenly body had something to feel up, or Heaven would be Hell. Then he would have to masturbate and then he remembered he would have nothing to masturbate with, for what in the Hell would a penis be doing in Heaven?

Vincent thought there would be a lot of old sayings that just wouldn't work in Heaven: " No pain, no gain," " What goes up, must come down," " Better late than never," That's a Hell of a note," " You can't take it with you," " It's hotter than Hell," "The only thing that is sure is death and taxes.

Vincent's mood was over as soon as he had laughed himself out. He was never going to make it to Heaven, anyway. He was going to the other place, where all his friends would be. His mother wouldn't be there, though. That was a sobering thought, and his sister wouldn't be there either. What could he do? He couldn't go to both places. And it was his belief that it was a one-way ticket. Maybe he should just have his body frozen for a future return to make things right. But he believed eternity would not be enough time to do that.

Vincent felt as old as an Antediluvian. He rose on unsteady feet, his thoughts getting darker by the minute; he could only see despair ahead. He left the bar, and headed for his wheels. His body ached, his feet, leaden. His bladder burned, and he felt bloated. He didn't know how soon he would get so ill he would not be able to get out and it worried him. Nothing could be as bad as not being able to get out for more booze.

When he got to his wheels he drove straight to the nearest liquor store so he could stock up. He bought another case of cognac and a bottle of Benedictine to sweeten it, just in case the cognac started to taste raunchy.

Vincent's depression grew deeper as he drove home. He hated his life and everything about it. Life meant nothing when one can't hang on to love. He had known great love, but it had always slipped away; it felt almost as if he had never had it. Had it all been an illusion? Torment raised a pain in his chest that creped up his throat, into his jaw, to his teeth, to his ears, swelling his tear ducts to overflowing.

When Vincent was at his front door, he had to find the keyhole with his fingers, for he could not see well enough through the tears. He sat the booze on the couch, and headed straight for Rachel's picture. He held it in his hand like an idol and that was what it was. He kissed it and cried her name. Vincent knew very well, even in his drunken state, that loving this girl so much was insane; at least not normal. So he guessed he was nuts. A sane man would not be in love with a woman a girl was going to be. To love the girl like a daughter at the same time was truly nuts.

Vincent had been sure to lose no matter what he did. The girl would not accept his fatherly love and by the time she got old enough for him, he would be senile, or dead. He gazed at her picture, torturing himself, drinking until he fell asleep sitting there. When he awoke due to a bladder alarm, it was twilight. After he relieved himself, the burning was still there. He thought it might be a virus, which was more comforting than thinking his bladder was haywire. Vincent felt like the walls were closing in on him. "Cabin fever," he had heard it called by old timers.

Vincent looked out the window to see if he could get away without being accosted. With the coast clear, he grabbed a bottle, stuck it under his coat, and made his escape. He almost tripped over Rags as the dog did a mad dash between his legs to get out of the house. Vincent felt guilty about the way he had neglected his little friend. They both got into the Hawk, and Vincent drove off like the Grim Reaper was after him, wanting to look over his shoulder like a fugitive, but he didn't look back, remembering Lot's wife. He headed straight for the beach and his favorite rock.

The tide had come in and the beach was gone, with the ocean splashing six feet below his rock. The spray was getting on him, and felt good. It was his favorite place, and he knew God must be there, but he knew he would not find favor with Him. He was not aware that God was looking for lost souls, not safe ones. The booze had put a mist between him and the truth he had learned in the study of metaphysics, but the truth was still there, and no amount of booze could wash it away,

Vincent was being purged of the sin that was in him. God was not doing it to him; he was doing it to himself, for he had a need to make himself suffer. He was not aware that he could purge himself by being and seeing good. His subconscious believed he had to see and do evil, and suffer for it to be purged. He was doing a thorough job of it; he had practiced it, he had been wearing the sackcloth since he was seventeen years old.

Vincent laid on the rock, lamenting over Rachel. He drank his cognac until he passed out, or went to sleep; it was getting hard to tell the difference. Vincent was on his back, but he rolled over, almost off the rock, on the ocean side. He rolled right to the edge and stopped, flat on his stomach. He stayed in this position until a breaker broke on the rocks below and splashed cold water right over the top of him. It startled him and he jumped the wrong way. He slid off the end of the rock, almost in the same way he had slid off the boat landing, head first.

Vincent was falling and was instantly sober. He had not time to think before the first pain had hit him, and his fear was greater than the pain. He was bouncing off the rocks with his arms out in front of him, trying to ward off the blows, but he was out of balance. The first bounce knocked the wind out of him, and then he bounced again; and then he was in the ocean. The same fear he had felt in the Sacramento River consumed him. For a moment he gave into it, like one accepting his fate, and then he fought for his life, thrashing, searching for something to grab onto.

Vincent heard another breaker coming, and he searched, frantically. Something touched his hand, and it felt like metal. He clung to it for life. When the breaker hit him, it felt like a wet giant had jumped on him. It pulled at him so hard he felt like it would pull his arms out of their sockets. He hung on, knowing that if he should let go, he would be a Neptune's corpse. When the breaker had gone, most of his strength had gone with it, but he struggled and climbed back up on the rocks, to the road, to the Hawk.

The dog wiggled, and whined all the way. Vincent opened the door, and sat behind the wheel, with Rags sitting next to him. He hurt all over, but knew nothing had been broken. It had been a miracle that he had not been knocked out. He shook his head, ruefully, for there had been his chance for the ultimate escape, but he had not taken it, for fear had ruled his will. He started to shake from the shock and cold, his teeth were chattering.

Vincent needed a drink, but the ocean had stolen his jug. When he got himself under control, he grabbed his flashlight, thinking the bottle might still be at hand, and he wanted to see what he had grabbed hold of. With the light he could see that it had been a "NO PARKING" sign that had been hit by a vehicle and knocked down to the beach. The cement end of it had been buried in the sand by the surf.

"That sign could have been anywhere!" Vincent exclaimed to himself in awe. He believed that God had saved him again. Then he got pessimistic and convinced himself that it had probably been dumb luck, for why would God want to save a worthless drunk? Right now he needed a drink more than anything, so he went back to the Hawk, for he hadn't seen his bottle anywhere.

Vincent's legs were weak, and he staggered. While his balance was off he twisted his right ankle and fell. He groaned and tried to get up, but couldn't. He tried to get into the Hawk, but he got a Charley Horse in the back of his right thigh. His shivering made the cramp worse, for he couldn't relax the muscle. The pain was so intense he cursed and groaned. He laid waiting for the muscle to relax, afraid to move, for the cramp was lurking, waiting like a demon for him to make a false move. Vincent moved his leg to see if he could, but he could feel Charley returning. His stomach was crawling with withdrawal worms, but he had to wait.

Vincent lay shaking, with teeth chattering for what seemed like forever. The asphalt was hard, his body hurt and his need for a drink made him try to get up. He had to be careful, for he couldn't pull the offending leg up underneath him, or put any weight on it, for the stress could pull the muscle back into a knot. Vincent managed to get up on one leg, and open the door of the Hawk. To make matters worse, his good leg felt like it was going to rebel and he just had to get off it. He couldn't get into position to sit, for he knew his leg would cramp in that position. He laid, face down, on the seat, and slid himself in. He laid with his feet sticking out the door, grateful there was no traffic.

It was about an hour before Vincent felt safe to move. He managed to get into a sitting position, but his leg still felt testy, too much to risk trying to operate the accelerator. He turned on the stereo, and tuned in some sad music. Vincent tired of it, turned it off and went back to some positively, negative thinking. Now Vincent was kicking himself for not taking the chance to escape all this bullshit; all this misery that life was all about. But he had been a coward. His mind was so screwed up on booze he didn't realize that it had not been cowardice, but the natural instinct to survive. He had saved himself, but for what?

Vincent finally was able to drive himself home. As soon as he made it through the door, he made a beeline to his cognac. He drank and waited for the shaking, and quivering to subside. In just a few moments the cognac was doing its job. He had another drink and went into his room to get out of his wet clothes. He had to strip to his birthday suit. He looked at himself in the mirror. His penis, shrunk from being cold, and wet, looked as impotent as a balloon that had lost its air. He put his robe on to cover his ugliness. After a closer look at himself, he realized he looked like he had been beaten. There were bruises, and lacerations on his face, and arms. His legs were also bruised, and skinned. He felt like he had been run over by an eighteen-wheeler. Vincent felt exhausted; he felt like he would die if he went to sleep, but he just had to. To die while asleep would not be so bad. He had an awful time trying to go to sleep, even with his eyelids feeling so heavy he could hardly keep them open, but he had to force them to keep them closed. The first part of closing went all right, but the last little slit seemed to be connected to a spring that kept them popping open. When Vincent did get to sleep, it was fitful with a duration of only a couple of hours.

The devil named "legion" awoke him, clutching at his innards, demanding fuel for the fire that was consuming him. His need popped his eyes open, and waking did not please him, for he would have liked to sleep forever. Vincent's mind was crystal clear and his world was a hostile place; there was nothing he wanted from it except escape. He was shivering, his teeth were chattering again; he was cold to the marrow of his bones. His heart was cold and his blood felt languid, almost frozen in its channels. He sat up, and grabbed his bottle; he drank a big slug, and it bounced. He just made it to the John before gagging with the dry heaves. He gagged until he thought he would turn inside out.

After his stomach had settled down, he made a drink, lacing it with Benedictine. It smelled good and he sipped on it, the sweet, tangy flavor went down easy. Vincent sipped himself to sleep. He slept for another two hours and awoke again, starting the whole scenario again. He repeated this act until six the next morning. It was time for the skid-row bars to open, the ones he knew in Oxnard. He liked to go to dives when he was in this condition; it was comforting to find someone who was in worse condition than he was, and misery loves company.

Vincent arose, tidied himself and had a few more drinks. He drove to Oxnard, parked, and went into a dive that would not have been inviting to most, but looked like an oasis to him. The odors insulted his olfactory as he walked in, but it gave him a perverse pleasure to degrade himself when he was in this condition. The joint was full of assorted bottle worshipers, a den of woe and false cheer. Some of the voices were suffering from years of alcohol erosion, sounding coarse, and irritating. One had reached a kind of attractive sound, like the voice of David Jannsen, the actor, one of Vincent's favorite.

One voice had reached a metallic sound; he was talking into a little black box via a hole in his throat. He was doing a good job, but sounded like a robot. Vincent watched him out of the corner of his eye as he walked over and sat next to him. The guy was smoking a cigar, drinking straight shots of whiskey, defying and tempting the grim reaper. He looked to be about seventy, going on fifty. His hair was gray and so was his face. He was talking about the good old days to a crony sitting next to him. It was a common subject for drunks, the good old days, but most of them had really been bad. They only seemed good, for today was even worse. For most of them their days were going to get even worse.

While the Tin Man talked, the bartender headed Vincent's way. He was a heavy dude, looked like a retired wrestler. He said not a word when he stopped in front of Vincent; he just waited for his order. He was probably afraid if he said anything he would have to listen to another sad story. He had a bored look on his face; he had heard all of the sad stories. Vincent ordered cognac with a water chaser.

"We don't have any cognac," answered the bored bartender, "Could your taste buds tolerate some Christian Brother's brandy?" Vincent didn't answer directly; the Tin Man had looked his way and their eyes had met. Vincent didn't say anything, he just gave the bartender an equally bored look, shook his head in the affirmative, pointing his finger at the Tin Man, indicating he was also buying him a drink, which the bartender brought.

"This one is on the governor," the bartender told Tin Man, and he pointed at the Captain, The Captain gulped his drink and chased it with water. Tin Man looked at his drink, took a sip, holding it up, as in a toast. "Thanks," he said," But I don't need any charity," "I don't give a shit what you need!" retorted Vincent, "I just wanted to buy someone a drink, anyone." Tin Man warmed to him then, and the Captain was sorry he had spoken to him, for now he was telling him his life story in nine hundred pages, through the metal box.

It was creepy, raising the hair on the back of Vincent's neck. He asked Vincent who he was. "I'm Captain Moon," he answered, hoping Tin Man would think he was strange and leave him alone, but Tin Man remembered being a corporal in W. W. 2. He proceeded to tell the Captain how he had helped to win it. All the Captain's sociability left him. He felt sorry for Tin Man, but sorrier for himself. He didn't want to listen, he just wanted to get drunk enough to live, or was it drunk enough to die?

CHAPTER 46

The Captain drank all day and night. The next morning when he awoke, he knew he was in trouble, at the tail end of his rope. His stomach was hurting, his bladder burning and he had a pain in his chest. He tried to belch the pain away, and the bloated feeling, but to no avail. Vincent tried to urinate, but could only dribble. He wished he had saved some of the catheter tubes, for he could have drained himself. He wondered where he could buy some tubing that would work; he was sure he could not buy catheters without a prescription. He knew regular tubing would not work; the end would be sharp. Catheters had rounded ends.

Vincent believed he had two choices; he could drink and die, or he could quit drinking and die. He had to decide which way would cause him the most suffering. Withdrawal symptoms made his choice and he drank. He knew that if he didn't die he would end up in the hospital. There, they would put him in bed and feed him through an I. V. Then they would give him drugs to ward off withdrawal, but they would not give him as much as he needed. They would give him enough to get him hooked on the drugs they were giving him, starting the whole damned merry-go-round again. Vincent wanted no part of that; he had had enough. He continued to drink, going deeper into depression, deep enough for death to become attractive, even tempting.

Vincent was aware that his bladder was swelling from the excess urine that could not find its way out. Vincent knew he would not be able to tolerate the pain, or the horror of waiting for his bladder to burst. He had always been terrified of internal bleeding and that would be the way he would die. With his mind warped by depression, he resigned himself to die, but he didn't know how to do it. A gun would disfigure him, for he would have to shoot himself in the head or risk a slow death. He had no poison, and knew he wouldn't be able to take it if he had.

In his warped sense, Vincent rationalized that he might be able to bleed himself to death if he could control it. He could not control internal bleeding, but he could control external. He drank some more as he thought about it. He wept as he realized he would have to die before seeing Rachel again and that was the worst punishment of all, but he surely deserved it. He got up and went into the kitchen. He pulled his French knife out of the rack. It was sharp as a razor; he had kept it that way with an oilstone, a habit he had learned while a cook in the service. Vincent sat on the floor by the couch with his bottle and the knife. He drew the edge of the blade lightly across the inside of his wrist, watching the tiny beads of blood form a trail. He tried it again on the other wrist, but he could not muster the courage to press harder on the blade.

Vincent drank some more in an effort to bolster his courage. He went back to the first wrist and pressed a little harder. Bigger beads of blood started showing. In a perverse way he was enjoying the desecration of himself. He moved to the upper side of his wrist and made some shallow gashes. He was getting bloody, but he knew it would take forever to bleed to death this way, at this rate.

Vincent looked to see if the scar was still there where he had branded himself with Greta's initials so many years ago. He had to strain his eyes to see it, but it was still there. His mind traveled back to the first time they had made love. He wondered where his youth had gone. Vincent knew it had gone down the drain and with no meaning whatsoever. He drank some more and dozed off with the knife in his hand, nestled in his lap.

Shelly was worried about Vincent. She knew he had been drinking, visibly, dissipating himself. She had a special feeling for him, knowing he was a kind, and good person, one who had shown much affection for her children, even though his obsession with Rachel had caused her considerable grief. She could not hold it against him. She knew how difficult and possessive love could be. Shelly's marriage had been that way. She had married when she was only fifteen because she had been pregnant. Shelly had been tired of her marriage for many years, but she loved Marcus. She knew that without her, he would have nothing, and be alone. This was not an ego thing on her part; it was just the truth. Marcus didn't make friends and he didn't want her to make any either; he was jealous of anyone she liked, including his own children. This was one of the reasons there was so much friction between Marcus and Rachel; he was jealous of her bond with her mother.

Rachel had been a premature birth; she had almost died. This near tragedy had formed a bond between her and her mother, attaching them with an emotional umbilical cord. Rachel was much like her mother, in looks and temperament. She had the same volatile, temper; she had the same vulnerable innocence, mixed with a defensive guile.

Shelly decided it was time to check on Vincent, so she went to his door and knocked. The door was ajar when she hit it and it opened, slightly. She pushed it a little further and called his name. None of his lights were on, and it was getting dark. He didn't answer and her intuition moved her forward into his living room.

At first Shelly didn't see him because of the dimness and because he was sitting on the floor. He had his back against the couch. She called again, but he didn't move. She could see him, now, see that he was asleep; he was snoring, softly. Shelly stood looking at him, waiting for her eyes to get use to the dimness. When her eyes adjusted, she spotted the knife resting in his lap. She turned on the light, and she cursed when she saw the blood. She was shocked, frightened and furious all at once. She had to resist the compulsion to kick him. She shook him, instead and not gently. Vincent jumped like he had been shot. His eyes had a frightened, animal look for a second, until he recognized her. He remembered what he had been doing, looked down at his mess, and cowered in shame. She grabbed the knife in anger.

"What in the Hell are you trying to do?" she shouted and he got maudlin. "I'm trying to die before I get sick," he answered," I don't want Rachel to see me this way." he wailed, "But I don't know why," he added," She doesn't care about me." Shelly was getting madder by the minute. She knew that if he did do himself in, Rachel would blame herself and she was already having enough trouble with her. "That is such bullshit" she retorted, vehemently. "She told me so." he cried. "For Christ sake!" she exclaimed, with her voice up several octaves," She is just a little girl. She doesn't know what she is saying; she doesn't even know what she is feeling. She has taken a lot of crap over you that she would not have if she didn't care for you. So don't you lay this load on her; she would never forgive herself. Is that what you want?" Shelly turned and left; she was so angry she was afraid she would kick him if she stayed. She took the knife with her, knowing he had others.

A little while later Shelly decided she would call Rachel and see if she could get her to tell Vincent that she still cared for him. She thought this would be the only thing that would help him. She went to the phone and dialed Rachel's number. It was Vincent's phone and had a long cord. When Rachel answered, Shelly told her Vincent was ill and needed her to tell him she still cared for him. Rachel was confused, for she had not really meant what she had said to him; he had pressed her at a time that was bad for her, and she had blurted it out, and had hung up to keep from saying anymore.

Vincent was still sitting on the floor; he was thinking. The thought had never entered his mind that Rachel would blame herself for what he had almost done. He was appalled by his own insensitivity, feeling even more remorse, and shame. He had to straighten himself out, but had no idea how. He fixed a drink and sat on the couch. He was trying to get his mind to function when Shelly handed him the phone.

"It's Rachel," she told him, and he was confused; he had been oblivious to her call, lost in thought. A flash of fear went across his haggard face. "Rachel?" Vincent asked, bewildered. "She wants to talk to you," Shelly told him and Vincent held the phone, staring at it, not knowing what to say. "Rachel?" he finally asked, meekly, "I'm sorry," she told him, with contrition," I didn't mean what I told you on the phone." "I only hoped you would love me someday," he told her, so emotional it was all he could do to speak. "I do." she told him, with her voice changing from contrite to sincere, a plea for him to believe, "But I just don't know how to say it to your face."

"I can say it to you, though," he answered," And I do love you, but you have always known that," "I know," she answered, apologetically. "I miss you something awful!" he exclaimed, but softly, his words inadequate to express his feelings. "Me too, she replied, and he wished he could crawl through the phone line to touch her. He was averse to losing contact with her, but Shelly wanted the phone. Vincent knew this episode had been painful for Rachel and Shelly was probably thinking the same thing, "I'll let you talk to your mother now," he told Rachel. "Thanks for caring, goodbye." "Goodbye," answered Rachel. With a sigh, Vincent surrendered the phone to Shelly, reluctantly. Shelly assured her daughter that Vincent would be all right, said a few more words to her and hung up the phone. She shook her finger at Vincent. "You straighten yourself out, so you will be well when she comes home!" she ordered on her way out. "I will," Vincent told her, sincerely, but with little conviction.

Shelly was gone and Vincent was alone again with the truth. He knew that will power and good intentions would not work; they had not worked in the past. His will power lasted for about an hour and then he had to have a drink for his nerves. He had a sip, but a sip was not enough, so he sipped until the bottle was empty. He went to the John to urinate, but had little success. The pain in his chest was worsening. Between the bladder swelling, and the alcohol, induced colitis, he was running out of room in his abdominal cavity to breathe.

Vincent suffered through the night and by the next morning he felt like he was having a heart attack. He was feeling like he was not getting enough oxygen, feeling like he might pass out. He knew he couldn't drive anywhere, or even walk out of the house, so he called an ambulance. He tried to be calm while waiting, breathing in short respirations, carefully, fearful of hyperventilating, which would make him feel worse.

Vincent didn't want to die, not now, not after Rachel had told him that she loved him. He prayed, for he wanted to live to see Rachel again, knowing she might blame herself if he did not live. He sat and waited; he could not lie down. He felt like he couldn't breathe in that position. He tried to involve his mind in the Twenty Third Psalm, but it was subordinated to his fear.

When the ambulance arrived, three attendants came to his door. They were polite, and professional, checking his blood pressure, and pulse right away, talking to him, calming him at the same time. They gave him oxygen and when they found he wouldn't be able to walk, they brought a stretcher and carefully put him on it. While they were getting him out the door, Shelly came. She was worried, and afraid for him, but tried to assure him he would be okay, that God would take care of him. Vincent thought this was odd coming from this woman who could rant the vilest language he had ever heard come out of a woman's mouth. He wondered what in the world was she doing talking about God. He was thinking this in a self-righteous manner.

On the way to the ambulance, Shelly's children watched. He was thinking there would be no secrets on this street, for everyone would know. He was trying to think good thoughts, but it was hard for him to think while on his back. It was even hard when he was feeling good. He grimaced at that thought, thinking that the only time he felt good was when he was drinking, or full of Valium. He would have sold his soul for a shot of Valium. He surmised they would be doing that soon and he'd be hooked on it again, as soon as it entered his blood stream. He didn't care at this stage. All he wanted now was escape from the suffering. In his heart he knew there would be no escape, only temporal relief.

Forever had passed by the time they had arrived at the hospital, where they took him straight to emergency. After the swollen bladder was discovered, the doctor put the catheter in him to drain him. Vincent was extremely nervous, but was told he could not have anything for it until after the draining. The pain that was in him was following the urine on its way out his penis,

"I'll bet that feels good," commented the doctor. "You better believe it!" exclaimed Vincent, but this was nothing new to him, he had been down this road before. The doctor closed the tube with a clamp. "We can't let it all out at once," explained the doctor, "It might cause you to go into shock." "I know," answered Vincent and the doctor looked at him askance. "You have been through this before?" he asked, with a raised eyebrow. "A few years ago", Vincent admitted, feeling ashamed. "For the same reason?" asked the doctor, incredulous, and he took the clamp off the hose.

The doctor had seen many drunks before, but he had never seen one with such a full bladder. Vincent shook his head in the affirmative, ashamed, thinking what a fool he must appear to be. The doctor shook his head in the negative. "If you don't stop this," he warned, "You will be wearing a bag on your leg for the rest of your life. And your life might be very short." He shook his head again and continued. "Your bladder came close to rupturing and if it had, you probably would have died, and a ghastly death it would have been."

Vincent cringed, thinking about it. He pictured it in his mind, feeling the blood filling his abdominal cavity. He blanched and the doctor noticed. He told Vincent they were almost finished. When the draining was finished, the doctor measured the urine, and shook his head, "This must be some kind of record," the doctor commented to the attendant. "I never saw anything like it," he answered. "You feel better now?" the doctor asked Vincent, " Better, but I'm awful nervous," he answered. "Have you had Valium?" asked the doctor, and Vincent told him he had, "I'll give you a shot in a few minutes," the doctor told him and left.

In a little while a nurse came and gave him a shot of Valium. She was pretty, which was a pleasant surprise; he had been expecting an ugly one, thinking it would be his luck. In a few moments the Valium was dissolving his withdrawal symptoms. He was aware of the price he would have to pay; he had been through this before.

Vincent knew they would be looking in his bladder with that awful instrument of torture, but he was at the point of not caring what they did to him, just as long as they kept him full of Valium and alive. He was aware the shot would wear off long before time for another and he would have to suffer between shots. At least he would be okay for a little while. A couple of orderlies took him to a ward next to I. C. U. He would be monitored. He heard one say he had been put on a seizure alert, but he didn't know what it meant and didn't want to know. They hooked him to the I. V. and the monitor, put side rails up on his bed and left.

Vincent wondered what the rails were for; they were about a foot high. He noticed they had been raised after pushing a button at both ends. He wondered if a seizure was anything like a convulsion and he worried about it. Vincent rose up, tried to lift the rail, not liking the confined feeling. It was a little like being in jail. He couldn't get the strength, or the coordination, to push in the buttons and down on the rail at the same time. Vincent gave up; he decided if he were going to escape, he would have to climb over the rail. Anyway, it was better than being in a straight jacket.

Exhaustion and the comfort of the Valium lulled Vincent to sleep. He hadn't slept for long when he was awakened and it was a rude awakening. The ugliest woman he had ever seen informed him it was time for his bath. She wasn't just big and ugly; she was meaner than a junkyard dog. She even had a mustache and he would have bet anything she had at least half a penis hanging between her legs. She looked like she should have been a drill sergeant. God was truly cruel sometimes.

"I'm too, tired to take a bath." Vincent complained. "That's alright, honey," she told him. She was enjoying herself, "If you are too tired to do it yourself, I will do it for you. Now won't that be fun?" "I'll do it myself," he retorted, hoping he would be able. She unhooked him from the I. V. and monitor and helped him into a wheelchair. She took him to a bathroom with a large tub with handrails. She ran the water while he waited. Vincent was praying she would let him undress himself, knowing he would not be a pretty sight. He knew his penis had probably shrunk out of sight. He didn't know why it shrunk so much when he was in this shape. Maybe it knew it wasn't good for anything at these times and was ashamed.

Even as bad as he felt, Vincent still wished he could have an erection. He missed the pleasant sensation every time his thoughts, or instinct, stimulated it. He was a sensual man; he did not want that to change. Vincent had realized, though, that sex was more trouble than it was worth, usually. He believed sex was just another form of escape, surrendering to body and orgasm. When it was over, one was left with nothing, having accomplished nothing, unless one was trying to cause a pregnancy. And in a short time one would just want to do it again; it was just like an addiction. Vincent knew he didn't have to worry about getting an erection with this nurse; she couldn't give him one, not even if he was healthy, not even if she was the last woman on earth, and he was to be shot at sunrise.

After the awful nurse had helped him and his wilted appendage into the tub, he was glad to be taking a bath, for he was sure he must smell like a whore house latrine, but he was weak, for the Valium was wearing off. When he was through with the bath, a male nurse fitted him with a catheter and bag and wheeled him back to his prison.

Vincent was feeling worse every day. The Valium wore off at least two hours before the next shot. He was spending much of his time going through withdrawal, watching the clock, waiting for his next fix. Again, he had traded the false god alcohol, for another, Valium. He knew neither of these gods had the power to save him; they would only prolong his suffering.

Death seemed Vincent's only escape from this dilemma. But he couldn't die and lay a guilt trip on Rachel. He couldn't die when he knew she loved him. He wouldn't be able to help her if he was dead. He had no escape; he would have to suffer and live through his familiar nightmare again. He didn't know if he could, for he felt like his substance was slipping away. It seemed like the only substance he had left was coming from a needle.

After three days Vincent was still on the I. V. He was feeling even worse, weaker. On the fourth morning the bed that was next to his was empty, the man had died during the night. That afternoon, another man moved in. He was an alcoholic, about thirty years old. His eyeballs were yellow and so was his face. His skin looked dry and leathery. The doctor had told him that his liver had almost stopped functioning. He had blond curly hair and would have been handsome had he been another color; yellow was not a good color for a face.

But he was still stronger than Vincent. He was a chain smoker and ate everything that was put in front of him. He didn't act sick at all; he just looked that way. Vincent knew different, though, this guy was more yellow than Spider had been when he had died. This guy was truly not long for this world, and there isn't any other. Steve was the guy's name. Vincent had heard his wife call him that when she came to visit him. She was pretty, petite, with curly, dark hair; it was obvious that she loved him. They talked constantly about their children. Steve told Vincent that all he cared about was raising his two sons and after he had done that he was going to go on one last drunk. Steve was just an empty container waiting to be filled. Vincent thought there wasn't much difference between Steve and himself, except Steve was yellow.

It was time for the stainless steel pistol to be shoved into his penis again and he was scared to death of that thing. It went easier this time, though, for they had filled his bladder with some kind of pain killing solution, but the stress had weakened Vincent. On top of that they had decided he needed to be purged; they wanted to take some pictures of his innards. They gave him the purging mix that night; it turned every thing in his bowels to a burning liquid, and he spent most of the night sitting on the throne. The next morning, before breakfast, even before his precious drug, they took him in for the pictures.

Vincent had to drink a huge glass of pink liquid that tasted like chalk before taking the pictures. By the time they had finished Vincent felt so weak he thought he would pass out. He needed the Valium even more, but they were not yet through with him. He was informed they were going to fill his bladder with water until he felt like he couldn't hold anymore; they wanted to see how well his valve was functioning. When they got him to the lab where it was to be done and they told him he would have to wait an hour, Vincent rebelled.

"There is no way you are going to do anymore to me until I have my shot!" he exclaimed," No way in Hell!" "But we have you scheduled," argued the technician. "Screw your schedule," retorted Vincent. "You don't have to get nasty about it!" answered the technician, with hostility, and Vincent reflected his hostility. "Screw you, screw this hospital, the doctor and screw the administration," answered Vincent vehemently.

After he had said it, they moved him in the wheel chair, back out into the hall and took another patient in. He sat for an hour, seething and cursing before the doctor came, and he was impatient with Vincent's attitude. "You are not the only patient I have," the doctor scolded, and Vincent was totally out of patience; he was tired of saying screw you. "Well up yours!" he retorted," You are the only doctor I seem to have, and I am the only one who knows how I feel, and if you don't care how I feel, well screw you with a capital S."

The doctor softened, knowing how Vincent was suffering, but it was his responsibility to wean him off the drug; he could see that Vincent had tolerated it about as long as he could.

"Try to relax," the doctor told him, apologetically, "I will have a shot brought to you right away." Thanks," answered Vincent with contrition, "I'm sorry I blew my stack." The doctor smiled, and walked away. In a few minutes a nurse came and gave him his shot of holy Valium. An orderly wheeled him back to the ward and back to his bed. In a little while he was dreaming he was walking with Rachel. She was an adult, as tall as he was. They were holding hands as they walked. They walked into a house; it must have been hers. Rachel asked him if he wanted some tea. He told her he did. They held hands every chance they got and talked like they were sweethearts. And then he awoke. What a disappointment it was to wake from such a sweet dream into harsh reality.

The shot of Valium was running out of steam. Vincent waited with dread. He wondered if he would ever escape from this squirrel run. He remembered the other times he had made it through this, but this time he felt worse, and he was older. But he had to hang on for Rachel. Someday she would grow into a beautiful woman and he wanted to be there to see her. Vincent had his shots for the rest of the day and night, suffering through the intervals. The next morning the nurse came with two capsules instead of his shot. Vincent looked at the capsules with disdain.

"What's this?" Vincent asked with alarm. "The doctor has changed you to oral medication, so you can give it to yourself when you leave," the nurse told him cheerfully. "Is it Valium?" Vincent asked, hopefully. "No, but it is a sister to it," she answered. Vincent was already into withdrawal and he had the sinking feeling of impending doom. There was no doubt in his mind that the capsules would be worthless; he swallowed them and waited for the confirmation of his suspicion. He waited and nothing happened, except for a bad taste in his mouth; the capsules had no affect on him. He was going deeper into withdrawal; he could feel what little strength he had left running out of him. Fear was clutching him like a demon.

Vincent tolerated it for about an hour and then he buzzed for the nurse; it seemed it took forever for her to get to him. He informed hey that the capsules had done him no good and he needed a shot. She told him she was not authorized to give it to him, but in three hours she could give him some more of the capsules,

"I will be dead in three hours" he exclaimed in distress, and he truly believed that he would. "I'm sure you are exaggerating," retorted the nurse, with little sympathy," Just try to relax," she told him, and she left. Vincent knew he was up the creek without a paddle. The more hopeless he became, the more agitated. He blanched, his blood pressure was rising. His pulse was erratic. He tried to get out of bed, but couldn't, for he was too weak. He thought it must have been the capsules; he felt worse than he ever had. He could feel his innards filling with hot gas; it felt like his gall bladder was pumping him full of it. It seemed like the more he belched, the more it pumped. He felt prickly sensations all over his body. He felt like he was not getting enough oxygen, but was afraid of hyperventilating.

Vincent wanted to press the buzzer again, but knew it would be fruitless. He gave in to despair and wept, but it only made him feel worse. He tried to think of God. There was no one left but God, but He seemed to be not relevant out there, or up there, somewhere. Vincent was certain that God had saved him before, but why had he saved him for this? Why? What was he going to learn from this that he didn't already know? Was he supposed to be learning to not be afraid of death? To trust no matter what? Maybe that was it, but he was afraid to die and he couldn't believe that he wasn't going to and he could not see why God would want to save him.

Laying on his back, Vincent began to feel weird, like his body was undulating and rising, "This must be it," he told himself, "This must be what dying feels like," Too tired to fight the feeling, he surrendered to it. He felt like he arose about a foot and was hovering above his Mattress. Vincent opened his eyes and it looked like he was. He wondered if it was an illusion. He exchanged that thought for one about death; he wondered how long it would take for oblivion and peace.

But Vincent didn't want oblivion, or peace, he just wanted to be alive. He just had to see Rachel again. Vincent turned over in mid air, grabbed hold of the edge of the mattress and pulled himself back down. Then he had a sinking feeling; he was sinking into the mattress. He closed his eyes and the feeling became worse. This was just too, frightening. Vincent frantically searched for the buzzer, and pressed it. He waited in terror, as he sank further into the mattress. He grabbed hold of the seizure bar, and hung on for life. Vincent felt like he was getting heavier. He felt like there was a huge magnet on the other side of the mattress, drawing him through it. He knew oblivion was on the other side.

"What's wrong?" asked the nurse, impatiently. "I'm falling through the mattress." he exclaimed in terror. "That can't be true," she told him, calmly, as she tried to free one of his hands from the rail so she could take his vital signs," Let go!" she ordered, and he did, holding tighter with the other hand. "Try to be calm," she told him as she was putting her paraphernalia away," While I go after the doctor."

Vincent cursed her under his breath for expecting him to be calm. How could anyone be calm while sinking into oblivion? "Screw it! Vincent exclaimed, weakly and he let go of the seizure bar and let himself sink. The sinking feeling changed to one of falling. He was falling into a black nothingness. Vincent felt as if his substance was separating, like his molecules were spinning off into space. He wanted to scream, but he was afraid the effort would drain him of his last drop of protoplasm, and he would vanish into oblivion.

CHAPTER 47

Rob Snowden, from United Metaphysical Research, had been worried about Vincent; he had not heard from him since their meeting. Rob's intuition had told him that Vincent was in a bad way, both mentally and physically. After some research, he had typed out a lesson he thought would help him with his problem. He had called Vincent's number and Shelly had answered; she had been cleaning Vincent's place in anticipation of him coming home. She had told Rob that Vincent was in the hospital and had told him which one. When Snowden found Vincent in an agitated state, he sat in a chair across from his bed. Vincent didn't see him and Rob didn't announce himself; he wanted to do some metaphysical work first. Quietly, he tried to image Vincent as God saw him, as a spiritual being, rather than a biological one. When this was clear in his mind, he started to recite the first part of his lesson, which was the Twenty Third Psalm, with the metaphysical explanation of it.

When Vincent thought he could stand it no more and was about to scream and vanish from the face of the earth, he heard a soothing voice; it was a man's, and it sounded vaguely familiar. He still felt like he was falling, but slower. "He maketh me to lie down in green pastures." said the soothing voice, "He leadeth me beside the still waters." He recognized these familiar words from the Twenty Third Psalm, and as he concentrated on the words, he stopped falling. Vincent let go of the seizure rail and the voice stopped; fear clutched him.

"Do you want me to read some more?" asked the voice. "Yes!" exclaimed Vincent frantically and the voice read on, but started at the beginning. Snowden wasn't sure Vincent had heard it all, and he knew its power. "The Lord is my shepherd; I shall not want," read the voice, but Vincent did want; he wanted a shot of Valium. "He maketh me to lie down in green pastures," said the voice, but he was in a hospital bed, and he was

477

angry with God for not being a good shepherd. He realized, though, that it was not God's fault that he had not followed Him. "He leadeth me beside the still waters," said the voice, and Vincent felt calm; this dumbfounded him. What was happening? Something was and he hung on to the voice, "Yea, though I walk through the valley of the shadow of death, I will fear no evil; for thou art with me." All fear left Vincent. "Surely goodness and mercy shall follow me all the days of ray life; and I will dwell in the house of the Lord forever."

The fear Vincent had felt was replaced with profound joy. Snowden had finished with the Psalm and was now telling Vincent how God loved him. He told him how God was the only cause, and all else was affect and affect could never cause. He explained to him that God only caused good; that anything that was not good had no cause, wasn't real. Rob told him neither alcohol, nor Valium, was caused by God, therefore had no power; its supposed power was illusion.

As Snowden talked, Vincent's toes started to tingle and the tingle moved up his legs and the strength was returning to his legs. Then the same thing was happening to his fingers and arms strength was returning to his arms. It was a strange feeling and frightening how quickly it was happening. Vincent sucked in his breath in amazement. Rob heard him.

"What's wrong?" asked the voice. "Nothing," answered Vincent, as he sat upright. He looked at the voice and recognized Snowden. "It's you!" he exclaimed, surprised. "How did you know I was here?" he asked. "Shelly told me," answered Snowden. "Why did you come?" asked Vincent. "I wanted to read you this lesson I had worked out for you." "Please finish it," pleaded Vincent, and Snowden read on.

While Snowden was reading, Vincent felt compelled to get out of bed. He pressed the release buttons of the seizure rail and lowered it all the way. What a thrill it was after being so weak and not able to do anything. Vincent got out of bed and stood on his feet, testing himself. He felt not like an invalid. By this time two of the regular nurses were watching him with their mouths agape and their eyes in wide-eyed, wonder. When Snowden finished with the reading, Vincent walked to the window with Snowden following. He looked out at the clear blue sky and saw what a beautiful day it was.

The doctor came into the ward. He was startled at seeing Vincent standing. He walked over to Vincent's bed. "Come and sit," he ordered," And I will have the nurse give you your shot." "I don't want to sit," replied Vincent," and I don't need a shot." Vincent looked out the window again, to the place where he belonged, out with the sky, and trees, the flowers, and the people; he could hardly wait. "You better get it now," warned the doctor, "It will be awhile before I come back this way." "That's alright," replied Vincent with confidence," I will not need it anymore." "Suit yourself," retorted the doctor, impatiently, thinking what a pain in the ass

Vincent was, all drunks were. Just a little while ago he had been begging for a shot. The doctor figured he would be begging again; he left in a huff.

"I want to go home now!" shouted Vincent at his heels. The doctor walked away without turning. "Maybe you shouldn't leave so soon," suggested one of the nurses. "Why not?" asked Vincent. "Maybe getting well all of a sudden like this was just a fluke," suggested the nurse, "Maybe it won't last." For a moment Vincent was frightened. "It was not a fluke!" exclaimed Snowden," God does not cause flukes. All metaphysical healings are caused by God and are permanent.

Vincent was certain that Snowden was right and the fear left him. He thanked Snowden, and asked the nurse to find the doctor, and get his release. He then asked Snowden if there was anymore to his lesson. Snowden said there was, and pulled some papers from his briefcase. He told him the rest of the lesson was there plus a list of books he should read. He told him when he had finished reading the books he should return to the research center and they would map out a road from sense to soul for him. Vincent's profound gratitude caused him to embrace Snowden and it was returned. After Snowden had left, Vincent gathered his things and waited for his discharge.

In his whole life Vincent had never felt so alive. He was certain that this sudden cure would lead him to the cure of the ailment that had kept him separated from Carla for all these years. He would read the books and return to the research center for his map for his journey from sense to soul before returning to Carla.

A month later Rachel had still not returned. Vincent had done all his reading and had his instructions from United Metaphysical Research. Thanks to God, he was ready to go home. He had talked to Rachel on the phone, and had told her he was going home, he told her he would visit her after she had returned to Ventura. He had given notice on his little house and now all he had left to do was go home. He had not told Carla he was coming home; he wanted to surprise her. He had not wanted to surprise her, nor himself, with any sexual surprises that were not healthy. He had pleasured himself to test for orgasm after affect. The bad feeling was gone.

During the drive home Vincent thought of the Tower, and how the puzzle had come together. The solid rock of the Tower's foundation was the firm conviction that God was real, that God was the only power, the only Tower builder. He would not have to re-build the Tower, all he had to do was clean it up so he could see it, and God would help him.

Some hours later Vincent was pulling into his San Francisco driveway. He was trying to think of something to say to Carla, but the door opened and Carla stepped out on the porch. He was struck dumb by his longing for her. She was surprised to see him, and joyful, for she had just been thinking about him, missing him. They walked into each other's arms oblivious to the dog's happy yapping. After the joyful greeting, Vincent put Rags out to pasture on the lawn, and led Carla upstairs to the bedroom to make his return official.

THE END

www.ingramcontent.com/pod-product-compliance
Lightning Source LLC
Chambersburg PA
CBHW051429260626
47162CB00001B/9